by Irving Stone

BIOGRAPHICAL NOVELS

LUST FOR LIFE (Vincent Van Gogh)
IMMORTAL WIFE (Jessie Benton Fremont)
ADVERSARY IN THE HOUSE (Eugene V. Debs)
THE PASSIONATE JOURNEY (John Noble)
THE PRESIDENT'S LADY (Rachel Jackson)
LOVE IS ETERNAL (Mary Todd Lincoln)
THE AGONY AND THE ECSTASY (Michelangelo)

BIOGRAPHIES

SAILOR ON HORSEBACK (Jack London)
THEY ALSO RAN (Defeated Presidential Candidates)
CLARENCE DARROW FOR THE DEFENSE
EARL WARREN

HISTORY

MEN TO MATCH MY MOUNTAINS

NOVELS

PAGEANT OF YOUTH
FALSE WITNESS

BELLES-LETTRES

WE SPEAK FOR OURSELVES (A Self-Portrait of America)
THE STORY OF MICHELANGELO'S PIETÀ

WITH JEAN STONE

DEAR THEO and I, MICHELANGELO, SCULPTOR
(Autobiographies through letters)

COLLECTED

THE IRVING STONE READER

THOSE WHO LOVE

"To look back and recollect the adventures of myself and my wife and daughter and sons, I see a kind of romance, which, a little embellished with fiction . . . or only poetical ornament, would equal anything in the days of chivalry or knight errantry."

JOHN ADAMS *to* ABIGAIL ADAMS, *February 10, 1795*

Those Who Love

A BIOGRAPHICAL NOVEL OF ABIGAIL AND JOHN ADAMS

by Irving Stone

DOUBLEDAY & COMPANY, INC.
Garden City, New York

To my wife

JEAN STONE

Minister without portfolio

"God grants liberty only to those who love it. . . ."

DANIEL WEBSTER, *January 26, 1830*

CONTENTS

Part One

LADY MOST COMPASSIONATE

BOOK ONE

A PURITAN IN LOVE

1

SHE sat in the center of the bed she shared with her older sister Mary, slim legs tucked beneath her, enjoying the early October sunlight as her hand moved across the letter paper. There was a French escritoire in a corner of the room next to her crowded bookcase of volumes from England but she preferred placing a blotting pad and inkwell on the dark tufted spread, writing vivaciously as the autumnal sun warmed her face and shoulders. Outside the window that faced the hills she could see her young brother Billy feeding his rabbits and geese, moving gracefully among them as he made quiet conversation.

She turned her eyes back to the letter she had just received from her cousin Hannah Quincy, who had married Dr. Bela Lincoln and was living at Hingham. She read a line from Hannah:

"Tell one of your sparks to bring you to see us."

She chuckled, two pleasant-timbred notes low in her throat.

"You bid me tell one of my sparks . . . to bring me to see you," she wrote. "Why, I believe you think they are as plenty as herrings, when alas! there is as great a scarcity of them as there is of justice, honesty, prudence and many other virtues."

There was ample reason for the popular Hannah to imagine that her cousin Abigail, nearly seventeen, would be surrounded by admirers. Certainly Hannah had been: Richard Cranch, now engaged to Mary, had been an interested visitor to the comfortable Colonel Josiah Quincy home backing on Massachusetts Bay; John Adams, the young lawyer from Braintree, had been there so frequently that, when he stopped visiting, the countryside rumored that one of them had jockeyed the other.

"Is Hannah that much prettier than I?" Abigail asked herself.

She scrambled to her knees, started to disembark from the center of the four-poster, then remembered that it was not considered proper for a clergyman's daughter to indulge in the vanity of the mirror . . . even though there was a tempting one over the chest of drawers. She laughed again with those two quick notes of self-amusement as she thought of the numerous times she had accidentally caught a glimpse of herself as she went past the glass.

She closed her eyes, visualizing her own face.

"Am I beautiful? Well, not exactly. But attractive, surely?"

There was a symmetry of bone structure, her high and agreeably curved forehead balanced by prominent cheekbones, a slender but resolute oval of jawline and strongly molded chin. Her mouth was small but full-lipped, with precisely set, small white teeth. Her eyes were the best part of her visage: large, a warm brown, luminously liquid and friendly under slender arched brows. Her nose . . .

She opened her eyes abruptly.

"O good Heaven," she cried aloud, "a Roman nose in a slender face!"

The nose was a miniature of her father's. If only it had been smaller, without the suggestion of a curve just below the hollow of the eyes. But then, she decided, what would a clergyman's daughter in the village of Weymouth do with classical beauty? Her skin was lovely: soft, a cream complexion, with high color in the hollows beneath the cheekbones. She liked her chestnut-colored hair, too; it was thick, alive with light as she brushed it back from her brows and temples. Right now it was pulled tight and tied with a blue ribbon at the base of her neck.

She returned her attention to the letter. Hannah had written, "Can we not remain friends through correspondence?"

Abigail recalled the lines by Dr. Young that she had read only the evening before:

A friend is worth all hazards we can run.
Poor is the friendless master of a world;
A world in purchase for a friend is gain.

She agreed with Dr. Young, the more so since she had never had a friend. Relatives, ah, yes! Her mother's family, the Quincys, who had settled Mount Wollaston in 1635, were a widespread clan with a dozen young girls and boys. Her father's family, the Smiths, who came from Charlestown, across the river from Boston, had not been quite that prolific, but there were her delightful uncle Isaac and aunt Elizabeth

Smith and their two sons. She was on close terms with both families, spending the summers at her grandfather Quincy's house and at least one month a year in Boston with her father's brother Isaac.

Why were friends so hard to come by?

For several years now she had yearned to be close to the young people around her, but it was difficult to have intimate friends when one lived in the parsonage and was the daughter of the leading citizen of the town. She knew everyone in Weymouth, had visited their homes with her father in times of sadness or celebration. Yet intimacy had been denied her, either to give or to receive. As the Reverend Mr. Smith's daughter she was expected to keep her own counsel.

Her father had tried to help. At teatime with its strawberry and quince tarts, and at Sunday noon dinner, or at Artillery Election, there were present the young men of Weymouth and the surrounding towns, as well as a fair share of the young clergymen of New England searching for wives.

Her mother had shielded her. Abigail was the little one of the family, slight in build, only a couple of inches over five feet tall, a sapling in a family of tall trees, with her big-boned, powerfully built father standing six feet two in his stockinged feet. Her mother and sister Mary were robust women with heavy-set shoulders and thick forearms and thighs, who reached up perilously close to the low ceilings of the parsonage. Even fifteen-year-old Billy was already a full head taller than she. The only smaller one in the family was her sister Betsy, but she was only ten.

"You're the runt of the litter," her father had said to Abigail affectionately, kissing her on each cheek; and she had not been hurt because she knew she was his favorite.

"You're delicate," her mother had decreed in her vigorous voice. "There's been so much consumption in the Quincy family. You're forever catching colds."

It was true she had had a lot of colds as a child, and an occasional bout of rheumatism. But as for being delicate: she gazed out her window to watch one of Billy's colts cavorting in the pasture.

"I'm about as delicate as that colt," she thought. "I can race all the way up Burying Hill and back and not be out of breath."

Very early in her childhood her mother had got it into her head that physical size was a measurement of strength. Abigail had been adjudged too fragile to attend the neighboring Dame School where Mary had studied for several years. On the afternoon of her eighth birthday Abigail had stood with her feet resolutely apart announcing to the family gathering that she was commencing Dame School the following morning. That had been nine long years ago, but she could still hear the silence in the sitting parlor and see the expression on her mother's face as she decreed that Abigail needed her health more than she did book learning.

That night as she lay stretched out taut in bed, her fingernails cutting into the palms of her hands, her father had come into the bedroom, lifted her from under the feather-filled comforter, carried her downstairs to his library, warm from crackling logs on the fire. He lit the brass lamp suspended from the ceiling, turned up the wick to fill the room with light. Parson Smith, warm in his own wool robe, settled in the leather armchair that was his special seat through the years, wrapped his arms about his eight-year-old daughter.

"Don't be unhappy, my little one. I've already taught you to read and write."

"Then you won't make Mother let me go?"

"A fight in a family never brings good."

"But I want to learn. That could bring good, couldn't it?"

"Hammer on the nailhead! Yes, knowledge is one of the permanently good things in life."

"You don't think I'm delicate?"

William Smith's eyes were like Abigail's: large, warm brown, but usually shielded, the brown veiled down to blackness as though the thoughts behind them were his own. Now they were shining.

"Inside yourself you're strong. That's the place where strength counts. Strength shows not only in how fast you can chop down trees."

There was a tinge of bitterness in his voice. His massive shoulders had hunched over. He looked the way he did when she saw him plowing the fields beyond the house, driving the horses forward with as much fury as though the devil was pursuing him.

"Then what am I to do?"

His body relaxed.

"We will get you the best education this side of Harvard College. But we must not let your mother know. She would be worried about the strain."

"What's a strain about studying, Pa?"

"I know, Nabby," he replied gently. "It's only for those who find books hard that study is all work."

"Like Billy?"

"Like Billy. For those who find moving through books as natural as walking over the hills in the spring, books are a refreshment and a delight. We have three good libraries in our family: the one here, the one at the Smiths' in Boston, and the fine collection at Mount Wollaston. Between your uncle Isaac, your grandfather Quincy and myself, slowly, slowly, we'll get you educated."

A *friend is worth all hazards.*

No one could help her there. She would have to earn them on her own.

"Ah well," she thought, giggling a little at her own seriousness, "our wishes give us not our wishes."

Her sister Mary called from the foot of the stairs.

"Nabby, Richard is here. Brought company for tea."

"Who?"

"That lawyer from Braintree. The one Mama doesn't like. They're tying their horses at the front gate."

She sprang off the bed with a lively bounce, shaping her high crown of hair with a backward motion of her hands, caught a reflection of her face as she went not too hurriedly past the mirror. Her eyes were sparkling mischievously. From behind the corner curtains she took a blue dress with crewelwork trim, slipped into it, buttoned the bodice down the front, straightened the ruffle across her bosom. It was the gayest dress allowed her, and made her feel saucy.

2

When the three sisters had protested against having to sleep and dress in the one room, the Reverend Mr. Smith built a partition which gave Abigail and Mary two thirds of the space, Betsy the other third. The big room was heated by a single fire, and so the wall of privacy could not come all the way to the fireplace.

Abigail crossed in front of the hearth and foreshortened partition, then Betsy's narrow segment of the room. She had a special rhythm for descending the stairs: one, two, three, quickly, then a pause on the fourth; fifth, sixth, seventh, even faster, then on the count of eight a little spring brought her evenly to the balls of both feet on the tongue-in-groove entry floor. She enjoyed the light touch. Her father said that since dancing was denied to a clergyman's daughter Abigail was defying convention by dancing instead of walking through life.

Mary was helping Richard Cranch off with his coat, stowing it in the entry closet that had been built under the stairs to handle the wraps and overshoes of the parishioners who came to wait their turn for counsel, sitting on the hard wooden bench just outside the Reverend Mr. Smith's library.

Cranch was English born, having come to Massachusetts with his sister and brother-in-law, the Joseph Palmers, sixteen years before, with substantial capital and knowledge about mining and hydraulics. An openhanded man, he liberally shared his information in endless technical discourses while courting Mary. He was formal, somewhat pretentious in manner, attractive except for his nose, which appeared to have been pinched in by a pair of strong fingers while still in the formative stage. He was as tall as Mary and almost as broad-shouldered. He had opened a factory for making glass, pottery, chocolate, stockings and whale-oil products in Germantown, a few miles around the bay from Weymouth, sold it after several disastrous fires, and then combined with other manufacturers to corner the spermaceti (whale oil) candle market. He had been generous with Abigail, bringing her the poetry of Gray, Dryden, Milton and Pope as holiday gifts.

Mary loved Richard.

"You can rely on him, Nabby," she confided to her sister the day she accepted Cranch's proposal. "He's always the same. You don't have to be afraid that next time you see him it'll be a different Richard."

"How comfortable."

"Oh, it is, Nabby. I'd hate to marry one man and discover there were ninety-nine others living inside him, with me never knowing which one was about to come in the front door."

"I think it could be exciting not to know which one was coming home," Abigail cried, her eyes twinkling. "That might make marriage a better guessing game than blind man's buff. Except that polygamy is illegal in New England."

Mary had shared Abigail's wit until she became serious about Richard Cranch. Since most jokes were undecipherable to her literal-minded fiancé, she had abandoned humor as an approach to life.

Mary and Cranch went arm in arm into the parlor. Abigail was about to follow when she caught a glimpse of John Adams standing in the library between her father's desk and a wall of books. He was holding two volumes spread wide, one in each hand, alternately sniffing one and then the other. His shoulders were hunched up toward his ears as a protective covering against the intrusion of an outside world. It seemed strange to see him standing so . . . consumingly . . . in the room she loved best in all the world; for here her father had fulfilled his promise, teaching her not only from the Bible and his extensive collection of sermons, but from the plays of Shakespeare and Ben Jonson, in between bouts of grammar, arithmetic, geography and such history books as *Discourse and View of Virginia*. Between the rigorous minds of her father, her uncle Isaac Smith and grandfather Quincy, and from her own natural thirst for knowledge which she slaked by exploratory reading, she had achieved a rudimentary education along with the valuable tools of logic and objective thinking.

"Whatever can he be doing?" she wondered as Adams returned two books to the shelf and selected two others. This was the first time she had had the opportunity to study this young man who usually squirmed if he thought anyone was watching him. Seeing him with enough of a side angle to catch the profile of plump jowls and rigorous set of stocky figure, she found him the exact opposite of the two men she loved and admired most, both of them tall, angular, powerful men, lean and spare: her father and her uncle-cousin Dr. Cotton Tufts.

She stepped into the room noisily. Startled, John Adams turned, a pink rise of color mounting on his plump cheeks. Then he held out both arms to her, an open book balanced in each hand.

"Did you know that you can tell which part of the world a book comes from, Miss Smith, just by the smell of its paper? This biography of Cotton Mather was printed in Boston, and it has a pungent smell of fibrous matting. This *Chronological History* was printed in London, and it has the fragrance of pressed wet rags."

"That comes as a bit of a shock, Mr. Adams."

"Why so?"

"I had imagined that it was the subject matter that made the difference in the bouquet. One of your lawbooks might give off the dank odor of a prison cell, while that volume of sermons on Father's desk could fill your nostrils with . . ."

"Brimstone!" he cried.

"Precisely."

He threw her a glance of appraisal.

They crossed the entry to the opposite door and went into Elizabeth Quincy Smith's handsomely furnished sitting parlor. The windows, two facing the front of the house, two at the side, were covered by lemon satin curtains. On the floor was a thick Brussels carpet, white ground with green leaves and lemon-yellow flowers. On the marble mantel over the fireplace, facing the front windows, were painted glass candleholders and bronze lamps for oil, flanked on either side by Wedgwood ornaments. There was a yellow damask sofa in the corner beyond the fireplace, a table between the side windows, now set for tea. Six comfortable mahogany chairs with upholstered seats were spaced gregariously around the room. Scattered about were Limoges figurines, gifts to Mrs. Smith from the members of the Quincy family.

John Adams dropped onto the sofa alongside the Reverend Mr. Smith, plunging immediately into discussion. It was about "The Weymouth Case." The two men were debating an issue which had been harassing Parson Smith as far back as Abigail could remember. When the First Congregationalist Church was founded in Weymouth in 1639, seventeen years after the village itself had been established, the Town Council granted a certain house and lands to the ministry. Ninety years later, when the Second or South Parish of the Congregationalists was formed, their minister had demanded as his legal right half of the lands of the original grant.

Abigail settled in one of the nearby mahogany chairs and watched Mr. Adams as he presented to her father a neatly marshaled array of legal arguments. John Adams had been coming into the house for more than two years now, drinking tea of a Sunday or on Militia Day. They had never become friends; in fact he had seemed to avoid her. Nor, for that matter, had she felt that John Adams liked her father. "Respect, yes," she thought; "liking, no." Yet he had continued to come.

She heard his voice rise in intensity as though he were reaching a focal point of his summary. She leaned forward so that she might hear, marveling that a man's voice, which was not particularly pleasant or interesting in an exchange of amenities, could grow in scope and character as his mind took over from his surface personality and he became immersed in the legal aspects of a case.

"Parson Smith, the original grant is clear. There is nothing in the document that says the holdings ever should be, or could be, divided."

"Mr. Bayley of the Second Parish won't agree."

John Adams turned on the sofa and gazed at Abigail soberly while he sifted his thoughts. She knew that he was looking inward, that he could not have told which of the three Smith girls he was seeing. When he turned back to her father there was a wisp of a smile in his serious, probing eyes.

"But would the Reverend Bayley say that the church properties should be divided between all the sects that open within the town borders? Anabaptists, Quakers, Separatists? Since this grant was a public one, each new clergyman would have an equal right, assuming Mr. Bayley's position to be correct, to demand a share of his property. Perhaps even the Catholics. The Reverend Bayley could end up with barely enough room to stable his horse."

William Smith struck his bony right knee a sweeping blow.

"By Jove, Mr. Adams, I think you've settled this interminable argument. Mr. Bayley will never sue me if he sees that he's establishing precedent to be sued in turn."

"Well," said John Adams, slumping on the sofa as though the wind had gone out of him, "it's good to win a case for a change." He added with a wistful smile, "Miss Abigail, do you think I might have a strawberry jam tart as a fee?"

When she passed the platter and refilled Mr. Adams's teacup she thought she saw a new look of respect in her father's eyes. But not so her mother, who rescued the tray from Mr. Adams and took it to Richard Cranch. Abigail mused:

"It's a good thing the minister's wife must be polite to all sorts of unacceptable characters."

"John Adams is nothing but a lawyer!" her mother had cried scornfully when her cousin Hannah Quincy's name was linked to his. "Lawyers are the most despicable group in New England. Everybody agrees. They ought to be outlawed."

"That's quite a pun, Mother," cried Abigail gleefully.

"Pun? What pun? You know I don't make jokes, Nabby. Massachusetts was a City on a Hill until they began allowing lawyers to practice their evil witchcraft."

"Massachusetts was never an ideal community," her father interposed mildly. "And Mr. Adams is not a witch. In fact there are moments when I find him almost intelligible."

"Intelligent? If he hadn't wasted his four years at Harvard College he would have become a clergyman. Isn't that what Harvard is for?"

Abigail did not know what Harvard College was for. Obviously it was not for girls, though her father had taken her last spring to hear the orations of the graduating class of 1761, after which they had picnicked on the bank of the Charles with the families of the young men.

The October dusk had begun to filter downward like fine rain. The room was darkening. Mrs. Smith lit the bronze lamps on the tables, then closed her curtains. This was the signal that the supper hour was at hand. John Adams rose to take his leave.

"You must stay for supper, Mr. Adams," said Mrs. Smith.

Abigail looked at her mother with admiration. Much as she disliked Mr. Adams, Elizabeth Smith would not violate the tradition of inviting to share supper all who were present at that hour.

She also noticed that, although Mr. Adams was surprised by her mother's invitation, he did not appear anxious to leave their company.

3

Her parents preceded them through the door in the parlor wall which led to the original house that had been built on these grounds, just below the first church on the hilltop, called "God's Barn." The cabin was a floor and a half, with a gabled roof and four small dormer windows at a height halfway between the big parlor and upstairs bedrooms of the main house, known as the Mansion, a large white wooden structure which the Reverend Mr. Torrey, a former parson of Weymouth, had built and attached to the cabin. The cabin supplied the family with a kitchen and dining room, two dormer bedrooms and a workroom in which Mrs. Smith had set up her looms. The walls were covered with grained wood panels.

Mrs. Smith took her seat at the foot of the long table, with the kitchen immediately behind her. Parson Smith took his at the head of the table, between the two windows that had been renovated to match the Mansion windows. Billy scrambled into a seat as far away from his father as he could get. Betsy sat next to her father, Mary and Cranch took the chairs with their backs to the brick fireplace, leaving the opposite side for Abigail and John Adams, in front of the sideboard with drawers and cupboards. Though the congregation had not yet approved the purchase of an organ for the church, the Reverend Mr. Smith had brought an old family piano from Charlestown. Over the piano, standing on a bracket, was a French clock. It was a friendly room; no family differences were permitted while food was on the table.

Phoebe, one of the Smith family slaves who had been brought into the parsonage at the death of the Negro Peg seven years before, was laying out platters of cold lamb in the kitchen, while Tom, who had been Peg's husband, brought in bowls of pudding, biscuits and milk. Tom, with a weather-textured face the color of rubbed mahogany and white hair standing up like stubble in a cut-over field of hay, worked by the parson's side at planting and harvesting time. He also served at table when there was company. Peg had cared for the girls when they were young; now short, plump, deep-voiced Phoebe had taken over. She had also become Tom's wife.

The penumbra of the suspended oil lamp bound them closely together as the conversation moved quickly to the favorite subject of the countryside since their newly crowned King, George III, had made his splendid first speech to the Parliament. A warm glow came over the room. They were Englishmen all, deeply devoted to their Mother Country, proud of their Empire. Their language was English, their thoughts and sensibilities, their fashions and much of their architecture, furniture, dishware, silver, their books of poetry, plays, politics, sermons were English; their music, their law, their Constitution, their cultural heritage. Massachusetts was a second home. England, though only Cranch had ever seen it, was the fount of all that was good and permanent in their lives.

There might be a family argument, such as the one that had started twenty-eight years before, in 1733, when Parliament passed the Molasses Act setting a high duty on all sugar and molasses imported into the colonies from the West Indies. Since Massachusetts converted the molasses into rum, one of its major exports, and these new duties would ruin the manufactory and most of the merchants along with it, Massachusetts had declined to pay any part of the tax. Smuggling was developed to a high and respected art. England had been indulgent, perhaps wincing meanwhile, but like a fond parent had not attempted to enforce the Act.

Harmony had prevailed until the year before when England issued to its customs officers Writs of Assistance, or general search warrants, which gave them the right to make a forcible entry into any ship's hold, warehouse, shop or home looking for contraband. Massachusetts, in high dudgeon, had cried:

"A man's home is his castle. So is his ship, dock, shop. The wind may enter, and the rain, but never the King!"

James Otis, most brilliant of Massachusetts' scholar-lawyers, had risen before the Superior Court and in a fiery speech denounced this calamitous piece of injustice. Everyone was convinced that England would withdraw the Writs. Massachusetts remarked on how sensible was their Mother Country, once she had been shown the error of her ways.

These occasional tiffs, always settled the way New England wanted them, strengthened the bonds of loyalty between Britain and her adoring if not always respectful colonies. If England sometimes felt that the colonies, in particular sententious Massachusetts, acted like spoiled brats, it was also true that they were precocious children and highly productive, pouring fortunes into the King's coffers through their external trade, rigorously regulated by England with a no-nonsense enforcement. New Englanders only misbehaved when they imagined that the parental government was attempting to invade their "political rights as free Englishmen."

As Phoebe and Tom passed the pompion pie and fruit, Abigail quoted admiringly from George III's speech those sections in which the King had promised to patronize religion, the British Constitution, the rights and liberties of all his subjects; sentiments, Massachusetts declared, worthy of a patriot King.

Now that supper was dispatched Mrs. Smith had fulfilled her duties as a hostess.

"There are some who are not proper Englishmen," she said. "Take that Samuel Adams, for example, always trying to foment trouble."

Her husband asked quietly, "Is he a close cousin, Mr. Adams?"

Abigail, sitting next to John, felt that he was not embarrassed. But she also sensed the fighting cockles were stirring within him.

"Not so close as cousins: we share an Adams great-grandfather. But as friends, close indeed. I love and admire Sam'l, even when I don't agree with him . . . which is nearly always."

"But what is there to admire?" Mrs. Smith persisted. "He has failed in business several times. Lost all his parents' bequest in the brewery. Now that he is a tax collector there seems to be a considerable sum missing from his accounts. So everyone says."

"Oh, admittedly, Sam'l is a poor businessman." His voice was more amused than irritated. Apparently John Adams could handle uncomfortable situations. "He wanted to become a lawyer, and he would have developed into one of the greatest legal minds. But you see, Mrs. Smith, Samuel's mother despised the law. There are some people who feel that way, you know, implausible as it may sound."

Mrs. Smith had the grace to blush.

"Sam'l is a superb political theorist and writer."

The Reverend Mr. Smith was now puzzled. He leaned across the table to bring his face closer to John Adams.

"But don't you find his theories incendiary?"

"Not necessarily, Parson Smith. Sam'l is only trying to accomplish politically what you have succeeded in accomplishing religiously: unchallenged and absolute independence."

"But we Congregationalists have many preachers with the same concept. How many Samuel Adamses are there?"

"Only one, the Lord be praised!"

This raised a laugh. Abigail asked:

"Then you agree with my father?"

"On the contrary. Not to have one Samuel Adams would be a cruel loss."

The Reverend Mr. Smith's skin was growing blotched.

"I feel I must repudiate your comparison between religion and politics."

"Why so? Do you allow bishops to control your congregation? Do you allow an English presbytery to send you pastors, dictate the articles of your faith? Assuredly not! My father was a deacon of the Braintree Congregationalist Church for twenty-five years. A more porcupinish congregation never existed. If a clergyman from Boston so much as told them what note on the wood whistle to use for their hymn, they'd tar and feather the man."

The mottles subsided and her father's eyes began to sparkle.

"Exaggerated. But true."

"That's how Samuel Adams feels about politics."

Everyone rose from the table, started for the sitting parlor. Abigail looked John Adams straight in the eye and thought:

"You've got spirit."

4

She awakened early on Saturday morning, shook Mary, who was a solid sleeper, then went quickly down to the kitchen where Phoebe had water boiling in cauldrons hung from hook pegs.

"You trapped you a fine day for your picnic, Miss Nabby."

"I did, Phoebe, didn't I?" She added cold water to the steaming water Phoebe was pouring into the tub. "But it was no accident. I wished it into being."

Phoebe withdrew to the storage porch to prepare a picnic lunch, leaving Abigail to slip out of her dressing robe, dip an experimental toe in the tub and then ease herself in, knees tucked under chin. While she scrubbed herself with the bayberry soap and a white flannel cloth she wondered how the larger members of the Smith family managed to fit into this battered ancestral bath each Saturday night. The oaken tub with its brightly polished copper hoops had become her measuring rod. She judged the growth of her slim legs by the height her dimpled knees rose above the water; and how miraculously, a few weeks short of seventeen, no matter how energetically she crowded forward in the tub she could no longer submerge her well-developed breasts.

Phoebe had put a towel in the baking oven to warm. Abigail stepped out onto the oval wool braided rug, draped the big linen towel around her, patted rather than rubbed herself so that the drying would not redden her skin.

"Phoebe, would you refill for Mary? She'll be right down."

The pleasant afterglow of the bath vanished as she went through the dining room to the sitting room and heard raised voices in the study.

"Why are you suddenly so friendly to Mr. Adams?" she heard her mother ask in her well-bred albeit stern voice. "I've not heard you enthusiastic about him before."

"No, admitted. Though I've been watching him."

Abigail balanced on one foot in the hallway. It was the first time she had heard her parents debate the virtues of a young man who wanted to come calling.

"Then how can you encourage . . . He's the son of a yeoman, and a lawyer."

"I would like Nabby to have friends. It's time, now that Mary is engaged."

"What has friends to do with going in a boat to Rainsford Island in the fall when the weather can turn bad? You know how easily she catches cold."

Abigail fled up the stairs to her room.

"What's wrong?" Mary asked, about to descend for her bath. "Your face is pale but your eyes are hot."

Of an even disposition, Mary was little given to alarums. She had served as a buffer between Abigail and their mother ever since the day Abigail, kept home from a sleigh ride because her mother felt she was not up to it, cried in vexation:

"There is only one of me, but there seems like six of her!"

Now she replied:

"Mother doesn't want me to go with you and Richard, though I can't tell which she objects to the more, Mr. Adams or the boat."

"I'll speak to her," said Mary in her reassuring tone. "Wear your wool stockings and goloe-shoes."

She sat on the edge of the worsted flannel sheet which Elizabeth Smith had taught her three daughters to loom, her natural good humor returning. Her mother loved her and would not want to bring her unhappiness. Since Abigail had long since determined never to allow her mother to condemn her to a life of seclusion and inactivity, why should she become upset?

The men rowed the flat-bottomed boat as far as Rainsford Island while Abigail and Mary sat together in the bow. The water was calm, though cool to her fingers as she dabbled them over the side. The two men were enthusiastic rowers, John Adams silent and obviously enjoying the exercise, Richard Cranch talking rhythmically while he stroked about the waterworks of the river Thames and how they conveyed water all around the city of London by means of cogwheels and pumps.

Every now and then the two men would drop a line. Since there were no bites they took the boat around the island and beached it. The girls found a flat stone surrounded by goldenrod and marsh rosemary. They spread Phoebe's lunch of chicken, cider and journeycake. After they had finished eating, Mary and Cranch went to search for specimens of seashells. John spread his coat by the edge of the bank just beyond the crop of three-year-old salt hay that the elder Adams used to buy for five shillings the load.

Abigail sat down on the coat, enjoying the view. The island was covered with flowers and rocks. Herring gulls cawed and screamed above them.

When John Adams mentioned one of the cases he was working on she turned to gaze at him.

"Why do people say the law is a dirty business?"

"Because it is!" She was astonished at his vehemence. "Take Braintree. You have never seen such illegal quacks as practice in that town. The ridiculous litigations have multiplied until the very stones cry out. There is a saying in our province, 'as litigious as Braintree.'"

"Why has this happened?"

"We have a multiplicity of pettifoggers who give out that they are sworn attorneys. Forgive me if I feel strongly, but last year one of them, Captain Hollis, tried to ruin my reputation after I proved to the town that he had never taken the oath of an attorney."

He was trembling with rage. She put a finger gently on the back of his hand.

"But he did not hurt you?"

The healing touch of her voice, even more than the tranquilizing finger, calmed him.

"No. I am determined to stay in Braintree and break up the strife these dirty dabblers in the law have caused. They incite the townspeople to sue each other. That is their crime. Some of them are so crafty they have absorbed the estates of our neighbors. Have you heard Justice Dyer's accusation? 'Lawyers live upon the sins of the people.'"

"That's probably why lawyers were prohibited in early New England."

"These men are not lawyers, Miss Abigail. They have never studied. Most of them are process servers who create suits out of tavern amusement. It's as though Dr. Cotton Tufts went about Weymouth encouraging people to eat poisoned foods so that he could charge them a fee for curing them."

"But if the law consists of what you call 'dirty dabblers and ridiculous litigations,' why would you want to practice it?"

Suddenly the agitation was gone from his body. Over his face came a warm glow. She observed that his eyes were like the surface of the sea, depending on the weather for their hue: pearl gray when clouds were overhead, cerulean blue in the bright sun, turning from green in the rain to purple in a storm: a changeable man who reflected shadings of mood as the ocean reflects the sky. He took a long breath, seemed to settle into himself.

"My inclination was to preach. I studied hard and gave a good deal of myself to the examination of theology. But in the end I was not convinced I could preserve an orthodoxy. No priest or pope has any right to say what I shall believe, and I will not believe one word they say if I think it is not founded in reason and in revelation. Every man has a right to speak and think and act for himself, in religion as well as politics."

"My father would not quarrel with that concept."

"I have an inquiring mind. At moments I found myself thinking like the Antinomians, and since one of the preachers with whom I boarded while teaching school was expelled by his congregation for Antinomian heresy . . ."

"In short, you were not called?"

He turned to look at her head on.

"I admire the law, Miss Abigail. Law is human reason codified. Law is justice. It guarantees our rights. Without codified law we would live like savages. True lawyers spend their time keeping people out of trouble.

When I decided to go into the law and apprenticed myself to Mr. Putnam, do you know what I asked myself?"

She smiled; no force she possessed could have stopped John Adams now. He had his short arms circled wide in front of him, the fingertips of the stubby hands almost touching, as though embracing a judge and jury.

"I asked myself, what rule must I observe to make a figure, to be useful and respectable? I set out with firm resolutions never to commit any meanness or injustice in the practice of the law. I laid out for myself a seven-year plan of study. I labored hard in my lawbooks for at least six hours a day to get distinct ideas of right and wrong, of justice and equity. I searched for the answers in Roman, French, English treatises on natural, civil, common and statute law. I tried to dig out of history the exact nature and ends of government, for all civilized government is based on equitable law. I compared the effects of governments in every age on public welfare and private happiness. I studied Seneca and Cicero, Vinnius . . ."

His voice rang out bold and clear. She felt a sense of pride within him. Yet suddenly a haze came over his eyes, his heavy head dug into his short, stout neck.

"That was quite a speech I made, wasn't it?" he asked, sotto voce.

"I was moved."

"So was I. At Harvard I belonged to a club of students and they often asked me to read at their meetings, especially tragedies. They said I had some faculty for public speaking, and that I should make a better lawyer than clergyman." His manner became ironic. "I have just entered the twenty-seventh year of my life and the sixth year of my studies in law. Twenty-six years of the animal life is a great proportion to be spent to so little purpose. My Latin and Greek are still imperfect . . ."

"You have the makings of a flagellant," said Abigail.

"I vow each night I will rise with the sun and read Littleton or Coke. But I sleep instead. I burn to pursue the mathematical and philosophical sciences, to study Locke, Montesquieu. I hunger to know more of ethics and moral philosophy, as well as English literature: Milton, Chaucer, Spenser, Swift."

"Then what do you do with your time?"

"I gallant the girls."

She stared at him in the sheerest astonishment, her brown eyes wide, her lips parted in incredulity. Then, simultaneously, they burst into hearty laughter.

"It wasn't true, you know," he murmured.

"What wasn't true?"

"That she jilted me. I never courted your cousin Hannah seriously. Oh, I might have, if Jonathan Sewall and Esther Quincy hadn't broken in on us one evening and interrupted a conversation."

He sprang up, began pacing a semicircle around his coat spread on the sand.

"That marriage would have depressed me to poverty and obscurity to the end of my life. She was a master of dangling, your cousin Hannah: she was wheedling Richard Cranch, Parson Wibird, me, at the same time that she was writing passionate letters of avowal to Dr. Bela Lincoln."

He stopped in his tracks. "True, I visited the Quincys so often that her family thought I was courting. My father put a stop to that. He said, 'This story about you and Hannah has spread so wide that if you don't marry her she could be said to have jockeyed you, or that you jockeyed her.' But Hannah kept assuring me that she didn't want to marry for five years; and even then didn't want costly things."

"So that's why you weren't frightened of calling?"

He had a disconcerting way of enveloping one's face with eyes that consumed everything in sight. It became impossible to look away from him.

"I had so little choice. Do you know that every man of rank and figure in this province is desirous that his daughter be married to a man who never saw her?"

"I did you an injustice, Mr. Adams," she replied. "I thought you had been hurt by Hannah."

"I did you an injustice too, Miss Smith. Two years ago I remember thinking, 'Hannah is fond and loving, but Parson Smith's girls have not this fondness, not this tenderness.'"

"But this is the very first time . . ."

"I asked myself, 'The Smith girls are witty, but are they frank, or fond, or even candid? No,' I said to myself, 'not fond, not frank, not candid.'"

"Truly, you astonish me!"

"Purposely. So that you can see what an utter fool a young man can be."

He sat down abruptly at her side, his shoulder hitting clumsily against hers. For a man who seemed plump, his shoulder was exceedingly hard.

She looked seaward, saw a gray bank of fog rolling in, shivered. John Adams asked:

"You're not angry with me for having such thoughts?"

Into her mind flashed a picture of herself at fifteen, a scrawny, flat-chested girl.

"I'm surprised that you thought seriously about me at all."

"Suffolk County is sparsely settled." He gave a derogatory chuckle. "Our Puritan ancestors said we had to marry in order to bring saints into the world. Since this is the one area in which I intend to remain orthodox, I was merely surveying the field."

Mimicking his high-pitched voice, she said:

"The Adams boy is a wit, but is he frank or fond, or even candid?"

"I'm too candid for my own good, Miss Abigail, it earns me enemies. I'm certain I could be fond too. But I've had so little opportunity."

Abigail had not heard Mary and Richard come up behind them. She was startled to hear Mary say:

"We'd better start back before it turns cold."

She scrambled to her feet. The mood was broken.

5

They ran into a wind that sprang up in the south; the waters of the bay turned choppy. Richard Cranch became so seasick that John Adams put them into Hangman's Island, two miles closer to shore. Cranch crumpled himself into a knot on the salt grass, promptly falling asleep. Adams found a spot partially protected from the wind, took off his coat and wrapped it around Abigail, the dark material bundling her up to the ears as he shyly managed the legerdemain of securing the coat about her shoulders without seeming to hold her in his arms. She was warm and comfortable, but the sun was beginning to sink behind the mainland.

"I know how uncomfortable Richard is," said Mary after a time, "but my mother worries. She probably has us drowned off Hough's Neck by now."

John got Cranch up, settled him into the bottom of the boat with his head on Mary's lap. Abigail, still with John's coat about her, sat at the other end of the boat, behind him, watching the play of shoulder and back muscles as he rowed the craft into the whitecaps. She had not thought of him as a particularly strong man. In fact, she realized, she had never thought of him at all until the previous week. Yet she marveled at the power with which he sent the heavy boat against the wind and spray. It was a picture that remained in her mind after she had settled under her warm comforter in bed, filled with her father's brew of hot tea and her mother's equally warm remonstrances against risking her health on such a foolhardy venture.

"You were right, Mama, it was late in the year to go out on the bay."

She was remorseful the following evening when she learned from Richard Cranch that it was John Adams who had come down with the cold. She felt again the body warmth of his coat as he had wrapped it around her.

"I hope it isn't a bad one."

"Only a bit of a rheum. But he's also complaining of a phlegmatic stomach and a colicky pain. He is a bit of a hypochondriac, you know."

"That surprises me."

"It's all that book reading he does. And the writing. Seems like he feels a duty to write two pages for every one he reads. Too much study sets a man's digestion on edge."

Amused, Abigail said, "I'll ask Uncle Tufts to brew a jug of his cold killer, if you'll be so kind as to carry it to Braintree on your way home."

She called to her brother Billy for company, then left by the front door, walking through her father's now dormant vegetable patch closed in by a picket fence, and out the swinging gate. Behind the unpainted wood barn two of the family cows had their heads hanging over the rough-timber railing. They strode the hard-packed earth road of North Street between Burying Hill and Great Oak Hill, past the Whitman house and the Meeting House to where Church Street angled off of North. Here her uncle-cousin Dr. Cotton Tufts had his office and crossroads store.

She stood for a moment, pushing the hood of her cape back off her head, gazed up at the clarity of the Massachusetts sky, lucidly bright and sparkling in the air that had been washed clean by a sunset shower. She felt intensely alive, inhaling the sweet smells of the lingering rain, the giant oaks on the hill above them, the sharp tang of the newly gathered haycocks at the nearby farmhouses: Burrell's on the short path to Mill Lane; Elisha Jones's old gambrel-roofed house across the field; James Humphrey's place a little way down Duxbury Trail. She caught the burnt smell of charred wood and hammered metal from Lieutenant Yardly Lovell's blacksmith shop beyond Burrell's, near the corner of Mill Lane.

She had a deep love for Weymouth. The village rather than just the parsonage was her home. She had been in every house a hundred times when the parson had had to call, sometimes for births, sometimes for deaths, or when her uncle Tufts had had to visit the sick and wanted company. She stood with her eyes closed.

"What are you got your eyes closed for?" demanded Billy.

"It's a special way to see, Billy. I'm tracing a map of Weymouth: straight south of us is the Hill Hollow, beyond it Whitman's Pond and Whortleberry Pond. On Plymouth Road, going out toward Monatiquot River, there's John White's, next to him Thomas White's, then the Arnold Tavern and across the road . . ."

"Why do you want to know all those houses?"

She opened her eyes. "They're part of our family."

"Not my family," said the fifteen-year-old boy explosively. "I got too much family already. I mean to get out of Weymouth."

"You will when you go to Harvard. How can you become a clergyman if you don't go to college?"

"I'd rather be dead!"

She saw tears in Billy's eyes and tried to take him in her arms. He wrestled free, stood gazing at her with hatred contorting his young face.

"I thought you was on my side. I thought you would help me against him."

"But, Billy, Father only wants to help you make the most of yourself."

"No, he don't. He wants to make me like him. But I won't be like him. I'm never going to preach to people. I don't like to be told what to do, and I won't tell anybody else."

"Not even if they need help?"

"No!"

"But you help the animals when they come to you."

"We're friends. We never make each other unhappy."

"And Father makes you unhappy? Suppose you wouldn't have to go into the clergy? Suppose I persuaded him to let you go to Harvard and become whatever you want?"

Billy managed a thin smile.

"Thanks, Nabby, but I'm not going at all. See if you can make Pa accept that, will you? 'Cause if not, I'm going to run away . . . out to the Ohio Valley."

"Don't be hard on him, Billy. It's not his fault if you're his only son."

"Well, it's not my fault either that you're all girls. So tell him to let me alone."

Billy turned and ran back along North Street. Abigail continued on to Dr. Tufts's alone, distressed. The blow would be severe for her mother, since all the male Quincys had gone to Harvard. But it was more serious for her father, who had hoped that his only son would one day take over his parish in Weymouth, inherit his carefully selected library of English and American sermons from John Donne to Jeremy Taylor.

Through the window she could see Dr. Cotton Tufts working between two tall candles, looking like a fourteenth-century alchemist. He was a tall man who was all knobs of bone covered by scant flurries of flesh as he hunched over his work counter grinding ingredients from his medicine jars in a stone mortar. He was a double relative to Abigail, an uncle by marriage on her mother's side, a blood cousin on her father's. Cotton's older brother had been trained by their doctor father; he in turn had trained his younger brother. Ten years before, searching Massachusetts for a promising place to begin his practice, Cotton had come to Weymouth to visit his uncle, the Reverend Mr. Smith, and his sister-in-law, Elizabeth Smith. He found himself in a plague of putrid sore throat so virulent that more than a hundred and fifty adults and children had already died. There was no doctor in the village. Cotton had a formula for fighting what he called "thin diphtheria." Seven-year-old Abigail, big-eyed, had watched him mix individual doses on Peg's table in the parsonage kitchen: snakeroot infused with two teaspoonfuls of India rum, followed by two teaspoonfuls of molasses and salad oil. Though only twenty and without medical practice, Cotton had dosed the village, tended the sick, routed the plague without another death. Not a body from Fore and Back rivers on either side of Great Hill at the north end, down the whole nine miles to Dense Woods and Great Pond to the south, but agreed that Weymouth had found its permanent doctor.

Abigail opened the front door, with its tinkling bell.

"You're working late, Cousin Cotton."

He looked up, still twirling the stone pestle in his long fingers. He wore spectacles, was almost beardless, with hollow cheeks and prominent cheekbones.

"I can always tell how you feel about me, Nabby, from your first two words. If you're being stern with me, it's 'Uncle Tufts,' but if you're happy with me, it's 'Cousin Cotton.'"

His cocoa-brown eyes and big lips, with the omnipresent crack in the center of the lower one, smiled their pleasure with her.

"Only the fashionable Boston doctors can afford to have their drugs ground by apothecaries. Just as they feel it's beneath them to perform surgery or extract teeth. That's barber's work, they say. So here I am at any hour."

Abigail took a swift look around the doctor's crossroads store. After a full decade of practice he still was not able to support his wife and child on his medical fees. The side of his store facing on Duxbury Trail was his apothecary shop: shelves stacked neatly with colored jars of bitter stomach worm drops, perfumes against deafness, aromatic elixers, pomatum to preserve the hair. Along the back wall were his rows of surgical instruments, the anodyne necklaces to help teething children, urinals, lancets, nipple shells. On the Church Street wall was perforce his general store, imperishables such as teas, spices, ginger, sugar, saltpeter, snuff, eating oils, sweetmeats. Difficult as times had sometimes been, Cotton had refused to accept perishables as his pay, drawing the line at becoming a butcher or greengrocer.

"I am a touch fatigued tonight, Nabby. There's dysentery out beyond Phillips Creek. Had me up three nights running. I bled them, put them on Indian physic and mullein root to drink with their boiled milk. It's just beginning to restore the mucus of their bowels."

"Would you have a cure for a cold?"

"Who's down in the family?"

She flushed, was glad that Cotton's candles lighted only the herbs and powders he was grinding.

"Not in the family. A friend."

Cotton rested his elbows on the rough plank counter.

"Might I ask: who is the friend for whom I'm prescribing?"

"John Adams."

"John Adams!" His mouth dropped open. "Why, that self-taught scientist never misses an opportunity to prescribe for me. Last time I found him coughing and sputtering I recommended Ben Franklin's advice: 'Fresh air helps cure, stale air causes cold.' Confound me if he didn't give a learned oration on how colds are caused by cold air, especially when a person is overheated."

Abigail fluted two low notes of laughter.

"Uncle-Cousin, you are the greatest doctor in North Weymouth, besides being the only one. But in this instance Mr. Adams could be right. He was overheated from rowing seasick Richard to Hangman's Island, and because there was a wind he took off his coat to wrap around me."

"Well, well, that's the first romantic gesture I've heard about John Adams since Cousin Hannah jockeyed him."

She started to say, "He wasn't jockeyed," but thought better of it. Cotton turned to the drawer under his surgical instruments, took out a handful of scrawled notebooks, searched for a formula to cure a cold. She knew him to be a formidable fighter. For the ten years she had been close to him the fight had centered on these pages of spider-fine writing in his commonplace books.

"No two doctors want to talk to each other," he told her woefully, "for fear they might spill their secrets, give another doctor the means to take away their patients. Each practitioner treats his own little body of knowledge as though it were private property, like a forest marked for ships' masts, and he has to fence out trespassers. The bigger their practice, the tighter they guard their prescriptions and cures. We have no schools to study in, no doctors' club where we can thrash out our common problems. We publish no books or pamphlets in which we can find prescriptions that have helped other doctors cure a sickness or stop an epidemic."

"Yet you had the right formula for throat distemper," she proffered.

"Only by sheerest accident, Nabby. When I was seventeen I heard about the doctor who mixed snakeroot with rum. I jotted down that formula in my diary. Without it, another hundred children, adults too, could have died in Weymouth."

She knitted her brows. "What you're saying, Uncle, is that a person in Hingham can stay sick, or even die, because the doctor in his neighborhood doesn't have a formula that is used to cure in Braintree?"

"Just so, Nabby. Each of us works in the dark, with maybe a tiny candle or two, until the Grim Reaper blows them out. If all the doctors in Massachusetts would combine their knowledge we could make medicine a science instead of a desperate guessing game."

"Has anyone tried?"

He grinned sheepishly.

"Well, no one of any consequence. Only me. I collar every doctor I meet, write letters. They think I'm a fool, trying to give away my heritage. I tell them: the more we give, the more we get. The last doctor I told that to said, 'Son, you missed your calling. You should have been a preacher.'" He searched his notebooks, clucked discouragingly. "Tell your Mr. Adams to go to bed for a day with a volume of Herodotus, strong beef broth and a jug of Barbados rum. Between the three, nature will cure him."

"He's not my Mr. Adams. And I doubt that he consorts with kegs of Barbados rum. He told me yesterday of an article he wrote for the *Boston Gazette* against taverns and rum drinking."

Cotton laughed heartily before making an effort to pull in his big lips. "I like John Adams. He's more variable than the New England weather, now blows hot, now blows cold. But he's a fighter, and I like a man with courage. If only he didn't think he was dying every other time we meet."

6

She sat in the family pew, the third on the left, her hands wrapped around the hot baked potato in her muff, her feet warm in the depth of the live-coal foot warmer which she shared with her sisters. This was the third of God's Barns since the congregation had been gathered in 1623. The first, on the hill above the parsonage, had burned down, the second had blown up when the town's store of gunpowder somehow got ignited. The air of the wooden plank building was so cold that she felt she was inhaling thin sheets of ice. Her mother, dressed in handsome ribbed velvet, held herself erect in the high pew enclosure, declining to share her daughters' baked potatoes or foot warmer in an effort to demonstrate that a clergyman's wife never feels cold in a Congregationalist Meeting House.

The men were across the aisle. Billy sat with Cotton Tufts, whose pew was at the rear of the forty-foot church because the Tuftses were recent arrivals in Weymouth.

"If there's anything I hate worse'n school," Billy had grumbled as he trudged at Abigail's side in the solid Smith phalanx making its way down North Street in its best clothes, "it's the Meeting House."

North and Church streets had been filled with parishioners holy walking, the women in their best black woolen dresses, the men in black coats, knee pants and black stockings, wearing round, broad-brimmed hats. Churchgoing was obligatory in New England: Abigail had attended every Sunday and holiday service since she was two years old and able to holy walk on her own feet. Only the dying did not make their way to God's Barn, for there were few sicknesses a good sermon could not cure.

"Now, Billy, Pa's the most considerate preacher in New England. When other clergymen take all morning for a sermon, he never turns his hourglass. Most pastors make us pray for an eternity; Pa quits after ten minutes."

" 'The Lord is not deaf,' " Billy mimicked his father's austere, no-flourish voice. " 'He can hear our prayers the first time we utter them.' "

"Wait till you move away," she admonished, "and get a 'hellfire and damnation' preacher who rants at you for six hours during the two Sunday sermons."

Billy had the good grace to turn a contrite face.

"I guess Pa's not bad in meeting. At least our tithingman never has to hit his parishioners with his fur-tipped rod to wake them up."

The Reverend Mr. Smith was a rare Puritan in that he was abstemious with words. In New England society, which still respected its sumptuary law, lived sparely and beneath its means, found virtue in doing without, the Puritans were profligate in their speech, rarely using one word where a dozen might be uttered. This eighth deadly sin made forebearance from the other seven almost tolerable. When they were studying together in the Smith library, William Smith had explained to his daughter that he considered himself an antidote to the excesses of Congregationalism. For this reason he refused to vote in town meeting. The Church *was* the State in Massachusetts, for only those who were saved, the members of the congregation, had the right to vote. He considered that what had happened in Salem, the beating and hanging of women as witches, was the poison of too much church.

"Love and charity are quiet subjects, Nabby, and so I don't have to go on endlessly at the top of my lungs, like the herb peddlers and fishmongers of Boston. The popularity of the great Boston preachers, Increase and Cotton Mather, was based on their ability to thunder from the pulpit. I don't like the sound of my ownsome voice that well. Besides, a quiet village like Weymouth doesn't have the unquenchable thirst for entertainment of a pleasure-mad Boston."

"Are you saying that sermon-listening can become a vice, like card playing or drinking flip?" she had asked.

"Surely it was for the first hundred years in Massachusetts. The ministers preached so long and hard that their congregations became possessed. They didn't have time or emotion left to do their work or raise their families. The shops and schools were constantly closed so the preachers could keep their followers in meeting. I can't see that our people have become more lustful or avaricious than the scourged ones who are constantly inhaling the fumes of hellfire."

"I think it's a virtue in you, Papa."

He had laughed, thrown a big arm affectionately about his daughter's slender shoulders.

"I have another virtue, Nabby. I'm an even better farmer than I am a preacher."

Abigail had seen him work from early spring planting to late fall harvesting, his broad, brawny figure clothed in homespun and high boots, guiding a plow behind the oxen, harrowing, pruning the apple and pear orchard, gathering in the crops. She could tell by the pride with which he built stone walls, enlarged the stables, cut down the virgin white birch and pine to make room for new orchards that he enjoyed the dawn-to-dusk labors.

William Smith had been the son of a prosperous sea captain and merchant family in Charlestown, across the river from Boston, one that had a superb silver collection. He owned a good farm there and had long been independent, having his boots and coats made by the best craftsmen in Boston, when the Weymouth deacons called the twenty-seven-year-old man to their pulpit, voting him £108 a year, plus five acres of firewood a year to be cut for him. In 1738, two years before his marriage to Elizabeth Quincy, he had bought their comfortable parsonage and surrounding lands for cash, preferring to own rather than be given a parsonage rent-free by the congregation.

She rested her eyes on her father, standing in his long black robe, freshly starched white collar and bands, behind the simple plank pulpit called a scaffold, which rested on a platform only a few feet higher than the floor of the church. When the Meeting House was being rebuilt the deacons had refused their pastor's suggestion that the square wooden enclosures of the pews, so high that only the tops of people's heads were in evidence, be painted and made shorter. The benches were as hard and narrow as pantry shelves. But one was not supposed to be comfortable in meeting; that was one of the many things that Abigail's Puritan ancestors had been positive about.

She listened to her father's bass voice as he preached from Hebrews 6:10: "For God is not unrighteous to forget your work and labor of love, which ye have showed toward His name."

She thought how alike the three so very different men, her father, Cousin Cotton and John Adams, were. All in revolt: her father as dissatisfied with the practice of clergymen as Cotton was aghast at the narrowness of doctors, and John Adams at what he called "the multiplicity of pettifoggers." At the time of the Great Awakening, a couple of years before she was born, when self-styled "Grand Itinerants" had rocked New England with revivalism, throwing congregations into convulsions and causing thousands at outdoor meetings to roll epileptically on the ground; with so many important clergymen, led by Jonathan Edwards, aiding the revivalists, William Smith had taken his stand against them at considerable danger to his job and calling. Joining with an association of ministers behind Charles Chauncy and subscribing to his book, *Seasonable Thoughts*, the Reverend Mr. Smith battled mightily in Weymouth to hold his congregation together in the dignity and grace of their religion.

Her father's voice announced the number of the closing hymn. Everyone rose, the hinged seats bouncing up with a clatter. Many of the hymns in the hymn book took a full hour to sing, but the Reverend Mr. Smith declared that he always picked the shortest because his parishioners were unable to carry a tune. Never had a congregation been so grateful for a derogatory remark.

As Abigail turned to leave her pew she saw John Adams, his round face red-cheeked, standing next to Cotton Tufts, who had been singing robustly. She was surprised to find him at Weymouth's service. She had not seen or heard from him since she sent him her cousin Cotton's prescription two weeks before. He obviously had not made the three-mile ride to Weymouth this morning for medical advice, he looked far too healthy.

By the time she had disentangled herself from the Sunday greetings John Adams had left with the Tuftses. She admitted that she was disappointed.

Late afternoon tea was social time in Weymouth. People came together to visit with friends and relatives, to eat from baskets of freshly baked cookies and trays of candied fruits and nuts, washed down by cups of aromatic Hyson or Congo. Tea was conducive to the exchange of news and to arguments over the immediate issues of the day, such as the forming of a new county to be set off from Suffolk, or how brilliantly young James Otis had defended the colonies against the noxious Writs of Assistance. On Sundays a high tea was served in the Reverend Mr. Smith's parsonage, replacing supper.

This was Mrs. Smith's finest hour. There were some forty parishioners scattered through the rooms: from the Humphreys, Lovells and Torreys from Back Lane to the north, to Deacon Josiah Waterman, who owned the land on both sides of the road from Whitman's Pond to the Hingham line, and the Bicknells, who lived beyond the Watermans at the end of Sheep Street. A good assortment of cakes had never been known to keep away company.

Elizabeth Quincy Smith enjoyed the pour. She sat at the head of her table with dignity and grace, her hair coiled regally on top of her head, proud of her Holland linens, the handsome English silver, the blue design of the Delftware tea service, an amply set though not ostentatious table, much of which had come with her as part of the generous Quincy dowry. Abigail marveled at the ease with which her mother poured precisely the right amount of tea into a succession of cups while gazing up at her guests and asking all the right questions about their babies, illnesses, crops and the current church needs which would make their way gradually from today's tea table to the bylaws of the congregation.

Though Abigail sensed that Weymouth was a bit awed by the stately, wealthy parson's wife, she also knew that her mother was highly regarded. If she permitted herself no close friends, neither did she indulge in favorites or enemies. From earliest childhood Elizabeth Quincy had trained herself for the exacting role of a minister's wife. Her demands on herself were rigorous to the point of being inexorable. Weymouth forgave her for her consciousness of being first lady of the community, and for going abroad in the only luxurious chaise in the countryside, because Elizabeth Smith, singlehandedly, ran a clothing factory for the poor, buying the wool herself, bringing in the needy to card, spin, weave the cloth, cut and sew garments, all in the room on the other side of the dining-room fireplace; and then took the suits to Boston to sell. She was brisk, able, devoted, giving generously of her time and energies, even as her husband tutored the poorer boys of the village without compensation.

Abigail crossed into the Mansion and saw Cotton Tufts come in with his wife, her aunt Lucy Quincy Tufts. She caught sight of John Adams before he saw her, and paused for a moment in the doorway connecting the two oddly joined houses to gaze at him. His wig was powdered, immaculately brushed and gathered tidily back behind his ears, making him look like an English judge on his woolsack. He was wearing a fine white linen collar, a wool coat and vest with long buttonholes and buttons cut with deep X's. She had never noticed him to be so well dressed before.

John Adams made his way to her with the quick, eager steps of the energetic small man, took her hand in his.

"Thank you, Miss Abigail," he cried in a voice loud enough for Cotton Tufts to hear, "for trying to get a cold remedy out of that quack cousin of yours."

"It's part of our family tradition, Mr. Adams, to help the afflicted."

He grinned at her. There was something about the way he pulled back his head that tightened his cheek muscles and gave his face, not a lean look, she admitted, not as her father was lean, but one of compact strength. There was a good deal that was attractive about his face: the strong dark eyebrows, the short well-formed nose, the disciplined mouth proportioned to the wide-set, clear eyes.

"It was Cotton who was afflicted today," Adams retorted. "He brought out his prescription books right in the middle of the roast goose and I felt impelled to tell him that some of his formulas sounded like witch's brew."

Cotton and her aunt Lucy joined them.

"Now isn't that just like a pettifogging lawyer?" Cotton demanded. "He thinks those mumbo-jumbo concoctions in his lawbooks will cure every evil known to man. But when he's faced with my scientific medical laws . . . Nabby, he has made me thirsty. Could we have tea?"

Mrs. Smith politely asked John Adams about his cold, while pouring his first cup. Pastor Smith promptly involved him in a discussion over the miserable printing of the Boston newspapers, John bemoaning the little progress printers had made since the Gutenberg Bible of 1456.

The slow dark of a Massachusetts night had fallen. The guests made their adieus, began drifting homeward, heavy cabashes tightened against a drizzle. Cotton and Lucy too, after their third cups, vanished. But not, Abigail saw, Mr. Adams. By the time her mother had poured him five cups he was the last remaining visitor. Mrs. Smith rose to her majestic height, several inches above that of her reluctant guest, and held out her hand.

"Thank you for coming, Mr. Adams. I trust you may be in Weymouth again before too long. If so, do give us the pleasure of your company."

For the second time that day Abigail found herself being disappointed. She had looked forward to another tête-à-tête with John Adams. She could not oppose her mother. But her father could. While John Adams was hastily setting his teacup on Mrs. Smith's immaculate linen tablecloth, William Smith said amiably:

"I'd like to consult Mr. Adams about some ramifications of the Weymouth Case. I know you've had a long day, my dear, and it's almost eight o'clock. Why don't you go upstairs? I'll join you in a few minutes."

The shoe was now on the other foot. Mrs. Smith could not oppose the pastor in front of company. She had been outflanked and did not like it. She bowed formally and went up the stairs.

The Reverend Mr. Smith chatted for exactly as long as it would take his wife to fall asleep, then rose and bade them good night. Abigail flashed her father an amused smile, wondering:

"How did he know that I wanted to be left alone with this young man?"

She threw a spate of lemon-colored cushions in front of the fire, sat with her legs folded under her, the lutestring dress spread about her in a circle.

"Would you like to bring in a couple of logs from the woodbox? It's on the porch behind the dining room."

John Adams brought in an armful of birch logs, indicating that he intended to remain a long time, or at least keep them comfortable. The logs were dry, quickly caught fire. Abigail motioned to a cushion beside her. He dropped down a little awkwardly, as though he were not accustomed to sitting on the floor. The flames behind the brass fender were soon high, enveloping them in their crackling light and warmth.

"I'm glad to see that your father doesn't dislike me."

"Mother doesn't dislike you. She just disapproves."

"On what grounds?"

"That you're not a clergyman."

"If everyone were a clergyman there would be no one to sit in the congregations. Is that what she wants for you?"

"Apparently my mother thinks the genteel life of a clergyman's wife is the proper one for me."

"You seem a robust young female to me," he blurted out.

She blushed at the frontality of the compliment, for his eyes had slid down her face to her bosom.

"Mr. Adams, is it allowable in law to answer one question by asking another?"

"Common procedure."

"Then don't you think that many of our disappointments arise from our forming false notions of things and persons?"

"By being romantic about reality?"

"Or by letting our imaginations impose on us. We create a fairyland of happiness out of fancy, and when we're disappointed we're not vexed at ourselves, but at the innocent person about whom we've spun our ideas."

"Does that mean, Miss Abigail, that you're unwilling to risk your happiness because life may not come up to expectations?"

"On the contrary, Mr. Adams. The person who can't bear a disappointment should not live in a world as changeable as this."

"There I agree!" He hitched his rather heavy posterior around with so much emphasis that several of the cushions under him went flying. "Where does this wisdom come from? A book? You're too young to have learned it from experience."

"Do you mean, am I parroting?" She leaned forward to gather in the wayward cushions, the firelight picking up the chestnut strands in her hair and the deep brown of her eyes. "That's a little hard to tell, isn't it, if one has consumed hundreds of volumes?"

"Honest, as well as intelligent," he murmured. Then she saw his eyes take on a bright mocking mischievousness. "At the beginning of this year I wrote a long essay of advice to several hypothetical nieces, instructing them on how to become perfect young women. Would you like to hear some of my learned strictures?"

"For your ideal girl? Yes, I imagine I might."

"One of my rules for their behavior in mixed company was that I would not have them be pedants in Latin or Greek or science, nor overly fond of talking. I suggested that when their opinion was asked they should give it, but only if they happened to know something the company was at a loss for; but they were not to turn the conversation to prattle about dogs or cats or servants, or any contemptible tittle-tattle of their own."

She threw back her head and burst into peals of laughter. He joined her, but a little wanly.

"I wrote in moral indignation that no man who is free, and can think, should rush blindfold into the arms of any such ladies who, though it is possible they might prove angels of light, may yet more probably turn out hags of hell!"

He had expected derisive laughter. Instead she felt suddenly sad, and there were tears smarting beneath her lids. She wanted to cup his round, childlike face in her hands as she sometimes did with her young brother Billy when he was hurt or bewildered.

"Is it that difficult for young men to grow up too?" she asked quietly.

"I didn't know. I thought we were the only ones who had to grope in the dark and pray that somehow we might meet a congenial soul."

7

The next word she had from him came from Boston, via Germantown, a postscript to a letter written by Richard Cranch to Mary. Writing to Mary, John Adams scrawled:

"My—I don't know what—to Mistress Nabby."

"No man more truly spoke his mind," she groused as Mary read the words to her. "He wants to send me some kind of regards, but since he doesn't know what he feels about me, what sentiments could he send?"

"Do you know your feelings about him?"

Abigail looked up quickly from the dressing table where she had been brushing her shoulder-length hair. Had she heard a note of reproof in her sister's voice?

"You're right, Mary. If I were writing I wouldn't know what sentiments to send either. John Adams interests me because he's complex."

"If you mean moody, he is that."

"Truth to tell, he hasn't grown up yet. When he does something childish he suffers."

"You're pretending to be mighty adult yourself, for someone only just turned seventeen."

Abigail had reached out for the letter. She read the rest of John Adams's message. After avowing that his good wishes were "poured forth for the felicity of you, your family and neighbors," a comparatively fresh emotion, she decided, since he had managed to conceal any real enthusiasm for the Smith clan during the two years of sporadic tea drinking, he then pretended he was jealous of her affection for their young King George:

"Although my allegiance has been hitherto inviolate, I shall endeavor all in my power to foment rebellion."

Written like a Braintree lawyer, she thought; with his emotion blanketed under convoluted, legalistic language. She was piquedly amused. Apparently his defense against young ladies was thin and vulnerable; he preferred not to expose himself to wounds. But then, she herself had expressed only the kind of interest careful young people vouchsafed to each other.

"Mary, how did you decide that Richard was the *one?* Father and

Cotton kept bringing young men to tea and Sunday dinner. When did you know that all the others were not, and Richard was?"

"Dear, you're bothering yourself unnecessarily. Love is as transparent as water. Richard and I both wanted to find someone to love and marry, and now we have. There's an end to it."

"An end?"

"There can be setbacks, of course. Richard's monopoly of the whale-oil candle market didn't succeed, but he is going to open a watch-repairing shop. Later we'll buy land and build a home as big as Grandfather Quincy's. Richard will be a deacon of the Church, a selectman . . ."

"Mary, you make it all seem so accomplished, as though it had already happened."

"We will live comfortably. Have children. Visit Richard's family in England. Accumulate beautiful things, like Mother's china and the Smith family silver. Nabby, all of this will happen to you exactly the same way."

When she was concentrating hard, Abigail pursed her lips and eyebrows.

"No-oo. I'd like to leave room for the unknown. My life may all be set down in heaven before I start it, but I shouldn't like to know every detail in advance."

"You'd suffer no surprises."

"Nor enjoy any!"

Mary pulled a warm flannel nightgown over her head, got into bed and cupped the wick of the oil lamp on the stand by her side.

"I don't mean to sound indecorous," she murmured as she worked her way down under the cold sheets, "but it's going to be a lot warmer on these winter nights sharing a bed with a husband than a sister."

Abigail could think of nothing to think about this comment. When Mary married and moved out, Abigail would inherit young Betsy in the sisterly bed. A husband in whose arms she could sleep, warm and loved, on winter nights, or any other nights, seemed a very long way off.

She was pleased to learn that John Adams had been included for the first time in the traditional New Year's Day dinner and reception at the home of her grandfather, Colonel John Quincy, patriarch of the countryside, for almost forty years the political leader of Massachusetts Bay Colony. Though he was now retired to his extensive farm and manor house, he was apparently keeping up his practice of knowing everything that went on in Massachusetts before it happened. Though John Adams had been a frequent visitor at the nearby home of the Colonel's cousin Josiah, where he had been friends with Hannah as well as Samuel and Josiah, Jr., both of them young lawyers, he had apparently never been invited to her grandfather's before.

Could her grandfather also know that John Adams had arranged to have a carriage at the Colonel's to take her, Mary and Richard Cranch to tea at his newly opened law office?

It snowed heavily all New Year's Eve, but with a late dawn a pale sun ventured out. Abigail was dressed in a new blue silk over a blue quilted petticoat, with a round neckline that did little to conceal her lovely shoulders. She wore a velvet hood over her hair. The Smiths drove in their sleigh the three miles from Weymouth to Braintree, past the two Adams houses sitting side by side in a sea of white silence on the Plymouth–Boston Road and continued on to Mount Wollaston, up a rising road lined with linden trees and a picket fence. The manor house overlooked the considerable land grant made to the first Quincy by the city of Boston in 1633. Abigail's grandfather had built this house in 1716, when he was twenty-seven, continuing to add graceful wings to his composite of all the English country houses he had admired.

Abigail's grandparents were receiving in their separate throne rooms, the Colonel, white-haired and hearty at seventy-two, in his superb library which ran the full length of the house at the rear, overlooking Boston Bay with its islands and lighthouse. From its windows the Colonel, aided by his ancient spyglass, logged in and out every brigantine, schooner, sloop and ship arriving from all the ports of the world. It was here that Grandfather Quincy, who loved politics above all other arts and professions, had taught Abigail from Plato's *Republic,* More's *Utopia* and Locke's *Essay Concerning Human Understanding.*

In the drawing room, furnished with colorful charm, sat Elizabeth Quincy. She embraced Abigail warmly, for they were confidantes and the most alike of any two temperaments in the widespread Quincy clan. Grandma Quincy had a native wit, a humor which Abigail had absorbed during her ten consecutive summers in this gracious house.

"Nabby child, there's a rumor abroad that a new young lawyer is coming for dinner. Would you have heard anything about that?"

"No, Grandma, you know Papa doesn't allow gossip in Weymouth. But I suspect Grandpa has heard about it."

"Yes indeed. He's just hoping the rumor doesn't reach your mother's ears."

They chuckled together: Grandpa Quincy had always been a little afraid of his daughter Elizabeth.

Abigail excused herself so that she could be with her grandfather when John Adams came in. He entered the library garbed in a scarlet grogram vest over a white shirt ruffled at the neck and sleeves. His light-colored, tight-fitting breeches came just below the knee, his fine white silk stockings shining like the silver buckles on his shoes. His legs were surprisingly long and well formed. He had obviously bought this outfit for the New Year's affair. His eyes were bright with holiday excitement. Her grandfather sprang up from his chair.

"John Adams! Welcome to this house. The sight of your face takes me back twenty years, when I was defeated for my command of the militia. Your good father, Lieutenant Adams, refused to serve under Joseph Gooch, who ousted me, and helped me to be re-elected to my command."

Abigail sat on a stool at her grandfather's knee while the two dozen men present, known in the Quincy family as the "loyal porcupines," plunged into a discussion of England's latest attempt to control the Bay Colony's trade. Abigail found politics a pleasurable environment. From the earliest age she had been encouraged to listen.

"Nabby, I've always maintained that man is a political animal. Can it be that woman is too?"

"Grandfather, you know the word 'man' is generic and includes woman. I've always believed that, even though Mother claims the opposite. She says, 'A man is a man and a woman is a woman, and they should never intrude on each other's sphere of activity.'"

"Your mother has a tendency to categorize. But life is not really a series of harsh alternatives: good and bad, right and wrong. Nor is there a rigid man's world and a rigid woman's world. They should overlap, intertwine. I always told your grandmother what I was doing and what my problems were. Her counsel was mostly right. Did it make her any the less feminine?"

By one o'clock the long tables of turkey and ham, venison and beef, preserved fruits, plum pudding with brandy sauce, apple cider and wine syllabub had been consumed. Richard and Mary, Abigail and John Adams slipped out quietly to the barn where the horses and snow-sled Adams had hired were waiting. Mary sat in front with Richard. Abigail found herself being enveloped in robes which John wrapped under her feet, then doubled around her.

"I promised your father I wouldn't let you catch cold."

"Are you always so attentive to duty?"

"Always, when it's pleasant. I deplore that part of Puritanism which says that a man is happiest when he is most miserable."

"Yet you once confessed that you have a capacity for making yourself wretched."

"Today, Miss Abigail, I am a pagan seeker after worldly pleasures. I've looked forward to this moment ever since I was sworn in at Superior Court in Boston and opened this first office in the house my father left me."

She felt the excitement of his voice, the timbre of pride as well.

It was a short ride from the Quincys' to Braintree, only a couple of miles. They stopped in front of the Adams houses, the one John's father had bequeathed him, and the other, occupied by his mother and two younger brothers. Abigail had often seen these two "salt-box" houses, set at an angle to each other a few yards apart, under elms and maples, at the foot of Penn's Hill. They were on the road from Weymouth north to Boston.

John unlocked the newly installed and painted door facing the road while Richard took the horses around to the barn. The girls stepped inside.

"Ah, this is beautiful," exclaimed Abigail.

"I hoped you would think so," John said quietly. "I put in that new door so clients could come and go without bothering the rest of the house."

Mary did not stop in the office but went through the tiny main entry foyer into the sitting room beyond, where she was joined by Richard. Abigail was alone in the office with John still leaning against the door he had closed behind them, devouring her with his eyes. For the moment she was absorbed only by this room and the unity and cohesiveness she found within it. She sensed that the stocky, sturdy room, a century old by now, with its freshly whitewashed walls, its old beams, heavy doors and random-length sanded plank floor, its deep brick, well-scrubbed fireplace, was a true reflection of the sturdy and immaculate man who had re-created it. This was a workroom, no question of that, desk and conferring table strewn with pamphlets, journals and sheets of paper meticulously filled by John Adams's hand.

"This used to be the kitchen of the old house," he explained when she stood before the fireplace; "before they added the leanter."

He opened the woodbox, put two four-foot logs on the hot bed of ashes from the morning fire. The dry logs caught, filling the low beam-ceilinged room with warmth and flame-light. In front of the fireplace was an oblong table with pewter cups for candles and pens. On either side were ronged, curved-back chairs for clients. On the wall opposite was John's desk with a level bookshelf at the back, a slanting top with a half-round guardrail at the bottom to hold his papers and notebooks. Above it, suspended from the central roughhewn beam, was a glass oil lamp. The wall was solid with bookshelves made from the same dark cherry wood as the furniture. This was the only room he had completely furnished, for he still lived across the yard with his mother and two brothers in the house where he had been born.

She went to his desk, picked up one volume after another as she murmured the titles aloud: *Spirit of Laws, Institutes of the Laws of Rome, Commentators on Justinian.*

"The tools of my trade," he commented.

She moved from the row of legal books to his wall of general literature. Many of the titles she knew, and some she had read, though not in their original Latin or Greek, as John Adams had: Virgil, Seneca, Cicero, Horace, Homer.

"You have a good library for so young a man."

"It is my primary need. But look at the large gaps in each field, not only law and politics, but history, philosophy, theology."

"It's interesting, the difference between you and my father. You had a whole wall of shelves put up . . ."

"I built them myself," he interrupted. "I'm a good carpenter. And one day I shall be a good husbandman, too, on these ten acres my father left me."

". . . while my father never puts up another shelf in his library," she continued, ignoring the interruption, "until he has already acquired the books to fill it."

"That's because he can afford a whole houseful of shelves, and I can't. I am pleased that you like my office."

For the first time she saw her companion in perspective. Somewhere in the back of her mind she had been thinking of him as a little man. In those nebulous images in which a young girl envisages her future love she had seen and felt a man towering over her. But John Adams, in his law office, among his books and papers and writings, dominated the room because he had stature. There were as many ways of being big as there were of being small. She was grateful to her host for having helped her make this difficult transition.

"I do more than like your office. I'm stirred. In some strange way it's more you . . . than you." She looked across the fireplace to where he was poised on the edge of a chair, asking softly, "You are not offended?"

"Only surprised that anyone could see through me so clearly."

"I don't at all pretend to see through you."

"Miss Abigail, out of this room I'm full of small talk and pretension; or I reveal myself as inflamed by ambition. Sometimes I despise myself because I have flavored everyone's food with my opinionation." He let out a long breath, leaned forward. "But here, in this room, I am a man alone, at work, who is fascinated by all thinking and writing, by the contrasting structures of the world in time and space. Do you know what Plato said? 'Studies cleanse the soul.' I'm not only going to learn everything there is to know about the law and the history of civilization, but also what the law properly must become. Here I am at peace. Yet I have not an easy moment without my pen in hand."

She sat back in her chair, her eyes dark and serious, her youthful face and slim body reflecting his intensity. She thought, "No man of his ardent conviction will remain long in Braintree."

Almost as though he had followed her thought, he said:

"There is so little to be accomplished here, as a country lawyer. All the big cases, the important issues, are fought in Boston."

"You have said that Braintree needs you."

"Yes, Braintree must have a trained lawyer to make the practice of law here an honest profession. But the cases are so petty. I go from reading Coke, Bolingbroke and Locke to defending people in tavern brawls, to suits over the price of a hat or boundaries to a cow pasture. It's a rare occasion when I can write a brief on universal principles. Like that case last August of young Prat, a fatherless child whose mother was unable to provide for him. He was only ten when she bound him over as an apprentice to a weaver *for eleven years*. His master covenanted to teach him to read, write and cipher, which he never did. Could I read you a bit of my final plea? I think it is the best I've written."

He went to the drawer under his desk top, took out a commonplace book of stitched pocket-sized leaves, protected by wrappers of marbled paper, began to read aloud in a voice filled with earnestness.

"'The law, gentlemen, is extremely tender and indulgent to such actions as these. For such is the benignity and humanity of the English Constitution that all the weak and helpless and friendless part of our species are taken under its peculiar care and protection. . . .

"'But, young Prat is to be favored for another reason: because the

English law greatly favors education. In every English country some sort of education, some acquaintance with letters, is necessary that a man may fill any station whatever. . . . We know it to be our duty to read, examine and judge for ourselves, even of ourselves, what is right. . . .

" 'The very ground of our liberties is the freedom of elections. Every man has in politics as well as religion a right to think and speak and act for himself. No man, either King or subject, clergyman or layman, has any right to dictate to me the person I shall choose for my legislator and ruler. I must judge for myself; but how can I judge, how can any man judge, unless his mind has been opened and enlarged by reading?' "

She sat back against the hard-ronged chair hearing his words reverberate inside the room. Or were they inside her heart? She began to grasp what this restless, energetic, ambitious, sometimes vain and pompous young man was after, and why he continually flailed himself for not reading more, studying harder, writing a clearer, more incisive English.

John Adams was after wisdom. That was the secret of him. Not information, about which a person can readily be satisfied, but the wisdom to understand the nature of the world and man, to transcend the particular to achieve the universal. It was a dedication, she sensed, that spelled the difference between a visitor on earth and one who meant to inhabit it. For all his shortcomings, John Adams was a man. No one, and nothing, would ever destroy that quality within him.

He studied her expression.

"You're being mighty eloquent behind those tightly pursed lips and snapping eyes. The room is full of your unspoken sentences."

"My thoughts are my own," she said gently.

"Then all we share now, Miss Abigail, is words. Perhaps when we become better friends we may share our thoughts?"

He had risen, was standing with his arms awkwardly at his sides, flexing his fingers in and out of his palms, his eyes luminous. Did he also seem like a man who was fighting back an urge to put his arms around a girl and kiss her?

She did nothing to help him or to deter him. It was up to him to know whether this was the proper time or place. As for herself, well, what girl did not think expectantly of her first kiss? She was past seventeen, she had never been courted. Was John Adams courting her? They certainly both seemed ready for something; but she did not know for what. Friendship? Assuredly that. Love? There she was not so certain.

Love had to be approached with caution. Any mistake could spell a lifetime of suffering.

He stepped back, turned away. Her eyes clouded.

"Congratulations, Mr. Adams."

"Well, he who fears and runs away will live to fight another day."

"Fight, Mr. Adams?" Her eyes were bright again. "I thought the word was hussle?"

His eyelids flared. "How would you know that term?"

"Everybody in Massachusetts knows it. It has been the cause of my father performing frequent hasty marriages."

He chuckled. "I remember the Sunday evening Bob Paine and Dr. Wendel took Kate Quincy and Polly Jackson into a retiring room. They laughed and screamed, and kissed and hussled, then came out glowing like furnaces."

"A man who spends much time gallanting the girls surely must have sometimes glowed like a furnace?"

He blushed. There was considerable cheek to become red.

"Guilty, Your Honor, but only of minor transgressions. My motto is, 'Let no girl, no gun, no cards, no violins, no dress, no tobacco, no laziness keep you from your books.'"

She thought, "This man will truly be wretched if he does not find someone who agrees that 'studies cleanse the soul.'"

A door slammed in the lean-to behind them.

"That will be my mother's Judah bringing tea. Shall we join Mary and Richard in the sitting room?" He linked his arm through hers as he led her to the door admitting to the foyer and the room beyond. "Do you know, Miss Smith, I like you in all the best ways possible. I also remember two urgent pieces of advice given to me some three years ago by Mr. Jeremiah Gridley, who had me sworn into the Inferior Court in Boston: 'First, pursue the study of law rather than the gain of it. Second, don't marry early. Early marriage will obstruct your improvement and involve you in expense.'"

She stopped abruptly, releasing herself from his grasp. Then, seeing his crestfallen expression, she realized that he had impaled himself on a heavy-handed pleasantry. She shook her head in mock despair.

"Mr. Adams, you are a most difficult young man."

"Don't be provoked with me, Miss Abigail; it's only myself I make difficulties for."

She stood on the threshold of the sitting parlor, seeing with surprise the charming atmosphere, the Staffordshire china set on the low table before the fire, with Mary leaning forward from a sofa, pouring four cups. She turned to John Adams. Their eyes probed each other's, silent, uncommunicative, searching. She thought:

"That might just possibly be true, Mr. Adams. But it's something I'm going to have to know for sure."

8

She was reading Samuel Richardson's *Clarissa: or the History of a Young Lady* when Billy knocked, then burst into the bedroom, his skin the color of an unripe lemon.

"You haven't quarreled again!"

"He won't let me quarrel. Just says, 'If I abdicated from my duty I'd be derelict all the rest of my life.'"

"So he would, Billy."

"But why is he making me horse-trade his misery for mine? He says he's got to tutor me Latin and Greek so I can pass the entrance tests for next year at Harvard. I told you, Nabby, if he forces me to take the tests I'll run away. You'll never see me again."

There was such despair written over his face, she feared he might carry out his threat. She got up, put both hands on his shoulders.

"I'll help you. Because if you ran away it would be a public repudiation of Father. But what do you intend to substitute for his program?"

"Someday I'll have money for my own farm."

"You should know Father will give up one plan only if you present him with a workable alternative."

"I just want to be let alone. Isn't that an alternative?"

"Not for an only son. We've got to shape a plan to placate him."

"Could you really do that, Nabby?" There were tears in his eyes.

"Next time Pa goes to Charlestown I'll ask him to drop me at Uncle Isaac's in Boston."

Late the following week Parson Smith announced his intention of leaving for Charlestown to inspect his parental farm and the lands he had set out in orchards. Since Abigail had spent one month a year with her uncle Isaac and aunt Elizabeth Smith, she had little trouble in getting her mother's consent to accompany him. John Adams heard of the visit through Richard Cranch. He came to tea.

"How fortunate!" he told her. "I must be in Boston for a hearing about the same time. Perhaps we could go walking together."

"I'd like to do that. Boston is so colorful, full of sights to delight the eye."

"Indeed, in Boston I find it hard to study. My eyes are diverted by carriers of wood, merchants, carts, horses, coaches, markets, sailors and my ears are so filled with the rattle-gabble of them all that I can't think long enough upon any one thing to pursue a thought. So I'll pursue you instead."

She sprang from the carriage on Queen Street, bade her father adieu and ran up the red sandstone walk lined by ancient trees to the front door of a handsome three-story house of white painted brick. She was admitted by one of her aunt's servants. She took a deep breath: this house, like her uncle's shops and warehouse, was permeated by exotic fragrances of the products brought home by the captains of his ships.

She stepped into the parlor with its rich Turkey carpet, teak wainscoted walls, heavily lacquered black chests, tables and chairs brought from China. There were tall windows overlooking a walled courtyard, a ceiling traversed by a beam encased in teak. From the center of the beam hung a multi-surfaced glass globe which her uncle told her came from Persia. In the room's convex mirrors were reflected the portraits of her aunt and uncle by John Singleton Copley. At the back of the house were extensive gardens, and beyond them the compound where her uncle Isaac kept his pets.

Her aunt Elizabeth came down the stairs, embraced Abigail warmly. She was a deep-bosomed, shortish woman with red cheeks and the pleasant manner for which her father, Ebenezer Storer, had been loved all over Massachusetts.

She led Abigail up to her own bedchamber, which she always turned over to her niece. Abigail protested that she did not want to put her aunt out of her bed, but Elizabeth derived pleasure from giving her niece pleasure. It was a plain room, with a four-postered canopy bed. The attraction for Abigail was its reading closet, into which was built a comfortable desk and bookshelves, with a window looking over the gardens and Uncle Isaac's zoo. Uncle Isaac had given her permission to keep up here her favorite books from his downstairs library, mostly personal recountings of travel, exploration and adventure which enabled Isaac to visit vicariously the countries from which he imported pitch, turpentine, cork, spices, ivory, cocoa. Here she had read Smollett's *Travels Through France and Italy*, Pontoppidan's *Natural History of Norway*, Pococke's

Description of the East, and had had her first glimpses into life in other countries and other ages.

Her uncle was an exact edition in miniature of her father, as though his parents had run out of material by the time they reached their ninth child.

"Uncle Isaac, I have come to have a confidential talk with you."

"If you're planning to open a shop or build a ship you couldn't have come to a better man."

"Other ways too, Uncle. It's about Billy. Papa's trying to make him over in his own image, but Billy's not the bookish kind. Papa says Billy must have a Harvard education. Billy says he'll run away. You managed without a college education, and you're acknowledged to be one of the most successful merchants in Massachusetts."

Isaac was highly pleased; though he loved his older brother he took inordinate pride in having done well without William's advantages.

"Now, Nabby, you're courting your defenseless uncle, which means that you want something special from me. Put your cash on the counter."

"What I'm trying to buy, Uncle Isaac, is happiness for Billy. He is so wretched at home. He's bright and honest, he could be happy here if you would take him in and apprentice him in your business."

"Does your father know you're doing this?"

"No."

"His feelings could be hurt."

"Yes, but if Billy takes off for the Ohio Valley, Pa will feel a lot worse."

"Truth to tell, I'd like a nephew to train." It was plain he was flattered by the idea that his brother William's only son would prefer to live with him and follow his example. "Though our young William and Isaac, Jr., are only six and twelve, their ma's already got them set for Harvard. Uneducated Billy and me could have a lot in common. Next time there's a contention at home, persuade your papa to bring Billy in."

John Adams struck the clapper on the Smith door shortly after noon dinner. It was a clear, crisp day, the pavement drying beneath their feet after a light rain. They walked rapidly but without haste, for they had no set plan. His arm was linked through hers, a little possessively, she thought, but she was content to have him act as her guide. Boston had been destroyed some ten times by fire. Each time it had been rebuilt with better taste and more durable materials. Now the third largest city in the colonies, behind Philadelphia and New York, it had two thousand structures and more than fifteen thousand inhabitants. Its physical formation was that of a misshapen kite, with Mill Pond on one side of the head of the kite, and the harbor on the other, the city lying broad across the mainmast, all the way from Barton's Point on the north down to Rowe's Wharf on the south, then narrowing quickly to its long tail, a thin strip of land called Boston Neck leading south to Roxbury.

At the Common they walked past the ducking stool for scolds and railers, with its little pond. The Beacon Pole towered above them. They turned downhill to School Street and King's Chapel, the first Episcopal church built in Boston.

"A factionsome people, these Bostonians," John commented. "They won't allow in Quakers, used to hang them on the Common, or Catholics, and they barely tolerate this one Church of England congregation. They'd much rather fight among themselves, finding it no doubt more pleasurable, and with fewer casualties."

One block north along Cornhill they came to Wharton & Bowes bookstore. John Adams confided, "This is where I dissipate my meager savings."

Two thirds of Boston's houses were of wood construction, several stories high, the other third of brick, substantially built and in good architectural style. The main streets were wide and well cobbled, but there were numerous narrow dirt alleys winding between them. The metropolis had long been the center of wealth for New England. Here the ships were built, sent all over the world to bring back the goods of the West Indies and the Orient, a small part of it legally declared, the major portion artfully smuggled past British customs so that profits were enormous, and great houses could rise on tree-lined Bowdoin and Scollay squares, filled with tapestries and works of art, the most expensive of furnishings.

"Can you get used to this tremendous noise?" Abigail asked.

He had to raise his voice in order to answer her, for there was a clatter of horses' hoofs on the stone pavements, exceeded only by the clangor of the cartwheels going by. Above this was the pleasant and melodious cacophony of the patent medicine peddlers crying their wares, the fishmongers hawking off of wet wagons, the farmers selling their milk out of cans on two-wheeled carts, the blackened chimney sweeps with their high, harsh calls, the town criers announcing the hour and the news, the bells summoning people to church, to meetings, to school, to fires; the clappers of hand bells being struck on both sides of the street by vendors with packs on their backs.

They continued along Cornhill Street, past the Town House to Faneuil Hall, which had burned out completely the year before, nothing but its red brick exterior walls still standing. This hall had long been the center of Boston, with shops at the ground level selling everything edible, wearable or usable; while above was the large hall where town meetings took place and every man who was "ratable at twenty pounds estate" had the right to speak his mind and vote. The rubble of the hall had been cleared out but there was no building going on except for the merchants who, promised free rent if they would rebuild their shops, were hollowing out the basement and street-level stalls.

John Adams had a whim to edge their way through narrow Damnation Alley into King Street. A few steps and they were in front of the Bunch of Grapes Tavern, where Mackril Lane came in. The shops in this neighborhood were filled with handsome merchandise, much of it recognizably English, Dutch, French, Italian, Spanish.

"Look at that magnificent coach with its six well-groomed horses and liveried servants," cried John as it tore down the street. "And over there, those men in their cocked hats and yellow and green waistcoats. I imagine London must be a good deal like this."

"It wouldn't be strange; we imitate them in all things."

"The city excites me as well as repels me. I don't think I would want to live here."

"I've often thought about it while staying at Uncle Isaac's. I'm more comfortable in a village where I know who lives in every house. I feel safe, that way. Here in Boston I might know a dozen persons, but all the rest would be strangers."

He hugged her elbow to him warmly.

"But do you know, being here with you, in this big impersonal city, is different from being with you any place else. For some reason it makes me feel closer, as though we were all alone, as you said, in a sea of strangers."

"I feel something of that too," she confessed. "It is as though you stand in a rather different light."

"Well, I'm glad the light of Boston is none too good," he grunted. "And particularly in this winding street. I don't think I show up too handsomely in the clearest light."

"We weren't talking about your features, Mr. Adams. We were talking about you as a person. If you won't misunderstand me, I'd like to say that I rather enjoy this new person with whom I've been walking through the streets of Boston."

"Yes. It's as though we have achieved some kind of intimacy that had been unattainable to us either in Weymouth or Braintree. In Weymouth I think of Miss Abigail Smith and Mr. John Adams as two quite separate persons, who come together when they can, to enjoy an hour or two of good company."

"And in Boston?" Her eyes were teasing him now.

"I'm serious. It's a kind of revelation, and a very happy one for me. I feel as though we had come to possess a little part of each other."

"Perhaps that's a good definition of friendship."

"Yes, my good friend."

"Is it possible that we could be friends? I would guess that's the most beautiful relationship in the world."

"Even more beautiful than love, Miss Abigail?"

"I don't know. I've not had love. Perhaps friendship is the core of love. Could that be?"

"It could be. Though I really know as little about love as you do."

She stopped in her path. Under the ruffle of the woolen cloth bonnet her eyebrows came together. Unnecessarily, she brushed back a strand of hair from her forehead. Her cheeks were flushed.

"What I meant to say was, if people are good friends and they love each other as well, wouldn't that friendship give another dimension to their love?"

"You mean enable it to survive difficult times?"

"Yes, I think that's what I mean. Give a man and a woman a broader base for pleasuring each other in the many phases of life."

They resumed their walk, out Long Wharf to where the volunteer Boston firemen were sending their jets of water high into the air, "putting out the moon."

"Easier than putting out Boston, apparently," Abigail observed. They retraced their steps, angled onto India Wharf where her uncle Isaac's cargo ships from the East tied up. The air was filled with smells of tar and salt brine.

"Are you getting cold, Miss Abigail?"

"I think I might do with a cup of tea."

The sun had begun to sink. She buttoned the top button of her cloak.

"That's within the realm of the possible."

They made their way south on Kilby to The Fort Street, then past the six ropewalks where crews of ropewalkers were moving back and forth weaving the heavy strands to be used in ships' riggings. Abigail had never been in this part of the town before. They walked slowly along Pearl Street into Cow Lane, found themselves only one square from the curving line of privately owned piers to which the Massachusetts merchants brought their rich spoils. They reached Purchase Street, where a substantial dwelling with gardens and orchard ran down to the waterfront.

"This is my cousin Samuel's house," he said.

"Is it?" She was genuinely surprised, for all the talk she had heard about Samuel Adams was that he was in seriously reduced circumstances. "What a beautiful property. Though a bit neglected."

"Everything is run down. That big building in the garden was the Adams malt house. Closed last year. The first Adams to come to Massachusetts, our common ancestor, was a maltster. I'm afraid Samuel is the last. He neglected his private business for what he calls public business. I told him we might be walking by. He suggested we stop in for tea."

"I should like to meet my mother's favorite ogre."

9

They were admitted by a Negro girl, with the two Adams children peering around either side of her, and a huge Newfoundland dog blocking the way. Samuel's wife had died almost five years before. The dog recognized John and led the way into Samuel's study. The desk was at the street window to admit the most possible light. Samuel Adams had become a familiar sight in Boston, his lamp burning half the night while he wrote and read, his profile clearly visible to the passer-by.

As Abigail came to the threshold of the book-lined room, its once luxurious furnishings now threadbare, Samuel rose with a hearty smile and came forward to greet her, reaching out both hands to take hers while they were still at her side. In these few seconds she saw that his hands and head shook with a kind of tremor, and that despite the fact that he was barely forty his big mop of hair was shot through with gray.

"It pleasures me to receive a friend of Cousin John's, Miss Smith."

"This is a happy surprise for me, Mr. Adams. Your cousin John didn't tell me until he had your door clapper raised."

He motioned her into a comfortable chair.

"For a time there I thought John was going to become a crusty old bachelor. I'm glad to see him gallanting the girls again."

"You're the one who needs a wife, Sam'l," John Adams rejoined.

Abigail sat studying Samuel Adams. She could see the family resemblance to John, though Samuel's nose was longer, the lips thicker, his face and neck thinner. He appeared to be about the same height and build as John and a man of considerable physical strength. She had heard him called "violent," "excitable," but he had the aura of a genial, cheerful man.

"Now, Cousin John, what woman would be so foolhardy as to marry me, in my predicament?" He turned to Abigail. "Miss Smith, you are listening to the worst businessman in Boston. When my father died he left me this house, a prosperous brewery and a third of his sizable estate. Now, only fourteen years later, I'm so poor my friends accuse me of wanting the wisdom to estimate riches at their just value."

"Precisely what are their just value, Mr. Adams?"

"A question that has confounded philosophers since the beginning of time. Cousin John, you're a lawyer. Answer Miss Smith."

"The value of riches, Sam'l, is to enable a twenty-six-year-old man to start printing a weekly paper, the *Public Advertiser*, as you did, and to fill its sheets with good political essays. I dare say the bills ran high?"

"Quite high."

"Well, one pays for one's pleasures. The value of riches is to be able to neglect your malt house and spend your hours in this delightful library contributing articles to the press about the tyranny of England . . . though I can't remember at the moment just what tyranny you were complaining about."

"You will, John," replied Samuel mildly, "when the issues arise again. But I'm happy to see you approve my poverty."

"On the contrary, I disapprove. You asked me to present your case to Miss Smith. But fearless and brilliant a lawyer as I am, I hardly think I could justify your tax-collection mechanics."

Tea arrived. Samuel smiled ruefully, swept aside a batch of manuscript pages and laid out the cups on his desk. It was a skimpish repast. John had been right: Samuel did need a wife. John took a sip of the scalding-hot tea, then turned to Abigail.

"As a Boston tax collector, Samuel is excellent in gathering the harvest from the rich. But he's much too tenderhearted to collect from the poor. . . ."

". . . who shouldn't have to pay any taxes," Samuel interjected.

"Well, you're arranging that! He uses the tax receipts from the rich to pay for the poor. Precisely how much are you in arrears, Sam'l?"

"If I could keep books I wouldn't have lost the brewery."

"Then give up this tax collector's job before you bankrupt Boston."

"How can I? That tiny salary is all we have to live on."

He was the first to laugh at the absurdity of his position. Yet, stripped as he was, Abigail had heard that he was one of the most beloved and influential men in Boston. He had formed one of Massachusetts' first political clubs to watch every move of the Crown-appointed governors and judges, and to raise opposition to whatever its members considered injustices. He was the undisputed leader of the young men of the city, particularly among the artisans and craftsmen, lending them money when he had it, finding them opportunities to advance themselves. He came by his position legitimately: his father had served Boston at the General Court, was one of the colony's strongest writers against England's usurping of colonial rights; and was a charter member of the Boston caucus which worked behind the scenes to get its own people into the political offices of Massachusetts. Samuel had been raised in the aura of controversial politics, the one parental gift Samuel had increased rather than dissipated.

As Abigail listened to the two Adamses discuss the politics of the Monday Night Club, which was attacking Governor Francis Bernard and Lieutenant Governor Thomas Hutchinson, she gathered that Samuel was basically a teacher. He taught the young people at the club; he taught through his newspaper articles; he taught at the taverns where his friends gathered at night, though he himself, a rigorous Puritan who wanted to turn pleasure-loving Boston into another Sparta, drank nothing at all. His opponents called him "Sam the Malster" and then "Sam the Defunct Malster"; yet he was so highly respected for his personal integrity that committees appointed by the Massachusetts legislature to draft papers came to the Adams residence on Purchase Street for advice, frequently remaining to have Samuel write the documents. Despite the fact that the only job he had ever filled successfully was inspector of the Boston schools, and that he faced a scandal over his tax shortages, his position in Boston was second only to that of James Otis in shaping opinion. Boston long since had learned that he was incorruptible, not only in terms of money but in rewards of position, fame or power. John had commented on their walk:

"Samuel has the greatest store of political wisdom in the colony. All of the brains and energy he would have used to make himself a great lawyer he is devoting to the study of politics."

"To what end?" she had asked, perplexed.

"To help him serve in the legislature, to become its Speaker, perhaps one day to become governor of the province of Massachusetts."

"Now, John, why would the King, or Parliament, appoint their worst opponent?"

"Because he's best qualified to know what Massachusetts needs to keep her people loyal to England and happy as colonists."

"His enemies claim that Samuel Adams will never be happy until he causes a revolution."

John's face had turned a brick red.

"Samuel has never put one line into print that says any such thing. I am a loyal Englishman. I love her law, her Constitution, her culture. I am proud to be an Englishman."

"We weren't talking about you, John Adams."

"Miss Abigail, if Samuel were preaching treason I would know it. He is preaching freedom. Mistakes are made in London as elsewhere: poor governors are sent to us because they have influence. Unworkable laws are passed because no one knows our special problems. Samuel sounds the alarm bells, puts out small fires so Boston won't burn down again."

Gazing now at this older Adams sitting behind his desk with a child leaning against each knee, saying, "Forgive me, but they get a story at teatime every day," his steel-gray eyes filled with fondness for his young, his clear strong voice bringing the characters of *Gulliver's Travels* to life, Abigail realized that a man's enemies are rarely his most objective biographers. And from the sweetness of his nature she surmised something that she could not have guessed: he was a man of piety.

He turned his gaze on her.

"Miss Smith, you've been surveying me and judging me. What decision has the court brought in?"

Embarrassed, she stammered. "No, I . . . well . . . yes . . . our private thoughts do make a noise, don't they? Everything I thought about you was good."

He turned to his cousin, said with a slow smile, "I like your Miss Abigail Smith. She meets one head on. But gently. Are you courting her?"

"According to my definition, yes."

"How is my cousin at defining things, Miss Smith?"

"Cautious . . . a little ambiguous."

Samuel laughed. "John, could she be saying you don't know your own mind?"

"No, Samuel, I think she is saying that we're both walking warily."

"I can't imagine why!" interrupted Samuel. He turned back to Abigail. "We Adamses are a loyal clan. If he should ever be bold enough to declare himself, and you foolish enough to accept, please do move into Boston so you can be near us. Cousin Adams and I could make a good team."

"At what?" John asked caustically. "Matchmaking?"

Amused at their tiff, Abigail said with a chuckle, "Your cousin and I have decided that we are country people. So, no matter whom we marry, I'm going to stay in Weymouth and John Adams is going to remain in Braintree."

"It saddens me to think that I'll never be able to give you another tea party in Boston."

It was past six o'clock and dark by the time they reached the Smiths' front door. The street was deserted at this early supper hour. They turned at the top of the stoop to say good night; stared at each other defenselessly. Then John reached out for her and they were in each other's arms. She felt his lips on hers: warm, sweet, profoundly stirring. It was long before they separated. Her heart was thumping, she could see his face only as through a mist. It was a rare silence for them. They looked into each other's eyes dumbfounded that they could possess such power each over the other. Then she stepped backward. He turned, walked slowly down the red stone path between the high trees, his shoulders hunched, covering his head protectively, weaving his way uncertainly to the gate and down the street.

She stood before the door of her uncle's house breathing deeply. After John had passed from sight she felt as though she had been staring down long dim corridors of the past, and at the same time into a sun of such brilliance that its light hurt her eyes. She murmured wryly as she crossed the threshold into the foyer:

"I doubt that my knees can get me up the stairs."

10

When she returned home everything was the same; but how different the world. Weymouth's air had a more exhilarating buoyancy; at every turn she caught some sharp moment of beauty: winter sunlight striking the stark white birches, the gulls arching overhead in scimitar formation, the houses huddling more companionably along Church Street, the earth springing resiliently under her feet. She was amused at herself: it was she who was exhilarated and resilient, who felt happy and companionable, walking in sentient aliveness.

"All this because of one kiss?" she chided herself.

Yet the intensity of her feelings had not receded; she was as stirred this very moment, brushing out her hair in quick strong strokes, as she had been at Uncle Isaac's front door, when all of life had seemed to turn over inside her bosom. Had it meant as much to John Adams, this one fierce kiss? It had been her first kiss. But he who had readily confessed to his share of hussling, had he kissed her cousin Hannah in the same fashion? Or any of the other girls of the neighborhood? After all, it was the custom of the countryside, even if being the clergyman's daughter had excluded her.

She replaced the brush on the table, stood looking into the flames of the fire Phoebe had started.

It was important for her to know just how John Adams did feel about what had happened in Boston. She felt strongly about him. She had no wish to go back to the days before that searing embrace, but neither could she expose her feelings to anyone who might be cavalier about them. She had imagined for herself a love mutually arrived at, a knowledge and emotion that seized and permeated both parties equally, at the same moment. Yet she had read enough poetry about unrequited love to know that this did not often happen.

John Adams did not leave her long in doubt. A few days later he came riding the three frostbitten miles from Braintree, arriving just after Phoebe had cleared the supper dishes. She thought she detected a raising of his brows as he caught sight of her in a dress of deep red wool cloth she had loomed herself. But it had been too fast for her to be sure, and within moments he had plunged into a political discussion with her father.

An hour passed. Rain had been falling, the sound of it insistent against the windows. Her mother rose, said, "Good night, Mr. Adams. I hope you have a cape to cover you?"

John also rose, the red from his cheeks flushing high into his temples at being so summarily dismissed.

"Now, my dear," the Reverend Mr. Smith intervened, "it's no fit weather for a man to plod three miles along a muddy road. Besides, it's early and I'm sure these young people are not as tired as we are." He turned to John. "If you don't mind waiting, it's likely to clear. I don't doubt Nabby will keep you company."

"Mr. Smith!" exclaimed his wife.

"You know where the woodbox is? Throw some fresh logs on, and warm yourself against the cold ride."

He took his wife by the arm and led her reluctant steps under the arch, through the foyer and up the stairs. Abigail sat quietly, an irrepressible smile tickling one corner of her mouth. Without looking up she said:

"Judge the size of the logs by how long you think the rain will last."

He shot her a swift look.

"There are other criteria," he murmured.

When he returned he had three stout cuts of pine in his arms.

"Going to be a long, cold winter," she said, mimicking the tone of the Weymouth farmers gazing up into slate-colored November skies.

He put two of the logs on the fire, poked at them energetically. Then he turned.

Again it happened. She had half risen from her chair, he had left the fireplace and taken a step toward her. Their arms were about each other, gripped tightly as though afraid to lose their newly found joy, their lips pressed together, hurting. She felt small held in his enveloping embrace; in his ardency he seemed to be trying to absorb all of her inside his own skin, her breasts were crushed against the muscled tautness of his chest, through the thicknesses of her petticoats she felt the firmness of his thighs.

That culminating kiss in Boston had been no accident, no meaningless trifle. Neither for herself nor for John. This was a language so clear that even though they had each other's lips locked in a twisting, twining, deeply drinking fulfillment of thirst, though her eyes were closed tight, she could see and feel that this was love declaring itself from the tops of their heads to the toes they were digging into the Brussels carpet, as though here they might take root and remain locked forever in passionate avowal.

They sat side by side, holding hands almost reverentially, on her mother's yellow damask sofa, their legs stretched toward the fire.

"When did you know?" she murmured.

"Never."

"Never!"

"I liked you. I admired you, I kept waiting for the moment when we could be together again. But knowledge? I had none."

"Then what happened?"

"I was standing on your uncle Isaac's stoop thinking what a wonderful day I had had with you, unlike any in my life. Then somebody, or something, gave me a giant push from behind . . ."

"The devil, as Phoebe says?"

"More likely God, who plans our fates in advance. Before I kissed you I was ignorant and alone. After it, I had knowledge, and we were two."

"How could you be sure? Perhaps you had only taken me by surprise. Perhaps I was gallanting you?"

"Knowledge, my adorable Abigail, transcends such superfluities. But you must have known a great deal too if you could persuade your father to sweep your mother's objections out of the room."

"My father can read my tone and manner as clearly as you read Blackstone."

"The good lady would approve me even less if she knew our relationship is slightly incestuous."

"John Adams, whatever are you talking about?"

"Us. My mother charted it through her Boylston genealogy. One of your father's grandmothers was a Boylston. That means that your great-grandmother and my great-grandfather were sister and brother."

"Oh, is that all? You had me frightened. My father says that all Massachusetts families are interrelated; and that's what makes them so cantankerous."

"You know, Nabby, I did your father an injustice. I thought he didn't like me."

After she had smiled at his use of her nickname, she asked, "Any reason?"

"Yes. My own guilty conscience. It happened about two and a half years ago, when I was having tea in this very room. I thought, 'Parson Smith has no small share of priestcraft. He conceals his own wealth from his parish that they may not be hindered by knowing it from sending him presents. He talks very familiarly with the people of his parish to gain their affection. He is a designing man.' I wrote it all down in my diary that night, in Braintree."

He rose from the sofa, stood with his back to the fire, his hands clasped behind him.

"That is the one stupid thing for which I must ask your forgiveness. I caught your father several times looking earnestly at my face. Because of the ridiculous things I was thinking, I imagined he did not care much for what he saw."

"I cannot answer for Father, not as to your appraisal of him, nor his of you. Knowing you both, now, if you will forgive my lack of timidity, I would assume they were in well-struck balance. As for your face, I like it."

He returned to the sofa. "If you like it, then I'm the most handsome man in New England. But you are lovely!" There was an exultation in his tone. "Your skin is exquisitely soft, your lips are red with the sweet wine of life, your teeth are pure white, more perfect than Copley could paint them. But I like your eyes best."

"Why? They're not specially big or liquid, like some of our New England girls'."

"It's going to take me a lifetime to answer that one, Nabby. Let's say for the moment that I love everything I see reflected there. No meanness or guile comes through. They don't make harsh judgments; they're never veiled. They warm me, their brown goodness and perception testify that life is good, and whole, and meaningful."

"Isn't it?"

"We'll make it so, dear soul."

He slipped to the floor, sat on the carpet before her and nestled his back firmly against her knees. She felt a stolidity in him, and security for their future. In his law office just a few weeks before she had not been certain. But could not love, when it came, be deeper and stronger for having had doubts, for having comprehended idiosyncrasies, shortcomings? This was the opposite of blind love: it was love with a compass. Poetry spoke of love as an enchanted oasis, where no cloud or invader could disturb one's ecstasy. What she had found was a kind of foreknowledge which would help to keep the relationship from being stripped by highwaymen. Assuredly her levelheadedness came straight out of her Puritan New England heritage: what her father called "the mature acceptance of the imperfectibility of man." Compassion was the key; and a profound sense of belonging, of the rightness of their love.

High among her feelings was the element of awe, almost of reverence for this man John Adams, who had enabled her to change from a gay, bright girl into a woman who was able to fathom the depth of passion. Time assumed the architectonic form of an onrushing symphony, of harmonies and melody that almost stopped her heart with their poignancy. The words "Love" and "God" came mystically close to being one and the same. How else could two strangers come together and solve between them the seemingly unravelable exigencies of human character?

There flooded over her a feeling of exultation. She thought:

"I have found a friend."

11

She came into a period of intense joy. Their pleasure in each other's company grew by the hour and embraced the miracle of one human being revealing himself to another in full confidence. They were not speaking about marriage, for this was the time for the burgeoning of love. For Abigail that spring was a paean to loving and being loved; lyrical days, ecstatic nights that opened new vistas of feeling for her. John Adams had told her, "My life is to be the law, not poetry." But these were poetic days, free of doubt, fear, responsibility, gloriously sun-filled.

Equally wondrous was the watching of herself revealed to her astonished self. She had entered a new world of physical excitement in which she trembled if John Adams so much as took her hand in his, put an arm about her shoulder. She knew something about the nature of physical love between a man and a woman; it would have been difficult not to, from the vantage point of a New England parsonage where so many "fornication marriages" were performed. What she could not have suspected in her own nature was how deeply she could be stirred as he clasped her in his arms and they kissed until their lips were bruised, and still their pleasure in each other remained unslaked. Every remote corner of her was magnificently aware, from the recess of her brain to the tactile tingling of her toes as John sat catercorner on the yellow sofa holding her to him, his strong, widespread fingers on the back of her head as they roamed each other's lips knowing that the basic strength of their passion for each other was so true and reciprocal that it could never diminish and certainly never end. A sense of well-being flooded over her. Whatever the years might bring forth, she knew that she would have the moral courage and stamina to match the need.

Their new relationship brought a number of changes. Weymouth began its busy rumoring about her suitor, and let it be known that it thought the Reverend Mr. Smith's daughter was courting below her station. John Adams rode over from Braintree two evenings a week, and on Saturday nights stayed with the Cotton Tuftses. They were his sole proponents.

Her home was her haven. Her sister Mary knew that she and John had fallen in love, though scarcely a sentence had been uttered about it. Mrs. Smith was giving a convincing performance of "Ignore it and it will go away." But her father knew that John Adams was not going away. Alone with him, Abigail and John felt free, without constraint, were able to hold hands and speak to each other affectionately. Her father returned their confidence by giving them refuge.

"Nabby, your mother is asleep by nine. After that hour the house is yours. Here, in the parlor. Or my library, if you prefer. All young couples should have this precious courting period alone. The only thing I ask is that you don't stay up past midnight. You must get enough sleep to stay well, or your mother will have a reason to fault me."

She put her hand affectionately on her father's arm.

"Thank you, Papa." She leaned up to kiss his cheek. "Can you know how much it means to me to have your approval? Not to have to be furtive? But I must say, my dear Reverend Mr. Smith, you surprise me. Couldn't you be excommunicated for this heresy?"

Her father's eyes grew troubled the way she sometimes saw him in the fields when she came upon him unexpectedly. He led her to the parishioner's chair across his big desk and sat down in his ministerial seat of judgment.

"My dear Miss Abigail Smith, as your pastor I have something to say to you. I could not voice my feelings in Meeting House but here in the intimacy of my study I can. In fact, as I love you, I must."

She sat still before his intensity, watched the furrows in his forehead deepen.

"It simply is not true that the Puritan disapproves of physical love, of passion between a man and woman. Neither is there truth in the thunderings from the pulpit that sexual love, except for purposes of procreation, is sinful. That it is evil, or ugly, the work of the devil, for which the participants will be fearfully punished by their conscience or their community. My dearest daughter, carnal knowledge between people who love each other is one of God's noblest works. The devil, if such there be, can debase love, if a woman gives her body for pay, or a man is aroused by intoxication or religious excess, such as we had in the Great Awakening. We Puritans are a hearty breed, though there are some who would destroy the joyous fulfillment of life. Of course I don't need to add that fulfillment must come at the proper season. After marriage you must never let your passion for each other die."

She dropped her eyes, unable to look at the unhappiness on her father's face.

"I want you to be happy in all ways, Nabby. The same act of love that creates children can continue to maintain a happy home for them. From a lifetime of reading scripture I have come to believe that this is God's will."

There were tears smarting behind her eyelids.

"Thank you, Papa."

She told none of this to John Adams; it was enough that he knew her father had given them sanctuary, sanctuary to talk quietly, explore each other's minds and spirits, and in between, as naturally as rain falls in the autumn, to fall into each other's arms as though this meeting of lips could attest to their shining worth and beauty in each other's eyes.

Once she asked:

"How many times do you suppose we have kissed?"

"I have given two or three million at least for each one that I have received. That puts the account immensely in my favor."

At midnight she walked him out into the cool starlit spring, watched him mount with the agile, compact grace of the strong little man, then slowly climbed the stairs to her bedroom filled with the ecstasy of loving and being loved.

Her sister Mary would be married to Richard Cranch in November. Until that time there could be no thought of her own marriage. Nor for that matter had John as yet taken her to Braintree to introduce her to his mother and two brothers. Occasionally he would write her an elaborate legalistic prank:

"I have taken the best advice on the subject of your billet, and I find you cannot compel me to pay unless I refuse marriage; which I never did, and never will, but on the contrary am ready to have you at any time."

He was not, of course; and she knew this even better than John Adams did. Impetuously as he was behaving in love he was totally conservative about such matters as money, a completed home and working farm, a secure legal practice before he could in all conscience marry.

"The gods must be jealous of me," he commented as summer drew on; "since I have fallen in love with you, I have fallen clean out of the courts. Oh, I have a few inconsequential writs. Now that I need money more than ever, and am making less, I have never been happier. Does that make good nonsense?"

Abigail was not in a hurry. It would be six months until Mary married. In all probability a year after that, when she was nineteen and John twenty-eight, they too would be ready. Since she intended to be married to John Adams for a very long lifetime, she cherished these carefree days.

"It means you think the world well lost for love."

"Not quite, dear soul: it means that love makes idiots out of men. Have you ever heard of a New Englander who was happy when he wasn't making money? That's as impossible as living without breathing. And just to prove how topsy-turvy my world has become I'm even spending money I'm not earning."

"Why, that is serious," she said, her eyes attempting to remain solemn while her voice mocked him. "We'll have to see if Cousin Cotton hasn't got a prescription to cure you."

"No, I prefer the fever to run its course." He gave her a sly sidewise glance. "My mind has been turning to husbandry lately. Could we ride over to Braintree on Sunday, after sermon? I'd like you to hear my plans."

The sun was hot in the hollows of the road but an offshore breeze refreshed them as they rode horseback into Braintree. John put up the horses in the unused and neglected barn; but no more neglected than the fields, Abigail saw as he led her downhill toward the creek. The house that John Adams, Sr., had willed to his oldest son had been rented until recently to Dr. Elisha Savil, whose wife was a double cousin of John Adams. The Savils had not wanted to keep up the acreage. Both banks of the flowing creek were overgrown with ginger bushes, willows, alders, dogwood and briar.

"I've hired a neighbor to cut out these bushes and burn them. After I clear that swamp down below I'm going to close it in with a stone wall and plant clover. See how poor this apple orchard is. I shall have the trees pruned, the dead stumps dug out. But first I'm going to buy posts and rails to fence against the road, the creek, my uncle Adams whose farm adjoins, and my brother Peter, who inherited our big farm."

"Fence against your brother? But you love him."

"Fences are like the law," he replied solemnly; "construct them properly and they breed honesty and justice. Every man knows where he and his fields stand. There's no chance for a stray horse or stray argument to bring on a lawsuit. I like fences."

They began to climb Penn's Hill. Halfway up they came to a spring which gushed through a crack in a large flat rock. She cupped her hands and drank of the water, finding it sweet and cool.

"It's supposed to have a wholesome quality," he told her, "because it issues from a mountain and runs toward the north."

Germantown and Hingham Bay spread out before them. White sails of small craft were visible on the water. John held her against him in the considerable breeze, and with one arm describing eloquent circles indicated where he was going to plant corn, potatoes, cabbages, where he would plant wild cherry trees because the fruit could be sold in the market and the wood to cabinetmakers. From the top of Penn's Hill they had a magnificent panorama of the islands in Boston Harbor, and a part of the city not concealed by Dorchester Heights.

"It sounds very ambitious. Won't it take considerable time? Are you a good farmer?"

"It will take time. As for my being a farmer, that was what I wanted to be when I was twelve. I loved my father dearly, and if farming was good enough for him . . . But Deacon Adams was a wise man; he made me finish my training and go to Harvard. Thanks to him I can now be a lawyer and a farmer, both. Each will lend me strength for the other; when I am tired and ill from too many books and courts I can renew myself plowing the fields."

"Very well, then, I shall be a farmer's wife. Billy showed me how to milk the cows, Phoebe taught me to make butter and cheese. I know how to salt down sides of beef and pork."

It was growing cool on the summit. They went with matching strides down the winding path, across the rickety footbridge over the creek, and through the back door of the lean-to into his office, where his mother's Judah had left pots of tea and hot water with their quilted covers, a tray with hot buttered muffins and blackberry jam. While Abigail poured, John brought down an armful of books he had recently acquired. She noted the glow of pride with which he held the volumes; how quickly he made the transition from yeoman to scholar.

In June he left to ride circuit, starting in Taunton. There was a suppressed excitement about him at the prospect of the journey, coupled with a mild melancholia.

"It's because I'm not likely to get any cases," he explained as he saw her dark eyes studying his countenance. "I'm still too young, unknown. The older lawyers will draw the clients. Yet I can learn a tremendous amount by watching procedures. There'll be little chance of sending a message, but I'll bring you back a full report."

Elizabeth Smith had yet to acknowledge that John Adams was courting or that her daughter was in love. With John gone, a good deal of the tension went out of her manner, the first unmistakable sign Abigail had had that her mother knew what was going on. And she felt contrite; the last thing she wanted was to inflict unhappiness on her family. She wished she could discuss the matter, but Mrs. Smith was not giving ground. In her opinion the battle was far from lost.

"Mother, I ought to start on my linen dowry. Mary's is complete now, and she has offered to help with mine."

"Of course, Nabby, we'll all help . . . when the proper time comes."

"Most girls begin at fourteen."

"You're still very young."

"At near eighteen?"

"It's really your health I'm thinking about, dear. All those hundreds of hours of work over the looms."

"I haven't had a cold for a year."

"Because we've protected you."

Abigail concealed a smile as she thought of how she and John had ranged the woods, climbed cliffs, spent long hours hunting, which he loved.

"In a few months now, Mary will be married. It's going to be my turn to think of a husband." When she saw the flash of pain cross her mother's usually controlled face, she leaned her head against the older woman's shoulder. "I too must have a home, and children, and a life of my own." Remembering one of John Adams's gamier descriptions, she asked, "You wouldn't want the temper and habits of stale virginity to grow on me?"

Mrs. Smith shuddered, stroked her daughter's hair over the back of the rounded head.

"No, my dear Nabby, I would not turn you into a spinster. I ask only two considerations: that you marry at the right time, for you; and the right man, for you."

"But will you trust my judgment?"

Elizabeth Smith looked at her daughter head on. Abigail pulled up to her full height, her brown eyes blazing. Had there been a mirror she would have seen that she was standing as tall and regal as ever her mother had. It was Mrs. Smith who backed down . . . momentarily.

"Very well, we'll start on your table linens and towels. Do as many as you can and we'll buy the rest in Boston."

"No, Mother. Everything that can be woven or sewn I shall do myself. So let me start weaving my sheets and pillowcases, and blankets too. If I am not to become a spinster, I must one day have a marriage bed."

Mrs. Smith turned away.

"Abigail, I know you think you are indulging in logic. But more and more you sound like a pettifogging lawyer."

12

It was a breathing spell, a time to be quiet within herself. Her thoughts were never far away from John. Nonetheless it was good to be alone for a while, to sort out her feelings after the months of tumultuous courtship; to be able to ride into Boston with Billy, help him get settled at their uncle Isaac's and watch him report for his first day of apprenticeship in their uncle's warehouse; to shop with Mary for her sister's copper pots and dishware; to spend companionable hours with her youngest sister Betsy.

She moved light-footedly about the house and farm, practicing those handicrafts she would need to manage her own home. Out in the kitchen she strung two long poles between chairs, and on them placed the candle rods from each of which hung eight wicks. When the tallow was melted in the pots she dipped in the wicks, then put them back across the poles to cool and harden, continuing to dip slowly to make sure they would not be brittle, until she had the size candle she wanted. Another day she made soap from the grease and wood ash that had accumulated, then added the proper amount of lye, letting the water and lye leak out into a tub, ending with one barrel of soap from six bushels of ashes and twenty-four pounds of grease.

Her mother helped her improve her technic of spinning flax and wool. Mary, who loved embroidering, taught her tambouring. Phoebe showed her how to make pickling fluids for purple cabbage, green walnuts, barberries, fish, and how to make her preserves so rich that they would not ferment or go sour if the paper covers were removed. Tom even showed her how to obtain quills for pens by putting a stocking over the goose's head so he would not bite. Her father trained her in salting cod and smoking ham and venison. She tried her hand at the boiling of a thick barley and beef soup, baked pies in the oven that occupied the brick side wall next to the open fireplace.

When John Adams returned some three weeks later, he too appeared to have enjoyed the separation; or at least he came home refreshed from the weeks of travel and the companionship of his young lawyer friends. They sat in a slatted swing in the cool of the back porch, facing the Weymouth hills. His lips brushed her soft hair back over the top of her ear.

"I'd forgotten how lovely you are, and what a joy to be with. Assuredly, you did not waste away pining for me. You're plump as a partridge."

"It's the tranquil life, Counselor. My father plied me with food, my mother with rest. They must have feared I was facing a rigorous winter."

"So you are, dear soul, so you are. Being in love will never be easy for either of us. But it's going to last. Is that a bad bargain to strike with the devil?"

"I shall have to consult my lawyer. Speaking of the law, how did you fare?"

A bemused smile lifted one corner of his mouth, then dropped the other.

"I earned nary a crumb."

"Since you don't appear unhappy, I'd guess you came back with some crumbs of learning?"

"Oh yes, I learned!" His voice rang out in the quiet night. "But about judges, rather than the law. It's as important to know judges as it is the statutes. Few of them have any legal training, particularly in the villages. Would you believe it, Nabby, not one judge felt obliged to give his reasons for ruling in a case? Case, did I say? I should have said chaos."

"You must take me through a day's litigation. At Taunton, for example."

John looked at her to see if she were serious. He was vivid of speech. His years of practice at writing down the events he had seen enabled him to re-create the boisterous color and clamor of the crowds gathered in town for market day: the lawyers, clients, litigants, accused all packed into stifling, boxlike courts; the constant movement of the country people with their morning's purchases in big baskets jamming into the court for the entertainment provided by their litigious neighbors. He told her about the judge who, in an allegation of riot against the King's government, had repeatedly stopped his friend, Robert Treat Paine, from exposing the King's witnesses.

"Would you believe it, that judge was unwilling that the sessions should adjourn for an hour to take the verdict of the jury, but would have had that jury kept together all night till the court should sit again the next morning?"

Though he appeared to have little law work during the summer, he did have one client: Braintree.

"The best possible client for a young lawyer," he assured her, "even though my services, like everyone else's, are free."

He enjoyed telling her about his work. The South Common had been leased over the years to various farmers, but the income was considerably less than the animosities incurred by those who applied for rentals and were turned down. Braintree also had need of continuing funds for new roads, schools and poor relief. John Adams was appointed by the freeholders of Braintree, along with two other inhabitants, to find a legal remedy for both problems.

"Our solution was simple: divide the South Common into such lots and divisions as shall be thought proper, and sell them at public vendue. The funds received to be set aside for the use of the town."

When the committee's report was accepted, John Adams was "appointed and empowered to draw conveyances and securities respecting South Common." He was pleased with himself, confiding to Abigail:

"This is good on two counts: it's the first admission by the Council that I am the only trained lawyer in Braintree. It's also a step forward to taking the place my father had as selectman. Oh, not for a year or two. I wouldn't want the older members to think I'm eaten by ambition . . . even though you know I am."

It was fall, and she was caught up in the frantic weeks of preparing for Mary's wedding, from the posting of the first bann on the publishing post through the Reverend Mr. Smith's wedding sermon: Luke 10:42:

"Mary hath chosen that good part, which shall not be taken away from her."

To the reception came a formidable portion of Weymouth: the deacons, elders, selectmen, old friends in the congregation, as well as a hundred assorted Quincys, Nortons, Smiths from all over Massachusetts. Phoebe and Tom directed a dozen serving girls who kept bringing in trays of smoked meats and game. There could be no dancing in a clergyman's house, but rum was as integral and respected a part of New England life as the salted cod; and as the bungs were blown on additional barrels the men recounted some of Suffolk County's bawdiest stories, a staple at weddings.

John Adams came to the parsonage with the Cotton Tuftses. He spent most of the afternoon keeping out of Mrs. Smith's view, then ended up by being thanked by her for saving Mary from being abducted by the young men of Weymouth. "Stealing the bride" was a favorite game in Massachusetts; if the men had got Mary to a neighboring tavern where food and drink were on the table, and musicians ready for a night of dancing, Richard Cranch would have been obliged to pay for the revelry, and Mary would have lost her wedding night. John's warning to Cranch got the couple off safely to their new home in Germantown.

"How did you learn of the plot?" Abigail asked.

"I can't expose my spy system. But I can tell you a story I heard in the room where all the gentlemen gathered 'to raise their spirits.' It was an old one of my father's that cropped up: Old Horn, a lawyer in my father's youth, made a business of jest and banter. He overtook a market girl on the Neck and asked her to let him jigg her. She answered, 'What is that? What good will it do?' Old Horn replied, 'It will make you fat.' 'Pray be so good then,' says the girl, 'as to jigg my mare. She's miserable lean.' "

When the last of the guests had parted, Abigail put on her heavy coat and walked with John to where his horse was posted. They kissed good night lingeringly. She wondered:

"Next year will I be going with him?"

13

Her father took down the partition in the girls' bedroom and moved out Betsy's cot. Betsy was a new-found pleasure for Abigail. She was an amiable child, not as stolid as Mary or as irrepressible as herself. Trailing along behind Billy as the baby of the family, Betsy had never had a chance to become close to her two older sisters. Now, moving into the four-poster with Abigail, she exclaimed:

"It's going to be nice to have a sister at last. Seems like I always had three mothers around here."

With Mary's marriage, Abigail found that the idyllic sense of timelessness was gone. She entered the lists against her dowry, a formidable packet of sheets in her disciplined handwriting which embraced everything her future family would need in the way of household goods for a solid ten years.

John Adams too became industrious, as was proper for a suitor of a girl next in line for marriage. He accepted one action of trover, another of ejectment, the probate of a will. With the turn of the year, into 1763, his journeyings into Boston began to bear fruit. He worked with the ablest of the Massachusetts attorneys, Jeremiah and Benjamin Gridley, Oxenbridge Thacher, Benjamin Kent, Robert Auchmuty, Jr., Samuel Fitch drawing up four rules to be presented to the judges so that no one would be allowed to practice in the courts who had not been sworn and licensed. He was jubilant.

"This makes our Bar a profession. It will give us a chance to establish standards of ethics as well as judicial procedures."

His elation was short-lived. He returned from Boston in the first week of February, his skin dark with frustration and rage.

"Jockeyed! One whiff of Otis's pestilential breath and our whole system was blown away."

"Your friend James Otis, who helped you get sworn in? You considered him the leader in politics as well as the law."

"Not any more. After Mr. Gridley read our rules to the court, calling them 'unexceptionable regulations, agreed upon by the Bar,' Otis rose and said he never voted for any such rules, that they were against province law and the rights of mankind. The judges threw out the regulations. Mr. Thacher spoke for the rest of us when he cried, 'Whoever votes for him to be anything more than constable, let him be Anathema maranatha!' "

She could not tell precisely when the change began, it was so subtle in nature. He was working extremely hard that spring, and if she saw him less frequently than before she knew it was because of his constant trips into Boston. He was as ardent as ever when he came to call; but all interest in a marriage date dropped out of his conversation.

Summer came on like a flash, hot and lethargic. Though John was frequently morose he was pleased when his essay on agriculture appeared in the July eighteenth issue of the *Boston Gazette* under the name of Humphrey Ploughjogger, since it was common practice to use a pseudonym. She knew that he was studying more conscientiously than ever, bringing books in his saddlebag when he came to Weymouth for the weekend visit.

She was neither a doubter nor a worrier. Since she had been in magnificent health from the instant she had declared, "I love," and been told, "You are loved," she possessed both the energy and tranquillity to walk away from any lessening of John Adams's devotion to their relationship. She gave no indication that he had come down from his high plain of ecstasy.

She knew that he worried constantly about money. Massachusetts was suffering financially following the end of the French and Indian War. Several banks had closed, money was scarce, only the most imperative cases were being taken to court.

"It isn't just that I can't seem to earn enough from the law," he replied to her hesitant question; "but that I have a dozen imperative places for every pound that comes in. The house needs paint inside and out. The leanter needs another room and fireplace at the south end. There's a sofa in the parlor and no furniture upstairs. The farm can't be self-supporting until I clear new fields, dig more irrigation ditches. Books keep arriving from England that I must buy. They're expensive, but I need them if I'm to know more than anybody else about the law. Sometimes it seems an endless road: my needs go up faster than my income."

She knew better than to solace him. This bitter process would go on endlessly, since his need to buy, to improve, to invest, to collect was as strong and came from the identical source as his need to know more than anybody else. For John Adams falling into the briars meant not merely having insufficient cash with which to eat and keep a roof over one's head; it meant not having enough money to put one's hopes for the future into effect . . . this very instant.

But forbearing as she was, he managed to upset her. One day in August when he had promised to come and visit, he failed to make an appearance or to send her a word of explanation. She worried that he had fallen ill; he had been complaining of a bad stomach, been taking vomits to purge himself and been dieting for weeks on milk and bread. But she also sensed that had he been ill he would have got word to her.

By the end of the day she was so upset that she was no longer certain whether he had said, "I will come to Weymouth on Saturday," or whether she had assumed it because he always came to see her on Saturday. She sat down at her desk in her bedroom and wrote him a letter:

"Weymouth, August the 13, 1763—My Friend: If I was sure your absence today was occasioned by what it generally is, either to wait upon company, or promote some good work, I freely confess my mind would be much more at ease than at present it is. Yet this uneasiness does not arise from any apprehension of slight or neglect, but a fear lest you are indisposed, for that you said should be your only hindrance. . . ."

She did not have long to wait for her answer. Cotton Tufts brought it on his way back from Boston. Her heart sank when she felt the formality of his tone. There was not even a salutation, the first time he had not used an endearing term. He had not come because an old friend had dropped in to spend Saturday and Sunday with him. He concluded by saying he would obey and come to Weymouth from Boston the following week.

She resented his use of the word "obey." He was going to come to her, not because no force could hold him back, but because she had commanded it! She quarreled with him inside her own head as she did her chores with quick angry emphasis. But by the following weekend her good sense had reasserted itself.

She thought nothing more of the affair and consequently was unprepared for his letter from Germantown, written in the guest room at her sister Mary's, the following Saturday morning. He had not continued on from Germantown to Weymouth because "the rowing and walking that lies between is a great discouragement to a weary traveler."

She was repelled by the artificial effort at warmth. Had it not been for his pathetic ending, "Your drooping J. Adams," she would have been sufficiently outraged to have a horse saddled, ride to Germantown and lace him down. Instead, she waited another two full weeks before she wrote:

"You was pleased to say that the receipt of a letter . . . always gave you pleasure. Whether this was designed for a compliment (a commodity I acknowledge that you very seldom deal in), or as a real truth, you best know. Yet if I was to judge of a certain person's heart, by what upon the like occasion passes through a cabinet of my own, I should be apt to suspect it as a truth. And why may I not? when I have often been tempted to believe that they were both cast in the same mold, only with this difference, that yours was made with a harder metal. . . . A. Smith."

The following week John arrived in a carriage to take her to the court in Worcester. The road was full of jutting rocks and deep holes. Abigail felt as though her head would be shaken loose. She mused:

"I hope there's no resemblance between this journey and matrimony."

Repentant, he leaned over to kiss her.

"You were right to reprove me, but an angel to do it so gently. You could have flailed me."

"I thought I had . . . in a ladylike way."

"Then please be gentle still once again."

"What about?"

"Our marriage."

"Is it imminent?"

"It's just too soon," he pleaded pitifully. "November, I mean. I need more time."

She turned a white face to him.

"John Adams, you are not a defendant. I'll thank you not to mention marriage to me again if you tremble at the prospect. I look on marriage as sacred. I have no intention of being jumbled into it on a road like this one."

"Nor will you be. I have good prospects for the winter and spring trials."

"I think we had better find our way back to love, first."

"I do love you, Nabby, and I always will, much as you shall sometimes regret it."

"I think I shall not," she said determinedly. "I never imagined you were perfect. But do you think you could droop a little less in the months ahead?"

14

They agreed on a February wedding date, only to have their plans abrogated by a virulent outbreak of smallpox. According to Dr. Cotton Tufts, the outbreak showed all the signs of being as lethal as the epidemic of 1721, when more than half of the population of Boston was infected. Out of that earlier epidemic had come some sizable good: Dr. Zabdiel Boylston, a cousin of Abigail's and a great-uncle of John's, had performed the first inoculations in Boston, spurred on by the leading clergymen, Increase and Cotton Mather, but opposed by all the other doctors in the city, as well as the selectmen, who had ordered him to desist on the grounds that such inoculations would spread the disease. Dr. Boylston, in a heroic act of faith, had inoculated his own two sons, aged six and thirteen, then some two hundred and forty others whose fear of the dread disease led them to accept his assurances. Almost a thousand who had refused inoculation had died of the disease in a few months. Only half a dozen of Dr. Boylston's cases succumbed. By the epidemic of 1752, thirty years later, more than a third of the city's population was infected, but of the two thousand who were now inoculated, the loss was so small that Dr. Boylston and the Mathers were acknowledged to have been right.

Abigail and John were having dinner with her cousin Cotton and aunt Lucy on a wind-driven January night, when Cotton made his announcement.

"An epidemic in Boston requires only a few hours on horseback to reach Weymouth or Braintree. John, you and I are in Boston every few days. We could bring the pox back here and infect everyone around us. There are two private hospitals being opened by qualified men in Boston. I'm going in for the whole treatment: inoculation, festering, diet and medicines, dry-up and convalescence. I think you should come too. Once the pox can't get me, I'll live to be a hundred."

"If you don't fall off a horse."

"Why should I fall off a horse, John? My feet reach the ground on both sides of the animal. When a man makes a poor joke about something I think maybe he's afraid. Nabby, I'm going to suggest to your father that I take Billy into the hospital same time I go."

"What about me, Cousin Cotton?"

Dr. Tufts stared at her, then muttered, "Well, no. Women don't get inoculated."

"But they catch the pox, and die of it."

"That they do."

"If it's so important for you and John and Billy and Samuel and Josiah, why not for Aunt Lucy and me?"

The doctor moistened his lower lip.

"Where would women go for the cure? The hospitals are only for men."

"I must say you disappoint me. Half of you is just as conservative as the doctors you keep fighting."

"It's true, I'm only half a hero. But even that's quite a lot, don't you think?"

She got up, went around the table and put her arms about her cousin's long, gooselike neck.

"Forgive me, dear Cousin."

John Adams had not been listening.

"You're right. Riding circuit as much as I do, I doubly need the protection. But I couldn't do it now, I have a couple of cases that have to be settled. By the middle of February . . . I'll take my brother in too. How long does the whole treatment take?"

"Depends on how cleverly you break out. Three to four weeks in the hospital, another two or three at home to convalesce, seeing nobody." He shot a quick glance at Abigail. "And I mean nobody! That confounded disease can be communicated even in its final phases."

Abigail had begun counting on her fingers, lying concealed in her lap. From his expression she could see that John Adams was also reckoning. Six to eight weeks would bring them to the middle of April.

The hospitals in Boston were filled, the number of doctors woefully inadequate. At one point the pox looked as though it had abated. Then it broke out again. Some twenty doctors were conscripted from the small towns of Massachusetts to come to Boston and inoculate.

Cotton Tufts went first, after dieting so strenuously that, as John remarked, he looked as though a puff of wind would blow him off his horse. But it was not until the thirteenth of April that John finally made the move to Boston.

"I'm sorry about all the delays," he explained. "I kept waiting to draw those writs. I wanted to put money aside for all the expenses."

"You couldn't know that they would never come to court."

"I'm not to be allowed to study or work. My letters to you will be my main diversion."

She did not realize how tautly drawn she was until she sat down to write to her cousin Cotton and report the news from the Tufts home. Her aunt had a toothache, and in any event did not care much for writing letters. She had asked Abigail to write to Cotton:

"I have been a very good girl since your absence, and visited your lady almost every day. She would have empowered me to have written to you in her name, but I told her I had no inclination at present to have . . . communication with any man in the character of a wife. Besides I who never owned a husband did not know how to address one."

She leaned back from her desk and mused:

"That isn't very nice of me. A stranger reading it might think I was complaining, which I am."

She fell into a reverie, fantasy dreaming that John Adams had not procrastinated. Was waiting a waste? It could not be, or what would happen to that wonderful word "patience"?

Their parting had been difficult, made the more so by John's troubled letters before he left Braintree. His office had suddenly become "a den of thieves and a scene of money changers." Apparently his neighbors were presenting bills on the theory that he was going to die. Only his last letter braced her. He ended it with his "esteem, love and admiration." These were words that could sustain a girl over lonely days.

Her mother was tender. Mrs. Smith came into Abigail's bedroom to find her writing. Abigail hesitated, pen suspended. Her mother was equal to the moment. She said:

"Tell Mr. Adams he has my good wishes for his safety."

Abigail impulsively threw her arms about her mother.

"You're kind and thoughtful. I love you."

"I love you too, my dear, though you have sometimes been a trifle dubious about it. I have only one favor to ask: that you make sure Tom smokes all of Mr. Adams's letters thoroughly before you open them."

"Mr. Adams is smoking them at his end too."

She began her inoculation in absentia, for John Adams fulfilled his promise to write her all the details. Dr. Perkins had used his lancet to divide the skin on his left arm for about a quarter of an inch, waited for blood to appear, then buried a thread infected with smallpox in the open channel. Lint was laid over the scratch, then a piece of rag, then a bandage. John's brother had had the same operation performed by a younger doctor named Joseph Warren, whom John described as "a pretty, tall, genteel, fair-faced . . . gentleman." They were left a quantity of red and black pills, then turned loose in the house where ten inoculated men were contained under one roof.

She sent him supplies of tobacco, fresh milk, apples. For his part he was successful in achieving "a short shivering fit and a succeeding hot glowing fit, a want of appetite," and all the smallpox he could boast of: "about eight or ten . . . two of which only are in my face, the rest scattered at random over my limbs and body. They fill very finely and regularly."

When he returned to Braintree he was locked in a room in his mother's house. It was difficult not to be able to see him, not even through a window. It was almost summer before they came together again.

He was bursting with energy, holding her securely against his chest, her head in the comfortable pocket under his shoulder as they nestled once again in the corner of the sofa in the parsonage parlor.

"Miss Adorable, first let's get the unpleasant things out of the way before we go on to the pleasant. You remember that some of my . . . well, opponents in Braintree, when I was going to Boston harassed me for money. That, and the costs of the hospitals in Boston . . . I have little left by way of tangible funds."

"Money! That's one spot that keeps refilling. Will it always?"

"No. I am going to build the most lucrative practice in Massachusetts. I have some important matters for the fall sessions of the courts. Let's begin our preparations at once. I'll select the heavy furniture in Boston for your approval. We will canvas the countryside for a good girl to come live with us and help you."

"When did you have in mind?" she asked quietly.

"Say . . . October? Late October. I'll be back on my feet by then, and we'll have everything we need to make a start."

"However you wish it."

The summer sped by quickly. Elizabeth Smith had stuck to her commitment and helped Abigail assemble her pewter tableware, glasses, bowls, silver mugs, a spinning wheel, andirons, bellows, skillet on legs so that it could stand above the ashes. John managed to scrape together enough money to choose for their north bedroom a high, covered bed, a matching chest of drawers, night table and chair, and small rugs to cover the two-foot-wide planks of the floor.

It was a difficult time to furnish a home. Goods were in short supply, for England and her colonies were not at the moment on the best of terms. In debt for considerably more than £1,000,000, in part from fighting the French and Indian War in Canada, England desperately needed money. In April of 1764 the Parliament had passed a Sugar Act, cutting the rate of taxation but setting up a customs apparatus to collect the monies.

Unhappy at this unprecedented severity on the part of its Mother Country, and concerned that its rights were being jeopardized, Massachusetts was retaliating by refusing to buy anything grown or made in England.

They had set their wedding date for October twenty-fifth. Abigail decided to spend the last couple of weeks in Boston buying her brass and copper kettles, materials for the window curtains. She would not buy any English materials because of the boycott. Neither was there very much of good American manufacture.

She received a letter from John written on September thirtieth. He had been unable to shop for the rest of the furniture because he had been called away on business, but he would send a man with a horse cart to Boston to bring back to Braintree her newly acquired possessions. He continued:

"Tomorrow morning I embark for Plymouth—with a disordered stomach, a pale face, an aching head and an anxious heart. And what company shall I find there? Why, a number of brawling lawyers, drunken squires and impertinent and stingy clients. If you realize this, my dear, since you have agreed to run fortunes with me, you will submit with less reluctance to any little disappointments and anxieties you may meet in the conduct of your own affairs. . . .

". . . My mother says that her Judah will do very well for your service . . . that she shall have no occasion for her this winter and that you may take her if you please and return her in the spring. . . .

"This last project is the most saving one. And parsimony is a virtue that you and I must study. However I will submit to any expense for your ease and conveniency that I can possibly afford."

It was obvious that he had fallen into a funk again and was frightened. What was he so miserable about, with his disordered stomach, aching head, anxious heart? Despite his frequent dietings and complaints he was as sturdy as an oak. What had happened then could only be that he had not earned as much money as he had hoped for. She sensed that had he had the courage he would have asked for another postponement, oh, for only, say, three or six months! Then assuredly he would have enough money. But this time too many arrangements had been made; he could not do so without hurting her. His pain was evident in every line of his letter, despite his expression of how sorely he needed her:

"Oh, my dear girl, I thank heaven that another fortnight will restore you to me, after so long a separation. My soul and body have both been thrown into disorder by your absence, and a month or two more would make me the most insufferable cynic in the world. I see nothing but faults, follies, frailties and defects in anybody lately."

The problem posed by his letter was the need for her to take his mother's maid, Judah, for the winter. They had been over this question before. Abigail had pointed out, quietly but firmly, that it was not a good idea. She could not retrain Mrs. Adams's girl to do things her way, the time was too short. She did not want to be beholden to Mrs. Adams for a servant; nor did she want in her house a girl who would go back and forth carrying tales. Judah would rob Abigail of her independence. She preferred to dispense with a servant altogether and do her own work until they could afford a good girl, like Rachel Marsh, who was a capable young woman seeking a permanent home.

John knew all this. He had agreed with her reasoning. Yet here it was again. Of course she would submit; this was not a matter to quarrel about.

The next day she received another communication, criticizing in harsh terms her exchange of his bureau and table for more expensive pieces. She sat down at the desk in the alcove of her aunt's bedroom. She loved John Adams, but she knew that she had to be frank and stern with him now:

"Boston. October 4, 1764—I am much obliged to you for the care you have taken about help. I am very willing to submit to some inconveniences in order to lessen your expenses, which I am sensible have run very high for these twelve months past, and though you know I have no particular fancy for Judah, yet considering all things, and that your mama and you seem to think it would be best to take her, I shall not at present look out any further.

"The cart you mentioned came yesterday, by which I sent as many things as the horse would draw. The rest of my things will be ready the Monday after you return from Taunton. And—then, sir, if you please, you may take me. I hope by that time that you will have recovered your health, together with your former tranquillity of mind. . . . A few things, indeed, I have met with that have really discomposed me; one was having a corrosive applied when a lenitive would have answered the same good purpose. . . ."

The letter placed in hands that would see it delivered, she went to bed, her teeth chattering with chill. Her aunt called in Dr. Joseph Warren, of whom John Adams had spoken so highly. Billy sat by her side trying to entertain her. Her cousin Isaac, Jr., a handsome fifteen-year-old, with fine blond hair, a sensitive face and beautiful green eyes, read to her in French. She enjoyed the music of the language, though her head was too hot to follow all of the meaning. Her uncle was intensely proud of his son, a brilliant student who had already announced for the ministry. When Isaac, Jr., had left the room, her uncle remarked with a pleased twinkle in his eye:

"I know it's bad manners to gloat, Nabby, but my brother William with all his education begets a son who hates books. Now me, without enough learning to pickle in a barrel, I get me the clergyman your father yearned for."

She obediently took Dr. Warren's pills and felt sorry about his frustration over the cause of her illness, which he could not find. She felt weak and low-spirited; she had lost considerable weight.

"Nabby dear, don't you think we should send word to your parents?" her aunt asked. "And have them postpone the wedding?"

"No, Aunt, I'll be better."

"But it's so close now, only a couple of weeks. Dr. Warren doesn't know what you've got."

"I know what I've got. And I will find a way to cure it. It was foolish of me to fall sick in the first place."

She had let John's despondency, his funks and fears, overwhelm her.

Her mind went back to the first day she had become interested in John Adams. She had been writing a letter to her cousin Hannah about the scarcity of her "sparks." She had recalled the line from Dr. Young's poem, "A friend is worth all hazards we can run." She asked herself, rather woefully:

"What hazards are open to me?"

Well, she had learned.

BOOK TWO

THIS THORNY BREED

1

SHE lay snugly in her four-poster with its ball-fringe curtains half closed to keep them warm against the drifting December snows. She could watch the flakes falling through the crack she had left open in the curtains of the far window, opposite her bed. The central beam of the low ceiling, stained to match the fireplace panel, ran straight above the middle of the bed to the window, which seemed like a porthole admitting to the white night. Pressing deeper under their protective quilt, she thought how much this bed was like a ship, sailing on its private sea to new ports.

It was past midnight and John was asleep, breathing rhythmically as she lay cradled against his back in the center of the big bed, her arm affectionately about his shoulder. Her head was high on the bolster and pillow; past John she could see the last logs he had put on the fire, burning brightly. Above the fireplace was the graining of the wooden panel she had discovered under a half century of smoke and blackening, and had stained a deep gray-green in harmony with the tile of the hearth. On the side walls were matching chests, over which she had hung English hunting prints. On either side of the bed there was a low dressing chair, and a night table with its candles and the books they had been reading before they went to sleep.

This bedroom was particularly precious to her, though she loved every foot of the cottage. She had learned from neighboring families in the six weeks she had been married that she was not the first Abigail to live here; she was the third since the original two-room cabin had been built on this spot in 1680.

"Nor, for that matter," she thought, "do I intend to be the last."

Behind her, in the corner, was the borning room, which she had turned into a small study and office for herself. Here she had placed the French escritoire and the mahogany bookcase her father had built for her, her forty volumes arranged neatly by category: Uncle Isaac's gifts of travel books, Grandma Quincy's novels, *Pamela, The Life and Strange Surprising Adventures of Robinson Crusoe*; Grandpa Quincy's political tomes, Machiavelli's *The Prince*, Bolingbroke's *Idea of the Patriot King*; her father's collection of sermons; and her selections on American history. She had modeled her study after her aunt Elizabeth's alcove, finding a similar curtain for the single window that overlooked the back yard, the well and pump, the barn and the turnstile leading to the older Adams house where John had been born. It was a snug retiring room where she could leave her letters, household accounts and books spread open on her desk.

She could not sleep for sheer happiness. She marveled at marriage, which dissolved the accumulated strains and restraints, the sense of standing still while moving through vacant time. The fulfillment of their love had been more meaningful than she could have dreamed. It had had in it elements of the sublime, and had soared, a magnificent blending in which spiritual ecstasy had been born of the marriage of the flesh. A man and a woman who loved totally were multiplied by infinity. It was one of life's gifts, this tender and profoundly stirring physical passion which each night swept them far out to sea on the hurricane that engulfed them; and then, the storm spent, allowed them to drift slowly, gently back to shore, to the protected cove where they could lie quietly at anchor, falling asleep in each other's arms.

Her thoughts went back to her wedding day. The second daughter in a New England family labored under the same difficulty as a second son; the first son went to college, the first daughter was tendered the big wedding. It was not that her parents could not afford to give Abigail as luxurious a wedding; it was simply considered unnecessary, in fact, not good form. There would be almost as many people invited, almost as much food and drink. But the exuberance, the hilarity, the proof that one could and would give a superb wedding party had already been manifested.

This Abigail had not minded. She had dearly loved Mary's wedding and had been content with considerably less by way of celebration. What she had minded was that, though the church was filled with her relatives, friends and neighbors, the feeling of delight at the marriage, present at Mary's ceremony, was missing from her own. Everyone wished her the best of fortune, but there remained the intimation that the attractive, high-spirited Miss Abigail Smith had not done the best for herself.

Unpredictably, her father's wedding sermon had gone askew. He was preaching from Luke 7:33, 34 and 35. When he read, "For John the Baptist came neither eating bread nor drinking wine; and ye say 'He hath a devil,'" there was a muted gasp, a craning of necks and turning of heads. Was the Reverend Mr. Smith excoriating them for not accepting John Adams? Or was he agreeing with them? The clatter of unspoken thoughts bounced off the bare wood walls.

John stirred, turned slightly. She leaned up on one elbow, peered down at his face, thoroughly relaxed in sleep. She recalled their conversation just before he had dropped off.

"How is Judah working out?" he had asked.

Judah was not working out at all; the girl did the scrubbing of floors, clothes and pots reasonably well. She resented being sent back and forth between the two houses. Abigail had learned that Judah had been the cause of a row between John's parents when his father, in charge of the town's poor, first brought the orphan girl home to live. She had no intention of perpetuating the tradition.

"Oh, she'll be all right," she had replied.

"Do you remember the girl, Rachel Marsh, you liked so much? I saw her guardian yesterday. Seems he has to bind her out to strangers."

"I had hoped she could stay where she was until you were ready. . . ."

"No need. I was wrong. I should not have forced Judah on you just to save a few pennies. I've already told my mother, and Rachel's guardian. We can bring her home after preaching tomorrow. Once I recognize an error I like to rectify it as quickly as possible. From now on, Mistress Adams, I'll practice the law and let you practice housewifery."

She had kissed him warmly. In this first contretemps of their marriage she had steered her craft successfully through a choppy channel.

"It's strange, all the things a man can find to worry about when he's approaching marriage," he said. "If I listed them for you, they'd run the length of a legal brief."

"Perhaps the man does the worrying before marriage and the woman after."

"Are you worrying?"

"I'm so happy it frightens me."

"For six years I tried to persuade Braintree that the purpose of a lawyer was not to cause trouble but prevent it or, at the very least, straighten matters out sensibly. I marry you, and overnight people believe me. Since being married to you I have the strength that I lacked in my fumbling, ill-poised years. Sometimes I'm hard pressed to understand the strange creature that I was. How odd that you should have loved me."

"I saw through your prickly shell."

"You were the only one who did."

"Could we perhaps say that marriage has agreed with you?"

"They say my thorns are pulled, that marriage has filed down my abrasiveness."

He held her to him with an affirmation so intense that it choked her, whispered against her ear:

"Because you love me, I love myself."

"Because you love me, I love myself," she repeated.

2

She awakened at first light, a thin slab of pale winter slicing in from the opening in the curtains at the east window. The house was silent about her. She loved it at this early moment when she could move unseen and touch things affectionately, inanimate objects that were peculiarly her own, walls, tables, silverware toward which she would be embarrassed to show affection after the workaday world was stirring.

The clapboard salt-box house with its single roof and brick chimney was only half as large and commodious as her parents' Mansion in Weymouth. Her father and mother had, unbeknown to each other, given her substantial gifts of money, her mother's offering being the larger of the two. There were also "sweetening" gifts, £5 or £10 from numerous aunts, uncles and cousins. But she was holding tight to her money. Braintree might take offense if she spent too lavishly or completed her furnishings too quickly. She was eager that her new neighbors accept her. The alterations she wanted to make, the several key pieces of furniture, were still in abeyance. Yet from her first entrance into this home as Mrs. John Adams, she had taken the modest cottage to her bosom with a fierce pride.

Warm in her padded blue banyan, a ribbon holding her hair which was pulled back from her forehead in a loose braid, she put a fresh log on the fire so that the bedroom would be warm when John awoke, then made her way down the narrow, sharply curving pie-shaped stairs, with their dangerously exposed edge from which one could fall onto the floor of the tiny foyer. Even on these steep stairs she danced her way up and down a dozen times a day.

In the lean-to kitchen the coals of the fire were still live under their fine coat of ash. She dropped on kindling, then two logs from the woodbox in the corner. When the water was warm she washed her hands and face with the scented soap her uncle Isaac had included in what he called his "round-the-world" packet for her new home.

The kitchen was a fairly new addition, long and narrow, its wood ceiling sloping sharply from the height of the inside wall to only seven feet where it met the wall facing the back yard. There was an eight-foot fireplace for cooking, with two baking ovens buried in the side bricks. The fireplace was splayed to throw the greatest possible amount of heat into the room.

This was the one room in the house which a bride was permitted to furnish to its last necessary detail. Abigail had installed her iron potato boiler, her forty-pound, fifteen-gallon pot for boiling vegetables, fry skillets, waffle iron and toasting forks, all with long handles; her oversized teakettle and gridiron; warming pans with covers, one- and two-quart skillets; brass and copper chafing dishes; the stumpy-legged bake-kettle, to be placed among hot coals; the dutch oven, open on the one side toward the fire, with its little door at the back; the "bread peel," a long-handled shovel and rack which she used to place food in the oven, kept by the oven side; and in the corner of the fireplace a group of three-legged trivets to raise or lower the pots the desired height above the coals.

She enjoyed the handling of her new copper pots and cranes. She frequently burned her fingertips, and needed practice in singing the hymns which were used as sound-dials to determine when eggs had been boiling for exactly three minutes, or a piece of beef had broiled over hot coals for four minutes. Yesterday morning she had sung the eight verses of the fourth Psalm too slowly and John's soft-boiled eggs had come out hard. The only clock in the house was the tall one in the sitting parlor.

John came into the kitchen looking sleepy, his hair rumpled, using his right index finger as a bookmark where he had stopped reading the night before. She cut a steak off the smoked ham in the cooler closet, placing it in a fry skillet as John lifted her hair by its ribbon and kissed the back of her neck. He dropped into a cane-bottomed chair next to the fire and watched her mix the batter for muffins, then slide a pan of them into the brick oven and begin to hum the lullaby which she would finish as the top of the muffins turned a golden brown.

"During the years I was a bachelor I vowed every night I would get up at dawn and read. Next thing I knew, the sun was on my face. Now that I'm a respectable married man I find myself studying *Institutes* by candlelight at six o'clock of a freezing winter. Could that be because I have an ambitious wife?"

"Or a noisy one. I always drop that bedroom log a little ostentatiously."

"Hardly necessary, my child. The instant you leave my bed I wake up lonely and forlorn."

"I haven't noticed you summoning me back lately."

"Well, a hot breakfast on a cold morning is one of the delectables of life. I find myself settling deeper into the role of a pampered guest. I welter in self-congratulations at my wisdom in having married you. . . ." He looked up at her wistfully. "And wonder why I waited so long."

"May I refer you to your own story of B. Bicknal's bride? 'In the morning she was amazed, she could not think for her life what it was that had scared her so.'"

She brought over to the hearth the drop-leaf table which opened as capaciously as a plump matron's bosom, when there was company, but closed as slim as a fifteen-year-old girl when there were just she and John to sit over a quiet meal. After breakfast they returned to their bedroom, made comfortable by her extravagance of the early morning log, and began dressing for meeting. Abigail wore her new velvet cloak and hat, long white gloves and goloe-shoes over her calimancos with their thin paper soles. John, who had shaved from a pewter bowl in the kitchen, proudly donned his shantung wedding vest as well as his broadcloth coat and breeches, the warm cotton stockings and the shoes with the shiny silver buckles. The last thing he put on was his white tie wig.

"It changes your character," she complained, looking him over. "Makes you look . . . official."

Holy walking on Sunday morning in Braintree was a gregarious exercise. The bell started ringing in time for those parishioners in the farthest house to reach the church, and it rang continuously until services began. Out in the Coast Road, which ran for five miles through Braintree, the Adamses joined the Seth Manns, and Veasey, the blacksmith. The snow crunched noisily under their high boots as they overtook the Samuel Curtises, while ahead they recognized the Fiske family, their closest neighbors to the north; and the families of the Millers, Cleverlys and Apthorps. Their movement up the road was like that of a swelling army, with a new group joining them every few yards, each with its squad of freshly scrubbed youngsters frisking ahead and shaping snowballs which they were not permitted to throw on the Sabbath.

Abigail exchanged greetings with her new neighbors, her arm linked possessively through John's. Braintree was her town and her home now; the phrase in the wedding ceremony "forsaking all others" had, alas, included her beloved Weymouth. It was only a three-mile journey between the two towns, but as far as allegiance was concerned it was equal to a journey of three thousand miles across the Atlantic.

There were subtle differences to which Abigail had to accustom herself. Weymouth was a natural boundary community: nine miles of narrow ribbon land, with Great Hill at one end and Dense Woods at the other, Mill River emptying into Great Pond, and Great Oak Hill above Duxbury Trail. Braintree was artificial; men had made it by putting rulers on a map and drawing four straight lines, a quadrangle except that its south base was too short and the line heading north, which ended at the abandoned ironworks on Monatiquot River, shot off on a right angle, leaving the northeast open to the waters of the inlets.

Their own house was only the distance to the top of Penn's Hill away from the man-made line which separated unsettled South Braintree from the well-populated North Braintree, where their Adams kin and friends lived. The two Adams houses were the last down the elm-bordered road toward the South Precinct line. Immediately above them was the Eleven Mile Stone, measured south out of Boston; then the Fiske house, across the road from which was Christ Church and the Episcopal burying ground. In a broad eddy of the road was their own Meeting House, beyond its burying ground, and across the road, the schoolhouse. A couple of hundred yards below was the town landing. Where the Coast Road swung sharply to the west were the Hancock house and Bass Tavern; on the road to the east, toward Mount Wollaston, were the Quincy mansions.

Braintree was twice as large as Weymouth, with some twenty-five hundred inhabitants, prosperous shipbuilding, fishing and tanning industries. She found it more worldly, with one of the largest general stores between Boston and Plymouth, the sign in the window advertising "Everything from a Paper of Pins to a Glass of Rum." The Braintree church was considerably larger and more solidly built than her father's Meeting House in Weymouth. The interior walls were painted. The Reverend Anthony Wibird's pulpit was spacious, with a comfortable chair, nothing like her father's "hanging pulpit." John Adams, Sr., had sat for years with his fellow deacons in the row of "old venerable heads on the forebenches." There were seats for men and women who came alone, divided by the center aisle. The main pews were sold or rented according to the prominence of the family and the amount they could pay. The ownership of a pew was one of a family's most valuable possessions. The Adams family's pew was to the left of the pulpit. The Reverend Mr. Wibird, standing above her, was a tea-drinking companion of John's.

What might have been a difficult transition came easily to her nature, stepping down from the position of first family of Weymouth to the modest social standing of the Adamses. The fact that her grandparents, John and Elizabeth Quincy, were the leading family of Braintree, and had been for forty years, raised her status not at all. When she married an Adams she became an Adams. Braintree expected her to behave like an Adams: modestly, as befitted her position. This was the reason she had not yet used her "sweetening gifts" of cash to put a railing on the pie-shaped stairs, a window in the storage room at the east end of the lean-to, or planking under the two open vaults of the cellar where she stored her preserves, salted meats and fish, cider and Madeira. It was also why she kept part of her dowry of linens and silver under cover, and asked John not to buy the corner "bowfat," a buffet she sorely needed for the sitting parlor.

After preaching they visited on the cold steps with their fellow parishioners, then made their way back south on the Coast Road. This time it was John Adams who held his wife's arm possessively against his blue wool greatcoat.

"Nobody needed their footwarmers or muffs in meeting today. The glow on your face flooded the Meeting House like an August sun. That congregation can be crotchety to new people, wives in particular. But the very way you walked into meeting and sat up so proudly, with your ear cocked a little to one side so you wouldn't miss a word of Wibird's sermon: he's been giving the identical one from Ecclesiastes 9:12 for years: warmed their hearts . . ."

"And their feet?"

"Much more difficult in December! . . . with the knowledge that you were proud to be a permanent part of Braintree. You probably earned me three law cases this morning."

"Now, John, you're not supposed to be mercenary on the Lord's Day."

They went directly from meeting to John's mother's. The members of his family had considerately given her a month to settle in, even though she had put the welcoming latchstring of the back door on the outside each day. But this was her day of arrival. She could tell from the meticulously set table in the old kitchen, now the dining room, even as their own old kitchen had been converted to John's law office; and by the tantalizing smells of celebration food seeping out from the lean-to kitchen: turkey, a savory dressing with roasted chestnuts, sweet potatoes baked in the back of the fireplace, cherry and pumpkin pies.

"Can I help, Mother Adams?"

"Things are mostly ready. You be the hostess for the boys."

The "boys" were Mrs. Adams's three sons. It was the first time Abigail had heard a note of affection in her mother-in-law's voice. She stood quietly studying the older woman, putting together the fragments she had heard about Susanna Adams, a Boylston by birth, who had been thought to be marrying beneath her when she chose John Adams, a farmer, cordwainer and shoemaker, the Boylstons being one of the first families of Massachusetts, with considerable property in Boston.

Susanna Adams was fifty-five, of medium height, on the portly side, with iron-gray hair, a youthful complexion and gray eyes steady and wide. Abigail had gathered that although John was fond of his mother he had felt the stronger allegiance to his father. He had once referred to his very first, bungled case, which he knew he should not have undertaken because he did not have the experience to draw the writ properly, as something he had been pushed into by the "meddling and cruel reproaches of my mother." Apparently Susanna Adams had fretted over money; although her husband was a conscientious worker, adding to their holdings, he could never achieve the status Susanna Boylston had married out of. John Adams, Sr., had been deacon, and captain of the Braintree militia, a selectman. Yet in the end, for all of his services and success, Susanna Boylston Adams too had come to believe that she had married beneath her station.

They sat down to dinner, the five Adamses, Peter Boylston in his father's place, saying grace and carving the turkey with a rugged doggedness, a heavy-built man, three years younger than John but appearing older because of a deliberateness of speech and manner. He had had three winters of learning in the Braintree public school. Once John went off to Harvard, Peter became his father's helper; strong, plodding, faithful, unresourceful. His thirty-five acres were beginning to show the first faint signs of running down. Twice in the first month of their marriage Abigail had heard John talk to Peter about new methods in husbandry, but Peter had said:

"I do everything like Pa done. That's good enough for me."

John commented to Abigail, "So it might be, except that he hasn't my father's natural feel for the soil. I try to give him the best information, to make up for his lack of instinct."

"But his acres can support a family?"

"He won't be able to save or buy new land. I've always felt guilty about this confounded primogeniture we borrowed from England. I get all the education I can use, and Peter gets little. It isn't fair."

"We must never allow that to happen to our sons. We must manage carefully so that even if we have half a dozen boys there will be funds enough for all to attend college."

His eyes flashed pleasure.

"An Adams dynasty, eh?"

John felt closer to Peter than to anybody in the family. That was why he had worked so hard to get him elected deputy sheriff of Braintree. Peter was also earning small cash sums by serving John's writs and those of John's lawyer friends in Boston.

The youngest Adams boy, Elihu, was twenty-three, lean, fast-moving, restless, excitement-loving. He had already moved out of the homestead to be independent, and was living in a cabin on the ninety undeveloped acres his father had left him in South Braintree. Elihu was entertainingly voluble. This Sunday he intermingled stories of Thankful White, who had agreed to marry him the following year, with tales of how he had joined the militia, made an estimate of its officers, and knew precisely how long it would take him to work his way up to a commission as subaltern.

Abigail let her eyes roam about the table. How different the four Adamses were, one from the other. And if Deacon Adams had still been here he likely would have been different from all the others. But wasn't that equally true of her own family in Weymouth? She wondered whom her own children would resemble, the Adamses and Boylstons, the Smiths and Quincys? Or perhaps a new breed made up of bits and pieces of the generations of Adamses and Smiths who had been born, married, had children, worked and died all within a few miles of each other.

3

From the first morning of their marriage there had been horses hitched to the post outside John's office, Braintree folk mostly, but her relatives too were bringing him legal matters. Her grandfather Quincy summoned him to Mount Wollaston to take over a badly muddled will; her cousin Josiah Quincy, though he had two sons who were lawyers, brought in a deed involving the sale of lands, remarking to Abigail when they were alone:

"Now that you have become an Adams, we have to make John a Quincy. That's how we box our family loyalties."

Her uncle Isaac sent word from Boston that he wanted John to write an agreement with some English exporters from whom he was buying. When John went down for the January court in Boston he was sought out by his old Braintree schoolmate, John Hancock, who had inherited his uncle's fortune and trading empire, and asked to straighten out a tangled shipbuilding affair. With Isaac Smith and John Hancock for clients, several other merchants asked John Adams to draw writs for them and argue before the court.

It was a gratifying beginning. Though the fees were modest, Abigail now felt free to use some of her own money on the house. By studying its structure she found that the original cabin was composed of the room that John now used as his office, with a six-foot fireplace, and a small chamber behind it. No cellar had been dug under this older part of the house. Along about 1716 two carpenter grandsons of the original settler had extended the front to include the parlor, and built a second bedroom upstairs as well as an attic.

John bought the lumber she required. She hired a carpenter to put a floor under that half of the cellar where she stored her foodstuffs. This finished, she built the railing to protect her stairs, then had a window cut into the east wall of the little room next to the lean-to, where Rachel Marsh had been installed. She built a buttery into the other end of the lean-to, and a cooler through which the cellar air could rise and keep her foods fresh. She replaced the small units of leaded glass in the second bedroom with larger panes, had the floor scraped, and then painted the fireplace mantel and the walls a bright color. Since John hoped to hire a hand to farm their nine acres she closed in half of the raftered attic to use as a bedroom.

These renovations completed, she bought a maple bed and bureau for the second bedroom, a set of comfortable chairs for the parlor, and recovered John's old sofa in a robust yellow fabric. She also acquired a deep, comfortable chair for John to read in before the sitting-parlor fire. At this point he appeared to be growing restive about the expenditures, so she stopped.

Money, between a husband and wife newly married, she discovered, is unexplored territory. Abigail had not had any money of her own because she had never needed any. Everything becoming to her life and station had been provided by her parents. She had not handled money herself, but she had learned from her mother what commodities should cost, and had often sat with her father while he painstakingly set forth his daily accounts: the expenses for building his barn, close to £300, with the itemized costs of three thousand nails, so many thousand shingles, feet of boards . . . and three gallons of rum to hearten the builders. Between his notation of how many children had died of the white throat distemper, and a quotation from a Hingham lecture which contained his lifetime philosophy toward religion, "I shall show the folly and madness of an intemperate zeal," she learned the price of ink powder, the cost of binding books, washing and shearing sheep, of tea, corn, rye, wheat, a load of wood (her father had paid with a load of hay).

She knew little about John Adams's income and family resources. He seemed constrained about revealing his savings. Evidently no one had been privy to his affairs before, and surely he had never let anyone else spend his money or have control over it. She recognized and respected his hesitancy: New England men fastened their pocket purses with garlands of thorns. Their larder was filled with wedding gifts of smoked hams and salted fish, barrels of apples and kegs of Madeira. She had little need of cash to buy the day-to-day necessities. She was prudent, spent from her own monies only after discussing the improvement with John.

John liked what he saw.

"Ladies are generally poor at money matters. But I'm not sure I'd want to get involved with you in a horse trade. I might come out with a lame nag, blind in one eye, the way Brother Cranch did with Greenleaf."

She knew he was teasing, but she replied, "I'm not shrewd, John, it's just that I come from a long line of successful merchants and landowners. They always lived well, but they were never known to spend a pound when they could make do with shillings."

He took her in his arms, kissed her fondly. "What a lottery marriage is! But we have to watch closely, to see how much we want for the house, for the farm, for savings. Let's keep our cash here, in this locked drawer of my desk, except what you need for the daily kitchen. At the end of the year we'll add it all up, cash on hand, money spent to live, to improve the house and farm, to buy what we need. I like to keep a daily account of ideas I've taken in. But fees? I don't think so."

Abigail was surprised. This was unlike him. She looked at him with eyes as brown as the rich spring earth. How much about John Adams had she truly learned during the courtship years? For the first time she fully understood the line from Benjamin Franklin's *Poor Richard's Almanack:* "Men and melons are hard to know."

Well, wedlock was as good a place as any to begin.

John came up from Boston after the end of January court quivering with excitement.

"You have been appointed chief justice of Massachusetts?"

"Even better. Come, sit by me and warm me. My blood is ice. Soon after I got to Boston, at the change of court, Mr. Fitch came to me and said that Mr. Gridley had something to communicate to me but I should keep it in sacred confidence."

She poured him a steaming cup of chocolate.

"When I waited on Mr. Gridley in his office he said he was determined to bring me into the first practice, and Fitch too."

"Oh, John, Mr. Gridley is the most respected lawyer in Massachusetts."

"He told me that he and Mr. Fitch proposed a law club, a private association for the study of law and oratory, and that he was desirous of forming a Sodality of himself and Fitch and me and Joseph Dudley, in order to read together. He loaned me Godefroy's *Corpus Juris Civilis.* We met the next night, agreed to begin our studies with the feudal law and Cicero's orations."

"It's like a law school. What you have wanted so desperately."

"We've agreed on a study schedule. We're to exchange our books, each buying volumes we lack. I'm going into Boston for a meeting every

Thursday. I tell you, Nabby, I expect the greatest pleasure from this Sodality that I ever had in my life."

She kissed him heartily to make up for an involuntary pang of jealousy.

"You haven't been doing much writing lately. I was getting worried that marriage might make you too concerned with fees."

"My conscience has been smarting. But out of this Sodality I'm certain to get some good legal papers."

Even Abigail was amazed in the ensuing months at the scope of his interests. He had always studied the background of each case that came to hand; now he was confronting not only the history of Western law but its philosophy, trying to get to the basic theories which underlay the statutes; how the laws had been shaped, developed, changed in their journey down the centuries and civilizations.

Each Friday when he returned from Boston, where he had stayed overnight with the Samuel Adamses, or his old friends John Hancock or Jonathan Sewall, she got a detailed account of what had transpired. He was not a hermit scholar who locked himself off in his study. When her chores were finished he called her into the office, or brought his books into the warm kitchen, spread them over the open-leafed table before the fire while she read or sewed, looking up occasionally to quote Rousseau, who called the feudal system "that most iniquitous and absurd form of government by which human nature was so shamefully degraded."

When he grew fatigued from his studies he read aloud from Shakespeare or Milton, because he and Gridley had agreed they hoped to see the Bar, as a consequence of this Sodality, achieve a purity, an elegance and a spirit surpassing anything that had appeared in Amcrica.

"I hope some part of that will come true, Nabby, because I'm beginning a dissertation on canon and feudal law. It's never been written in this country."

She met the optimistic gleam in his eye with one of her own. A third month had passed, and she was now certain. She was in circumstances.

"I'm certain you're coming into a creative period. In fact, you're already in it. I have a surprise for you."

He looked up from his copy of A *Treatise on the Social Compact* and asked with a shy smile:

"What makes you think it's a surprise?"

"How could you know?"

"You told me."

"I did no such thing. I didn't even tell my mother when the family rode over from Weymouth last week."

"I knew the instant you did. Your eyes. The first month they gazed at me with adoration. Then a new element crept in: awe. It was as though I had suddenly assumed Godlike proportions."

She laughed deep in her throat, a madrigal that burst out of her when she was deeply content.

"Are you happy about it?"

He put his arms about her, kissed her gently.

"I'm very happy . . . with everything you do."

"You took the news calmly. Is that because it's the common fate of brides to be extended?"

"I take all important things calmly. It's only the unimportant that throws me into a furor. Now listen quietly while I read you something I have just written, so that our first child may be born with a fine prose style."

His voice was high and unmusical, but he was reading sentences of such intensity that she shivered.

" 'The struggle between the people and the confederacy . . . of temporal and spiritual tyranny became formidable, violent, and bloody. It was this great struggle that peopled America. It was not religion alone, as is commonly supposed; but it was a love of universal liberty, and a hatred, a dread, a horror of the infernal confederacy . . . that projected, conducted and accomplished the settlement of America.

" 'It was a resolution formed by a sensible people, I mean the Puritans, almost in despair. They had become intelligent in general, and many of them learned . . . but they had been galled, and fretted, and whipped and cropped, and hanged and burned. . . .

" 'After their arrival here, they began their settlements and pursued their plan both of ecclesiastical and civil government in direct opposition to the canon and the feudal systems. . . .' "

He looked up at her.

" 'I always consider the settlement of America with reverence and wonder, as the opening of a grand scene and design in providence, for the illumination of the ignorant and the emancipation of the slavish part of mankind all over the earth.' "

She sat beside him, her eyes gazing back upon him, thinking:

"He is a species all to himself. My life will never be dull."

4

It seemed to Abigail that John too was in circumstances, growing heavier with work each day. Now that he was rising at five each morning to write by candlelight, extending and revising the scope of his essay, the Braintree Town Council appointed him to a committee to divide and sell the North Common. He and two neighbors, Niles and Bass, hired surveyors and chainmen, working for several weeks.

"We've been rambling over rocks and ruts, through swamps and thickets, but finally we made our division and made the lot plan. One night next week we're going to handle the auction mallet ourselves as vendue masters, and we hope to sell everything. I have two lots picked out for us, and part of the Rocky Run pasture."

She went to the auction in the Meeting House. People came in from miles around to bid and buy. John did a good job with the mallet, then turned it over to Bass and Niles while he wrote the deeds, collected the monies and made sure the bonds for the remaining payments were collectible. Her distant neighbors, some of whom she had not yet had an opportunity to visit, congratulated her as she left the Meeting House.

"Are they congratulating me because I'm in circumstances or because you sold every last lot?" she asked.

"Both. I couldn't do your job, and you couldn't do mine."

They enjoyed another minor triumph. John was elected surveyor of highways by the town meeting, a dubious honor, since Braintree's factions had been rowing about their roads for several decades. The problem, explained John, was as simple and ancient as man. Nobody wanted to pay the taxes to have the roads rerouted, repaired, kept in good condition.

"Or rather, they can't agree on who should pay what share of the taxes. The Pennimans use the roads to haul their crops to market, and their heavy wheels cut them into ribbons. The Thayers use only a light carriage. The Allens ride only horses. The Billingses are on foot, to attend town meeting or visit their friends and relatives."

She watched him go about solving his problem in terms of his own character rather than Braintree's; collecting the highway laws of the surrounding towns, the one from Weymouth secured by her father, those from Milton, Hingham, Dorchester. He inquired in the several towns which part of their laws worked and which parts did not, analyzed

Braintree's particular needs, then wrote his own proposal. When he offered his statute it made such solid sense that the town gave him unanimous approval.

She teased:

"How does it feel to be a lawmaker?"

"I feel such a flow of spirits as I've rarely known. To write a good contract or will, that's gratifying; but to write a good law, that a town can live by, that's magnificent. I hope I have many opportunities to write laws. When they work they're as precious as poetry."

"Won't the public weal call for new laws every season? No one will be able to put you down."

But she was wrong. Someone did.

It was Samuel Adams who carried the calamitous news up from Boston, bringing with him his bride, Betsy, and a portmanteau for staying overnight.

Abigail was staggered by the changes in Cousin Samuel. When last she had seen him he had been shakily slow-moving, though still under forty. Samuel was now dressed in a neat coat and breeches, was wearing a modest wig, his linen was fresh even after the ten-mile ride from Boston; but more important, he moved and spoke like a vigorous youth. The tremor was almost entirely gone.

After she had installed them in the second bedroom, Rachel brought in tea. They sat chatting in the lingering April dusk. Abigail asked after the children.

Samuel looked fondly at Betsy.

"I swear, Abigail, this larcenous wife of mine has completely stolen my young."

"Now, Sam'l," murmured his wife in her plain, pleasant voice, "extravagance is afforded only to the rich."

"And who is richer than I? Lieutenant Governor Hutchinson? John Hancock? Abigail's uncle, Isaac Smith? Preposterous!" He turned to Abigail, his radiant smile lighting the sitting parlor. "I've married a witch. In these months of marriage I've earned precious little, you'll allow me that boast, yet Betsy has decked us out in new apparel; the house is painted, the furniture has new coverings."

Abigail turned to her new cousin-in-law. Elizabeth Welles was twenty-eight. She came from a family of mechanics and had had no dowry, which explained her late marriage to an impoverished widower with two children. Betsy's plainness was of the most attractive kind; scrubbed, clear skin, hair pulled back severely from her brow, features that clearly stated they had been set in her face for functional rather than decorative purposes: a short, abruptly angled nose through which to breathe, frugal lips with which to talk, irregular though gleaming white teeth with which to eat. But ah! those eyes, thought Abigail, they are not merely in Betsy's countenance to see with, they are there for all to look deep into her soul and know how dear and precious this woman is.

Samuel thanked Abigail for the goodly tea, then got down to business, the reason why he had ridden up to Braintree to spend a couple of days with his young cousin: a packet had arrived in Boston Harbor that morning, thirty-four days out of Liverpool, with an official copy of the Stamp Act passed by the Parliament.

John cried, "I can't believe it! The Parliament hasn't the right to tax us for their revenue purposes. They know that better than we do."

"Not any more, John. Here's a copy of the London paper with the full Bill. Read and passed three times. Now the law of the Empire. Every clearance paper of a ship that enters or leaves our ports must have a stamp on it. Every newspaper issued must carry a stamp; every almanac, pamphlet, sheet of writing paper; every indenture, apprenticeship, bill of sale; every writ served, will signed, or decision handed down in the courts must have the proper stamp affixed to be legal. The stamps, printed in England, are on their way here."

John's face was ashen. When he finally broke the fury-laden silence, his voice was as hoarse as though he had been shouting inside himself.

"That means we either give Britain the right to absorb more and more of our earnings, until we have been reduced to serfs; or we refuse to buy the stamps, closing down our shipping, manufacturing, the selling of goods, publishing, the seeking of redress or justice in the courts."

"The courts!"

"Yes, Nabby. If we refuse to buy stamps for the papers needed in court processes, the courts will have to close. Without courts to enforce the law, there is no law, no matter how many guards patrol the streets. And without law there can be no organized society."

"You still have nine acres," she said, trying to lighten the mood. "Parliament can't stick a stamp on every turnip that sticks its head above ground."

Betsy flashed her a grateful smile. The men were sunk too low to be amused.

"Well then," she said resignedly. "John, didn't Prime Minister Grenville protest for a full year that he did not want a Stamp Act, that we could raise our assessment in our own way? What went wrong?"

"Everything," replied Samuel Adams, "and nothing. It's part of the struggle that has been going on for a long time, and will never end. That is, until we put a stop to it."

"Now, Sam'l," John admonished, his first shock wearing off. "Let's go back to the Writs of Assistance, and James Otis's speech against them. That was in February of '61. Seems to me it began then."

The Writs of Assistance were part of the mercantile theory under which England governed its Empire. England wanted all of its colonies to be secure and prosper; but first and foremost England had to grow rich and powerful. All raw materials and manufactured goods had to be shipped to England before they could be sold elsewhere in the world. They also had to be reshipped in English bottoms with English crews. Massachusetts could produce raw materials, ships' masts, iron or leather, but could not manufacture woolen cloth, hats or steel. Thus England, under its Navigation Acts, controlled the trade of the American colonies and of Massachusetts.

As compensation, England provided her colonies with bounties to produce things wanted in England: masts, hemp, pitch, indigo, and protected them from the French in the north, the Spanish to the south.

The system had worked extraordinarily well. The mercantile controls had never been considered as taxes. In Massachusetts the Molasses Act of 1733 was winked out of existence, at worst costing the shippers 1½d. per gallon to bribe the customs collectors when the smuggling got difficult. Wages were high, work was plentiful, profits were gratifying and, if any man grew tired of Massachusetts, there were millions of virgin acres to the west, free for a man's taking. Few bothered to quarrel with their prosperity or ask embarrassing questions . . . except Cousin Samuel, of course, gazing on them now with canary feathers on his lips.

"It worked after a fashion," Samuel said, taking up the thread, "until the end of the French and Indian War in '61. The year you fell in love, my dear young cousins, and began a new era for yourselves, marked the end of an old era for Massachusetts. For America, actually. When England defeated France and secured Canada for herself, she decided we should help pay for the costs of that war, as well as the costs of maintaining ten thousand of her soldiers here. That's when they decided to enforce their duties. But how did we illiterate Bostonians spell the word 'duties'? T-a-x-e-s. And we refused to pay them. For the first time since the Pilgrims and Puritans set foot on Massachusetts, men asked, *'Have they the right to tax us, free Englishmen, without our knowledge and consent?'* "

"But they didn't make it work," John replied. "I was in the Council Chamber of the Town House when James Otis rose to attack those Writs. It's a day I'll never forget. A great fire in the hearth, and around it the five judges in their robes of scarlet English broadcloth, large cambric bands and tie wigs; Lieutenant Governor Hutchinson at their head as Chief Justice, at a long table all the barristers at law in Boston." He smiled self-consciously. "I was twenty-five, the youngest barrister there, and fairly bursting with pride. Otis had accepted to plead for the merchants. Great fees were offered, but Otis cried, 'In such cases I despise all fees.' "

He bounded up from his chair. "Let me get the notes I took that day. Otis stopped the British from meddling with us for two years."

John returned to the parlor.

"Otis was like a flame of fire as he started off. 'This Writ is against the fundamental principles of law. An act against the Constitution is void. An act against natural equity is void. Special Writs to search special places may be granted to certain persons on oath, but I deny that the Writ now prayed for can be granted. It is directed to every subject in the King's dominions. Everyone with this Writ may be a tyrant. A tyrant in a legal manner also may control, imprison, or murder anyone within the realm. . . .' "

John set his papers down. Abigail rose, went into the kitchen to help Rachel get supper started, then she brought in a tray with four glasses of Madeira, toasting Betsy and Samuel and diverting the subject from politics.

But only momentarily. They went to preaching the next morning, where Samuel sang out in his charming voice the hymns he loved. He was strict in his religious observances; prayers had to be read before each meal, passages from the Bible read with the children at bedtime, the Lord's Day spent in meeting. Perhaps it was his new bride, perhaps the zeal he showed in singing and reading scripture after the Reverend Mr. Wibird, but the Braintree congregation, which only a week before would have looked on Samuel Adams as an incendiary, today stood on the steps to ask concerned questions about the Stamp Act. Why had the Prime Minister changed his mind and forced it on the colonies? How seriously could it hurt them?

As the four Adamses walked home, Samuel said with a chuckle,

"That's a new role for me: consultant on the acts of Parliament. Mighty pleasant."

"You're taking an unconscionable lot of pleasure out of our troubles with England, Sam'l," Abigail commented.

Samuel took little enjoyment from answering a question directly. The oblique approach gave him an opportunity to entertain himself.

"Increase and Cotton Mather had all the fun in the Puritan pulpits. Boston was prostrate at their feet. What can a Congregationalist clergyman tell a congregation in these times? Be pious, stay away from balls and feasts, don't deck yourself out in finery like a whore . . . Sorry, Cousin Abigail! No, all the diversion has gone out of being a preacher. Politics is going to be the most exciting profession in Massachusetts for the rest of our lives."

"Betsy, take your husband in hand," John chided, "and tell him we're not seasoning our roast goose from his political pepper pot."

Betsy smiled. "Samuel, my dear, let's be good guests so Cousin Abigail will invite us back again."

Rachel had moved the table into the parlor before the fire, opened it to its widest, and set it with Abigail's best dowry linen, glasses and silver. The four cousins sat together in family comradery. But after the hot apple pie, and with the men's pipes stuffed with Virginia tobacco, Samuel went back to the purpose of his visit.

"John, I need your counsel. As a lawyer, I mean."

"Sam'l, I'm happy to see you're keeping business in the family."

"How can we best defeat this Stamp Act? By disobeying it? By smuggling our papers without the stamps? Or by closing down every business that requires the stamps?"

"They'll never enforce it, Sam'l. It will disappear, like the Writs."

"You're being shortsighted. These acts are only effects. The basic causes of conflict remain."

"What conflict?" asked Abigail. "My father always said we're the best-governed colonies that history has ever known."

Samuel rose, began pacing her Turkey carpet.

"Granted. We have been. For two reasons. When England attempted anything we didn't like, such as the Molasses Act, we smuggled past it. When she tried to make us pay an annual wage to her Crown-appointed officers, we categorically refused. She was too busy and successful in her trade and wars of conquest to bother about us. She indulged us as we do our bright but spoiled children. But we've grown up. England has gone heavily into debt to drive the French out of Canada. She's going to insist that we share the cost. Most important, this new King and Parliament are determined to do something not attempted before."

Abigail took the bait. "What is that?"

"I will tell you. They are finally determined to set forth their legal rights and constitutional powers over us. This, my dear young friends, will be fatal. To them, not to us!"

Now John was perturbed. He sprang up, jerkily began pacing in front of Samuel.

"Sam'l, that's fighting talk. We've always allowed Britain its legitimate rights: the right of their Crown-appointed governors to negative our elected officers for the Massachusetts Council; to tell us in whose bottoms we could ship; to have our fish, lumber, raw iron sent only to them, and to buy our finished products only from them. We've grown, we have no poor or unemployed, as London has . . ."

"Cousin John, sit down, I'm the one who gets roiled about politics. You are the calm objective barrister. Granted. Three thousand miles of ocean made it easy and respectable to shrug off their oppressive laws. But what happens now that Parliament is determined to tax us, not on our world shipping and trade, but on our *internal* affairs? What about the Stamp Act? Suppose you agree to pay England a tax for every legal paper you draw, and they keep raising the tax each year . . . ?"

"We won't pay it! Parliament has the right to regulate our external trade, as it does for the entire Empire. It cannot tax us without our consent. Only the colonies can tax themselves."

Samuel licked his lips with the tongue of polemics.

"Parliament says the tax will be only a small amount of the cost of maintaining their troops to protect us . . ."

"We can protcct ourselves. We have our militia."

". . . only a small part of the cost of driving out the French and opening the whole American continent for settlement by our people."

"We had soldiers on the Plains of Abraham too. Now, Sam'l, stop goading me. England has never tried to tax us without our representatives agreeing to the tax. We'll let no outsider tax us."

"Why, Cousin John, how can Mother England be considered an outsider?"

"You both stop goading each other," cried Abigail. "This is our first family visit, not a political debate."

Several of the young couples of the neighborhood came in to tea. Abigail sat at the head of the table, looking up and talking to each of her guests as she expertly poured the right amount of tea into each cup. After tea Samuel and Betsy thanked them for a lovely visit, invited them to come and stay with them in Boston, and left.

On the way up to their bedroom Abigail asked John:

"Can Samuel be right?"

"No-oo, I don't think he's right. Or at least not wholly. We are children, as he said, and children are subject to discipline. But we've lived alone so long now, and governed ourselves so well, we won't take kindly to harsh controls. Yet England has the best government on earth; her politicians would not be so foolhardy as to stir up a tempest."

"I think Samuel wants trouble. Or am I misjudging him?"

John's eyes turned dark. "What we call trouble, Samuel calls freedom. He's agitating for freedom."

"From what?"

"England."

5

As the weeks passed and she grew larger she let out the cord on her wrapper. She found it strange but exhilarating to feel life inside her. The movements became stronger, occasionally one of them would hurt, but she was more than compensated by being able to watch the kicking of her child. Her only discomfort was when she tried to sit upright in one of their cane-bottom chairs. She solved this by settling tailor-fashion on the sofa, her legs tucked under her as she had when she used her bed in the Weymouth parsonage for letter writing.

In the cool of the morning and evening, when John was riding circuit, she went for a walk across the fields and down the creek, sometimes with John's mother or brother Peter. Everyone was kind to the point of solicitousness. Her own family came to visit: her parents, Mary and Richard Cranch, her sister Betsy.

When she grew too heavy to move around easily she sat with a book or journal on her lap, unopened, trying to read the future instead of the past. It was a time to wait, a woman's time. She had moments of panic when she wondered if she would know how to care for the baby if it got sick. What if it weren't born normal, if it had eleven fingers or toes? But she was healthy, young, she felt loved and important. The fearfulness vanished. During the calm happy days she pondered how to raise the child. She wanted it to be independent, but she realized that both she and her husband were strong characters who would impose disciplines on their young. They would be good students, male or female, she was sure of that, who would be trained to take their proper place in New England.

She did not miss John when he rode circuit or spent the night in Boston at a meeting of the Sodality. It was a period of tranquillity similar to the first time he had gone circuit riding after they discovered their love for one another, an interlude in which to gather one's hopes and energies for the next onslaught on life.

Her thoughts were interrupted by the sharp tattoo of the clapper being raised and dropped against its metal plate in the front door. She opened it to find James Otis and his sister, Mrs. James Warren, standing on the granite platform below her doorsill. She recognized them at once, for John had described them in his picturesque images.

Mercy Warren introduced herself, said, "My brother and I wanted to meet Mrs. John Adams."

"What a happy surprise. I was just wondering with whom I was going to drink my dish of tea."

"So were we," said Otis with a laugh. "We've jolted the ten miles from Boston. Is John at home?"

"No, sir, he is not. But please allow me to offer you the convenience of his home."

She led her guests into the parlor. James Otis was forty, had been married for ten years (some people said he had married out of loneliness over the marriage of his sister Mercy) and had three children. Mercy was several years younger, the wife of a prosperous Plymouth planter and mother of four sons.

Having made her guests comfortable, Abigail instructed Rachel to bring in a spacious tea. Then she sat herself opposite the brother and sister, observed that nature had seemed to reverse its normal procedure, making James the more attractive of the two, with strong features in a broad, oval face, high, rolling brow, eyes wide-spaced and brilliant, proportionate mouth and chin, an alert, perceptive intellect that showed through his every expression. Mercy was tall, flat-chested, inclined to angles where her well-padded brother had an amplitude of curves. She had the same high brow, but it was over-dominant in her more slender face; the nose was too long and thin. Her eyes were large and luminous.

James had permitted Mercy to share his tutoring by their uncle, considered an erudite man in Massachusetts even though he had inexplicably gone to Yale for his education. After James was graduated from Harvard, he had taken his sister under his wing and reviewed with her Raleigh's *History of the World.* At her brother's insistence Mercy started writing poetry, essays, drama.

James Otis was mercurial. He wrote and published prosodies in Latin and Greek as a scholarly diversion from his exacting legal and political tasks. But no one could ever know what bizarre act or self-destructive folly to expect from him next. His wrecking of John's hope to establish a standard of legal ethics had been totally senseless and had brought down on him the bitterness—temporary, for all feelings about James Otis had to change as abruptly as his moods did—of the New England Bar. In some circles he was known as "The Walker" because he walked out, inexplicably, not only on the Massachusetts General Court and Boston town meeting, but on parties of his chosen friends in his own family residence in Barnstable. He was also a brilliant polemicist, writing pamphlets, newspaper articles, speeches against the Crown officers whenever they impinged on colonial liberty, which in James Otis's opinion was every time they so much as breathed.

Abigail poured the Lapsang souchong, a smoky tea which her uncle Isaac imported, and passed the trays of hot buttered muffins and little cakes. Otis then plunged into an analysis of the Stamp Act, as perturbed as Samuel Adams had been.

"We are obliged to shift the centrum of our thinking. Up to now we have tacitly agreed that England has the right to regulate our external trade but not our internal affairs. Now all such distinctions have proved to be spurious. Without giving us a proportionate number of representatives in Parliament they have no right to legislate over us in any way. Once we grant that right, *and we never have!* we are lost. It's too late for Americans to become a slave race. Almost a century and a half too late! Freedom is an intoxicant, far more powerful than rum. We are verily addicts in Massachusetts."

He rose, excused himself to visit a nearby client, and left Abigail and Mercy alone. Abigail was happy to become acquainted with Mercy Warren. Although the female Quincys were sent to Dame Schools, and continued to read poetry and novels, none of them had developed the fascination for politics which Abigail had inherited from her grandparents. Mercy Warren was the first woman she had met, aside from Grandma Quincy, who found politics exciting and who had been trained to write.

"Not writing for the sake of art," Mercy explained. "Writing to be useful. If James says he cannot reach the people with his pamphlets, then I'll try to stir them through a poem. If he has no way to dramatize the wrongdoings of Governor Bernard I can present him as a character in a play. Then all who read will know the nefariousness of his conduct."

"And see him portrayed on the stage?"

Mercy was quiet for a moment.

"Alas, no. The Puritans of this colony will never allow a theatre with actors. You were too young to take notice, but our General Court passed an act back in 1750 to prevent, and I remember the wording of the law, it was so painful to me, 'the mischief of stage plays and other divertisements which encourage great expense, discourage industry, tend to increase immorality, impiety and contempt for religion.' Mrs. Adams, have you ever heard such horrendous nonsense?"

She did not wait for a reply.

"With all our great English plays available, Marlowe's *Dr. Faustus*, Ben Jonson's *Alchemist*, Shakespeare's tragedies. I would hate to sound unpatriotic, but do you think we Puritans left some of our good sense back in England when we took ship?"

"The witch hunts in Salem proved that we could create a more burdensome religion than we fled from."

"Abigail, have you tried the pleasures of writing?"

Abigail flushed.

"I will confess that I take great joy from filling a blank sheet with ink and lines."

On his return from circuit, despite the hot June sun, John's face looked peaked.

"Have your cases not come on?" she asked.

His eyes flashed. "Indeed! I gained my cause, much to the satisfaction of my client. The Plymouth Company has engaged me. I've agreed to come every year to the Falmouth Superior Court to handle their law."

"What a lovely present to bring home. The Plymouth Company has a great deal of causes."

He sprawled in his big chair before the cold hearth.

"You know how I am charmed by travel: it raises a flow of spirits in me. Those roads in Maine! Where a wheel has never rolled from creation! From Falmouth to Pownalborough is a wilderness, encumbered with the greatest number of trees. My horse kept flouncing and blundering among the roots and stumps. When we did arrive anywhere there was no inn, just a house offering a bed or two for a half dozen of us, and fresh out of rations."

"All heroes arrive home lean and hungry. Our cellar is full of nourishment, and although you'll still have to sleep three in a bed . . ."

He seemed to look at her for the first time. A few moments before she had untied the tight bow at the nape of her neck and shaken her hair loose about her shoulders; the westerly sun, shining through the windows, lighted its variety of rich browns. He buried his face in its abundance, murmuring how good it was to be home with her. He kissed the corners of her mouth, then her eyelids, quoting from *Poor Richard:*

"'A ship under sail and a big-bellied woman are the handsomest things that can be seen!'"

Rachel came in with a pitcher of apple cider. He drank thirstily as he told Abigail of his stop for a meal at Samuel's house in Boston before riding the last leg up to Braintree; of the possibility that Benjamin Edes, who owned the *Boston Gazette,* might publish his essay on canon and feudal law. Of his meeting James Otis, who had congratulated him on his choice of a wife. Otis's own wife was the imperious daughter of a wealthy merchant, close to the Crown officers. She despised her husband's activities, called them vulgar and treasonable. They were not treasonable, but some of Otis's and Samuel's ideas were radically new. "Think of it," exclaimed John, "they have persuaded the elected Massachusetts Assembly to issue an invitation to the other twelve colonies in America to meet in a Congress to evolve a scheme to stop the Stamp Act."

Abigail was impressed.

"A Congress? Has that been tried before?"

"Once. The Albany Congress in 1754 to help fight the French and conciliate the Indians." He told her how Benjamin Franklin had set forth the Albany Plan for the thirteen colonies to have a voluntary general government, with each electing delegates but retaining its own authority over internal matters. The federated government was to have the power to levy taxes, build forts, purchase Indian lands, raise an army . . .

"The King and Parliament killed the plan?" she asked.

"Alas, so did we. Each colony was afraid its independence would be threatened by the others. But this plan of Sam'l's and Otis's is so simple, it's a stroke of genius! The other colonies are all equally stirred up.

You see, Nabby, England has never treated us as subjects before. If we act together, the Parliament and Ministry will retreat. If we're going to prevent them from behaving like bad Englishmen we have to act like good Englishmen and keep the Empire free."

"I understand," she answered gravely. She was surprised to find tears smarting behind her lids. "Our child has to be born a free Englishman. That's the most honorable title the world has to bestow."

Samuel and Otis had come up with a second ingenious scheme: to create Committees of Correspondence, groups of Massachusetts men who would write letters to people in the other twelve colonies with similar interests, even though they were strangers, stating the case against the Stamp Act in the strongest possible terms, sending pamphlets and articles from the *Gazette*. The recipients would be urged to answer, and to write of their own accord to men they heard about in other colonies, fellow clergymen, merchants, shippers, doctors, lawyers, craftsmen, to build a network through Massachusetts, New Hampshire, Rhode Island, Connecticut, New York, New Jersey, Pennsylvania, Maryland, Delaware, Virginia, North and South Carolina and Georgia, of hundreds, ultimately of thousands of men who wanted to prevent the destructive bill from becoming law.

And, before the month was out, still another plan.

Working behind the scenes, they had brought together a group which called itself the Loyal Nine. It was a committee formed for action. What action? No one was sure. The time and the needs would dictate the pattern. Otis and Samuel could not belong because they were elected members of the Massachusetts General Court. The Loyal Nine, in addition to Benjamin Edes, who would afford them the voice of the *Gazette*, were solid men, prosperous shopkeepers and skilled artisans who had never been engaged in controversy. Their headquarters was at Chase and Speakman's distillery on Hanover Square. Their meetings, like the Letters of Correspondence now beginning to crisscross the colonies, were secret.

John agreed to attend a meeting the next time he rode down to Boston.

6

Returning from holy walking, Abigail set the dinner table in the parlor, laying out her best linen tablecloth and napkins. Jonathan and

Esther Sewall were coming to visit. This was the couple who had broken in on John and Hannah Quincy when John had been about to stumble into an unpremeditated declaration of courtship. Esther Quincy was Abigail's cousin, twice or thrice removed, Abigail was not good at figuring the removes, six years older than Abigail. Jonathan, seven years older than John, was one of John's dearest friends, going back to his schoolteaching days in Worcester.

They were a beautifully matched couple, Abigail thought, as she opened the door to them, and exclaimed over Esther's draped gown of flowered jade silk brocade, with shoes of the same fabric. Esther and her sister Dorothy, who was being courted by John's schoolmate, John Hancock, were the beauties of the Quincy family. She was vivacious, had an infectious sense of fun-making, and, though she confided to Abigail that she had not read a book since she fell in love with Jonathan, was nevertheless a shrewd observer of human antics. Jonathan had taken to the study of law rather late, yet he had become one of the ablest lawyers in Massachusetts, building a lucrative private practice. He had also found favor with the Crown and was in line for appointment to the office of attorney general. His uncle, Stephen Sewall, had been chief justice of Massachusetts Colony. Abigail had heard rumors that Jonathan aspired to his uncle's eminence.

It was a gay dinner, Jonathan and Esther bubbling with a wonderful zest for life. Sewall was a prankster; while at Harvard, he had thrown a rock through a window, aimed, accurately, to land in a professor's bed. Esther was filled with family gossip, the current stories of the countryside: of Aunt Nell, who broke two teeth at dinner and to avoid exposing herself swallowed them; of Mr. Reuben Burrell, who made a barrel of soft soap and left it in the lean-to, just over the well, only to have the floor give way.

Jonathan confided to them, "I work all day with intense concentration. When work is over I like to laugh. A hearty laugh is the most wonderful gift in nature. I greedily reach out for it. I don't laugh because something funny has been said or done. *I laugh first*. Out of that laughter comes the wit to be funny, the incisive insight, the laconic barb, the extraction of the absurd from the skein of events."

However, after dinner Jonathan Sewall turned serious.

"John, I came to divert you from any further opposing of the Stamp Act. This is a perfectly legal and valid Act of Parliament. You can't hurt the Act, it goes into effect on November first. But you can hurt yourself. In fact, you already have."

"I disagree, Jonathan," replied John mildly. "The Stamp Act is a beginning. The power to tax is the power to absorb. Soon Parliament could absorb all we have."

Jonathan turned to Abigail. "It won't disturb you if we discuss this?" He was solicitous; his own first child had been stillborn, and he would not want to upset her.

"No, Jonathan, not if you both discuss the matter impersonally."

He turned back to John.

"Look at the record of England. In our hundred and thirty years in America, who has been the giver and who the taker? England has poured millions of pounds into the colonies to help us develop. Are they unreasonable now when they ask us to pay only twenty-five per cent of the cost of maintaining their troops? Making our northern border secure has practically bankrupted Britain. They are so heavily in debt that the English pay far more taxes than we do. These are our own people, our own government, calling on us for help in a time of crisis. We have played fast and loose with even their simplest requests: smuggled, falsified bills of lading, defied their laws. And how has the Crown, the Ministry, the Parliament done? Quieted our tantrums, removed restrictions that we screamed were oppressive or onerous. . . . Where else in the whole recounting of empires has a Mother Country been so indulgent? Why can't we take our share of responsibility at the family board? Are we to go down in history as poverty-stricken in all the ethical and moral qualities our clergymen preach to us in meeting? Great God! I can barely stand my image in the morning shave. I, for one, want to pay my share to remain a free republican Empire. We bleat about freedom but we will not contribute one farthing to keeping that freedom alive in the world. Our Empire is beset by enemies: France, Spain, Holland, Russia would all like to blow our great navy out of the sea and strangle us until we capitulate and become their subjects and serfs. But will we offer to help? Or even agree to modest demands for our assistance? Assuredly not! Do you know what that makes us, John?"

"What?"

"Monsters."

There was a painful silence. Sewall's voice had risen. He glanced at Abigail, continued in a quieter tone.

"I know I'll never convince Massachusetts of that, Brother Adams; not with your friend James Otis and your cousin Samuel filling our people with hate and sedition."

"Now, Jonathan, let us leave off with name calling. Otis and Samuel are doing what they believe must be done, same as you are."

"You are one of my dearest friends. You know that I love you, Brother John."

"Yes, Brother Jonathan."

"Then let me beg you, with all the passion and eloquence I can command, not to join the ranks of the malcontents. England deserves better of you. As you love England, and you love her as I do, obey, be loyal in her troubled times so that her strength will be multiplied. Prove that Boston and London are one and the same cities, occupied by true brother Englishmen."

John too studied Abigail's expression. She signaled him to go ahead.

"I would make any sacrifice to prove that, Jonathan, except that which is self-defeating. We do not help England by letting her destroy our rights. Once we give up our legal right to govern our internal affairs, to exact our own taxes, as a people, and as colonies, we are no longer of any value to the Empire let alone to ourselves. We can be good Englishmen by fighting for our political rights with the same resolution the barons did for their Magna Carta in 1215, and the Long Parliament from 1640 to 1660 for their independence. We best serve England by remaining strong. We remain strong by allowing no man to weaken or absorb our constitutional and statutory guarantees. This is one ground on which I cannot yield."

Jonathan sighed.

"There is one thing more I must tell you, John. I can only pray that you will listen. *This is a dangerous course.* To refuse to obey the laws of England is to commit treason."

"Now, Jonathan," Abigail interposed, "John is simply refusing to cooperate with an unconstitutional act. That cannot be called treason."

"Perhaps it does not begin as such. But that is the way it will end. And what will be the consequence for you? Loss of your legal practice. Indictment . . ."

"O Heaven, Jonathan, they can't imprison the quarter of a million people in Massachusetts Bay Colony."

"All our people? No. But the leaders? Yes. Otis, Samuel Adams, the Loyal Nine, all can be arrested. . . ."

Abigail flashed a sign to her husband that she had had all she wanted.

"Thank you, my good friend," said John as he rose abruptly from his chair. "I know you want to protect me. But what man can be protected against himself? I will not practice in a court that demands tax stamps, sent from England, on our every legal paper. Nor will many of the others. We shall simply close the courts. That is defiance, agreed; but not treason. If I cannot engage in an honest quarrel over principles with my Mother Country, then I had best be an orphan. Arrest, trial, imprisonment . . . none of this will happen."

To Abigail's surprise, Jonathan's eyes filled with tears.

"Oh, my dear friends," he cried in anguish, "I hope so. I passionately hope so!"

Her child was born the following day, July fourteenth. At the first signs that the time was near, John removed the desk and chair from the borning room, replacing them with the hard cot the midwives favored. Sometimes women were obliged to spend days, even weeks, in their borning rooms, but Abigail pulled vigorously on the leather straps the midwife had attached to the bottom of the cot. The child itself seemed vigorously eager to be born, and after a short series of labor pains she gave birth to a girl, red of face and damp of scraggly hair, but perfectly formed. Once she was sure of this, Abigail dropped off peaceably, and slept around the clock. When she awakened she asked John, who came quickly at her call:

"Are you disappointed it's not a boy?"

"I always hoped for a daughter. We have many years ahead to have sons."

"What shall we call our little one?"

"Why not Abigail? It's a name I'm partial to. And apparently there's been an Abigail in every generation of your family."

"Which one of us is to come running when you call?"

"Both. The master of the house has the right to expect that."

Her high excitement vanished as the loss of the infant within her was uncompensated by the baby in the crib. Then the baby began to nurse. She spent wonderful hours with the babe at her breast, enveloped by a deep sense of being a link in time, all pasts and futures meeting here with the child in her arms. A sense of exhilaration filled her as she gave up the life sustenance on which countless generations had been nourished. She wondered if there were any experience that could equal the miracle of creating a human being out of one's own blood and bone and sinew. Could it ever be possible for a man to know this total feeling of accomplishment? She gazed down at John's sleeping face and pitied him the deprivation.

Now came the parade of friends and relatives, from Weymouth, Boston, Charlestown; relations from the outlying Smith, Boylston, Quincy and Adams clans, the deacons from Weymouth who had officiated at her own christening, twenty-one years before. Little Abigail was dressed in a white lawn christening gown and coat, wrapped in a soft woolen blanket and taken for her first holy walking in her father's arms, trailed by the several dozen relatives. Abigail remained behind, dressed in a pale green robe she had fashioned and sewn in the intervals of John's absences. When John kissed her good-by, he murmured:

"You're more beautiful than ever."

She too thought her skin clearer and whiter, her hair a deeper chestnut and shinier, her eyes and lips more moist, with a smile continually, almost involuntarily, hovering about both. As for her figure! It seemed to her the slimmest, most graceful in the world . . . by comparison.

She directed Rachel to set up the table in the sitting parlor, to bring in trays of hot "groaning cakes" traditional for the occasion, and the kegs of wine John had been storing in the coolest part of the cellar.

The baptismal party returned home, joined by a group of the Adamses' neighbors. Gifts were shyly presented: pincushions with designs made with inserted pins; pressed quilts for the baby's trundle; cool white sheets for summer; flannel sheets for winter, woven like oriental cashmere; petticoats of fine linen; silver spoons; little sacks with gold coins tied inside. The wine was poured and toasts drunk to the two Abigail Adamses. Abigail whispered to John:

"We Smith girls produce daughters, first time. I can earn a little variety if you'll be patient."

"Great events are in the womb of futurity."

"John Adams! Punning is a low form of wit."

"Remember, my love, what John Cotton wrote: 'It is true of women what is wont to be said of governments: that bad ones are better than none.' Could I not say the same for my jokes?"

As soon as she was able she joined John for tea in his office where he was spending concentrated hours writing his essay on canon and feudal law. The door to the road stood open for a breath of air. Slowly she grasped his intent: to describe the birth and growth of political freedom through a historical study of laws, constitutions, charters; and conversely, how those freedoms, in certain ages and civilizations, were lost before the onslaught of emperors, tyrants, war lords, ruling classes, religions. His purpose was to crystallize the political rights Massachusetts enjoyed, and to delineate the subtle methods by means of which they might be stripped away.

They spent the warm summer evenings on the porch outside their kitchen door, and here John brought the table from inside the lean-to, lit an oil lamp and read to her from the day's writing, his voice high, strong and pulsating.

He had started his essay by quoting one of her favorite authors, Dr. Tillotson: *Ignorance and inconsideration are the two great causes of the ruin of mankind.* Then he read his own words:

"'In the earliest ages of the world absolute monarchy seems to have been the universal form of government. Kings, and a few of their great counselors and captains, exercised a cruel tyranny over the people, who held a rank in the scale of intelligence in those days but little higher than the camels and elephants that carried them and their engines to war.

"'By what causes it was brought to pass that the people in the Middle Ages became more intelligent in general would not, perhaps, be possible in these days to discover. But the fact is certain, wherever a general knowledge and sensibility have prevailed among the people, arbitrary government and every kind of oppression have lessened and disappeared in proportion. . . .'"

He put down his papers, glanced at her. She asked quietly:

"Why are you letting it be published anonymously?"

"This way we keep out personal rancour."

"Since important ideas need to be stated, why shouldn't men sign their names and defend their point of view?"

He frowned. "In political disputes attacks proliferate. A man would spend his whole time defending himself."

She settled into the pleasant routine of being a mother, wondering why she had ever worried about the intricacies of bathing her baby, the period of weaning, the care of colic. Everything came quite naturally. Nab was a healthy child and, providentially, slept a solid twelve hours. Providentially, because John could not contain his energies. He told her about his next scheme while they trudged across rock-strewn fields to the abandoned ironworks, closed down a full hundred years.

"There's only one way to let the Ministry and Parliament know how strongly we feel about this, and that's for each town meeting to set forth written instructions to its representative in the Assembly. I'll petition for a special town meeting in Braintree."

She smiled to herself. His plan was written plain across his face.

"And you will have yourself appointed to the committee that is to write them?"

John threw back his head and laughed heartily.

"Smart, my Nabby. And beautiful too," he answered. "As soon as the meeting approves the idea of Instructions, I will quietly produce my document, so irrefutably reasoned that the others will find nothing to add or take away."

They picked their way carefully across the rotted plank bridge to stare down into the primitive blast furnace, its crumbled stones piled about the rusted power wheel. After a moment she looked back at her husband.

"My Machiavellian friend. If you keep up at this rate of intrigue you are going to be chief justice of Massachusetts."

"It's not intrigue, dear soul. It's vision. Recognition of a need and a resolve to do something about it. Far better than any other man in the community could do it. Would you say that is presumptuous of me?"

"Oh dear, no. Besides, we all know that the man who is willing to do the work gets the job."

It took him only a few days to rough out a draft of the Instructions.

"You know, Nabby, there's no such thing as true waste. Those simple laws I wrote for the Braintree highways, and then the series on canon and feudal law, have taught me how to write these Instructions."

He took his gun and went hunting, inviting her to read the manuscript.

"In all the calamities which have ever befallen this country, we have never felt so great a concern or such alarming apprehensions as on this occasion. Such is our loyalty to the King, our veneration for both Houses of Parliament, and our affection for all our fellow subjects in Britain, that measures which discover any unkindness in that country toward us are the more sensibly and intimately felt. And we can no longer forbear complaining that many of the measures of the late Ministry and some of the late acts of Parliament have a tendency, in our apprehension, to divest us of our most essential rights and liberties. . . .

"We take it clearly therefore to be inconsistent with the spirit of the common law and of the essential fundamental principles of the British Constitution that we should be subjected to any tax imposed by the British Parliament because we are not represented in that assembly in any sense. . . ."

John went about Braintree seeking signatures to his petition from "respectable inhabitants." When the meeting was called to order he was asked to speak first because he was responsible for the gathering. He pleaded for an Instructions Committee to be appointed. He was appointed to the committee. When he read his draft to the other members at Mr. Niles's house, it was approved without change. The next meeting accepted the resolutions "unanimously, without amendment."

7

News in Massachusetts had a curious facility of seepage through the air, the earth and the sea that was the main roadway for so many of its towns. Whatever happened in Boston was known almost instantaneously in Salem and Ipswich to the north, Concord and Worcester to the west, Duxbury and Plymouth to the south. There were people traveling in every direction, yet even the swiftest couriers could not account for the near simultaneity with which the violence in Boston permeated the atmosphere of Massachusetts, so that Abigail learned the full detail in Braintree even while John was absorbing the shocking news in a neighboring village. He returned home at once, riding his horse at top speed.

Boston, called one of the most disputatious towns in the New World, was said to enjoy violence for its own sake. The Puritans were not and never had been a peaceable people, not even among their own parishioners. But this was the first time that the city had seen a mob surging through its streets intent on mayhem, if not murder, and a wanton destruction of property.

Abigail stood in the open doorway to greet him. They exchanged a sober nod, went directly to John's office to piece together the ingredients of this story which could disrupt the plan of their lives.

"Whose version comes first?" she asked.

"Yours. Braintree is closer."

"The way it came to us: a mob was formed at Newbury Street near Deacon Elliot's in the morning. Some thousands of people marched through the streets carrying an effigy of Andrew Oliver, and hung it from a tree, the one under which the Loyal Nine has been holding meetings."

"It's called the Tree of Liberty. Oliver's appointment as stamp distributor must have arrived from London."

"I think not. I gathered that this was in preparation, to prevent him from accepting the commission when it does arrive. After hanging the effigy the crowd went to the Town House, where Governor Bernard, Lieutenant Governor Hutchinson and the Council were sitting. Then pressed through the streets to Oliver's dock, where they tore down his new building. Razed it to the ground. Didn't leave a stick."

"I heard it was his house they destroyed."

"No, not yet. First they leveled his office, where he would distribute the stamps. Then they went to his house, beheaded his effigy by his front door, carried it to the top of Fort Hill and burned it on a bonfire of the wood and timbers from his office on the dock."

She insisted on going out to the kitchen for a towel wet with water from a jug in the cooler for him to wipe the caked perspiration and dust from his face.

"All right," she said, "now you can tell me the rest."

Their voices fell to a whisper, as though they had become part of the conspiratorial act.

After burning Oliver in effigy the mob had returned to his house, destroyed the furniture, ripped the handsomely grained wood wainscoting from the walls. They had then stoned Lieutenant Governor Hutchinson and the sheriff, the only two men in Boston with sufficient courage to try to disperse them. Oliver's house remained standing, though gutted.

"But only until tomorrow, according to my information," said John. "A committee is calling on him in the morning to demand his resignation as stamp distributor. Will he agree? He will . . . unless he wants his house leveled as his office was, and maybe his *corpus* instead of his effigy burned on Fort Hill."

"John, surely they wouldn't commit murder!"

"A mob calls its action retributive justice." He rose, walked to the window overlooking the Plymouth Road, and asked hoarsely, "Besides, who is *they?*"

"The mob."

"Who organized the mob?"

"The Loyal Nine? Or Loyal Ninety?"

He came jerkily back to her side.

"And who organized the Loyal Ninety?"

She gazed at his face, pale and contorted as he stood above her. She made no attempt to answer.

"Cousin Samuel. James Otis. So did I. . . ."

"You, John? But you met with them only once."

"I helped provide a motivation. What happened today was an uprising. Against constituted and constitutional authority. Uprisings don't happen by accident. Ideas, arguments, appeals create a political climate. First a mob has to feel it has cause. This conviction comes from the people who provide the emotion, the logic, the ammunition, the belief that they must act this way. I wasn't alone, but the first installment of *The Canon and Feudal Law* set out to convince them that the right was on our side, and that by acquiescing to the Stamp Act we would be destroyed."

"Politically then, yes. But assuredly you didn't urge anyone to violence."

"Politics, dear soul, is not a quiet philosophy to be mused upon in monastic cloisters. More men have been killed through politics than religion or the smallpox."

He was sweating profusely.

"Now, my dear, aren't you taking rather too much credit, if I may use a strange word, for what happened?"

"Yes. But I had to make it clear to myself that there is no *they* in this matter. There is only *we*. This is not the end of violence, it is the barest beginning. We have to face the fact that we too are involved, and responsible."

They sat in silence. Jonathan Sewall's stern warning blocked like a third party between them. Outside all the music of late summer was in the air: men harvesting in the fields, animals stomping in the cool of the barn, carts on the road carrying produce to market; the smith, the tanner, the cooper hammering and cutting under the trees that shaded their shop fronts.

Feeling suddenly ill, she gripped John's bulky forearm for comfort. "We were wrong, weren't we? To tear down Oliver's office, vandalize his house, stone the lieutenant governor . . . ?"

He sat with his hands clasped low between his legs, his head down, chin on his chest. When he looked up his eyes were flecked with purple.

"Oliver has been attacked. Is there any evidence that he ever placed in a false light the character of our people, our principles in religion or government? Is there any indication that he ever advised the Ministry to lay internal taxes upon us? Or solicited the office of distributor of stamps? No, there is not. Then the blind rage of the rabble has done him irreparable injustice."

He paused.

"On the other hand, let me ask a question. While it is true that Oliver's brother-in-law, Lieutenant Governor Hutchinson, is native-born Massachusetts, has he not grasped four of the most important offices in the province: lieutenant governor, chief justice, judge of probate, president of Council? Oliver has one of the greatest places in government. Instead of preventing the fears and distress of our people, they have acted in combination to prevent us from discouraging the ministers in London from these rash, mad and dogmatical proceedings with the Stamp Act. Now we're all blind, Massachusetts and London alike, and we've begun to strike out like savages."

Unable to contain themselves within the four walls, they walked down the road as far as the attractive Borland house built by a retired West Indies sugar planter. They stopped at the Reverend Mr. Wibird's cottage for tea. It was filled with the musty smell of hundreds of disputatious theological pamphlets strewn helter-skelter over tables, chairs and floor. The minister was one of John's oldest friends, incongruous to gaze upon, with a crooked body, his head and chest listing in one direction, his hips and legs in the other.

They returned home through the warm dusk. Back from the road they could see the first oil lamps being lighted in their neighbors' houses. The air was full of the scent of hollyhocks.

John went into his office. She found him standing before the clean-swept hearth. Tumultuous thoughts were reflected in his eyes, a bitter expression on his lips.

"In my allegiances I can justify what happened yesterday. But in that part of my mind in which I am a lawyer, no. The law which does not defend your opponent will have vanished when it's your turn to need it. That's why the three-letter word 'law' is in some ways equal to the three-letter word 'God.' It's the only human concept that protects us all equally, with a hard-nosed stubborn justice. If I want to preserve order for myself I have to preserve law for my enemy. Many a man down through history has stood in the midst of ashes and cried, 'Look, I have won! I am the victor!' Over what? He has destroyed himself in the midst of his triumph and he did not know it."

"But what of uprisings, John, and revolutions? All through history submerged people have risen to ravage and kill in their fight for freedom."

He paced the office.

"Injustice is illegal. Laws that result in slavery must be overthrown."

"By force?"

"Not until all legal means of revoking them have been exhausted."

"And the enslaved people exhausted too! Oh, John, aren't we on crumbling ground?"

"Troubled, yes; crumbling, no. Sometimes a show of strength is needed to change an oppressive law."

"And shows of strength, as in Boston, can lead to violence. Violence is illegal. Therefore the only way to overcome laws we don't like is by illegal acts that we like no better? Ah, my dear, you are caught on the horns of a dilemma."

"Sharp ones." He smiled ruefully.

Though Boston quieted, Abigail felt that a subtle change had come over their lives. John refused to pull his remaining three articles out of the *Gazette*. The second installment was published five days after the violence. Although John Adams's name was not signed, many of the group who were now calling themselves Patriots knew who the author was.

"I'll soon be out of a job as a lawyer," he confided. "I shall post my books, put my accounts in order, diminish our expenditures . . ."

"They've already stopped. Not the smallest coin goes out of my hands."

John rode into Boston every few days to confer with his cousin Samuel, James Otis and the other lawyers with whom he worked closely: Gridley, Thacher, Auchmuty, Samuel Quincy, William Browne, Samuel Fitch, Benjamin Kent. Each time he came home with a bland expression. Yet she sensed strain. The city had forgiven Oliver for having his house vandalized; yet Boston was restive. Lieutenant Governor Hutchinson was still putting up opposition to any official Massachusetts Bay Colony protest being sent to London. Time was getting short, there were only two months until the Stamp Act became legal, and it took that long even in the best of weather for a packet to reach London and return. Nine of the colonies had agreed to meet in New York for a Stamp Act Congress. However, the meeting was not to be held until October, too late to get the courts open for the November sessions.

When John seemed reluctant to discuss politics with her for fear of upsetting her, she convinced him that such talk was more natural for her than talking with her Braintree neighbors about how to keep the servant girls from squandering the food stores.

"Massachusetts must stand bluff," he told her. "We stood bluff in

1732 when the English Ministry passed the Hat Act, denying our hatters the right to export their beavers. It was never enforced."

"What happens, John, if both the colonies and Parliament stand bluff?"

"There are remedies. James Otis has published a brilliant pamphlet, *The Rights of the British Colonies Asserted and Proved.* He suggests colonial representation in Parliament. Everyone on this side favors it as a splendid solution. We're even discussing the possibility of an American nobility."

"You'll be Lord Adams and I'll be Lady Adams! Will you serve in the House of Lords?" She went through a lighthearted pantomime in which she placed a tiara on her head, curtsied to King George III.

"The only place I want to serve is in the Massachusetts Superior Courts," he grumbled. "I have a family to support. I've never seen anyone with the appetite that young Nab has."

Boston was too impatient to stand bluff. August twenty-sixth word came up the road that violence had broken out again.

A mob had gathered on King Street, rallying around a bonfire. On instructions of Ebenezer Mackintosh, a cobbler from the South End, they had broken into two groups. The first party went to the house of William Story, registrar of the Admiralty, where they destroyed a considerable portion of his private and public papers and set about systematically tearing out the inside of his beautiful Georgian home. The second group went to the home of Benjamin Hallowell, comptroller of the customs, a cousin of John's by marriage. Here they smashed the windows and doors, the sash and shutters, the exquisite French and English furniture, working their way to the wine cellar and emptying its contents down their dry and thirsty throats. They gathered up the considerable library and papers of Mr. Hallowell and carried them off, no one knew to what end.

There was the sound of horses' hoofs coming along the road. The rider stopped, tied his mount to the hitching post outside the Adams house and entered. It was Josiah Quincy, Jr., Abigail's young cousin, on his way home to Mount Wollaston. He was a plain-looking man, cross-eyed, warmhearted and lovable, popular with everyone. A shaft of sunlight crossed John's office; it picked up the strain on the face of young Josiah.

"The mobs combined," he reported, "and went on to Hutchinson's home. You've never seen such a mess. Every one of the eighteen windows facing on Garden Court Street has been smashed. His paintings have been taken, £900 in cash, and all the clothing and silverware. They even cut down his trees! Where will they stop?"

Abigail shook her head in despair at the peculiarly Bostonian form of bloodletting, pulling down the houses of one's opponents.

"You have no idea what they did with Hutchinson's papers," Josiah cried; "they pulled his files out into the street, dumped them into the water and mud and trampled on them. You know that he's been assembling documents for a second volume of the *History of the Colony of Massachuset's Bay?*"

"He's the Crown's best man, but he writes solid, readable history."

There was a painful silence. Abigail said, "I hear Rachel in the kitchen. Let me have her prepare some food for you."

"Thank you no, Cousin Abigail. Father and your grandfather Quincy are waiting for a report too."

Though a sizable portion of the citizens present had been part of what her cousin Josiah called "the rage-intoxicated rabble," the Boston town meeting passed resolutions strongly deprecating the violent proceedings and called upon the selectmen to suppress such disorders in the future. Lieutenant Governor Hutchinson, who emerged with dignity and courage in the face of his shattering losses, labeled the mob as one "ripened in ebriety."

John returned from Martha's Vineyard. He and Abigail talked about the Boston violence. He groaned:

"Why do the mobs always find the most exquisite homes to destroy?"

"Probably because the most beautiful homes belong to Crown enthusiasts who are in power, and consequently have the most money with which to build and furnish them. Or does that sound cynical?"

"Not cynical, just hard fact, I guess."

Rachel was rocking Nab in her cradle. The girl had heard enough to be upset. Abigail spoke to her, assuring her that no trouble would come to Braintree, and the girl went about her tasks.

Not so Abigail, who made several trips to the garden to pick fresh herbs, to the well to draw cool water, enjoying the orderly physical chores because there was considerable turmoil in her mind, and many questions she could not ask her husband. Was the mob truly an unnamed, unfaced crowd to John? Did he know who had plotted to have the bonfire built, to notify Boston of the time and place? Who had determined the houses to be attacked? Was he undertaking more responsibility for these "shows of strength"? Were they on the path to the deep end of treason Jonathan Sewall had predicted?

She would simply have to wait for the answers. Waiting was an activity peculiarly available to women.

Despite the fact that Samuel Adams's Instructions for Boston had been published some three weeks ahead of John's, forty Massachusetts towns followed John's line of argument, patterning their protests after his. The Braintree Instructions also had been published anonymously, but the authorship was one of the worst-kept secrets in Massachusetts. Cousin Samuel Adams could have had something to do with that, Abigail realized, when Samuel stopped over for a visit en route to a country meeting.

"I'm prouder and more pleased than you are," Samuel whispered to her when John went to his office to finish a paper Samuel would take with him to the meeting. "We Adamses make quite a team."

"Samuel, what is going to happen?"

"Stalemate. The stamps have arrived, but they're locked up in Castle William, where Governor Bernard has fled. The Stamp Act Congress in New York passed a strong resolution proving to Parliament that we colonists can work together when our rights are endangered. In a few days our Assembly is going to report to the governor that practically every city and hamlet in Massachusetts rejects the law."

"Do you really think Bernard, or Hutchinson, will yield so easily?"

"If that law goes into effect, no merchant in Massachusetts will buy from England. None of our ships will clear port to take raw materials to Liverpool. Patience, dear Cousin. This is a battle we can't lose if we stay in it together."

"Oh, I have patience. It's a quality all mothers share."

Samuel's heavy head shook a trifle as he tendered her his wistful smile.

"We're all mothers now, bringing a new political child into the world. Remember how our children used to be named Hope and Charity and Faith? This new baby is called Independence."

When she hesitated to answer, he said:

"The birth of ideas is a part of Genesis too. The Lord's second week of work, after the first six days during which He created the sun and moon, the land and the sea, the fish, the serpents, the animals and man. New ideas are more rare than children, more difficult to germinate, to bring into life with sufficient vitality to survive. This time we have just such an idea, one of the most important ever born."

"Independence? It's all of that?"

"All of that! It is not only in Boston that we care about such matters. Do you know what Governor Bernard recently admitted? That our country people talk of revolting from Great Britain in the most familiar manner, and declare that though the British forces might possess themselves of the coast, and maritime towns, they will never subdue the inland! What do you say to that?"

"I say quite outright, Samuel, that I'm frightened, that I cannot grasp your 'Independence.' John isn't working to achieve a war. He's working to re-establish our rights as Englishmen."

"England won't let us. There isn't one man in the Ministry or Parliament who has ever visited America. Our friends in London, the great Pitt, Burke, will never prevail. This crisis is not a war, it's a battle, the first of a long and bloody campaign. I may be a poor maltster but I'm a good political soothsayer."

"You're a good political proselytizer, Sam'l, that's what you are. You're trying to proselytize people into a new political faith. You're going to get yourself burned at the stake as a political Antinomian if you're not careful."

"Ah well, I always longed to be a martyr." Samuel kissed her on the cheek. "But I'll never make it. I'm far too ordinary a soul. But John here, he fits the role perfectly. I can just see him, sitting on top of a huge bonfire, scribbling away at a tract to prove that burning at the stake is illegal."

"Now what was all that?" John demanded from the doorway. "Why am I sitting on top of a bonfire, writing a tract . . . ?"

Abigail shivered. "Your cousin has a grisly sense of humor."

8

As November first approached, the people of Boston fell into a frenzy. There were street meetings, bonfires, parades, speeches. Children remained out of school, business was at a standstill, the air carried dust particles laden with frustration, vituperation, intimidation. On their assembly ground in Newbury Street, under the Tree of Liberty where Oliver, and now Chancellor of Exchequer Lord Grenville, were hanged in effigy, the Loyal Nine renamed themselves the Sons of Liberty. In Weymouth, the Reverend Mr. Smith abandoned a lifetime philosophy that preachers should stay out of politics; Dr. Cotton Tufts took time out from his practice to help write the Weymouth Instructions to the legislature.

Governor Bernard had been forced to proclaim that no stamps would be distributed from their cache in Castle William. Oliver was made to reiterate that he would not serve as stamp distributor. The Admiralty Court judges had been pushed into the position of saying they would call no cases without juries, as the Stamp Act provided. The Council arrested no Bostonian no matter what he did, having been warned after the arrest of Ebenezer Mackintosh that the Boston militia would not protect their beautiful Custom House should it be attacked.

Swept up as Braintree was in its rejection of the Act, still the action was in Boston, ten miles away. Abigail was grateful for the subtle difference. Calm was a quality she needed, for John was totally involved, spending much of his time in Boston in an effort to keep the Massachusetts courts open. But in the end he and the other lawyers were defeated. He returned from Boston on the last day of October, spent from sleeplessness, and depressed.

"Nothing?"

"Nothing. London knows now that nine of our colonies have joined to resist the Act. The Massachusetts Assembly has presented a solid front of opposition to the Council. But the courts close tomorrow, to remain closed until Parliament admits defeat. How long? A month . . . a year . . . a decade . . ."

"There'll be a goodly number of people in mourning tomorrow."

He looked up with a bitter smile.

"Quite so. Governor Bernard called the Council and ordered out the militia. The first militiaman to appear on the street had his drum smashed. End of militia. All the church bells will toll in the morning and Lord Grenville's effigy will again be hanged on the Tree of Liberty. In the afternoon he will be cut down, paraded through the streets to the gallows, hanged again, and then cut to pieces."

"I thought theatrical plays were illegal in Massachusetts?"

He missed the edge of sarcasm.

"Everything's illegal now. We'll have to shut down the whole colony. Except for the farms." He looked up, life returning to his frame. "I'll clear one of those wood lots I bought in Hemlock Swamp, then that pasture lot in Rocky Run." He slumped back in his chair. "Until the rains start, anyway."

She took the rum punch which she had asked Rachel to mix strong, and handed it to him.

"This will revive your moral courage as well as slake your thirst. Now you will have that winter of study you've been wanting."

"I don't know, Nabby. Study shouldn't be something we escape into as a court of last resort, to save us from the gallows of boredom. A man should go to his books tremulously, as he does to his bride, anticipating almost uncontainable pleasures. . . ."

"Then behave like your Puritan ancestors and take a grim pleasure out of the pain of acting virtuously."

That brought a mild laugh. She helped him pull off his heavy riding boots. He went into the kitchen where Rachel gave him a pan of warm water to wash his hands and face with, then his feet. Refreshed, he sat down to eat his boiled dinner with appetite, but by nighttime he had fallen into lethargy again, which deepened the next day when the church bells of Braintree were tolled lugubriously.

Watching him, Abigail mused:

"John is carrying this baby Independence of Sam'l's mighty hard."

One week passed, then another. Waiting, she now learned, can sometimes be a man's portion. John read fitfully, cleared some of his land; but he was sunk in abstraction, his mind focused on near-paralyzed Boston where his presence could no longer serve a useful purpose. Boston Harbor was locked tight, no British merchandise either entering or being shipped out.

"Don't you find it strange," he asked Abigail, "that no copy of the law or member of the commission has arrived? It's now two weeks after the Act went into effect. These failures give me a rise of spirits."

December fell. There was a plain of snow, white enough to blind one's eyes. Abigail decided to abandon penury and buy them the few American-made necessities that would ease their days. They rode in the Adams family sleigh over almost obliterated roads to Mount Wollaston to hear about what Grandfather Quincy called "the meatiest brawl we've had in these parts in years." The sound of sleigh bells rang out for miles across the countryside.

The Reverend Mr. Smith leaned across Colonel Quincy's library table on his knobby elbows and gathered in the people around it even as he leaned forward from the pulpit to gather in his congregation.

"It was a clash of clergymen, really," he explained. "Something we Congregationalists have tried to avoid in New England."

The Reverend Mr. Gay, preaching in Hingham, had maintained that the ancient weapons of the Church were prayer and tears, not clubs, and he advised submission to authority. There was almost an uprising on the front steps of his Meeting House, his people claiming that he would do very well as a stamp distributor. The Reverend Mr. Smith retorted by preaching from his Weymouth pulpit from the text "Render therefore unto Caesar the things which are Caesar's, and unto God the things that are God's."

"I recommended honor, reward and obedience to good rulers," he told them with flashing eyes, "and a spirited opposition to bad ones. Along the way I apparently interspersed a good deal of animated declamation upon a rather touchy subject these days: liberty."

The weeks in December evaporated. Neither the Superior nor Inferior courts adjudged the Stamp Act valid. The probate office was shut, the Custom House shut, all business at a standstill. John alternated between bouts of writing and grumbling. Each few days he would bring her some pages from his commonplace book, or suggest that she come into the office and look at material freshly written for a new series he hoped to publish in the *Boston Gazette*. She stood, frequently with Nab in her arms, surrounded by his lawbooks and the smell of his tobacco, the strong ink and sometimes damp paper, feeling an emanation of her husband as strong as any physical sense she experienced in their intimate embraces.

She read part of an attempt to answer "William Pym," an Englishman who had published an article in the *London Evening Post* in which he stated that "a resolution of the British Parliament can at any time set aside all the charters that ever have been granted by our monarchs," by writing: "If ever an infant country deserved to be cherished it is America; if ever any people merited honor and happiness, they are her inhabitants. . . . They have the most habitual, radical sense of liberty and the highest reverence for virtue. They are descended from a race of heroes who, placing their confidence in Providence alone, set the seas and skies, monsters and savages, tyrants and devils at defiance for the sake of religion and liberty. . . . Yet this is the people, Mr. Pym, on whom you are contributing for paltry hire, to rivet and confirm everlasting oppression."

Abigail admired her husband's writing, even on those occasions when it was dominated by invective. But his grumbling was of a very different nature. She had read in one of her books on English history that "the English have always had a persecution mania." Sometimes this seemed to her to be true of an Englishman by the name of John Adams. He said to her as she lay in bed with her hands locked behind her head listening to him:

"The Bar seems to me to behave like a flock of shot pigeons. They seem to be stopped, the net seems to be thrown over them and they have scarcely courage left to flounce and flutter."

"Have you tried persuading them of this?"

"Indeed. I am getting myself disliked. But I'm convinced that if we signed a collective petition, with our legal and constitutional reasoning affixed, that would give us sufficient force to oblige the governor and the attorney general to allow the courts to be opened without their blasted stamps."

Little Nab stirred restlessly in her trundle. John took a log from the woodbox, dropped it abruptly into the fireplace, sending a shower of sparks against the screen. He stood leaning against the mantel, gazing down into the flames and talking in a dry toneless manner which she recognized as his voice of despair.

"This long interval of indolence and idleness will make a large chasm in my affairs, if it should not reduce me to distress and incapacitate me to answer the demands upon me. . . . So sudden an interruption to my career is very unfortunate for me. I was but just getting into my gears, just getting under sail, and an embargo is laid upon the ship. Thirty years of my life are passed in preparation for business. I have had poverty to struggle with, envy and jealousy and malice of enemies to encounter, no friends, or but few, to assist me, so that I have groped in dark obscurity till of late, and had but just become known and gained a small degree of reputation, when this execrable project was set on foot for my ruin as well as that of America in general and of Great Britain."

She was not unused to the attitudes of self-abrogation. She had had premarital training during the years she went about with her father, listening to the community of Weymouth pouring out its tales of woe. Even in her younger years she had surmised that there was a considerable difference between the male Puritan and the female. The women, she had found, were gentler and more stable, wiser in their estimates of passing moods and events. The men liked to complain; to attack themselves in the process of attacking their neighbors and general conditions. It had sometimes seemed to her as though Congregationalists found it an implicit part of their religion periodically to damn themselves and their neighbors, if not to perdition, at least to considerable soul-raking.

"It is," she thought, watching her husband's bent and suffering back, "the Puritan's peculiar form of debauchery. We're not supposed to drink anything more than an occasional rum punch or a glass of wine. We're permitted to smoke only in moderation, and to attend the theatre not at all. Adultery is punishable by death, and fornication by whipping, putting in the stocks and cropping of the ears. We're not allowed to charge usurious rates of interest or excessive prices for our goods. The sumptuary laws are rigid, we can't wear jewelry or expensive laces. It's part of our religion not to worship material goods or to display our wealth ostentatiously. Aside from his love for his wife and children, his home and profession, the Puritan is hard put to find passing pleasures. It isn't so strange, then, that the poor man has had to turn inside himself to create a combination of battleground and Globe Theatre. I could pity them, if they were not already so rich in their own self-pity."

Nor had John Adams's courtship of her given the lie to any of her assumptions.

"My dear," she cried, "are there *no* encouraging omens? Our merchants have had mail from the London manufacturers that they have stopped buying from, pledging their support. Not one Crown officer has been willing to issue the stamps or open the Admiralty Court without a jury."

He turned about, took a deep breath.

"Yes, there are good signs. When Oliver's commission finally arrived a couple of days ago, he was made to walk to the Tree of Liberty and publicly repudiate his office. My old friend, Attorney General Auchmuty, bless him, has had the courage to advise both the shippers and the Crown officers that our ships must be allowed to clear the harbor without stamps. The Custom House may open . . ."

"Then mustn't it follow that the courts will open too? If ships can clear without stamps, why not writs?"

Within a matter of days the Custom House did open, as well as the ports. Ships long tied up and loaded with cargo sailed for England. Immediately a meeting was held in Faneuil Hall whose sole purpose was to get the courts open. The following day when Governor Bernard entered Town House to meet with the Council, he passed a placard hung in the entrance room:

Open your Courts and let Justice prevail,
Open your Offices and let not Trade fail.
For if these men in power will not act,
We'll get some that will, is actual Fact.

They had finished their midday dinner when there was a sharp knock at the house door. Abigail opened it to find a constable standing there with an official-looking document in his hand.

"Are you Mrs. Adams, ma'am?"

"I am Mrs. John Adams."

"I am a constable of the town of Boston. I have a letter for your husband from Mr. William Cooper, the town clerk. Kindly summon your husband so I may put this notice in his very hands."

John took the letter, signed for it. He tore open the wax seal, unfolded the paper and read aloud:

"Sir: I am directed by the Town to acquaint you that they have this day voted unanimously that Jeremiah Gridley, James Otis, and John Adams Esqrs. be applied to as Counsel to appear before His Excellency the Governor in Council, in support of their memorial praying that the courts of law in this Province may be opened. A copy of said memorial will be handed you on your coming to town. I am, sir, your most obedient hum. sert.,

"Wm. Cooper, Town Clerk."

He turned to his wife wide-eyed.

"What reason would induce Boston to choose me, at a distance, and unknown as I am?"

"Oh, I think I might manage to find some reasons. Jeremiah Gridley, for instance, or Samuel Adams. Or your essay on canon and feudal law, so good that even the *London Chronicle* reproduced it as the outstanding statement of the American point of view. . . ."

"Oh, don't mistake me, I'm not so astonished that I'll turn down the honor. In fact, if you'll tell Rachel to heat some water, I'll have a bath and ride into Boston immediately. But, Nabby, when I think of some of my reflections yesterday, part of which I committed to writing, I can't help but wonder whether Lord Bacon wasn't right when he spoke about the secret, invisible laws of nature, communications and influences between places that are not discoverable by sense."

"John dear, the Boston town meeting needs a lawyer, not a metaphysician. How could you be thinking any different from what the meeting was thinking? You've all been in the same stewpot for months now. I'll set out your finest raiment."

9

John Adams was something of a force of nature: on the rebound from the depths he gathered the momentum to sweep everything before him. If in the process he sometimes left his wife exhausted, that was an integral part of the marriage contract she had signed, and which was safely deposited in John's file. There was nothing about her husband she would change. Pulling a loose thread could unravel the fabric. She devoted her time to her daughter, now going on six months, a bright but placid child with her father's wide face and plump figure, and eyes, too, that were coming more and more to look like John's. Either stolid or serene, Abigail could not determine which.

When he returned she found him ruminative. They pushed forward in the knee-deep snow to the top of Penn's Hill, trying to find their old trail, the intense cold making the breath come out of their mouths like thin white smoke. Helping her upward, John allowed as how he had done reasonably well. They had been heard in the evening, in the candlelit Council Chamber, with Governor Bernard in his purple robes and purple-tinged wig. The governor had surprised them by demanding that they speak in sequence, each presenting a different aspect of the case. Gridley and Otis had quite naturally asked their junior associate to begin the argument.

"And so I did, but I was cold. Colder than this December air. I think they were expecting an impassioned speech, but I was juridical. So were we all three. But between us we said everything the case demands."

It was Christmas week. A second heavy snowstorm blanketed the countryside. On New Year's Day, Cotton and Lucy Tufts came to them from Colonel Quincy's traditional party. Because of his constant traveling of the roads of Massachusetts to build his book of medical prescriptions and to persuade the profession to form a Sodality in Boston, Cotton had contact with more doctors than any man in the colony.

"Most of them are Patriots, to use your term, John; but a surprising number still cherish association with England. They studied there, or their fathers or grandfathers did. A disproportionate number are Church of England, as are so many of the squires around Mount Wollaston. They believe King, Ministry and Parliament can do no wrong. Since no stamps would be required to cure putrid throat, why should they raise a fever over them?"

The following day John drove their cattle through the deep snow to Dr. Savil's watering hole. He returned at dusk, red-cheeked, invigorated by the walk. With him came his brother Peter.

They ate before the cooking fire in the kitchen, the warmest spot in the house. Peter was a defensively silent man, speaking only when spoken to. His virtue for Abigail was his devotion to John, whom he loved blindly and without a jealous bone in his yeoman's body.

After dessert, John announced that he thought the time had come for him to run for selectman and take his father's place in the Braintree town meeting. Would Peter help him? He was friends with most of the young blades in town. Could he line them up?

Peter's eyes gleamed. Abigail sat with her hands in her lap while the brothers dissected the Braintree vote. Five selectmen were to be chosen, all five of the incumbents were running again. To win, John would have to dislodge one of them. John's old enemy, Thayer, the tavern-owning lawyer, still controlled the meeting. His clique would be against John. Cleverly, the leader of the Church of England group, who had not dared to vote publicly against John's Instructions but who had resented them, also would be against him. John could count on the votes of the people who liked the Instructions, liked the way he had handled the highway laws, the sale of the Common lots.

"Best I count noses," said Peter. "Election is early March. Time enough. Only one trouble . . . Thayer buys votes. All a man wants to eat and drink at his tavern."

"We know those people in advance." John's voice was sharp. "Ignore them. Work inside your own circle. If the young men back us . . ."

"We see. Eight weeks is time enough to clear a field and plant clover. I start tomorrow."

Peter would have only thirty or forty strides over the snow to the door of his own house. John banked the fire.

"What do you think?" she asked.

"When Peter says 'we see' that is an outburst of enthusiasm. Do you suppose he is so reticent because God supplied me with such an unholy quantity of words? Do I use up the whole Adams family allotment?"

Time has a texture. Each period of waiting looms its own design. For Abigail, this one was shot through with golden threads, for John's reports of his activities in Boston were sanguine. He was sought after by individuals and groups he had not known before. When he went to dinner at Nick Boylston's, a cousin on his mother's side, and there met another cousin, Benjamin Hallowell, the comptroller of customs whose home had been wrecked, Hallowell violently attacked Samuel Adams and James Otis but intimated that John's conduct in the Patriot cause had been judicious. When he spent an evening with the Sons of Liberty at Chase and Speakman's distillery, with John Avery, Jr., a distiller, Thomas Crafts, a house painter, Benjamin Edes, printer of the *Boston Gazette*, Stephen Cleverly, a brazier, Joseph Field, a ship's captain, George Trott, a jeweler, he was accepted as able but objective counsel, an antidote to James Otis, who raged about Boston talking feverishly, not all his observations in the best interests of the Patriots.

Governor Bernard appointed Lieutenant Governor Hutchinson's younger brother, Foster Hutchinson, who was willing to preside without a batch of stamps between himself and the woolsack, to open the Inferior Courts and attempt to unfreeze the hundreds of legal entries and actions.

Work came to John on the very day the court opened, not only in Braintree but in Boston, where strangers sought him out to write their writs and handle their cases. He put aside his political articles, again made room on his long table and desk for his clients' affairs. Abigail had said to her sister Mary, in the innocence of her youth, "It might be entertaining to find that one's husband was a hundred different men." Certainly one of the two or three she liked best was Lawyer John Adams, hovering over his legal papers with the concentrated joy of a man who has made himself an expert.

"Oh, God, it's good to work at my profession again!"

"You never stopped."

"Isn't it a lovely sight, all these scrawled pleadings? You know, Nabby, there's mighty few pleasures in life to equal doing one's job. It is an act of love. Even so plebeian an activity as making money . . . A man has to go for a number of months without earning to appreciate how important it is. We must not worship wealth, but money isn't an inanimate object that one prays to. When I plead a case I'm exchanging my skill for a new dress for Nab, or a halved beef. I like to earn. I like to acquire. It's as wrong to despise money as to worship it."

"You'd have a hard time getting an argument on that sentiment in Massachusetts."

Each Sunday after holy walking, Peter stopped at the house to report progress. He was working quietly but steadily in John's behalf. Her uncle Norton Quincy, who had taken his father's place as selectman, stopped by for tea and to talk of the factions in Braintree.

"Niece, will you vote on March third? One vote, two, might make the difference."

"How many other women will be voting?"

"A few. Widows mostly, who inherited the family farm or house. No intent to pry, but you have a ratable estate of £20, haven't you? Or £50 personalty?"

She figured in her mind her dowry of cash, furniture, silver, pewter, fabrics.

"Yes, Uncle, I surely have chattels worth £50."

"Then you should vote. Establish your right, early."

The entire town assembled for the hundred and twenty-sixth anniversary of the founding of Braintree. Samuel Niles was chosen moderator, Elisha Niles clerk and treasurer. The six major candidates loaned their beaver hats, to be spaced down the length of the Meeting House alternating on the railing of either pew, each with the name of the candidate affixed. Each freeholder stood below the pulpit, had his name checked off a list, was handed five ballots. John had the right to vote, as did the other candidates. The voter went down the center aisle, dropping his five ballots into his chosen felt linings. Abigail concentrated on John's hat, trying to keep count. Norton Quincy had said that for the first time in his memory of Braintree this was not a local election but had colony-wide implications—the Anglican Church members were trying to defeat Deacon Penniman for his Patriot services. The Patriots were eager to dump Major Miller, leader of the Anglicans, who had condemned the agitation.

John returned to sit beside her in the Adams pew. The six hats were collected, carried up to the pulpit and put in a line facing the meeting. The moderator took the ballots out of each hat. The clerk recorded them. Abigail glanced about. It was not good form to express either pleasure or pain over these non-partisan, non-paid offices, yet she sensed an undercurrent of feeling and, toward the end of the ballot counting, a low murmur building.

Her uncle Norton Quincy, as everyone expected, drew the largest vote: one hundred and sixty. Deacon Penniman came along nicely with one hundred thirty. Cornet Bass would have done well except that his followers withdrew for refreshments and failed to vote. Major Miller fell by the wayside. One more than half the people present voted for John, a respectable showing for a neophyte.

John had to remain for the annual business: choosing tithingmen, fence viewers, sealers of shingles and leather; to discover an effective means to get the fish called "alewives" up the Monatiquot River. Abigail whispered, "Congratulations," and walked home to set up refreshments, to lift her elbow high in pouring the rum into the punch, a trick she had learned from her grandmother Quincy, "to get a celebration started right fast."

Letters and papers trickling in from London indicated that Parliament was going to debate the Stamp Act again. Still, Lieutenant Governor Hutchinson refused to open the Superior Courts.

"I have to admire him for his consistency," cried John in a voice that indicated no admiration whatever; "where British-born Bernard is vacillating, confused, our native-born Hutchinson anticipates our every move and is frightened by nothing, not even those Boston mobs. Like every convert, he's more orthodox in his thinking and procedures than a member of the royal family. He has been a tower of strength to the Crown. He'll be our next governor."

"God help us."

"And God help him. He's a man too proud to compromise."

The next morning a message reached them from Weymouth that the Smiths' Tom had died. He was old, the Reverend Mr. Smith had inherited him from his own father. John hitched the horse to the carriage and took Abigail to the parsonage. That afternoon they stood on Burying Hill while Tom was put to rest. Back at the parsonage, Abigail sat in the kitchen with Phoebe.

"Phoebe, my father says he won't buy another man; he thinks that has to stop now; but he told me to ask if you would like us to advertise for a free man in the Boston paper. Father is putting it in his will: when he dies, you'll be free."

The newly widowed woman stared out of tear-swollen eyes.

"Free? Who I got if'n I free? Where I go if'n I free? Tom is free. When I die I's free. Ain't no other way for any'n us."

As a selectman John found himself overseer of the poor, assessor in charge of highway surveys of the roads leading to the connecting towns, inspector of boundaries and of schools. He enjoyed the public office because it gave him a chance to delve into the law and history of other towns to see what would work best for Braintree.

When the report came of the official act of Parliament which rescinded the Stamp Act the Adams and Smith families assembled in Grandfather Quincy's library overlooking the bay. He was still paterfamilias of all political action.

Colonel Quincy cried, "Let us rejoice that we have been vindicated, but let us not gloat. We have not defeated anyone. We have simply persuaded our homeland to see the light."

Boston was some twelve miles from Mount Wollaston; Grandpa Quincy's voice of reason could not carry that far. The Sons of Liberty and the Patriots decided that Boston should put on a riotous celebration. Samuel insisted that John and Abigail come in to participate.

"Aunt Elizabeth has been asking us to visit with them," said Abigail.

"I can take care of some business quietly on the side."

They never got to see the Boston celebration. Nab developed a cough. At first Abigail thought it was a bad catarrh, but when she started continuous paroxysms of coughing, Abigail recognized it as whooping cough. She promptly came down with it herself.

John came down with his own malaise. He returned from the Braintree town meeting at which they were to elect Braintree's representative to the Assembly for the colony of Massachusetts, his face bloated. To her question of what had gone wrong he replied:

"I guess you could call it a case of whooping mortification. All the towns around us threw out their assemblymen who had supported the Stamp Act and elected those who had been most active in opposing it. But not ours!"

She rocked Nab's trundle, thinking:

"He said he did not want to be in politics. He said he wanted to be a private counselor, to study and write. Then why is he so bitterly disappointed?"

As if reading her thoughts, he said sotto voce:

"Frankly, I didn't want the job. But I did think the town meeting should have given me a vote of confidence."

"John, isn't that visionary? Town meetings rarely concern themselves with gratitude."

He remained silent, his short legs spread apart, his eyes cast down. After a moment he looked up.

"It's unworthy of me to have my pride so easily mortified. The same complaints I made to you I made in my diary. I'm going in now and ink them out. If and when I want to get into politics in a serious way I shall work at it as I do at the law."

He went into his office, to pick up his pen and scratch out six lines of hurt pride. Bemused, Abigail took a fresh cloth to moisten Nab's face, and hummed *Little Sally Waters, sitting in the sun,* which her mother had sung to her. Instead of the words of the song, she sang:

"Arsy-versey, that husband of mine. Full of all the weaknesses and frailties that the flesh and soul are heir to, but quickly seeing his sins, and atoning for them."

10

Young Abigail was a year old and walking a little, putting one foot before the other in a charming pigeon toe, her chubby-knuckled hands holding onto her mother's finger. She was bright-eyed, observant. She continued to be a miniature of her father: plump face, changing blue eyes, stocky body, John's strong but muscle-bound gestures. Abigail chuckled.

"You know, John, a woman has to be careful when she marries, for at least one of her children will remind her of her husband every time she looks at it."

John Adams was not the only one to take a political fall. James Otis, after being elected, was cast out of the Speaker's chair by the governor. In retaliation, the Assembly dropped Lieutenant Governor Hutchinson and Peter and Andrew Oliver as councilors to the governor, electing a Council of Patriots in their place. Governor Bernard negatived four of them, made the two Houses "a most nitrous and sulphureous speech," which John reported to Abigail when he returned from Boston.

He also told her about the law cases. William Douglass was charged by a Dutch girl with being "the father of a bastard child born of her body." The King vs. Francis Keen was about a stolen cask of molasses. The King vs. Mary Gardiner was a case of a "common scold, quarreler and disturber of the peace." Punishment: putting her into the ducking pond.

"All these cases weren't mine actually, but I took notes on the reasoning and skill of the attorneys."

"Was there no good news, John?"

Yes, there had been. At a meeting of the Bar at the Coffee House, her cousin Josiah Quincy, Jr., had been admitted to the Inferior Court. They had passed regulations to insure the experience of the young lawyers who were "swarming and multiplying" in Massachusetts: four years had to pass before those admitted as lawyers could wear the gown of the barrister. The Bar was setting up standards of excellence, and they had agreed to haul barrators into court.

Every newspaper and pamphlet, every public and private letter arriving from England continued to breathe a spirit of benevolence. The utmost delicacy was being observed in all the state papers. Even the resolve of the House of Commons and the recommendation from His Majesty concerning indemnification to the sufferers was couched in the most alluring language.

"You agree with King George's request that all damage be paid for?" she asked.

"Yes. By appropriation of the Assembly. Now," he concluded, "we can live in peace again. I don't think I was born for controversy. It cuts up my insides with a dull knife. And it lands me in all sorts of equivocal situations, such as now, when I find myself disapproving so much of what Cousin Sam'l and James Otis did in fomenting the mobs."

She too was happy for the peace. She was in circumstances again. Her cousin Cotton had recommended that she try to keep her pregnancies two years apart. Her Puritan family and friends had evolved a method of having only as many children as they wanted and, barring accident, fairly close to when they wanted them. Her sister Mary was three years older than she; she was two years older than Billy; Billy was three and a half years older than Betsy. Her sister Mary had had her first child three years before and was still not in circumstances. Mercy Warren had confided that, although her second son had been born only a year and a half after the first, they had waited three years for the next one, and two more for the fourth. As closely as she could figure she had conceived in the month of October, which meant that her children would be born two years apart.

John rejoiced when she told him.

She carried well, a mild nausea in the early morning, sleepiness in the afternoon. By the time she got into loose-fitting clothes she had butterfly-like movements within her. An inner glow of happiness made her eyes mystically luminous. John became increasingly tender as she grew more and more extended. There was an old wives' tale in Weymouth, she told him, that if you grew big all around it was a girl; and if you grew straight out in front it was a boy.

"Keep growing straight out!" he admonished.

He rode circuit, again trying cases of little consequence, the feuds endemic to New England which frequently provided the only excitement and entertainment the countryside could count on. In many instances the suits sprang from passion, from rivalries for town office, from defamation; town quarrels and jealousies that had been fought for twenty years, impoverishing both sides.

"Why are our folk so corrosive?" he complained.

"Father says it started when our people first came over. They examined each other's personal lives relentlessly for years to make sure that a man was truly 'saved,' before they admitted him to their congregation. That when the Puritans were 'gathered' they made a covenant with the Lord binding themselves to expose every last sin of their own conscience . . . and everybody else's, as well. He says our forebears, bless or blast them! were hopeless pryers, meddlers, spies and informers. When the first congregations were formed, and they needed 'seven pillars' to make a church, seven men had to survive public interrogation unknown this side of the Spanish Inquisition. Heaven may have been their dearest country, as they claimed; and they did, God knows, create an independent republic in each tiny community; but by 'opening their spiritual condition to each other' they created a special kind of Congregationalist hell which no other religion could have conceived. My father has worked hard to put an end to vicious gossip and intrusions of privacy. He says, 'Live in peace with your neighbor or find yourself another preacher.' That's why our Weymouth people are so much less in court."

"It's not money I like to take. But if I don't handle the case someone else will. Look at this purse of gold coins: a beginning patrimony for our son." Resignedly he added, "I'll take them up to the attic."

Over the lean-to there was a sharp-angled space, and in it a concealed ladder that led to a secret attic. In this attic, through which the brick fireplace passed, there were two loose bricks. Inside was a hollow space which they called the Adams Specie Bank. Here John deposited all of his earnings except the portion Abigail kept out for house expenses.

He killed a cow for their meat, lopped and trimmed the walnuts and oaks. Wanting to open the prospect of the house, to let in more sun and air, he cut down the irregular misshapen pines; now they could see clear to the creek. In the evenings they sat before the parlor fire while he read aloud to her from Hume's *Political Discourses.* On rainy days he worked on an essay, *Who Are to Be Understood by the Better Sort of People?* an answer to Jonathan Sewall, who under the name of "Philanthrop" had been publishing a series of articles in the *Boston Post* on what a great governor Bernard was for Massachusetts.

Again she had an easy birth. As she lay on the hard cot in her borning room she thanked God for her good fortune, as well as for the beautiful son, long, skinny, red, looking like a collection of bones inside a sausage casing. John was beside himself with joy. He kept bringing her gifts: flowers, a lace handkerchief, a finger ring, material for a robe of sapphire-blue brocade.

Two days after the birth of the boy, her grandfather Colonel John Quincy died at Mount Wollaston. She was excused from attending the burial. When John returned he said:

"We thought you might like to name him after the Colonel."

She brushed away her tears, answered with a smile:

"John Quincy Adams. Yes, I would like that. Grandfather Quincy was a good man. With our son carrying his name, he remains alive."

She looked down at the babe sleeping in her arms.

"Welcome, John Quincy, to the Adams family."

Her first feeling, after the elation of giving her husband a son, was one of pride. Though she had desperately wanted a boy she had never been sure that she would be able to cope. She felt she would know all the answers to a daughter quite intuitively. It would be like having a new doll to play with after one had outgrown dolls, the chance to dress the child prettily, tie her hair with ribbons. A daughter was a continuation of her own, known life; a son was pure adventure.

She was certain that he would become a strong young man. She liked the idea of having more strength in the house and in the family, even though it would be a few years before he could manifest that strength. She would not dress him in elaborate clothes but leave him free to roam the farm, learn to hunt and fish with his father. Nab would stay at home, help with the chores and the younger children. Johnny would turn outward, be independent, forced at an early age to accept a man's responsibilities. Even at the age of a few weeks he seemed overwhelmingly male, and her love, though not greater than for Nab, was of a different, more exciting kind. She felt that perhaps the most important thing, when having a son, was to love your husband. Then the boy was free to become his own man, as independent as his father.

And now that she was taking care of Johnny, she was amused that she had ever been fearful of doing so.

John's itinerary for the rest of the year was already established: to Plymouth in July; August was reserved for the Suffolk Superior Court in Boston; in September he would attend the Worcester and Bristol courts; in October, north to Plymouth again, then back to Cambridge;

November at Charlestown, her father's home place; December at Barnstable, and Plymouth for still a third time.

Her weekdays were filled with countless tasks. After supper she sat in John's office reading the Boston papers and out-of-town gazettes since he had asked her to keep up with the news. But the Sabbath was lonely. Lying in her bed at night, her head high on the bolster so that she could see Nab in her trundle and the baby in his cradle, she knew that John had to build his practice; they had to establish a competence with which to raise and educate their young. But it seemed a high price to pay.

Their desire to live outside the realm of controversy was shattered within two months of the boy's birth. John had warned Abigail that the language of the Repeal Act had left the door open for further conflict, but she had attributed this to his legalistic reading of parliamentary procedures. Now Chancellor of the Exchequer Charles Townshend, as acting head of the British Ministry under George III, steered four new bills through Parliament. They provided for revenues from the American colonies. A special Board of Customs Commissioners was set up in Boston to collect the fees that would be charged against commodities brought into American ports, and which could be imported only from England: paper, glass, painters' colors, tea and many others.

As far as could be gathered from the first English newspapers reaching Boston, Townshend based his reasoning on the concept that the colonies had fought the Stamp Act because it was an *internal* tax, a tax on the everyday processes of American living. The Townshend Acts would be *external* taxes, paid on transported merchandise only, the monies collected to be used to pay Crown officers in America. They had been paid by the colonists up to this point, which gave the colonists a measure of control. The new Board of Customs Commissioners would have the legal weapons to collect the taxes, as well as the power to close established ports and open new ones. They could hire vessels and employ as many new customs officers as they thought they wanted to collect the customs charges. Boston was to be headquarters for the new commission. The Acts also set up four new Admiralty Courts, in Halifax, Boston, Philadelphia and Charlestown, with the right to search and seize and try Americans, without a jury trial, and before judges appointed from London.

It was only sixteen months since the furor over the Stamp Act had died down. John returned hurriedly from circuit, laden with Boston and New York newspapers.

"The New York Assembly has been suspended," he cried. "What has been its crime? General Gage demanded that the Assembly provide barracks, funds and supplies for British soldiers to be quartered on them without their consent. New York refused. And now the Townshend Acts dissolve the assembly until it obeys General Gage! If Parliament can abolish the New York Assembly, then why not Massachusetts? And Virginia? And Pennsylvania?"

He was trembling with rage.

"These Townshend Acts are worse than the Stamp Act. They are more dangerous than the Writs of Assistance in '61. They were to raise revenues. These also discipline and control the colonies, curtail our self-governing rights. If our legislatures don't themselves pay the governors and judges, they will never heed a word we say."

In Boston the Sons of Liberty were crying, ". . . we'll be wading through seas of blood, though stunned with the awful roar of cannon."

Tears smarted behind Abigail's eyes. John came to the low chair on which she was rocking agitatedly and put a firm hand on her shoulder.

"We are no longer novices. We will know how to handle ourselves more quickly this time."

She looked up at her husband with a quizzical smile at the corner of her lips.

"I thought 'we' were out of politics."

"This isn't politics, my dear. Politics is running for office, being elected a member of the legislature. This is survival."

"And survival means conflict. It has from the beginning of time."

"So it has: resist or succumb. If Parliament can pass acts which quarter troops on New York without their consent; if they can turn Boston into one huge custom house to control the imports and exports of all thirteen colonies; if they can tax us to raise money to pay the wages of their officers; if they can deprive us of our trial by jury; if Parliament can do all this, *what can they not do to us*? We are not allowed to elect representatives to that Parliament. How then can we continue to allow it to pass regulations against us? All boundaries are down between London and Boston. Their acts will have clear sailing straight across the Atlantic . . ."

He stalked his office, heavy boots leaving tracks across the polished planking.

". . . unless we build fences. New England is made of stone. We'll gather and dump and build a breakwater a thousand miles east."

"I believe you can!" she said. "This *is* politics. You don't have to be elected; you're a volunteer. Your eyes are snapping. There's high color in your cheeks. You're like a man rescued from ennui, willing to be thrown into an arena bristling with wild boars."

He blushed, which further heightened the flame on his cheeks.

"I will confess. In my blood I feel there is no distinction between politics and law. I am practicing law; I am practicing politics. As barrister I work for an individual; as politician I work for a colony."

"As a barrister you are a private man, you and your family. As a politician you are public property, like the Common. Everybody can graze their cattle on your grass. Every conflict that arises involves you. You are no longer solely ours, Nab's, Johnny's, mine."

"Would you bid me stay out?"

She met his gaze straight on.

"No, John. We're small, we three dependents of yours, and not of much use in a fight; but we'll follow you down the trail as far as it goes."

BOOK THREE

THE HIDDEN AND THE REVEALED

1

NEW Year's Day of 1768 was family day at the parsonage in Weymouth. Billy, now twenty-one, a gangling youth who still looked sixteen, seemed pleased to be home. At the end of dinner they pushed their chairs back, though it was tight quarters with the family table extended to seat thirty. The talk turned to the Townshend Acts.

The tone of the contest had changed, for the Ministry had chosen the five new customs commissioners extremely well: Charles Paxton had experience as customs commissioner of Boston, John Robinson had been a collector of revenue at Newport, Rhode Island. William Burch and Henry Hulton, just arrived from England, were reputed to be determined to make the Acts work. John Temple was a native Bostonian. So well indeed had the Ministry chosen that the Sons of Liberty, now a Boston-wide organization growing out of the original Loyal Nine, became equally determined to enforce a boycott not only of the to-be-heavily-taxed glass, paper, paint and tea, but of everything raised or manufactured in England.

Abigail had spent a considerable part of the latter months of 1767 alone, while John spent more and more time in Boston at political meetings, and with businessmen seeking him out as counsel, particularly former clients of Jeremiah Gridley, who had died a short time before.

Suddenly from across the table Isaac Smith blurted:

"John, when are you and Abigail moving to Boston? Sooner or later you will have to. You could double your practice in the city."

Abigail and John gazed at each other. They had been wondering about this same question, yet dreading to face it. Forces beyond their control were making the Braintree residence less and less tenable. If they lived in Boston John would not be obliged to beat up and down the roads, sleeping in unaccustomed beds, sometimes too tired of a Sunday even to make the long journey home. She recalled his remark when he had reached home one evening as exhausted as his horse:

"I've ridden so many hours and miles that I'm coming to believe that the bottom of me is more important than the top."

For her own part, she loved the cottage, but the move would mean that John could spend twice as much time with her and the children.

"We wouldn't like you to take Abigail and the babies ten miles further away," commented the Reverend Mr. Smith, "but the energetic young men of every country have moved to their capital, to London, Paris, Rome . . ."

"Home is roots," declared John. Then he rushed on impulsively, "But what plan of reading or reflection or business can be pursued by a man who is now at Pownalborough, then at Martha's Vineyard, next at Boston, then at Taunton, presently at Barnstable? What a dissipation that is."

Agreement murmured around the table.

In the carriage going home Abigail said seriously, "I feel at home in a village. But we must move into Boston, mustn't we? We have no choice."

"We have a choice, dear one; yet all the arguments are piling up in front of the Boston courts. Nabby, let me grope my way forward."

She pulled her coat tighter about her.

"Very well, let us grope."

"Madam: to what object are my views directed? What is the end and purpose of my studies, journeys, labors of the body and mind, tongue and pen? Am I grasping at money or scheming for power?"

"No."

"I am tossed about so much from post to pillar that I have not leisure and tranquillity enough to consider distinctly my own views, objects, feelings. . . ."

Panic clutched her.

"We won't sell our home, our farm?"

He transferred the reins to his left hand, put his right arm about her securely.

"We will never sell our home. We will have it to come back to, for the summers and holidays. Or when we grow weary or sated with the life of a big city."

Her heart stopped pounding.

"For a moment there I felt as though I was about to be blown across the fields like a dry bush."

They decided not to lease until spring, when the wet season would be over. John asked his friends to find him a few possibilities. When the list was ready, Betsy, close to eighteen now, came over from Weymouth to stay with the children. John took Abigail into town. Aunt Elizabeth gave them her bedroom.

It took several days of trudging up and down stairs, weighing drawbacks against advantages. Finally she chose a pleasant house on the southeast corner of Hillier's Lane and Brattle, across the street from the Brattle Square Church. It was a two-storied brick house painted white, called the White House. It faced the open square, separated from the next house by a wide passage filled with shrubs and tall trees. Faneuil Hall and the Town House were close by, a few minutes' walk for John over the cobbled Brattle Square, with moss growing between the stones, and then through Dock Square.

John left the choice to her, though he added:

"Check the inventories carefully. I'd rather not have to haul in wagonloads of supplies. If we could leave the Braintree house as it is . . ."

That decided her. There were more luxurious houses available, but the one on Brattle Square was the most completely furnished. The entry hall was spacious, with a wainscoted staircase. In the parlor facing the square were nine straight-backed chairs about the walls, two easy chairs before the fireplace, a stand-up clock and a marble table. There was a cream-colored carpet and cream curtains at the windows, a room not unlike her mother's in Weymouth. The smaller sitting room had hunting prints on its walls between copper candle brackets, a broad mahogany desk held a glass lamp, there was a solid wall of bookshelves. John returned from a newly rented office opposite the Town House to find her here.

"Of course you've guessed this will be my study. I won't attempt to cart in my whole library, only the books I shall need."

She smiled indulgently. "The books you don't need have yet to be printed."

They examined the dining room, with its glassware in cabinets. In the center of the room was an oval mahogany table with eight chairs upholstered in red velvet. The kitchen proved to have been the repository not only of the original Jeremiah Allen estate, but also of the British customs officer who had leased it before them. Apparently he had decided that it was cheaper to leave certain things behind than to box and ship them to England: pewter dishes, colanders, skillets, trivets, dripping and frying pans.

Arm in arm they walked through the back door to the rear garden. The pump was just outside the kitchen door; a cistern held ten hogsheads of water. Hidden by a trellis were twin outhouses painted white. The garden had been advertised as "fit for housekeeping." The gardener had planted peas, beans, radishes, turnips, squash and spinach.

"We'll be eating our own fresh vegetables all summer," said Abigail.

John stopped in the path that led to the carriage house, took her in his arms.

Back in Braintree John announced that he could no longer serve as selectman. The town meeting gave him a vote of confidence.

They moved into Boston in April, Abigail indicating the clothing, linens, foodstuffs from their cellar they would take with them. John took care of the carting. She chose for their bedroom the freshly painted second-floor room on the corner, with one window overlooking Hillier's Lane and two windows on Brattle Street. There was a fireplace, a four-poster trimmed in yellow mohair, and a marble-topped chest with a pair of china pitchers and bowls.

She put Johnny in the adjoining room with Rachel to look after him. Young Nab, now approaching three, was sad when she was given a room to herself across the hall. She was a precocious child, serious of manner, with a memory for nursery rhymes which she sang to Johnny. The fourth bedroom at the end of the hall would be for family and friends visiting Boston.

The day after they moved in they went to Purchase Street to pay their respects. Samuel was in his study, writing before the fireplace in a worn but clean white shirt. Though James Otis was the leader in the legislature, Samuel was now drafting most of the protest papers that were being sent to England.

"How sweet of you to yield to a cousinly request and move into Boston," he cried.

"Now, Sam'l, that was six years ago you asked."

"No matter. Time was coined to be spent. Welcome to Boston, hotbed of sedition. If I remember rightly, I offered you a tea party if you would come and be my neighbors. Betsy, is there tea?"

Betsy was wearing a simple black dress that made her skin and eyes seem to shine.

"Now, Samuel, you know we never have tea at five in the afternoon. That's a British custom, and you don't like anything British."

Samuel put down his pen.

"Good. Bring in the no-tea, with the no-cakes. And bring in that no-child of mine." Only Hannah was at home. Samuel, Jr., was already attending Harvard.

"We are not interrupting those inflammatory letters you've been writing?" John teased dryly.

"Pretty effective, though. Miss Abigail, did you read the messages the House sent to the Ministry, to the Earl of Shelburne, the Marquis of Rockingham and Lord Camden?"

Betsy brought in tea. Abigail took a cup of the fragrant Chinese tea from Betsy's hand, a slice of lemon, cut a sliver of sugar off the cone, then returned to the badgering game with Samuel.

"Let me see one of those letters you drafted for English consumption."

Samuel fished among layers of papers, came up with a bite.

"You have a treat in store," he said, "after being obliged to read your husband's dry treatises. Let me read you a couple of lines:

" 'There are, my lord, fundamental rules of the Constitution which it is humbly presumed neither the supreme legislative nor the supreme executive can alter. In all free states the Constitution is fixed; it is from thence that the legislative derives its authority; therefore it cannot change the Constitution without destroying its own foundation. If, then, the Constitution of Great Britain is the common right of all British subjects, it is humbly referred to your lordship's judgment whether the supreme legislative of the Empire may rightly leap the bounds of it in the exercise of power over the subjects in America any more than over those in Britain.' "

"You don't do too badly," contributed John, "for a man whose mother wouldn't let him become a lawyer. The city Adamses write a mighty flowing line."

"We shall see," answered Samuel. "I think you've come to Boston at exactly the right moment. We need you."

2

The exterior pattern of her life changed abruptly with their move into Boston. The newly arrived Adamses were invited to a different home each day for a party to celebrate their becoming Bostonians. Samuel and Betsy led off with a crowded buffet for fifty, including James Otis, Benjamin Edes, John Avery, Jr., and many other merchants and craftsmen among the Sons of Liberty. No other wives were present. The men surrounded her in excitedly talking groups, for was she not the wife of one of their chief spokesmen? And were they not now in a dripping pan over an even hotter fire? Most of them assumed that the Adamses had moved into Boston the better to fight Parliament.

When the last guest had departed and Abigail had embraced Betsy for her heroic effort, she turned to Samuel.

"Sam'l, I know you will pretend this was a political dinner. But you're not fooling me. There wasn't a man here who doesn't have legal work to be done, one time or another."

Samuel ducked his head as he did when he was caught out.

"One bad businessman in the family is enough. I have to make sure Cousin John's practice flourishes or we'll lose you again to the remote frontier of Braintree."

Uncle Isaac gave a dinner for them, inviting his fellow shippers and merchants with their wives. They were elegantly gowned, their hair coifed in elaborate fan-shaped structures. John's fellow lawyers entertained for him: Robert Auchmuty, Jonathan Sewall, now solicitor general for the Crown, Samuel Fitch, Benjamin Gridley, nephew of Jeremiah, John Lowell, Francis Dana. Abigail's cousin Josiah Quincy, Jr., invited in his young friends to a Saturday night supper. John Hancock, still courting Dorothy Quincy, gave a formal party, with a string quartet playing Bach. For this occasion, which would see the wealthiest Boston society turn out, Abigail had gone to a Boston dressmaker and ordered a gown of red silk brocade with a low neckline showing her beautifully rounded shoulders. The gown had bouffant sleeves, three-quarter length, ruffled at the edges; the deep V of the neck was outlined in ribbon to the pointed waist. Her shoes were made of the same red silk fabric, with high wooden heels.

As she tied the strings of her petticoat and stepped into the gown she commented:

"I'm glad you moved into town to build a more lucrative practice, because I've already spent all that extra money you plan to earn."

John regarded his wife's figure with unabashed admiration.

"Only now do I realize what a scrawny thing you were when I married you. There's nothing like a husband to make a wife curvacious."

Abigail examined herself in the full-length mirror, glad that the affluent owner had installed one, and that she no longer felt so guilty over the stricture that it was sinful to seek pleasure in a mirror. John was right. Her bosom was fully developed now; the nursing of the two babies had given them a rounder, more mature shape. The mirror confirmed that she was still slim, the heavy silk making her seem longer in the hips and legs.

"I'm glad you're pleased with the gown. It cost a king's ransom."

"Elementary investment, Miss Abigail. Boston will know I have an extravagant wife. As a result they will bring me their best law cases."

They subscribed to the Tuesday evening concerts at Deblois's Concert Hall on Queen Street, where they heard vocal and instrumental music. The programs were titled "Select Pieces by the Best Masters," of whom Handel was the favorite. The hall was reputed to have the best organ in America for religious music. Once a month there was a Grand Assembly, with good music for dancing but bad wine and punch for refreshment. Plays were illegal, yet actors came to Boston to read *The Beggar's Opera* or *Love in a Village*. Though the reading of the librettos was awkward the arias were charmingly sung. They took Nab to see the lion on board the sloop *Phoenix* at Long Wharf, and to a shop which had a musical machine that played a combination of notes. On warm days they drove with friends to Fresh Pond or South Pond where they picnicked, the men fishing while the women chatted about housewives' problems.

Her greatest pleasure was to take long walks through the streets and their lore. John, the perennial student, was gathering stories of the houses of the city and of the people within them. She liked to walk down to the Old Feather Store. The man who put up this building in 1680 had had the idea of mixing fragments of glass bottles in with his wall plaster and putting ornamental figures on the surface. Here Thomas Hollis kept the main apothecary shop of Boston. The triangular warehouse, located at the Town Dock near the head of Market Street, was a building of towers, one in the center and at each angle of the pointed slate roof, each capped with a stone ball on iron spires.

One of John's favorite walks was a circular stroll among the taverns.

They would go first to the Lamb Tavern where the stagecoach to Providence was now stopping; then continue on to the neighboring White Horse and Lion taverns, which served as meeting clubs and political centers as well as drinking establishments. From the Town House she could see the towering masts of the ships in the harbor.

She fell into the pattern of the city wife. It was not considered proper for her to do any of the housework or cooking. Betsy Adams secured her a robust third cousin as a cook. A young boy kept the stoop and yard. In the early mornings Abigail shopped on the docks for fish just brought in, or went to the stalls at Faneuil Hall for fresh beef or lamb. Fruits, milk, butter and eggs were vended at the house, live poultry came through the streets in baskets balanced on either end of a pole across the farmer's shoulders. Young Nab enjoyed the morning pilgrimages among the food shops, and Rachel was proud to be walking home with a wicker basket of eatables on her arm.

The city was at fever pitch. The Patriot *Boston Gazette* fulminated against the Townshend Acts, while the Tory *News-Letter* and *Weekly Advertiser* called down a pox on the Patriots' heads. Bostonians with no stomach for politics, and Abigail was surprised to learn how many there were, read the neutral *Chronicle* or the independent *Evening Post.* On the street corners there were knots of men arguing so heatedly that she sometimes had to step off the curb into the street to avoid their gesticulations.

The gratifying part of their introduction to Boston was her growing sense that John's activities for the Patriots had not alienated the Loyalists. At the reception given for them by Esther and Jonathan Sewall, in their neighboring home on Brattle Street, most of the people holding office under the Crown—Andrew Oliver, Hallowell, Joseph Harrison, Edmund Trowbridge, John Temple, as well as a number of the wealthier merchants who were loyal to King and Parliament—told Abigail and John how delighted they were to have them in Boston. Abigail gathered that John Adams had been forgiven for his Braintree Instructions and the appeal before the Assembly for Massachusetts Bay Colony, because his tone had been quiet and he had based his opposition on the Massachusetts charter. It was also known that he believed that all who had suffered damage during the rioting should be compensated.

Jonathan said to Abigail, as they took a stroll through the lovely Sewall gardens:

"Lieutenant Governor Hutchinson really wanted to come today."

Abigail gazed at him wide-eyed.

"That strains my credulity."

"Truly, he asked me to express his regrets. He admires John's talents. I'll confess that Governor Bernard ignored my invitation. But I know that once I bring John and Bernard together they will become friends."

The Otises also entertained for them. James Otis had come to visit one evening. He was built like John, plump, with a touch of jowl. His wide-spaced eyes reflected his quickly changing moods. He had such enormous magnetism that his silence filled the room fuller than most men's conversation.

"I have come seeking a favor."

"Granted," said John.

"I'd like you to come to my home for dinner this Sabbath after preaching."

"It would be our pleasure."

"Only possibly. My wife refuses to entertain my friends. I vanish when she has hers."

"Then why ask us?" Abigail was puzzled.

Otis looked her squarely in the eyes.

"Because I think she might accept you two. Even though you are Patriots. She mentioned she had heard nice things about 'the new Mrs. Adams in town.'"

James Otis had married Ruth Cunningham within a few months of his sister Mercy's marriage to James Warren. She seemed to have been the last woman in Massachusetts he should have selected.

". . . or who should have chosen him," Abigail rejoined when John told her of Otis's unhappiness at home. "I hear she's a beauty."

"Undoubtedly. But an imperious beauty. Otis describes her as a High Tory. She reads him unmerciful lectures about the filthy rabble he is consorting with, the vulgar unwashed he is attempting to lead, the disgrace he has brought upon the proud name of her dead father, and how he'll end up on a gibbet for high treason if he doesn't come to his senses."

"Why didn't she marry a Crown sympathizer?"

"Why didn't he marry a Patriot? How can we explain who marries whom? It's my guess that friction at home, as much as anything, has been the cause of the irritability that is breaking up his fine mind."

"I hadn't known it was breaking up."

"I am inclined to believe that it is the days of icy silence in his own home that cause him to launch into hours of excitable and eccentric talk. He grows the most talkative man alive. No other man in company can find space to put in a word. Agreed there is brilliance, much knowledge and humor in his conversation, but he grows narrative like an old man. He's only a year or so over forty."

"John, wasn't he always eccentric? His sister Mercy has told me how at a country dance in their Barnstable home James played several dances on his violin for them, then at the height of the stomping held his violin high in the air, cried out, 'So Orpheus fiddled and so danced the brutes,' and ran out of the house."

Ruth Otis's home was exquisitely kept. Abigail got along splendidly with the three Otis children, Elizabeth, Mary and James III. Mrs. Otis, though reserved, seemed to accept her as a near equal. During dinner the men mentioned the H.M.S. *Romney*, a fifty-gun warship that was riding at anchor in the harbor with its heavy guns trained on Boston. Mrs. Otis beamed her approval, which threw James Otis into a bitter denunciation of Lord Hillsborough, who had ordered troops into Boston, and of General Gage, in charge of His Majesty's troops in North America, who was preparing to send several companies of redcoats from Halifax to Boston to help enforce the Townshend Acts. Ruth Otis froze, became silent, a silence that was too painful to be endured. Immediately upon leaving the table Abigail and John departed. The experiment had failed.

Their introduction to Boston rounded itself out in a day they were not likely to forget. A note arrived from Jonathan Sewall asking if he might "come to noon dinner, alone; something wonderfully urgent."

He was flushed with pleasure as he sprang jauntily up the four steps from the pavement. When dinner was finished he thanked Abigail elaborately, then asked:

"John, could we go into your office and talk?"

"If we don't, Jonathan, you will explode like a firecracker right here in the dining room."

Abigail went into the kitchen for a few moments to give the cook her instructions for the evening, then retired to her bedroom. It could not have been more than a half hour when she heard the front door slam and John come heavy-footed up the stairs.

He slumped into a cane chair, unbuttoned his waistcoat and loosened the broad knot of the cravat at his throat. Then he explained that Jonathan had been promoted to attorney general of Massachusetts. He had come at the request of Governor Bernard to offer John the Crown position of advocate general in the Court of Admiralty. He grinned sheepishly, but underneath she perceived an element of tension.

"As Sewall tells it, Governor Bernard and Lieutenant Governor Hutchinson agreed that, in point of talent, reputation and consequence at the Bar, I was best entitled to the office."

Her head spun. Advocate general! It was a proud office. In the past it had been held by some of the men John admired most in Massachusetts history. She knew how lucrative the offer was. The advocate general was permitted to carry on his private practice, indeed had his major time for it. John often had told her these offers of Crown appointments were "a first step in the ladder of royal favor and promotion."

They sat in silence. It would have been impossible for either of them to anticipate such a development. She dared not look at him or trust her voice to speak. She sensed the profound implications of the decision. It was his to make, and his alone. After a few moments he continued:

"I told Jonathan that I was sensible to the honor done me by the governor but that I had to be excused from accepting the offer."

Breath came back into her lungs. She had felt she knew what his answer would be; but how could one tell, even a wife, how a man would respond to an offer that put aside uncertainty and guaranteed cases, honor, money?

"He asked what my objections were. I told him that he knew my political principles, that the system I have adopted is that of the Patriots in opposition to any royal or parliamentary encroachments on our legal freedoms."

She turned to him a face radiant with pride.

"Jonathan refused to take 'No' for an answer. I tried to explain to him that the British government was persevering in a system wholly inconsistent with my ideas of right and justice. How then could I place myself in a position in which my duty would pull me one way and my political convictions the other?"

"Surely he could see the logic of that?"

"On the contrary, he thought I was being idiotically illogical. The governor had sent word that he knew my political sentiments very well but that I would be at full liberty to entertain my own opinions uninfluenced by the demands of the office. The governor said he believed in my integrity."

He walked over to the bed, where she had been resting, stood there.

"You knew, of course, that I could not accept. With the Townshend Acts hanging over our heads it would be my job as advocate general to prosecute our friends, perhaps even our relations. I'm sorry, my dear. It was our first chance to become rich and powerful. There may never be another."

She rose, put her arms about his neck and held him fiercely.

"Let's not be sorry. Let's go down and open the very best bottle of Madeira that's ever been smuggled into Boston."

3

She could tell from one quick look at John Hancock's face and figure as he stood on her doorstep that he was bringing disturbing news. Hancock was considered the most meticulous dresser in Boston, avowing that the major purpose of clothes, aside from covering one's nakedness, was to bring pleasure and color to the town. Abigail did not think this ostentation or vanity. Why should not a man of social prominence dress as well as his money and good taste would permit? But on this late afternoon as she opened the door to his knock, she saw that his beautiful apple-green coat and lace collar were awry.

John Hancock, some fifteen months younger than John Adams, had attended Mrs. Belcher's and Mr. Cleverly's schools with him. Hancock's father had died and the boy was taken in by his father's brother Thomas. The Boston Hancocks were among the richest merchants and shipowners in New England; and were childless. When Thomas Hancock died in 1764 John inherited most of the vast estate: £80,000, huge areas of land in Massachusetts and Connecticut; ships, shops, wharfs, warehouses.

John Adams and John Hancock had been close friends for the three years they were at Harvard together. Hancock took his Master's at seventeen, spent the next six years in a rigorous apprenticeship under his uncle in the Hancock countinghouse, and at the age of twenty-seven had to take charge of the world-wide operation. He had made his mistakes, lost some money, but now was in firm control of its intricacies. In spite of the great fortune he had to risk John Hancock had joined James Otis, Samuel Adams, Dr. Joseph Warren and Josiah Quincy, Jr., to fight the Stamp Act. However he had so vigorously disapproved of the mob violence that Samuel Adams had had as difficult a time convincing Hancock that the end justified the means as he had John Adams.

"The remarkable thing about Hancock," John observed, "is that the inheritance of that tremendous fortune has made little change in him. He was always steady, punctual, industrious, an indefatigable man of business. And he is generous with his money, a rarity among the rich in Boston."

"In New England."

"On Pope's Day in November 1765, when the North and South End crowds agreed to unite, Hancock paid the costs at the Green Dragon for the evening's food and drink. True, he had a bounden audience for his first political speech, but it was an eloquent appeal to resist England's destructive taxation. He has also loaned Samuel money to straighten out his tax records."

John Hancock was not a particularly handsome man: long, retroussé nose, very high forehead which set the relatively small chin somewhat out of proportion. His eyes were clear though rarely reflecting intensity; he had strong black eyebrows and thin lips. It was a good face, characterized by intelligence but not intellectual force. Abigail and John thought him attractive. His detractors called his face "contradictory and weak." It was true that it sometimes took him an unconscionably long time to make up his mind.

Now John Hancock was in trouble. There was a dew of perspiration on his usually placid brow. He was breathing heavily from a perturbed half-run from his wharf. John Hancock never came on business when a messenger could run the errand, so Abigail knew there must be mischief abroad.

"Mrs. Adams, my pardon. It is not my custom to break in so unceremoniously."

"Mr. Hancock, please do come in. Mr. Adams will be back any moment. Could I get you a cold refreshment?"

"Indeed. Any refreshment would be welcome after these past hectic hours. Mrs. Adams, my sloop *Liberty* is now anchored under the guns of H.M.S. *Romney*, a prisoner of war!"

Abigail swallowed hard.

"Had you time to get your cargo off?"

Hancock shot her a swift, sideways glance to see if she were gulling him. Satisfied that she had heard nothing, he replied:

"That's what the conflagration is about. When the tide-waiter, Mr. Kirk, came on board to assess our cargo for duties under the Townshend Acts, my purser locked him below in a cabin while my men at the wharf unloaded her."

"O Heaven!"

"You may say so. None of this was done with my knowledge, of course."

They exchanged a look of guileless innocence. She heard John's energetic steps coming across the cobblestones of Brattle Square. She went to the door to admit him. He too was out of breath and disheveled.

"Well, Brother Hancock, for a man who disapproves of riots, I must say you instigated a lovely one this afternoon."

"Ah, then you were on the docks."

"Wasn't all of Boston? I never saw such an assembly."

"Suppose you gentlemen sit down and stop circling each other around my carpet."

She pulled the Chinese silk tassle hanging by the parlor door to summon Rachel. "Please get the gentlemen a draught of cold cider."

Then she listened as the two men spoke of the happenings, neither one waiting for the other's sentence to be finished. Boats from the man-o'-war *Romney* had rowed into Hancock's dock, cut the *Liberty's* moorings and towed her out to the lee side of the *Romney*. Hancock's workmen retaliated by hurling stones at the customs officers. The ensuing uproar attracted an ever growing crowd which, learning that the Crown authorities had committed an aggressive act against Massachusetts, went wild with rage, breaking the sword of the inspector of imports, seizing and dragging a Custom House boat through the streets and burning it on the Common. They then set off for the houses of the comptroller and inspector, breaking every window in the buildings.

Hancock put an arm affectionately about John's shoulder.

"You'll represent me, of course?"

"Of course. How much is the *Liberty* worth?"

"Many thousand pounds. Why?"

"Because the Crown apparently intends to hold the boat until they collect the full duties, plus punitive damages."

"Can you keep them from doing that?"

"*I* can't. But our Constitution can. The Townshend Acts are illegal, hence the seizing of the *Liberty* is illegal. We'll seek punitive damages from the Crown for malicious mischief."

Hancock's face brightened. He put his scarlet velvet cap on his head, rebuttoned his white satin embroidered waistcoat.

"I feel vindicated already. Do me the honor of coming to dinner on Sunday, Mrs. Adams? Brother Adams, sharpen up those lawbooks of yours. Until tomorrow!"

Abigail saw that her husband did not share Hancock's sense of relief. He asked her to help him out of his black broadcloth waistcoat and leather shoes. When she asked how serious the matter was he replied:

"More than Hancock realizes. Bernard and Hutchinson are very clever. They didn't seize the *Liberty* for smuggling. The Madeira had already vanished into Boston. They caught him loading tar and oil without a Customs Commission permit. On a technical legality, they've got him."

"You mean, they've got the *Liberty*."

"Precisely. They're in process of declaring the *Liberty* contraband. In addition the Crown officers plan to sue our friend for £100,000 in old tender."

"But that's the wealth of Croesus."

"It's the wealth of John Hancock. If the Crown can collect. The fine is all out of proportion. It may be a fiendishly clever scheme to frighten us. I'll know more when I get to court."

Suddenly they gazed at each other in terror.

"May God save our benighted souls! Abigail, do you know what would have happened if I had accepted the office of advocate general?"

"Yes." Her voice was hoarse. "You would now have to prosecute John Hancock, confiscate his *Liberty* and his fortune."

The sweat broke out on John's face.

"Nabby, if ever in my life I should be tempted to fight on the side of money or power instead of my friends, please remind me of this fatally close call."

"I'll remind you. But what was close about the call? You rejected it out of hand. Now take yourself a tub. We're going to Nick Boylston's for supper."

John was not to be diverted. He had suffered the shock of a man whose sane legal training had come into collision with an opposing reality.

"For the first time that we know, England has used a man-of-war to force its will on Massachusetts. If today the Crown has used one of its battle fleet, will they tomorrow use soldiers, cannon?"

By seizing the *Liberty* the Crown had endangered the liberty of every man, woman and child in the thirteen colonies. In terms of symbolism it was neat. Very neat indeed.

A meeting was called for "Liberty Hall," the area under the Tree of Liberty in Hanover Square. Abigail asked if it would be taken amiss if she went along.

"I mean, will there be ladies present?"

"There are frequently women in the crowds, and since they don't throw stones it's safe to assume they are ladies."

It was a warmly pleasant mid-June morning. Most of Boston was abroad. So many people came to the area that the speakers could not be heard from the tree. An official town meeting was called for that afternoon at Old South Church. Abigail and John walked with Mercy and James Warren straight down Newbury or No Smoking Street until it became Marlborough Street and led to the Old South, with its tall spire, the brick building painted a light color. They found seats in a side pew.

James Otis was chosen moderator. A hush fell over the hundreds who crowded the aisles, sides and two tiers of balconies. Otis thrust home each point: the Townshend Act taxes had been imposed without their knowledge or consent; dutiful petitions had been sent to their most gracious Sovereign, but instead Boston had been invaded. . . .

It was the first time Abigail had heard a number of the Patriots speak. There rose to the podium Dr. Joseph Warren, Samuel Adams, Benjamin Church, Dr. Thomas Young, John Adams. Each spoke to a special point of reference: that many of the laws of Parliament were extinct, that Governor Bernard must remove the *Romney* from the harbor, that the customs commissioners who had fled to the *Romney* for safety be taken off the ship, that the *Liberty* be returned to Mr. Hancock; that Parliament answer their petitions. James Otis was elected to head a committee of twenty-one to write and present a petition to Governor Bernard. John Adams was nominated to a committee to write the Boston Instructions to the General Court.

"I'm going to hang a sign outside our house: John Adams—*Instructions Writer*," he whispered.

"No false modesty, my friend. You know you're proud as a peacock."

"But not so beautiful."

He held her firmly under the arm as they walked up Cornhill through Dock Square and past the Brattle Street Church. John read Nab a story from Aesop's *Fables* while Rachel prepared tea. Nab repeated the tale to Johnny, now nearly a year old. John began writing. His Instructions were addressed to the Boston representatives, Otis, Samuel Adams, John Hancock and Thomas Cushing. Abigail read behind him, picking up the wet pages from the floor as he dropped them off the flat desk. He seemed to be writing effortlessly.

"After the repeal of the late American Stamp Act, we were happy in the pleasing prospect of a restoration of that tranquillity and unanimity among ourselves, and that harmony and affection between our parent country and us, which had generally subsisted before that detestable act. But with the utmost grief and concern we find that we flattered ourselves too soon, and that the root of bitterness is yet alive. . . . We have the mortification to observe one act of Parliament after another passed for the express purpose of raising a revenue from us; to see our money continually collected from us, without our consent, by an authority in the constitution of which we have no share. . . .

". . . it is our unalterable resolution, at all times, to assert and vindicate our dear and invaluable rights and liberties, at the utmost hazard of our lives and fortunes; and we have a full and rational confidence that no designs formed against them will ever prosper."

There was more, but this was the essence. No one in London reading these Instructions, neither King George III nor his ministers nor the Parliament—and they would be read as soon as the fastest packet could carry them there—could ever think of America as weak, indecisive or cowardly. If the men in London were indeed blood brothers of the men in Boston then the Townshend Acts would be repealed immediately. There was no longer any doubt in Abigail's mind, after listening to the meeting in Old South, that John Adams spoke for Massachusetts. Samuel Adams and James Otis would say that he spoke for the other twelve colonies as well. Samuel had told her that England was creating a wholly new species: the American.

She piled the tea dishes on a tray, took them back to the kitchen, then returned to the sitting room. Pushing aside a curtain, she stared out at the square where some boys were beating metal hoops across the cobbles, and asked herself, "What is an American?" She did not know. It had to be a great deal more than merely a man or woman who happened to be born on the new continent. She herself had been raised as an Englishwoman. If a foreigner had been blind enough to ask her what she was, had asked her father, or her cousin Cotton, or Uncle Isaac, each would have replied with pride and affection: "An Englishman."

But so many disturbing things were happening that they staggered the mind. She had learned not only that George III's first speech to Parliament, which had made her love her new sovereign for his wisdom and honesty, had been written for him by the Earl of Bute, but that George III was incapable of feeling such paternal and rational sentiments for the colonists. Reports from England said that he was passionately against any conciliation with the Americans; that he was narrow-minded, arbitrary, ignorant; yet strong enough to force his views on his ministers. The great ministers Pitt, Burke, Shelburne, among the ablest statesmen of the age, were out of favor and out of office. She felt defrauded. The colonies would have to go it alone.

John had written of the British Parliament as the supreme legislature *in all cases of necessity*. . . .

Was he suggesting that the colonies had the right to decide for themselves which cases were necessary and which were not? If so, Parliament was the supreme legislature only in those instances where the colonists decided the laws were proper. In the past four years they had declared that neither the Sugar Act nor the Stamp Act nor now the Townshend Acts were necessary. Rather, John Adams was writing in his study, while she stood in the parlor watching a milk cart clatter across the cobbles, these Acts were unnecessary, illegal, destructive, invalid, void: hence not to be obeyed.

James Otis had said at town meeting, "To relinquish the security of life and property without a struggle is so humiliating and base that one cannot bear to think of it."

Neither John Adams nor the men he worked with would accept humiliation and baseness. They would rather fight. They had to fight. There was nothing else their characters would allow them to do.

She turned away from the window. A soft dusk was falling. Rachel had lit the oil lamp on John's desk. As Abigail stood in the doorway watching her son and daughter playing on the floor, her husband's hand moving swiftly and surely across the paper, she asked herself:

"Is that what an American means? A man who will fight? Who must be independent or die?"

She felt her throat choke up. The peaceful world in which she had grown up was gone. The world into which she had married, become a wife and mother, was full of conflict.

4

The summer was a hot one. They were able to go home to Braintree for two or three days at a time and sleep in their own beds. The man whom John had hired on shares to work the farm was bringing up a good crop of clover. There would be a modest profit from their produce.

It was here that she became certain she was in circumstances again. She was not pleased with herself, for it was only a year since Johnny had been born. She had intended waiting another full year. Somehow during the confusion of the move into Boston . . .

John was working in his lawbooks all the time. Boston felt that the Townshend Acts would be sustained or rescinded, depending on the outcome of the *Liberty* decision. She knew that she was merely a convenient and discreet ear for him to talk at. Even if her answers missed the mark they stimulated him to cry out, "No, no, you fail to see the implications of . . ." and proceed to his analysis.

"This is a truly painful dilemma, Nabby. Do I push for an immediate trial while the law is still new, and tempers in London are on trigger; or, as I think would be better, do I wait until Parliament feels the weight of our petitions and the British merchants begin suffering from our own non-importation agreement?"

"Time was your ally in the Stamp Act."

"Yes, but what happens to my client in the meanwhile? It was John Hancock who hired me, not Massachusetts Bay Colony. The Crown has Hancock's *Liberty*. He loses heavily because it's tied up. There is a rumor they may even sell it. An advocate has rigid responsibilities to those whom he represents. Yet if Hancock demands an immediate trial, and I lose because I allow his judgment to supplant mine . . ."

"Hancock trusts you. Besides, there are other considerations. Unless we get rid of the Townshend Acts Mr. Hancock is largely out of business."

"I'll have to risk it. Our real opponent here is not the local Customs but the Ministry. If I can get their laws thrown out of the Massachusetts court Parliament can have no choice but to revoke. I shall tell Hancock what I'm doing and why; but I shan't solicit his opinion."

The *Liberty* trial was put off until the November court at John's urgent request. He left to travel the circuit and earn a living from litigious New England. Abigail could not shake off a feeling of excessive fatigue. There were lots of simple reasons: the late summer heat was oppressive; the formal demands of Boston social life, which she could not neglect even when John was out of the city. She missed the farm with its trees and running brook.

The political brawling between Governor Bernard, the Massachusetts legislature and the Boston selectmen kept the city tense. A circular letter written largely by Samuel was moving about the thirteen colonies asking the colonists to work together in the struggle against England. The British Secretary of State for the Colonies, the Earl of Hillsborough, was so outraged that he ordered Governor Bernard to have the Massachusetts Assembly "rescind and repudiate the letter." The Assembly refused. Bernard was instructed to dissolve the legislature. Since they could no longer meet as the official Assembly of Massachusetts the Patriots now met unofficially. Letters went out to every town in Massachusetts asking them to send representatives to a convention in Boston for September 22, 1768.

John was unhappy about the convention, afraid that the hotheads among them would get themselves involved in actions which might prejudice their petitions or even lay them open to charges of treason. He sent a messenger to Purchase Street asking Samuel to come to see him.

Samuel arrived, walking at an easy pace. Abigail had never seen the two cousins quarrel. John was stern when he warned Samuel to keep his convention within legal bounds. As Advocate Adams he had a precedent-making case to try not only for John Hancock but for Massachusetts as well. He did not want to have the Crown officers further inflamed against them because of what the convention did.

"What I'm trying to say, Samuel, is that I should like to fight one war at a time. Have your meeting if you must, but don't make my problems more difficult."

Samuel was unimpressed. "If Bernard can intimidate us he can also intimidate the judges of the Admiralty Court. Every show of strength helps you. If the citizens don't like a law they have a right to throw it over, the way refuse is thrown overboard on ships at sea."

"It helps," put in Abigail, "if you don't throw the garbage into the wind."

"Now, Cousin Nabby, I have a hard enough time wrestling with your legalistic husband."

"She is quite right," replied John; "if your convention grows mutinous, I'll get it right back in my face when I rise in Admiralty Court. I want to settle these Townshend Acts as unconstitutional. I don't need any of your Bostonian window smashing to help me."

John's anger failed to ruffle Samuel.

"*Your* Bostonians now, Brother John. Remember? You've thrown in your lot with us rough trodders of the cobblestone streets. You're never going to get away."

The first defeat was John's. The Customs Commission sold Hancock's *Liberty* without notice or compensation to its owner. It was a substantial loss to Hancock and to the prestige of the Patriot cause. Boston felt the fault was clearly John Adams's; somehow he should have found a law or a procedure which would have rescued the ship. Hancock himself assured the Adams family that he was content to wait for settlement of the larger issue in November, the issue of the £100,000 fine.

Not so the Crown. John was in Springfield engaged in a cause between a Negro and his master. Abigail had just dated a letter to her parents October first, when she looked out the window of John's study and saw a regiment of redcoats drawn up in Brattle Square. Her first panicky thought was that they had come to arrest John. Then she realized she was being foolish. These were General Gage's troops, come to Boston by ship from Halifax. The fleet had arrived in Boston Harbor two days before, bringing two regiments and artillery to the barracks at Castle Island. Earlier that morning eight armed ships, with their tenders and cannon loaded in case Boston resisted, had landed one thousand soldiers at Long Wharf and marched them with fixed bayonets, colors flying, to the Common.

The drums and fifes were making a shrill percussion as the soldiers marched into place. She saw how smartly uniformed they were, white straps crossed over their red coats, new guns, bayonets, powder horns, fully equipped for war.

"But against whom?" she asked herself. "Against Boston? We have no army. No one I know owns a gun, except for hunting. For what purpose do they camp in front of my door?"

It was Samuel Adams who answered, coming late in the afternoon with fresh-baked sugar buns Betsy had made, and a cannister of redolent tea bought, he hastened to explain, before the non-importation agreement. As they drank the tea and ate the buns Samuel explained:

"When we heard there was a regiment bivouacked under your window, we thought you might like company."

"Oh, they're well behaved. So many of them are young boys I hardly think they've begun to shave yet."

"They will," said Samuel with a grin, "if they stay here long enough to enforce the tariffs."

"Can they, Sam'l?"

"They can try. But if the colonies remain firm? No. How are they going to get the money? By shooting us? Not unless Parliament passes death taxes as well. So enjoy the fife-and-drum music. Everybody likes a parade."

A day later John returned. Abigail saw him from the parlor window coming through the square, ignoring the redcoats, pretending they were not there, just as the soldiers refused to see him as he walked across their drill formation, up the sidewalk, and into his house. He was red with rage.

"I see you have company."

"Yes. They bring their own musical entertainment."

"They're too kind. Have they caused you any trouble?"

"Nab and Johnny think you sent them for their entertainment."

The mention of his children drained the outrage from his face.

"Forgive me, I was so upset I forgot to greet you. How are my young?"

"Jonathan Sewall warned me the day would come when you would prefer an attack on England to kissing your wife."

"They are not mutually exclusive." He took her in his arms. The fife-and-drum corps in the square chose that moment to burst into *Fair Rosamond*. The Adamses' pleasure in being reunited was spoiled by the sharp barking orders of the officers moving their several hundred soldiers across the cobblestones to their billets in Faneuil Hall.

Abigail commented, "John, the soldiers aren't in the least bit hostile. They look as though they might like to be friendly, given half a chance."

"They're not here to like us, Nabby." His voice was harsh. "They're here to put us down, the moment they're given the order."

"But we are English, and these are English troops, the same ones we fought with on the Plains of Abraham against the French."

"Admitted. But this war is not for us, it's against us. I never thought the Ministry would be so stupid as to turn Boston into an occupied town."

"Governor Bernard says they're here solely to preserve the peace."

"And how does he define peace? Doing things the way he and Parliament say we must?"

"Come, dear, have a glass of port wine to quiet you. Was the circuit a success?"

"The food was inedible. The beds were lumpy. I got soaked crossing rivers. Once I was lost in the woods half the night. In short, I missed my wife and children, my bed and board. Otherwise the trip was a success. There were writs and cases aplenty at each court." He chuckled. "I won my share, more than, I guess, and brought home a pouch of money big enough to take us through the *Liberty* case."

There was an outburst of song beneath the parlor windows, accompanied by the music of violins and flutes. John was one step behind her as she moved aside the curtain.

"In God's name who are they?"

"Friends. I would guess the Sons of Liberty. There's Dr. Thomas Young and William Molineux."

"And look who's lurking at the rear of the singers. Cousin Sam'l."

The group sang *In Freedom We're Born, and in Freedom We'll Live; Liberty Song* and *Yankee Song*:

"Corn stalks twist your hair off,
Cart-wheel frolic round you,
Old Fiery dragon carry you off,
And mortar pessel pound you."

After the third madrigal Abigail cried:

"Invite them in, John. Bring that new keg from under the stair well. I'll get out the glasses."

Their home was filled with the Sons of Liberty, laughing, pounding each other on the back, demanding:

"Mrs. Adams, don't we make sweeter music than the British? Every day they bombard your ears with the thunder of their drums, we'll come at evening to offset them with the honey of our voices. Only way we can beat 'em right now."

5

Abigail slept little the night before the trial. John kept bouncing about in the bed, rehearsing his case before the morrow's court. She looked a little wan in the morning when the bell began clanging vigorously to summon the litigants. John could barely swallow his breakfast, he was in such a hurry to get started. His eyes were flaming. He donned his best outfit, the white wig combed out wide in puffs over his ears, the white shirt and lace collar fitting doggedly tight under his chin, the matching black waistcoat and greatcoat with the big crosshatched buttons and wide slit buttonholes, the broadcloth breeches and dark stockings. His barber had come to the house before breakfast to give him a close shave and powder his wig while John breathed through a paper cone.

"You're looking your best this morning, Advocate," she teased.

"I'm not going to win cases on my appearance. That's why I've read more law than any man since Jeremiah Gridley. And this morning I'm going to need every last word of it; for it's my interpretation of our Constitution against the King's, Ministry's and Parliament's. I can think of a few simpler adversaries for my first big public case."

There was a throng standing in the square before the Town House. Abigail had a moment to wonder why all these people were outside instead of jamming the big Council Hall upstairs. She soon found the answer: Governor Bernard had outmaneuvered them by putting the trial in one of the small downstairs rooms ordinarily used by the clerks of the Admiralty Court. A temporary podium had been installed with a woolsack, a worktable for counsel and less than a hundred chairs . . . every one already occupied. Abigail saw Esther Sewall sitting at one side with the wives of several Crown officers. Since John had refused the position of advocate general and no one else had been appointed, Jonathan Sewall had been ordered by the Crown to prosecute John Hancock and the *Liberty* case. Abigail walked toward Esther, who moved over to make room for her. John joined Sewall at the desk below the judge's rostrum.

The court guardian cried out, "Rise, all ye present, rise! His Honor, the judge of His Majesty's Court of Admiralty. God send you a good deliverance!"

Abigail saw that the judge in the long white wig was Robert Auchmuty, an original member of John's first Sodality. Then, in the moment before Judge Auchmuty deposited his somewhat reluctant bulk on the woolsack, Abigail saw the backs of two heads, dearly familiar. The Reverend Mr. William Smith and Dr. Cotton Tufts had taken the long ride in from Weymouth that morning, starting before dawn in order to be present and counted when John Adams rose to speak for Massachusetts.

Jonathan Sewall presented the opening for the Crown. His gestures and tone were restrained. Yet he would not plead less than his full case; and some of his strictures against John Hancock stung like hornets:

The basic rights of an Englishman arose out of his basic duty: to obey the law. If Massachusetts did not approve the Townshend Acts, then the colony must work to have them repealed, as Englishmen had since the Magna Carta. "We have enjoyed our gracious sovereign's protection, as well as his justice. Let us then behave like self-respecting members of the greatest nation on earth, and not like brawling mobs from the North and South Ends on Pope's Day." The Empire had evolved the best possible means of making laws; and of rescinding laws. The Parliament must make these decisions, and not each individual merchant of Boston who might be tempted to replace his conscience with his counting ledger. . . . The days of smuggling goods into the colony must be put aside. The time had come for Massachusetts to become one of the brilliant gems in the diadem of the British Empire. "Let us then conduct ourselves as Englishmen, proud of our legal heritage, proud to undertake our responsibilities as equals in the noblest Empire on earth."

Sewall had established a mood. Abigail watched the crowd stir and move in their seats as people will who have been flagellated.

There followed a silence while John Adams shuffled his papers, apparently in no hurry to counter with his opening statement. Judge Auchmuty waited as long as he could, then called for Counsel to rise and present his case. Even now John took as long as he could, wanting to let Sewall's words recede. When he began, Abigail could barely hear him though he was not more than thirty feet away; but with a few sentences his voice took on strength. First he specified the statute of George III through which the prosecution had indicted, labeling it a "hardship statute." Then, his head back, his tone strong with authority, he made his legal analysis to the court, to Judge Auchmuty, to Massachusetts, to the other twelve colonies, to the King, Ministry and Parliament three thousand miles and two months of rough weather away.

"Among the group of hardships which attend this statute, the first that ought always to be mentioned, and that ought never be forgotten, is . . ." He turned about to face the hundred men and women packed into the clerk's room for a moment before turning back to Judge Auchmuty. ". . . that it was made without our consent. My client, Mr. Hancock, never consented to it. He never voted for it himself, and never voted for any man to make such a law for him. In this respect, therefore, the greatest consolation of an Englishman suffering under any law is torn from him. I mean the reflection that it is a law of his own making. Indeed, the consent of the subject to all laws is so clearly necessary that no man has yet been found hardy enough to deny it.

"The patrons of these Acts allow that consent is ncccssary; they only contend for a consent by construction, by interpretation, a virtual consent. But this is only deluding men with shadows instead of substance. Construction has made treasons where the law has made none. . . . Arbitrary distinctions . . . have always been the instruments of arbitrary power, the means of lulling and ensnaring men into their own servitude. For whenever we leave principles and clear positive laws, and wander after constructions, one construction or consequence is piled upon another until we get an immense distance from fact and truth and nature, lost in the wild regions of imagination and possibility, where arbitrary power sits upon her brazen throne and governs with an iron sceptre."

John paused. The audience again shifted in its seats, this time with a sigh of relief. John Adams had replaced the mood created by Jonathan Sewall with one of his own choosing. The next part of his case was personal, that the impounding of the *Liberty*, the confiscation of her cargo and imposition of a tremendous fine for omitting to secure a license created "a great disproportion between the crime and the punishment."

He attacked the Townshend Acts for enabling the case against Mr. Hancock to be tried in an Admiralty Court, "not by a jury, not by the law of the land, but by a single judge." Was it not directly a repeal of Magna Carta as far as the American was concerned?

When Jonathan Sewall jumped to his feet, declaring that Parliament had decreed this kind of case must be tried under common law and therefore Advocate Adams was entitled to no rights of cross-examination of the Crown's witnesses, Judge Auchmuty ruled that Mr. Sewall was right on the point.

He banged his gavel and rose, declaring: "His Majesty's court is adjourned. Hearings will be continued."

Then he swept out of the clerk's room, his long black robe trailing him.

Over the heads of the hundred people standing between them, Abigail and John Adams stared at each other, agasp.

There were few days throughout that winter that John was not, as he complained to Abigail, "dongled out of the house by that tyrannical bell." He was grumpy with himself and the world. He was right in charging that "the officers of the Crown were determined to examine the whole town as witnesses." He grew weary of what he called "this odious case," but in rebuttal had to summon the whole town for his own interrogatories. By Christmas it seemed clear that nobody on the Crown side wanted a decision, not Bernard, not Hutchinson, not the five members of the Customs Commission, not Judge Auchmuty, and not Advocate General Jonathan Sewall. It appeared to the Adamses that the Crown officials were afraid of the verdict going either way, and were waiting for outside events to render the trial obsolete.

"In that sense it could be considered a victory for you, John," Abigail consoled; "they'll not fine Hancock that £100,000."

"Nor yet declare him innocent. I'm trying to convict the Townshend Acts by acquitting Hancock. They are not going to let me do it."

"The Crown has not seized another ship."

"No, but the English navy is impressing more and more of our sailors."

She too walked about off balance. She was not carrying this baby as she had the other two. The sense of life was quieter within her. She had pains in the groin and abdomen and in her legs each night which kept her from sleeping. She detested illness, a residue of her mother's preoccupation with her alleged delicacy, yet she had been aware of real distress during the increasingly cold months of October and November. It was almost impossible to keep the house warm, even though John had built a second coal house in the back yard. The winds came off the bay, screeched across Brattle Square, seeped under doors and through window frames.

Frightened, she questioned her sister Mary, who had moved into Boston from Salem, and who visited nearly every afternoon. Then she sent for Dr. Joseph Warren, who had inoculated John for the smallpox four years before.

"I know you've attended when midwives weren't available."

"A doctor doesn't do much then, Mrs. Adams. He just stands by."

"Then you can't help me?"

"I'm not qualified. But if your husband would not object to an obstetrician examining you, there is one such man in Boston. Dr. James Lloyd. He's a New Yorker who was trained in England. He attended lectures on midwifery by William Smellie and is the first physician in America to practice obstetrics on a scientific basis."

Dr. Lloyd was forty, a long-faced, balding man who puffed out his natural hair to simulate a wig; wise, with sad eyes, and the biggest nose she had seen since the Weymouth parsonage. He asked her a good many questions, seemed to recognize the symptoms but would make no commitment. "I have several midwives in whom I have confidence, but it would be better if you consent to my being present at the birth. I can then take the best possible care of you and the baby."

"Of course, Doctor."

Early one morning at the end of December, when her labor began, she sent for him. He performed his first vaginal examination, searching for the posterior and anterior fontanels.

"The baby is lying on its back. That isn't the most favorable position."

The water broke early, but as the hours of the long day passed she was unable to gather the momentum for the crescendo of pains needed for a good expulsive labor. The first midwife to arrive asked for a feather, put pepper on it and waved it under Abigail's nose. She sneezed several times.

John and Dr. Lloyd sat up with her all night. She was only half conscious. The relief midwife who came shortly after dawn fastened straps onto the bottom bedposts for her to pull on. Just before noon the midwife changed the leather straps to tied sheets. Each of the women held one of her legs, begging her to bear down. She was at the end of her strength now, but realized that if she gave in both she and the baby would die. She made one monumental effort, more with will power than physical strength. In this act the child was born.

Dr. Lloyd took the infant. Through a haze Abigail saw that he was having trouble getting it to breathe. He did not cut the umbilical cord, but instead laid the infant flat on the bed beside her and breathed into its mouth at intervals. When this was insufficient he began compressing and squeezing the baby's chest. Then he held the little girl by her feet, rubbed her back, struck the soles of her feet sharply. Some fifteen or twenty minutes after the birth the baby gave a gasp. Everybody in the room cried out with joy. When the child's breath came regularly he cut the umbilical.

"Everything is fine, Mrs. Adams, both you and your daughter. Go to sleep now. You've earned a long rest."

It was a gray period for the Adamses.

She recovered her strength slowly. She felt well but tired, and so it could be only a matter of time before she was back on her feet. Her relatives and friends deluged her with kindnesses, letters, gifts. But Susanna was a puny baby. She did not move much, was content with a minimum of milk, and instead of crying lustily as Nab and Johnny had when they wanted something, only whimpered. Dr. Lloyd insisted that many puny babies grew into buxom children.

John spent his days in the gloomy room of the Admiralty Court with Judge Auchmuty and Sewall examining endless witnesses. Not a single spectator put in an appearance any more. His other cases were neglected.

"Surely Mr. Hancock will pay you a fair fee?"

"Of course. But I should be handling the affairs of a hundred clients. Tomorrow still once again I shall move to have the case thrown out."

She held his hand as tightly as though it were her only grip on the outside world.

6

At the end of the winter their house on Brattle Square was sold out from under them. They were offered first purchase but they were not certain they would want to own a house in Boston.

On the first pleasant day of spring she took Nab and Johnny for a walk up King's Lane and then north along Cold Lane toward Mill Pond. The redcoats, who had been confined to barracks during the weeks of rain and snow, were once again at attention in Brattle Square. On her right as she walked with her face in the pale yellow sunshine, holding a child by each hand, she saw the Green Dragon Tavern used by the Sons of Liberty as their headquarters. About fifty yards from Mill Pond a house she had always admired had a freshly painted sign in one of its front windows: FOR LEASE. It was a handsome all-wood structure, two-storied, with dormer windows. It had just been given a coat of cream-colored paint. There were twenty sash windows facing south and west, admitting the most light and warmth. She felt a rise of excitement.

At dinner she told John about the house. He had heard that it belonged to a Mr. Fayerweather. He promised to bring the key from the agent. By four he was back.

She responded to the house the moment she entered the front door. There were eight main rooms, seven of them fire rooms, with much larger hearths than on Brattle Square. The house was freshly painted throughout, the furniture ample. My. Fayerweather had a touch of gaiety in his nature, for the sitting room was painted a light blue, the furniture upholstered in a deeper blue silk, the family room was a pale green with cream curtains, the dining room cedar, and the library wood-wainscoted to match the entrance hall and wide flight of stairs. The house had a tight, weatherproofed feeling.

"Mr. Fayerweather not only has good taste," Abigail observed, "but everything is so clean. Many of the heavy pieces are newly covered. Bring me an inventory, and I'll inspect it room by room." She paused. "Is the rent high?"

"Yes. Somebody has to pay for all this fresh paint and plaster." He smiled at her. "But it's worth it if you'll be comfortable here."

The next morning she liked it even better. The bedrooms were spacious, with inside shutters and window seats covered with gay cushions.

Their bedroom had a marble hearth and mantelpiece. The beds were all comfortable, with a few nice pieces scattered about: a small desk and bureau in one room, a wardrobe and table in another. There were windows overlooking Mill Pond to the north, West Church to the west. The library downstairs had adequate bookshelves.

Early Saturday morning John took Abigail and the three children to her aunt Elizabeth's. By nightfall he came back to retrieve his family and move them into the new house.

John initiated his office by writing a new set of Instructions for the Boston legislature against the continued presence of British troops in Boston.

May and June were delightful months. John bought a small boat and frequently took them sailing. There was a refreshing breeze off Mill Pond when the days waxed hot. She found herself enjoying pleasures which had become a burden to her: long walks through the streets at dusk, dinner parties with their friends, picnics in the country with Susanna in a woven basket.

There was encouraging news from London. Agents and friends wrote that a movement had arisen in Parliament to repeal the Townshend Acts. What was described as "a considerable section of the Cabinet" appeared to support the view that compromise with the colonies was in order. Lord Hillsborough, Secretary of State, sent a circular letter in which he declared that the Cabinet "entertained no design to propose to Parliament to lay any further taxes on America for the purpose of raising a revenue." A number of Boston's merchants, knowing that the non-importation agreement would become invalid the instant the Townshend Acts were repealed, began ordering shipments of British goods to fill their long-empty shelves. John cautioned Hancock to draw up lists and send them to his agents in London with the instruction that the merchandise be shipped only after the repeal.

The two months of respite were heaven-sent, for in June John came home from his office near the steps of the Town House with his face once again ashen, his manner preoccupied. To Abigail's query, he replied:

"Every lawyer, if he practices long enough, reaches the time when he must defend men against the charge of murder. I'm starting out not with one life to save but four."

"Who killed whom, and why?"

"You've just summed up the entire case. Ask Rachel to pour me a cold tub. I've been simmering all afternoon. James Otis brought me the case;

the General Court starts and he is busy with committees there. He was most unlucid about it."

"Not that unlucid, if he brought the case to you."

John smiled wanly. "Thank you, dear soul. You have reduced my temperature ten degrees."

Rachel fed the children. Abigail then gave the girls the evening off. She and John donned the silk robes her uncle Isaac had imported from China. On evenings such as these when they were alone they had their supper of pot cheese, fresh-baked bread, sweet butter and cooked fruits on the kitchen table as they had in Braintree. Relaxed now, John told her the story of the four sailors being held in the bridewell on Beacon Street, near the Common, since the county jail had burned down. They were charged with murdering Lieutenant Panton of His Majesty's frigate *Rose*, a charge with political implications equal to those of the *Liberty*. John's expositions were a blessing for Abigail.

The four sailors had been sailing on the American brig *Pitt Packet*, out of Marblehead. On the return voyage from Europe, when only six or seven leagues from its home anchorage, the *Pitt Packet* had been stopped and boarded by an armed party from H.M.S. *Rose*, led by Lieutenant Panton. The lieutenant demanded that the crew line up on deck. Corbet, a sailor, recognized the action as an "impressment," or seizure under which they would be forced to serve in the British navy with its brutal discipline of flogging and near slavery. He and three of his companions holed up in the forepeak. Lieutenant Panton, searching the ship, found them there.

"Come out, ye dogs!" he cried.

To which Corbet replied, "I know who you are. You are the lieutenant of the man-of-war, come to deprive me of my liberty. I and my companions are determined to stand on our defense."

A British midshipman fired his pistol into the forepeak, shattering a bone in the arm of one of the sailors, who was holding a musket. Corbet, standing at the entrance with a harpoon in his hand, marked a line in the ship's cargo of salt, crying, "If you step over that line I shall consider it a proof that you are determined to impress me; and by the eternal God of heaven, you are a dead man!" Lieutenant Panton calmly took a pinch of snuff from his box, then crossed the line in the salt and attempted to seize Corbet. Corbet threw the harpoon straight into Lieutenant Panton's jugular. He died instantly. Reinforcements from the *Rose* boarded the *Pitt Packet*, arrested the four sailors, delivered them to the sheriff in Boston under formal charge of murder in the first degree. If Corbet were guilty of murder, his three companions would be considered equally guilty. All four could be hanged.

"But if they were defending themselves?" Abigail murmured.

"Precisely. Impressment of sailors is the vilest crime being practiced by any government today. It's also the most illegal, and has been for sixty years. Yet the English have been carrying on this practice, whipping men through the fleet for alleged disobedience, shooting them for attempted escape. This has been a running sore in the colonies for decades. Perhaps we have a chance to put an end to it."

"How, John?"

"First, I'll demand a jury trial. I have a stronger case than with the *Liberty*. If I fail to get a jury and it goes to an Admiralty Court, my first question will be whether impressment in any case is legal. If impresses are always illegal, and Lieutenant Panton acted as an impress officer, Michael Corbet and his associates had a right to resist him. If they could not otherwise preserve their liberty, they were within the law to take away his life."

"John, are there ever any important dull cases?"

"Yes, routine business matters, the kind that pay for the work and worry involved in these political cases. For who is to pay me a fee here? The four sailors? They have nothing. Mr. Hooper, the owner of the brig from Marblehead? It is better in cases having strong political implications to keep one's motives pure. I would never want to be a suspect patriot."

John's study was spacious, overlooking a side yard of shrubs and elm trees. He told her he was going to confine his routine legal affairs to his office and handle the Panton case here at home: "To keep my papers unmixed, and my thoughts too." Since each of the four accused sailors had to plead separately he was obliged to draw the papers four times over, each with many pages of citations, statutes, opinions from the laws of Henry VIII and William III.

He groused about the number of nights he had to sit up late, transcribing the pleas four times.

"Couldn't I be your amanuensis? If you'll give me the differences in personal detail, and indicate where I should write them . . ."

"I can use you better as a librarian. If you would hand me down the *British Statutes-at-Large*, Wood's *Institutes* . . ."

He turned a thoughtful face to her.

"If I'm to put an end to impressment, a publication of this case might be of considerable utility. I want to bring a variety of useful learning into it. I think a book I wrote would sell."

Amused at his commingling dedication to an ideal with an eye half cocked at a potential sale, about as good a description of a Puritan as one could set forth, she chuckled to herself.

"If erudition can win cases, my dear, your four sailors are already celebrating their release at the Dragon Tavern."

"Erudition won't do it alone. But I've got them stalemated. You see this volume, *British Statutes-at-Large?* I sent to England for it just as we were married. It was a terrible extravagance at the time, since I was earning little. I think it is the only copy in Massachusetts. But that extravagance is now going to save four lives."

"All by itself?"

"Yes. Now listen to this: it's from 6 Anne, c. 37 s. 9. 'No mariner or other person, who shall serve on board or be retained to serve on board any privateer or trading ship or vessel, that shall be employed in any part of America, nor any mariner or other person being on shore in any part thereof, shall be liable to be impressed or taken away, or shall be impressed or taken away, by any officer or officers, of or belonging to any of Her Majesty's ships of war, empowered by the Lord High Admiral, or any other person whatsoever.' I tell you, Nabby, even if I can't procure a jury I shall confound Hutchinson."

She had rarely seen him so ebullient over his prospects. He looked considerably younger than his thirty-four years. He invited her to be present at his triumph. His plea went off brilliantly, showing the weeks of intensive care; but before Jonathan Sewall could answer, Chief Justice Hutchinson rose and announced that the court would adjourn to the Council Chamber. Abigail could see that John was literally struck dumb by the court's refusal even to consider his plea for a jury.

The Adamses returned home. Friends and sympathizers fell in all afternoon with protests and a crop of green rumors. By nightfall word had spread that the court had agreed to a jury trial.

"I don't think Jonathan wants those four men convicted," said Abigail.

"No decent man would. And Jonathan is one of the finest I've known. But when you take pay from the Crown you do the Crown's work."

He kept Abigail awake most of the night, pacing the room, staring out the window at the star-studded night. By dawn she was exhausted so remained at home. He was back by midafternoon.

"John, what could have happened? Surely there has been no time to plead . . ."

"No plea! I had my books opened to their citations. I had scarcely risen and said, 'May it please Your Excellencies and Your Honors, my defense of the prisoners is that the melancholy action for which they stand accused is justifiable homicide, and therefore no crime at all,' and pushed the *British Statutes* over the table toward the Bench, when once again that jack-in-the-box Hutchinson sprang up and moved that the court be adjourned."

"What reason did he give?"

"None. He handed it down like a papal bull. The judges obeyed." He tore off his high choker collar. "The whole town is dismal, expecting a death sentence in the morning. My glass bubble was burst! All the inflammable gas escaped from my balloon, and down I dropped."

"Now, dear, you're mixing your metaphors."

"I caused my own undoing by my vanity. I had the spine of the *British Statutes* pointed at Hutchinson like a harpoon. He must have known the statute against impressment was in there. The case is over."

It was a sad ending after the high hopes. No one came to call. The streets seemed deserted. A pall hung over the town.

It was almost midnight when John said:

"I must go to the jail and comfort the four men, convey the feeling that someone cares about them even if they are to die. What else can we offer them? Just . . . brotherhood. A poor sop, in the dark of night. . . ."

"You have put in almost two months of unremitting labor."

"Yes, but I walk out of the bridewell to my bed, to my wife, a hot breakfast. They walk out to a sentence, and ropes dangling from a gibbet. Who is responsible, the sailor who threw the harpoon or the lawyer who failed them?"

"Can the jailor make tea?"

"We don't import tea any more."

"Then I'll cook some of ours. You can carry it in a pot."

"Brew it strong, Nabby. It'll give us all courage."

The next morning she insisted on going to court to hear the verdict.

She had never experienced anything like the solid sheet of gloom in the courtroom. When the four sailors were brought in by their jailors they blanched at the sense of horror. They stood at the Bar before their fifteen judges including Bernard, Auchmuty, Commodore Hood of Her Majesty's Navy, and "certain counselors from Massachusetts." Governor Bernard Hutchinson rose and, with a forbidding frown, pronounced:

"The killing of Lieutenant Panton was justifiable homicide, committed in necessary self-defense. The prisoners are acquitted and shall be released."

Abigail sat stunned. So did the rest of the courtroom. Then Judge Robert Auchmuty bounded up from his chair and in a constricted voice announced:

"The judgment of the court is unanimous!"

Pandemonium broke loose. People were shouting, laughing, crying, embracing the four sailors who stood unbelieving in the midst of this outburst of joy and relief. Abigail, trying to push her way forward to congratulate John, had her hand wrung by total strangers, was kissed on the cheek by a succession of familiar female faces she could not place. But there was no reaching John. He was being mobbed by friends pounding him on the back, lauding him with the most extravagant praise.

It was like that for the rest of the day, hundreds of people calling, bringing their wives and children, offering flowers, sweets, books, keepsakes. Jonathan and Esther Sewall came too, though they stayed for only a moment. Esther told Abigail:

"No man likes to be beat. But Jonathan is proud of John tonight. All Boston is."

When they were alone John asked, rubbing his thick fingers over his tired eyes:

"Proud of what? I was never allowed to present my case. Hutchinson was afraid that, if I did, all American sailors would fight and kill before letting themselves be impressed."

"But it was you who forced him to the decision. Your defense will be available now in any colony should the English attempt impressment again. Don't be chagrined. You are the hero of the day. Enjoy it!"

It was delightful being the figure of the hour. The number of toasts drunk to them would have filled Boston Harbor. Men swept off their hats as she passed in the street. The women beamed. Merchants rushed forward to greet her, elbowing aside their clerks. Even in the meat, fish and vegetable stalls the news was whispered that this was Mrs. John Adams. She was given the finest cuts, the best-looking fruits and vegetables, the most attractive fish in the catch.

John was in Falmouth. He had hoped to be back in Boston in time for the July court, but at the end of the month he sent her two letters by friends, saying that although he had won three of his clients' actions there remained some sixty more on the docket.

"Nothing but the hope of acquiring some little matter for my dear family could carry me through these tedious excursions."

With this she had to agree, for every time they managed to put by £100 of savings a political case arose which absorbed John's attention, their income fell off and their savings were used up in the day-by-day maintenance of a house and a life in Boston. All they hoped was that the controversial times would allow them to maintain the precarious balance.

Governor Bernard had been recalled to London for "conferences," a word which John described as a euphemism for retirement. When his ship sailed, the bells were rung, guns were fired from John Hancock's wharf, the Liberty Tree was covered with flags, great bonfires were lighted in King Street and on Fort Hill. The Massachusetts Assembly had been petitioning King George III to "remove Sir Francis Bernard forever from this government." Boston was certain it had succeeded.

Business was good. Although the non-importation agreements were still hurting there was enough work to warrant a clerk, and so John took in a pleasant-mannered young man by the name of Jonathan Williams Austin, who had just been graduated from Harvard. Since there was no other legal training available, he felt it his duty to make it a teacher-apprentice relationship. Ten days later he was importuned by an old friend, John Tudor, to take in his son as well.

"What shall I do with two clerks at a time?" he groused to Abigail. "What will the Bar and the world say? That I am being pretentious?"

"You can give them as good a legal education as they're likely to find in the colonies."

"That's the rub, my dear. My own sense of honor, conscience, if you like, will demand that I give them intensive training; not only in the books, but in the procedures in court, about which James Putnam bothered to teach me nothing. Putnam preferred arguing religion."

"You'll make a better master for having been inadequately trained as an apprentice."

"I do like to teach. Sitting in my great chair at school, I used to consider myself as some dictator at the head of a commonwealth. I could discover all the geniuses, the generals, the politicians in petticoats, the divines as well as the fops and buffoons. To fire a newborn soul with ardor for learning! At that time I thought the world could afford no greater pleasure."

"Then sign young Tudor's papers. It will be good practice until Johnny is ready."

"Johnny! Do you really think that little devil will turn out to be a lawyer?"

"If you instill in him a love of the law."

He took off his coat, shed his neck lace. His eyes were dancing now.

"I'd like another lawyer in the family. That idea gives new spring to my nerves and a quicker circulation to my blood. Perhaps we could found a dynasty of Adams lawyers. I'll assure you of one thing: by the time Johnny dons his robe he'll have at hand the best single law library in these thirteen colonies."

She marveled at the power of love. Five minutes before he had come home worried about the possibility of taking on two clerks. She had suggested that one day he might be training his own son, and lo! here he was kissing her warmly, enchanted with the idea of building a great law library for the two-year-old to use.

Her only concern was Susanna. Going on eight months, the child still had not acquired any real strength. In spite of the warm summer air and clear sunshine she was yellowish in color; and despite advice from Drs. Tufts, Warren and Lloyd on how to stimulate a baby's appetite with special foods, she was a poor feeder, rarely taking enough nourishment to stouten her thin flame of life. The doctors had told her that the baby would catch up, but now she was beginning to worry. A gentle melancholy settled over her, a feeling that somehow it must have been her fault. She had not given Susanna a good beginning: she had been too tired while carrying the baby; exhausted the infant in the long difficult labor. Even now she was helpless; she did not possess the wisdom or skill to bring her daughter a sense of survival.

The months of heat passed, an early cold set in; the baby was fading before their eyes. Susanna died during the first week in February. Nothing in particular happened; her little life simply flickered out as would a small taper that had reached its end.

Abigail went into her bedroom, threw herself face down on her bed and wept into the pillow. After a time the tears were spent. She fought her way back to a reconciliation with fate. Self-pity was a sin. Neither was the escape of self-flagellation vouchsafed to her: for in truth what could she have done otherwise while carrying and giving birth to Susanna?

She must accept it as God's will, difficult as this was to do. It was the first time His hand had been turned against her. But that too was improper thinking. A great many children died in New England, they were stillborn or failed to survive the rigors of the first winter. God in His abundance gave; and God took away. She had two magnificently healthy children. She must be grateful for His past blessings, and for those of the future. . . .

She sat up on her bed. It was not a thing they would easily forget, but there was the compensation, particularly strong for a woman, that she could re-create within herself to replace the loss.

John said nothing. She could judge the depth of his mute suffering by the fact that he would not speak Susanna's name.

When she returned from the cemetery she set her mind resolutely toward the birth of the next child.

It took a mindless accident, implicit in the temper of the times, to close the door irrevocably on the past.

The first step in the tragic sequence was the killing of the eleven-year-old son of a poor German immigrant. Christopher Snider was part of a group of boys hanging around a crowd that was threatening Theophilus Lillie, who was importing from England. His shop, near the New Brick Meeting House, was being lampooned by a caricature head mounted on a pole. A neighbor of Lillie's, Ebenezer Richardson, known in the neighborhood as an informer to the Customs, tried to have the pole pulled down. The crowd drove him into his house under a barrage of dirt and stones. Richardson picked up the musket by his front door and fired into the crowd, hitting young Snider in the chest.

Abigail heard the mournful tolling of Boston's bells; they intermingled in her mind with the funeral of her own child, the dull pain over Susanna transferring itself to the towheaded eleven-year-old who had become the martyr of Boston. She joined the mourning without making any effort to separate her grief. Only Dr. Joseph Warren's stern warning kept her out of the funeral march.

Not so John. On his way back from Weymouth he stumbled upon the cortege forming under the Liberty Tree.

"First I warmed myself at Mr. Rowe's," he told her that evening, "these Massachusetts roads in February! Then I joined the funeral cortege. A vast number of boys walked before the coffin, followed by men, women and carriages. My eyes never beheld such a funeral. The ardor of the people is certainly not going to be quelled."

They bundled up in greatcoats and walked to the bookstore, where John Mein maintained a circulating library for those who were able to pay his fee of £1 8s. a year. They selected a novel, then came back for supper before the fireplace in John's study, something they had not done since the death of Susanna.

7

The following Monday evening, not long after John had left for a meeting of his Sodality at Henderson Inches's house, there was a new ringing of the bells. Only a fire of great magnitude could call forth the ringing of every bell in Boston. She sprang out of her rocker, called to Rachel to get the children ready, and ran up the stairs to the third-floor dormer windows which gave a view over the city. She could see no flames or smoke anywhere. She summoned the yard boy and sent him to find out what was happening. He returned with a wild tale of shooting and killing at the Town House.

John came home shortly.

"It's what we have been anticipating," he cried. "The belief has been that the redcoats were under orders not to fire; and so a mob with sticks and clubs broke up two companies of them a few days ago. One soldier fired over their heads. This time, they fired into the crowd. Three are dead. A fourth man is reported mortally hurt. The crowd had dispersed, taking the dead and wounded with them, by the time I reached the Town House. I will know more in the morning."

They awoke to a strange stillness. Gone were the noises of a city awakening, cooking, hurrying to work or to school. The delivery carts, hucksters' cries, the hum of activity from the center of the city and from the docks were missing. It was as though they had arisen in a community of the dead. Abigail fed John a breakfast of bean porridge, ham and biscuits, fearing that the days ahead might leave little time or appetite for meals.

He kissed her cheek, admonished, "It would be better if you did not leave the house."

She heard his footsteps returning up Cold Lane, then mounting their outer steps. It was a strange tempo, one she did not recognize. "Pushing forward with reluctance," she thought. He had come home early in order to acquaint her with the situation; yet he was averse to starting. He seemed to be struggling to contain himself, at the same time it was apparent that he had become personally involved. She thought:

"After being married to a man for five years you can hear every word of his silences."

Finally he said, "Put on a warm coat and let us take a turn about the garden."

There were wide paths among the trees, leafless now, with snow covering the roofs of the carriage and coal houses. They had walked only a few feet when he began.

"It will take weeks, perhaps months, to sort out all the truth. At least a hundred people are telling the story differently."

He held her arm against him in a hard grasp as he discussed the tension that had existed in the city since the redcoats had been garrisoned there, the minor clashes between the Bostonians and the soldiers, the constant exchange of insulting expletives, the unrelieved passion over the death of Christopher Snider. The redcoats, feeling themselves beleaguered, were going faster to their bayonets and guns.

This was powder aplenty, but precisely which of several incidents set it off he had had difficulty in ascertaining. The facts were certain. During the evening the Bostonians had formed in crowds. The soldiers were engaged in "driving" or moving swiftly through the streets on exchanges of guard duty. The first outbreak occurred on Brattle Street where a sentinel, stationed at Boylston's Alley across from his barracks, challenged three or four young men who wanted to pass. There was a fight in which one of the Bostonians received a minor head wound.

Roaming street crowds were alerted. Thirty or forty men in Dock Square armed with canes and sticks, many of them American sailors spoiling for a fracas, tried to get through to the barracks. Turned back by the troops, they re-formed, then surged into King Street. There was a British sentry in front of the Custom House. Some of the young boys taunted the sentry, crying, "There's the soldier who knocked me down!" Others shouted, "Kill him! Knock him down!" They pelted him with icy snowballs. The sentry loaded his gun. The bells of the town started ringing, first Old Brick, then Old South. Another boy cried, "The lobster is going to fire!" The sentry cried, "Main Guard!" Six soldiers of the Main Guard stationed at the Town House at the end of King Street came on the double. Captain Preston reached his detachment as the crowds poured into King Street Square from Pudding and Crooked lanes, Damnation Alley, Cornhill and Royal Exchange. The soldiers formed a semicircle in front of the Custom House. Sticks and curses flew faster, the crowd screaming: "Fire if you dare!"

One of the soldiers, Montgomery, had his gun hit with a stick. He was knocked down. The crowd converged on him. Somebody yelled, "Fire!" Montgomery, struggling to his feet, fired into the crowd. Seven other soldiers fired in succession from right to left. Three men were killed instantly, five more were down on the cobblestones, wounded.

The crowds fell back. The soldiers held their ground. The Bostonians moved forward to pick up their dead and wounded. The soldiers, thinking this another attack, raised their guns. Captain Preston went swiftly down the line striking the gun forelocks with his hand. He then ordered his men back to Town House. . . .

John had been walking her hard and fast. Suddenly he turned, saw the tenseness of her expression.

"You look chilled through and through."

"Rachel will bring us chocolate to your study."

He lighted the kindling under the logs in his fireplace. Fingers of flame licked the outer bark. He sat down with his legs stretched out stiffly toward the fire, maintained silence while they sipped their chocolate. Then he sat up straight and said in a resolute voice:

"I have accepted to help defend Captain Preston and the eight soldiers who were involved in last night's killing. I will be representing the Crown."

For an instant she too was still. Shards of emotion collided in her head, bosom and stomach, she could hardly tell which.

"You volunteered?"

"No. Mr. James Forrest, the one they call the 'Irish Infant,' came to my office. I knew him a little; he is a prosperous merchant, friendly to the Crown people but an honest fellow. With tears streaming from his eyes, he said, 'I am come with a very solemn message from a very unfortunate man, Captain Preston, in prison. He wishes for counsel, and can get none. I have waited on Josiah Quincy, Jr., who says he will engage if you will give him your assistance. Without it he positively will not.' "

He rose, stalked agitatedly behind her chair.

"I engaged. I had no hesitation in answering that counsel ought to be the very last thing that an accused person should want in a free country. That the Bar ought in my opinion to be independent and impartial at all times and in every circumstance. But he must be sensible this would be as important a cause as ever was tried in any court of the world, and that every lawyer must hold himself responsible not only to his country but to the highest and most infallible of all tribunals for the part he should act. He must therefore expect from me no art or address, no sophistry or prevarication in such a cause; nor anything more than fact, evidence and law would justify. Captain Preston, he said, requested and desired no more; and that he had such an opinion, from all he had heard from all parties of me, that he could cheerfully trust his life with me, upon those principles. Upon this, Forrest offered me a guinea as a retaining fee. I accepted it. This also means I shall defend the eight soldiers."

"Will it be possible for Boston to understand," she asked warily, "after blood has been spilled, the principle of law that every man is entitled to a defense; and that a lawyer is under obligation to provide that defense?"

"Just as difficult as it is for Boston to understand that Cousin Samuel and his Sons of Liberty have been whipping up the crowds to too high a state of tension, toward that point where a crowd becomes a mob. It's going on this very moment, in every block, every street, every shop, tavern and home, to make people believe that Captain Preston and the soldiers committed cold-blooded murder."

"And you don't think they did?"

"It's going to take a considerable time to find out. But first I shall go before the court and ask for a postponement until next fall. If the soldiers were tried right now, there isn't a jury in Massachusetts that wouldn't convict them."

There was a determined clapping on the front knocker. It was Abigail's twenty-six-year-old cousin, Josiah Quincy, Jr. When he was excited his left eye crossed so close to the high-ridged, bony nose as to seem to have disappeared, the dimple in his chin became crevice-like. But his youth, his ardor, his warmth filled any room he entered. He went directly to John and hugged him before he turned back to proffer his amenities to Abigail.

"Cousin Adams, you have done a noble deed. I could not have entered this case without you there to make us solid and respectable. I have just visited Captain Preston in prison. I made the most explicit declaration to him of my opinion of the contests of our times, and that my heart and hand were indissolubly attached to the Patriot cause of my country."

"You are young, Josiah, and Massachusetts will forgive you this case because of your youth."

"The rest of Boston will be nothing compared to my father," cried Josiah. "I shall be fortunate indeed if he still allows me to carry the family name."

"Since your brother Samuel is solicitor general for the Crown," observed Abigail, "perhaps he will be the prosecutor. That will avenge your family honor."

"*Our* family honor, Abigail. You're a Quincy too."

"At the moment she has enough to contend with, being an Adams," declared John.

Josiah had no sooner left than Samuel Adams arrived. He looked at them with the benign inscrutability of a wise and wily Chinese philosopher.

"I wish you weren't engaging for this case, Brother Adams."

"Because you think I shouldn't?"

Samuel said in his gentlest voice, "It's just that I'd like a conviction."

"Samuel, you don't want those eight soldiers hanged!"

"Oh dear, no. Violence is against my nature. We just want to prove that Boston was justified. I'm going to oppose you all the way on this."

He departed, leaving behind him the scent of Betsy's strong soap.

"What will he do?" Abigail asked.

"Nothing that either of us could expect. That's the only predictable thing about Sam'l: his unpredictability."

The last term of His Majesty's Superior Court of Judicature began in a week. John spent his time seeking legal precedents with which to secure a postponement. Whatever changes in attitude he may have encountered at his office or in the Town House he kept to himself. He made no comment and showed no signs of agitation. For her own part it was as though she had suddenly been transplanted to a foreign city, or had overnight become another person. The people she had been dealing with every day showed no emotion; neither did they show recognition. The shopkeepers, butchers, fishmongers no longer tipped their hats or greeted her by name. Neither did they neglect her, or show hostility. After a couple of days she caught her first clue. Describing how her neighbors walked past her on the street as though she were not there, she said:

"They're treating me *anonymously*. They don't hate me, they're not bitter, it's just that they haven't the faintest inkling why you are doing this to them."

"Make no issue of it," he counseled. "When this trial is over it will be better if no harsh words have been exchanged. Then nobody will have anything to be forgiven for, including us."

Boston for the next few days was like the stories Parson Smith had told about the hysteria that prevailed when religion was paralyzing the community, the preachers thundering damnation and redemption for four and six hours a day, the shops closed, the schools shuttered, the people walking the streets in a trance. Now it was dominated by another word with precisely the same number of letters: *politics*. There were meetings, fiery speeches, bitter denunciations of the redcoats as cold-blooded monsters who had shot down innocent, peace-loving patriots whose only crime was to believe in freedom.

"The Sons of Liberty are waging a brilliant campaign," John admitted. "Except for the Crown sympathizers, who are locked in their homes these days and keeping the shutters down on their shops, this city is on fire to hang everybody it can get into the docket. If that last injured man, Patrick Carr, dies, I'm afraid the sermons on Sunday will be an incitation to riot."

Carr died that night. A new revulsion swept over Boston. John decreed that they would not leave the house over the weekend. But Monday's publications were worse than Sunday's sermons. Paul Revere had drawn a series of five blocks, shaped like coffins, with a death's-head and the initials of a victim scratched on each, which was used to illustrate the *Boston Gazette's* story of what was now called the Boston Massacre. Boston was being induced to believe that a contingent of British soldiers, lined up in solid rank, fired point-blank under the orders of Captain Preston's upraised sword, into a crowd of genteel, well-dressed Bostonians, including women, out for a peaceable stroll in Town House Square.

"Mr. Revere must know that this drawing will multiply the hatred and violence in the air," said Abigail.

"He wishes to imprint the stigma of massacre on every mind; to so inflame Boston that the judges will fear for their lives if they grant me a postponement tomorrow morning."

The hearing was held in midafternoon. John's face, when he returned, was tired but not beaten.

"The case was put over until fall."

"How good."

"Samuel bundled up his entire dinner party of Patriots and brought them in a body into the court. You never saw such a scene. They bullied, threatened, demanded that the trial start immediately."

"How did you defeat them?"

"They defeated themselves. The louder they harangued the more the judges were convinced that no fair trial could be held at this time. Right in the middle of a passionate Son of Liberty speech the presiding judge cried, 'Case put over!' The Bench emptied before the Patriots could collect their wits. Truth to tell, I got out of there rather quickly myself."

She laughed.

"Now, John Adams, don't tell me you *ran* out of that courtroom."

"Ah, no. That would not have been dignified. Let us just say that it was the fastest *walk* Boston has ever beheld."

8

It was as though the John Adamses were living behind a moat.

Abigail came to realize how blissful mere anonymity had been, for now she became *that* Mrs. Adams. The tradespeople turned surly. She stopped going into the bigger shops entirely. The round of friendly parties and outings ceased altogether.

She did not feel abandoned. Her sister Mary came over nearly every day. Her parents visited, then her sister Betsy. Nevertheless she found it strange that few of the lawyers in John's Sodality, who had agreed that he was duty bound to take the case, dropped by their house any more. John said he saw them at the office and at Town House; that they sent their friendliest greetings. But for some reason too obscure for her feminine mind to grasp they apparently did not want to be seen going in or out of Mr. and Mrs. John Adams's house.

John had his own problems. He was trying to round up and interrogate the hundred eyewitnesses to the actual shooting. The search and the questionings occupied endless wearisome hours. His law practice fell off, though she had to learn this from her own sources.

"Is Boston revenging itself on you, John?"

"I think not. There's very little shaping up for the July court. The Bar and the clerks universally complain of the scarcity of business."

He pushed aside a batch of evidence on his desk, opened the window wider for more air.

"I have eight human lives to concern myself about. If I do nothing more this year than save them, I shall be content."

"You believe you can?"

"If I am able to impanel an unprejudiced jury. That possibility becomes more unlikely by the day. It's that new Paul Revere engraving, largely: *The Late Horrid Massacre in King Street*. Edes and Gill have been advertising it in the *Gazette* for eightpence, until I can hardly imagine there is a home in Boston without a copy on its sitting-parlor wall. Revere knows that his picture is false. But if I attempt to interfere . . ."

"Could I? We've ordered several silver pieces from Mr. Revere. Shall I make a small purchase at his shop and see if I can persuade him to withdraw?"

"Bring up the subject only if it is relevant."

"There are ways of making anything relevant."

The next morning she walked to Revere's shop near the docks. It had a low ceiling with blackened beams, small leaded windows. Paul Revere came forward to meet her, a short man, stockily built, with dark eyes and a broad mouth in a flat appealing face. Plain, without education, he wore no wig and was girt around with a leather apron. He bowed, even seemed pleased to see her, a rare treat in these days of isolation. She ordered a salt shaker she had been wanting. While Revere was making a rough sketch in charcoal she said:

"I hear you have talent, Mr. Revere, in setting down whole scenes. Streets, people, houses, even the dogs."

"Ma'am, I get pleasure from drawing things."

"I hear you did a sketch of King Street after the shooting."

"By God! I did. Would you like to see it? Keep it right in my desk."

She studied the engraving for a moment, then said:

"I understand your print is selling extraordinarily well?"

"Near to six hundred copies. That's a pretty smart number. There's my first pull, on the wall."

Abigail studied the original alongside the engraving.

"You made a number of changes."

"Improved it."

"In the original the bodies of Attucks and Gray are close to the soldiers. In the engraving the crowd is at a distance."

"Art, Mrs. Adams. Pure art."

"Because it's more true?"

"Because it's more useful."

"Is that the criterion of art, Mr. Revere, usefulness? I would have thought the criterion might be truth."

"This is a special art. The art of politics."

"Ah, I see. Politics has joined the great arts of literature and painting."

"Do you know how Samuel Adams defines politics? 'The art of the necessary,' he says. Mighty right, he be."

"Do we serve our own best interests when we pervert evidence to convict men we don't like?"

Revere ducked his head into massive shoulders.

"We got nothing agin those lobster-backs, Mrs. Adams. We just say it's illegal to quarter troops on Boston."

"I agree. But what happens, Mr. Revere, if you help establish a precedent for convicting men on contrived evidence, and then somebody contrives against you?"

Revere scratched his scalp vigorously with the blunt end of his crayon.

"Who's goin' to accuse me of anything, Ma'am? Besides, if someone tells a pack o' lies against me in court, I got friends can tell taller lies and get me off."

She had lost. She paid Revere a deposit against the salt shaker, approved his design and left the shop, the bell tinkling behind her as she closed the heavy wooden door.

She reached home to find Samuel Adams, Dr. Joseph Warren, Josiah Quincy, Jr., John Hancock and James Otis toasting each other with John's rum punch. To her raised eyebrows John quickly explained that Captain Scott, commanding Hancock's *Haley*, had just arrived from England with the news that Lord North, the King's Prime Minister, had guided a bill through Parliament which rescinded the Townshend Acts, dropping the taxes on all imports with the single exception of the tax on tea.

"Why tea?" she asked.

"Possibly because every last soul in New England drinks tea. Britain knows it is indispensable," replied Samuel.

"It goes deeper than that," said John. "Parliament has retained the preamble to the Acts whole. By preserving the tax on tea they are reminding us that the list can be broadened or extended at any time they see fit."

Boston never took up the celebration. A few days later a town meeting of freeholders in Faneuil Hall voted to reject the British concessions with an "unalterable resolution to support the non-importation agreement."

As John had predicted, when Samuel Adams struck it was from a most unexpected quarter. But it did not come until after Abigail had given birth to her second son, whom they named Charles. He was a robust boy who cried fast and loud and was hungry from the instant of his birth. She thanked God for His goodness.

It was the sixth of June, a warm clear day, with a slight tang of salt breeze in the air. She came downstairs later in the afternoon to find John stretched out like a corpse on the sitting-room sofa, holding an ice pack which he kept moving over his face and forehead. This was a sight she had not seen before. Her first impulse was to laugh.

"John, whatever in creation could have happened to you on such a delightful day?"

"The worst. I was sitting in my office correlating the evidence of a dozen witnesses when a messenger came in with a paper from the town meeting. It informed me that I had just been elected by the Boston freeholders to represent Boston in the House of Representatives and the General Court."

"But that's wonderful! Grandfather Quincy was a representative for years, and a member of the General Court, even the Speaker."

John stared at her hollow-eyed.

"I went down to Faneuil Hall immediately, and in as few words as possible tried to tell them of my insufficiency to fulfill the expectations of people. They listened to none of it. They thought it was false modesty. Then I accepted. But it gave me no joy."

"For Heaven's sake why not?"

He cried out in anguish:

"When I accepted this seat in the House of Representatives, my dear partner, I thereby consented to my own ruin, to your ruin, and to the ruin of our children."

He put the ice pack back over his face. She realized what was disturbing him. The job of representative paid no salary; it absorbed most of a man's time and left him free for little other work. John would become occupied by politics almost to the exclusion of a law practice. She knew what this would do to their diminishing store of gold coins. They had received no fee for the Panton case. There would be little further fee for the defense of the eight soldiers. A few more of these honors and they would be in Cousin Samuel's situation. She burst into tears, but stopped almost immediately. It was foolish to decry their fate when it had been leading them upward every step of the way. She walked over to the sofa, took the ice pack from John.

"I'm willing in this cause to run all the risks with you. We'll place our trust in Providence."

Suddenly she saw the incongruity of the situation.

"It's absolutely impossible. The Bostonians hate you! They couldn't possibly have elected you to represent them."

"The final ballot showed that I had more than four hundred votes out of something over five hundred."

"But how could that be?"

"Samuel Adams. . . ."

She sat down in the nearest chair.

". . . He happens to think I write the best Instructions, laws and amendments in Massachusetts. He decided that he needed me in the General Court to fight for the Patriots, Captain Preston and the redcoats or no, and so there I am. A strange way to begin my political career, is it not?"

"You began your political career when you wrote the first highway laws for Braintree. Politics is a road through a quagmire; once you get on at the beginning there's nowhere to get off except at the end. And you're a very, very long way from the end."

She had said the wrong thing. He slumped back down on the sofa.

"Before I engaged in this Captain Preston case I had more business at the Bar than any man in the province. How are we going to get through the thorns and leap all the crevices before us? My health is too feeble to handle this mass of work, these months-long trials without any compensation, or at best a few guineas, and then the endless quarreling with the lieutenant governor, the Council and England, when I have a family to support. I'm devoting myself to endless labor and anxiety, and all for nothing except a sense of duty."

Abigail repressed the smile twitching at the corners of her lips.

"To good Puritans like you and me, duty is a short cut to heaven. John, as your partner, I have an offer to make you. My proposal is that you worry about Captain Preston and the trial, the House of Representatives and the General Court. I will take over the worrying about your enfeebled health and the food for our enfeebled family."

The trial of Captain Preston opened at the end of October. That of the soldiers was scheduled to follow on November twenty-seventh. The Sons of Liberty were grimly determined to convict the soldiers, but John sensed a lessening in their drive against the captain.

"Would you know why, John?"

"Yes, I would. If Captain Preston gave the order to fire, then he alone is responsible. The soldiers had to obey his orders or be considered mutinous. His conviction would give the soldiers immunity."

As the trials grew closer he found that meat did not agree with him, then fish, then the cabbage family of vegetables, then the fresh fruits of the summer and fall, then sweets. Abigail asked Dr. Cotton Tufts about him when Cotton rode in from Weymouth. Cotton's hair had grown gray at the temples, which made him look almost handsome for a winsomely homely man. He laughed softly at the question.

"Cousin, you married a plump man. John could go without food for a year and not come out as skinny as I am. When he complains, 'My stomach hurts,' he means 'I'm afraid I'll be inadequate and lose.'"

On the morning of Preston's trial a strange thing happened. Jonathan Sewall, who was posted to prosecute, disappeared from Boston. Samuel Quincy was appointed in Sewall's place; he would be appearing against his brother, Josiah, Jr. One of John's oldest friends, Robert Treat Paine, was also named for the prosecution.

"Good luck," Abigail murmured as John left the house.

The following day was the anniversary of King George III's accession to the throne. Abigail, who had been up half the night listening to John's summary of Samuel Quincy's opening statement, was almost jolted out of bed by the fleet in the harbor firing its heaviest guns. The salute started with the commodore's ship and came down the line through the captains of each ship according to their seniority. They were answered by salvos from Castle William and the Battery guns. It was, Abigail thought, an inopportune time to show off so much power.

Defense witnesses of good character testified that Captain Preston never uttered the word "Fire"; in fact had tried to prevent the shooting and get his men back to quarters. The judges: Benjamin Lynde, John Cushing, Peter Oliver and Edmund Trowbridge, gave their opinion that Captain Preston was innocent, a verdict with which the jury quickly agreed.

"It's the veriest prologue," John told her when he returned that evening. "If the soldiers fired without orders, they alone are responsible for their acts. That puts the burden on us of proving that their acts were justifiable homicide."

"It does seem as though there ought to be some gentle times, when we can play with our children and enjoy our love without being harassed from without."

"These are harassed times, Nabby. But if I can conduct my case properly I can accomplish a great many different purposes. Save those lives; convince England that it must withdraw its soldiers and Boston that it must eschew violence. That's the only way we can earn a permanent peace. It's my dearest hope that with an acquittal the Ministry will lift the last of the taxes. Then we will be back to happier days, when we can be friends of England."

She slipped her fingers into his, whispering:

"May God rest His hand on your shoulder."

9

The trial of the eight soldiers was to be held in the Council Chamber on the second floor of the Town House, a noble room with high ceilings, tall and stately windows. It was a gala day in Boston. The city streets were filled with carriages, each laden with groups sitting forward and back. All night long country carts had been rumbling in over the cobblestones. The ancient ones, crowding up the staircase of the Town House, were saying that this was the most important day the Massachusetts Bay Colony had ever known. The benches, more like comfortable pews, were filled by the time Abigail entered the room. The army officers led by Colonel Dalrymple, who had first landed the troops on the Boston waterfront, were resplendent in scarlet coats with black boots that came up to the knee over light breeches. The officers, swords hanging from their sides, wore their appropriate shoulder ornaments, and gold braid around the rim of their hats, a splotch of color which easily dominated the Council Chamber.

Abigail noted as she made her way toward the front of the room, where seats had been reserved for the wives of counsel, that the Bostonians, male and female alike, had also decided that they must make the best possible impression. The most resplendently attired were John's distant cousins, Mr. and Mrs. Thomas Boylston, the wife in a blue satin dress with white ruffles, and blue and white polka-dot collar, a magnificent white lace hat tied under her chin, Thomas Boylston in a gray grogram with a dark green broadcloth vest.

As she gazed about she picked out a purple velvet dress with silver buttons; several pin-striped corduroy suits with waistcoats in black for the conservative, and gay colors for the social-minded. Dr. Joseph Warren was handsomely garbed in a thin-striped corduroy suit of matching coat and breeches. Abigail herself was plainly though not too demurely gowned in a brown wool brocade buttoned to the waist. Her sister Mary wore a blue worsted. Her aunt Elizabeth was in crimson damask with fine lace ruffles.

A section had been reserved for the craftsmen and mechanics. They wore their traditional leather breeches, black or buff colored, gray yarn stockings and plain white shirts. Some few wore colored vests with brass buttons. Their wives wore wool dresses, dark in color, and the traditional elbow-length gloves.

The lawyers took their seats at a long table beneath the bench. John had had his wig freshly powdered. He had a new black robe which covered him completely. Although Josiah Quincy, Jr., had been admitted to the Superior Court and was entitled to wear the robe, he refused to do so as a protest against the "pomp and magic of the long robe." He was wearing a simple black outfit and a white shirt with a side band around the neck.

The judges entered wearing scarlet broadcloth robes imported from England, their luxuriant wigs falling in curls to their shoulders. The court stood.

The accused soldiers were summoned by the clerk. They filed in, heard the charges read against them, pleaded "Not guilty." They were in their uniforms, immaculate, the white pants tucked into the black boots which came midway to the calf, their coats red with intersecting white bands across the chest from shoulder to waist. Each was carrying a black felt three-cornered hat and had been provided a new wig, tied in back with a black ribbon. Only the prison pallor and fear on their faces exposed them.

The clerk cried, "God send you a good deliverance! The jury will be called."

Twenty-five prospective jurors were brought in from a side room. John rose, said, "My lord, the prisoners have agreed that one of their mates, Corporal William Wemms, shall make the challenges for them all."

John and Josiah, Jr., had been working with the soldiers for months. On instruction, Wemms challenged for cause four jurors who lived in Boston. They were dismissed. Another dozen were challenged peremptorily and dismissed, their fates having been decided by John's copious political files. Eight more prospective jurors were brought in and three were sworn. When twelve men were finally agreed upon and seated, Abigail saw that they all came from the surrounding small towns: Roxbury, Dorchester, Braintree, Dedham, Milton, Stoughton and Hingham.

The lawyers' table was three feet in front of and below the array of scarlet-clad judges; beyond them was the witness box, a discreet six feet from the judges. The attorneys were now bade to rise. It was not often that Abigail had a chance to see her husband plain. She was comforted by what she saw. John Adams was cool and quiet in his manner. All along he had told her that he was not for one side or against the other but rather he was for law and justice, assuredly man's greatest hope on earth. He was a rational man who had resolved to put the trial in its proper perspective as a case in which fact and law, not passion or prejudice, would prevail. He seemed to Abigail to have behind him the authority of two thousand years of Western law, as well as the dignity of a self-respecting man who meant to practice honestly and well a noble profession. No one looking at him now in his incorruptible faith and courage could have any concept of how harrowed a man he had been.

She turned her gaze to the other side of the counsel table and saw her older cousin, Samuel Quincy. She knew what the Sons of Liberty were saying around Boston, that slow-moving, slow-speaking Samuel, now thirty-five years old, was a mediocre lawyer; jealous of the success of his nine-year-younger brother, Josiah, Jr. That Samuel, aside from taking care of the Quincy affairs, had secured little law business in Boston, while cross-eyed, lovable Josiah, with a flashing mind and spirit, had been adopted by the Sons of Liberty and the Patriot merchants and was enjoying a bright success. Since Samuel Quincy could get nowhere with the Patriots, since his name and solidity were needed by the Crown—or so the Sons of Liberty said—he had been taken up by the governor and the customs commissioners, offered the job of solicitor general with assurances that he would rise high in King George's favor. Abigail knew enough of her stolid cousin to be convinced that he had not aligned himself with the Crown for money, but rather for a place in the sun.

Josiah was standing alongside of John. Neither John nor Abigail thought he was half as good a lawyer as Boston had decided. By the same token they did not believe that Samuel was as mediocre as the Sons of Liberty were trying to establish.

"Give Sam Quincy the time and he'll find the law," said John. "He'll never amaze you with his knowledge, but nobody is going to break any contract or will he draws."

Samuel made his opening statement. John's judgment of the man proved sound. He did a painstaking job of getting at the basic substance of the prosecution's case and in eliciting pertinent evidence from his witnesses about the shooting of the dead and wounded men.

For a week each side abstained from rhetoric, trying to build a solid structure of fact. Each evening after the five o'clock closing of court Josiah came to the house to work with John until midnight. After the children had been put to bed Abigail sat in the study crocheting or sewing as the men dissected the day's statements, tracked down precedents and set up the pattern of examination for their own witnesses.

Samuel Quincy summed up for the Crown. Brother faced brother.

First he laboriously built the reliability of the prosecution's witnesses and their testimony. Next he reiterated the identity of the prisoners and their participation in the firing, then he expounded:

"It is a rule of law, gentlemen, when the fact of killing is once proved, every circumstance alleviating, excusing or justifying in order to extenuate the crime must be proved by the prisoners, for the law presumes the fact malicious until the contrary appears in evidence. There is another rule I shall mention also, and that is that it is immaterial, where there are a number of persons concerned, who gave the mortal blow, all that are present are in the eye of the law principals. This is a rule settled by the judges of England upon solid argument. . . . The laws of society, gentlemen, lay a restraint on the passions of men, that no man shall be the avenger of his own cause, unless through absolute necessity, the law giving a remedy for every wrong. If a man might at any time execute his own revenge, there would be an end of law. . . . I shall therefore rest the case as it is, and doubt not but, on the evidence as it now stands, the facts against the prisoners at the bar are fully proved. . . . From the force of that evidence, you must pronounce them GUILTY."

Then began the interrogation for the defense. By the end of the week eighty-two witnesses in all had gone upon the stand to tell their stories. Each side was reporting a totally different shooting. The piles of notes and records grew higher on John's desk, as they must have on Samuel's and Robert Treat Paine's. John and Josiah knew every line on the pages that brought forth the tiniest conflict or contradiction in the prosecution's testimony:

The witness Bridgham said he saw one of the accused, a tall man, Warren; then admitted that he saw another man belonging to the same regiment who looked so like Warren as to make him doubt whether he had seen Warren at all. One witness said it was the soldiers who were doing the pushing. Following witnesses said that there were fifty people near the soldiers, pushing at them, and a crowd of sailors with clubs, urging the crowd to violence, with people huzzahing and whistling, crying, "Damn you, fire! Why don't you fire?" A defense witness, Mr. Davis, swore that he heard Gray, who had been killed, crying, "I will go and have a slap at them if I lose my life." Other witnesses swore that Gray was in liquor, that he ran about clapping people on the shoulders saying, "Don't run away, they dare not fire."

James Bailey, a witness for the prosecution, admitted under cross-examination that some of the mob around the sentry were throwing pieces of ice as big as fists, hard enough to hurt any man. He also admitted under John's prodding that he "saw the mulatto seven or eight minutes before the firing, at the head of twenty or thirty sailors in Cornhill, and he had a large cordwood stick." That Attucks wanted to be the hero of the night, to lead his army with banners, that he had formed them in Dock Square and marched them up to King Street with their clubs.

John cried:

"If this was not an unlawful assembly, there never was one in the world."

Court adjourned at five o'clock on Saturday afternoon. The jury was kept together. On Monday morning John and Josiah would begin addressing the jury with their final pleas. He and Josiah had agreed to work separately in drawing up their summations. Abigail had her husband to herself on the weekend. He confided that he would not write out his speech because he needed the power of spontaneity. He worked far into Sunday morning, but made her go to bed at midnight. He awakened her at seven so that they might dress and go to church. After the preaching he returned to his desk. It was a sight she never tired of, seeing him working at the top of his energy, his eyes sweeping the books, his hand moving with strong open strokes across the page.

At nine o'clock on Monday morning December 3, 1770, the city of Boston prepared for judgment day. Abigail found twice as many people jammed into the Council Chamber, filling in the areas around the judges' rostrum and lawyers' desks, in the aisles and at the back where there were no seats. People were standing quietly, almost immobile, on the stairs and in all of the clerks' rooms and smaller rooms of the Town House. Outside on King Street for the two blocks from the Town House up to the Custom House where the shooting had been committed, they knotted into little groups, some talking, most silent, waiting for a result.

Josiah Quincy, Jr., opened the final plea for the defense. His argument fell inside the boundaries of his talent and his temperament; he appealed directly to the sympathies, to the heart and soul of Boston and Massachusetts, pleading for mercy. It was not his task to address himself to the body of involved and contradictory evidence. That was John's job. Abigail remarked Josiah's gift of rhetoric. There was absolute silence in the big room, for his magnificent voice was weaving a spell.

"Permit me, gentlemen, to remind you of the importance of this trial as it relates to the prisoners. It is for their lives! If we consider the number of persons now on trial, joined with many other circumstances, it is by far the most important this country ever saw. The eyes of all are upon you. Patience in hearing this cause is an essential requisite; candor and caution are no less essential. . . . Nay, it is of high importance to your country that nothing should appear on this trial to impeach our justice or stain our humanity. . . ."

Abigail saw the jurymen stir, move to a more comfortable position not only on their hard bench but also in their consciences. She remembered how the two men had searched the lawbooks for this ultimate line:

"Instead of that hospitality that the soldier thought himself entitled to, scorn, contempt and silent murmurs were his reception. Almost every countenance lowered with a discontented gloom and scarce an eye but flashed indignant fire. . . . The soldier had his feelings, his sentiments and his characteristic passions also. . . . The law had taught him to think favorably of himself. Had taught him to consider himself as peculiarly appointed for the safeguard and defense of his country. How stinging was it to be stigmatized as the instrument of tyranny and oppression!"

There was a low murmur; this was the one indisputable fact emerging from the trial. Boston had bitterly resented and hated the British soldiers from the first foot set on Dock Street.

"Can anyone think it is duty to espouse the part acted by those assembled in King Street? I think not; but lest my opinion should not have weight, let me remind you of an author whom I could wish were in the hands of all of you . . . I allude to the third letter of the 'Farmer of Pennsylvania' to his countrymen. 'The cause of liberty . . . is a cause of too much dignity to be sullied by turbulence and tumult. It ought to be maintained in a manner suitable to her nature. Those who engage in it should breathe a sedate yet fervent spirit animating them to actions of prudence, justice, modesty, bravery, humanity and magnanimity!' "

This was a clever ruse, Abigail knew, to bring the influence of their favorite writer on the members of the jury.

Josiah went as close to the jurymen as the protective railing would allow, and in a moving voice recited:

"The quality of mercy is not strained;
It droppeth like the gentle rain from heaven—
It is twice blessed;
It blesses him that gives, and him that takes."

John was to begin his appeal immediately after noon dinner. Abigail knew that it was only a figure of speech that a person could have his stomach up in his throat, but that was precisely where she felt hers to be. When they returned to the Council Chamber it appeared that few of the people had moved, though doubtless some of them had gone out for something to eat or drink.

John Adams rose from the counsel table, circled it and took up his position halfway between the judges and jurors, presenting the exact opposite picture of Josiah Quincy. He had a stern air about him, like that of a schoolmaster. It was not for John to appeal to the sympathy of the jurors, to bring tears to their eyes. It was for him to separate the mass of evidence, so much of it contradictory and implausible; to throw out the irrelevant, the prejudiced, and to leave the starkest of architectural forms, the unadorned structure of plain, believable and irrefragable fact. Abigail knew John's thinking: it would serve only half of their purpose to save the lives of the eight men on the basis of pity or sympathy. It would resolve nothing for the future.

No, John Adams, standing there stockily in his long robe, with his uncurled white wig puffed about his ears, his eyes big and hard in his plump face, was going to make no concession. The jury and the court would settle this case in the manner prescribed by law, hewing close to judicial procedures. When this trial was over no Bostonian was going to be able to reproach him with having played them soft and loose. He wanted an acquittal from Boston and Massachusetts as much as from the jury.

He began to speak. His voice was neither big nor resonant. His manner ceded nothing to the well-dressed people in the courtroom or to the several thousand less well dressed gathered outside.

"May it please Your Honors, and you, gentlemen of the jury . . . As the prisoners stand before you for their lives, it may be proper to recollect with what temper the law requires we should proceed to this trial. The form of proceeding at their arraignment has discovered that the spirit of the law upon such occasions is conformable to humanity, to common sense and feeling; that it is all benignity and candor. And the trial commences with the prayer of the court, expressed by the clerk, to the supreme judge of judges, empires and worlds: 'God send you a good deliverance.'

"I shall now consider the several divisions of law under which the evidence will arrange itself. That action now before you is homicide; that is, the killing of one man by another. The law calls it homicide, but it is not criminal in all cases for one man to slay another. Had the prisoners been on the Plains of Abraham, and slain an hundred Frenchmen apiece, the English law would have considered it as a commendable action, virtuous and praiseworthy. . . . The law divides homicide into three branches; the first is justifiable, the second excusable, and the third felonious. Felonious homicide is subdivided into two branches; the first is murder, which is killing with malice aforethought, the second is manslaughter, which is killing a man on a sudden provocation. Here, gentlemen, are four sorts of homicide. . . . The fact was the slaying of five unhappy persons that night; you are to consider whether it was justifiable, excusable or felonious; and if felonious, whether it was murder or manslaughter. One of these four it must be."

The judges frowned. The jurors began to perceive that there would be no easy way out for them.

"Gentlemen, the law has planted fences and barriers around every individual; it is a castle round every man's person, as well as his house. As the love of God and our neighbor comprehends the whole duty of man, so self-love and social comprehend all the duties we owe to mankind, and the first branch is self-love, which is not only our indisputable right, but our clearest duty. . . . It is the first and strongest principle in our nature; Justice Blackstone calls it 'the primary canon in the law of nature.'"

John now turned to his organized notes, beginning a dissection of the evidence from both sides. It was relentlessly logical, stripping away the hysteria, the improbable and the impossible, cutting out the interested lies. He concluded:

"If you are satisfied that the people, whoever they were, made that assault with a design to kill or maim the soldiers, this was such an assault as will justify the soldiers killing in their own defense. . . . You must place yourselves in the situation of Wemms or Killroy, consider yourselves as knowing that the prejudices of the world about you were against you; that the people about you thought you came to dragoon them into obedience to statutes, instructions, mandates and edicts which they thoroughly detested; that many of these people were thoughtless and inconsiderate, old and young, sailors and landmen . . . that they, the soldiers, had no friends about them . . . with all the bells ringing to call the town together to assist the people in King Street, the people shouting, huzzahing and making the mob whistle, as they call it . . . crying, 'Kill them! Kill them! Knock them over!' heaving snowballs, oyster shells, clubs, white birch sticks three inches and an half diameter, consider yourselves in this situation, and then judge whether a reasonable man in the soldiers' situation would not have concluded that they were going to kill him."

John paused for the burthen to sink into the jury's mind. They had been chosen as reasonable men. The law clearly stated that if a reasonable man concluded that his life was in danger he had the right to protect himself by striking back.

"In the continual vicissitudes of human things, amidst the shocks of fortune and the whirls of passion that take place at certain critical seasons, even in the mildest government, the people are liable to run into riots and tumults. There are church quakes and state quakes in the moral and political world, as well as earthquakes, storms and tempests in the physical. Thus much, however, must be said in favor of the people and of human nature, that it is a general if not an universal truth that the aptitude of the people to mutinies, seditions, tumults and insurrections is in direct proportion to the despotism of the government. . . ."

This was the John Adams Abigail liked best: the man who could move from the particular to the universal; who, like a good historian, could expand the area of a trial from King Street to the world.

"To your candor and justice I submit the prisoners and their cause. The law, in all vicissitudes of government, fluctuations of the passions, or flights of enthusiasm, will preserve a steady undeviating course. . . . Without any regard to persons, it commands that which is good and punishes evil in all, whether rich or poor, high or low. 'Tis deaf, inexorable, inflexible. . . ."

The listening silence was so intense that Abigail could hear the courtroom breathe.

"On the one hand it is inexorable to the cries and lamentations of the prisoners; on the other it is deaf, deaf as an adder, to the clamors of the populace."

He turned full face to the courtroom.

"May God send us all a good deliverance!"

The jury was out for two and a half hours. John had moved back to sit with Abigail and her family. They talked of the Cranch and Adams children, of Billy's engagement to Catharine Louisa Salmon from Lincoln.

When the jury returned to the box John went to stand with the prisoners. The jurors revealed little, but it was obvious by the manner in which they sat upright on their benches, the way her father's congregation did while he was preaching, that each had followed the stern dictates of his Puritan conscience.

She craned forward to hear the clerk. The hundreds in the Chamber joined her. The clerk of the court announced:

"Six of the accused: not guilty! . . ."

Abigail sat unmoving. A hubbub broke against her ears.

"Matthew Killroy and Hugh Montgomery: guilty of manslaughter."

She saw John throw both arms ceilingward to gain the attention of the court. There was a common-law custom which could save Killroy and Montgomery from prison.

"My two clients pray the benefit of clergy."

The sheriff was obliged to bring in a brazier. He returned with a branding iron, put it into the live coals. The entire courtroom rose. First Killroy proffered his thumb. He was branded. Montgomery then stepped forward, reached out a hand at the end of an untrembling arm. The brand was applied. The clerk cried:

"God has sent you a good deliverance!"

The case was over. The eight soldiers were free. The sheriff took them out a side door. John joined Abigail. They walked together down the center aisle. The spectators did not so much move physically as shrink back inside themselves to make room for the Adamses to pass. No one spoke. No one smiled. Abigail had in her nostrils the faint odor of burnt flesh.

The Adamses too had been branded.

10

She found it hard to understand her new status. The first stage of anonymity had gone; nor did they any longer live in a fortress, beyond a moat. They were now perhaps the most notorious people in town. The Crown sympathizers were delighted with the verdict but they did not venture to approach the Adamses. Boston neither condemned nor approved, a segment of the city feeling the verdict was the best of several bad solutions, particularly with the redcoats now locked up in Castle William, and the eight men who had stood trial returned to England. Abigail simply had the feeling that they no longer belonged here, that Boston was thinking:

"You're an Englishman who must have come from London to defend the soldiers. You got them off. Why don't you go back home?"

John was too utterly spent to care or even to discuss the aftermath of the trial.

What awoke him out of his apathy was an article in the *Boston Gazette*, published five days after the verdict and signed "Vindex." The verdict was declared a bad one: the evidence had clearly pointed to the guilt of the soldiers; the victims had done nothing wrong; the Bostonians were in no way at fault. More articles were promised, one in each week's publication, to prove that a "gross injustice had been done to the town of Boston."

John turned from the newspaper, rubbing his fingers over his face, leaving behind streaks of the fresh print.

"I thought the case was closed," he muttered hoarsely.

"John, we've become pariahs. Boston doesn't know what to do with us."

"The *Gazette* does: damn us to perdition. Now who would write such an article, pile fuel on the fires?"

John returned from the *Gazette* office looking dazed.

"Cousin Samuel?" she ventured.

"Yes. Who else?"

"How could he justify such an attack?"

"Easily. He was there. Told me the attacks had nothing to do with me. That I had conducted a superb defense. He's proud of me! He's even glad the prisoners are free . . ."

". . . but?"

". . . but it doesn't serve the Patriot purpose for Boston to have been wrong. When he finishes his series of articles it will be perfectly clear to Massachusetts that Boston was innocent and the soldiers guilty. In that way, says Samuel, both of us will have accomplished our desired results."

They sat in silence. John asked how long they had been living in Boston.

"Nearly three years."

"What have we to show for it?"

"Baby Charles."

"We could have had him anywhere. For my work this past eight months I've been paid eight guineas. How much savings do we have left?"

"Very little."

"Then I must ask the question. What have we gained by moving into Boston? We hoped to earn more money, to secure our children's future. We have nothing to show. As a representative to the General Court I have already served on a dozen committees, helped to write the Assembly's resolutions, correspondence to England and to the other colonies, helped in the plans for the encouragement of the arts, agriculture and manufactures. Yet Boston has turned from me. . . . We hoped to spend more time together, but this succession of political cases, the *Liberty*, Lieutenant Panton, now the eight British soldiers, has used up so much of my time and strength that I have nothing left for the rest of you. Why can't we go back to our home in Braintree?"

A long sigh escaped her, as though someone had taken a hundred-pound sack of barley off her shoulders.

"We can, John."

"There are so many years ahead. What good does it do us to remain in this alien city? I'll give myself this much, I've helped achieve some important results. We've put an end to the seizure of our ships. Impressment has been rendered illegal. We've saved the lives of eight soldiers. Yet we're outcasts. The more we triumph, the more harshly we're attacked."

"Then it's settled," she murmured. "We'll go home. We'll walk across the fields, pick fruit from our trees, bathe with the children in the brook, climb Penn's Hill at sunset, enjoy a perspective on the world."

She slipped into the shallow angle of his arm as though it were a haven.

BOOK FOUR

SPREAD OUT THE HEAVENS

1

How much simpler Braintree was to grasp: the elm-shaded main road, the little group of houses, school, churches, artisans' workbenches. Behind the road were the farms, each family known to her as in Weymouth. She was happier in a small town because she could hold all of it in her mind. She had moved into Boston at twenty-three, still a young girl, though she had been married for three and a half years. She had returned after another three years feeling that the experience had turned her into a mature woman.

As she moved about her cottage, untying the carpets that had been rolled and roped at either end, removing the rough sheets wrapped about her furniture, scraped off the heavy oiled paper that had been pasted to the inside of the windows, she found the composure to ask herself the meaning of the lightning-like reversals in their fortunes. Was the fault their own? Due to inherent weaknesses in their character? It must be so for them to have risen so far and fallen so fast. Yet where in their more than six years of marriage had they failed themselves or Massachusetts Bay Colony? It was a few months short of ten years since she had come dancing down the steps of the parsonage to find John Adams standing in her father's library; yet it seemed as though iron cartwheels had passed over the rough cobbled streets of an entire lifetime. She asked her husband if he felt this.

"I know quite clearly *what* has happened to me," she confided, as they sat over a simple supper in their kitchen, the pots, fryers, cranes having been polished to a high sheen and returned to their duty in the fireplace. "But do I know *why*? So often I feel as though I have no control over our fate."

He pushed aside his half-empty bowl, leaned forward toward her with elbows on the opened table leaf, stocky fingers interlaced.

"You mean that circumstances seem to happen to you, instead of you happening to them?"

She flashed him a grateful smile.

"It's almost as though I stood defenseless against northeasters. Isn't there some way we can avoid being buffeted by the world?"

"Beleaguered, in fact."

He filled his pipe, puffed away thoughtfully.

"In all fairness to ourselves, dear soul, we must remember that we always had the right of decision. We were never helpless pawns on somebody's chessboard. If it had been in our nature to join the Crown Tories I could have become advocate general of the Admiralty Court and begun our climb up the royal ladder of favor. Should we have accepted that post?"

"I'll pass that as a rhetorical question."

"Agreed. When James Forrest pleaded with me to defend Captain Preston and the eight soldiers I could have replied, 'Regrettably, I am overcommitted.' Had I done that, you would have looked back on my years of glorying in law and justice as hypocrisy. Following one's principles is costly business. It has us back in this leanter eating pot cheese and stewed fruit instead of attending a formal ball in Boston."

She knitted her eyebrows and lips tightly.

"Forgive me for pursuing this, but I suffer vertigo if I find myself stranded halfway up a cliff."

"Throw me a rope."

"You say that we exercised the right of decision? Twenty years ago you could have accepted the position of advocate general because we were all peaceable Englishmen together. Ten years ago you could have defended a group of British soldiers without becoming a pariah because there had been no Townshend Acts. Doesn't that mean that we are making our decision inside a set of circumstances superimposed upon us?"

Having difficulty sitting still when an argument began plumbing the depths, he paced the length of the kitchen, stopping to stare sightlessly into the room where Rachel Marsh had lived so long. Rachel was now married to the artisan with whom she had "walked out" in Boston. He returned to the hearth and stood with his back to the fire, hovering above Abigail protectively.

"What you are saying, Nabby, is that every man is part of his times. All too true. We live in an age of ferment. The best we can hope for are periods of calm. I doubt we will ever know truly tranquil years. The yeast is all about us, changing the air we breathe, the ideas we absorb, the values and loyalties that are being baked up larger than life from the flat dough we put in the oven when we were young."

"What you are telling me, John, is that we have already etched the design of our lives. That the happenings of the past six years have not been haphazard, or imposed from without, but arise out of a combination of our own nature and our own age."

"Yes. One could possibly be master of one's fate in a quiet era, but perhaps an era only looks quiet in retrospect. Perhaps for the people who had to trudge their way painfully through it, it was filled with turmoil. Your father was called to Weymouth in a quiet time; but soon he was embroiled in a religious war, trying to put down the revivalism and hysterias of the Great Awakening. He had to fight the battle of separation of State and Church. Your cousin Cotton was born into a quiet time, but since his twenty-first birthday he has been fighting a one-man war against secrecy in the practice of medicine. It is the human condition."

She garnered strength from his solidity.

"I accept that, John. And it's important for me to know it. I need to eliminate the shock, the loss of perspective at every turn of the road. I don't want to keep crying out, 'Why is this happening to us?' "

He looked away from her.

"We all hope to reason ourselves into composure. It's the first law of nature. We yearn to understand our roles in the unfolding drama. What lies at the base of the mystery? Ourselves, and history. The past never goes away; it returns garbed in different raiment, yet in materials we have helped to card, loom, cut and sew. The future is a protective attire that will clothe our nakedness at the same time it exposes us to the winds of adversity."

He reached behind him for an apple, tossed it to her. Her face broke into a delighted smile as she quickly reached up and caught it. They spitted the apples on sharp sticks, took down knives and spun the apples in a continuous circular movement, the peel rolling off like a swirling red ribbon.

"Now, would you answer something for me?" he asked.

"Yes."

"Could we go to bed? Sometimes I got so homesick for this cottage it was like a sharp physical pain: for this intimate kitchen, for my office, for the sofa in the parlor; but mostly for my conjugal bed. I never sleep anywhere as I do there."

She laughed.

"In a world that changes so swiftly, it's good to know that some few things remain constant."

Later, while John slept with his face buried deep in a pillow, she rose, lit the two lamps on her desk above which she had affixed a small mirror. The light was bright enough to tell her the truth as she faced her reflection.

Her chestnut-colored hair seemed to her as rich as when she had brushed it down over her shoulders in the Weymouth parsonage. Her eyes were still luminous with a vibrant expectancy. Her skin was not as radiant as she remembered it from her courtship days, yet despite the harsh Boston climate it was unblemished.

She leaned closer to the glass. There were no lines in her forehead, nor the beginning of wrinkles at the corners of her eyes. She pulled back her lips to examine the small, beautifully white teeth; how good that there was an embargo on tea, for drinking too much hot tea scorched the enamel off one's teeth. Her nose! Not time nor fortune would ever improve that direct inheritance from her father. Sometimes, as when John called her a plump pigeon, it seemed more in proportion than when her face, as now, was its usual slender oval.

She pulled tightly behind her the flowered calico night rail with the high-collared neck, and surveyed the outline. The nursing of four children had not enlarged her breasts, but they no longer had that fresh bursting quality. She deliberately committed the sin of pride as she relished the continued slimness of her body, the small waist, the flat abdomen, the long slender legs; and prayed that she might always remain physically attractive. The early Puritan preachers would have damned her. But not her father.

She slipped back into bed and lay quite still, her hands at her sides, staring up at the ceiling. In these hours of happiness and tranquillity in their cottage where she had come as a bride six and a half years before, she asked herself to what degree she had been right in her youthful conception of what love and marriage would be.

"If I did not contest every step of the way with John, and suffer so intensely over his causes," she thought, "if I could be detached: loving, sympathetic, but without involvement, would my love be more idyllic, more romantic?"

Or was this a delusion? For any wife? Either she was one with her husband, suffering with him, or they were a separated two. She did not want detachment even if it were possible, given John's volatile nature. She preferred exhaustion to being excluded. Non-involvement would mean the loss of love.

Nor had John failed her on her childhood dreams. His feelings fluctuated, he was moody, gyrated through all manner of cycles, now scaling the mountain peak, now wallowing in ocean deeps. But not in relation to her. He knew that what he did was motivated by himself alone. In his recurrent bouts of self-loathing, it never occurred to a New Englander to blame his wife for his troubles. He had been too well trained from infancy to be a flagellant, flailing himself with birch branches of self-criticism and deprecation, to try to sneak out from under his own culpabilities. The Puritan husband might be difficult but he would not be impossible. She took comfort from that.

2

At home John Adams was a bit of a great man. Braintree did not need to be acquitted of inciting a massacre as Boston had. One evening a week he was obliged to go to Brackett's Tavern to discuss politics with the men who used it as their gathering place, for here they had planted their own flourishing Liberty Tree. Ebenezer Thayer indicated the extent of his capitulation by coming to Sunday tea, hat in hand, to ask John if he would take on his young son as a law clerk.

"You're now the first lawyer in the province, Mr. Adams," said Thayer. Abigail could not repress a tiny smile as she poured, for this was the process server who had hurt John by calling him in open court a "petty lawyer."

John accepted Thayer's son, a boy in delicate health. Abigail thought that showed a largeness of spirit. John replied that Boston too was showing largeness of spirit. On his trips into his law office he had found new clients awaiting him. The act of moving away had apparently been salutary.

Braintree's hero worship was short-lived. Samuel Adams persuaded John to campaign for him for the office of register of deeds for Suffolk County. Braintree put up a local candidate, defeating the two Adamses decisively.

"They're crowing like dunghill cocks," John complained. "I've reaped nothing but ridicule and contempt for my efforts, and afforded all the Church of England gentry a stick with which to beat me."

She had been suffering from a series of winter colds. The May sun was warm and healing. She took early morning climbs with John to the top of Penn's Hill, then returned home by way of the meadow. Walking over their fields was like swimming in the ocean and emerging to feel the rhythm of the waves in her body; for the earth had its tides too, pouring upward in physical emanation not only through the ripening crops but through the soles of her feet, calves, thighs, groin, belly, chest and brain. The earth did not belong to her, but she to the earth, a mating unknown to city dwellers who had to scuffle along cobbled streets.

She dressed and took the children on horseback to visit their uncle Peter and his two babies. Their uncle Elihu now had three. In the afternoon she sat out in the yard as the children played; at dusk she fed them, took them up to bed, read a final tale from *The Renowned History of Giles Gingerbread.*

John too wanted to lie low, bank his fires.

"It's the old Mosaic law, Abigail, called the sabbatic. Every seventh year one should lie fallow."

"Perhaps we ought to use some of our marsh-mud compost on ourselves? Think of the extraordinary harvest we could produce."

"My opponents already claim that I have too large an element of manure mixed into my ideas."

It was good to be able to make jokes together. In Boston they had lived in deadly earnest. Here John's most pressing problem was to clear a plague of caterpillars out of the trees and build a stone wall against Deacon Belcher's horses and cows which had been fattening on the Adams crop of English hay. He planted peas, parsnips, beets, carrots, cabbages, onions, potatoes, and bought additional calves, piglets, sheep, chickens, geese for their barnyard.

"And just in time," Abigail observed. "Unlike the first time I came to live in this house, the cupboard is bare. When the fruits come ripe and the berries, I'll make our year's supply of jellies and jams. If you'll bring up my barrels from the basement I'll scrub them and let them dry in the sun. Then, when the runs are good, I'll salt down cod, shad, mackerel."

"Goodwife Adams," he murmured; "and Yeoman Adams. I've hired two hands to cut several acres of firewood from our lots on the Common. When that's all neatly stacked I'll move those piles of manure out onto our fields."

"Then all we will need is a charming rain and we'll sprout emeralds."

A succession of young girls had been offered for work. Now there came two whom she liked. The first was Patty, a remote Adams kin; the second Susy, a Braintree girl of good antecedents who had been left homeless. Both girls needed training as well as dowries with which to secure husbands. Patty, fifteen, was tall, blonde, with an omnivorous appetite. She loved food wildly so Abigail trained her to cook for the family. Susy was described by her guardian as "fanatical clean." Abigail trained her to become the housekeeper. The girls moved into the room at the end of the lean-to. That left Abigail free to care for the children.

How different in appearance and temperament three children born of the same parents, within a short time of each other, could be! Nab, almost six, and doing well in Dame School, was still a pudgy child, neither pretty nor graceful. She had a strong personality: reserved, literal-minded, with an astonishing sense of family responsibility for so young a girl. If she rarely laughed or even smiled, she did everything she could to keep the family happy. Abigail sometimes had the feeling that little Nab was taking care of her.

John Quincy, almost four, favored his mother in appearance: oval face, widespread, all-consuming eyes, rounded chin and forehead, with a swift intelligence, sopping up books as though they were games or sweetmeats.

"He's going to be a genius," his father declared.

Charles, a year old now, was an ingratiating clown. When one of the cows calved he insisted on visiting "Bosse" a hundred times a day. Barely able to toddle, he led the family a merry chase over the farm, providing droll stories and laughter for them.

John observed, "Look at Peter, Elihu and me. Could you imagine three such different men being raised in one household?"

"Isn't it time to have the Adams family for Sunday dinner, babes and all?" she asked.

After preaching, Peter came with his Mary and their two children, Elihu with his Thankful and their three. John's mother came across the yard with her second husband, John Hall. John had become reconciled to her remarriage, though he was not happy about it. There were now fourteen Adamses. Elihu continued to be the gay member of the clan, his sole topic of conversation his promotion in the militia. He still lived in his rude cabin, raising only enough crops to feed and clothe his family. He emphatically did not want more rooms or furniture or goods.

"Why bake for tomorrow?" he asked. "Bread gets stale."

Peter was now working two farms, his own thirty-five acres, inherited from his father, and his wife's farm surrounding the former Crosby Tavern which had become their home. He had grown heavier, slower of movement and speech. He had set forth for himself a ten-year plan. He was already a surveyor of highways; next he must become constable, then committeeman to solve the fish problem in the Monatiquot River, then selectman. He seemed happy but tired. The reason became manifest when the men lighted their pipes and cracked nuts for the women.

"John," said Peter, "two farms is too much for one. I want to sell Papa's farm. Will you buy?"

"I'd like to buy, Peter, and run these two farms together."

"Good. It's agreed."

"Not so fast. We have to set a price. Then I have to save the money. I don't have it now."

"We'll take your note."

"I've already given a series of notes for those adjoining pastures of Elijah Belcher. The fences are in a ruinous condition and require a large expense for repairs. But in a year or two . . ."

In the midst of their serenity John became tense. She insisted he tell her why.

"Very well. Our cause is going downhill. The Patriots are out of favor. Since Hutchinson was appointed governor, I have become his whipping boy. He called me one of the few remaining discontents: 'the seditious writer at Braintree.' He claims that the continuing clamors in the newspapers come from me. A number of our former friends have taken Crown positions. Otis has been bought off with a sop and is declaring that we must observe Hutchinson's wishes. Hancock is tired."

"Why must this affect you personally?"

"Some are saying that I fought the Crown Acts only because of a personal feud with Hutchinson. It's not easy to have one's motives impugned. Everywhere I go in Boston and on circuit I hear insinuations that I was the cause of our troubles. I tell you, Nabby, it eats my insides out."

"I can see that it would. John, I've heard that in Connecticut they have fabulous mineral springs. Why not try them? They could bring you a recruit of spirits."

He rode off excitedly to drink the mineral waters, leaving her to teach the children how to milk Bosse and to coach them from a new edition of the *New England Primer* in which she had learned her alphabet. Nab had long since memorized from A: *In Adam's Fall, We sinned all* to W: *Whales in the Sea, God's Voice obey;* but Abigail still refused to teach her young the dismal X and Y: *Xerxes did die, And so must I; While youth do chear, Death may be near.*

Noisy busy Boston receded from her thoughts. There had been times when she had been offended because women were described as mere domestic beings. Now she was content to take care of her children and dairy. She sat under her vine and apple tree in peace, enjoying the fruits of their labor. Though she was still smarting from what she described as "the unnatural treatment this poor America has received from England," she took pains to teach her children that England was their Mother Country. She told them that America was better calculated for happiness because the people were more equal, "there being none so immensely rich as to lord it over us, nor any so abjectly poor as to suffer." Yet she could be stern about England too:

"It is better never to have known the blessings of liberty than to have enjoyed liberty and have it taken from us."

Samuel Adams did not believe in a sabbatic. As soon as John got home from Connecticut he arrived with Betsy for a visit, portmanteau of linen in one hand, sheets of notes in the other. They had come, Betsy confided, for the purpose of having Samuel apologize for his Vindex articles.

"I've persuaded him," she said, "that Vindex sounded too much like Vindictivedex."

After supper in front of the kitchen hearth Samuel said:

"John, you were right to acquit the soldiers. I was also right to acquit Boston. Only an irresponsible handful precipitated the massacre."

"'Massacre' is a propaganda word."

"Even though the soldiers were provoked, when we lose five in dead from quartered troops that's a massacre. But," Samuel smiled, "Brother Adams, you know we never fired an arrow at you. All we did was wrap Boston in a soft cocoon. She may need it, one day soon. We're never going to be on opposite sides of an issue again. I promise, Abigail."

"O Heavens!" she cried.

They had been in Braintree a short time when a case arose which would have repatriated the Adams family in the big city. John was to argue against a Crown customs agent who had been caught extracting more money from the merchants of Massachusetts than the law designated. This time he was defending the colony. Again he won. The plaudits were instantaneous.

"People said it was the finest speech they had ever heard, equal to the greatest oration ever spoken in Rome or Greece. Nabby, what an advantage to have the passions, prejudices and interests of the whole audience in a man's favor. They will convert plain common sense into profound wisdom and wretched doggerel into sublime heroics."

The fall harvest was good, the barn was filled with hay and clover, her cellar with apple butter, pickled vegetables, oysters, nuts, barrels of salted fish. The winter's firewood was stored, the window cracks sealed against rain and wind.

Their family's harvest was fruitful too. The children were as brown as berries. Johnny had been taken hunting by his father and was learning how to shoot. Nab proudly rode her own mare over the countryside. There was a growing collection of cash in the Adams Specie Bank behind the loose bricks in the concealed chimney. John called it salt for their porridge. At night they sat before a wood fire, John studying Sir Thomas More's *Utopia* while she read Molière's plays in an edition sent to her by Mercy Warren from Plymouth.

In December she conceived. She was happy to be in circumstances. This would be a Braintree child. Perhaps a second daughter to round out their family.

The winter passed. Her parents and vivacious sister Betsy came frequently to visit. Mary and Richard drove up from Boston in their sled. Billy brought his wife to introduce her to the Smith clan.

Catharine Louisa Salmon was not a pretty girl; her teeth were uneven and her skin sallow. She was educated considerably beyond her husband, had a more incisive turn of mind. She was intensely religious, while Billy hated all churches. Despite these differences Billy appeared happy and outgiving for the first time that Abigail could remember. Catharine Louisa had been deeded as a wedding present by her mother and stepfather a farm and one of the oldest houses in Lincoln, at the fifteen-mile stone northwest from Boston, between Lexington and Concord. Billy was farming sixteen acres in barley and corn and thirty-five acres in grain and grass. He had borrowed a goodly sum from his father against the homestead and farm. With the money he had bought herds of cows, sheep, swine, not to mention chickens, ducks and rabbits, from the sale of which he was making a good cash living. Catharine Louisa was also in circumstances.

John left to ride circuit. She watched him go, knowing how much he dreaded the small-town courts, the feud cases, the primitive accommodations, the riding through all-day rains or snowstorms. His first letter came from Plymouth:

"I wish myself at Braintree. This wandering, itinerating life grows more and more disagreeable to me. I want to see my wife and children every day, I want to see my grass and blossoms and corn every day. I want to see my workmen, nay, I almost want to go and see the Bosse calves as often as Charles does. But above all, except the wife and children, I want to see my books."

She gave birth in September. The child was a boy. They named him Thomas Boylston. The disappointment at not having a second daughter was driven from her mind by the demands of the lusty infant who, his father declared, had been born with the notion that the world owed him food, shelter, warmth. Bald, blue-eyed, fat Thomas Boylston's vitality was infectious.

"My father hoped for a lot of grandsons," she exclaimed. "Maybe one of my three will become a clergyman and take over his congregation."

John became restive. He spent more and more time in Boston, sometimes handling sixty to seventy cases in one court session. The sheer volume of writs and briefs obliged him to sleep over at one relative's or another's: Uncle Isaac's or Cousin Samuel's or her sister Mary's. Sometimes he would work until midnight, sleep on his office couch until dawn.

She picked a quiet moment, when Tommy was a month old, to sit beside him at his flat worktable.

"John, what are you brooding about?"

He started, guiltily. Then he reached across the table to cover her hand.

"I haven't wanted to disturb you."

"Out with it, what have you done?"

"Bought a house."

"In Boston?"

"You don't mind, Nabby? We must go back. I can't carry on my work from here."

She was thoughtful. "We've had a year and a half of blessed peace. I've known that this stay was only a respite. How badly we needed it, and what great good it has done."

He murmured, "You're very nice to take it so calmly."

"I'll pack up my four little ones."

"As well as your pots and pans, beds and chairs. We're going to live among our own things this time. Then perhaps we may feel that Boston is home."

"If it must be."

She chuckled, two notes low in her throat.

"We'll have our farm to come home to when we need caterpillars in the trees, worms in the corn."

3

The house stood on the corner of Queen Street, where Cornhill poured in its cobbles to make a small square in front of the Town House. It was a gem of unpainted brick, severely tailored in its lines, smaller than either dwelling they had rented, and now they had four children to fill the rooms.

To Abigail this spelled coziness, particularly when John's flat table, desk and several hundred books were moved into a front room to make his office. Each of the six rooms was a fire room. Nab wanted Tommy in her room, which left the second bedroom for the two older boys to share. Patty and Susy, both excited at the chance to live in a big city, had dormer rooms on the third floor. There was a double-sized kitchen, with an added lean-to and walk-in hearth. In the back of the house was an orchard, a well and pump shaded by two green elms, two matching painted privies, outhouses for ice, wood and carriages.

The sitting parlor was larger than the one in Braintree. When she had placed her "bowfat," her yellow sofa, low-lying tables and hard-backed chairs about the room, precisely as they had been in Braintree, her mind was at ease.

As she was unpacking some of John's papers her eye was caught by a quote from a Major Martin, who had been in John's office earlier that day:

"Politics are the finest study and science in the world. . . . They are the grandest, the noblest, the most useful and important science in the whole circle."

She turned away, stood with her head down, breathing heavily.

Sunday morning they went holy walking with their two oldest: up Cornhill across Dock Square and into the familiar Brattle Street Church and the pew they had bought several years before. Their neighbors greeted them as though they had seen them on these wind-swept stone steps only the Sunday before. They were polite, friendly, with a puzzled veil before their eyes; something had happened between them and the Adamses but they could not remember exactly what. There was no round of dinners or receptions.

"Why should there be?" John demanded, half to himself. "We're not novices in this Bostonian religious order."

Early each morning John walked to his office across the street to work with his three young clerks. After noon dinner he remained in his library at home, using his reference library to document his procedures. He occasionally lost a difficult case; but as the Boston and circuit courts had come to concede, it was difficult to best Lawyer Adams on his accumulation of historic precedents or the writing of his briefs. He was admired, and hired; but there were moments when she realized that they were living on the periphery of Boston society.

"I've never been happier than I am at this moment," exclaimed John. "My resolution to devote myself to the pleasures, the studies, the business of private life is a source of ease and comfort to me."

Their closest friends were Samuel and Betsy Adams. Samuel's time was employed in the public service. Betsy was still turning pence into pounds; she had given the house on Purchase Street a new roof and newly glassed windows; the interior was freshly papered. At one of her dinner parties the John Adamses found a resplendent group: John Hancock, Elbridge Gerry, Josiah Quincy, Jr., William Phillips of the Patriots; Jonathan Sewall, and the young Hutchinsons, Elisha and Thomas, Jr., of the Crown adherents; Thomas Cushing, who stood halfway between the two.

Samuel knew of every conflict in Virginia and North Carolina, as well as the closer ones in Connecticut and Pennsylvania. He was almost singlehandedly maintaining the Committee of Correspondence which looked toward the creation of a colonial governing body which could represent all of America in the contests with Britain. To Governor Hutchinson this was an act of treason.

"But is it illegal?" John chuckled, riding home in their carriage. "How can the governor keep people from writing letters to each other, exchanging the news of the day?"

"John, how does Samuel earn what now appears to be a quite good living? As a member of the Massachusetts Assembly he receives no salary."

"None. It's volunteer work, same as selectman."

"Then?"

"I don't know, but I could venture a guess: he's probably on John Hancock's pay list, and those of other Patriot merchants. Samuel was their strongest voice in ridding them of the Townshend Acts. They're smuggling tea successfully. Even if they lose one chest in three their profits are enormous. They see Samuel as important in keeping them free."

Troubled, she asked, "John, are we equating freedom with profits?"

"It's one manifestation." Stubbornly. "Men must be free to run their shops and farms, to earn for their families as well as to vote, speak, write their laws."

"Agreed. It's just that I think we make a better figure talking about preserving our natural God-given or Social Contract rights than our balance ledgers."

John laughed heartily.

There were times when her husband seemed to be two men living under one panoply of skin. He spent the last day of the year writing an overdue letter to Mrs. Macaulay, the British historian, complaining that the prospect before them was gloomy; the system of a mean and a merciless administration was gaining ground upon the Patriots every day. That night, New Year's Eve, at the Cranches', he fell into an argument with an English gentleman over the attempts of the Crown to apprehend the Providence, Rhode Island, burners of the *Gaspee*, a Crown revenue cutter rumored to have been converted from John Hancock's *Liberty*.

"There is no more justice left in Britain than there is in hell!" he cried. "Sometimes I wish for war, that they might be brought to reason or ruin."

She was astounded at his speaking so violently. He himself was sick with self-reproach by the time they reached home.

"Nabby, I cannot but reflect on myself with severity for those rash, raw, awkward expressions. A man who has no better government of his own tongue, no more command of his temper, is unfit for anything but child's play and the company of boys!"

The following morning he was ebullient. Gone were his worries over the dead and dying Patriots; gone was his self-castigation over his own acrimony. He arose humming a tune, bussed his wife heartily, pronounced at the breakfast table:

"This year will be a pleasant, cheerful, happy and prosperous one for us."

Groggy over the transition, Abigail murmured:

"For a man with a troubled conscience you must have slept remarkably well."

"Troubled conscience? I?" He turned to his four children with raised arms, the palms of his hands turned outward, at the absurdity of the query. "My dear Miss Abigail, you are not only my wife but my mother-confessor. Your listening absolves me. I then sleep like a woolly white lamb. Did you know that absolution for your husband would be part of your job as a wife?"

"Frankly, I did not. If I had known I might have been frightened. But then, if every girl knew what older married women know . . ."

He was in a gay mood.

"Are you suggesting to your four wide-eyed children, sitting there with blackberry jam all over their pretty faces, that you're sorry you married me?"

"O Great Heaven, no! Does a sailor refuse to go to sea because there will be storms? I'm only thankful to the Lord that He waits to afford us knowledge until we're too deeply entrapped to use it as a tool to break out."

John's prescience of the coming year proved sound. Britain had internal problems. All attempts to raise money from her hotheaded colony through taxes on products shipped in were abandoned, except for the face-saving gesture of retaining the right to tax tea. Why tea instead of glass or paint no one knew. Perhaps because paint and glass could be manufactured in New England. The Americans were fanatical tea drinkers. It was food, medicine and solace to them; they would always have to import great quantities of it. Since tea chests were eminently smuggleable, and were now being purchased for the greater part in Holland and brought in by American ships, the colony was provided with its own face-saving device. The only controversy keeping the political pot brewing was the Resolves of the Committees of Correspondence circulating through the towns of Massachusetts under the heading, *A List of Infringements and Violations of Rights.*

At the end of the first week of January 1773, Governor Hutchinson met with the elected Assembly and protested the grievance letters. The American colonies, he claimed, had been settled as part of the British Dominions; they were subject to the supreme legislature of Britain. There could not be two supreme authorities.

"Everybody is behaving so politely," John confided to Abigail, "that I think there can be no reason why I should not go and hear the Council's reply."

Abigail looked dubious.

He reported back to her the scene in the Town House. The twenty-eight-man Council, elected by the Massachusetts Assembly, had offered a reasonable answer to the governor's charges, and assured Hutchinson that they had no such touchy idea as independence in mind. However the Council felt it its duty to "exculpate the people from being the cause of the discontent in the Province, and charge it to the acts of Parliament." They denied the supreme power of Britain, because where people were controlled by unlimited authority they must emphatically be slaves.

The winter weather was foul but the political climate remained clement. John was involved in only one conflict. It was concerned with the appointment and payment of judges. He wrote a series of letters to the *Boston Gazette* in which he argued that the common law of England forbade judges to have appointment for life; that if the colonists did not pay their salaries they would be totally subservient to the Crown. Abigail noted that her husband signed these letters with his own name. This was not controversial politics, this had to do with systems and traditions of law.

For his efforts he was elected by the Massachusetts Assembly to the Council. He did not want the appointment, but when Hutchinson negatived him, he went wild with rage. The only way she could quiet him was by insisting that the children needed a few days on the farm. He agreed for their sake, working out his fury by building a dry stone wall. Within a day or two he was exulting in the fine crop of grass he had secured from the spring rains and from his obviously excellent recipe for compost.

John and the Patriots were further embittered against Hutchinson when they learned of his letters to London urging the Ministry to send in sufficient military might to crush Boston. These letters had fallen into the hands of Benjamin Franklin, who dispatched copies to John Adams, Samuel Adams and Thomas Cushing to warn Massachusetts, but explicitly directing that they not be published.

They were published, of course. John swore that he had not given them to the printer. It might have been Cushing, but more likely it was Samuel, who recognized their inflammatory value. From the instant of publication in pamphlet form the issue was joined: either Governor Hutchinson would be driven out of Massachusetts or he would drive out the Patriots. John reassured his wife, blandly:

"In my opinion there is not enough spirit on either side to bring the question to a complete decision. We'll oscillate like a pendulum for years to come. It is our children who will see revolutions of which we can form no conception."

She shivered. "Cold comfort."

4

The trouble with face-saving, she perceived, was that nobody saved much face. Late that summer while John was engaged in the mysterious case of Ansell Nickerson, charged with the murder of three or four men on a vessel, whom Nickerson claimed were murdered by boarding pirates (John got him off, but confessed to Abigail that he did not know whether Nickerson was innocent or guilty), the British Ministry was engaged in proceedings with the East India Company, a British firm which had accumulated seventeen million pounds of tea in its warehouses. When the news of the passing of a new Tea Act reached Boston by packet, it aroused a storm among the Patriots.

"Why a Tea Act?" asked Abigail.

"It's simple," John explained. "Under British mercantilism all products raised anywhere in the Empire must first be shipped to England, where they are taxed. Take tea, for example. The chests are then transferred to another British bottom and reshipped to the colony, to be taxed a second time at the port of entry."

"In other words, our tea traveled twice the distance, took twice as long to reach us, and cost twice as much."

"Approximately. And was profitable to the British. That is, until Holland tea began to compete. The thousands of Englishmen who had invested their savings in the East India Company learned that their company had a deficit of £1,000,000; that their stock had fallen to half its value; that a bankruptcy of the East India Company could start a panic throughout Britain. The owners put pressure on the government to allow the East India Company to ship their tea directly to us from China and India. Even after our merchants paid the 3d. a pound customs duty, it would then cost less than the Holland-bought, smuggled tea. The British imagined we would want the cheap tea so badly we'd throw our political scruples into Boston Harbor."

"That would mean more tea for everybody, and no more smuggling!"

"It would also mean accepting the British right to tax us without our consent. No Patriot can buy this tea."

"You don't think we will?"

"Who is *we*? Benjamin Faneuil, Jr., Joshua Winslow, Elisha and Thomas Hutchinson, Jr., have been named consignees. They'll pay the tax happily, expecting a fortune in every shipload."

Abigail asked thoughtfully, "Don't the other *we* have to buy from them before they can purse those profits?"

"We can have either cheap tea or expensive freedom."

Fractious Boston was beaten to the punch by outraged Pennsylvania. John brought home a copy of the *Pennsylvania Gazette* of October twentieth, with its set of Resolutions: the duty imposed by Parliament upon tea landed in America was a tax on the Americans, levying contributions on them without their consent; the express purpose for which the tax was levied, for the support of government, administration of justice and defense of His Majesty's dominions, had a direct tendency to render assemblies useless; a steady opposition to this ministerial plan was absolutely necessary to preserve even the shadow of liberty.

The protest meetings and denunciations at Old South and Faneuil Hall echoed the outrage in 1765 when the Stamp Act officers were brought under the Tree of Liberty and forced to resign the commissions they had not yet received. But now, at the beginning of November 1773, the men who were to receive the shipments ignored the demands of the Patriots. When Boston pulled down the offices of Oliver and sacked the houses of Hutchinson and Hallowell, there had not been one soldier to protect the property. Now there sat in Boston Harbor several British men-of-war; two regiments of redcoats were quartered in Castle William.

John declared glumly, "At town meeting tomorrow we'll adopt the Philadelphia Resolutions and ask the appointed agents of the East India Company, for the sake of their own characters, as well as the peace and good order of this town . . ."

He was whistling in the wind.

"I know they won't resign. After eight years of unremitting work we're weaker than when we started."

Boston fumed. The tea importers refused to ignite. Faneuil, Winslow and the firm of Richard Clarke and Sons spread the word that tea would be on sale at a price so low as to dissolve all opposition in its aromatic flavor.

On November seventeenth it was announced that the first ships loaded with tea, the *Dartmouth*, the *Eleanor* and the *Beaver*, were due, that the arrival of the *Dartmouth* was scheduled for Sunday when the people would be at preaching.

Abigail and John emerged from the Old South on Sunday morning after hearing Dr. Cooper's sermon to find crowds pouring down the streets to the docks where they could see the *Dartmouth* swinging at anchor in a stiff northerly breeze. Captain Hall had anchored his ship at Griffin's Wharf, just a block from Samuel Adams's house.

"That is not going to improve Samuel's disposition," said Abigail as they joined the hundreds of Bostonians jamming Flounder Lane and the haulage area between Belcher's Lane and the wharf. "John, surely they won't attempt to unload on Sunday, the Lord's day?"

He turned about abruptly.

"Then let us go home before our duck gets his wings singed."

Nab and Johnny were as curious as they were hungry. Six-year-old Johnny, who had a keen interest in happenings, asked:

"Papa, what do we want them to do with all that tea?"

Abigail, spoon-feeding Charley with walnut and bread-crumb stuffing, turned to the master of the house.

"The best question yet. Answer all us five youngsters, Papa."

John puffed with pride.

"There's no role I enjoy more than being the omnipotent savant at my own dinner table. We want the tea to turn around on the next tide and float itself back to England."

"Good thing tea leaves don't get seasick," observed Abigail.

The children giggled. John was serious.

"We'll have a decision soon, because if a cargo is not unloaded in twenty days after arrival it can be confiscated by Customs. When the other ships arrive we'll see one of three courses of action: they'll put back to sea, and that will be the end of the Tea Act; they'll forfeit their cargoes and that will be the end of the Tea Act; or . . ."

"Or?" asked Abigail. When he did not continue, she proffered, "Or they'll attempt to land the tea."

John's eyes were vague.

"They wouldn't be so sinfully foolish."

Samuel Adams came to report the results of the meetings of the selectmen and the Committee of Correspondence. A mammoth meeting was to be held the next day at Faneuil Hall. John Hancock announced that although he was colonel of the Corps of Cadets he would categorically refuse to use his young Bostonians to protect anyone rash enough to unload tea. Josiah Quincy, Jr., arrived to tell them that the other two ships were due on Friday, and that the owner of the *Dartmouth* had agreed to turn his ship around and send it back to London with its cargo intact.

John asked Abigail to break out a cask of Madeira. A few moments later Dr. Joseph Warren was obliged to water their wine by adding that Governor Hutchinson had announced he would not issue clearance papers for any of the three ships to leave the harbor until after the tea had been unloaded and delivered to its consignees.

Abigail did not attempt to suppress a wry laugh.

"We've spent years perfecting the art of smuggling tea *in*. Now we have to find a way to smuggle it *out*."

They were awakened shortly after dawn on Monday morning by a message from Samuel reminding them to come to the meeting at Faneuil Hall.

"If not for this Tea Act I think Samuel and the Sons of Liberty would have perished from desuetude," said Abigail.

All normal business was suspended. Abigail dressed in her green wool and green shoes. Although the day was full of foreboding there was a festive quality in the air, with the ringing of the bells, the sound of excited voices as the people passed before their windows. As they reached the street they saw a poster pasted to the wall of the Town House. Abigail read aloud:

"*Friends, Brethren, Countrymen! That worst of plagues, the detested* TEA, *shipped for this port by the East India Company, is now arrived in this harbor. The hour of destruction, or manly opposition to the machinations of Tyranny, stares you in the face. Every friend to his country, to himself and posterity, is now called upon to meet at Faneuil Hall at nine o'clock this day (at which time the bells will ring), to make a united and successful resistance to this last, worst, and most destructive measure of administration.*"

She murmured, "Sounds like the mellifluous prose of our cousin Sam'l."

"This is what is known as Patriot prose. I can name you a dozen men in Boston, myself included, who could have composed it."

By ten o'clock Faneuil Hall was jammed. There were faces from Weymouth, Braintree, Hingham, Milton. She did not know how many the hall held, but she felt there must be two or three thousand people crammed into it.

Abigail listened intently as Samuel's motion that the tea be sent back was unanimously adopted. But the crowd had grown so dense that the meeting was adjourned until three that afternoon at Old South.

That night a volunteer watch of twenty-five armed men stood guard over the ship to make sure no tea was smuggled in. The next morning Abigail returned to Old South for the most impassioned meeting yet, set on fire by the arrival of the Suffolk County sheriff with a proclamation from the governor:

"All inhabitants at this meeting are violating the good and wholesome laws of the province. We warn, exhort and require them, being unlawfully assembled, forthwith to disperse."

Hisses filled the big church like steam. Owner Francis Rotch and Captain James Hall of the *Dartmouth* agreed that the tea would be returned without touching land. The applause was so thunderous that the factors for the *Eleanor* and the *Beaver* had little choice but to rise and pledge their word. Samuel Adams was appointed head of a committee to write to the Massachusetts seaport towns, as well as to Philadelphia and New York, to report this success.

One of the problems of success is its inherently transitory nature. The *Eleanor* and the *Beaver* arrived with their cargoes. Their owners kept their word not to land the tea or pay duty, but Governor Hutchinson refused them permission to sail and, to prove that he was not standing bluff, ordered the Castle William cannon loaded and manned. Admiral Montagu placed two gunboats athwart the harbor, close in to the three tea brigs.

The shipowners had been put straight on. If they did not unload within the specified twenty days they would lose their cargoes. If they tried to run before the wind the British gunboats would blow them out of the water.

"Something will be resolved soon," said John.

"Do you already know what the resolution is to be?" she asked teasingly.

"We smoke more rumors here than we do cod. I must leave for Plymouth court tomorrow."

The town kept itself in order through armed patrols in the streets; but the fever was mounting. There were meetings every day. Companies of armed redcoats from Castle William were making forays into the neighboring towns.

On the last day before the *Dartmouth's* tea would be confiscated, about £5,000 worth, two thousand people gathered in the Old South. Abigail was sitting in a rear pew. Seven thousand people engulfed the church, surrounding it on all sides. Owner Rotch of the *Dartmouth* was ordered to ride out to Governor Hutchinson's home in Milton and demand written permission to sail that night. He was to return immediately and report.

Abigail grew cold and tired, despite the fiery speeches being made from the lectern. She would have liked to walk the one block up Cornhill to her home for a dish of tea. But it would have been impossible to push her way out of the church.

It was an hour past dark before Rotch returned. A signal was sounded, aisles cleared for him to reach the altar. The church was lighted by flickering candles. There was strain on every face.

"Nothing!" cried the owner. "The governor will not grant me a pass. The tea will be landed and confiscated at dawn unless we pay the duty tonight!"

Samuel Adams rose, his arms extended in the candle shadows for silence. He said in a tightly controlled voice that yet filled the big church:

"This meeting can do nothing more to save the country."

An Indian war whoop sounded from the floor of the church. It was answered from the galleries, then from the outside stoop. Abigail was literally picked up and swept into the bitter cold of the street. There before her unbelieving eyes she saw some fifty men, their faces stained with paint, covered by Indian blankets, hair coiled and collected Indian style, brandishing hatchets.

More whooping Indians poured into the street in front of the church. She was unable to accept the insane idea that a painted, armed Indian tribe had invaded Boston.

Then she gazed intently at one of the chiefs who was forming his braves into files, two abreast, holding up his arms for silence. There was something about the broad mouth in the flat face, the sturdy figure and muscular gestures that reminded her of . . .

"Not really," she whispered to Betsy, "Paul Revere?"

"Come along. Only we must be quiet."

There was now a swelling body of Indians, two hundred at least. Betsy's arm through hers, she moved silently along, pushed forward by the crowd behind her: through Milk Street, a right-angle turn into Pearl, then down Pearl to Griffin's Wharf where the tea ships were moored.

She stood on the cobblestones at the head of Griffin's Wharf while the Indians were ferried in small boats to the *Dartmouth*. One could hear only the muffled sound of oars in the dark night. Through the blackness she could see the Indians climb up rope ladders on either side of the ship. They disappeared from view; then there came the sound of heavy burdens thudding onto the wooden decks, the concentrated sound of hatchets breaking up the chests, the light splash of the tea as it hit the water.

It took perhaps an hour to scuttle Captain Hall's cargo. After the tea the chests too were thrown into the harbor. No one came or went among the crowd huddled in itself in the icy air. Then, as on a signal, the Indians transferred to the *Eleanor* and began the process anew.

Questions pounded through her head. Who had organized this expedition? Who had decided it should be an Indian raid? How could they have been so thoroughly trained and disciplined?

Then her mind turned as cold as her frozen toes in their paper soles. Where were the British soldiers who had been moving through the city for days, bayonets attached to their guns? Was it possible they did not know this attack was taking place, that for two hours now, with the Indians having dumped the *Eleanor's* tea, already boarding the *Beaver*, with as many as seven thousand people assembled in the largest crowd in Boston history, and only a few armed Patriots posted at the end of the wharf, not one guard or soldier had turned in an alarm? Who had silenced them?

For that matter, where were the crews of the three ships, that not one had appeared or made the slightest protest? Ashore? Asleep? Drunk? Dead?

Where was the British navy? It was true that the fort of Castle William was three miles offshore, but this was a piercingly clear winter night in which sounds would carry over water. How far? Certainly as far as the two men-o'-war posted close by to keep the *Dartmouth* from smuggling itself out of the harbor!

Could it be that His Majesty's army and navy were unwilling or unable to counterattack? It was no less credible than the fact that thousands of pounds of tea were awash in the harbor and nearly three hundred and fifty battered chests bobbed about on the waves while the Indians were ferried ashore, made silent but triumphant flourishes of their hatchets and disappeared.

Betsy commandeered her across to Purchase Street and the Adams house. She lit a fire in Samuel's office, put water on to boil, then took off Abigail's shoes and warmed the numb toes in her limber fingers. Samuel came in while they were sipping mugs of chocolate so hot it burned the fuzz off their tongues. He seated himself by Abigail's side, put an arm about her shoulder.

"Sister Abigail, I'm happy you were there. What you saw and heard tonight you will remember all your life."

"That I will, Samuel, that I will."

"May I tell you a few things I'm particularly proud about? There was a great deal of valuable merchandise on those ships, easily available. Nothing was touched. The ships were not damaged, neither below nor on deck. One padlock was broken; we have already replaced it. No one was injured. It was a peaceable demonstration by a peaceable people."

"What about the tea, Samuel?"

"The East India Company has millions of pounds to spare. The customs duties will not be paid because the tea was not landed. The ships can now be loaded with paying cargo and put to sea. The battle is over. We have won."

5

First light seemed to darken the room further. The house was piercingly cold. She rose, wrapped a blanket around her, went from room to room dropping logs on the embers, securing blankets about the shoulders of her sleeping children. In John's office she sat at his desk to write a reassuring note to her parents. The ink had frozen in the inkwell.

John arrived at midmorning, blue with cold but his eyes radiant. She took him directly to the kitchen hearth. He reported that a few men who had tried to take some of the tea that was lapping the shore had been roughly handled; that a British man-of-war had already sailed for England with the news of the night's happenings.

"I tell you, Abigail, this is the most magnificent movement of all. There is a dignity, a majesty, a sublimity in this last effort of the Patriots that I greatly admire. The people should never rise without doing something to be remembered, something notable and striking. The destruction of the tea is so daring, so bold, so firm, and must have such important consequences that I can't but consider it an epoch in history."

"There's a question that kept me awake half the night. Where were the troops and ships? They could have stopped this tea party instanter."

He looked away. "Why ask me? Ask Colonel Dalrymple or Admiral Montagu. They're both fine officers, and one more angry than the other this morning. Admiral Montagu has written to the lords of the Admiralty that he could easily have prevented the execution of the plan but was never called on for assistance."

"Could it be that Colonel Dalrymple and Admiral Montagu were powerless to interfere without instructions from Governor Hutchinson, and he on his hilltop in Milton, too far away to give the necessary orders?"

John grinned crookedly.

"Perhaps he was willing to spill tea but not blood."

A figure loomed in the kitchen doorway, encased in a black cape and an equally black scowl. It was Jonathan Sewall, hovering over them like a tempest, his face drawn. Abigail thought, "Nobody slept in Boston last night."

"Jonathan, come in," she said gently. "Will you have a cup of this miserable-tasting coffee? I doubt if New England will ever get used to it."

Jonathan glared at John, said with a lashing voice:

"Apparently you would just as soon spill blood as tea."

"I didn't say that, Jonathan."

"Last night's excursion was an attack upon property. Another similar exertion could produce the destruction of lives. You don't deny that many of your self-named Patriots are bloodthirsty?"

There was nothing left of the humor of Jonathan Sewall, the prankster, the man who proclaimed, "I laugh first; out of that laughter comes the wit to be funny"; the man who exalted the laconic barb, the extraction of the absurd from the skein of events.

"I won't deny it, Jonathan. Many persons wish that there were as many carcasses floating in the harbor as chests of tea."

"But whose corpse, John Adams?" cried Sewall. "Yours?"

There was a painful silence during which John had the grace to blush. Then he answered:

"If necessary. I have drilled and stood guard with our militia. But, Jonathan, the question you're really propounding is: was the destruction of this tea necessary? It was absolutely and indispensably necessary. They could not send it back, the governor, admiral, collector and comptroller would not suffer it. It could not get by the Castle or the men-of-war. To let it be landed would be yielding to the principle of taxation by Parliamentary authority; losing all our labor for ten years, subjecting ourselves and our posterity forever to Egyptian taskmasters: to burthens, indignities, to ignominy, reproach and contempt."

Sewall's voice was grim. "Brother John, Sister Abigail, I have loved you as I have loved few friends. Let me plead your cause as I have never pled before: Britain is determined on her system. Her power is irresistible. Every foot of Boston will be occupied by troops, and the harbor by ships of war. Soon! Very soon! John, she will destroy you, as she will destroy everyone who remains in opposition to her measures."

John looked to Abigail for permission to continue. It was not a request lightly made, she knew; for they were at the Rubicon. Then he put a hand on Jonathan's shoulder.

"My dearest friend. I know that Britain is determined on her system. That very determination determined me on mine. For us the die is cast. Swim or sink, live or die, survive or perish with our country. That's our unalterable determination. I see that sooner or later we must part. You may depend on it, this adieu of our two families united by blood as well as affection is the sharpest thorn on which I ever set my foot."

They embraced. They parted. It was the first division inside their circle of family and friends. She was filled with a sorrow akin to the death of Susanna. This loss of a childhood cousin and a close friend was like dying a little. How many different kinds of dying one could do while still remaining alive.

Heroics have their aftermath. Boston felt let down. Abigail took cold. She made up for her inactivity by writing letters approving the attack on "tea, that baneful weed . . . this weed of slavery"; but sent back to Mercy Warren her copy of Molière, exclaiming, "Molière is said to have been an honest man . . . yet all pictures of life are not fit to be exhibited upon the stage." In her New England heritage property values were as sacred as moral values; she was uneasy because in some undefined way she was contradicting herself.

She drove out with Cotton Tufts to Weymouth to spend a few days between Christmas and New Year's with her parents. She had no sooner entered the parsonage than there was such a tremendous fall of snow that the world became a single white plain, the roads impassable. It was the first time she had been away from her husband and four children; she felt dislocated, as though cut adrift from the past ten years, and reverted to childhood. Homesick, she wrote to John:

"I never left so large a flock of little ones before."

A woman with four children and a husband she loves is staked to the earth. She was even glad when word reached her about a small domestic crisis at home: she had inadvertently taken with her the key to John's linen drawer. She sent it into Boston by one of her father's hands, expressing the hope that John had thought to remove the drawer above the locked one, so that he could get at his clean shirts.

She returned to Boston hilarious at being back with her brood. Lying in the warm security of his arms, she told John about the new boarder at the parsonage, young John Shaw, who was teaching school in Weymouth and sleeping in Billy's old room. Her sister Betsy seemed to like Shaw; at least they were arguing literature and politics with considerable heat, a good beginning for a romance in a clergyman's household. He told her of how he had taken the four youngsters sleighing out at the Neck, and they had covered the sailboat until spring came around. Mostly his news was about Boston itself.

"The Patriots and the Sons are still celebrating what they claim is a smashing victory. Hutchinson and the Crown group think we're going to be bombarded to the ground. The middle group, men like our merchant friend John Rowe, say we'll have to pay for the tea and provide a formal apology."

"What do you think?"

"That we have been caught in a conspiracy since the day we were married: on the part of Bernard, Hutchinson, the Olivers. Bernard was recalled; Hutchinson will be summoned to London in disgrace for not protecting the tea; Lieutenant Governor Andrew Oliver is mortally ill. I am drawing up impeachment papers against Chief Justice Peter Oliver to rid ourselves of him."

She was silent for a moment.

"What about London? We won't know what they're doing until it's done. Then what is our recourse?"

"What it has always been: to fight with every weapon at hand."

He stroked her hair as he frequently did in troubled moments.

"England has the experience to resolve these problems amicably. We are English to the core: in our speaking, thinking, feeling; an indispensable part of her family. It would require the most astounding combination of talents, genius, in fact, to conjure up the array of repressive actions that could drive us out of the Empire."

"Apparently she has that genius."

"If only Parliament would allow us to elect and send representatives from each of the colonies, to debate the laws they pass against us."

The Patriots were taking considerable abuse for dumping the tea. Benjamin Franklin, who had been living in London for years as a colonial agent representing Massachusetts, Pennsylvania, New Jersey and

Georgia to the Crown and private business as well, wrote that he deplored carrying matters to such an extremity as, in a dispute about public rights, to destroy private property. One Parliament member was quoted as crying, "The offense of the Americans is flagitious. You will never meet with proper obedience to the laws of this country until you have destroyed that nest of locusts." King George III observed, "We must master them or totally leave them to themselves and treat them as aliens." The American Tory papers said that Boston should be treated as Carthage had been.

At the end of February John bought his brother Peter's farm for £440. Abigail asked if they could afford it.

"No, we cannot afford it," replied John doggedly. "I bought a house in Boston, a pew in the church, a boat. I've spent an estate in books, in improving our ten acres."

"Then I fail to follow your reasoning."

"We can less afford to let it go. Someone else may buy. I've wanted it ever since we were married. With that extra thirty-five acres we can make a living off the soil. The earth does not fail to produce at every crisis the way the law does."

Boston stood bluff. There was little else to do. Everywhere they went people hotly discussed tea while drinking coffee. Business fell off sharply. John had so few cases he went to Ipswich but stayed away from the Plymouth court. There was even less government, for the governor had prorogued, or dismissed, the meeting of the Massachusetts Assembly before it could gather.

6

At the beginning of May the *Harmony* arrived with news of the Boston Port Act. Abigail had gone to Weymouth to be with her ailing mother and to patch up a quarrel with Betsy, who had been the victim of some gossip about her conduct with John Shaw, the boarder at the Smith parsonage. Abigail had written Betsy a strongly worded letter of caution about protecting her good name; and had invited her to Boston for a long stay. Betsy's reply flailed Abigail.

"You cannot think how much I was astonished to be told that I had excited fears in some of the family. . . ."

This was the first quarrel Abigail had had with her sister. She knew the relationship had to be repaired at once. Her letter had been prudish and moralistic, and when she remembered her magnificent hours alone with John before the fire in the sitting room where they had exchanged what John had called their "million kisses," she was ashamed of herself.

She read her copy of the Boston Port Act with her father in his library. The Act was so appalling that the Reverend Mr. Smith cried:

"It's like reading the details of your own death sentence!"

There was no other way to describe the calamity that had befallen them. The port of Boston was to be closed. No ship, except a British man-of-war, might leave or enter. General Gage, in charge of British troops in New York, was to be military governor of Massachusetts. Several regiments of troops were to be moved in. Governor Thomas Hutchinson was summoned to London.

Boston was stunned by Britain's reprisal.

Abigail returned to the city to absorb the hailstorm of bad news that reached them in the following weeks. Boston would live under martial law. British troops were to be quartered on the inhabitants. Town meetings were abolished throughout Massachusetts. Selectmen could not call their constituents together without leave of the governor. The King alone could appoint the Council, the Superior and Inferior Court judges. The local sheriffs were to be chosen by the military governor. In effect, Parliament had rescinded the Massachusetts Bay Colony Charters of 1628 and 1691 under which the colony had governed itself from the moment its first ship left England.

Marblehead, fifteen miles north, was to be the new port of entry. Boston was to be crushed: if no goods or food could be brought in by ship, everything would have to be carted across the narrow Neck by land, a Neck easily blockaded by British troops. Boston would slowly starve to death, its people, its business, its culture. It would be abandoned.

"If that is what the British intend," commented Abigail, "we'll have to board up our house."

"No, Abigail. Everyone must stay. Don't imagine from all this that I am in the dumps. Far otherwise. I can truly say that I have felt more spirits and activity since the arrival of this news than I had done before for years. I look upon this as the last effort of Lord North's despair."

"But what about Boston?"

"The town of Boston must suffer martyrdom. It must expire. Our principal consolation is that it does so in a noble cause. It will probably have a glorious reformation, to greater wealth, splendor and power than ever."

Cotton Tufts visited them for a few days while he bought up all the medications he could find before the English source dried up. On the second morning they heard a tremendous cannonading from Castle William and the warships in the harbor.

"That's for General Gage, landing at Long Wharf to take over his duties," said Cotton, his eyes behind his spectacles owl-like in their somberness.

They went into the street. Colonel John Hancock in his resplendent buff and purple uniform was leading his handsomely accoutered cadets as an honor guard for General Gage, who was followed by companies of even more handsomely outfitted redcoats, en route to what had been the Town House but now, through Samuel Adams's efforts in the Assembly, was renamed the State House. Colonel Hancock, Boston's socially acceptable Son of Liberty, went into the Council Chamber to be part of the welcoming committee.

John led her back to the warm fire in his office. Scattered over his flat desk were papers relating to a New Hampshire–Massachusetts land dispute, and the impeachment of Chief Justice Oliver. Her experienced eye saw that there were no new writs, contracts, briefs. He followed her glance.

"There is no prospect of any business in my way this whole summer. I don't receive a shilling a week."

"Then we should be home to work our farm."

"We'll send word to Brackett to bring in the wagon."

They reached Braintree in glorious June sunshine. The children were out from early morning. John worked in his cornfields, preparing for several freights of marsh mud to be brought in to fertilize his hay and the grasses of his meadow. Then he decided to leave for Ipswich, York and Falmouth for the opening of the courts.

"Whatever there may be, I must try to get my fair share."

He drifted about the courts of northern Massachusetts, barely getting enough work to pay for his bed and meals, or for oating his horse. The only release for his loneliness was long letters to her, sometimes written twice a day:

"My refreshment is a flight to Braintree to my cornfields and grass plots, my gardens and meadows. My fancy . . . is continually with you, and in the neighborhood of you; frequently takes a walk with you, and your little prattling Nabby, Johnny, Charley and Tommy. We walk all together up Penn's Hill, over the bridge to the plain, down to the garden."

She taught Nab and Johnny to churn butter and make cheese. Charley's domain was the feeding of the chickens and ducks.

She led a second life: after dark, when the house was quiet about her, she went into John's office to read the newspapers from the other colonies. England had closed the port of Boston on June 1, 1774, as the law had stipulated: hardly a rowboat could have wiggled its way through the formidable line of ships of war, the *Tartar*, the *Magdalen*, the *Lively*, the *Tamar*.

Never in their lifetime had she or her neighbors lived such an illegal existence. Town meetings had been prohibited by the Regulatory Acts, to take effect August first, but Braintree had already changed the name of its governing body to the county meeting, and begun holding sessions. The Boston town meeting had been abolished, but on his way to Maine, John presided at a meeting where the Boston representatives voted not to pay for the jettisoned tea. In Charlestown reports described how jurors refused to take the oath from the Crown-appointed judges, and so the courts were adjourned. Townspeople obeyed their old sheriffs, ignoring the Crown appointees. Massachusetts could not cause the warships in Boston Harbor to vanish, but beyond that almost every stricture of the Regulatory Acts was negatived by the citizens.

A strange oversight had failed to outlaw the colony's elected Assembly, the body to which John Adams had been named to serve on its high-placed General Council or Cabinet, and from which Governor Hutchinson had negatived him. The Assembly had met in Boston and been told that it must move to Salem as prescribed by the Acts. Meeting in Salem, the Assembly promptly called for a Congress of all thirteen colonies.

General Gage cried:

"Illegal! Assembly dissolved!"

It was too late. The Massachusetts Assembly claimed that its call for a meeting of committees was legal.

The Congress was patently based on the earlier Stamp Act Congress which had been called by Samuel's Committees of Correspondence, and would again meet in Philadelphia. The first Congress had been attended by nine colonies. How many of the colonies would send representatives this time? Here at home every town and hamlet pledged support and physical help for stricken Boston. How many of the other twelve colonies would consider Massachusetts' plight their own?

A letter arrived from Ipswich with a mysterious but enthralling line added almost as a postscript:

"I want to be at home, at this time, to consider about dress, servant, carriage, horses, etc., for a journey."

She sat with John's letter in her hand, her heart pounding audibly in her ears. What kind of journey? Where could he be making a journey that would require dress, servant, carriage?

It had to be Philadelphia! The Congress!

She sat leaning precariously forward on the parlor sofa. First came pride: John Adams had earned his right to represent Massachusetts. Then came fear: since General Gage had prorogued the Massachusetts Assembly could its representatives be considered seditious? If so, John Adams would be in a critical position: trial by jury for such cases had been abolished, all American-appointed judges removed. He could be sent to Halifax for trial under a British Admiralty Court, or to England, taken out to the *Canceaux* or the *Lively* and under sail before she even knew that he had been seized.

As pride had subsided, so did fear. Now she began to think about the more practical implications. The journey to Philadelphia took at least two weeks. How long would such a Congress have to sit? Another two weeks, two months, who could tell? She dreaded a long separation. Yet she knew that she would overcome that dread before John came home.

As she moved about the countryside, alternating the children for company in the carriage, she found the zeal pot boiling over. The news was heartening.

Virginia, which had not participated in the Stamp Act Congress, had this time stepped forth even before hearing from Boston. The moment the House of Burgesses learned of the Port Bill, Thomas Jefferson proposed, and the House adopted, a strong resolution declaring June first "a day of fasting, humiliation, and prayer"; asking for divine intervention to avert the heavy calamity, "to give us one heart and one mind firmly to oppose, by all just and proper means, every injury to American rights." When the Crown governor of Virginia dissolved the House of Burgesses, the members met a few days later, called themselves an Association and wrote a denunciation of the Boston Port Act as "a most dangerous attempt to destroy the constitutional liberty and rights of all North America," stated that an attack upon one colony was an attack upon all.

As newspapers reached the countryside from Providence and New York she found that they too were calling for united action in the emergency. One grim determination ran through all the articles: an insistence that the Boston Port Act and the Regulatory Acts be repealed.

John came home from his circuit riding with no more shillings or pounds in his pocket than he had departed with.

The Massachusetts Assembly had voted each of its five representatives, Thomas Cushing, James Bowdoin, Samuel and John Adams, Robert Treat Paine, £100 for expenses to cover the costs of horses, carriage and servants to Philadelphia, as well as their bed and board. No one would receive a salary.

"Who pays for those outfits you're having tailored for Philadelphia?" Abigail asked.

"We do." He blushed. "Massachusetts can't cut a lesser figure than those *élégants* from New York and Virginia."

"I should think not! Fortunately the spring gave us fine falls of rain. Our harvest of corn and hay should be good. I'll sell them in Boston."

In a rare departure, he was unconcerned about their domestic economy while worrying about the political economy . . . and his own limitations. Mercy Warren wrote that she was proud for Abigail that John had been appointed. Her husband James, as a member of the Assembly, had insisted upon it. Warren wrote from Plymouth characterizing the coming Congress as an assembly of "as great dignity and importance as any, either ancient or modern, that ever met. . . . I presume the greater part of you will be masters, learned in politics . . . prophets replete with the true spirit of prophecy, and statesmen both wise and upright."

The Congress was set for September 1774. In the meantime Boston suffered as the city's normal supplies were cut off. John was appointed to a committee to collect donations for the relief of the Bostonians. As the fruits and vegetables came ripe, Abigail filled a wagonload, supplementing it with eggs and cheeses. The British were still allowing food to cross the Neck. John and one of his hired hands drove the wagon to town and turned over the food to the committee. They also stopped at the Cranches' and Samuel's to leave supplies.

The John Adamses were suffering a more subtle distress. In early July, while writing home from the circuit, John told Abigail of the scenes of violence he was encountering. At Falmouth a mob broke into a Tory's house, rifled his papers, terrified his wife, children and servants. In other towns Crown sympathizers were being tarred and feathered. People who disagreed with the Patriots, or claimed that Boston had earned the shutting of its port by the ruffianism of its Tea Party, had their property destroyed by infuriated crowds.

When he returned home he cried:

"I burn with resentment and indignation at such outrageous injustices. We can't get rid of bad laws by terrorizing wives and children. Jonathan Sewall reproached me at Falmouth with the Latin phrase which translates as 'who does through another, does himself.' He implied that I was as guilty as any of the people actually participating in the attacks. Above all he was thoroughly angry because I accepted the role of delegate to the Congress. He claims that by my attendance in Philadelphia I will be a renegade, setting my foot on a path from which there can be no turning back."

He got up, walked about.

"I set my foot on that path a long time ago, probably when I heard James Otis give that sheet of fire speech in 1761 against the Writs; but surely by 1765 and the Stamp Act—I lay awake all that night."

"Worrying?"

"Wondering. About an idea I've had. To write a history of the contest between Britain and America. Beginning, say, at the accession of King George III to the throne; or perhaps the approval in Massachusetts of Governor Bernard."

She smiled to herself.

"Worrying?" he teased.

"Wondering. Whether you would rather make history or write it."

As his departure for the Congress approached they crossed their verdant fields, climbed Penn's Hill. The sunset flamed rose and indigo to the west; straight ahead they saw the sailboats and green islands bobbing in the bay.

"Nabby, I must say I feel my own insufficiency for this important business. I confess myself ignorant of the characters which compose the court of Great Britain as well as of the people who compose the nation. As comprehensive a knowledge of arts and sciences, especially of law and history, of geography, commerce, war and of life is necessary for an American statesman at this time as was ever necessary for a British or Roman general."

"You're as well trained as anyone in our colony."

"Perhaps. But our New England educations are quite unequal to the production of such great characters."

If he lacked sufficient education to consider himself a young Demosthenes or Pitt, he assuredly did not lack for advice. "The best is from my old friend Joseph Hawley, of the General Court," he told her. "He warns me to be patient, moderate, and to have courage. Most important, he believes, is that since this is the first continental conclave in ten years, everything tending to create disgust or strangeness, coldness or indifference, must be carefully avoided."

"He is a wise man," she observed.

"He warns us Massachusetts men against arrogance and superiority. We are not to offend delegates of other racial stocks or religions. He fears that in the other colonies there is the feeling that the patriots of Massachusetts try to dictate; that we assume haughty airs, from inward vanity and self-conceit."

"Do you, John?"

The sun had set. Dark was falling. He put an arm about her shoulder. They wound their way down the familiar path.

"It's been said that our character is as good as our disposition is bad. I have no conceit about myself. As a breed, we are insular; we believe our religion is the only one, that our New England culture is greater than the rest, that we are the only truly moral people in the world."

"You mustn't even *think* such things in Philadelphia."

"No. We can either achieve freedom by living with our fellow colonists, different as they may be; or live subservient to Englishmen, similar as they may be."

They came past the parental house, saw his mother and Mr. Hall supping in the kitchen. Just outside the door to their own lean-to she suddenly threw herself into his arms.

"John! Three to four months without you! All the children to care for, the two farms, our debts. You must accomplish good things to make up for it all."

He kissed her, almost penitently.

"I'll try, dear soul. I'll do everything Joseph Hawley says I must. I'll think of you and the little ones, and I'll be the humblest man on God's green earth."

7

On Tuesday afternoon, August 9, 1774, she went to Boston for the ceremonial departure. As they drove along the dock she got her first sight of an occupied city. The tight ring of warships froze her blood.

The flagship lay between Long Wharf and Hancock's Wharf; the *Tamar* was at the mouth of Broad Sound, the *Lively* stood at anchor off Governor's Island, the *Canceaux* was between the Charlestown and Winnisemmet ferries, with the *Halifax* across the Charles River.

Uncle Isaac said grimly:

"Permit me to take you on a tour of Britain."

In their winding walk through the city they saw the Royal Welsh Fusiliers encamped on Fort Hill. The 4th and 5th Regiments, mostly Londoners, had pitched their tents on the Common. The 38th and 43rd Regiments of redcoats, their ranks apparently made up of north Englanders, bivouacked in the plain by the workhouse. A stop at the Boston Neck revealed an advance party of the 59th, en route from their debarkation at Salem, preparing to dig fortifications so that Boston could be isolated. The walk back in the fading sunlight to the Smith house on Beacon Street was silent and glum.

Company fell in after supper. Their friends too were subdued. The group about the cleared supper table, cracking nuts and sipping Madeira, seemed hesitant to put their thoughts into words. Was the Congress seeking independency? Were they trying to throw off only part, or all, of the rule of King George III and the Parliament? Did they intend to form a permanent American government made up of the thirteen colonies? John said quietly:

"We are meeting in Philadelphia to find answers."

But if her husband was tentative, there was one man at the table who seemed clearly unsympathetic. It was her young cousin Isaac Smith, Jr., now twenty-five, about to graduate into the ministry; a well-read, well-spoken young man of impeccable manners who had made the most of his education and his journey to England. He was of medium height and build, with steady green eyes and blond hair which kept falling over his brow. He sat with one eyebrow cocked quizzically, as though listening to a discussion between strangers. Covertly watching him, Abigail found this disturbing. Her uncle Isaac and aunt Elizabeth were ardent Patriots who had given liberally of their time and money to every movement espoused by the Sons of Liberty.

Josiah Quincy, Jr., came in late. He had been ill the year before and Dr. Cotton Tufts, fearing it to be the deadly Quincy tuberculosis, had sent him by ship to Charleston, South Carolina. Josiah had recuperated in the warm sunshine, and then enjoyed a leisurely trip overland on horseback. Now he looked tanned, his eyes wonderfully alive. Josiah went up to the bedroom, with the alcove of books and the desk at which Abigail had studied during her yearly visits. John closed the door.

"Josiah, are you ready to sail?"

"In about a month."

"Good. It is a delicate mission. Try to persuade the ministers and members of Parliament that we're not irrational men, or congenital hotheads, as Bernard and Hutchinson have portrayed us. Persuade them that we want to rejoin the family board and that our purpose at the Philadelphia Congress is not to pick a fight but to pick a peace that can last."

"I'll do my best, John."

John turned to his wife.

"You, Abigail, and Josiah's wife, are the only ones aside from the committee who know why he's going to England. If the British learn in advance that he represents the Congress, they'll arrest him or ship him back on the outgoing tide."

He turned back to Josiah. "Your best will be good enough for us. You carry a great name; you defended the King's captain and soldiers; you're an able attorney. You have charm, money, and you're a gentleman. That combination should prove irresistible to the British."

They slept poorly. The night was hot and airless. The separation ahead lay heavy on their minds. They said their farewells at dawn. It was a commingling of joy and sadness.

There was nothing sad about Boston, glittering in the clear bright morning air. It was a day of celebration. The city had donned its preaching clothes and assembled in the square behind the State House to give their delegates a rousing send-off. Abigail mused that the ceremonies were taking place where the soldiers' killings had occurred four years before. Boston had repudiated John; but today he was leaving for Philadelphia to represent all of Massachusetts in a General Congress. Where would the next spin of fate land them?

The entourage of coach and four, with mounted and armed guards riding ahead, and four Negroes in livery behind, was about to depart. She found herself shaking hands formally with Robert Treat Paine, murmuring good wishes. They would pick up Thomas Cushing in front of his house on Bromfield Lane, near the Common. James Bowdoin and his wife were both ill, and he could not leave. It was Samuel Adams who was the sensation of the festivities, for he was dressed in claret-colored broadcloth and fresh white ruffles, a gold top to his cane, a glossy hat on his head. On the gold of his cane and glistening cuff links was stamped the emblem of the craftsmen of the Sons of Liberty, who had contributed this resplendent outfit. John held her hand for an instant longer than the others had, nothing more; then the four men were in the coach, there was a cracking of whips, a rising shout from the crowd.

Arm in arm, Abigail, Betsy Adams and Mary Cranch followed the carriage, moving slowly as the cheering, waving throng fell back. Fifty to sixty horsemen, handsomely mounted and groomed, waited as a guard of honor in front of the Adams home on Queen Street to escort the delegates to Watertown. The three women were swept along by the crowds past King's Chapel to the Common. People lined the sidewalks waving handkerchiefs and hats, crying out good wishes from their windows and doorways.

It was a stirring moment when the parade passed the whipping post and found the encamped regiments of British redcoats banked loosely along the street edge of the Common. The Bostonians halted. All cheering ceased. The Massachusetts committee peered out at the British soldiers in silence from their carriage, two sitting forward, two aft. The soldiers, far from home, come to hostile country for they knew not what purpose, stared back, not angrily, but all of them, committee and soldiers alike, uncertain, touches of fear and pride mixed into their confusion. In this silence, broken only by the sound of horses' hoofs and carriage wheels on the cobblestones, could be felt almost palpably in the clear hot near-noon August air the wondering of just where these jobs would lead these men, viewing each other in this confrontation; and just what their resolutions might finally turn out to be.

Or so Abigail and Betsy told each other over an appetiteless dinner in Samuel's house. Betsy asked:

"Does your food taste salty?"

"Am I gulping tears? Yes. I dared not show them."

"No. Samuel and John would have been ashamed."

"Perhaps not, Sister Betsy. There may be a time or two before our respected husbands return from this journey that they'll shed a tear or two of their own."

Later, over supper in the back garden of the Smith house, Isaac, Jr., surrounded by eulogies of the Sons of Liberty, lost his patience and commented adversely. Abigail saw pain cross her uncle's face. Afterwards, she knocked on Isaac's door. At his bidding she entered.

"Isaac, we were friends during the years I visited here. Later we corresponded, we exchanged French books for study."

Isaac pulled a chair around to his desk for her, then said in some surprise, "But, Cousin Abigail, why should you doubt it?"

"From what you said at supper."

"About the Sons?"

"Yes."

"Surely you know of their excesses, their raids, their tar-and-featherings."

"They don't change the validity of our position."

"I'm sorry, Cousin," Isaac broke in, forking back his blond hair with his fingers, "I don't see the validity. I think you may be surprised, if it comes to war, how many of our family and friends will remain with the British. Orthodoxy in politics is, I am sensible, fully as necessary a qualification for the ministry at this day as ever was orthodoxy in divinity. If I am reputed as an heretic in either, I cannot help it. I hate enthusiasm and bigotry in whatever form they appear. But I am willing to submit to censure. The greatest friends of their country and of mankind have frequently met with the same hard fate. I am not indifferent to the good opinion of those around me, but I cannot in complaisance to others give up the independence of my own mind."

"No one would want that, Isaac."

"Into what times are we fallen, Cousin Abigail, when the least degree of moderation, the least inclination to peace and order, the remotest apprehension for the public welfare and security is accounted a crime? What sort of cause is that which dreads the smallest inquisition?"

"We don't dread a facing up to our shortcomings. All of the colonies are sending good men to Philadelphia."

"Our cause, you tell me, is in very good hands. I do not dispute it. But is it not also in bad hands? Have not bad men brought us to a state of the greatest extremity and hazard? And may not the violence and temerity of such men precipitate us into measures which the united efforts of the good cannot prevent?"

He rose from the desk at which they had been sitting, and stood by the window with his back to her.

"Nabby, I hope you don't conceive of me as wanting in affection for my country. It is true, I have not exclaimed too loudly against the cruelty, the injustice, the arbitrary nature of the late Acts of Parliament as others have done. My age, my particular profession in life, my connection with the seminary of learning, would have forbidden me to do so. No one, however, wishes less to see them established. At the same time I must freely own that I had rather calmly acquiesce in these, and an hundred other acts proceeding from a British legislature, than be subject to the capricious, unlimited despotism of a few of my own countrymen, or behold the soil which gave me birth made a scene of mutual carnage and desolation."

She remembered John's line when he came to a parting with his beloved friend Jonathan Sewall:

"This adieu is the sharpest thorn on which I ever set my foot."

Isaac was a sharp thorn for her.

8

She returned to Braintree and the farm which was now her responsibility. The two hired hands John had left behind were experienced workers but not inclined to crowd too much accomplishment into any one day's work. She had been taught that "the foot of the owner is the best manure" and so she was in the fields shortly after dawn, took the cattle out to graze in the morning, bringing them back at dusk, milked the cows, churned for butter and cheese, letting the children help feed the poultry and the hogs.

John had asked that she get two cuttings from the hayfields, but a drought was drying up the ponds and creek.

He had warned her before he left that he would not risk his letters to the sometime post traveling between Philadelphia, New York and Boston because the British could intercept them. She endured it as long as no word reached Boston from Philadelphia except the newspaper accounts of the magnificent reception the delegates received in every town they passed through, with the story of the wining, dining and toasting, a journey of two weeks which had already stretched to more. But when Samuel Adams's son received a letter from his father, and Mrs. Thomas Cushing received one from her husband, she became unhappy. Each day the children squeezed into a chair beside her, or gathered on her lap, demanding:

"Where is Papa tonight? When will he come home? Send him our duty."

She wrote to him almost every day, pouring out her day's work, thoughts, feelings, the stories of the children, the crops. It was an enormous help to be able to write.

Nab attended Dame School but John Quincy, now past seven and avid for book study, was a source of concern. She had been instructed by

John not to neglect the boy's education. When the local schoolteacher, Joseph Crosby, resigned, she and Johnny read to each other from Rollin's *Ancient History*. She set forth writing exercises each night, but she had no organized course in which to instruct him.

She found it feasible to settle two problems at once. There were now four clerks trying to train themselves in John's small office in Boston, though there was nary a writ. So she brought up to Braintree John Thaxter, Jr., and Nathan Rice. They had a room in the parental house in which to work and sleep, and ate their meals with her. John Thaxter was nineteen, a Quincy cousin, son of her aunt. He was a mild, pleasant chap who readily agreed to tutor John Quincy in Latin, Greek and history.

Her mother becoming ill, she visited Weymouth every few days. Mary Cranch came laden with burdens: Richard was still failing at everything he tried, losing more and more of his original family fortune, with seemingly no way to convert his technical knowledge and skills into profit. Cotton Tufts never lost an opportunity to stop for a chat.

By the end of August she saw that she would not get her two cuttings of hay. She was unhappy, not so much about the lost money as the fear that John might think she had failed him.

Deep in the night, with Nab sleeping in her bed, Tommy in the trundle alongside, the two older boys in the bedroom across the hall, she went to her desk in the alcove and poured out her tumultuous feelings.

"The great distance between us makes the time appear very long," she wrote.

It really should not matter whether he was five miles away or five hundred. Yet when he was riding circuit she could visualize him in the little towns, in the courts, or with their friends; although she longed to have him home she had felt no severe cutting of ties. Now, with John in the midst of scenes totally strange to her, surrounded by men she did not know, there was no way to keep her thoughts linked to his.

"The great anxiety I feel for my country, for you and for our family renders the day tedious and the night unpleasant. The rocks and quicksands appear upon every side. What course you can or will take is all wrapped in the bosom of futurity. Uncertainty and expectation leave the mind great scope. Did ever any kingdom or state regain their liberty, when once it was invaded, without bloodshed? I cannot think of it without horror."

In spite of the bleakness of the nights and the excruciating Sundays, her long hours out in the open doing simple physical tasks brought her full physical strength. How anomalous it was to feel so well at a time when she was the loneliest of her life. Yet she needed her strength, for she was surrounded by turmoil. The Crown sympathizers of Mount Wollaston were bitter about John Adams's attending what they called "that treasonable conclave" and took no pains to conceal their hatred. When the Regulatory Acts were introduced, which denied the right of choice of jurors to the towns, the resulting outbreaks and closing of the courts only gave them further proof that Massachusetts was incorrigible.

There were those in Boston and Braintree as well, moderate folk, who were now convinced that the hotheads of Boston had willfully brought this trouble down upon them. Some former Patriots were saying:

"What does it matter under whose rule we amass a deal of money?"

Blood and temper ran high on both sides. Isaac, Jr., ran into trouble straight off. His first two sermons in Boston pleading for obedience to the Crown had had him banished from those pulpits. Preaching engagements in several small towns where he might have found a parsonage were canceled. The ill will generated by the son fell on his mother and father as well, affecting his father's long-established business.

Lieutenant Governor Oliver was forced to resign by a none too gentle crowd of four thousand Patriots. The councilors to the governor, who had always been elected by the Massachusetts Assembly but were now appointed by Governor Gage, were obliged by their outraged communities to refuse the post. General Gage mounted cannon on Beacon Hill, dug breastworks in the city. People who had stood in the middle, refusing to take sides, grew frightened and sought shelter with the British. One of the first was Thomas Boylston, wealthy merchant and a relative of John's mother. Mrs. Hall came through the back door of Abigail's kitchen pale and distraught.

"It's obvious the British must prevail."

"Mother Hall, may I remind you that your son is at an American Congress in Philadelphia?"

"What would happen to Thomas Boylston in the event the British troops should be obliged to leave?" demanded Mrs. Hall, pursuing her own thoughts.

Abigail replied stiffly:

"I dare say the same thing that would happen to your son in reverse. His properties would be confiscated. He would be written down as an enemy of Massachusetts. If he were out of the country he might not be allowed to return. Just as John, if transported to London for trial, might never be able to get back to his home and family."

"It's a frightening gamble," sighed the older woman.

"Thomas Boylston may be gambling. We are not. We're fighting for principles. But I wouldn't worry about him. He has ships to load his wealth onto if he has to flee."

"Abigail, bitterness doesn't become you."

"I am sorry, Mother Hall. But my husband has been gone a long time. I have not heard one word from him about his health or well-being. My whole life and my four children's are committed to my husband's position. So perhaps you'll forgive me for being partisan."

John's mother leaned out a hand, patted back the hair over Abigail's ear. The two women had rarely engaged in shows of affection.

"John is fortunate. He found a woman who could love her own family yet immerse herself in her husband's."

"My father would cane me out of the parsonage if I ever intimated that I am a Smith or a Quincy first, and an Adams second."

It was becoming commonplace for family conflicts to be staged in many a seemingly tranquil New England household. At Mount Wollaston there gathered in the library of Josiah Quincy, Sr.'s home half a dozen Quincys and their kin. From this room there was a magnificent view of the bay, the hills with their orchards, the fields ripe for harvesting.

Abigail knew that Josiah, Jr., would sail in a few days on the *Boston Packet* for England. He was discussing the political impasse with his older cousin, Norton Quincy, quoting from a speech written by Jonathan Shipley, Bishop of St. Asaph, intended for Parliament. Everyone turned to listen.

"'North America is the only great nursery of freemen left upon the face of the earth!'"

Abigail commented, "How wondrous for us in our difficulties to know that people in England also believe us to be right."

Samuel Quincy, Josiah, Jr.'s brother, agreed. His wife Hannah, a robustly forthright woman, cried out:

"If you admire the speech why don't you admire the sentiment?"

Samuel gazed expressionlessly at his young law clerk, Sumner, also a relative.

"I do."

"No, you don't," his wife snorted, "or you wouldn't still be consorting with the Crown crowd."

"They have a right to counsel."

"Let somebody else counsel them. I say it's time we left the Episcopalians. If this ruckus gets worse we'll have nobody to talk to but redcoats. There's never been a Quincy didn't stick by his clan, and I'm not aiming my husband should be the first."

Samuel bowed his head.

"This is not a Pope's Day brawl. We began English, we'll end English. Our children too."

Josiah, Jr., quietly broke the news that he was sailing for England. His father, who had almost disinherited his son for defending Captain Preston and the British soldiers, exploded vocally and physically.

"Why would you want to do that? The Patriots will say you're running away. The Tories will claim you're being sent back to be hanged."

Abigail and Josiah, Jr.'s wife exchanged a glance of commiseration.

At the beginning of September there came two simultaneous events that rocked the colony as hard as though its collective stores of gunpowder had exploded. General Gage somehow managed to drop on a street in Boston a letter he had received from Brigadier General William Brattle, commanding officer of the Massachusetts militia. The letter was passed from hand to hand, then published in the *Gazette,* and Boston learned that Brattle had traitorously advised General Gage to break every commissioned officer in the colony's militia, thus leaving it without leadership; then to use his troops quickly to seize the colony's gunpowder by commandeering the supply from each town.

On the same day news arrived of Parliament's Quebec Act. Intended to placate their French Canadians in Quebec and to guarantee their rights of Catholicism, it contained a provision which turned New England wild with fear: Quebec was to extend to the Ohio River on the south and the Mississippi River on the west, all to become part of Canada. This meant that Americans moving westward would become Canadian subjects and live under French civil law. Eventually the existing colonies would be surrounded by the Catholic Church. They would also lose millions of acres of rich, virgin lands to Canada.

Abigail threw herself into the work of the farm and the caring for her four children; it helped to close out the external angers. As the drought continued its depredations, she wrote wryly to John, "My poor cows will certainly prefer a petition to you setting forth their grievances and informing you that they have been deprived of their ancient privileges."

Some brightness came from Philadelphia, the first word she had had of the meetings. It did not come from John but from a newspaper brought to her by Betsy Adams. John had discussed with her the first and perhaps unbridgeable problem of the Congress: religion. How were delegates of so many religions going to work together for a common cause when they hated, persecuted and tried to eradicate each other's religions?

Samuel Adams had solved the problem. When the question arose of who should give the opening prayer, Samuel had risen and said:

"I am no bigot, and can hear a prayer from a gentleman of piety and virtue who is at the same time a friend to his country," adding that he was a stranger in Philadelphia but had heard that Mr. Duché deserved that character, and therefore he moved that Mr. Duché, an Episcopal clergyman, might be desired to read prayers to the Congress. The motion was seconded and passed.

The Reverend Mr. Duché had prayed so fervently for all men, and all Americans, that the delegates had been welded into a cohesive body, a tradition for religious unity woven into the texture of the Congress. After the Quebec Act the Church of England group in Braintree had attempted to move their Episcopalian churches nearer to the Congregationalists for protection against the impending Catholic settlements to the south and west. Samuel Adams had subtly changed all that; in Philadelphia Congregationalists and Episcopalians were working together, side by side not only with Quakers, Unitarians and Anabaptists, but with Catholics as well. Betsy Adams, her face shining with pride, asked Abigail:

"Perhaps this bodes well for the future?"

Abigail assured Betsy that it did; but events were moving too fast for anyone to feel assured. Massachusetts had been without a legal government since General Gage dismissed the Assembly. The Boston town meeting, which had had no legal right to convene, had met and voted to send representatives to Dedham to form a Suffolk County government. The Committee of Correspondence had written to other Massachusetts counties urging them to set up county governments and at the same time refuse to disband their town meetings. Each town had formed its Committee of Safety.

Abigail watched all this being accomplished with rapid sure-footedness, as she reported to her husband, for New Englanders had been governing themselves in their congregations, in their town councils, in their assemblies and in their elected members to the General Court since their first ships landed. They had had royal governors over them, their rights had been defined by their charters; sometimes the Crown appointees had been troublesome. But Massachusetts had evolved its own *modus operandi*, prospered, and helped the British Empire to prosper. For some ninety per cent of their activities they had governed themselves.

"And that," Abigail concluded to Betsy, "is what we're doing now. It's as natural and necessary to us as breathing. General Gage can close the port of Boston, Parliament can deprive us of our assemblymen, selectmen, judges, jurors. But we'll go on governing ourselves. How do you tell a seventh- or eighth-generation freeman that he can no longer be free?"

"You can't," said Betsy. "That's why our brace of Adamses is at Philadelphia."

"And, Betsy, if I don't have a letter from my half of that brace, I shall hitch up a horse to the carriage and go to Philadelphia to get one."

The following day she heard the noise of tramping men and ran to the window overlooking the Coast Road. It was a company of militia, about two hundred strong, marching in ragged file with rifles slung over their shoulders, their faces grim. They were dressed in long loose-fitting shirts, some of them in buckskin even on this hot September day, wearing the heavy boots used in the fields. They continued down the road to where Braintree's supply of powder was stored. Soon they were on their way back. She stood at the open window and waited.

"Mrs. Adams, would you care to have some of this powder?" cried the officer as they came abreast.

"Thank you, no, Captain."

"There are too many Tories in this town. That's why we had to move it. It'll be hid secure, now."

Word had gone down the line that this was Mrs. John Adams, wife of their delegate to the Congress. Each militiaman saluted or waved or, if his arms were full of powder sacks, smiled. She did not know these men or even what town they came from; but when she turned from the window her heart was beating hard in her chest. What would have happened if a company of General Gage's redcoats, come to capture Braintree's powder, had met this company of Massachusetts militia bent on preserving that powder?

A few days later she sank into John's office chair in front of his worktable, began to read the letter she had just received. First she had to see his closing lines. If he sent love, all was well for her. If not, the information from Philadelphia would have little significance. Even with the sound of the militiamen fading down the Coast Road the important thing in life for her was to be loved.

He sent that love, "with the tenderest affection and concern."

Tears sprang to her eyes. It seemed a lifetime since she had bade him farewell in Boston. But now she knew again that she was wanted. She was needed. She was loved. How terrible and wonderful to be a woman.

The letter had been written at the end of August when John was still some forty miles from Philadelphia. She gathered the four children in the office, seated them about the table in the client chairs.

"Nab, the first word is for you. Papa sends his tender love and asks that you write him a letter, to be enclosed in my next."

"I will, Mama, but my thumb is still sore. Papa won't like my writing."

"He'll like it. Johnny, the next is for you. Papa says he is glad to hear that you're so good a boy as to read to your mama for her entertainment. He asks that you stay out of the company of rude children."

Johnny looked perplexed.

"Tell Father I will, as soon as I can find any."

"Next is for the little ones." She rose, went to the other side of the table. "Papa says, 'Kiss my little Charley and Tommy for me.'" She kissed them, and they kissed her, Charley crying, "Write Papa we kissed you back."

"I will. Now listen carefully, all four of you, to Papa's last paragraph because I want you always to remember it.

"'The education of our children is never out of my mind. Train them to virtue, habituate them to industry, activity and spirit. Make them consider every vice as shameful and unmanly. Fire them with ambition to be useful, make them disdain to be destitute of any useful or ornamental knowledge or accomplishment. Fix their ambition upon great and solid objects, and their contempt upon little, frivolous and useless ones. It is time, my dear, for you to begin to teach them French. Every decency, grace and honesty should be inculcated upon them.'"

When she had finished, Nab asked with a frown on her plump red-cheeked face, "Ma, why doesn't Papa wait to tell us all that when he gets home?"

"Perhaps because when he's so far away you all seem more precious to him. And he is lonesome for you."

She heard the faint sounds of drops on the windowpanes, ran out of the office door and stood in the road letting the rain fall on her parched face. It was a saturating downpour, the grasses would be revived, though it was too late for a second crop.

9

John's second letter came more quickly. The opening lines were inexplicable to her.

"When or where this letter will find you, I know not. In what scenes of distress and terror, I cannot foresee. We have received a confused account from Boston of a dreadful catastrophe."

Then she remembered: a rumor had been bruited about that General Gage had opened artillery fire on the city and many people had been killed. She put the letter down, sick with sympathy for him, immobilized three hundred miles away, not knowing whether his wife and children had been caught up in the violence. Then she scanned his writing swiftly, hoping for a date of return. All he could tell her was that no one could leave Philadelphia until the business of the Congress was completed; and that it was "the general disposition to proceed slowly." He urged her that if there should be hunger and distress in Boston to write to as many of their friends as possible to take asylum with her, particularly Betsy Adams and Mrs. Cushing. He asked her not to be concerned about him.

"There is in the Congress a collection of the greatest men upon this continent in point of abilities, virtues and fortunes. The magnanimity and public spirit which I see here makes me blush for the sordid venal herd. . . . There is such a spirit through the colonies, and the members of the Congress are such characters that no danger can happen to us which will not involve the whole continent in universal desolation, and in that case who would wish to live?"

The air and the hours became filled with portentous happenings. The alarums came on swift horses from Boston, vanishing as quickly in the direction of Plymouth or Taunton. The Sons' spy system was so penetrating that Paul Revere, who had become the Patriots' most energetic and resourceful courier, was riding one of his fast horses to the outlying towns while General Gage and his staff were making the decision as to which towns would be raided for their stores.

Mercy Warren came for a visit bringing her manuscript of a play she was writing, a satire on Lord North and other English political figures.

Brilliant of mind and tongue, Mercy heaped scorn on the English writers being quoted in the press as saying that Bostonians were a mercantile class, "a tumultuous and riotous rabble, who ought . . . not trouble themselves with politics and government which they do not understand."

The Suffolk County Convention, meeting under the leadership of Dr. Joseph Warren in Stoughton, Dedham and Milton, passed a series of Resolves, a copy of which was brought to her by Joseph Palmer, her sister Mary's brother-in-law, who had been selected to represent Braintree. Abigail read the Resolves carefully: no obedience was due from Massachusetts to any part of the Coercive Acts; any attempt to enforce the obnoxious measures would be resisted; a severance of trade relations with Britain was recommended, and a refusal to pay monies to the county treasurer until the government of the province had been returned to a constitutional base; a pledge to "pay all due respect and submission" to all measures the Congress should suggest "for the restoration and establishment of our just rights . . . and for renewing that harmony and union between Great Britain and the Colonies, so earnestly wished for by all good men."

Paul Revere carried the Suffolk Resolves to Philadelphia in the incredibly fast time of five days. In a letter brought back to her by Mr. Revere from John she learned that the Congress vastly applauded the Resolves. It had been unanimously resolved "that this Assembly deeply feels the sufferings of their countrymen in the Massachusetts Bay . . . that they most thoroughly approve the wisdom and fortitude with which opposition to these wicked ministerial measures has hitherto been conducted, and they earnestly recommend to their brethren a perseverance in the same firm and temperate conduct. . . ."

Copies of the Suffolk Resolves and the Congress' adoption of them had been printed in Philadelphia and rushed back to Boston by Revere. Abigail felt a foolish pride at being the first in Massachusetts to know of the delegates' unity. It was the Congress' first public statement of policy.

John had written in his letter "My dear [redacted]," and then heavily inked out the word; but not heavily enough to evade the eyes of a lonely wife: the word was "charmer," she was sure, and it gave her such sharp pleasure that she had to sit down to savor it. She understood why he had decided to ink it out: if the letter had fallen into unfriendly hands such a personal token of affection could be used to ridicule the Adamses. But that one blotted word made up for the fact that Brackett, their hired man, was imbibing freely of rum in the Braintree taverns after work, that she had to wait up for him each night and talk quietly to him until his tongue thickened and he stumbled up the stairs to sleep.

Rumors proliferated like worms in the corn. Braintree was accused of maltreating its Church of England residents. She attended a clandestine town meeting called to issue a statement that no Episcopalian had been treated illegally. An alleged uprising of Negroes in Boston, armed by the Tories, was taking to the roads to slaughter Patriots. She wrote to her husband in disgust at such hysterias:

"I wish most sincerely that there was not a slave in the province. It always appeared a most iniquitous scheme to me—fight ourselves for what we are daily robbing and plundering from those who have as good a right to freedom as we have."

She received a worried letter from John directing her to bring his office furniture, books and papers back from Boston, and the remaining two clerks, Hill and Williams, as well; to take them into the house, providing they paid for their board. She questioned a dozen Quincys before she became convinced that it would be safe to leave the law office and its two young clerks where they were, for a while at least.

John's clerk, Hill, rode up from Boston with a letter that had been left at the office. A line jumped out of the short sheet:

"If it should be necessary to stay here till Christmas or longer in order to effect our purposes . . ."

Her first reaction was concern rather than disappointment: there was a contingent of redcoats in Plymouth, with every town and village in Massachusetts forming new militia companies. Able-bodied men worked, ate and slept with their guns within arm's reach. The most repeated line in New England was the one John had brought back from circuit about the Reverend Mr. Moody of York:

"He enjoyed intimate communications with the Deity, but always kept his musket in order."

This had been true of the Puritans and Pilgrims since the day they landed in America: without both their God and their guns they would have perished.

Her father sent her a note telling her that he was going to Lincoln to visit with Billy and Catharine Louisa for a day. Wouldn't she like to come along? He would call for her in his carriage at seven the next morning.

They crossed the Charles River at Watertown, took the rutted wagon road west, then went through the sparsely settled center of Lincoln to the intersection of the Bay Road. Lincoln was not quite a village, for it had never been laid out deliberately as a town, with a central Meeting House and burying ground, a tavern, a general store and shops centered around a Common. It was rather a joining together of outlying farming districts of three abutting towns, Concord, Lexington and Weston. The center was made up of parcels of farmland donated for the building of a handsome white church with a tall steeple. There was a tanhouse but no gristmill as yet; a few farmhouses faced the center, with twenty graves straggling unevenly uphill in the burying ground. A level stretch between the Meeting House and the topmost graves was known as the Old Training Ground where the local militia drilled.

They drove another two miles up the road to the knoll on which stood the house, shaded by a giant elm, that had been deeded to Catharine Louisa. It was said to be the oldest house in Lincoln. Originally only one room deep, it was now quite spacious, of two stories. Its outstanding feature was a huge fireplace made of soft brick taken from the clay beds of the farm, twelve feet square in the cellar and with a chimney known as Ten Commandment style because it was shaped like Moses's two tablets of stone. Catharine Louisa had made the house colorful with calico curtains at the windows and bright Turkey rugs on the floors.

While Billy took his father out to show him the pond he had dug for his animals, the extended barn for his nine milch cows, Catharine Louisa set the heavy wainscot chairs she had inherited around the eight-legged table in her sitting parlor. She had a servant to help with the children; Billy had bought an experienced young Negro in Boston to do the farming while he took care of the livestock.

"Billy's content," exclaimed Catharine Louisa. "He's saving money to open a general store. Oh, not now, we have only a hundred families in Lincoln, and they trade in Concord or Lexington. But in about five years. Folks hereabouts like Billy. He's been elected lieutenant of the militia."

Billy was exultant over the Middlesex militia. Only three weeks before British soldiers had seized several barrels of gunpowder in Charlestown, and two fieldpieces from Cambridge. Several hundred militiamen from Concord, Lexington and Lincoln had marched on Cambridge, part of them under arms, ready to fight if they encountered redcoats. Patriots in Boston were certain that more of such sudden swooping by the redcoats could be expected.

"That's why we're preaching emergency call," Billy told them, his eyes gleaming with pride. "I have the right to summon once a week."

After dinner he drove them into the center, parked the carriage alongside the church, ran up the stairs of the belfry and began ringing the bell as though the whole of Middlesex County had caught on fire. Instantly the farms and houses around the center erupted men with flintlocks, adjusting their knapsacks and cartouches, running for the level area between the Meeting House and the highest graves in the burying ground. The first squad was assembled in a matter of moments. The next wave came from the farms south of the center toward Flint's Pond, the tanners in rolled-up shirt sleeves, leather aprons hung around their necks, running in their lightweight work slippers, their arms and faces covered with brown splotches of the oak bark and tannic acid from their vats. Next came the farmers from the Bay Road, near Billy's; they had thrown down their tools where they were working in the fields, tied the reins of their horses or oxen to the nearest stump, caught up gun, powder horn, cartouche and knapsack at a dead run. Lastly came the men who had been in Brooks's or Hartwell's taverns on the Bay Road, some of them riding two on a horse.

In only a few minutes the Lincoln company was complete, some forty men ready to march and to fight. Billy was standing with his right arm in the air, having tied a green ribbon across his chest between his coat and waistcoat. The captain, wearing a pink ribbon, was inspecting his forty-man company, checking the flintlocks, occasional bayonet, shot bags. Billy stood at one flank, the ensign, with a blue ribbon across his chest, at the other. The inspection finished, the captain barked an order to Lieutenant Smith. Billy rushed to the center of the company.

"Shoulder firelocks! Forward march!"

He came sweeping across the drill ground toward Abigail and their father, holding his flintlock securely across his chest while the men stepped sharply behind him, each man with his musket pointed. When the company reached the corner by the church, Billy cried, "Halt! Take aim! Fire!" All rifles were raised. Some of the men went down on their knees to steady their guns. Aim was taken, triggers pulled. But there was no noise, no bullets. Powder was too rare and precious to be wasted on maneuvers.

"Besides," murmured the Reverend Mr. Smith, "they don't need practice. We've all been hunting since we were old enough to tote a gun."

On the way home from Billy's they decided to stop over in Boston to get a look at what was going on. The Neck was fortified but not completely blockaded. American soldiers who had fought in the French and Indian War ridiculed the fortifications as mud walls. Abigail asked her father why they were so poorly built.

"Because not one of our artisans will help. The British appear not to have brought any engineers."

"Why would they need engineers to subdue peasants in a wilderness?"

Dozens of people were gathered about the passage in the wall, some weeping, some arguing angrily, their lifetime possessions in their arms or on little carts and saddlebags: frightened Tories trying to get into Boston for safety, the more cautious Patriots trying to get out. Though the British officers were beginning to think of all Congregationalist ministers as traitors, having labeled them "the black clergy," they were still permitting them to move about freely. A lieutenant passed them through.

She could not believe her eyes. In the four months of the blockade of Boston Harbor the British had managed to convert a noisy, brawling, vivacious city into a dying hamlet. The misshapen kite which was Boston's physical structure lay broken on the ground. Gone were the coaches with their matched horses and liveried servants; gone the elegant gentlemen in their cocked hats; gone the cacophonously pleasant noises of the patent-medicine peddlers, the fishmongers, the blackened chimney sweeps, the town criers announcing the hour and the news, the bells of Old South and Brattle. Gone were the farmers with their cans of milk filling the jugs of servants on the house stoops; gone were the fashionably dressed women shopping for the latest imports from London and Paris; gone were the itinerant tinkers, the hundreds of carts and horses' hoofs thundering over the cobblestones.

There were few abroad: British soldiers marching to their change of the guard; Bostonians moving quietly along the streets, staying close to the buildings, apparently not looking at anything very closely but actually spying out every move made by each company and division and individual soldier of the occupying force.

She turned to her father as they came through Brattle Square.

"Father, I view Boston with much the same sensation that I should the body of a departed friend."

"Your friend is unconscious," remarked the Reverend Mr. Smith grimly, "not dead."

"Look, Faneuil Hall is closed. I used to buy my fruits and vegetables from those stalls on the street, and my meats inside. And how can those beautiful houses look so run down in so short a time?"

Her father threw her a stern glance.

"Nabby, you've never seen an occupied city before. Wait until the soldiers are quartered in private homes. They'll leave the brick and timbers standing, but that's about all."

When Abigail had been embraced by her uncle Isaac and aunt Elizabeth, and had had time to wash up from the journey and join the family in the sitting parlor, they had hot coffee with plain buns. Everyone hated the coffee but derived pleasure from the fact that it was not Bohea tea. When her father left to visit with Mary, Abigail asked, "Could we go for a walk, Uncle Isaac? It's safe, isn't it?"

"Oh yes. During the day," he replied. "The troops don't bother the civilians much, except when they're drunk. They fight more among themselves than they do with us. I guess we can't deny them their acknowledged Christian pleasures."

Though it was late, the September afternoon was still warm when they went out. They walked past the Adams house on Queen Street. It was locked and boarded as they had left it. Several of the King's best regiments were now in the streets, marching sharply and in flawless step to the music of *Yankee Doodle*, returning to headquarters or to take ship to Castle William. Uncle Isaac had made himself an expert in the regimental costumes; she gathered that he had done so for specific purposes.

Most of the soldiers had on a cocked hat with a low crown and a broad brim caught up in front and back. The grenadiers wore a cap with a high brass or black metal front piece. The infantrymen were in leather skullcaps, also faced with metal plates. All the coats were scarlet, each company or regiment being distinguished by the color of its lapel or the embroidery around its buttonholes. The King's own regiments had blue facings, the 5th Northumberland Fusiliers gosling green, the 24th South Wales Borderers willow green, the 54th Dorsetshires a variation called popinjay green. The drummers and fifers were in grenadiers' bearskin. On their arms was a line of chevrons up to the shoulder. These musicians were the peacocks of the British regiments; apparently not more than two soldiers could march anywhere, even for a change of guard duty, without the fifers and drummers preceding them.

Uncle Isaac explained that these were the old and traditional regiments which were officered by good men and kept in excellent condition. Then, turning sharply off King Street and heading toward the group of taverns in which the Sons of Liberty had held their meetings, he commented:

"Now you will see the common British soldier. He has no tradition, his commanding officers are slack and disinterested. They despise the Americans, maintaining they could slaughter every militiaman in the colony in one day if General Gage would give them the order to march. They're homesick. They miss their English entertainment and public houses; though the regimental officers are entertained by the Tories no home will receive these men."

They had made their way down to the docks. The line of British men-of-war was still there. The wharves were deserted except for the few boats transporting sailors to and from the warships. There was not one topsail of an American merchantman. It was forbidden for the Americans to so much as row a scow to Dorchester or run a ferry across the Charles River to Charlestown. Even transporting bricks or wood or cattle from pier to pier was forbidden.

The ropewalks where she had first gone with John and seen the men weaving the strands that were used in their great sailing ships were deserted, but there were a number of workmen on the docks and the streets.

"What are they working at?"

"They're repaving the streets. Repairing the docks. Any public task we can find. They're mechanics or artisans thrown out of work. We have plenty of foodstuffs brought in from all over New England. The fishermen of Salem and Marblehead are contributing a portion of their catch. Colonel Israel Putnam drove in a whole herd of sheep from Connecticut. But our selectmen decided that no man should draw food from the common fund without working for it."

They were passing a group of laborers resetting cobblestones. The men glared at them.

"Whom do they hate?" she asked. "The British, or the selectmen who are making them labor for their food?"

"I can't dissect the anatomy of hate. As you can see, it fills the air of Boston."

"I can feel it and smell it."

"It makes your eyes tear, your lungs cough and your stomach want to retch. We'd better move on home now before dark falls. The troops will be off duty, and with money in their pockets."

She holy walked with the Smith family to the Brattle Street Church. Out on the square the British soldiers raced their horses in noisy contests.

When they left the church and walked into Dock Square they heard the heavy muffled beat of drums, the impact of marching boots. Past her, as she stood frozen before the locked door of Faneuil Hall, went some of England's finest bands and regiments, and midway down the troops a terrifying sight: a man tied by ropes to keep him upright in a four-wheeled cart, his entire body, head and face covered with wet black tar. Sticking to the tar was a covering of white feathers. As he was trundled by Abigail could see only two holes in the face; they were his eyes.

She gazed at her uncle in terror. "Why?" she whispered.

"We'll know tomorrow. We'll take his deposition."

She felt ill. Isaac put his hand under her arm, holding her erect.

"They learned this charming lesson from us. Last January I saw a Boston mob tar and feather John Malcom, a Tory. When he had barred himself into the second story of his house, brandishing a sword and loaded pistol, a crowd put ladders up to his window, dragged him out, stripped him to the waist, painted him with tar and dumped two pillows of feathers over the tar. Then they put him in a cart and hauled him all over Boston, out to the gallows on the Neck, then to the Liberty Tree, up to the top of Copp's Hill. There must have been a thousand of us following that procession, and truth to tell we did nothing to prevent them from flogging Malcom at every stop. When he tried to remove the tar and feathers his skin came off in patches."

He became quiet for a moment, then murmured wistfully:

"Sometimes I hear my son's voice saying, 'There isn't much to choose between us.'"

That night, lying awake in bed, she thought, "Isaac, Jr., said there was not much to choose between them." But there was. Everybody had to make a choice. It did not mean that one was always right. It meant that right was on one's side.

10

On the first of November when the crops were in, she sat in her borning-room office with her account books open before her. In one pile she had her bills: the taxes to be paid on their property in Braintree, church dues, Brackett's wages, installments due on the Queen Street house in Boston and on Peter's farm. In a second pile she had her estimates of how much food they would need until the following summer: of fruits, vegetables, fish, meat, flour, barley, cider. A third list contained the items to buy: sugar, spices, coffee, Madeira. The fourth list was the difficult one: how much of her crops would have to be sold to cover her debts, buy the remaining necessities and still supply the several wagonloads of foodstuffs to the Boston Committee for distribution. She would have to release some of the meat and vegetables she had hoped to store in the cellar for her own brood.

Uncle Isaac got her fair prices.

She paid their bills. There was no cash left over for the Adams Specie Bank, but neither would they face 1775 with debts. Perhaps John would be able to practice a little law to bring in the cash that would be needed for the children's medications, for the needles and thread, pins and cambric for the family clothing.

She had no sooner completed her accounts than John came riding up, as exhausted as his mount but hilarious to be home. He looked in excellent health. The only hazard of the road, he assured her, was the enthusiastic reception committee in each city and hamlet prepared to stage triumphal dinners for the returning delegates.

"The enthusiasm of every colony for the Congress was deeply gratifying," he told her as he unpacked an abundant crop of papers. "Several times a day I begged off from a celebration on the grounds that my poor abandoned wife and children were desolate without me."

"So we were," she exclaimed.

He lighted a fire in his office hearth. The cold room was warmed. They sat side by side on the backless bench before the flames, arms about each other's waists. It was good to be together again.

"Miss Abigail, you're plump as a pigeon. And all the while I thought of you as pining away for me."

"Every time I felt lonely I found myself in the kitchen, eating. Isn't that strange? I would have thought that I would skin down to a skeleton."

He embraced her.

"I'm so happy you didn't."

They had a frolicsome supper, with the children opening their gifts and hearing some of Papa's anecdotes of life in the strange fascinating city of Philadelphia. John moved Tommy's trundle across the hall, then laid the fire in their own bedroom. He was wanton with the big logs, keeping the room warm and filled with flamelight. It was wonderful to make love again.

"Of tangibles, we don't have much to brag on," he confided later, telling her about the Congress. "But the fact that fifty-six men from twelve different colonies and a variety of geographic areas, religions, cultural and economic backgrounds worked together harmoniously, compromising our differences, accepting defeat when the majority vote went against us: that hasn't happened since the Agora of Athens, the Senate of Rome, the Hansa towns of Germany in the Middle Ages. It promises more for the future than anything we achieved in terms of specific resolves."

He jumped out of bed, slipped his feet into his cotton slippers and stood in front of the fireplace in his ankle-length nightshirt, energetically rubbing the heat into the small of his back.

"We had been offered two meeting halls, the State House and the newly completed Carpenters' Hall. Some fifty of us met at City Tavern and walked to Carpenters' Hall. We saw at once that it was built by master craftsmen. There was a large meeting room downstairs, beautifully paneled, another room for committee meetings, in between a long hall for caucusing. Upstairs was the Library Company of Philadelphia, the one founded by Benjamin Franklin, with all its books neatly categorized in cases behind wire mesh. The general cry was, 'Accept!' We thereby accomplished two master strokes: dissociating ourselves from the King's government, which had always met in the State House; and letting the craftsmen of America know we represented them, not only rich planters or merchants."

She sat up straight, propped against the bolster, urging him to describe the delegates. She tucked her hair behind her ears with both hands as she frequently did when she was intrigued by a prospect before her.

"Close the curtains and bolt the door so that our ancestors won't know that we're putting on a theatrical," she chuckled.

"The gentlemen from Virginia appeared to be the most spirited and consistent of any. There couldn't be a culture more different from ours in its context, but at every disputed point we saw eye to eye and fist to fist. Richard Bland is a learned, bookish man. Peyton Randolph is large, well-looking. Patrick Henry proved to be our greatest orator. He said he had no public education but at fifteen he was reading Virgil and Livy. Richard Henry Lee of the Virginia group is tall and spare, a masterly man. I can't say all that much for the Connecticut delegates. Roger

Sherman has a clear head and sound judgment, but when he moves a hand in anything like action, Hogarth's genius could not have invented a motion more opposite to grace. Eliphalet Dyer is long-winded and roundabout, obscure and cloudy. By contrast sixty-seven-year-old Governor Hopkins of Rhode Island, after the business of the evening was over, kept us in conversation till midnight. Over Jamaica rum and water he gave us wit, humor, anecdotes, science and learning from the Greek, Roman and British history.

"The New York men interested me greatly. John Jay is a hard student and a good speaker. James Duane is sensible and learned, but a cold speaker. He has a sly, surveying eye, a little squinted; sensible but at the same time artful. Mr. Alsop is a soft sweet man but unequal to the trust in point of abilities. Another of that New York group, Philip Livingston, is a great, rough, rapid mortal. There is no holding any conversation with him. He blusters away. The Pennsylvania group is split. John Dickinson is a shadow: tall, but slender as a reed, pale as ashes. He's a modest man and very ingenious as well as agreeable. He has an excellent heart and the cause of his country lies near it. I can't say as much for his confrere John Galloway, because Galloway is just where the Hutchinson faction was back in 1765 when we were trying to get a repeal of the Stamp Act. Thomas Mifflin of Pennsylvania is a sprightly and spirited speaker, but Samuel Chase goes to extremes. He speaks warmly, is violent and boisterous yet of a temper naturally quick. . . ."

The room was crowded with the delegates standing two and three deep around her bed. She could see every figure and face, hear the voices, listen to the contests, how they disagreed, how much each was willing to sacrifice of his own colony and his own well-being for the good of all the colonies.

"John, I won't be able to close my eyes all night for the excitement of thinking about those men."

With which she fell asleep instantly and did not waken until late the next morning. John had already had porridge with the children. She found the five of them excitedly rearranging his office. John was in his best advocate black. The children's eyes were dancing with excitement.

"Where are you all going, to a second Congress?"

"We're going to school, Mama!" cried Nab.

"Papa's the new schoolmaster," added Johnny; "we gave him a contract like he had at Worcester before he became a lawyer."

Only Charley was unhappy.

"This is not a school. It's the law."

"You mean law *office*," his sister corrected.

"It's the same."

"Charley is right," said Abigail. "I'll bring down that new map of Massachusetts Colony I bought from Henry Knox. John, you have some prints in your desk; put up the ones of Julius Caesar and Cromwell."

"Since the courts are closed there can be no more law offices. I hereby proclaim, through the authority vested in me by the Congress, that this room ceases to be a law office and becomes the Adams Latin School!"

She went into the kitchen to get a cup of coffee, leaving the younger two children sitting before their slates, chalk in hand, the older two opposite them with paper, ink and pen; and their father at the head of his worktable about to begin the first session of his one-room school. She knew by the expression on John's face that this was no game invented to amuse the children. He was in deadly earnest, having written out a schedule: writing, reading aloud, arithmetic for the two hours of the morning; history, philosophy, science for the two hours in the afternoon between tea and supper.

She tended her chores, returned to find Tommy memorizing the alphabet from the *Primer*, Charley tracing over a picture of some chemical apparatus John had brought home from Benjamin Franklin's library, Johnny and Nab writing essays on the meaning of the first chapter of *Pilgrim's Progress*. Abigail took a seat at the rear of the room, contentedly netting a purse, the first time she had picked up the work in several months. Her eyes lowered, a little smile at the corner of her mouth as she listened to Charley and Tommy intone their lessons, she ruminated:

"Endurance. That's what we all need, in copious quantity."

Suddenly she heard the silence. She looked up to see her husband and children watching her. As though at a signal they bounded out of their chairs crying:

"Happy birthday!"

From their hiding places behind the bookshelves and from the crannies of John's high desk they brought forth their presents, tendered them, one by one: a copy of Laurence Sterne's *A Sentimental Journey*, a scarf, a blue netted purse, an exquisite lace handkerchief, and from John a package containing the five volumes of David Hume's *History of England* for which she had longed. All of the gifts had come down the road in his saddlebag.

"Dear Charmer, I made it home for your birthday! When I think of all those testimonial dinners I passed up just to be with you when you celebrated the ripe old age of thirty!"

Outside there was the sound of carriages coming down the road, several of them apparently having met at an agreed rendezvous: first her mother and father and Betsy, with the Tuftses from Weymouth, the Smiths, Betsy and Samuel Adams and the Cranches from Boston, Billy and Catharine Louisa from Lincoln, and lastly the Quincys: her uncle Norton, Josiah, Jr.'s wife, Samuel Quincy and his wife.

Patty and Susy were now able to take out the ducks they had been covertly preparing and pop them into the bake oven.

When they sat down to dinner, John at the head of the table, Abigail at the foot, nearest the kitchen, John said:

"Count them, Nab. One relation for every year of your life."

A few days later John was elected to represent Braintree at the first Provincial Congress in Cambridge. Abigail rode to Boston with him. She asked:

"John, do you think this Provincial Congress will elect delegates to a second Congress?"

"Yes, but I'm not likely to be one of them," he assured her. "We've agreed that a new set of delegates should attend each sitting. That way each colony will have a body of men with friends in the other colonies accustomed to working out our common problems. If the need should arise for a central government to rule all thirteen colonies, we will have the trained men and the precedents established."

It took a couple of days to learn how wrong John's predictions had been. The Massachusetts Provincial Congress admired the way its delegates had performed and re-elected them to a second Congress—if King George and Parliament should make it necessary for them to meet again. John Hancock was elected to replace James Bowdoin, who had been kept from the Congress by illness. John was penitent about forcing a second separation on Abigail.

"I'm not going to let all the months until May be unhappy," she replied stoutheartedly, "because you might have to leave again. I've developed the capacity for chopping time into oblong blocks, the way we cut ice out of the river in winter. If only you would build me a time house, right next to our ice house, for storage."

They settled down to a winter of companionship, abetted by the rains from the northeast followed by a blanket of white snow. It would take four to five months to learn Britain's reaction to the Congress' petition of grievances.

A month past her birthday, John brought home the December 12, 1774, issue of the *Boston Post Boy*. His skin was as green as his troubled eyes as he pointed out an article signed "Massachusettensis." It was written without hysteria or name calling, but step by step it was a logical devastation of the Patriot position. The theses built up over the years by James Otis, Samuel and John Adams and their associates concerning the rights and constitutional privileges of the colonies were subjected to a brilliant dissection.

"It could be written by no one but Jonathan Sewall," said John. "No one else has the lucidity, the wit, the convincing penetration that have always marked Jonathan's style."

He read aloud, " 'When a people, by what means soever, are reduced to such a situation that everything they hold dear as men and citizens is at stake, it is not only excusable but even praiseworthy for an individual to offer to the public anything that he may think has a tendency to ward off the impending danger.

" 'The press, when open to all parties and influenced by none, is a salutary engine in a free state . . . but when a party has gained the ascendancy so far as to become the licensers of the press . . . the press itself becomes an engine of oppression. It is too true to be denied that ever since the origin of our controversy with Great Britain the press in this town has been much devoted to the partisans of liberty. . . . The changes have been rung so often upon oppression, tyranny and slavery that, whether sleeping or waking, they are continually vibrating in our ears; and it is now high time to ask ourselves whether we have not been deluded by sound only.

" 'My dear countrymen, let us divest ourselves of prejudice, take a view of our present wretched situation, contrast it with our former happy one, carefully investigate the cause, and industriously seek some means to escape the evils we now feel and prevent those that we have reason to expect. . . .

" 'Will not posterity be amazed when they are told that the present distraction took its rise from a threepenny duty on tea, and call it a more unaccountable frenzy, and more disgraceful to the annals of America than that of witchcraft? I will attempt in the next paper to retrace the steps and mark the progressions that led us to this state. . . .' "

"Jonathan means to do a whole series!" she exclaimed.

"If I know him he has the series already written. One for every week's issue until the arrival of Parliament's decision. He plans to have our people prepared to accept defeat as the wise and constitutional solution. I'm going to answer him, argument for argument. Just as long as he continues to publish his essays there will be an essay in the *Gazette*."

"The war of polemics," Abigail murmured. "I like that form best: the clash of the heavy armor of ideas and philosophies."

John shook his head in mock despair.

"I still use excessive language, too many words cluttering up my central theme. But I know more history than Jonathan, and more about the structure of government."

They faced the challenge of Jonathan's weekly papers which became the talk of Massachusetts for the six issues before John could get his first essay completed to his satisfaction and published in the *Gazette* under the pseudonym "Novanglus." He first stated the crux of Jonathan's case against the Patriots: the claim by the Patriots that all men by nature are equal; that kings are but the ministers of the people; that their authority is delegated to them by the people.

Then he made his reply:

"These are what are called revolutionary principles. They are the principles of Aristotle and Plato, of Livy and Cicero, and Sydney, Harrington and Locke. The principles of nature and eternal reason. . . . It is therefore astonishing that writers who call themselves friends of government should in this age and country be so inconsistent with themselves, so indiscreet, so immodest, as to insinuate a doubt concerning them. . . .

"This writer is equally mistaken when he says the people are sure to be losers in the end. They can hardly be losers if unsuccessful, because if they live they can but be slaves, and slaves they would have been if they had not resisted. So that nothing is lost. If they die, they cannot be said to lose, for death is better than slavery. If they succeed, their gains are immense. They preserve their liberties. . . ."

He was like a man possessed, as though the freedom of America rested on his shoulders. He made no change in his schoolmaster role except to start the children earlier, in the kitchen by candlelight, over their bowls of cereal and hot milk. He went into Boston only to buy or borrow the reference books he needed, the files of pamphlets and newspapers. His eyelids grew red, began to burn from reading far into the night.

"You know, John, you're gaining ground on Jonathan. People are saying that you are constructing the most tightly knit justification of the colonial point of view thus far written."

He looked up from his ink-scrawled notes, dark rings under his eyes. "That's what it has to be, on the day the decision arrives from Parliament."

He had published only three of his series when King George accused Massachusetts and the other colonies of disaffection. When Abigail read the speech in the *Massachusetts Spy* she sat down and wrote with a trembling hand to Mercy Warren:

"The die is cast. Yesterday brought us such a speech from the throne as will stain with everlasting infamy the reign of George III, determined to carry into execution 'the acts passed by the late Parliament, and to maintain the authority of the legislature over all his dominions.' The reply of the House of Commons and the House of Lords shows us the most wicked and hostile measures will be pursued against us. . . . We will rather choose no doubt to die the last British freemen than bear to live the first of British slaves . . . this now seems to be all that is left to Americans."

When John returned from Boston that night he set about reassuring her.

"Nabby, King George had not yet seen our petition from Philadelphia. We must wait for the King and Parliament to answer our petition. I have another four essays blocked out. Let's do our job day by day. It's the only means we have of shaping the future."

She thanked him for calming her, then went into the kitchen, swung the kettle over the fire and, when it boiled, poured them stiff rum toddies.

King George did not bother to answer the petition.

The second continental Congress would commence its proceedings on May 10, 1775.

John published his twelfth article and prepared to return to Philadelphia.

11

It began like any other day in mid-April, after the warmest winter Braintree could remember. The children had been restless during the early school hours, moving their chairs closer to the east windows and settling the warming sun over their shoulders like a gold-threaded cape.

Now they were down by the pond, Charley's feet already wet as he splashed about, Nab trying to keep in line the flotilla of baby ducks wobbling along in the wake of their flagship mother. John was planting potatoes four in a hole, and Abigail was churning butter on the back stoop, the sun sentiently warm on her hair lying loosely over her shoulders.

It was a germinal day, the fields showing bright rows of green, the fruit trees rampant with flowering buds, the sky a brittle, powder blue: the kind of weather in which man stands ruminatively by, letting the earth burgeon with its bounteous fruits.

But not for long.

The tall clock in the sitting parlor had worn its nine o'clock face before she came out on the porch, not quite an hour before. Now she heard the sound of thundering hoofs coming along the Coast Road, and a man crying out hoarsely:

"Fighting! Fighting on the Lexington Green! Regulars fired on our militia! Men dead and dying! Fighting, fighting . . . !"

In the angle between the two Adams houses she saw the rider go by, hatless, his clothes mud-spattered, his face caked with sweat and dust, his horse covered with lather, foam dripping from the bridle in his mouth.

John came running with all his might. He grabbed her by the arm.

She called out to Patty to go down to the children at the pond. She and John ran across their yard. The road was filled with people running toward the Meeting House. Around them as they moved swiftly along the road were their neighbors, the Curtises, the Fiske family, the Millers. The Braintree minutemen, formed only the month before and like similar groups in every town in Massachusetts pledged to be in complete formation within one minute, were streaking in from the forges, shops and taverns; the tanners, flour millers, coopers, cordwainers, the nearby farmers with their flintlocks, powder horns and knapsacks. The courier returned from South Braintree followed by whole families two and three to a horse. As they neared the Meeting House they saw the school emptying, the heavy-booted boatmen and fishermen surging up from the town landing; militiamen hurrying from Bass's Tavern and the group of houses scattered around John Hancock's old home. The entire town was gathered, in every state of dress and half dress, including the Quincys from Mount Wollaston.

The four companies of minutemen had already shaped up in front of Brackett's Tavern, Captain Seth Turner's company from South

Braintree forming rank under the Tree of Liberty, the three companies of Colonel Benjamin Lincoln's regiment lined up in the Old Coast Road. The crowds before the Meeting House and Brackett's, only a few feet apart, merged in the road.

Everyone crushed toward the courier. The air was cut, torn and twisted, but silent.

The courier began his recital. The crowd hung on every word, leaning forward toward the rider like a forest of white birches under a whip of wind.

At nine-thirty the night before, acting under General Gage's orders, a detachment of grenadiers and light infantry numbering close to a thousand men had shaped up their ranks at the foot of the Boston Common, between the drunkard's block and the pillory, embarked in long boats to cross the Charles River, and disembarked at Phips's farm. From there they were to take the Menotomy, Lexington and Concord road, surprise the countryside and capture the sizable store of arms at Concord, twenty-one miles away.

The Sons had not been idle. Dr. Joseph Warren summoned William Dawes and Paul Revere and, in the name of the Committee of Safety, ordered them to warn the countryside as well as John Hancock and Samuel Adams, who had been attending a meeting of the Committee of Safety and were staying with the Reverend Mr. Clarke in Lexington. Dawes left at once, before the troops had begun embarking; Revere paused long enough to have two lighted lanterns hung in the Old North steeple to warn Charlestown that the British were beginning a sortie by sea. Revere was then rowed to Charlestown, where he started off on a fast horse, awakened Captain Hull of Medford's minutemen to spread the alarm, continued on the road, pounding and awakening every family on the way including the village of Menotomy, reaching Lexington about midnight while the British were still midway in their ferrying.

Revere went direct to the Reverend Mr. Clarke's house to waken Samuel Adams and John Hancock and get them out of danger of capture. The bell of the church was rung, loud and commanding. The Lexington minutemen, a hundred and thirty strong, assembled on the Green fully armed a half hour after midnight. They remained in drill formation for an hour in the intense cold. Since there was no sign of the British they were dismissed to their nearby homes and to the taverns for those who lived too far. Captain Parker sent out scouts to keep him informed. It was not until four-thirty in the morning that the fourth scout managed to escape being captured and returned to Lexington with the intelligence that the British troops were but half a mile away.

Sixteen-year-old William Diamond beat his drum in a strident summoning. The minutemen poured out of the homes and taverns. Seventy-seven men lined up in a double row, flintlocks at the ready, powder and ball jammed into place. Scattered around the Common, also at the ready, were the rest of the fighting men.

At first light, five o'clock, six companies of British infantrymen arrived in Lexington under the command of Major John Pitcairn, lined themselves up in battle formation at the edge of the Green. Major Pitcairn told the Americans to lay down their arms and disperse. Captain Parker cried:

"Stand your ground! Don't fire unless fired upon!"

The two armies stood facing each other a hundred yards apart. Visibility was fragmentary, but good enough for Captain Parker to see that he was hopelessly outnumbered. He gave the order to disperse. The men started to move, though slowly. Then it happened. Someone fired a shot.

"Who was it?" a Braintree voice cried out.

"We don't know," the courier replied. "Likely the British, but some say as how it was a minuteman behind a wall. Then the British fired a volley. Our men were unprepared, half turned away. Eighteen fell. Eight are dead. Ten others hit bad."

The women began to weep. A man at the rear shouted:

"Didn't we fight back? Didn't we kill some of those bloody lobsterbacks?"

"Scattered shots. Hit nothing. Our ranks broke. The men ran. Left the field to the British. Their main contingent poured up on the Green under the command of Lieutenant Colonel Francis Smith, the band playing, the redcoats cheering their victory. The townspeople gathered up their dead and wounded. The British moved on through Lexington up the road to Concord where our supplies are kept."

The courier ran the back of his hairy hand across his parched lips and was off. The Reverend Mr. Wibird led a prayer for the dead.

The militia officers caucused. All four companies were ordered into day and night duty. They would await further news before moving out for Lexington. Scouts were sent down the Coast Road toward Boston, to Mount Wollaston and Weymouth to watch from the hills in case General Gage decided to invade by the sea. The meeting was dismissed so that the alarm companies could get their flintlocks, powder horns, ammunition, knapsacks.

Abigail and John walked home stunned. Tumultuous thoughts pounded like crashing waves inside their skulls. Eight Massachusetts men had been dropped in their tracks by British guns: was this an accidental skirmish, or would they live in the midst of a battlefield? In a few days John would be leaving for Philadelphia. What effect would the killings have on the temper of the Congress? Would the delegates become more determined to resist, or be convinced that the British were invincible?

In swift succession the emotions surged through Abigail's bosom: pity for the dead and wounded; hatred and rebellion against trained troops that fired on villagers; uncertainty over what the future held; fear that her world would be set on fire; chagrin that the minutemen had been routed; apprehension lest John Adams be blamed because of his inflammatory "Novanglus" articles for encouraging men to stand, to resist, when they had neither the training nor the equipment to defend themselves. And lastly grief; grief for the families of all the stricken.

Peter Adams came to the house red-faced with mortification. Elihu Adams was wild with anger. Their commanding officers had decided to keep their minutemen in Braintree. If General Gage's strategy was to subdue Massachusetts in one sweeping offensive, his troops would soon be coming up the road from Boston. Braintree must stop them, block the road to Plymouth.

A courier brought a report that the militia of a dozen surrounding towns were converging on Concord and Lexington. But the Braintree men could not reach Concord, even in a forced march, before dark. Still best to stand guard here.

"When there's fighting," cried Elihu, bitterly disappointed, "you go where the fighting is. You don't wait for it to come to you."

Peter was less tempestuous.

"John, no matter what the British do at Concord they can't barrack there. They got to march back to Boston. If it's too late to help at Concord, why can't we cross to Menotomy or Medford and intercept?"

"Bide your time," he advised. "We'll know very quickly where our men are needed most. This road is urgent to the British. We must wait."

Yes, thought Abigail, but for what? More battles? For the minutemen to stand up and fight? That also meant falling down and dying.

Did the eight dead men laid out in eight houses in Lexington care any longer about shibboleths of freedom and liberty? Was it better to have fought and died than never to have fought at all? How could she say, when she was not a soldier risking death?

People fell in, friends, neighbors, relatives. Abigail put out food. Few touched it. Elihu and Peter brought up a demijohn of rum from the cellar. The men kept their pewter cups filled. The alcohol neither relieved their intensity, loosened their tongues nor changed the expression in their apprehensive and at the same time angry eyes.

By now, or within a few hours, there would be as many Massachusetts militia between Lexington and Concord as British regulars. Some of their kin and neighbors had been killed. If they were shot at would they not shoot in return? Unless they fought, all was lost. All essays, speeches, resolutions could be given to the wind. King George III, his ministers, Parliament, would despise a feeble adversary. After a decade of opposition Massachusetts would be ground into the dust. In the concluding paragraph of his last article in the *Gazette*, published only two days before, John had proclaimed:

"The Massachusetts Company came over to America and brought their charter with them. As soon as they arrived here they got out of the English realm, dominions, state, empire, call it what name you will, and out of the legal jurisdiction of Parliament."

If it were true, as reports coming to them from every part of Massachusetts Bay Colony testified, that the "Novanglus" essays had persuaded the majority of the people that Parliament had no right to tax the colonies in America, or enforce Coercive Acts, then this was a revolution because men had become convinced that they had the right to resist. Captain Parker of the minutemen on the Lexington Green, uncertain of his position and unwilling singlehandedly to start a war, had ordered his men not to fire. But how long would officers issue this command? And how long would their men obey it?

The next news reached Braintree five hours later.

Young Samuel Prescott of Concord, courting in Lexington, had heard just after midnight of the advancing troops. He left on his horse with Paul Revere and Dawes and rode home to warn his village. Revere and Dawes were captured on the way. Only Prescott got to Concord. En route he went off the road a short distance to awaken Sergeant Samuel Hartwell. Mrs. Hartwell ran across the fields to warn their neighbor, Billy Smith. Billy raced on his fastest horse for Lincoln, rang the alarm and had his company assembled in one minute, plus dressing time. Newly elected Captain Smith then marched his men the four miles to Concord. His Lincoln company was the first outside militia to reach the neighboring town.

When Prescott reached Concord and gave the word, Amos Melven rang the alarm. At two o'clock in the morning three companies of minutemen and a reserve alarm company formed in front of Wright's Tavern. Feverish hours were spent removing the stores of powder, lead and flints from Concord homes, Meeting House and taverns to farms in the country. When an advance British unit reached Concord kegs of powder were still being hidden behind country houses, musket balls, flints and cartridges being put in barrels in attics and covered with feathers.

The main body of the British reached the center of Concord at seven o'clock. No minutemen were on the Common to greet them, but more than two hundred militia were deployed on the ridge overlooking the town. The British sent out flankers of light infantry. The militia retreated north to a second ridge. The grenadiers began a house-to-house search. At seven-thirty Lieutenant Colonel Francis Smith ordered seven companies of his light infantry to the North Bridge, causing the militiamen to retreat across the Concord River.

By nine o'clock the colonials had been reinforced by groups from Carlisle, Chelmsford, Westford and Littleton and now numbered over four hundred men. When the British in Concord set fire to the Town House and to Reuben Brown's harness shop, they believed that Concord was being destroyed, decided the moment had come to march to the rescue. As they came down the ridge the British pulled up the loose planks of North Bridge and fired three shots of warning.

The militia continued to come on. A redcoat fired into the militia, injuring two men. A volley was shot by the leading British company. Two militiamen fell dead. Major Buttrick of the militia, next in command, cried:

"Fire, fellow soldiers, for God's sake, fire!"

The militia obeyed. It was their first fire. Three redcoats fell. The British troops broke formation, scattered, fled back to Concord and their main contingent.

Sensing revenge for Lexington, the militia started to follow, but Lieutenant Colonel Francis Smith had come up with reinforcements. The British seemed confused, unwilling to attack or retreat. At ten in the morning they returned to the Concord Common. There they had stayed.

Her brother Billy had volunteered to lead his Lincoln minutemen across the North Bridge to disperse the redcoats, the very offer proving the will of every man in Massachusetts to fight with and for his neighbors.

Two hours later a new dispatch rider reached Braintree. From this point on there were riders and couriers every half hour.

The British companies had remained in Concord for two hours, until noon, resting the men who had been on the nightlong march, confiscating mattresses with which to carry their wounded back into Boston. When they left Concord the militiamen on the ridge, seeing that they were making for Meriam's Corner, took a short cut through Great Meadow. Other groups of minutemen and militia were already at Meriam's Corner, having come in from Billerica and Reading from the north, from East Sudbury to the south. By this time the British were outnumbered.

Again the firing and fighting appeared to start accidentally.

The British crossed a small bridge at Mill Brook. The last grenadier over, in anger or exasperation, fired his gun. Taking this as a starting signal, the American militia swarmed in from both sides of the road and from behind, and opened fire. Two redcoats were killed, a number wounded. A half hour later at Brooks Hill the militia from Sudbury attacked. Under cover of the attack the colonials took a short cut over Tanner's Brook and into the woods beyond. Here they dug in behind trees and stone fences. When the British came into the woods they were met by heavy fire. Eight of their soldiers fell dead. A considerable number were wounded. Now the first three militiamen died in their tracks when British flankers came from behind.

The next hour and a half, from one-thirty until three, was a debacle for the British. Fresh companies of militia arrived from Framingham and Woburn eager to be part of the battle. The British were exhausted, their ammunition running low, impeded by the growing number of wounded.

The collapse of the British troops took place at Fiske Hill, just inside Lexington, where the Lexington militia had been waiting for almost ten hours to avenge the deaths and wounding of their townsmen. They poured on an attack from all four sides.

Many British fell. The wounded were abandoned by their comrades, who started running through Lexington and across the Green in total disorder. The rout would have been complete except that their officers ordered them to halt or be shot. Desperate, they came to a realization that they faced either death or capture at the hands of the despised local militia; the most serious defeat of a British army in its long history.

The exultation in Braintree was uncontainable. The cottage was jammed with men and women who laughed or cried without knowing which they were doing. This was the great day for Massachusetts, the day when they had proven themselves to be men, demonstrated that no one could put them down.

Then news came up the road that this glorious victory had been snatched from their hands.

Lord Percy had been dispatched from Boston at nine o'clock that morning with a thousand fresh troops, including in their ranks seasoned battle veterans of the marines, as well as two heavy cannons. But that was only part of the tale. Lord Percy had had to take his thousand men through Cambridge to reinforce the beleaguered troops. There were six separate roads leading out of Cambridge, only one or two even indistinctly marked. The Patriots had been informed that the British had no maps. Cambridge was warned. At a hasty gathering the people had agreed to lock themselves in their homes and not budge out until the redcoats were gone. The road signs were removed, leaving the six roads indistinguishable threads through the woods. If by accident a Cambridge resident were to be found or caught by Lord Percy's men and asked the route to Concord, he was to point in the opposite direction, to Phips's Landing.

At noon Lord Percy and his rescue battalion reached Cambridge. They stood immobilized. At that moment a young man had come out of Harvard College, walked onto the Common, directed Lord Percy down the right road to Lexington and Concord.

Did anyone know who the informer was? No, except that he seemed too old to be a student. He was being sought.

When Lord Percy reached a point a half mile east of the Lexington Green his ranks enveloped the desperate, fleeing redcoats. Lord Percy trained his two cannons on the Americans, gave the troops a half hour to rest, then began the sixteen-mile retreat back to Boston.

The battle was far from over. The Americans flanked the British from both sides of the road, firing from behind houses, barns, trees, walls. Englishmen fell, some killed, some wounded. That they were not totally destroyed in the cross fire was due to the fact that the American flintlocks were not effective for precise aiming beyond a hundred yards. In their eagerness to get a closer shot at the retreating British, the militiamen sometimes forgot the redcoat flankers, who came up behind them and did some sharpshooting of their own. The most devastating battle took place at Menotomy where twenty militiamen were caught in and around the house of Jason Russell, trapped between the regulars and the flankers. Eleven had been shot to death. A few yards farther down the road a furious burst of American fire on an exposed British company killed twenty of the redcoats and wounded many more.

It had been sundown by the time Lord Percy led the remnants of his harassed and decimated troops into Charlestown where they were safe under the guns of the British warships. But so had the Americans come in, from as far north as Salem and as far west as Pepperell. Probably five thousand of them. Here in Charlestown General William Heath and Dr. Warren decided to organize the militia under a permanent military structure. They posted sentinels along the roads as far as the Charlestown Neck. The British, in comparative safety at the base of Bunker's Hill, secured an armistice with the selectmen of Charlestown so that they could be transported back to Boston by His Majesty's ships.

By morning the Americans were still there, having cooked their supper around communal campfires, wrapped themselves in blankets and slept beside their flintlocks.

Boston now lay under siege by the Massachusetts militia.

12

The information came to the Adamses quietly. A Weymouth man who had been visiting in Watertown brought a confidential message from Deacon Joseph Palmer, Mary Cranch's brother-in-law. Palmer, a member of the Committee of Safety from Braintree, had been in Watertown for a meeting of the committee when news reached him of the firing on the Lexington Green. He had sent out dispatch riders, north through Massachusetts to mobilize the militia, south through Connecticut to New York.

Deacon Palmer reported that the informer who had guided Lord Percy to the Lexington road was Isaac Smith, Jr. The news would be in Boston by now. The young clergyman might be in need of immediate defense. Who other than his kin by marriage, John Adams, should undertake it?

Abigail gulped bitterly several times before she could speak. A look at John's face reassured her. She turned to her neighbor, asked:

"Will we have trouble getting through Boston Neck?"

"Some, ma'am. But the British command is paralyzed with shock. The guard at the fortification seems without orders. There's pandemonium, hundreds of people milling in and out with cattle, wagons, carts of furniture. But any time now the walls could be closed."

Queen Street was dark, the ancient trees closing in the red sandstone walk with deep shadow. But there were lights in the downstairs rooms of the three-storied white brick house. The younger son, William, his eyes red with crying, admitted them. The family was in the sitting parlor, curtains pulled over the tall windows. In the glass globe suspended from the ceiling, in which she had formerly seen reflected the Turkey carpet, the Chinese chairs, the teak wainscoted walls, she saw instead the stricken faces of her uncle Isaac and aunt Elizabeth.

No greetings were exchanged. Though the Smiths had not sent for the Adamses it was apparent that they were expected. The air of the sitting parlor, tinged with its faint Chinese incense, was tense. Isaac, Jr., appeared to be the only unperturbed person in the room. His sea-green eyes were clear and cool, his fine ash hair neatly combed back from the ascetic brow. Apparently he expected John to begin the questioning. But John sat in silence, waiting to be invited into the discussion. Abigail began.

"Cousin Isaac, did you give the correct directions to Lord Percy and his troops to make their way to Lexington?"

"Yes, Cousin Abigail."

"Might I ask why?"

"Because he asked me."

"Did you know that Cambridge had agreed not to give him directions? And that if an answer had to be given it should be misinformation, directing him to Phips's Point?"

"No."

Abigail turned to his parents.

"Then Isaac is not guilty of violating any agreement."

"That makes no palpable difference," replied Isaac serenely. "I would have answered the question truthfully no matter how many instructions had been issued in Cambridge."

John spoke for the first time, but gently.

"Why would you have done that, Isaac?"

"I vowed when I was ordained a clergyman to tell the truth at all costs."

"At all costs to others?"

"To myself."

Abigail interposed. "Scripture tells us that there are times when silence is the proper moral stance."

"Withholding the truth when you possess it is a form of lying."

His father cried in anguish, "How could I have raised such an insufferable prig?"

He raised his arms over his son's head, fingers intertwined and clenched as though he were going to use them as a club on the finely shaped head. John interjected a legalistic question.

"Isaac, you didn't go out deliberately to meet and inform Lord Percy?"

"No."

"Suppose you had seen Percy from your window as he gazed perplexedly at the six different roads; would your moral duty have obliged you to leave your room and rush to his side?"

Isaac remained silent.

"What I'm trying to say is that your being on the Common at that particular moment was an accident. Accidents should not control our lives. When asked that question, you could simply have turned on your heel and walked away."

His father screamed, "There are fifty Americans dead and another forty wounded or missing, not to mention a hundred British dead and two hundred wounded or missing because of you."

His son's voice was calm. "I didn't kill those people, Papa. If the militia had not resisted there would have been no shooting. I'd be glad to nurse their wounds, help them to recover."

"You've done quite enough for them already! And for all the others who will be killed and maimed because you pointed the direction to a war."

"No, Papa, I tried to point away from it. Nobody is going to believe that in Massachusetts. But I ask one thing of you: don't think of me as a murderer. These battles have been building up for ten years, ever since the Stamp Act, which you led the fight against, John Adams. Your hand is as much on those Lexington and Concord triggers as mine. So are the fingers of all the Patriots. I tried to preach peace and was ostracized from my own church. I'm still preaching peace, and have to flee for my life!"

"Every man is entitled to a defense," said Abigail. "Perhaps you were so involved in your studies that you did not know the British have been trying to capture each town's supply of powder?"

"I knew their troops were moving through the countryside, but not their purpose."

John bounded up from his chair.

"Isaac, I think we're coming to the crux of this situation. Please understand that we are here to help you."

"I don't need any help."

"Apparently you do. From what I gather . . ."

Isaac, Jr., interrupted. "That's what I've been telling you all along: a mob knows no ethics except mindless force."

"That's not the point of issue here, Isaac. Do you approve of the British troops marching out to the surrounding Massachusetts towns in order to capture their caches of gunpowder?"

"Yes."

"Why?"

"Because if there is no gunpowder there can be no shooting. If there's no war no one can get killed."

"Quite a few people got killed yesterday because you gave proper directions to Lord Percy."

Isaac, Jr.'s face, which had been pale, now flooded with dark blood.

"I reject that assumption categorically. The killing was started by Lexington militiamen and British soldiers. It was continued by British soldiers at the bridge at Concord, and militiamen who followed them back along the road, shooting at them." He became more angry than Abigail had ever seen him. The strictly moral approach to his problem vanished.

"The Americans had one purpose in mind: to kill. They had been killing all down the line from Concord to Lexington. It's just as tenable to say that they would have killed the remaining seven hundred British soldiers as to imagine that they would have taken them prisoner. If you want to make this a legal case, then I can make an equal point that my directions to Lord Percy saved hundreds of lives."

Abigail walked to her cousin's side.

"Is it your thesis that no responsibility whatever rests with the British in these battles?"

"None. Or little. The Parliament passed laws in London. We in Massachusetts refused to obey them. We have been drilling minutemen for months with the idea of resisting. The British raids could have had one purpose only, to capture the powder so there could be no physical conflict. I spoke out against the so-called Patriots for committing acts of violence. Now apparently I've called down that same violence on my own head."

He looked at them steely-eyed.

"Very well. You have been the prosecutors, judges and jury. What is your verdict? Am I to be hanged from the gallows on the Boston Neck?"

"Isaac, we're trying to save you."

"From what exactly, Cousin Abigail? From the mob, or from my own moral righteousness?"

"If you tell Boston that you approve of the British having marched to take our stores, that you would help them again, you will never be able to live in this country."

"I don't intend to."

Isaac's mother rose slowly, put her arms around her son.

"My dear, what plan is in your mind?"

"No plan, Mother. I'll simply board the next ship that leaves Marblehead for England."

His father cried, "Isaac, don't you see that's an admission of guilt? You'll be called a Tory!"

Isaac turned to Abigail. "You told me I would bring great unhappiness upon my mother and father. You were right. But what have you proved? That violence has its inner logic that no amount of truth can conquer. I love my mother and father. I do not want to do them harm. But one always has to make choices. I know you would have done anything to help me if I could have offered you the slightest opportunity. But you must see that I cannot." He turned to his parents. "Don't be unhappy for me, for I shall not be unhappy for myself. I'll find a way to preach or teach in England, and make a life for myself there. When all of this unpleasantness is over, and old wounds have been healed, perhaps I'll come back."

He bowed formally to John.

"Please spread the word around Boston that my parents tried hard to make me see the error of my ways. Then perhaps Boston will forgive them."

He left the room.

They sat mutely in the sitting parlor, listening to the footsteps in the room above as Isaac, Jr., threw books and clothing into traveling boxes. Then he came thumping heavily down the stairs. He went out the back door. In a few moments they heard the hoofbeats of his horse carrying him away.

Abigail sat with her eyes tightly shut. They had lost the first member of their intimate family. Would he be the last?

The answer came as she and John stood at the front door, unwilling to leave their aunt and uncle so soon, yet knowing that the British might close the fortifications at the Neck by dawn. Isaac and Elizabeth urged them to make haste. There was the sound of a man hurrying up Queen Street, mounting the stairs. Isaac opened the door. There stood a dispatch rider. Abigail did not recognize him. Her uncle Isaac did.

"Yes, Jeremy, what is it?"

The man stood twisting his round hat before him in jerky, circular movements. He said in a constricted tone:

"Sorry to be the one. Your nephew Billy Smith . . . He was killed. At Concord. Leading his Lincoln company across the bridge."

BOOK FIVE

WOMAN IN THE TENT

1

THE April sun was up, weak with uncertitude, by the time they reached Lincoln and Billy's house. There was no one about. From the front porch they heard the groans of a wounded man. Abigail cried:

"They said Billy was dead!"

John pushed open the door. The horrendous suffering of the injured man filled the house. Catharine Louisa came forward, blood staining the front of her cotton frock. Abigail ran toward the room off the lean-to whence the cries were coming, pulled up sharply at the open door. On the bed, his scarlet coat with its facing of regimental colors half ripped off, was a young British grenadier.

Catharine's servant, Anne, came in, wiped clean the jagged bullet wound over the heart, applied a fresh bandage. The grenadier opened his eyes, said between gritted teeth:

". . . gold sovereign . . . lining my coat. When I die . . . take it."

Catharine said from the doorway, "You're not going to die. We've sent for a doctor. We'll nurse you."

Abigail stared at her sister-in-law's face. There was no grief in it for a lost husband, only compassion for this young lad with the corn-colored hair and azure-blue eyes. She gazed uncomprehendingly at John; he too was stunned. Abigail went to her sister-in-law.

"Billy?" she whispered.

Catharine's plain face became transfused with pride.

"He's a hero, Sister Abigail."

The stricken man was burbling low in his throat. Catharine dipped a cloth in a bowl of cold water, wiped the perspiration off the soldier's forehead. Abigail felt sick at her stomach. Was this the way Billy had died?

"Anne found this soldier in the field at daybreak. She and the hired hand carried him to the house."

"Catharine Louisa, Billy! What about Billy? Please tell us."

"He's gone on to Boston with his company. Going to stay with the Massachusetts militia until they drive the redcoats out."

"But the Concord bridge? The captain who led the company across was shot. We heard about it in Boston last night."

"That was Captain Isaac Davis from Acton," replied Catharine Louisa sadly. "He was given the order instead of Billy. Felled by the first volley."

The sudden personal relief made Abigail faint. She felt John's hand under her arm leading her into the dark sitting parlor.

"Billy is all right, Nabby. It was a mistake. Many people heard Billy offer to clear the bridge. Then the firing started. Evidently no one realized it was Captain Davis who led that first counterattack."

Tears came to her eyes. John held her face against the rough fabric of his waistcoat.

"And that poor boy in there. Half his chest gone," she sobbed. "God help us all. How terrible that I must be grateful for Billy's life while that English lad is dying in agony just a few feet from us."

"Dear soul, many men died yesterday. Many lie as desperately wounded as this boy. More will die. War and death are synonymous."

She raised her head.

"For the love of God let us not hate these men who are sent here to kill us and whom we will kill in turn."

Catharine came in with bowls of hot porridge. She handed one each to Abigail and John, then asked as though suddenly surprised:

"Why have you ridden all the way to Lincoln?"

John answered quickly:

"To make sure Billy was all right."

"That was thoughtful of you. But Billy can take care of himself. He's a good soldier. Sister Abigail, please eat your porridge. You look exhausted."

She could not swallow the nourishing mush. From the lean-to came the crying of the grenadier, a sobbing that filled her with unendurable pain. Not until this very moment, seeing the shattered boy in the place of the reportedly dead Billy, had she realized the full flesh-and-blood implications of John's long struggle: John's, and hers too. Men would have their breasts ripped open, many would die, many mothers, sisters, wives, children would be bereft and would grieve. And the most that one could pray would be:

"Not mine, dear Lord. I entreat Thee, not mine."

They reached Braintree at midafternoon. She went to bed early, slept fitfully until the following dawn. When she put a hand out for the reassuring touch of her husband she found him gone. She donned a warm robe, brushed her hair back from her forehead, went down the steep sharp steps to John's office. The door was open. He was writing by lamplight on his flat table.

"John, you lost one whole night's sleep. Why didn't you rest this morning?"

He kissed her cheek. There was high color in his face.

"I had a few hours. All I needed."

"Something has roused you. Come into the kitchen and tell me while I start breakfast."

He put wood on the fire while she took eggs from the cooler, turned the fry-skillet toward the flames. He worked the wheel of the herb crusher to secure flavoring for his omelette, then held the long-handled toaster over the fire with its slices of bread.

"I'm going to that camp. Retrace every step of the route from Concord through Lexington to Cambridge. Collect the data. Not only from the officers and the men who did the fighting, but the householders along the way. No one else will think to do it, and we're going to need this record for the future. To fix responsibility. To learn how we can win the battles we must fight. The Congress will want to know all this. You won't mind being alone for a couple of days?"

"Someone has to be the historian. Besides, I'm drained of all feeling."

He returned a few days later with a cold and fever. She put him to bed, plied him with her cousin Cotton's original prescription of strong beef broth and rum, then demanded news of Billy.

"He's in high fettle. Even with their dead and wounded the spirit of the people on that Concord–Lexington road is stronger than ever for independency. Enthusiasm for our cause is high at our camp. Dr. Joseph Warren told me that nine thousand of the militia have dug in. The British troops are now prisoners in Boston. They'll never get out again, except to sea."

His eyes clouded.

"But our men are sleeping on the ground, without tents or sufficient blankets. The only food is what is brought in by volunteers from the nearby villages. No latrines have been dug. The stench is overpowering. There's an abundance of preachers, but except for Cousin Cotton and a few Boston doctors, there is no medical help, no drugs, no one to nurse them. We need a whole medical organization, and nothing has been started."

She brought him breakfast in bed. He was a natural talker as well as eater, able to combine the two arts without loss of a rhythmic word or mouthful. Although the Massachusetts Provincial Council had appointed two commanding generals, William Heath and Artemas Ward, the militiamen insisted upon remaining in their home-town companies and would take orders from no one but their own elected officers. Soldiers without permission or notice came and went; they were under no obligation to remain. There were no facilities for bathing. Some of the men who managed to get under a roof had caught infectious diseases because of the overcrowding, and were buried nearby in too shallow graves. The British army had women along to wash the clothes, but after two "fire ships" were drummed out of the American camp, no other women were allowed in.

Powder and shot were scarce. The officers had no way to replace them. There was no money or authority to buy supplies. Individual militiamen who still had a little cash were provisioning themselves and their friends. It was an army with the will to resist, but little else. Unless the local militia companies were absorbed into a Massachusetts Army, the Massachusetts Army into a New England Army, the New England Army into an American Army composed of troops from all thirteen colonies, with commanding officers appointed by the Congress; unless the Congress could then raise money, guns, powder and shot, food, clothing, tents, blankets, this beginning army would disintegrate.

"And then the contest will be lost," John said mournfully, sipping boiled milk to stop up his bowels. "King George III, his ministers and the Parliament are determined to crush what they call our 'rebellion.' They have the wherewithal: an army, a navy, central authority, organization, millions of pounds in cash with which to provision their men and pay them wages."

He insisted on getting out of bed. She wrapped a wool blanket about his shoulders, watched him as he paced the room, his round face perspiring from the fever, dark circles of anxiety under his eyes. Samuel Adams and John Hancock were already in Worcester; Robert Treat Paine and Thomas Cushing had left for Philadelphia. John should be leaving at once. She thought:

"Perhaps if I asked my father for the loan of his one-seat sulky?"

She knew he would feel better once he could get a purchase on the problems of that chaotic army camp. His eyes were overbright from something beyond fever.

"Abigail, we must have an army with the best officers and marksmen of every colony combined. All of us from Massachusetts want it, and the Virginians equally. We must also have a single command. We have good New England men experienced from the French and Indian War: Ward, Thomas, John Whitcomb, Joseph Frye, Israel Putnam. But wouldn't it be unwise to appoint a New England man to command? Someone from the outside could represent all thirteen colonies. Then all men would serve under him."

"Do you have such a man in mind?"

"I'm going to try to persuade our Massachusetts delegates to vote for him. He's a Virginian. Sat in the House of Burgesses for fifteen years. A soldier and officer from his youth, a lieutenant colonel at twenty-two, General Braddock's aide, later colonel and commander-in-chief of all Virginia forces. He owns a large plantation at Mount Vernon but is the most modest, amiable man I've met. He's a natural leader for the field, emanates poise, dignity and inner strength. If we could have him as general of an American army it would cement the colonies."

"Has anyone been proposed?"

"Prior to Lexington and Concord we had no need for a commanding general. Now we must have our best talent to mold those militiamen of ours into an integrated army and to organize the thousands of other soldiers we will need. We have little room for mistakes. George Washington is the man who can do it."

He stopped his pacing.

"If I could persuade Bass's son to come along and take care of me I'd leave for Philadelphia at once."

"I'll send Johnny across the fields to fetch him, then ride over to Weymouth. The upholstered seat of my father's sulky is comfortable, and you could close yourself in against the weather."

2

Two days later, April 26, 1775, he was gone, ensconced in her father's light carriage, the wheels higher than the horse's back, his trunk strapped on top, young Bass riding alongside. She and John had agreed that separation from Britain after Lexington and Concord was inevitable. Yet it was a blow, leaving an aching void. Nothing could be the same after the loss of their Mother Country. Abigail was heartsick at no longer being an Englishwoman.

She poured out her feelings through her pen to Mercy Warren:

"Our only comfort lies in the justice of our cause. . . . O Britain, Britain, how is thy glory vanished, how are thy annals stained with the blood of thy children."

It served no purpose to look back. If they had lost the dearest country on earth they had no choice but to create another dear country in its place. Massachusetts Bay Colony alone was too small and weak to stand as a nation among such giants as Russia, France, Spain and England. The thirteen colonies, with their common origins and common interests, if they could achieve union, could give birth to a country that could stand free. They would all have a hand in creating it.

She was not ignorant of the difficulties. John had shown her his journal detailing the differences, dissensions, jealousies, feuds and quarrels among the fifty-six delegates, the deep-seated reluctance of some of the men to leave the British Empire, men in front of whom the word "independence" could not be uttered for fear they would quit the Congress. Yet in most lesser matters they had managed to debate freely, respect one another's points of view and abide by a majority vote. Each delegate had had to swallow his disappointment on some matter important to him and to his colony: how conciliatory they should be to King and Parliament; how much control they would have to give up to the Congress. By the same token each delegate had achieved some measure of the hope for the "recovery of their just rights and liberties" which he had carried with him over the hundreds of miles along strange, rutted roads.

John left for the second Congress with a consuming purpose: to achieve political unity of the thirteen colonies. Lexington and Concord would help his cause immeasurably. He would work for union; but a majority of the colonies had to agree to union before union could begin.

She heard a carriage turn into the entrance before her house. She opened the door to find her cousin Hannah Quincy Lincoln standing there. It was Hannah Lincoln to whom she had been writing fourteen years before, sitting with her legs under her on the bed in the parsonage in Weymouth when Mary called from below, "Nabby, Richard is here. Brought company. That lawyer from Braintree."

Hannah's husband, Dr. Bela Lincoln, had died two years ago. Hannah, childless, had returned to the home of her father, Josiah Quincy. Though she had lived in nearby Hingham, Abigail rarely saw her. There was a story abroad that Dr. Lincoln had not got along with the ubiquitous Quincy family. Hannah had not even come in to witness the trial of the British soldiers in which her oldest brother, Samuel, had prosecuted, and her youngest, Josiah, Jr., had defended. Now it was rumoured that Hannah was considering marrying a brother of Abigail's aunt Elizabeth Smith. If that happened, Hannah would come into Abigail's family on her father's side as well as her mother's.

Hannah walked into the parlor and sat on the edge of Abigail's yellow couch, hands clasped tightly in her lap. She was no longer the pretty, flirtatious girl Abigail remembered. There were radiating cartwheels of wrinkles at the corners of her eyes though she could not yet be forty, but she was still attractive, with the well-modeled Quincy features.

"It's my brother Samuel I've come about," explained Hannah. "The Lexington–Concord battle has decided him. He's leaving for England with the first sail."

"I'm sorry, Hannah. I heard him quarrel with his wife about it."

"That's why I took the liberty of asking him to meet me here. I wanted to spare my father. The loss of my older brother at sea, the absence of Josiah, Jr. . . ."

"My house is yours, Hannah."

She brought them both a cup of chocolate. They sat in silence sipping the sticky sweet liquid. Then there was a solid knuckle-rapping on the front door. Abigail admitted Samuel Quincy. He and Hannah gazed at each other. Abigail asked:

"Would you like to speak privately?"

"No, stay," replied Samuel. "You're family."

Hannah wasted no time on the amenities.

"Samuel, one of our brothers died upon the seas."

"I will not die at sea. I have many years to live."

"You will say that your body is sound; but the sick in mind call for more than Aesculapian aid."

"Sister, are you suggesting that everyone who wants to go home is sick in mind?"

"Cousin Samuel, you bade me stay," commented Abigail. "May I then suggest that this is your home? We were all born within ten miles of this room."

"Home is where your loyalties lie, Cousin," Samuel replied gently. He turned back to his sister. "The list of lawyers who will be leaving Massachusetts for England in the coming months is long and impressive. Jonathan Sewall follows me almost immediately. Benjamin Gridley, nephew of Jeremiah Gridley, John Adams's mentor, is leaving. So are Andrew Cazneau and William Browne, judges of the Superior Court. Cousin Abigail, I have heard your husband say that Judge Browne was never a Tory. Two other lawyers who have worked alongside John, Robert Auchmuty and Sampson Salter Blowers, won't be far behind; nor will Daniel Leonard, one of John's oldest friends. Nor Samuel Fitch, whom John recommended to succeed Jonathan Sewall as advocate general. Not to mention Timothy Ruggles and William Brattle. Sister, can we all be sick in mind? I have just mentioned half of the best lawyers in Massachusetts Bay Colony."

Abigail was aghast at this list of names. She could not believe it. Hannah held Samuel by the heavy, rounded shoulders.

"Samuel, let it not be told in America, and let it not be published in Great Britain, that you fled from your country, the wife of your youth, the children of your affection, and from your aged sire. Samuel, for the love of God, arouse from your lethargy, let reason take the helm, disregard all greatness but greatness of soul. Do not call what I have said impertinent, but ascribe it to the anxiety of a sister really distressed for you. Your country is a land flowing with milk and honey; inequity of all kinds is punished; its religion is free from idolatry. Would you leave it for a country where evil works are committed with impunity? Can you take fire into your bosom and not be burned?"

Samuel took his sister in his arms.

"Hannah, it's long since settled. I sail on the next tide. My possessions are aboard. I came not to be converted but to embrace you with farewell."

He was gone. Hannah sank into a chair.

"I failed! I could not find the right words."

Abigail put a hand comfortingly over her cousin's clenched fist, the knuckles showing white.

"There are no right words, Hannah. There are only the words and arguments we believe in. In all these years I've never heard any convinced person, on either side, be swayed as much as one inch or one syllable. They are wrong, terribly wrong, but nothing will ever prove it to them, not even our independency. They are the truly lost souls in this conflagration. No one will want them, neither England nor America. May God have mercy on them."

3

When John was away at the first Congress she was the only Braintree woman whose husband had gone off to the wars; for that was how she thought of him, as a soldier encamped in Philadelphia fighting the kind of war he knew best how to wage. Now many of the surrounding farmers had joined the besieging Massachusetts Army that was keeping General Gage and his troops confined to Boston. Their wives, although their husbands were only a few miles away, missed them as sorely as Abigail did John at three hundred miles' distance. A comradery sprang up between Abigail and these women. Braintree men did not look with favor on their women visiting, except after preaching. The men drank at the taverns, played checkers at the general store, went hunting and fishing, drilled with the militia, ran foot races on Artillery Election Day. Their wives stayed home, from first light to first dark their lives a continuous stream of chores. Idle hands were unknown. Few of them could read, since the men believed that education addled a woman's simple brain.

Each afternoon now the women met in a different home to drink coffee and exchange news of the Massachusetts and British armies. They traded recipes, remedies for children's croup. Each goodwife had a patchwork quilt in her kitchen or parlor on an oblong stretcher, three feet off the floor, at which several women sewed while Abigail read to them from the latest newspapers. Abigail set up a stretcher in her own sitting parlor with chairs around the four sides for the women to huddle companionably while quilting on the odd-shaped random patches sewed into a potpourri of color.

She looked forward to this social hour, the women dressed in their white caps with the encircling white ribbon, their long curls falling forward over their shoulders as they leaned over the quilt, the full-necked dresses with puffed sleeves and long full skirts of light blue or gray wool from their own looms, the linen collars and cuffs freshly washed and pressed. Susanna Baxter was seven months in circumstances, Theodora Billings five; both were quiet women. The Clark women, Hannah and Mary, entertained with droll gossip. The oldest was Ann Savil, whose husband, Dr. Elisha Savil, had rented this house before John inherited it and remodeled it to give him the first law office in Braintree. A number of Adamses fell in: Elihu's Thankful, Peter's Mary, Mehitable, a cousin; as well as the bright young Thayer wives. Soon other women of the neighborhood asked if they might join. Deborah Wild's husband was a fence viewer, Sarah Spear's a surveyor of highways, Debora Mann's a fire ward.

When they discussed the Congress the townswomen turned to Abigail. Was there any chance to better their own lot, as women and wives, now that the colonies had a Congress?

"Can we get something for the ladies?" Abigail asked. "Assuredly, it's time."

The wives all talked at once, but that did not hamper clarity. Everyone knew the story. Women were treated as vassals; their dowries and property came into the control of their husbands; they had no suffrage unless they owned substantial property; and they had no voice in church. They could go nowhere, do nothing without their husbands' consent, not even make decisions about their children. The law and the courts put full power in the hands of the husbands, too many of whom were arbitrary and cruel. Sarah Arnold, whose husband, Moses, had lost a hand in the explosion of a gun, said softly, stitching her words into the conversation as she sewed connecting thread through two patches:

"It is the purpose of the Congress to pass laws, is it not?"

The women sewing patches or working at the quilt-stretch fell silent.

"Yes, in certain fields. But this Congress is concerning itself with independency. And provisioning our army."

"Nothing about personal lives?"

This cry came from a middle-aged woman whose husband had held a series of positions for the town, culler of staves, sealer of shingles and leather, but who was known as a tyrant in his home.

"If we remain English," Abigail said quietly, "we shall have to live under English law. If we become independent we can make our own laws."

Susanna Belcher spoke up. She was a thin-faced woman, blunt in manner, educated by her male relatives as Abigail had been.

"We must find a way to tell the men in Philadelphia what laws we women want."

"I have thought about it," Abigail reassured her. "When my husband comes home I shall be our advocate."

The women returned to their homes at midafternoon. By dusk militiamen began arriving for supper and lodging for the night, traveling singly or in small groups, down the road from Plymouth, Taunton, Barnstable, up the road from Cambridge, some on their way to join their town companies, others going home for a day or a week to farm.

They came into the Adams house ragged and filthy, with several days' beard growth, garbed in smallclothes, breeches fastened below the knee, coarse stockings and cowhide shoes. Their coats and waistcoats were overlarge for the warm weather, dyed in every color that could be pounded out of oak bark or sumach. Some wore long linsey-woolsey pants, others loose calico frocks. The officers had swords made by their local smithies. The soldiers carried every manner of weapon: old French guns captured at Louisbourg in King George's War; Spanish guns seized in Havana decades before; the heavy queen's arm, taken during the conquest of Canada. Every man was his own armorer and arsenal, for few soldiers could fire let alone provide the powder and ball for his companion's weapon. They introduced themselves to Abigail:

"Private Eb Netcher, Bridgewater militia, ma'am."

"Sergeant Menk, Duxbury, rejoining."

By nightfall there were a dozen or more eating from the fifteen-gallon pot of stew into which she threw anything available: corn, barley, potatoes, pieces of beef or pork or mutton. Each held out his pewter dish while Patty ladled, then gave him a hot biscuit. Patty was tireless, loved the activity and company, helped Abigail search out food in the countryside when the Adams larder ran low.

After eating, the soldiers washed their bowls and spoons at the yard pump, put them back in their knapsacks, exchanged bits of news with Abigail, left letters on John's desk to be given to the next man going to their town, then took their blankets and flintlocks to the barn and slept in the hay. When men began arriving without equipment, Abigail gathered up the blankets and mattresses she could requisition. When there were too many for the barn, the men stretched out in rows in the kitchen or John's office, using their hats for pillows. Those returning from the camp at Cambridge sometimes asked permission to wash their shirts, underwear and socks that had not been off them for weeks. She supplied each with a dab of soap from her cellar barrel.

The severe problem was the sick ones, trudging in from the Roxbury or Cambridge camp with sore throat, body rashes, dysentery. Abigail had neither the knowledge nor medications to treat them. Dr. Thomas Phipps came in each evening before supper, and Cotton Tufts scoured the countryside to keep a supply of medicines in a special box-cabinet he installed in the Adams lean-to. All Abigail could do was give them comfort and company, saving for the seriously ill the delicacies of a boiled egg, a cup of milk, a piece of roasted chicken, a dram of rum before sleeping. In the morning they ate a dish of corn-meal porridge or hasty pudding, shouldered their knapsacks, bandoleers, guns and were gone, murmuring their thanks.

"Kindest regards to your husband, ma'am."

"Tell him to do good by us in Philadelphia."

By seven the house was empty, windows and doors opened to draw off the fetid night odors, the floor broomed, kitchen scrubbed, made ready for that afternoon's influx, ten or fifty, she could never know in advance.

The second house, for which she was still paying Peter when she could scrounge up any cash, she used for the distressed inhabitants of Boston, Patriot families who had secured permission to leave the starving city but had nowhere to go. General Gage had promised to let them take out their personal possessions, yet when they reached the fortifications at the Neck the guard stripped their carriages and carts, threw out the furniture, confiscated the valuables, leaving many of them with little but the clothes on their backs.

Every Braintree household was taking in all the refugees it could hold. Some of the families had three and four children, but there could never be more than one room to a group. Abigail settled them into the sitting parlor, the attic, the barn. During the emergency John's mother and Colonel Hall went to live with one of Hall's sons in order to release one more room. Abigail's sister Betsy came whenever she could, arriving in the parsonage farm cart loaded with food for Abigail's communal pot.

Betsy was not happy these days; she had not been on good terms with her family since she had permitted rumors to get started about herself and the impecunious twenty-six-year-old schoolteacher, John Shaw. Abigail had met him a number of times, an ethereal chap with light brown hair and eyes, a good teacher and student who had done well at Harvard and had announced that he might one day become a clergyman, though he was not in the slightest hurry to be ordained. Weymouth had not taken to him, perhaps because he had Calvinist leanings. John had liked his candor, but the Reverend Mr. Smith's congregation decided he had shown folly and imprudence in proposing to Betsy so quickly, with no means of support. Betsy defended him hotly, saying, "I do not think there is one in this family that will pretend they ever heard him say anything which the most jealous prude could blame." John Shaw had to move out of the Smith house.

"Betsy, what shall I do with these poor refugees? They ask for a night and stay a week. Now I have to turn away exhausted people with no place to sleep. I can tell from their faces that they don't believe I haven't another inch of space."

"We'll put up a sign: *Rooms by the night*. You harbor the families their first night out from Boston, when they desperately need lodging and friendship. By morning they must move out to farther villages."

"Have you looked at their faces when they're told to move on? Many of them feel that the farther they go the smaller chance they will have of getting back."

Before he left John had told her:

"Keep your spirits composed and calm. Don't suffer yourself to be disturbed by idle reports and frivolous alarms." Then he had added, "In case of real danger, of which you cannot fail to have previous intimations, fly to the woods with our children."

Each day had its alarm. The Quincys on the bay had to flee their homes several times a week because the militia outlook observed British transports approaching. One Sunday morning she arose at six to learn that Weymouth had fired its alarm guns; her father's church bell had been ringing continuously. She sent an express rider to Weymouth, but her mother and father reached Braintree soon after, followed by the families living near the parsonage. Three British sloops and one cutter had come out from Boston, dropping anchor just below Great Hill. It was reported that three hundred redcoats had landed and were marching on the town. Her aunt Lucy Tufts had ordered her bed thrown into a cart, climbed in and been driven by her boy to Bridgewater.

The Braintree militia, Elihu and Peter among them, were off on the double to save Weymouth. Within a few hours two thousand soldiers of Suffolk County had converged there. However what the British had wanted to capture was the hay on Grape Island. The militia took to boats, drove off the British, burned the hay. Elihu was exultant.

"They had to run. It proves we can stop them anywhere. Sister Abigail, help me get a commission in the Massachusetts Army."

"Elihu, your mother is violently against it."

"That's because she never got over that scare about Billy. But Billy didn't get killed."

Abigail turned away, gazed sightlessly out the west window over her ripening fields. Someone in the family had perished, but he had not been given a soldier's burial. Kind, lovable, loyal Josiah Quincy, Jr., had spent the wet, freezing winter in London, gaining friends for the colonies and their cause. But Dr. Cotton Tufts had been right about the tuberculosis. Josiah had not survived the voyage home, dying within sight of the Massachusetts coast. He had done his job, his diary proved as much, though vital information had died with him because it had been too confidential to set down in writing.

Even during Josiah's funeral rites in the family home on Mount Wollaston there had come warning cries from the sentries posted on the hill. British troops were about to be landed upshore. The women fled, Abigail taking Josiah, Jr.'s thirty-year-old widow and three-year-old son home with her. Abigail Quincy's burden was a heavy one, for her daughter had died just a few days before. Yet she engaged in no lamentations.

"I'll be able to raise my son with wonderful memories of his father," she said to Abigail. "And I won't quarrel with the Lord's decision."

Abigail turned from her reverie to Elihu Adams.

"John wrote me asking whether you or Peter intended to take a command in the army. He said he would leave you to your own inclinations and discretion, but if you should be inclined, you should apply to Colonel Palmer and Dr. Warren."

Elihu beamed with joy.

"Would you write to Dr. Warren for me? He has the most influence."

"I'll do as you want. But, Elihu, don't lay the responsibility for this on John. Your mother would never forgive him."

"Nobody's responsible for nobody else, Sister Abigail. We all got a right to do what we want to do."

She sat at her desk in the borning room writing to Dr. Joseph Warren:

"A brother of Mr. Adams's, who has been a captain of a company in this town, is desirous of joining the army provided he can obtain a berth; he would prefer a major's to any other."

The note finished, she thought:

"Are we indeed not responsible for others? John knew that Josiah, Jr., had a weak chest. Should he have stopped him, while believing him the best man for the delicate task in London? Should I stop Elihu when he wants desperately to fight, because his mother trembles for him? But have I not trembled because my husband might be captured, tried for treason? I have never tried to stop John. Should I have?"

She sighed:

"We get all the questions to ask, and none to answer."

4

The next British shot was fired by a writer parading in the grand uniform of an English general: "Gentleman Johnny" Burgoyne, playwright by profession and soldier by necessity. He had recently arrived with Generals Henry Clinton and William Howe on the *Cerberus*, sent by George III to quell the rebels. Burgoyne asked before entering Boston Harbor, "How many regulars in Boston?" "About five thousand," came the reply. Burgoyne exclaimed, "What! Ten thousand peasants keep five thousand King's troops shut up? Well, let us get in, and we'll soon find elbow room!" Burgoyne was convinced that all that was needed to disband the militia army at Roxbury and Cambridge was a proclamation, but a proclamation so brilliantly written that the locals would see the folly of their uprising and sue for forgiveness. General Gage allowed Burgoyne to compose the proclamation.

Abigail got her copy in Braintree on a Tuesday morning. It had been printed in Boston the day before, on June 12, 1775. Burgoyne described the Lexington–Concord battle as the outrage of the King's troops being attacked. He ridiculed the militia and its "preposterous parade of military arrangement, affected to hold the army besieged." In order that not too many of the militia should be killed, the British mercifully offered pardon to everyone except the archtraitors, Samuel Adams and John Hancock. Braintree's Patriots were hurt that their representative, John Adams, had not also been proscribed.

The effect of the proclamation was to infuriate the New Englanders, make the besieged British in Boston look ridiculous to themselves as well as to New England, and arouse new recruits for the Massachusetts ranks. And just in time. Within two days news reached the Provincial Congress sitting in Watertown that Generals Gage, Clinton, Burgoyne and Howe had agreed on a course of action. They would attempt to control the two sets of heights overlooking Boston and the only two avenues of attack, Dorchester Heights and Bunker Hill, which overlooked Charlestown and its Neck. Then the British would be safe. They could not be invaded by the militia, or bombarded if the colonials unearthed some artillery.

The news of the plan reached the Provincial Congress by a circuitous route. British officers were talkative; a New Hampshire man, visiting Boston, was told the details of the British proposal. Knowing no Patriot in Boston to whom he could impart his information, he took it home with him to Exeter. Here he confided his news to his selectmen. The next morning Exeter sent a courier to Watertown. Two days later, June fifteenth, the Committee of Safety met, decided that since the British plan called for the fortification of Bunker Hill on the eighteenth, the militia would beat them to it.

All day of the sixteenth there was movement, suspense, an air of impending happenings. Word reached Braintree that Harvard College was emptying its library. No one knew exactly what was going on. Even so, Abigail comforted herself, she knew more than the British, for complete as was the American spy system inside the British army, just as complete was the blockage of any intelligence that might seep into General Gage's headquarters about the activities of the rebels.

She went to sleep Friday night anxious and uneasy. There were no soldiers billeted with her. The outward movement of militiamen going home had ceased. All those headed for the camp were in a hurry to push on.

At four in the morning the air of the graying dawn was shattered by the firing of a gun. By the time a second shot was heard she was out of bed, dressing hastily by candlelight. With the third cannonading she had Johnny up. He slipped into his clothes and together they ran through the fields, across the bridge, up Penn's Hill to its summit.

"What's happening, Mama?"

"I don't know, Johnny. But those were a ship's guns firing, I'm sure."

"At what? They can't reach our camps at Cambridge or Roxbury."

"Something else has happened. We'll have to wait for more light."

They did not have to wait long. The big guns began firing again. Somewhere over Boston she could see the shells exploding, first a ball of fire, then smoke blown by the wind. Behind each burst was another battering of the dawn by the noise of additional guns firing at regular intervals. The mound of sky over Boston was alight, torn and dissected.

Then came a lull. The sun had risen. It was a clear day, without fog or cloud, warm on one's face.

"Come, Johnny, we'll go down to the house. The little ones will be up."

"Has it stopped for good, Mama?"

"Hard to tell. We don't know what started it. There should be a dispatch rider with news for us before long."

There had been a number of skirmishes before this. The militia had captured a British boat when, after a raid on Hog and Noddle's islands on May twenty-seventh, the schooner *Diana* with four four-pounders and several swivels was grounded and then abandoned by the British. The Americans had boarded her, carried away what plunder they could and then fired the hull. But never before had she heard a cannonading of this intensity. Were the British preparing a major attack? If so, this road would be one of the main battle lines.

As she crossed the field to her house she saw people standing in the road, others hurrying to the Meeting House or to Brackett's Tavern.

There were tasks to be accomplished. The first was to send one of the hands to Elihu's house in South Braintree to tell him that if the firing grew more serious she and the family would come to stay with him. Then she saw that Nab, Charley and Tommy were properly dressed, preparing for each a bundle of clothing to last the emergency. Next a supply of food had to be packed into baskets, stored in the farm cart, the horse hitched to it, ready to leave at an instant's notice.

It was eight o'clock by the time this was done. She kept the solemn-faced children outside the kitchen door. As the clock in the sitting parlor chimed its eight count, the bombardment grew, a solid and continuous cannonading, as though all eight of the British men-of-war in the harbor had formed a tight scimitar around Boston and were firing their hundreds of nine- and twelve-pounders as fast as the gunners could load them. The house shook, the windows rattled, pots fell off their hooks in the fireplace. A Delft plate, exposed on top of the bowfat, crashed onto the wide wooden planks.

The children ran in from the yard, their eyes wide with terror. Her brother-in-law Peter thrust himself hurriedly into the kitchen, carrying his flintlock and knapsack.

"We're moving up to the Roxbury fortifications, Sister. Whole company. If the redcoats come out the Neck, we'll fight 'em there. We'll keep scouts coming down the road, soon as we know what to tell."

"I'll wait word, Peter."

"There'll be time aplenty for you to move the young. All five Braintree companies will be on our road. Bring the horse and wagon out of the barn, keep 'em under the big tree. Then, at the warning of the bell, you'll be gone like a shot. I sent Mary and the kids to Elihu's. Wait there, all of you, until Elihu or I come for you."

"Agreed. Good luck!"

He ran the few steps to John's dry rock wall, vaulted it and was gone. The alarm company, the old men and the boys, were stretched out between Brackett's Tavern and the Meeting House.

Abigail took the children into John's office, told them to take their accustomed seats about the clients' table. The constant roar of the cannon was distressing. She was hardly able to make herself heard as she read to them from the *Puzzling Cap*.

"It's all right, Ma," Johnny said comfortingly. "We'll just sit quiet until we have to go."

She sat with her head down, hands in her lap, waiting.

The sun was rising high in the sky and the day growing warm when she heard a great outcry, threw open John's door. The first of the express riders had stopped at the Meeting House. The bell was not ringing. That meant the redcoats had not yet come out the Neck. It was safe for her to go down the road.

The women of the town were there, those with whom she had visited, sewed, who had helped feed and shelter the soldiers these past two months. On the porch of the Meeting House were two of the elder selectmen, and the courier talking excitedly to her uncle Norton Quincy. Forming the outer ring of the crowd, all faces turned upward, was the alarm company.

"It's not what we think," Norton Quincy cried out. "The British are not attacking our men at Roxbury or Cambridge."

"Then what is it?"

The expression on her uncle's face was crossed between puzzlement and awe. His voice carried piercingly.

"It's us. We carried the fight to them. Our men from the Cambridge camp, three regiments, eight hundred men, assembled on the Cambridge Common a little after six o'clock. Down the line toward Charlestown they picked up another two hundred Connecticut men. When night fell they came to the Charlestown Neck and took the road that led up to Bunker Hill. Built a fort there. The British cannonading tried to knock down our breastworks. Not a shot has touched us. We command the heights. Return to your homes, all but the militia. We'll communicate the news as quick as it reaches us."

It was not until one-thirty in the afternoon that the fully equipped British soldiers, with guns, bayonets, hundred-pound knapsacks and blanket rolls on their backs, disembarked from North Battery and landed on the Charlestown peninsula. The small boats carried only a few men at a time, and it would be three in the afternoon before the more than fifteen hundred redcoats for the first two attack waves reached the Charlestown shore to begin their assault.

At midday there had come frightening news: the Massachusetts Army, which had committed some thirty-five hundred of its men to the building of the fortifications and their defense, had made a fatal error during the blackness of the night. Instead of digging their trenches and erecting their breastworks on Bunker Hill they had somehow settled on Breed's Hill, lower down the slope. Had they fortified Bunker Hill, and the British attack proved too strong, the Massachusetts Army could have retreated down through the Charlestown Neck to safety. But Breed's Hill was an inescapable trap. The British had only to land their troops around the hill to surround the Massachusetts Army and come at it from all sides. Being encircled, the militia would have no possible way to escape.

Boston's entire population, Tory and Patriot alike, was on the rooftops and surrounding hills to witness the battle. The Tories were reported to be exultant. The Massachusetts Army had made the kind of tactical error a raw peasant army could be expected to make. By nightfall the siege of Boston would be lifted.

"Ma, would you want to be in our house in Boston," Johnny asked, "so you could watch it?"

"I don't know, Johnny. Let's go back up Penn's Hill. Maybe we'll be able to tell something from the firing."

Reaching the peak, they looked over the lower green-treed knolls to the north to the milk-gray waters of the bay. Great volumes of black smoke were funneling heavenward. Abigail caught her breath sharply.

"They've set fire to Charlestown!"

British warships lying off the coast were still lobbing in fire shells. Abigail and her oldest son stood hand in hand, pressed against each other's side while a giant furnace of red flame leaped skyward. Charlestown would be leveled to ashes: her father's parental home, all his parents' possessions, their barns and orchards, the church and Meeting House.

For the first time in her life Abigail Smith Adams cursed her ill fortune at not being a man. Then she could have been on Breed's Hill, gun in hand, ready to fight when the waves of redcoats came up the slopes.

She heard the fast firing of guns: sharp, short volleys, sounding with utter clarity across the flawless summer day. She had no way of knowing whose guns they were, or who was being hit, for her view of Breed's Hill was cut off by an intervening range. But from the gunfire she could guess that a major battle was taking place.

The firing stopped as abruptly as it had begun. A heavy silence fell over the countryside. Abigail could see the white gunsmoke streaming across the sky.

She put her arm about her son's shoulders. The quiet could only mean that the British had encircled Breed's Hill and captured it. If there were more firing, then perhaps all was not lost.

She stood listening with every fiber of her ears and mind. At last it came, perhaps a half hour after the first sustained volley, another crescendo of shooting; then another silence; later a third, lighter firing, but sustained longer. Then, with the dusk, utter silence.

She stumbled down the well-worn trail, Johnny leading her across their fields, under the trees and into the kitchen. Once again she would have to sit by her hearth and wait.

It was almost midnight before the full story reached Braintree, brought in by Peter, Elihu and a courier, dirty, hungry. It was as miraculous as it was incredible:

The British had been unable to encircle the Americans.

As soon as it became light Colonel William Prescott on Breed's Hill had seen the militia's mistake and known that he could be outflanked. He started his men building a breastwork down the hill to the water. Here there were rail fences and a stone wall. The British charged this left flank, hoping to come up behind the redoubt, but the fire of the Americans behind the fences and improvised earthworks was so deadly that after two attacks they abandoned the plan.

Whole lines of redcoats, their white belts crossed on their chests, heavy packs on their backs, now made a frontal assault up Breed's Hill. The Americans, waiting behind their fort of earth and sticks, their guns resting on logs or a parapet for steadiness, followed orders not to shoot until they saw "the whites of their eyes." When the British came close enough the Americans opened fire. Whole lines of British soldiers went down, dead or shatteringly wounded. Most of the British officers had been killed at the opening fire. Those who had escaped the blast fled down the hill. There they were strengthened by fresh companies; again sent up Breed's Hill in a frontal assault; and again mowed down by the American fire. Only in their third attempt, toward sundown, when they had been allowed to shed their packs and had found the Americans almost out of powder, had they been able to breach the walls, get into hand-to-hand combat with bayonets, and at last drive the Americans out of their fortifications and off Breed's Hill.

"Then the British beat us?" she cried.

"They have the fort and the hill," said Peter glumly.

"But at what cost!" cried Elihu. "God, we came close to wiping out their whole army. They said we wouldn't fight. We fought them into the ground. Into their graves. They'll be burying their dead for days. Musta been a thousand of their best troops killed and wounded; practically all their officers are in Boston right this minute, while doctors amputate their arms and legs."

"How many of ours?" Her voice was low, apprehensive.

There was a silence. The courier took up the burden.

"We don't have the count. Killed, wounded, captured, maybe two hundred, maybe three. We got most of our wounded off the hill in good condition. But we needn't have lost any. We outfought them. We drove them off, time and again." Angrily, not looking at anyone: "We made mistakes. Bad ones. We had troops on top of Bunker Hill watching the battle; they never came down to help. Fresh companies were supposed to move in from Cambridge to relieve. They could have made it from Roxbury in time. Orders got fouled. No one knew who was commanding. Some of our men refused to cross the Charlestown Neck because of the fire of the guns and ships' cannon. The men who did the fighting had been there all night working, and all day waiting, with no food or water, no good supply of balls or ammunition. If a few more companies had come to help, if there had been even one more round of ammunition, we could still be on top of Breed's Hill."

5

The roar of cannon was still constant at three the next afternoon, Sunday. Abigail and the children had slept fitfully. It was expected that the British must attack again soon. The militia, at its alarm post in Roxbury, had marched at daybreak to Prospect Hill expecting a major encounter. The children were frightened and restive. Abigail set them to chores. Nab made gingerbread men with a cooky mold, the two younger boys put apples on a prong and pared them, Johnny carved on a wooden grain shovel. Abigail went upstairs to her desk and wrote to John.

"Dearest Friend. The day, perhaps the decisive day, is come on which the fate of America depends. My bursting heart must find vent at my pen. I have just heard that our dear friend Dr. Joseph Warren is no more but fell gloriously fighting for his country, saying better to die honorably in the field than ignominiously hang upon the gallows. . . . The race is not to the swift, nor the battle to the strong, but the God of Israel is He that giveth strength and power unto His people. . . . 'Tis expected they will come out over the Neck tonight, and a dreadful battle must ensue. . . . May we be supported and sustained in the dreadful conflict. I shall tarry here till 'tis thought unsafe by my friends, and then I have secured myself a retreat at your brother's who has kindly offered me part of his house."

The British did not come through the Neck that night; they were occupied in burying their dead, reorganizing their decimated regiments. Elihu got a commission as captain and left for the army camp at Cambridge. Peter remained behind as an officer of a Braintree company which would engage if the British attacked along the Boston–Plymouth Road. The Massachusetts Army had little powder with which to defend itself, but the British morale was shattered, the Americans had proved neither cowards nor peasants nor fools, but adversaries worthy of respect. General Clinton was reported to have said about the British capture of Breed's Hill:

"A dear bought victory, another such would have ruined us."

As a result of the battle, Abigail had an unexpected visitor: her cousin Esther, Jonathan Sewall's wife. She had always been one of the prettiest of the Quincy girls, with her light blue eyes and golden hair. Harassment lay across her slender features like a lace veil.

Abigail led her upstairs, took John's bedroom chair into her office, placed it close to hers at the desk. Esther gazed about the cubicle, then rose, examined the bedroom as though it were all of Massachusetts.

"Abigail, Jonathan is planning to flee. To Halifax. Or London. I don't want to go to England. I want to stay here. With my family and friends. But I don't know who is right and who is wrong! I know you can't understand that because you read the newspapers and magazines. You discuss these things with your husband, and you're able to make judgments."

"So are you."

Esther broke into tears, the first time Abigail had ever seen her cousin lose presence.

"The last time I read a printed word was before I met Jonathan. After he began courting me I stopped thinking about all serious matters because I was so happy in love. And then when we were married, and I had a home to set up, children to bear . . ." She interrupted herself. Abigail saw terror on her face. "It's all right to do anything, no matter how frightening, providing you know what you're doing. Abigail, can you understand how terrible it is not to know why any of these things are going on, or who is responsible, or any part of what is going to happen in the future? I'm afraid."

Abigail took Esther's hand in hers. "We're all afraid," she said sympathetically.

"I've had a wonderful time. Now it's all going to be destroyed."

"That's not necessarily true, Esther."

"I can't make him go alone; he and the children are my life. Cousin Samuel's wife is strong. She maintains that Samuel has been stupid to leave his friends and relatives on the Patriot side. But that's not true of Jonathan. He prospered, he had power, high position, money. How could I tell him he's wrong? If I'm giving up everything I have here and going to a strange world, oughtn't I to know whether we're right or wrong in what we're doing?"

"It would help, Cousin Esther. But if you've made no critical judgments during these last ten tormented years of Stamp and Sugar Acts, of the Boston Port Bill and Coercive Act crises, there's nothing I can tell you now to enlighten you."

"Then I will just have to go?"

"Apparently you will, Cousin, apparently you will."

Abigail sat unmoving, immersed in her memories of Jonathan's visits to their home to warn them of the implications of their position. He had been a true prophet: the times had been torn asunder, relative had been separated from relative, friend from friend. There was grave peril everywhere. But it was Jonathan Sewall who was fleeing, rather than John. That must be bitter for him to bear.

The reports reaching Braintree from Boston were full of despair. The British had taken over all the homes left empty by the Patriot refugees. There was no more firewood. Slowly the supplies of flour had vanished, then salt, sugar, eggs, poultry, milk. There was fresh food only for the wounded. Nineteen wounded Americans were thrown in jail and allowed to die there. Even the Tories who had set themselves on rooftops to watch the colorful spectacle of the redcoats marching triumphantly up Breed's Hill to victory were now shorn of hope.

Her brother Billy had received a captain's commission in the Massachusetts Army and was in camp at Cambridge. Her father came for a visit. He had lost everything in Charlestown, yet what he was feeling was not a sense of loss so much as of righteous fury.

"I give my possessions gladly," he cried, resting his big tired frame on her short yellow couch. "It is but a drop in the bucket. What can any American do but fight to the death when he has the picture of Charlestown before him? The few militia we had in the town to secure our right flank can never justify their burning down a whole village."

The first good news was that the Congress in Philadelphia had appointed a single command. John's campaign to have the Virginian, George Washington, appointed head of the army had been successful, though it had taken adroit handling to assuage the Massachusetts delegation, which wanted a New England commander. Within a day of General Washington's arrival in Cambridge to take over the Massachusetts Army, Abigail received a letter he had brought to her from John.

On July fifth, which flashed hot at sunrise, Cotton Tufts stopped for coffee en route to the Roxbury camp where he was going for a day of medical service.

"Cousin Cotton, could I ride along?" she asked. "I've never been."

"Glad for the company."

They found the camp in near chaos. The soldiers from Massachusetts and Connecticut regiments were only half clothed, having lost their clothes at Breed's Hill. A hurried attempt at fortifications had been made: an abatis across the Boston Road, earthworks thrown up on either side, close to the George Tavern, a second built up the Dorchester Road by the burying ground. The one solid structure was a fort on the hill near the Meeting House. The men were poorly armed, there was no organization for cooking, sleeping or medical care; but latrines had been built and many of the officers were marching and training their home-town companies.

Abigail was standing just inside the defense wall of felled trees, their branches and trunks pointed downroad for an attack from the British light horse, when she saw a man come riding across the fields at the head of a small group of officers. She recognized him from John's description. John had prepared her to entertain a favorable opinion of him but, watching the new commander-in-chief as he greeted his fellow officers, she remarked to herself that he carried his dignity with ease. He was uniformed in a blue coat with buff facings, impressive epaulettes on his shoulders, buff waistcoat and breeches, with a small sword at his belt, black boots coming just under the knees. Although he presented a majestic figure of a man, there was modesty marked in every line of his face.

When General Washington dismounted she saw that he was a foot taller than most around him, with huge shoulders, chest and thighs. His head seemed small for so statuesque a body; yet his face was writ large too: a heroically modeled forehead, thick slashing eyebrows over wide-spaced consuming eyes; a jutting bony nose, even more Romanesque than her father's; wide, flat cheeks, and the biggest granite-like chin she had ever laid eyes on.

While he moved about the scant fortifications, Abigail found herself thinking of John. What fantastic opposites the two men were! Washington was a man of action, one who had led troops and fought the ever changing face of the enemy since he was a youth. She would be the first to admit that John Adams had none of Washington's grace or assurance. John was short, stocky, filled with a thousand transient flights and moods. Yet if John could not lead armies, probably George Washington could not have evolved the political concepts and historical precedents which had crystallized the thinking of New England.

Abigail recognized Henry Knox, their fat bookseller friend. Though he was a civilian volunteer, Knox was trying to utilize all the books he had read about the uses of artillery. All he lacked was artillery. He saw Abigail, moved quickly to introduce her.

"General Washington, it is my pleasure to present Mrs. John Adams, wife of the Congress delegate from Massachusetts."

Washington took off his hat, bowed. He would hardly have to be told who John Adams was, since he had been on the floor of the Congress when Delegate Adams nominated him to be commander-in-chief. His smile was brief but warm, lighting up the countenance for an instant.

"Mrs. Adams, my great pleasure. You received the letter I carried from your husband?"

"I did, General, and I thank you for your kindness. How does Mr. Adams in Philadelphia?"

"He is the hardest-working delegate there; but his spirits are high."

"That means he is well. I thank you for the reassuring words. I'm certain you know by now, General, that every tongue applauds your appointment, and every arm is extended to receive you."

"My three days in Cambridge has taught me that. But these good wishes must be converted into powder, guns . . ." He looked with a frown creasing his forehead at the makeshift defenses set across the Neck. ". . . engineers, artillery. But I must not burden you with these problems, Mrs. Adams, they properly belong to your husband in Philadelphia. When you write to him, be so kind as to convey my warmest regards."

The immediate effect of General Washington's rigid reorganization of the two camps at Roxbury and Cambridge was the invoking of martial law by the British in Boston. This squeezed out almost the last of the Patriots. They flooded the roads that fanned out from the city with their meager remaining possessions, seeking shelter. The Isaac Smiths had rented a house in Salem, Betsy Adams moved to a cottage in Dedham.

Braintree was jammed to its attics. Among Abigail's neighbors the Veaseys had taken in three full families, each with several children, the Basses, Etters and Savils had each taken two. Abigail was able to house six families in the two houses, including the Cranches. Richard had once again lost his business in Boston. The George Trotts, remote cousins of the Adams family, were taken in by Peter's wife, Mary, but when she took to bed with labor pains it was Abigail's turn to give them refuge. She moved John's stand-up desk into the sitting parlor, his table into the kitchen, then carried his books and papers up to their bedroom, after which the Trott family slept in John's office.

The Cranches found a small house to rent near Christ Church. Abigail and Mary set up looms in their kitchens similar to the ones on which their mother had trained them in Weymouth. The quilt sewing stopped. The army needed thirteen thousand wool greatcoats for winter and there was no one to supply them except the housewives. The twenty Adams sheep were shorn, the wool carded, spun, woven, the coats cut big and warm. Like the others in the neighborhood, inside each was stitched a name, *Abigail Adams, Braintree. Mary Cranch* . . . Since the homespun coats were offered as a bounty for men who would volunteer for eight months' service, the women knew that each coat meant another soldier.

John's future kept her stumped. An acquaintance by the name of Collins informed her that she must not expect to see him until the spring.

"Spring? That's a good eight months away!"

The following week she had a note from John saying that it would not be more than a month before he returned. Her head spun; better not to think of John at all but to immerse herself in the thousandfold tasks of keeping a half dozen families alive and fed.

Early in August a courier brought word that Elihu Adams was down with dysentery at the camp in Cambridge. He had been ill for a week. Mrs. Hall went to nurse him. The next day Elihu died. He had commanded a company of militia and apparently had the makings of a good officer; but now he was dead without firing a shot. Abigail was in the midst of arranging with Peter to take their farm wagon to fetch him when word reached her that John was in Watertown giving a report on the Congress to the Massachusetts legislature. He would go directly to the camp, bring Elihu's body back to Braintree.

It was a sad reunion. Elihu was buried in the new cemetery near his home in South Braintree. John sat crushed, head down, arms crossed over his shoulders and hands straining to pull his body into the smallest possible bundle of misery. When he spoke it was without raising his head.

"Why do the gayest of heart go first?" When she could think of no answer he continued hoarsely: "He was as simple and good-natured as a child. All he wanted from life was a commission in the militia. I could not refuse him help in getting it. How could I say, 'We all must fight, but not my brother.'"

She saw the tears come down the line in each cheek, hover for an instant at the beginning wrinkles at the corner of his mouth and then drop, one by one, onto his chest. She had never seen him cry before, not even at little Susanna's death. She turned away, stood hunched over in silence, allowing him the privacy of his personal grief.

6

John's mother took Thankful and the three children to live with her, which released Thankful's house for the Trott family. John put his office together again. He had been on short rations and could not get enough sleep. Abigail had all she could do to keep her four young from swarming over him and waking him.

"Pa," Charley demanded with the long rolling *r* he gave the word, "are you home for good?"

"Alas! It's only an adjournment. We have to be back in Philadelphia on September fifth."

Nab cried, "Oh, Papa, no! That's only three weeks!"

John consoled them.

"Three weeks more than nothing. Otherwise you wouldn't have seen your poor old father until spring planting. Isn't this three weeks better?"

"If I may speak for my brood," replied Abigail quietly, "it's a whole lifetime better."

They spent the days inspecting and working the farm. The dry weather had given them a lean gleaning, but Isaac had managed to cut a fair crop of hay. John complimented her on the fine condition of their animals, the orchards and the vegetable patches which she and the children had irrigated by hand.

"John, how much of the food that we've raised shall we keep at home, how much do we send to the army?"

"Half and half. Congress is issuing bills of credit to pay customary prices. How are we on money?"

"We don't owe anything."

"Goodwife. I have all my vouchers for expenses. Spent well over the hundred pounds advanced. Our legislature will compensate me."

"Let's walk up to the top of the hill. There might be a breeze."

There was a breeze, and shade under a broad oak tree.

"Is this where you watched the battle of Breed's Hill?"

"Yes. At least the gunfire, and the burning of Charlestown."

"What you saw that day determined everything the Congress has done since. Prior to June seventeenth there was still a strong reconciliation group, headed by Dickinson of Pennsylvania. We actually drew up and signed another olive-branch petition to England."

She settled back against his shoulder, feeling the greatest of all security: having her husband with her. It was an integral part of their friendship that John treated her as he did his colleagues in the legislature, organizing in clear terms the contests, defeats and accomplishments of the Congress in its second sitting. This was one of the things that made his absences endurable: that one day she would learn everything that had happened.

Pennsylvania had added several new members to its delegation, including Benjamin Franklin, who had returned from England and who had promptly been asked to set up a postal system for the thirteen colonies. He did, and was named Postmaster General. A delegate from a parish in Georgia had finally attended, so that now all thirteen colonies were represented. Peyton Randolph had withdrawn from the presidency because he was Speaker of the Virginia House of Burgesses, and John Hancock had been elected president.

"The things we accomplished," John confided in his high excited voice, "were important because the thirteen colonies agreed to do them together. We set up commissions to treat with the Indians. We adopted measures to organize an army of fifteen to twenty thousand men and, after making General Washington commander-in-chief, chose generals from every geographical section. A committee was appointed to raise £6000 for gunpowder. We voted ourselves the power to issue two million Spanish milled dollars for defense. Twelve colonies pledged themselves to redeem these bills of credit. The evening we heard from Breed's Hill—Bunker Hill, the report said—was for most of us the hour in which America was born as a nation. Yet even then we were held back by conservatives like Dickinson. . . ."

"They will not accept independency?"

"That piddling genius gave a silly cast to our whole doings. We ought to have held in our hands the legislative, executive and judiciary of the whole continent, and have completely modeled a constitution, raised a naval power, and opened all our ports wide; arrested every friend to the British government on the continent and held them as hostages for the poor victims in Boston. However, I understand that the Congress must not split asunder. We must move slowly, if we are to fight as a united people."

They spent idyllic days rambling over the countryside, through fields and meadows, watching their children splash in the brook, taking a picnic supper up to Penn's Hill to eat out of pewter plates on their laps while watching the flaming sunsets settle into rose, vermilion, purple. The war seemed to be at a complete standstill. Neither was there a scintilla of law business at hand, though the Massachusetts legislature had petitioned the Congress to lay out a form of self-government for Massachusetts which, among other things, would get the courts open again.

They spent a day in Weymouth with the Smiths. Her father had turned into a white-haired Jeremiah who wanted no part of reconciliation. He and the tall almost fleshless Cotton Tufts made a fiery team as they visited the army camps and neighboring villages, dispensing preaching and paregoric in ardent dosages. Her mother had been up and down with an unnamed illness, but when the Adamses came to midday dinner with their four grandchildren, and the Cranches with their three, Mrs. Smith dressed in her most beautiful gown. John restaged some of the more dramatic debates of the Congress for them. Later, Mrs. Smith took Abigail aside.

"Abigail, I want you to know, in case I don't get another chance to tell you: your husband was right about the law and lawyers. I was wrong. The words that John speaks bring happiness to your father and me. We think that dogged mind of his is going to help create a beautiful new country."

Abigail put her arm affectionately about her mother's shoulders.

"If a man can create love in an unawakened girl, that's already a new world. Anything he accomplishes after that she assumes to be quite logical and natural."

The only rift in their three weeks of honeymooning came as one of those strokes of ill fortune against which John had tried so hard to defend. On July 24, 1775, in Philadelphia he had written notes to Abigail and James Warren, giving them to a visiting lawyer by the name of Benjamin Hichbourn to deliver. Hichbourn had been intercepted by the British at a ferry near Newport, Rhode Island. Instead of dropping his confidential letters into the water, he had allowed the British naval officers to take them from him. Unlike the sparse, uncommunicative, "safe" letters Abigail had been receiving, this one had contained the unburdening of the overworked, distraught moment.

The Tory owner of the *Massachusetts Gazette* published the letters in her journal. The fat was promptly spluttering in the fire of every kitchen in Massachusetts, for John had labeled John Dickinson, as he had to Abigail, a "piddling genius," accusing him of being a timorous conservative who was frustrating the entire Congress. What was worse, John's revolutionary writing and pleading before the Congress was now exposed to the world:

"The business I have had upon my mind has been as great and important as can be entrusted to one man, and the difficulty and intricacy of it is prodigious. When fifty or sixty men have a constitution to form for a great empire, at the same time that they have a country of fifteen hundred miles' extent to fortify, millions to arm and train, a naval power to begin, an extensive commerce to regulate, numerous tribes of Indians to negotiate with, a standing army of twenty-seven thousand men to raise, pay, victual and officer, I really shall pity those fifty or sixty men."

The effects were galvanic. Some of John's associates were angry with him for exposing the considerable differences in the Congress. Others, since some portion of the Patriot side was still hoping in a remote corner of its mind for a reconciliation with George III, were politically embarrassed by the naked clarity of John's will to create a powerful army, navy and central government which would take its place in the world as an international force.

Not all of Abigail's neighbors in Braintree were able to digest such strong meat. The Church of England members cut her dead. A few of her friends, who had been part of the sewing circle, failed to call. Their husbands were timorous: it was still not altogether discreet to associate with avowed enemies of His Majesty's Government.

Word reached the Adamses that the original letters had been sent to London for study and publication, all of which would confirm the impression created by Governor Bernard in England of that "damn Adams, every dip of his pen stung like a horned snake."

Samuel Adams was delighted by what he called "the deliciously timely exposure." He and Betsy made the journey from Dedham to congratulate John for setting forth in the strongest possible terms the position and direction of the Congress.

"It was nice of you to come all this way, Cousin Sam'l," Abigail said. "I would have thought you two Adamses saw enough of each other in Philadelphia."

"Hardly get to exchange salutations," Samuel replied. "We serve on different committees."

He was looking well, growing younger, Abigail thought, as his lifetime dreams were being fulfilled. The slight palsy had vanished, there was fine color in his cheeks, his eyes sparkled; for this Congress in Philadelphia, this emergent nation as John Adams had so indiscreetly pictured it in his intercepted letters, was more surely the work of Samuel Adams than any one man. Abigail said so.

"Always excepting King George III, of course," interjected John. "Or Lord North."

Abigail listened to the cousins bantering each other, thinking how considerably both men had grown since she first saw them together in Samuel's house in Purchase Street. Thirteen years had passed since their first cup of tea together. Samuel had said to her, "It pleasures me to receive a friend of Cousin John's, Miss Smith. Move into Boston and we'll have another tea party." He had kept his promise, God knew, making the port of Boston one huge dish of cold tea.

She glanced at her husband talking animatedly with Samuel about the Articles of Confederation and Perpetual Union which Benjamin Franklin had suggested that the Congress be turning over in their minds. Both Adamses had approved the structure, and so had the

Virginian, Thomas Jefferson; but he had maintained that the plan would shock the "timid members." Abigail gathered that both John and Samuel believed the Articles of Confederation could succeed right now. If they did not create the perfect government at least they would establish a workable framework inside which the colonies would have room to experiment. What she also gathered from their tone was that both men were determined not to quit the next meeting of the Congress until America was independent; and had its own central government.

"But a government we can defend, Sam'l," said John. "All we have now are the packets and sloops that men like John Hancock and Isaac Smith built. How can we be independent or defend ourselves if we don't build warships and mount cannon on them to outshoot the British?"

Samuel turned to Abigail, said with a slow ingratiating smile:

"A persuasive man, your husband. He wanted George Washington to command our troops. I can't count how many hours he caucused with me. But he was right. Now your husband wants a navy. No one else I ever heard in Philadelphia talked about our building a navy. But do you know something, Cousin Abigail?"

"Yes, Cousin Sam'l. We'll get our navy. That is how I reconcile myself to letting John go for four months at a time, with me alone to tend the farm and family."

John had no sooner gone from home, to stop in Watertown for a couple of days of conferences before proceeding to Philadelphia, than Isaac, the hired man, went down with dysentery. His groans from the attic were so heartbreaking that Abigail, Susy and Patty took turns nursing him. Within two days Abigail herself was in bed with a violent attack. When Nab saw how ill her mother was she demanded:

"Mama, shouldn't we send someone to Watertown for Papa? He would want to know if you were so sick."

Abigail thought for a moment.

"I need him, Nab, but I'm afraid to bring him back to Braintree. This epidemic is spreading. Give me a dose of the Indian physic and boil some mullein root in milk for me."

Her attack abated. She was no sooner on her feet than Susy went down. Abigail managed to get two of her neighbors to carry Susy to her guardians' home, but within a matter of hours little Tommy came down, and after him Patty. Tommy turned from a hearty, corn-fed boy to a lean and wan child within a few days. Patty grew worse. Before long she had a mortification and broke out in putrid sores. Her dysentery was so uncontrollable that there was no way to keep either her body or her bed clean. After each visit to the room Abigail suffered a spell of vomiting.

The house became a hospital. Every bed was occupied by someone in torment. But each house was the same now: Mrs. Randall's child was not expected to live, someone was down in the Belcher and Brackett and Miller homes, the Reverend Mr. Gay was dying and the Reverend Mr. Wibird was seriously ill.

The epidemic moved on to Weymouth. No one knew what caused it. Dr. Cotton Tufts had sixty to seventy cases which he tended before he himself was stricken. The news that caused her to come running to Weymouth was that her mother was prostrate. Betsy and Phoebe were competent nurses but they had worn themselves thin with night and day watching.

Abigail made the trip back and forth from Braintree to Weymouth each day, spending twelve hours with Tommy and watching over her own brood, then driving in her chaise to relieve Phoebe and send her sister to bed for rest. Tommy recovered. His face soon became too fat for his eyes to see out of. In Weymouth her mother kept wasting away, even though Cotton Tufts had managed to import some prickly pears from Virginia to heal her excoriations.

For four Sabbaths there was no preaching in the Braintree Meeting House. Abigail ran out of medicines. She wrote frantic letters to John, "Be kind enough to send me one ounce of turkey rhubarb. . . . I should be glad of one ounce of Indian root. So much sickness has occasioned a scarcity of medicine."

With the children well she arranged to spend a couple of days in Weymouth. She slept in her old bed over her father's library. The first morning she went down to the kitchen to brew a cup of tea and took it up to her mother's room. Her mother appeared asleep. Abigail put her hands gently under her mother's head and raised it. Her mother swallowed a few drops, gasped, fell back on the pillow, then opened her eyes for a piercing look that went straight to Abigail's heart. She lingered on for a few hours, with the Reverend Mr. Smith praying by her bedside. By dusk she was dead.

They buried her on Burying Hill. The whole town came to mourn her. That night when Abigail lay in the darkness with the curtains of her childhood four-poster drawn, visions of her early years surrounded her. She realized how good a mother Elizabeth Smith had been, how well she had trained her daughters, how adroitly she had mixed understanding and affection with discipline. As a young girl she had frequently been in revolt because her mother would not allow her to go to school, had considered her delicate of health. Yet she knew that many of her strengths came from her mother's watchfulness, her assiduity in instilling religious principles into her children, and faith in God, preparing them for the rigors of adult life. Her mother had never been a burden; she had made no personal demands on her children.

Abigail already missed her. She hoped that she could be that good a mother to her own young, that they too in the years to come might mourn her in the dark of night and feel forlorn because an integral and ever constant portion of their lives was gone. She felt older because she had no mother alive in the world.

The Reverend Mr. Smith seemed to be taking his wife's death with Christian fortitude; but a day or two later he came to Abigail with tears streaming down his cheeks and said:

"Child, I see your mother, go to what part of the house I will."

His face had grown old, lined deep and dark. She sat at the table with him and forced herself to consume quantities of food so that he would eat along with her. But it was futile. His bones stared out at the world from beneath his loose-hanging clothes.

She reached home exhausted in body and spirit, seeking rest and consolation. But Patty died in her arms. She buried the young girl in the Braintree cemetery among several generations of Adams tombstones, then trudged back to her house along the rain-bogged road. Josiah, Jr., Elihu, her mother and now Patty had all been laid to rest within a few months.

To divert her, Josiah Quincy invited her to his home for dinner with Benjamin Franklin. She donned her black mourning gloves. Franklin was beloved in the colonies, one of the few Americans to have gained recognition among the scientists and learned societies of Europe. Without formal education but with an original and creative mind, there was almost no field in which he had not made a lasting contribution.

He was standing in a far corner of her cousin's library overlooking a turbulent October sea. Since he was engaged in conversation with half a dozen guests, Abigail had an opportunity to study him for a moment. He wore his hair down over his ears and coat collar, a straggling uneven length but balancing the rounded bald brow. He was built big in every respect, head, sloping cylindrical shoulders and massive forearms, the broad chest and by now expansive stomach enclosed in a frilled shirt with a soft white collar, and covered by a wrinkled velvet waistcoat and outer coat of brown broadcloth. The big eyes stood wide open, their expression mildly interested. Abigail knew him to be a year short of seventy, but the only sign of age was the loosening flesh of jowl and neck.

Introduced by Cousin Quincy, she found him social though not talkative.

"But when he speaks, something useful drops from his tongue," Abigail observed.

The Congress' hope for union was based on an original Benjamin Franklin idea. His Plan of Union had been adopted by the very first Albany Congress of 1754, twenty-one years before. A staggering amount of what was good in Philadelphia life had been born in this ingenious brain: the first public library, city hospital, police, lighting and street cleaning, philosophic society, academy for the education of youth, experiments on weather, electricity. His *Poor Richard's Almanack* was widely quoted.

Franklin spoke to her of John's contributions to the Congress.

"I'm proud of Mr. Adams's work, Mr. Franklin," she replied, "but there are times when I miss him sorely."

"No more than he misses you, I venture."

"My husband is absorbed in his tasks, he is meeting with people. I live like a nun in a cloister. Since he went away I have not been in any other house than my father's and sister's."

"Then why not come to Philadelphia for the winter? It's been my home for over forty years. You will find it a city of learning and culture."

"Philadelphia! The idea intrigues me. Mr. Adams describes it as elegant. He particularly likes the way all the streets are exactly straight and parallel to the river. But alas, I must be at home for early planting."

Franklin's smile was serene.

"Politics and planting. A combination begun by Cincinnatus five hundred years before Christ."

7

She had reconciled herself to spending the holidays without her husband, when a few days before Christmas he thundered up to the house on a rented black stallion. His hat and cape were covered with snow. Abigail was astonished to see him.

"But, John, we heard the Congress was not going to adjourn."

"Nor did it. I simply rose in my seat and asked for a leave."

He had brought books for the children as Christmas presents, and for Abigail all of the articles that had vanished from her life when the Boston port was closed: packets of pins, worth their weight in gold doubloons, needles, calimanco and binding for shoes, Barcelona handkerchiefs.

Late that night with the children finally asleep and a fire crackling cheerily on the hearth, they nestled content in each other's arms in their marital bed. John confided:

"Those pins and handkerchiefs are a poor present, desperately as you need them. My dear girl, I'm convinced I've been asking too much of you."

"Have I been complaining in my letters? I hadn't meant to. You ask for the news, and so little of it is good these days."

He threw aside his warm cover, took up his favorite stance before the fire, legs spread wide, his right hand clasping his left wrist behind his back.

"Abigail, you're carrying the whole burden on your shoulders. No, it's true. Mine has been no sacrifice. I've traveled the colonies, working with excellent men and stimulating minds, been in the cauldron of fascinating conflicts and issues. I've worked long hours, but without the thousandfold obligations you wake up to each morning."

She raised herself on an elbow to see him the better. This declaration was hardly in character.

"I think I should give up the Congress for next year, stay home and run the farm, as well as educate the children. Things have not been easy for you."

She studied his face, squinting her eyes as though to sharpen the impression, then rose, pulled a cane-bottomed chair up to the fireplace. Her hair was loose over her shoulders, her eyes big with wonder at this unexpected development. A quizzical smile tipped the corners of her mouth.

"Have some things gone wrong for you, John? I mean, that would impair your usefulness in Philadelphia?"

"The Dickinson letters, of course. Dickinson doesn't speak to me, and his friends oppose my every move. There's bad blood between my old friend Robert Treat Paine and myself because I backed James Warren in their quarrel. I tried to stop the Massachusetts Council when it appointed me Chief Justice, knowing Paine would be offended."

The fire made visible his every shade of expression.

"But that's not why you want to resign?"

"No. I simply think it's my turn to care for the Adams family. My conscience will not permit me to think otherwise. In a year or so, when we're comfortable and secure again, I can return to Philadelphia."

She closed her eyes so that she could repeat to herself all he had said and listen to his tone. She detected no note of heroics or self-pity. His motive seemed genuine, come from a loving heart.

"John, are you giving me a choice?"

"Yes."

"If you leave now, won't that invalidate most of your work? Then my having been alone so much will have been a real waste. Are there men in the Congress who can do your job as well as you?"

He squirmed, unlocked his hands from behind his back and crossed them over his chest. False modesty was not an ingredient of his nature.

"There's a kind of historical-legal argument I can make on the floor of the Congress or in a committee report as well as any man in the colonies. . . . Let me get my journal from the office."

He was out of the room and back in an instant. He raised the wick of the oil lamp and began reading from his memorandum book, bound in red-brown leather. His voice communicated all the impetuosity, the clangor, the days and weeks of economic debate and personal conflict; by it she was transported as though on the wings of a giant bird to Philadelphia. She could see him walking backward and forward in the State House yard with his fellow delegates trying to persuade them that his plan for foreign trade was not "wild, extravagant and romantic," but could get foreign ships into American harbors past an understaffed British navy, with powder and other imperatives; and by the same token that American ships loaded with raw materials could slip through the sievelike British blockade and earn the colonies their buying-cash. That an American fleet had to be built "at the Continental expense" to capture valuable prizes and cargoes, and a corps of marines organized as fighting men for the American ships. That a state government had to be formed in each of the colonies for a "full and free representation of the people," and that each should "establish such a form of government as in their judgment will best produce the happiness of the people, and most effectually secure peace and good order." That they must build a Continental Army with permanent officers and bounties large enough to encourage men to leave their farms and forges; and that the Congress must provide for the army on the basis of sound money backed by silver and gold, not the paper money that had already depreciated so badly that no one would give goods for it. . . .

His voice went on, but she had stopped listening. Every word he said was his justification for continuing in the Congress. He could not really believe that she would permit him to resign because she was facing problems at home? The times were hard, everyone was living in the midst of difficulties, of a thousand niggling tasks.

She reached out to turn down the light, went to him, put her arms about his neck and kissed him hard on the lips. Then she murmured:

"Return to your Congress, John, but please, while you are writing your laws in Philadelphia: *we want something for the ladies!*"

They spent a busy month together. John took her with him on a trip to the Massachusetts Council in Watertown where he explained the delays and hesitancies of the Congress in achieving agreement on independence, and to Cambridge, where at General Washington's insistence he gave his opinion that New York was as much within Washington's command as Massachusetts, that New England troops could be sent to protect that city against capture by its plentiful Crown sympathizers or by invading troops.

But mostly they stayed at home. John worked on a number of committees, wrote, as a member of the Massachusetts Council, a proclamation for the legislature which would reopen the Massachusetts courts. Although there had been occasional tales of trespass, of "outrage committed by wicked and disorderly persons" in the fifteen months that the courts had been closed and law enforcement along with them, there had been little disorder beyond the tavern brawl. Each community had governed itself by common consent, the selectmen and deacons settling disputes. John confided:

"This is going to be a one-man composition. What a joy not to have to pass it along to committeemen who would rewrite the whole thing. See if you like it:

"'The frailty of human nature, the wants of individuals and the numerous dangers which surround them through the course of life have in all ages, and in every country, impelled them to form societies and establish governments.

"'As the happiness of the people is the sole end of government, so the consent of the people is the only foundation of it, in reason, morality and the natural fitness of things. . . .

"'It is a maxim that in every government there must exist somewhere a supreme, sovereign, absolute and uncontrollable power; but this power resides always in the body of the people. . . .'"

To Abigail it was moving prose; it was also revolutionary political thinking. Nowhere in the known world, not in Europe, Asia, the Near East did such governmental power reside "*always* in the body of the people." This was an American idea, evolved on this new continent.

"'The Great and General Court have thought fit to issue this proclamation,'" John was reading, "'commanding and enjoining it upon the good people of this colony that they lead sober, religious and peaceable lives, avoiding all blasphemies, contempt of the Holy Scriptures, and of the Lord's Day and all other crimes and misdemeanors, all debauchery, profaneness, corruption, venality, all riotous and tumultuous proceedings, and all immoralities whatsoever . . .

"'And all judges, justices, sheriffs, grand jurors, tithingmen, and all other civil officers within this colony, are hereby strictly enjoined and commanded that they contribute all in their power, by their advice, exertions and examples, towards a general reformation of manners, and that they bring to condign punishment every person who shall commit any of the crimes or misdemeanors aforesaid . . . and that they use their utmost endeavors to have the resolves of the Congress and the good wholesome laws of this colony duly carried into execution.'"

When he had finished she gave him the compliments he thrived on, then twitted him:

"You know, John, if you achieve a world as perfect as you have outlined, with all debauchery, corruption and crime vanished, you will at the same time have abolished any need for courts."

"As long as there are men to make laws there will be men to break them. That's why the judicial has to be as strong as the legislative and executive in our states as well as our central government."

But if the ideas and documents were surging forward in continuous conquest, the military was not. There had been little action over the winter, while General Washington attempted to organize his troops and arm them. His only success had been in sending out fast, armed schooners to capture British vessels, thus providing his troops with some of the muskets, flints and rounds of shot they badly needed and Congress could neither manufacture nor buy.

Because Canada looked like a rich prize for a fourteenth colony as well as security on the northern border, an attack was planned by the Congress in Philadelphia. General Washington dispatched Colonel

Benedict Arnold with a strong force from Cambridge to march northward along the Kennebec River toward Quebec. The highly able Connecticut-born Arnold had been trained in the French and Indian War as early as 1757, and along with Ethan Allen, leader of the Green Mountain Boys, had captured Fort Ticonderoga near the Canadian border the previous May. The second arm, based in Ticonderoga under the popular Irish-born, but now American, Brigadier General Richard Montgomery, was to move his forces from Champlain to attack Montreal, and then join with Colonel Arnold to conquer Quebec.

The entire force was so badly mauled by British soldiers, sailors and French-Canadian militiamen in trying to take that citadel that Montgomery and sixty other officers and men were killed, Colonel Arnold injured, and over four hundred taken prisoner. It was the first total defeat for the Americans. As the six hundred survivors stumbled down into New England that winter and early spring of 1776, the morale of the colonies was seriously depressed.

A few weeks after John had set out for Philadelphia she received from him a pamphlet published in Philadelphia called *Common Sense*. It was not signed but from the lines of the introduction she was sure he had written it:

"The cause of America is in a great measure the cause of all mankind. Many circumstances have, and will arise, which are not local but universal, and through which the principles of all lovers of mankind are affected. . . . Security being the true design and end of government, it unanswerably follows that whatever form thereof appears most likely to ensure it to us, with the least expense and greatest benefit, is preferable to all others."

But as she continued to absorb the devastating attack on the divine right of kings, the evils of monarchy, of hereditary succession and a dissection of "all the crowned ruffians that ever lived," progressed to the "Thoughts on the Present State of American Affairs" with its ringing, eloquent cry for separation and the bold demand for the creation of a new country, which had long been the "asylum for the persecuted lovers of civil and religious liberty from every part of Europe," she realized that a new voice had arisen in the land, one that spoke every bit as clearly and persuasively as John Adams.

New England thought it the work of John Adams. She tried to persuade their friends and relatives that he was not the author of the masterly philippic.

The next traveler's tale was not as flattering, but also needed denying. The story spread with more virulence than the dysentery: John Adams and John Hancock had turned traitor and fled to England. The charge, as far as Abigail could fathom, started among the Braintree Tories and was communicated through their Church of England members. Plausibility was lent the report by reciting the name of the man-of-war on which they sailed, the identity of the captain, the types of luggage each man carried, the hour of departure, how much of the Massachusetts legislature's expense money they had absconded with, the private papers of the Congress they had stolen and were turning over to the British Parliament for publication.

The scandal sprouted like a yard weed for nine consecutive days. Once again people were embarrassed to talk to her, their eyes moving up to the bird cages and iron tubs suspended from the ceiling when she walked into the general store. Some few revealed their rejoicing by glancing at her with sly pleasure.

On the morning of the tenth day the four children confronted her at the breakfast table. They had just come out of a caucus in the upstairs bedroom. The night before there had been fights in Brackett's Tavern. Isaac reported:

"Several men were dragged out with great threats for reporting such scandalous lies."

"Mother," said Nab, the oldest and hence the spokesman. "We want to ask you a question."

"Yes?"

"We want a straight answer," said John Quincy.

"Where is Pa?" blurted Charley, crimson-faced.

"In Philadelphia."

"How can you be sure?" This was young-lawyer Johnny again.

"Because he wouldn't be anywhere else."

"That is not an answer, Mama," her daughter cried.

Abigail opened her arms for her two little ones, spoke over their heads to the older two.

"These are only rumors you've been hearing."

"Some people believe them." Her daughter's cheeks were flaming.

"I know, Nab; the gaping vulgar. They will believe anything bad about a person. These stories were spread to injure your father and Mr. Hancock, to hurt their reputations and our cause." She turned to Johnny. "I have no *legal* proof; I can only tell you that Papa loves his family, he loves Braintree and Massachusetts and America. Remember what *Poor Richard* says: 'A lie stands on one leg, truth on two.'"

Then Bass returned home after accompanying John to Philadelphia and installing him in his quarters. That put an end to the immediate slander; but Abigail lay awake that night alternating between chills and flashes of fever over the maliciousness of man. Malignity had an omnipresent army of trained troops. The higher one rose, the better one served, the more devastating would be the attacks. It was a fate inherent in the character of public life; and that was the only life John Adams desired.

8

March was raw, the earth hard-crusted. She spent much of her time before a roaring fire, prodigal of wood; sewing, reading, doing her best to carry on John's course of study for each of the children. She yearned for spring when the sun would begin to turn warm, the farm awaken from its winter sleep. If the British troops did not overrun their land she could plant barley, bring in cartloads of fertilizers, walk down the rows with the sweet smell of overturned loam in her nostrils.

Mercy and James Warren were frequently on the road between their home in Plymouth and Watertown. Mercy spent several days with her, writing her political plays, keeping Abigail briefed on the activities of the legislature and General Washington, neither of whom had to lie dormant as had a farmer's wife because winter was an obdurate season. Washington had recommended a massive attack on the British troops before spring brought them reinforcements from Britain. The Council had urged patience; there was not enough gunpowder. Washington ordered Henry Knox to Ticonderoga to bring down the artillery pieces which had been captured there the previous May by Benedict Arnold and Ethan Allen. It was a near impossible assignment, but Knox, who was not yet an official member of the army, did not know that. He only remembered that Washington had said, "The want of them is so great that no trouble or expense must be spared to obtain them."

Knox left Cambridge with no help but his brother William. In Ticonderoga he sorted out the fifty-nine usable cannon, howitzers and mortars from the worn-out mass of weapons. Rounding up a scow, piragua and bateau, he loaded and floated down the lake to Fort George some hundred and twenty thousand pounds of artillery, flints and boxes of lead. At the fort Knox built eighty-two sleds, bought eighty span of oxen. Utilizing soldiers and hired civilians, he loaded slender hundred-pound pieces and the dumpy ones weighing five thousand pounds. They now had to move three hundred miles over "roads that never bore a cannon before." Knox took his train through forbidding evergreen forests and over the Berkshire Mountains where there was no road whatever, just endless canyons, precipices, deep valleys. They nearly froze from the cold, lost and then recovered two cannon that were drowned falling through the ice of the Hudson. Men quit, animals gave out, the snow failed, the sleds broke. But not Henry Knox. Inexhaustible, a two-hundred-fifty-pound mountain of cheerful dedication, appointed a colonel by Congress while he was in the depths of his dangers, he succeeded in bringing every last piece of his artillery back to his commanding officer.

To conceal the fact that he was going to fortify Dorchester Heights overnight in the same kind of effort that had fortified Breed's Hill, General Washington ordered Colonel Knox and his six hundred artillerymen to lob shells into the British works adjacent to Boston, without tearing up the city.

Abigail had her own vantage point, Penn's Hill, from which to watch. The nights were clear and she could trace the trajectory of each firing. On that first night she tried to keep an accurate count: the Americans fired eleven shells from their heavy mortars, and thirteen from the eighteen-pounders, shells which Henry Knox, in the midst of his heroic trek, had ordered shipped from New York to Cambridge.

The firing continued for three nights. Then on the morning of March fifth a courier brought the galvanizing word that Dorchester Heights had been fortified in a brilliant operation by three thousand teamsters, artillerymen and covering troops. Some three hundred wagons had carried up chandeliers, tied bundles of sticks. Ditches were dug, axmen cut down orchards to provide the abatis; barrels were filled and made ready to roll down upon the enemy. By dawn six separate fortifications had been built, three thousand fresh troops moved in to relieve, quantities of food, water, powder and balls distributed. The work was done so silently, even with the long lines of wagons moving back and forth, that at sunrise the British were astounded to find that the Dorchester fortifications towering above the fleet could blast their ships out of the harbor.

A deathly silence hung over Braintree the rest of the day. No one visited or worked. The little town was gripped in an excitement as intense as the one on Dorchester Heights and in Boston. Everyone asked himself, "What will the British do?" They responded by cannonading for two hours from their warships. The shots fell short of the forts. Now they either had to storm the Dorchester fortifications, where the carnage could be far worse than on Breed's Hill, or they could evacuate their troops and ships before Henry Knox's cannon blew them out of the water. General Washington had organized and executed a masterly job of work.

Once again the British redcoats embarked in small boats from which they were transferred to transports; but they were late. They lost the tide. A storm arose. While their attack was delayed, George Washington added six twelve-pounders to the hilltop, strengthened his fort, exhorted his troops to avenge the deaths of their brothers at Concord, Lexington, Breed's Hill. Four thousand troops at Cambridge were poised to pour into Boston if the British tried to swarm over the Dorchester forts. Peter Adams was with the Braintree militia at Dorchester Neck prepared for an attack by the British regulars.

The British never attacked. Their decision was made to evacuate Boston. A flag of truce was sent to General Washington with a message: General Howe agreed not to destroy Boston providing Washington would not fire on the fleet.

The usually phlegmatic Peter returned almost incoherent with pride. He related his story to an admiring wife, mother and sister-in-law in Abigail's kitchen.

"I saw four bombs flying over me at one time like comets! Our brave colonel said, 'The man that turns his back on the enemy, I swear by all that is good and sacred I will shoot him. I give you the same liberty to kill me if you see me flinch.' The blaze of bombs don't terrify us any more. I tell you, I was one of the hardy heroes!"

It was a victory of such stunning proportions that Abigail found it hard to believe until some days later she stood with her father on the hill above Josiah Quincy's house at Mount Wollaston and watched the British ships dropping down the bay, the packets carrying fleeing Tory families. Shepherding them were the men-of-war and troop transports heading out for sea. She did not try to blink back the tears of joy. Her father put an arm about her shoulder. They stood together on the crest of the hill, a cool wind blowing against their fevered brows. Abigail turned her pale face and dark brooding eyes up to her father.

"We were wrong. Breed's Hill was not a defeat. It was a victory. It was the memory of Breed's Hill that made the British surrender and move away."

The Reverend Mr. William Smith held his daughter close to him.

"The first half of what you say is right. The second half is wrong. The

British haven't surrendered. They have decided to choose their own battlefield. Sound military strategy. This is not the end of war."

Cotton Tufts would not allow her to visit Boston where the smallpox was raging. Only those Massachusetts militiamen from the Cambridge camp who had pockmarks were permitted to take over the city. Cotton promised to bring her back the news of what had happened there.

"Cousin Cotton, I simply must be inoculated. The children too. Couldn't you do it right here in our home?"

"Not safe, Cousin. But we'll be opening hospitals in Boston as soon as we can put down this epidemic. I'll see to it that you're cared for."

"Would you stop by a housewright, name of Crane, and ask him to send me a report on our house on Queen Street?"

"I'll bring his report myself."

So he did, the following night. Abigail sat him before the kitchen fire, heated some food while he pulled off his boots and washed in a bowl.

"First, Crane inspected your house. It has been occupied by a British doctor of a regiment. The things you left in it, your furnishings, curtains, rugs are all gone. The house is very dirty, but no damage has been done to it structurally."

"You mean it's still a livable house? I can't believe it. Why, it's like a new acquisition: a property which one month ago I could not value at a shilling."

Cotton gazed at her over the top of his spectacles.

"I warn you, Cousin, it's going to take quite a lot of scrubbing."

"I'm determined to get it cleaned as soon as possible. When the pox is cured I'll go into Boston and rent it. We need the income. Now please tell me about the city."

He mopped his plate clean of meat gravy with the rusticoat potatoes, stuffed his pipe with John's tobacco, leaned his cane chair precariously on its two rear legs.

"I must say some individual Englishmen discovered a sense of honor and left rent for the houses they occupied. Not your house, unfortunately. Others left sums sufficient to repair the damaged furnishings. John Hancock's house was well cared for, but our cousin Samuel Quincy's house and furniture were mercilessly torn up. I don't think there was any order to be destructive. It appears to have been a matter of individual taste. Some men are gentlemen, others are pigs."

By the next morning stories about Boston swarmed up the Coast

Road with the density of warblers wheeling south for the winter. The British had spiked their cannon, but an astonishing number had been left in good and usable condition. Colonel Henry Knox promptly acquired them, then set about repairing the hastily mutilated artillery pieces. The shops, warehouses and private homes of the Patriots had been ravaged, but unmovable quantities of British stores had been left behind. The thousand fleeing Crown sympathizers, unable to carry all their furniture on board the jammed vessels, had left enough to replace a considerable portion of the wrecked, burned or stolen Patriot furnishings.

Abigail wrote to John how differently she felt now about the approach of planting time from what she had felt only a month before with the redcoats in Boston.

"We knew not then whether we could plant or sow with safety, whether when we had toiled we could reap the fruits of our own industry, whether we could rest in our own cottages, or whether we should not be driven from the seacoasts to seek shelter in the wilderness; but now we feel as if we might sit under our own vine and eat the good of the land.

"I feel a *gaieté de coeur* to which before I was a stranger. I think the sun looks brighter, the birds sing more melodiously, and nature puts on a more cheerful countenance. We feel a temporary peace, and the poor fugitives are returning to their deserted habitations."

With the foreign enemy departed the talk was that the next major battle would be mounted in New York where the British had their strongest forces. Abigail turned her attention to the domestic enemy: man. She wrote to her own private legislator at the Congress:

"In the new code of laws which I suppose it will be necessary for you to make, I desire you would remember the ladies and be more generous and favorable to them than your ancestors. Do not put such unlimited power into the hands of the husbands. Remember all men would be tyrants if they could. If particular care and attention is not paid to the ladies we are determined to foment a rebellion. . . . Give up the harsh title of master for the more tender and endearing one of friend. Why then not put it out of the power of the vicious and the lawless to use us with cruelty and indignity with impunity? Men of sense in all ages abhor those customs which treat us only as the vassals of your sex. Regard us then as being placed by Providence under your protection and, in imitation of the Supreme Being, make use of that power only for our happiness."

John answered immediately. Engaged in a struggle to put food in the soldiers' stomachs, guns in their hands and blankets over them at night, he replied that Abigail's plea for an extraordinary code of laws for the ladies had amused him:

"We have been told that our struggle has loosened the bands of government everywhere. That children and apprentices were disobedient, that schools and colleges were grown turbulent, that Indians slighted their guardians. . . . But your letter was the first intimation that another tribe more numerous and powerful than all the rest were grown discontented. This is rather too coarse a compliment but you are so saucy, I won't blot it out.

"Depend upon it, we know better than to repeal our masculine systems. Although they are in full force, you know they are little more than theory. We dare not exert our power in its full latitude. We are obliged to go fair and softly, and in practice you know we are the subjects. We have only the name of masters, and rather than give up this, which would completely subject us to the despotism of the petticoat, I hope General Washington and all our brave heroes would fight."

Abigail managed to get in the last word, which she thought was the least she could do after promising her quilting coterie to speak up for them.

"I cannot say that I think you are very generous to the ladies, for whilst you are proclaiming peace and good will to men, emancipating all nations, you insist upon retaining an absolute power over wives. But you must remember that arbitrary power is like most other things which are very hard, very liable to be broken."

9

It was summer before she went into Boston to have herself and the four children inoculated. Some houses and shops had been leveled by bombardment from Colonel Knox's artillery and the British men-of-war. A number of buildings remained as burned-out hulls. Several hundred of the city's wooden buildings had been pulled down to afford firewood for the English soldiers' messes, each street resembling an old crone's mouth with teeth missing. Most of the trees on the Common had been chopped down, as well as the beautiful shade sycamores lining the sidewalks. The Tree of Liberty had been reduced to a mere sitting stump. The Old North Chapel, built in 1677, had vanished for fuel.

Abigail's Brattle Street Church had been used as a barracks, its insides gutted. She found the Old South in the worst condition; the British hated it because so many of Boston's decisive town meetings had been held there, including the one immediately preceding the Tea Party. The pulpit and benches had been hacked out and carried away, then the church had been converted into a riding stable with dirt and gravel on the floor where the cavalry had jumped their horses at full speed over practice bars. The handsome pews had been converted into pigsties. The books and manuscripts of the church library had been fed into the winter stove to keep the gallery spectators warm. The parsonage had been completely obliterated.

As she made her sad, circuitous way through the town Abigail saw that the scattered British fortifications had been left intact when General Washington led his army of nine to ten thousand men overland to New York for a showdown with General Howe. The fortifications at the Neck had been so strongly built that the remaining Massachusetts troops, twenty-five hundred of whom General Washington had left behind to guard New England against surprise attack, believed that they could not have been forced without fearful loss of life. Two of the redoubts appeared well constructed, but even to her unpracticed eye the shallow ditches over Beacon Hill and the thin line of barrels filled with earth on Copp's Hill could have served no purpose other than to frighten off attackers.

Many fine houses were still abandoned, or not yet lived in. The removal of the hundreds of Tory families had made a discernible difference in the number of people in the markets and shops. Some of the stores and warehouses had been so shamelessly looted by the departing redcoats that they had not been able to reopen. In the business district many of the signs and names of proprietors were new to her. As she moved toward the docks she found that all wooden fences had been knocked down, familiar warehouses and wharves had vanished from sight.

It was good to hear and see familiar big-city sights: the woman with a basket of live eels on her head, the man with a pole across his shoulders with a basket on either end, one containing live ducks, the other fat live chickens; the hawkers of almanacs, brooms, mops; the dustman, the chimneysweep, the scissors grinder, the street sign like a closed lamp reading Barber and Peruke Maker, the shoemaker's sign over his door with one tall boot in the center.

Yet Boston was saddened; it had lost its bustling air of activity, of exuberance, of joyous growth. People moved quietly through the streets. Gone were the magnificent English carriages decorated with gold scrollwork and vividly painted scenes, pulled by six matched horses; gone were the men accoutered in the highest English fashion, in gay cocked hats, matching gold buttons and buckles. Gone were their wives and daughters resplendent in their fashionable French gowns with the silk shoes and parasols to match. Boston's Patriots stood out in their austere black.

She passed the homes of old friends and relatives who had fled: Samuel Quincy, Jonathan Sewall, Thomas Boylston, Daniel Leonard, Samuel Fitch and Robert Auchmuty. She saw unfamiliar children playing in their front gardens. In a few of the stately brick homes which had not yet been appropriated or sold, windowpanes were knocked out, front doors stove in. The material damage could be repaired, but not so the loss of native-born families who had been caught up in a civil war.

Her own house on Queen Street provided the worst shock. One of the rooms had been used to keep poultry in, another to store coal, another salt. The building was so damp that parts of the plastered ceiling were falling down. The wallpaper was moldy and hanging in strips. The wooden floors were mildewed. The children's bedrooms were in pitiful condition, with broken windowpanes that had let in the spring rains. As they stood looking about them, their faces reflected bewilderment, sadness, rage. Their comments on the British would have made King George's ears turn carrot color.

She hired two laborers to clean out the dirt, and a wagon to cart it away. Then she threw open the doors and windows to the warm sun, went on an inspection tour through her once lovely home with the children carrying pen and ink, and Nab a book to write in. They stood in the center of each room while Abigail made her repair estimates. The floors would have to be torn out and replaced, the ceilings and walls stripped and freshly plastered, the wood panels of John's office sanded and stained. The work could not be done under £50; nor did she have the capital with which to pay for it.

They made their way to her uncle Isaac's house. The Smiths were still in Salem but had offered their home to serve as a hospital. Here Abigail found the Cranches with their three children, her brother Billy's daughter from Lincoln, her sister Betsy, with Phoebe to help nurse them; Cotton Tufts's son, Cotton, Jr., John Thaxter, Abigail's cousin and John's law clerk; Uncle Isaac's daughter and four Smith servants to cook for them all. Each family had brought its own mattresses, beds, blankets, a cow, hay, firewood and food. They named the house the Smith Family Hospital. Everyone slept in orderly rows, like soldiers in a barrack.

Boston was crowded with patients who had come in from the surrounding towns. Dr. Bulfinch arrived at the house to give the seventeen injections. Even the youngest children behaved well. Now they would have to wait patiently to find out which were the fortunate ones who would break out with eruptions. There was considerable bragging and betting among them as to who would break out first, and in how many places. The nature of the inoculations had changed considerably since John had gone into Boston before their marriage to earn his immunity. Then he had been locked into his hospital from the instant of the first injection; now Abigail and the children would be allowed to roam about the city and visit friends until the first eruption burst forth.

The next afternoon she received a packet from Philadelphia. Enclosed in the envelope with two letters from John were a number of sheets in his strong, emotionally uneven and yet precise handwriting. The manuscript was headed:

A *Declaration by the Representatives of the United States of America in General Congress assembled.*

She read:

"When in the course of human events it becomes necessary for a people to advance from that subordination, in which they have hitherto remained, and to assume among the powers of the earth the equal and independent station to which the laws of nature and of nature's God entitle them, a decent respect to the opinions of mankind requires that they should declare the causes which impel them to the change."

She exclaimed, "Independency!"

She ran out of her aunt Elizabeth's bedroom where she was quartered with Nab and the two younger boys, cried up her family and rushed downstairs to the sitting parlor, Johnny at her heels.

She waited until everyone had assembled, the adults sitting on the chairs and sofa, the nine children on the floor in a semicircle about her before she explained.

"This is our declaration of independence. The one we've been waiting for for two years. Listen to how beautiful it is:

" 'We hold these truths to be self-evident, that all men are created equal and independent; that from that equal creation they derive rights inherent and unalienable, among which are the preservaton of life, and liberty, and the pursuit of happiness; that to secure these ends, governments are instituted among men, deriving their just powers from the consent of the governed; that whenever any form of government shall become destructive of these ends, it is the right of the people to alter or to abolish it, and to institute new government, laying its foundation on such principles and organizing its powers in such form, as to them shall seem most likely to effect their safety and happiness.'"

Everyone began asking questions at once. She restrained them to read portions of the indictment against Britain. Then she came to the last paragraph, the one for which she had been seeking. She read slowly and carefully to the roomful of family:

"'We therefore the representatives of the United States of America in General Congress assembled do, in the name and by the authority of the good people of these states, reject and renounce all allegiance and subjection to the kings of Great Britain and all others who may hereafter claim by, through, or under them; we utterly dissolve and break off all political connection which may have heretofore subsisted between us and the people or parliament of Great Britain; and finally we do assert and declare these colonies to be free and independent states, and that as free and independent states they shall hereafter have power to levy war, conclude peace, contract alliances, establish commerce, and to do all other acts and things which independent states may of right do. And for the support of this declaration we mutually pledge to each other our lives, our fortunes, and our sacred honor.'"

Her heart pounded in her bosom; pride in what all the colonies working together had accomplished; pride in her husband's authorship of what she judged must be the most important document ever written on American soil. How completely this declaration justified all her struggles to preserve the family and its well-being. With this accomplishment John could be content, return to his home and to the practice of the law.

The same evening the printed version of the declaration arrived in the city. Abigail procured a copy and found that, although there had been a number of stylistic changes, the meaning and significance of the text were unaltered except for the deletion of John's page on the abolition of the slave trade. The omission saddened her, but she grasped that it must have been a compromise to gain the consent of the Southern colonies.

The town readied itself for the greatest celebration of its history. Abigail was showered with congratulations and praise. Though her arm was sore and she had recurrent headaches, no pockmarks had yet shown. The nine young ones awoke sick each morning, each having a puke, after which they felt well for the day.

It took Boston five days to prepare for the ceremonies. On the Thursday morning of July 18, 1776, after hearing a good sermon, she went with her family into King Street. Fieldpieces had been set in place before the State House. The troops which had not left with General Washington to defend New York were lined in company formation under arms. The soldiers were ceremoniously bathed and shaved, their clothes washed and pressed for the momentous occasion.

The Patriots of Boston were jammed into the square. A group of men came out on the State House balcony; army officers, selectmen, members of the Massachusetts legislature. Colonel Crafts called for attention, raising his papers high in the air. A hush fell over the crowd. The colonel began to read in a clear booming voice which filled the square:

"'When in the course of human events it becomes necessary for one people to dissolve the political bands which have connected them with another, and to assume among the powers of the earth the separate and equal station to which the laws of nature and of nature's God entitle them, a decent respect to the opinions of mankind requires that they should declare the causes which impel them to the separation.'"

Every word rang out in the clarity of the hot July day. Abigail, who now knew the declaration by heart, listened to her own voice instead: a recapitulation of her years in Boston, the accomplishments and the failures, the pattern of her life in Braintree without John.

Colonel Crafts read in great rolling tones the last of the declaration, "'We, therefore, the representatives of the United States of America, in General Congress assembled, appealing to the Supreme Judge of the world for the rectitude of our intentions, do, in the name and by authority of the good people of these colonies, solemnly publish and declare that these United Colonies are, and of right ought to be, free and independent states. . . .'"

There was a cry from the balcony:

"God save our American states! God save the United States of America!"

There were three tumultuous cheers. The church bells of Boston began to ring, the guns of the returned American ships in the harbor fired in salutation, the cannon from the forts responding. The platoons of soldiers lining the long square wheeled and marched up to the State House, the residents giving way. Mr. Bowdoin stepped forward on the balcony, cried:

"I propose a sentiment: stability and perpetuity to American independence!"

The King's Arms were taken down from the State House, burned in King Street.

Abigail gathered her children close to her, her arms encircling the four.

"If your father was with us he would say, 'Thus ends royal authority in this state.' Nab, I congratulate you, you are now a free and independent American."

"Thank you, Mama."

"Johnny, Charley, Tommy, I congratulate you, you are now free and independent Americans."

"Thank you, Mama."

"See that you stay that way."

"We will, Mama."

10

Betsy Adams invited her to tea. The British had so badly knocked about the house on Purchase Street that Samuel rented the Robert Hallowell house from Massachusetts, which had appropriated it as Tory property. It was not as sumptuous as the home of Comptroller of the Customs Benjamin Hallowell, which a mob had sacked eleven years before; but Samuel had furnished it richly with Tory furniture released to him by the General Court in lieu of his unpaid wages as clerk of the House two years before.

"Come into Samuel's new office," Betsy said with a deprecatory laugh. "I've brought all his books and papers back from Dedham. Tea is almost ready."

"Tea" was a euphemistic term which had meant literally anything for the past two years: coffee, chocolate, punch, raspberry leaves, loosestrife, goldenrod, dittany, blackberry leaves, yeopon, sage. But when Betsy came in with the tray and set it down on Samuel's desk by the window Abigail's nostrils were assailed by the most delicious of scents.

"Betsy, you can't mean it? Real, honest-to-God tea!"

"Isn't it wonderful? Samuel sent me a canister of green tea by Mr. Elbridge Gerry."

Abigail turned away from Betsy, who was too busy pouring to have seen her expression. If Samuel could send Betsy a canister of tea, why could not have John? After all, Mr. Gerry had stopped by the Isaac Smith house to bring her greetings from John. He could have carried a second package in his saddlebags.

"I've been simply famished for a taste," Betsy exclaimed, handing a steaming cup to Abigail, "but I wanted to wait until you could join me."

Abigail's jealousy vanished. She leaned over to kiss Betsy on the cheek. The two women sat with their cups in hand inhaling the fragrance with glazed eyes. They took a first sip, purred with delight, rolled the fragrant liquid around in their mouths in sensual ecstasy, swallowing as slowly as possible to make it last longer.

"This baneful weed," Abigail murmured, "is really a bracer."

"That's why we have had so much sickness these past two years," Betsy agreed. "There's never been a dysentery or distemper that tea couldn't cure."

They took a second, tentative sip. Again a beatific bliss came over them, as though tiaras of diamonds had been placed upon their heads.

"We must look like a couple of tavern frequenters," said Betsy.

" 'Tipplers' is the word. Do you suppose it's as sinful to be a tea addict as a rum addict?"

"I'm certain. Our preachers taught us that everything we enjoyed was sinful. Another cup, Cousin?"

"By all means, Cousin."

An hour later Abigail rose, all of her complexities dissolved in aromatic well-being. On the way to the door she asked herself:

"Will Betsy share some of the tea with me? Oh, not half, that would not be right; no, not even a quarter, that too would be profligate. But perhaps a tenth? One little bowlful which, hoarded scrupulously, could last for a month or more?"

Betsy made no such offer. It never occurred to her.

When Abigail received a letter from John saying, "Gerry carried with him a canister for you," she caught her breath.

"O Heavens, Mr. Gerry gave the tea to the wrong Mrs. Adams!"

First she apologized to John, in her mind, for failing to send her any tea. Next she asked the Lord to forgive her for the sin of envy. Then she went on to the main problem of how to get her tea back. How best to break the news? She hoped Betsy would not be embarrassed or too saddened by the loss. As for trying to figure out a subtle approach, she did not think Betsy would require that.

Then a stabbing thought came. Since there had been a mistake made, and Betsy believed the tea to be hers, should she not share with Betsy? Oh, not half, that would not be right. No, not even a quarter, that would be profligate. But perhaps a tenth? One little bowl which, hoarded scrupulously . . . Surely such a cousinly gesture would ease the awkwardness of the situation?

Betsy blinked hard, though only once. She went and got the canister from her kitchen and placed it firmly in Abigail's hands. Then they both burst out laughing.

"Cousin Betsy, let me prepare a good strong cup in your kitchen."

"Fair is fair. I brewed a pot for you when it was my tea, now that it's yours you can brew one for me."

When her uncle Isaac came in from Salem on business Abigail asked him to come with her to her Queen Street house. He made a close inspection, checked her figures, ruminated for a moment, head on chest.

"Should I try to get the house repaired now, Uncle Isaac? I can get £25 a year rent. In all candor, we need the money."

"We all do, after our losses. The British pulled down two of my warehouses for firewood. But materials and workmen are scarce. Prices are high. You'd have to stay here to supervise."

"I wouldn't want to do that."

"When do you expect John?"

"It should be soon. He's been gone more than six months."

"Let him hire the workmen and supervise. He'll get more done for less money, and the responsibility won't be yours."

As the pox eruptions began to appear, Nab became ill. Johnny and Richard Cranch broke out but felt quite well in spite of it. Then Abigail and Mary Cranch erupted at the same moment. Abigail felt all sorts of mysterious happenings within her while the pox worked its way out, but they were both able to go about. All of the children were doing cleverly except Tommy and Charley, who were being obstinate. Tommy was inoculated a second time, after which he proudly produced a dozen spots. Charley had three inoculations, none of which took. He finally immunized himself by catching the pox from a neighboring boy with whom he was playing, and became so ill with burning fever and delirium that for forty-eight hours his life was in danger.

The Smith Family Hospital had been a success. Its occupants began making their way back to Weymouth, Lincoln, Salem, Braintree. Before Abigail could leave, Samuel Adams reached home, worn out from his seven months of intensive work. John had written that he was fearful of Samuel's health and that he should have gone home months before. His hair had turned from smoke gray to streaked white, the tremor returned to his head and hand. He stretched out in his chair without books or freshly written pages on his desk, a sure sign that Samuel was spent.

"I worked no harder than John," he declared when Abigail backed Betsy in remonstrating against his having exhausted himself. "He's up at four in the morning to work with the War and Ordnance Board, then goes directly to the Congress to participate in our debates on the Articles of Confederation until three or four in the afternoon. He then works with the committee to design a seal for the United States until supper, and after supper he meets again with the group writing laws about the confiscation of British property. After that he writes in his room until midnight."

Abigail was shocked. "No long walks through the countryside, no horseback rides?"

"There isn't time. Besides, he's saving money by not keeping a horse in Philadelphia. Poor economy, Cousin Abigail. You should send him a horse."

She chuckled. "By Benjamin Franklin's new postal system? How is John bearing up under the strain?"

"You know my cousin better than I. He gets the same catharsis from complaining about his health as Catholics do from confession. If he can talk about how much his eyes burn, of having a constant cold, of overwork, of the fiercely hot weather, the pains go away. I haven't answered your question, have I? Cousin John was never better. There are many fine minds in the Congress but he probably accomplishes more in terms of our basic documents than any one other delegate."

She felt an inner radiance.

"You can't know the sense of pride all five of his dependents felt when we read his Declaration of Independence."

"John did not write that. Thomas Jefferson did."

She thought she had misunderstood.

"How could that be, Sam'l? I have the original draft, in John's handwriting."

"What you have is John's copy of Jefferson's draft. John was on the committee and made some suggestions. But Thomas Jefferson of Virginia wrote it. Based on his Preamble to the Constitution of the State of Virginia."

She burst into tears. Betsy came to her, wrapped a comforting arm about her. The tears stopped as quickly as they had started.

"I've been guilty of vainglory, haven't I? It is important only that it has been written. And joyously accepted."

"Evolved from a century and a half of people living alone on a new continent, learning painfully how to govern themselves," Samuel added wearily.

After a hearty tea she went back to her uncle Isaac's, climbed the stairs to her bedroom, took the Declaration from the desk in the alcove and once again read the glowing prose.

"Mr. Jefferson's Declaration is a work of sheer genius," she exclaimed to the walls around her.

The United States of America had declared its independence. Now they would have to earn it.

11

They returned to Braintree on September second, secure against the pox, considering themselves lucky that no one had been left with pits on his face. The same could not be said about the countenance of the infant republic which was erupting "cleverly" in a series of withdrawals and routs. Starting with the battle of Long Island, the bad news straggled into Boston and Braintree like dazed victims of a bombardment. Abigail's father had been right, the British had not run away; they had decided on a more strategic campaign. General Sir William Howe now commanded the largest British army ever sent abroad: thirty-two thousand trained and immaculately equipped men, including the armies of Generals Clinton and Cornwallis centering around New York; ten thousand English soldiers who had arrived with Vice Admiral Richard Howe's formidable fleet; ships of the line and heavily armed frigates in lower New York Bay, as well as an additional eight thousand Hessian mercenaries, the first of nearly thirty thousand hired by George III from his numerous cousins among the German princes. To oppose this force General Washington had ten thousand disciplined Continentals, with another ten thousand short-term militiamen whose muskets or fowling pieces had been taken from over their fireplaces at home. During the late summer of 1776 they were best known for their drinking, wenching and deserting in pleasure-prone New York, disaffection center for the thousands of fervent Crown sympathizers who controlled considerable areas of New York, New Jersey and Pennsylvania.

On August twenty-second General Howe, under cover of his brother's ships, had embarked fifteen thousand men from Staten Island to Long Island, followed by five thousand Hessians. General Washington, under instructions from Congress, split his army between Manhattan Island and Long Island, fortifying Brooklyn Heights and other strategic areas in an effort to keep the British from capturing New York. After reconnoitering to learn Washington's weaknesses, General Howe launched a well-planned attack. At every point Washington's army was surprised, outnumbered and outmaneuvered. The American casualties were fifteen hundred. If General Howe now attacked the main American force inside the Brooklyn fortifications it could mean the loss of half the American army for, as at Breed's Hill, the Americans had left themselves no escape hatch except the East River to drown in.

Howe did not attack. Reinforcements arrived, including the 14th Massachusetts from Marblehead. In a withdrawal manned by the Marblehead seamen, Washington under the cover of night moved his entire army by boat back to New York. The first British sentry arrived at the ferry at a four-thirty dawn to find the last boat carrying George Washington to safety.

Abigail spoke for all hard-pressed Patriots when she wrote her husband:

"If we should be defeated I think we shall not be conquered. A people fired like the Romans with love of their country and of liberty, a zeal for the public good, and a noble emulation of glory, will not be disheartened or dispirited by a succession of unfortunate events. But like them may we learn by defeat the power of becoming invincible."

This mystical faith was sorely needed in the months to come, when defeat followed defeat, with Washington's regulars and militia fleeing in panic as the British grenadiers invaded Manhattan after a two-hour naval bombardment, New England men participating in the rout. The disgrace in New York was partially atoned at Harlem Heights in mid-September when Washington, infuriated by the arrogant fox-hunting sounds made by the pursuing British, maneuvered troops to their side and rear, badly mauling a cocky British contingent. The New England men repatriated themselves at the heart of the battle, and the small symbolic victory permitted Washington to withdraw his army northward without stampede or disgrace. The general was not winning the war, neither was he losing it; but that was cold comfort to the people of Massachusetts who had been at war a year and a half now, since Concord, the withdrawal of the British from Boston Harbor their last semblance of a victory.

It was heartening news that the Southern states had organized their regiments and begun to build fortifications along the coast. There had been no major clashes as yet: the North Carolina Tories attempting to capture Wilmington had been driven off, and the long bombardment of the fortified Sullivan's Island, protecting Charleston, had failed because the British ships ran out of supplies and had to return to New York. From all reports coming in by letter and newspaper, the waging of the war still lay in the future.

The Adamses' main problem now, as John agreed through correspondence, was finding a way to get him home. An examination of the calendar on his desk showed that it was a full eight months since they had bade each other good-by. She had fallen unwittingly into the position of the wives of Boston sea captains who had their husbands home for one month out of the year.

John was doing his best to get leave, but he was now the only Massachusetts delegate still working with the Congress. He kept writing to James Warren, Speaker of the Assembly, urging the legislature to increase the number of delegates so that a new man could take his seat. Abigail followed through on John's request, but the legislature adjourned. When it met again it approved John Adams's idea, though the members passed no resolution to replace or free him.

John also begged her to send him a horse so that he would have a means of getting home. He had no money with which to buy or rent a horse in Philadelphia.

Nor did Abigail have any in Braintree. The harvest was mediocre because she had not been able to hire extra hands for the time she was in Boston. Of the short sums she received she first paid her taxes, then £34 as a next-to-last installment on the decaying house on Queen Street. That left her with little cash to tide them over the winter, but she spent all of it to send young Bass to Philadelphia with two horses. She wrote:

"I know the weight of public cares lie so heavy upon you that I have been loath to mention your own private ones."

She told him how much it would cost to put their Boston house in repair. Then she described his boat, lying rotting at the wharf; one more year without care and it would be worth nothing. The big family farm of thirty-five acres which they had bought from Peter was no longer paying its way. Either John would have to farm it himself, or it would have to be rented out. There were no debts but neither were there any coins in the Adams Specie Bank. She and the children ate well off the farm and the dairy; they could make their own clothes, cut firewood for warmth. Nothing more.

Yet with Bass safely in Philadelphia, John still remained. It was then she grasped that there was a third force, in addition to the Congress and the Massachusetts legislature, chaining John Adams to his desk: himself. As chairman of the Continental Board of War and Ordnance he had made himself the one delegate in contact with all elements of the army and its needs, evolving a *modus operandi* for securing the materials once he could persuade Congress to appropriate the money. His were the plans and insistences for the formation of a permanent army; for the stabilizing of the currency; for the securing of treaties with European countries which would acknowledge that the United States of America was an independent country; for securing money, powder, cannon, engineers, food and ships from abroad. He was concerned with the movement to build men-of-war, to arm cargo ships for the taking of prizes. His *Thoughts on Government* was the basis of discussion for the new state governments. He was on the committee to deal with spies and traitors; to pass on promotion of officers; the manner in which battles were waged; General Washington's conduct of the war.

From where she sat in faraway Braintree it appeared that through hard and continuous labor John Adams had become an Atlas, balancing a whole world of work on his broad shoulders, his contributions indispensable during the difficult period of transition when there was much desertion from the army, many battles lost through poor leadership, much greedy profiteering on the part of Patriot suppliers at the expense of the fledgling country. He could never leave until he considered his work in reliable hands.

Was this vanity on John's part? She did not believe so. She believed it was a sense of duty. She had written to Mercy Warren, "Our country is as it were a secondary God, and the first and greatest parent." If she felt this strongly, how must John feel?

John did not leave Philadelphia until October 13, 1776, thirty-eight days after Bass had reached there with the horses. The two weeks' horseback ride across Pennsylvania, New Jersey, New York and Massachusetts refreshed him. From the moment of jumping off his horse, of embracing Abigail and the children, the house glowed with so much of his joy that it lighted the rooms and their faces as though there were bright fires burning in every hearth.

The snows came early in November. She and John lay snug and secure in their four-poster, its ball-fringe cover half closed to keep them warm. Through the far window, through the partially opened curtains, she could see the white flakes drifting downward. More than ever her bed was like a ship returning to home port with its hold filled with a precious cargo of peace and contentment. She remembered her nuptial night in this bed and how she had thought what a miracle marriage was, sweeping away the accumulated strains and restraints. Not even John's reelection to the Congress disturbed them now, for the legislature had accepted his proposal to appoint additional delegates, any two of whom sitting in the Congress would be legally empowered to speak for Massachusetts. This meant that at the most John would have to spend only two or three months away.

He stirred in her arms.

"Are you awake?" she whispered.

"No," he murmured, "I'm asleep. I'm dreaming that I'm home in my own bed."

For a moment her voice felt locked in her throat, then she asked:

"John, do you think we might have another baby? I've been thinking about it these long months."

"My dear, have you found some occult meaning in the figure five not possessed by the figure four?"

"Yes. If it's a girl."

"Oh!" He tipped her face upward so that he could see her eyes. "You want another daughter. You've never forgotten Susanna."

"Have you, John?"

"No."

"You would have to make me one promise."

"Name it."

"That you would be home for the birth. That I wouldn't have to go through the childbirth alone."

"You have my word."

The law courts of Massachusetts had been reopened and as Abigail was able to testify from having entertained the judges for dinner when the court sat at Braintree, and the following night the lawyers, the returns were lucrative. The young lawyers who had come to the Bar while John was in Congress were reaping fortunes from handling "prize" cases, the capture of British cargo vessels laden with goods. John's former law clerks were piling up hundreds of pounds in fees.

"And I can't handle even one small case," John mourned.

"I don't understand why. You could have the pick of the litigations."

"I'm still Chief Justice of the Massachusetts Superior Court, even though I never sat. And I've just been re-elected a delegate to the Congress."

"You said you were resigning your position as Chief Justice."

"Yes, shortly."

"Then why not now?"

"I have to wait until a successor is chosen. And I must not become involved in private cases while I have public causes to plead. I know by maintaining my legal virtue I keep the Adams Specie Bank full of cobwebs instead of coins. Come into Boston with me tomorrow. I'll start repairing the house and bring my boat into a warehouse for scraping and painting. Then we'll be able to rent the house and sell the boat."

"I don't mean to intrude into your private affairs," she said with a wry smile, "but would you mind telling me what you're planning to use for legal tender?"

"Money. Several lawyers and merchants who have owed me for years are suddenly prosperous. The war. And scarcities. Since they are growing wealthy off our Massachusetts tax notes I think I'll do a little legal leveling by charging them interest on their debts."

"Usurious rates."

"Preferably. And the legislature has promised, come January, to repay all my expenses, plus a little item they call services."

"Would that by any chance mean wages?"

"It does when we engage our hired hands. Let's wait and see."

Everyone kept his promise. By the second week in January, Abigail was able to inform her husband that she was in circumstances. He congratulated her, then showed her the sum he had collected from the long-owed debts, as well as a draft from the legislature for £226 6s. 2d. covering his nine months of service for 1776. They sat at the clients' table while he studied his expense books for the year.

"I can't for the life of me tell whether this figure represents my outlays, or if there are a few pounds left over for 'services.' I sometimes forget to write down my expenditures, let's say for writing paper or candles or a stable bill. Each time I add my total costs I find I have £5 to £10 less than my figures say I should."

"Figure by previous years. What about 1775?"

He went to his locked desk, took an account book out of a pigeonhole. "Here: from April to August my expenses were £34 8s. From August to December they were £127 7s. 10d. I made two trips that year."

"Even so, they add up to something over £260. Then how could £226 for nine months of service include a wage?"

He sighed. "It couldn't. Maybe £20 because I scrimped and denied myself. Enough to pay the wage of your hired hand."

"That's quite an equation!"

"No, they're right. If public service becomes profitable, too many people will want the jobs for the wrong reasons. Thus far we've all been volunteers, which meant we could work ourselves ten times as hard as anyone employed. But the new law eases circumstances a little: we delegates are to be paid twenty-two shillings a day as wages. Not the wealth of Croesus, but it will pay for the new baby."

Her eyes sparkled.

"A fair bargain. Your labor for mine."

"When are you expecting?"

"Sometime in July."

"I have to leave in a few days. But I'll plan to be home by April or May."

"Please. The last weeks drag so and it's difficult to get around."

He left everything shipshape so that she would have a minimum of responsibilities before he returned. He had brought in a carpenter to make necessary repairs to the barn and cellar, hired two hands for the year, bought seed, salt hay to fertilize, re-stoned the fences, pruned the orchard, sharpened their farm implements. He took £100 with him, left the rest, after he paid the repair bills for the Boston house, in her hands.

He wrote to her every day or two, long amusing letters, telling her all the humorous anecdotes related by his garrulous barber. He confided little about the progress of the Congress, but she knew he was keeping up his journal and she would read the descriptions when he returned. With the British now threatening Philadelphia, the delegates moved to Baltimore, meeting in a converted tavern. John wrote that he found Baltimore a very pretty town surrounded by prosperous farms, the scenery being enhanced by the fact that all Crown sympathizers had been banished from the landscape. He complained about the monstrous prices, and of the streets being dirty and miry. However he was happy about the way the Continental Army was filling up, and the exemplary manner in which Maryland followed Congress' strictures in setting up its government. If a few days should pass without a message from him she went up to her office and read again the dozen letters piled on her escritoire and felt her own spirits as high as his.

She put an advertisement in Gill's *Continental Journal* for February sixth and thirteenth, renting the house on Queen Street to a Mr. Willis, a printer and good tenant, for £22 per annum.

Then a mid-February snowstorm set them between six-foot banks. The horses and sleds could get through so there was a lot of visiting with the Cranches and her father and Betsy in Weymouth. Braintree and Weymouth were filled with their own three-month militia who had deserted because of the continuing smallpox. There was no flour or rye to be bought, the butchers offered only the poorest cuts. Boston was on the verge of bread riots because the bakers would sell only one loaf to a family. Abigail had to put the children on short rations until one of her uncle Isaac's ships came into Boston Harbor with a cargo of flour, part of which John had ordered and paid for while he was home.

She felt completely well. There were occasional troubles to be sure: Johnny fell ill, and Cotton Tufts could not determine what it was. Tommy got worms and lost most of his flesh until Abigail managed to have John send her a box of Dr. Ryan's wafers. Their cow, Ruggles, was lost on the ice. Her sister Betsy notified them that she was going to marry John Shaw now that he had been ordained. This upset the Smith family, for Betsy had stoutly denied when John Shaw was obliged to leave the Smith home three years before that she loved the man. Apparently they had been meeting or writing in secret during this time. John wrote that he was delighted by the news; Abigail declined to forward John's good wishes on the grounds that Betsy had deceived them. Betsy did not seem to notice the omission, she was too busy with her preparations for housekeeping. The Reverend Mr. John Shaw had been ordained in his first parsonage at Haverhill, and in the fall they were to be married.

New England was awash with seasonal rumors: the Congress had tied the hands of George Washington so that he could not fight. The Congress had made General Washington a dictator. England had proposed a new treaty and terms to the Congress. The New England soldiers were cowards who ran from battle. . . .

Her brother Billy, in his uniform of a captain with the newly formed marines, arrived with Catharine Louisa to stay overnight before he sailed on the *American Tartar*. James Warren came by to compliment her on how well the farm looked. Richard Cranch gave up watch repairing and bought a nearby farm. Two hospitals opened in Braintree for the inoculation of soldiers, Cotton Tufts working in one of them. The only upsetting news was the death of a friend in Boston, a Mrs. Howard. Abigail wrote to John:

"She was delivered of a son or daughter . . . yesterday week. A mortification in her bowels occasioned her death. Everything of this kind naturally shocks a person in similar circumstances. How great the mind that can overcome the fear of death! How anxious the heart of a parent who looks round upon a family of young and helpless children and thinks of leaving them to a world full of snares and temptations which they have neither discretion to foresee nor prudence to avoid."

The snows disappeared, the sun lengthened. By the second half of April John was involved in shaping the Articles of Confederation under which the thirteen states would become a unified nation. The delegates, returned to Philadelphia because the British threat to capture the city had not materialized, were undergoing a protracted battle to achieve a compromise under which a central government could be strong enough to protect the separate states but not so strong as to bleed them of their local and legal rights.

She completed her sixth month; the child was wonderfully active, keeping her company. She knew by now that John would not be returning as he had said; nor could she hold him to his promise to return for the birth. If some matter of urgency failed because he had to quit in the heat of the contest, she would never forgive herself. Nor would she want John to be able to reproach her by thinking, "You really did not need me. I could have finished my job."

She wrote thanking him for his many letters, "consolation to me though a cold comfort in a winter's night," and then by indirection freed him to remain at his task. "As the summer advances I have many anxieties, some of which I should not feel or at least should find them greatly alleviated if you could be with me. But as that is a satisfaction I know I must not look for . . . I must summon all the philosophy I am mistress of since what cannot be helped must be endured."

May and June passed quietly. In July she began "not feeling well" as she reported to her sister Mary. Memories of her friend Mrs. Howard obtruded themselves despite her efforts to dispel them from her mind. Cotton Tufts was summoned from Weymouth. He must have ridden his horse at breakneck speed to arrive so quickly, but there was no sign of it as he came into the bedroom. He looked considerably like the Reverend Mr. Smith: tall, brown-eyed, furrow-cheeked.

"What's your complaint, my little cousin-niece?"

"Headaches. My vision is blurring. There's a swelling in my ankles."

"Sounds usual. How is the baby?"

"Kicking."

"You're expecting in about a week?"

"About."

"Let's stay in bed. Keep off the stairs. I'll round up some new books for you to read."

Though her legs had begun to swell she was moderately comfortable, reading Smollett's *The Expedition of Humphrey Clinker* and Oliver Goldsmith's *The Vicar of Wakefield* in its small two-volume edition. Cotton Tufts came in each afternoon to visit. Once, sitting opposite Abigail at the front window of the bedroom for a breath of air, he saw the whole imprint of the baby's foot through her lightweight robe.

"That baby's in a hurry to get herself born."

"Cousin Cotton, you're more heartening than a draft of John's rum punch."

"Cheaper, too," he laughed, "now that we're not importing molasses from the West Indies any more."

That night she was seized by a severe shaking fit. There was no clock in the room, and she would have been unable to time the seizure, so violent was its nature, but she surmised that at least three minutes had passed before she quieted. A heavy veil settled over her senses. She fell into a deep sleep. When she awakened at dawn it was like struggling upward from the floor of a dark lake. Only then did she realize that what she had fallen into was not sleep but a coma. When Dr. Tufts came in at noon she told him about the convulsion.

"Cousin Cotton, I think the baby is dead."

Cotton did not answer, but gazed at her over the top of his spectacles, the furrows deep in his forehead.

"Your eyes seem to be focusing all right, Cousin Abigail. Any blurring?"

"None."

"Good. And the headache?"

"It's gone."

"What about your ankles?"

She set aside the light linen sheet. "The swelling is down."

"You're all right. The child probably dropped into a better position for birth."

"Do you think the child could be taken from me now?"

"With those horrible instruments? Certainly not. They kill more mothers than they save. Give yourself a chance for a normal birth."

"Please ask Mary to summon the midwife."

When Mary came back she scolded Abigail gently. "You've let the vapors take hold of you."

"I hope so."

On the evening of July tenth a letter from John was brought to her from Boston. She forgot her misgivings, got out of bed and wrote him a cheerful letter, telling him of what a good season they were having on the farm, and that her labor pains had begun. She returned to bed and slept well.

At midmorning she gave birth. Her sufferings were sharp and short. She listened for the baby's cry.

There was none.

She raised herself on one elbow. The first thing she saw was that it was a girl. A pretty one. But the skin was a bluish gray. The midwife was pounding the child's behind and chest. She heard someone come running up the stairs, saw the blur of Cotton Tufts go past the foot of her bed, place his mouth on the baby's mouth and begin breathing into her.

It was no use. Neither the doctor nor the midwife could feel any pulsation in the umbilical cord or the child's neck vessels. Death had been due to compression, the child's chin pressing on the cord caught between the chin and chest.

Mary was dry-eyed, helping the midwife care for Abigail. But Cotton gripped his big underlip with his upper teeth so that Abigail would not be disturbed by the sound of his weeping. When he had regained control of himself he dropped on one knee by the side of her bed, took her hand in his long fingers, begged her forgiveness.

"I'm a doctor. I'm so ashamed of my ignorance. When you first told me of your alarm I should have been able to help you. There might still have been time to save the child. How could you have been so sure when I still thought she was alive?"

She answered wryly.

"Because the baby was in me, not you. When I quieted, it was because the struggle within me was over."

She was heartsick. When Nab was allowed into the bedroom and learned the news, the girl broke into convulsive sobbing. Mary wanted to take her out of the room. Abigail said:

"Let her stay. We will comfort each other. Nab, come here, my dear, and weep on my shoulder."

The dead child was named Elizabeth and buried in the Adams plot. Her father, sister Mary and John's mother accompanied the Reverend Mr. Wibird to the burying ground.

Five days later Abigail went to her desk to write John a letter, feeling that she must reassure him in her own hand that there was nothing he could have done for her by being home.

Cotton Tufts entered the room. She put down her pen and turned her face full upon him.

"Would you please answer me one question with complete honesty. I should not risk having another child, should I?"

"Your life has been in danger twice: with the birth of Susanna, and just now with Elizabeth. I think you should not risk it again."

She was silent for a moment.

"I knew that had to be the answer. From the moment I heard no cry. God has been good. He has given me four wonderful children. I think He does not mean for me to have more. I would be ungrateful if I did not thank Him for His bounty and accept His judgment."

She turned back to her desk, picked up the pen and wrote:

"Join with me, my dearest friend, in gratitude to Heaven that a life I know you value has been spared and carried through distress and danger, although the dear infant is numbered with its ancestors. . . . I have so much cause for thankfulness amidst my sorrow that I would not entertain a repining thought. . . . Adieu, dearest of friends, adieu."

12

It was fortunate that she regained her strength so quickly, and that she had a desire to trudge through the loam of her fields, her head in the ninety-two-degree hot sun; for the hundred-dollar bounty offered by the Braintree selectmen and Massachusetts legislature for soldiers had stripped the farms of help. The corn and English grain were abundant, but her recently acquired Negro had left in the midst of haying. The three-day cycles of heat, punctuated by days of rain, threatened to foreshorten the apple crop. Richard Cranch was farming successfully in his first year. When he found a hand who was willing to work for a few days he sent him to Abigail. So did her father and Cotton Tufts; at the height of the harvesting they both worked in the fields with Abigail and the children, getting the crops into the barn. Dairy products were scarce and expensive. Abigail earned considerable sums for her milk, butter, cheese, eggs and poultry.

At night she studied the maps, trying to place the American and British troops, following their movements, skirmishes, battles from the potpourri of information that reached her and was printed in the journals.

Even as she had been suffering her own personal defeat in early July, the American army had suffered a series of crippling blows in the north. "Gentleman Johnny" Burgoyne, whose mellifluous prose talents had so ably consolidated the Patriots by calling their militia a "preposterous military parade," had left Canada with a well-organized and provisioned army of nearly ten thousand soldiers and a hundred and forty cannon. He recaptured Fort Ticonderoga from Major General Arthur St. Clair and his poorly armed Continental regiments by fortifying a hill just above the fort, even as General Washington had driven the British out of Boston by fortifying Dorchester Heights with Henry Knox's cannon from this same Ticonderoga. On July 7, 1777, he had whipped the rear guard of the fleeing Americans at Hubbardton, Vermont, and started his drive toward Albany and Manhattan, where he planned to join up with General Howe's army in a pincer movement.

General Washington was not doing any better with the main American forces in Pennsylvania. Here at the battle of Brandywine General Howe with fifteen thousand men engaged Washington's forces of eight thousand Continentals and three thousand militia. Howe outmaneuvered Washington, sending half of his force against the American rear, crumpling its right flank because Washington had concentrated his men for an attack on center. The Americans fought stubbornly until sunset, then fled northward leaving a thousand casualties on the battlefield.

It was a major loss. Now, on September twenty-seventh, Sir William Howe occupied Philadelphia without a struggle. This time the Congress fled to York, Pennsylvania. General Anthony Wayne, preparing to strike the British rear, was surprised by a night attack at Paoli near Valley Forge. Almost his entire detachment of several hundred Americans was bayoneted to death in a massacre. On October fourth Washington marched on Germantown in hopes of surprising and crushing Howe's army of nine thousand regulars; he almost broke through Howe's lines, but Cornwallis moved out from Philadelphia with reinforcements and inflicted heavy losses on the Americans, including one regiment taken prisoner. Washington then managed to get the main body of his men out to safety, but it was still another crushing blow.

The news of the defeats and slaughters was like a bayonet thrust to the heart of Abigail Adams and all the men and women loyal to the Patriot cause. After each setback a pall would settle over the countryside like a leaden, suffocating black cloud. The Patriots cried out their unremitting hatred for the Tory companies fighting alongside the redcoats, Hessians and Indians. She had lived through the honest soul-searching of men such as Jonathan Sewall, Isaac Smith, Jr., and Samuel Quincy who had preferred to leave the country rather than fight against England. For her this was a sad error but an honest one. For native-born Americans to join the British—Burgoyne used six hundred of them in the battle of Bemis Heights—and kill other native-born Americans was a kind of fratricide that was totally incomprehensible. The Crown sympathizers of Christ Church were proclaiming that their husbands and sons too were dying bravely for their convictions, but it was too roiled a political sea for any safe passage of the frail bark of logic.

By nine o'clock her eyelids would grow as heavy as her spirits. She would climb the steep twisting stairs to her bedroom, sleep with all the windows open hoping for a breeze, and to dream, sometimes of John coming home and greeting her coldly.

When she received a letter and learned that John was at York, eighty-eight miles from Philadelphia, her major wonder about the town was whether it was eighty-eight miles closer to home or farther away. John informed her that he was now living in an area so totally German that they conducted their school and sermons in their own language, and a man could live his whole life there without learning a word of English.

Each day was a mixed bag. Her cousin Hannah Lincoln married Ebenezer Storer, her aunt Elizabeth's brother; that was a good marriage. Her sister Betsy married her Reverend Mr. John Shaw and moved into her new home and pastorate at Haverhill. In Abigail's opinion this was a poor match. Richard Cranch's brother-in-law, Deacon Palmer, led a militia army into Rhode Island to mount a major attack, but withdrew without a fight, and Palmer came into disfavor. Then news came from the north of a smashing success, with General Burgoyne surrendering an entire army of five thousand men, arms and equipment to General Horatio Gates at Saratoga, New York.

This was the greatest victory of the American troops. Abigail took her daughter into Boston "to join tomorrow with my friends in thanksgiving," as she wrote John that night, "and praise to the Supreme

Being who hath so remarkably delivered our enemies into our hands." The fort at Red Bank, New Jersey, on the Delaware River was defended with what John described as magnanimity; a bold British attack on Fort Mifflin across the river in Pennsylvania was repulsed, and two British men-of-war were set on fire. John, for whom some of the sheen on General George Washington had worn off between the defeats of Long Island and Germantown, wrote Abigail in confidence:

"Congress will appoint a Thanksgiving, and one cause of it ought to be that the glory of turning the tide of arms is not immediately due to the commander-in-chief, nor to Southern troops. If it had been, idolatry and adulation would have been unbounded, so excessive as to endanger our liberties."

A couple of weeks later she learned her brother Billy's ship, the *American Tartar*, was captured with all hands. Billy was sent to Newfoundland as a prisoner of war. Because the reputation of the British for treatment of American prisoners was a wretched one, when Catharine Louisa brought the report to Braintree, Abigail put on a cheerful face.

"My dear sister, you yourself have said that Billy can take care of himself. Unpack your portmanteau and enjoy a few days' visit."

November was stretching toward its end before John reached Braintree, just a month short of a year after he had left, in early January. She had not thought she would speak of their stillborn child, but they were awkward together after their first embrace, John's eyes not quite meeting hers. She realized then that the loss of the infant would have to be discussed to dispel the sense of guilt harrowing the air between them. She stood primly, her hands clasped in front of her.

"I should have been here with you," he cried. "It leaves a gnawing accusation in my mind."

"There is one in mine too. Was there something I did wrong, or might have done better? I'm sure every mother feels that when her child is stillborn."

He put both arms supplicatingly about her waist. His hair had fallen over his brow. She brushed it back with the palm of her hand, feeling the perspiration on his forehead.

"I do not reprove myself. And neither must you. It would have been a comfort to have you here; but it could not have changed the little one's fate. We must love each other the more for our deprivation."

He put his cheek on hers.

"It was never *you* that I might love the less," he murmured; "it was myself."

He had been home a very short time when she saw that this was a different John Adams from the one who had come home from his four previous sessions of the Congress. The way he firm-footed about the house; the manner in which he planted his papers in their proper places in his office; the lists he drew of their supplies after his inspection of the cellar, the dairy, the barns, portrayed a man who had come to a decision.

The six Adamses sat crowded, elbow to elbow, at the table before the fire in the kitchen, happy to be locked in so tightly together. John and Abigail made toasts to the little ones by raising their cups of the first New England rum made from the cornstalks of their fields.

"Children, I have presents for each of you. Can you guess what they are?"

"Books!" cried the four in unison.

John appeared crestfallen.

"Now how could you have known so sure?"

"But, Papa," cried Johnny, "you always bring us books."

"You've brought me some kind of a present too, John," murmured Abigail, "but I can't quite make out what."

"It's the gift of myself, for whatever that may be worth. I have finished at the Congress. The Articles of Confederation have been agreed upon. The Department of War and Ordnance is organized. Younger men can handle the work better than I. I will not accept re-election." His mind was set, and they could tell it. "From now on I shall only be a dealer in small politics."

"What about large politics?" Abigail asked. "Under your Articles of Confederation doesn't our central government have to have ruling officers?"

"To be sure. But I'm not one of them. By seven in the morning I shall be back to my practice of law. I've earned the right to work for us for the same four years I've worked for the common cause."

"Amen!"

They came together after their separations as friends and lovers. The quality of renewed delight in each other was a miracle they could count on; their faith that nothing between them would or could be changed.

"We are fortunate," Abigail observed when the night had grown late and still they could not bear to part again, even into sleep, but remained awake filling the absence of the eleven months with all their outpourings of thought. "Our affection will never grow thin. We both need love. With it everything is possible; without it we are nothing."

The stars paled, the first tint of gray dawn lighted their east window. John rose, slipped into his warm robe, dropped another log on the fire, covered Abigail to the chin with blankets.

"I'll keep the children entertained. Sleep until you've had your fill."

"What about you, John, don't you need sleep too?"

"No. I'm too happy to be home. I want to arrange my lawbooks, sort my papers, send out word to Suffolk County that Advocate Adams is back in his office and clients are welcome."

She slept until noon. When she came downstairs she found several men sitting in her parlor, the spill-over from John's office. His old clients had not forgotten him. Within twenty-four hours he had new clients ambitious to engage him. Abigail made the men comfortable not only in the sitting parlor, with a warming fire bright in the hearth, but in her kitchen as well, serving hot toddies. "Our own cornstalk rum," she explained triumphantly.

"I have applications from all quarters in the most important disputes," John announced with pleasure smeared over his face like jam.

"How could it be otherwise, Advocate? You've accomplished your youthful ambition to become the first lawyer at the Braintree Bar."

He chuckled. "Even at the Suffolk County Bar. Do you remember reading about Elisha Doane's ship, the *Lusanna*? It's a Cape Cod vessel but was carrying British papers and selling whale oil in England. It was captured by a New Hampshire ship and taken into Portsmouth as a prize. The captors claim the ship now belongs to them and the cargo as well. Doane wants me to defend and get back his vessel."

"It sounds interesting."

"With a fortune involved. But it means I will have to be away for two weeks to plead the case." He turned to his oldest son. "Johnny, hurry up and become a lawyer, then you can take care of all the clients who come to the office while I'm away."

"I'm willing, Papa."

"And what about you, Nab, wouldn't you like to be the first woman barrister in New England?"

"No, Father. I think it will be simpler if I marry one instead."

John cried, "Marriage! How old are you, young lady?"

"Twelve and a half."

He turned to Abigail, asked wide-eyed, "Isn't that a bit young for a girl to be talking about marriage?"

"Marriage is a woman's profession," replied Abigail. "The earlier she starts thinking about it, the better she will be at her job."

13

She spent the days reading and sewing before the fire and going out with the children each afternoon to sled on Penn's Hill. It was a period of tranquillity, of inner thankfulness that the master of the family was home to take responsibility off her shoulders. The children commented that they had not seen her look so well for a long time. As an exercise in luxury she had the worn yellow couch in the sitting parlor recovered.

It was a short reprieve. At mid-December, while John was at Portsmouth for the *Lusanna* litigation, a messenger from York delivered three letters into her hands. The first two were from John's fellow delegates, James Lovell and Daniel Roberdeau; the third was from Henry Laurens, who had recently replaced John Hancock as president of the Congress. She cut under the wax of Lovell's letter first, had to read only a line or two to have her felicity-bubble burst before her eyes.

"I am charged by all those who are truly anxious here for the best prosperity of our affairs in France to press your acceptance of the commission which has this day been voted you. The great sacrifices which you have made of private happiness has encouraged them to hope you will undertake this new business. . . . Doctor Franklin's age alarms us. We want one man of inflexible integrity on that embassy."

She made her way to a sunlit chair by the west window. What could the letter mean? With a shaking hand she opened Roberdeau's letter.

"Your domestic views of happiness was not consulted on this occasion, but the necessity of your country for your talents, which being devoted to her service, I expect a cheerful acquiescence with a call so honorable, which I doubt not will prove a lasting honor to you and your connections as well as a blessing to these states. . . . I would advise your taking French books with you and a French companion. . . ."

Her eyes were wet by the time she got the third letter open, but she did not need clarity to see that this was an official letter:

"SIR,—I have the honor of conveying under this cover an extract from the minutes of Congress of the present date, which certifies your election to be a commissioner at the Court of France. . . . Permit me, sir, to congratulate with the friends of America upon this judicious appointment, and to wish you every kind of success and happiness.

"I have the honor to be with very great respect and esteem, sir, Your humble servant, HENRY LAURENS, *President of Congress.*"

In the short time it had taken her to read these few lines she had plunged into the depths of despair. After only two weeks of reunion there was a plot to rob her of all her happiness. The journey to Europe would be for an unlimited time, full of risks and hazards. Her life would be one continuous scene of loneliness, anxiety and apprehension.

There was no fire in her cold bedroom and she was too desolated to light one. She removed her dress, crawled between the blanket and quilt, closed the curtains of the bed and drew the quilt over her head to blot out the exterior world. But she wrestled with that exterior world mightily through the night. There was no question that John's appointment was for the public good. He had been on the committee to draw up a "Plan of Treaties"; and he had written the original documents under which the first commissioners had been sent to Paris. No, the appointment was a logical extension of his work. One of the most important factors in the winning of the war could be a series of treaties with Britain's archenemy, France, which would bring to America the desperately needed food, tools and machinery to set up their own manufactories, the powder, arms, artillery, money, trained officers, engineers, ships to end the conflict.

As the long hours of the sleepless night spun themselves out she found this to be the most excruciating conflict she had ever endured. The Congress was far enough away, two weeks of hard riding; and there had been danger of the delegates being taken by General Howe's army. But Paris, France! More than three thousand miles, two to four months for any completed trip or answering of letters. Treaty making was slow, tedious business; John could be gone for . . . years!

Wretched, already feeling abandoned, she wept until she felt the soaked pillow beneath her. The still hours of the night and one's lonely bed were a merciless battlefield where one could hope for no succor. Then, exhausted, deep in the dark forest, she began the long hard climb out of the quagmire of despair to the open albeit rock-strewn road in the sunlight.

It had never been her role to put restraints on her husband. She had, instead, worked to leave him free to act for himself. The honor of this important embassy was the surest possible sign of the high regard in which the Congress held John Adams. It would be both humiliating and destructive to her pride to allow it to be said that John Adams had refused an important post because his wife would not let him accept, as well as a mockery of the self-government which he had spent the last three years helping to create. How could she nullify the years of suffering and sacrifice she had already endured? Indeed, her major capital, she smiled ruefully, seemed to be her vested interest in her sacrifice!

She rose, lit the candles in the double-jointed candleholder over her desk, lowering the bottom half so that the light shone more directly on the pages of her Bible. She picked up her magnifying glass, quickly found the passage for which she was searching in Judges 5:24–27:

Blessed above women shall Ja'el the wife of Heber the Kenite be;
blessed shall she be above women in the tent.
He asked water, and she gave him milk;
she brought forth butter in a lordly dish.
She put her hand to the nail,
and her right hand to the workmen's hammer;
and with the hammer she smote Sisera,
she smote off his head,
when she had pierced and stricken through his temples.
At her feet he bowed, he fell, he lay down:
at her feet he bowed, he fell:
where he bowed, there he fell down dead.

She was Ja'el. She was Sisera. With the carpenter's mallet in her right hand she must find the place for the mortal blow to everything within her which would be the enemy of her husband. She must pierce her own forehead so that everything weak and selfish would lie at her feet, helpless in death. Then, and only then, could it be said of her:

"Blessed above women shall Abigail the wife of John be;
blessed shall she be above women in the tent."

In her gathering strength she realized that there was no end to the road on which they had set their feet in a conjugal partnership thirteen years before.

She lit the fire on the hearth, cracked the thin layer of ice in the washbowl, splashed her feverish face and brow with the shocking cold water. She put on a robe, went silent down the stairs, read the stately clock at near three in the morning, put some kindling on the glowing under-ash of the fire, swung the kettle over the fresh spurting flames. When the water was boiled she indulged herself with a good pinch of tea from the canister John had brought home and drank the invigorating Souchong scalding hot.

Self-knowledge is hard won; admission of incontrovertible fact is even harder come by. By the time the tall grandfather clock chimed four she knew that John Adams would accept the commission. By the five-chime she knew that she too must insist that he go to France to negotiate the treaties. Very well, if she could not stop him, and could not let him go, what was the answer?

It was dawn before she reached her solution; and when it came, halfway through the third cup of the annealing tea, she wondered how she could have been so obtuse, allowed herself to suffer so greatly in reaching the decision.

Nab came into the kitchen, sleepy-eyed but anxious.

"Mama, I looked for you in bed. You were gone."

"I've been here since three."

"You look better. Even with a little smile. Mama, what was in the letters?"

"Your father's appointment to Paris, to write treaties with the French."

"Papa is going?"

"Yes."

Nab was a stolid character who kept her feelings to herself; only rarely did she verge on tears.

"And leave us alone again?"

"No, Nab, we're going with him."

"All of us?"

"Yes. Providing his tenderness will suffer us to accompany him. Wake Johnny, I want him to take these letters to Boston to Uncle Isaac's."

Nab ruminated for a moment.

"Mama, you always said you were afraid of an ocean voyage."

"Terrified."

"Then why have you decided to go?"

"Because the terrors of the unknown are no greater than the terrors of the known."

John was back in time for the Christmas party Abigail had planned for the combined Adams, Smith and Quincy families. She concealed nothing from him as she recounted her journey from Dante's pit of the Inferno out to the habitable periphery of Purgatory. He listened attentively.

"I heard at almost the same moment you did. At the trial of the cause at Portsmouth Mr. Langdon came in from Philadelphia and, leaning over the bar, whispered to me that Mr. Deane was recalled and I was appointed to go to France. I did not take it seriously because at York, when Elbridge Gerry told me that he wanted to propose my name for France because Silas Deane's conduct on the Joint Commission had been so intolerably bad as to disgrace himself and his country, and that the Congress had no other way of retrieving the dishonor but by recalling him, I told Mr. Gerry that it was beyond discussion.

"Then I found the letters at Uncle Isaac's. My first thought was for my beloved wife and children. My next was that I know little French and certainly not enough to deal with the French King and his ministers. The dangers of the sea, the sufferings of a winter passage, had little weight with me. The British men-of-war were a more serious consideration. The news of my appointment and the order to the Navy Yard in Boston to fit out the frigate *Boston* to take me to France will be known in Rhode Island where the British navy lies. Our Tory spies would keep the British aware of my departure. . . ."

"*Our* departure," she thought.

". . . On the other hand how can I refuse such a commission when General Washington and the pitiful remnants of his army are moving into a freezing camp at Valley Forge, and he has had to write the Congress that his men have not 'a moiety of a shirt'?" He looked up sharply at her. "You knew I would accept."

She nodded.

"You have always encouraged and animated me in all dangers and perplexities. I knew you would not fail me now."

"Did you also know I was coming along, with my four young trailing behind me?" she asked.

He seemed a bit startled; then he smiled.

"Immediately after Christmas we'll begin investigating."

Christmas was hilarious, with relatives and children packed into the house like cod salted in a barrel. The twenty-three adults and eighteen children took up every inch of space in John's office, the sitting parlor and thirty-foot-long kitchen, all set with tables. Abigail, convinced that it would be a long time before she could be with her family again, spread out a feast in the best tradition of her mother's holiday meals: roasted turkeys with chestnut dressing, a suckling pig, broiled fish, bacon, peas, custard, preserved fruit. She served no wine since General Washington had banished it from his table as an economy measure, but everyone loyally drank the cornstalk rum and declared it equal to the best West Indian product.

The next day John rode up to Boston with Samuel and Betsy Adams to begin inquiries about what was involved in taking his family to France. He did not return until the following evening. He was tired, his eyes clouded and lips twitching. Not until he had lighted his pipe and stretched his legs out toward the fire did she ask:

"John, is it that much more difficult than we imagined?"

"No-oo. Just in some aspects."

"Important ones, I gather."

"Yes. In an adventure like this everything is important. The consequence of a capture would be a lodging for me in Newgate. The spirit of contempt and vindictive rage with which the British are conducting the war forbid me to hope for the honor of an appointment to the Tower as state prisoner. Their Act of Parliament would authorize them to try me for treason and execute me."

"What about your wife and children?"

He turned his face from hers.

"No one in Boston knows."

"There are other problems?"

"All the mundane concerns. The Congress will pay my expenses: passage, the proper clothing, food on board, servants, proper supplies, the maintenance of lodgings in Paris, all legitimate costs to make our commission successful."

"Surely we can eat along and sleep along?"

"No, my dear friend, it doesn't work that way. First we must pay for your passage, and the little ones', at the regular rates. . . ."

"But you told me the *Boston* is a twenty-four-gun Continental frigate. Since this is a government ship and not a private one, why would we be obliged to pay fares? We would not be adding to the expense of the crossing."

"Captain Samuel Tucker is a commissioned officer in the American navy. However the *Boston* will be carrying all the paying passengers it can hold. The government needs the money."

"I see." Sadly.

"We must bring on board ship all of our food and drink for the journey: six sheep, eighteen chickens, forty to fifty dozen eggs, fresh slaughtered beef, pork, barrels of apples, of cider, twenty loaves of sugar, dried fruits, box of butter, cheeses, corn, flour for baking bread, cases of rum, Madeira."

"We have all that," she replied calmly. "What we don't have we can barter for."

His face cleared. "You're right, we have all that, thanks to your management of the farm. But clothes . . . We must have new clothes, fit to be worn in Paris, perhaps even in royal circles."

"We can barter for materials, refurbish what we have. There will be some fees, rents . . ."

"Yes, I'll be collecting some fees for my few weeks of legal work, perhaps enough for the passages. I won't grow discouraged again."

The children were wildly excited over the impending adventure. Nab worked by her mother's side, sewing and assembling the foodstuffs. Johnny was the quietest, but also the one who knew most exactly what life abroad would mean for him.

"Papa, will we have a chance to travel? I'd like to see Italy and Spain."

"Easy does it. We haven't left Braintree yet."

"That's what interests me most, Papa, foreign countries. Uncle Isaac loaned me his travel books, I brought them home in my saddlebags yesterday with the mail."

"Shades of my childhood," Abigail exclaimed, nostalgia enveloping her. "You're reading the same copies of Pontoppidan's *Natural History of Norway* and Pococke's *Description of the East* that I did."

Difficulties cropped up at every step. They could not find a responsible tenant for their house and farm. If they rented to someone they did not know or trust they could return to find it a shambles. John's mother suggested that they lock it up; she would watch over it. But they sorely needed the rental money. They also found themselves unwilling to rent the other thirty-five acres to the tenant they already had because he had not done well and wanted the farm for next to nothing. John was able to conclude only the smaller legal matters he had undertaken; the rest he had to turn over to other lawyers; hence the fees were modest because he had given only temporary service.

The cost of making clothes for the six of them proved outrageous. Cambric was up to forty-five dollars a yard, thread unbelievably expensive. If they were going to rent the house furnished they would have to buy mattresses, blankets, pillows, dishes, pewterware for the journey. Congress had voted him an adequate salary, about £2000 a year, but he could collect no part of the money until he had returned from his mission. . . . John worried constantly about her suffering should they be captured.

By mid-January Abigail knew that she was defeated. John was still struggling, trying to collect bad debts from past debtors, desperately seeking ways to assemble money without borrowing it. There simply was not enough to meet their needs, not by half. A ship's captain just in from France confided that setting up a household in Paris was even more expensive than in Massachusetts.

They lay in bed that night, each on his own side, rigid.

"It won't work, John."

"It's my fault. If I had practiced my law, had put aside a couple of thousand pounds . . ."

"You will have to go alone. It's the only solution."

He maintained bleak silence.

"Is it not, John, the only solution?"

"The only prudent one."

"And we do have to be practical?"

He was silent.

"Very well. We will remain at home. As we have these past eleven months."

He turned his head to her but did not put out a reassuring hand.

"Can you endure it? The mails will be months late. Many letters will be lost. We will know nothing about each other, whether we are well, even alive."

"I know what I will suffer. I've rehearsed enough. I will live and endure as best I can."

"The children will be disappointed."

"We will console each other."

In the morning when they informed the four youngsters, Johnny looked up unperturbed.

"I'm going."

"No, Johnny, we've decided."

"I've set my mind to it. I'll be Papa's companion. He should have one of us with him."

"You would be a fine friend for me, Johnny. But what about your mother?"

Abigail gulped. Johnny performed a thousand services for her in addition to being their post rider. She would miss him. He gave her company and sympathy when things went badly. He was a companion, too, for the other three children. It would give her two of them to worry about so far away.

The boy turned his face up to her, pleading.

"Mother, you will let me go, won't you? I could learn a great deal. I will get a good education. There's none here to have. You said so yourself."

She gazed about at her family. They were watching her, silent, big-eyed.

"Yes, Johnny, you can go."

She turned and left the room. It was the hardest decision she had ever made.

In the middle of February she stood alone on the peak of Mount Wollaston, the wind whipping her hair as it carried the *Boston* over the horizon to the northeast. Her heart was heavy. Through her mind surged the lines from Judges:

She put her hand to the nail,
and her right hand to the workmen's hammer;
and with the hammer she smote Sisera,
she smote off his head,
when she had pierced and stricken through
his temples.
At her feet he bowed, he fell, he lay down.

Part Two

SPREAD OUT THE HEAVENS

BOOK SIX

LANDSCAPE OF HELL

1

THE conversion of John's law office into a crossroads shop was complete. On the clients' table Abigail displayed her boxes of white gauze, handkerchiefs, colored ribbons, feathers, mittens and gloves, French glassware, Dutch paints. Husky little Tommy, reaching toward his ninth birthday on this stifling July day of 1781, had moved his father's lawbooks off the shelves, wrapped them in old copies of the *Boston Gazette* and stored them in the attic. On the shelves Abigail displayed the rolls of materials recently arrived for her from Europe: calico and chintz, Barcelona linens, Bengals, nankeens, Persian silk, woolens, colored lutestring. She had taken John's papers out of the stand-up desk with its myriad pigeonholes, labeled and tied each group and fitted them in neat piles in an attic trunk. The pigeonholes now had fresh labels, each a convenient bin for bundles of pins, Mogul playing cards, artificial flowers, squares of sealing wax, Bohea tea.

Standing in the open doorway to the Boston–Plymouth Road, through which customers could come without disturbing the rest of the house, Abigail surveyed her shop with satisfaction. Tommy came to her side. He had none of John Quincy's brilliance as a student and little of Charley's infectious humor, Abigail valued him as the most practical of her three sons, slow and methodical in his work but dependable for the completion of any task begun.

"It looks real nice, Ma."

"Better than selling over the kitchen table, Tommy. You did a fine job of helping me. So did you, Nab."

"I'm glad you're pleased, Mother, because I'm not."

Abigail made a sharp appraisal of her sixteen-year-old daughter. Nab had grown, since John's departure, from a child, dumpy and plain-faced, who resembled her father, into a slim, long-legged beauty with deep blue eyes and a crown of chestnut hair, with ripe-peach skin, full red lips and gleaming white teeth. In her preoccupation with the war, running the farm and assembling this merchandise, Abigail had not looked objectively enough at her daughter, with her high proud breasts and slender hips, to realize that Nab was now fully grown and likely to be the catch of Suffolk County. One thing she had noticed: as her daughter matured she had become more ingrown, keeping her thoughts and emotions to herself. She moved with a regal dignity that came straight from her grandmother Smith.

Nab had worked hard to make the shop attractive. Abigail was caught by surprise at the disapproving tone of her daughter's voice.

"Why aren't you pleased, Nab?"

"Because I resent our becoming petty shopkeepers."

"What does the word 'petty' refer to: your mother, or the goods we are selling?"

"Mother, you're quibbling. I just don't think it's dignified for the family of an American minister in Europe to be selling rows of pins and yards of calico out of their home."

"I like having a store," cried Tommy, red in the face. "Keeps company falling in."

Abigail answered her daughter.

"Were your father at home practicing law we would be comfortable. He prefers to serve his country abroad, on a modest wage. If I am to keep our farm and house together, put aside money for the three boys to go to Harvard College and keep us out of debt I must raise cash in any honest way I can."

"We could do without things. I don't mind being genteelly poor, but I cringe every time I see you measuring out cloth on Father's conference table."

"Nab, we're all shopkeepers of one sort or another. Your uncle Cotton sells his doctoring services. Your grandfather Smith's goods is religion and faith in God; your father sold writs, wills, appeals to judges and juries."

"But it does us so little good, Mother. Half the shipments that Father orders are lost at sea. These last rolls of calico reached us wet and mildewed."

"We'll sell them," Abigail interrupted; "they are dry by now."

"Yes, but for what price? How do you know what to charge for things when you never receive an invoice? Have you ever figured how much of your merchandise lies at the bottom of the Atlantic Ocean . . . ?"

Abigail came to the table to gaze head on at her rebellious daughter, already taller than she.

"That's why I don't figure, Nab."

She went to the open door and stared out at the oppressive granulated heat of midsummer. She had been able to get no money from the Congress for John's services even after three and a half years. At first he had permitted her to draw modest drafts on him in France or Holland where he was attempting to negotiate a loan for the United States; but the summer before he had urged her not to draw any more bills as he had no money either.

Taxes were the crushing burden, so onerous that tenants were threatening to walk off the farms, Abigail's included. Many owners were trying desperately to sell. In recent months Abigail had had to pay a sixty-dollar tax on land they owned in Milton, in addition to a parish tax of fifty dollars; state, county and town taxes to provide beef and grain for the army; for hiring a Braintree man for six months in the service, thirty dollars. Her days were spent in scrambling to assemble the necessary dollars. Her taxes were so high and so numerous that she knew not which way to turn.

Inflation caused by the printing of paper money had made a further shambles of savings and property values. Beef sold for eight dollars a pound, mutton nine dollars, rye at one hundred and thirty-three dollars a bushel, molasses at forty-eight dollars a gallon, coffee twelve dollars a pound, tea ninety dollars, corn one hundred and fifty dollars a bushel. Nightmare figures made bearable only because merchants were bidding for her cheese at ten dollars a pound and her butter at twelve. There was no question in her mind but that the inflation could be a more deadly enemy than the British; the quest for independence might fail in the field of prices rather than battle. How could the Congress, which had no assets to begin with, arm and provision an army at prices distended a hundredfold?

She had three sons growing up who would have to be educated, a daughter who must be provided with a respectable dowry. She owed them that much; they must not reach adulthood with what would normally have been their patrimony eaten up by taxes and inflation. And so she tried to accumulate the necessary dollars to buy farmlands for each of her young in the newly opened region of Vermont. A farm spelled personal independence. Sometimes she felt like a beaver trying to build a dam across a torrent.

She turned back to her daughter.

"Nab," she said gently, "when you have a husband and children of your own you'll do things more plebeian than shopkeeping to help your family. But I understand your reluctance, and I'll not call on you to sell to customers."

"I'll sell, Ma, when you can't," Tommy offered. "I like to keep shop."

There was the sound of a carriage coming up the road. The coach, as lavishly decorated as Abigail remembered from her days in Boston, was drawn by matching bays. The carriage stopped before the open door. Two ladies were handed down by grooms. Boston ladies, from the finery; apparently neither had ever heard of the Sumptuary Laws. The taller of the two was dressed in a stunning silk gown open in the front to show an embroidered flowered petticoat. A gold necklace matched two gold jangling bracelets on her wrist. The short one had her hair thickly powdered and pomaded under a wide hat with a tall feather. They belonged to a clique of newly rich in Boston whose husbands or protectors were acquiring fortunes by profiteering off the government and the army.

The taller of the two women said:

"Mrs. Adams, we heard from a secret source that you just received a shipment from Paris."

"From Amsterdam, more correctly."

"But you do have French goods?"

"French is all the fashion now, you know," the smaller one added.

Abigail showed her stock proudly; it had been acquired after months of heartbreaking losses through seizure on the high seas, theft, unexplained disappearance. Tommy brought down the materials from the shelves, the black silks, figured lawn, then opened the drawers of his father's desk to show the smaller objects. The women were interested only in the boxes on the table.

"We want everything to make us gay," the pomaded one cried, gathering up batches of ribbons and feathers.

"This green umbrella is divine, I'll take it," cried the taller one.

"Only the Lord is divine," Abigail murmured under her breath, adding up the bill.

Their coachman carried out the purchases. When it came time to pay, the two women brought forth rolls of paper money.

"I'm sorry," said Abigail, "but we paid for the goods in hard money. We cannot take soft."

"You'll take whatever kind of money we offer," said the taller woman, with an edge to her voice. "It's coin of the realm; my friend says so."

"Then tell your friend to pay his bills with it. Tommy, bring back our bundles from the carriage."

"Oh no," cried the short one, on the verge of tears; "we've searched all Boston and they've nothing so fine. Amanda, stop being shrewd. Pay her in sterling. You know we brought more than enough with us."

Amanda paid in coin. The two of them flounced out the door. Abigail turned from watching them being handed into the carriage to see Nab standing at the opposite door, grim.

"They humiliated themselves, dear, not me," she murmured in self-defense.

She had underestimated her daughter. Nab came to her mother and kissed her on the cheek, the first such demonstration Abigail could remember in quite a time.

"Mother, from now on we'll divide up the customers. You take the gentry, and let me handle these whores."

"Nab! Not in front of Tommy! Wherever did you learn such a word?"

2

When John was at home, time did not exist for her as a separate or discernible entity; it was fluid, days pouring effortlessly into nights, weeks into the months: the continuous flow of life. With John away, as he had been for three years, time became a solid; each hour was a hill, each day a ridge, each week a peak, each month a mountain range. From every ridge or peak, panting and exhausted, she would look behind her to see how far she had come, what steeps she had already conquered, never suspecting that there was a still higher range ahead. When she caught her breath, and her heart stopped pounding in her chest, she would begin her climb of the next Himalaya. She said to herself:

"I shall reckon over each week as it passes, and rejoice at my hard-won victory each Saturday night."

It was a method of blocking time into endurable segments. The prospect of another whole month without her husband might have overwhelmed her, but she was capable of living for a week without him, gathering the strength to face the new week by checking off the past one as accomplished. She knew all too well the line:

They also serve who only stand and wait.

Women, too, clasped on their armor at dawn, surged forth to sanguinary battle, swords flailing about them, bombs bursting over their heads. Had Milton's standing and waiting meant quiet acceptance? To wait courageously month in and year out took a courage peculiar to wives and mothers, no less arduous than the adventuresome sorties in which their husbands risked their lives.

John and John Quincy had no sooner disappeared over the horizon on the *Boston* than news reached her that Benjamin Franklin had been stabbed to death by British agents outside Paris; and that the next victim designate was Commissioner John Adams. The reassurance of her family that John was safe now because he would be on guard only intensified the nightly terrors which enveloped her.

The fact that the stabbing of Franklin had been an invention brought only an instant of relief; for on its heels came the report that the *Boston* had been captured by the British and taken into Plymouth, England, the captain and crew imprisoned. John Adams was in the Tower of London. There was no information as to what had been done with ten-year-old John Quincy. Nor did the detailed story in the New York newspaper allow for disbelief.

She lived in fear and anxiety, yet refused to give up to despair even with the curtains of the four-poster closed about her for privacy. Everything was tinged with uneasiness, the air she breathed, the food she ate, the reassuring words she spoke to Nab, Charley and Tommy.

Toward the end of June she heard from her uncle Isaac that a Captain Welsh of the *Boston* was in town with word for her from John. The *Boston* had indeed been captured by the British, but on its return journey. Her husband and son were safely in France, living at the abode of Dr. Benjamin Franklin in Passy.

The children would not let her go into Boston alone. Charley cried:

"Ma, you're too excited. I can handle the horses better."

She acquiesced. They found Captain Welsh at a shipping office. He was a square-rigged ruddy man, plain-spoken but polite.

"Captain Welsh, you have letters for me?"

"Begging your pardon, ma'am, I had. All at the bottom of the sea now."

She moved a step closer.

"Captain Welsh, kindly explain yourself."

"Drat it! We were captured! I had your husband's letters, some written on board ship, some from France. But I had to drop them into the Atlantic. My own papers too."

She left the office, her head bent. They rode home in silence. The loss of the letters was a blow. The diary of his passage and arrival in Europe would have contained sustenance more nourishing than food. At the four-mile stone she recovered her perspective, said consolingly to her young:

"Your father and Johnny are safe in Paris. God has sent us a good deliverance."

In July his first letter arrived from Paris. She read it savoringly, sat down at her desk and wrote:

"Shall I tell my dearest that tears of joy filled my eyes this morning at the sight of his well-known hand?—the first line which has blessed my sight since his four months' absence, during which time I have never been able to learn a word from him or my dear son. . . ."

She abided perforce the haphazard existence which her well-ordered mind detested. She could get no help for the farm, nor anyone to lease it. There was no school or teacher available in Braintree for the boys; to board them in an outside school would cost forty dollars apiece, which she did not have. She insisted that Nab spend some months in Boston with her uncle Isaac and aunt Elizabeth, reading in their library, enjoying whatever cultural life the city afforded. The lack of knowledge of what John was accomplishing in Paris to make this separation meaningful had a paralyzing effect on her will. She dragged through the hot, airless summer almost as heavily as when she had been carrying the last little girl. Nor was there much consolation in writing to him, for she had already written thirty to forty letters and as far as she knew the whole lot of them could be in the salty brine, along with John's to her.

John's letters, when they finally arrived, one batch on the *Alliance* in mid-August, another in early October, were unhappy. He had received no mail from her. The letters were obviously part of a series and referred to matters about which she knew nothing. But of one thing she could be certain: he was frustrated over his role as a commissioner in Paris.

By the time he arrived, the three American commissioners, Benjamin Franklin, Arthur Lee and Silas Deane, had already concluded two treaties with the French. Their Foreign Minister, Vergennes, had signed them in the name of King Louis XVI. The treaties recognized the independence of the United States and made provision for the shipment of needed supplies and materials: guns and powder, uniforms, beef, ships. Franklin was so beloved by the French people and the court that through his wit, warmth and brilliance he could wangle practically any thing in the possession of the French for the American cause. John perceived that there was no need for three commissioners, and forthwith recommended to the Continental Congress that they appoint one man the commissioner, Benjamin Franklin. That this would leave no place in Europe for Commissioner John Adams had not seemed to bother him.

Since he had no diplomatic work to do he thrust himself into dull but imperative tasks. There had been no copies kept of letters to the Congress of transactions carried on by the commissioners themselves, or by the American agents and factors who had drawn on the Commission's French loan in order to purchase goods in France. He put a stop to this, and even more quickly put a stop to the practice which had brought Silas Deane into disgrace, that of carrying on private and profitable business deals while representing the United States. Although the Congress had not provided John with a clerk, as it had Franklin and Lee, he attempted to set straight the financial record of the monies that had been received by the commissioners, and what actually had been purchased and shipped to the United States. Blessed or cursed with a New England fanaticism for honesty, he finally managed by a torrential outpouring of letters and accounts to set straight the books and affairs of the Commission.

Surprisingly for a man of his nature, he was being most diplomatic in the matter of the Commission. Urged to plunge into the controversy over Silas Deane, he declined, contenting himself with attempts to straighten out Deane's tangled affairs. He found himself in the midst of a protracted quarrel between Franklin and Arthur Lee, both able men dedicated to the cause of the United States, and exercised the kind of tact which the Puritan was accused of having been born lacking. On the Fourth of July he gave a dinner for the Americans in Paris which went a long way toward bringing them together on a friendly basis.

This was almost the last service he could perform, despite the fact that all three of the commissioners were searching in Europe for places to borrow money for their new country. Abigail received word from Philadelphia that the Joint Commission had been dissolved, even as John had recommended; Franklin was to be minister to France, Arthur Lee minister to Spain. There was nothing left for John.

The war itself, which had begun so close to home that she had seen the smoke and fire, had moved to other parts of the country. On June 18, 1778, the British had evacuated Philadelphia. General Washington trailed General Clinton toward New York. The two major armies had engaged at Monmouth Courthouse. Though there had been no victory for either side, the fine showing of the Americans reflected the months of training at Valley Forge under the Prussian drillmaster Baron von Steuben, who had joined Washington as a volunteer in February 1778. Von Steuben had arrived with letters of recommendation from Franklin and from French officers who knew about his training as a captain on the General Staff of the expert Prussian army.

Comte d'Estaing, commander of the French fleet, arrived in North America shortly after, and attempted to capture Newport, Rhode Island. Washington sent troops by land to help. A gale caused serious damage to the French ships, which limped into Boston Harbor for repair. There was harrowing land action in Pennsylvania and central New York. Colonel John Butler, with Tory volunteers and Indians, came down from Canada and struck the Patriot Army. The Americans were massacred at Wintermoot; Wilkes-Barre was razed and the Wyoming Valley in Pennsylvania devastated. When the Tories struck at German Flats in September, the Americans under Lieutenant Colonel William Butler retaliated by razing the Six Nations' town of Unadilla. Three years after the war had begun the skirmishes and battles added up to a war of attrition.

The Congress, having voted to dissolve the Commission, did not send its instructions to Paris until January of 1779. John could have been home with his family, practicing law in his office, eating supper at his kitchen table and sleeping in his own bed. The months were sodden, not merely with the torrential rains and then the snows of winter but with the fact that she and her husband were being held apart senselessly. She did not know what to do about their strained financial affairs or their land. If ever a home, a family and a farm needed its master, it was here and now, in Braintree.

The involvement in her personal plight sometimes caused her to lose sight of the grandeur of the Revolution, the heroic struggle of her neighbors and the emergence of the young, embattled nation. Exaltation was not a tent in which one could find shelter by night and day. Nor was all sacrifice on the same level. She saw hoarding, profiteering, desertion, indifference at the same time that other men were dying in battle. Thousands in the army and navy were away from their homes for a year or more at a time, forced to neglect their families and farms, shops and crafts, paid in deteriorating paper script. Wives, mothers, children were left to survive as best they could, knowing that any hour might bring word that the man of the family had been killed, or was dying in some remote fever-laden camp. Braintree, with only three thousand in population, provided six hundred men to help fight the war. There was hardly a neighboring family but had lost a husband or son: the Adamses, Basses, Belchers, Bracketts, Glovers, Newcombs, Pennimans, Savils . . .

It was not unnatural, she knew, in the midst of anxiety and harassment for courage to fail, for resolution to flag. No Patriot of New England would give up the contest; yet these were bad times. She would not pretend that her heart and her hopes did not sometimes plunge to the depths of despair. But she had the recuperative power to shape up for herself the enormity of what the American people were trying to accomplish: freedom for themselves, and the precept of freedom for an entire world. The United States of America had been the first country in centuries to cast off the shackles of arbitrary rulers and to declare that all rights of those who govern must be derived from the governed. It was such a unique and blindingly brilliant vision that she had difficulty in finding the right words with which to explain it to her children. Here, in this thin scattering of settlements along the Atlantic coast a new civilization was dawning.

3

She was happy when John Thaxter, her young cousin who had been John Adams's law clerk, returned from his job in the office of the Secretary of the Congress in Philadelphia to resume his law studies. He could live with them and again tutor her young. He was willowy as a reed, with tousled hair, spectacles, and a quiet, almost withdrawn manner, except when he was teaching. The boys did well under his tutelage. For Abigail, it was like having a young brother in the house.

The women of Braintree continued their Sodality. Susanna Baxter and Theodora Billings, who had been in circumstances during the earliest meetings in the days of Lexington, Concord, Breed's Hill, now had several children each. The Clark women, Mary and Hannah, had not lost their drollery but were hard pressed to exercise it on the happenings of these days. Several of Abigail's relatives were missing, Dr. Savil's wife Ann had become too old to move about, Peter's Mary was ill, Elihu's Thankful had remarried and moved away. They met for an hour twice a week in Abigail's sitting room, their hair freshly brushed and faces scrubbed, the white lace collars and wristbands lost to the war, each carrying a few cookies, a pinch of tea or a mug of cider, sitting about on the sofa and chairs in an irregular circle, heads down over their crocheting. They sought and gave counsel as well as comfort; here their ills and burdens were lightened by sharing. They could speak their minds without fear of criticism or danger of having their words bruited about. Several of the women had husbands or sons serving on American fighting vessels, for Braintree had long gone down to the sea. Mrs. Newcomb, who helped Abigail in the house, and Billy's daughter, Louisa Catherine, who had come to live with Abigail, liked to serve the ladies.

The Smith family had suffered its first casualty: Billy. Released from the British prison in Newfoundland, he had taken to drinking heavily, had either failed to report back to the marines or, having done so, been discharged for habitual drunkenness. When he drank he gambled; when he gambled he lost. Strangers holding Billy's chitties appeared at the farm in Lincoln. When they learned that Catharine Louisa was penniless, they moved on to dun Abigail or the Reverend Mr. Smith. Abigail paid when she could, Billy's father when he would.

Not that Billy had disappeared completely. He would return to Lincoln for a week or two each year, staying just long enough to leave Catharine Louisa in circumstances, then he would be reported drunk in one town or living with a woman in another. He never showed his face in Weymouth or Braintree. Catharine Louisa came to visit Abigail once a month, bringing her three other children. She held her head high in spite of the fact that her only income was what her father-in-law sent her.

Abigail suggested, "Sister, we must try not to be hard on Billy. He was a good husband and father until the war came."

"Yes, he was that."

"Something happened to him in prison. Something was lost from his character, the way our soldiers lose an arm or leg from their bodies." She put an arm about Catharine Louisa's bony shoulders. "Sister, may I intrude with some intimate advice? Do not bear him any more children. It's cruel to you and to those you have. The farm returns to your ownership in my father's will, but you already have a flock of young ones to feed and raise."

Catharine Louisa turned her long, sallow face to Abigail, said:

"Sister, forgive me, but I sometimes think Billy really did die on that bridge at Concord. How much better it would have been for him . . . and us. Captain William Smith, the hero of Concord, loved and respected by everyone. Sometimes I wish that in the dark of night, and then I get out of bed and pray on my knees for God to forgive me."

Ten months elapsed between the time Congress dissolved its Paris Commission and John returned briefly to Braintree. Though he brought the good news that Spain, which had the third largest navy in the world, had joined in the war against England in an effort to revenge past defeats and regain such conquered territories as Gibraltar and West Florida, he came home under a personal cloud. The Continental Congress had passed a resolution severely censoring all the commissioners for their "suspicions and animosities" abroad. He was in a fury. On what grounds could the Congress have condemned him? She suggested he write for copies of the proceedings. In the meanwhile she took pleasure in her son Johnny, who had grown two inches in height and equally in poise. Massachusetts, which had been limping along on its colonial charter, elected John to its state Constitutional Convention. He was named to a committee of thirty, which contracted itself into a committee of three, James Bowdoin, Samuel Adams and John; which named John Adams a subcommittee of one to write the document.

Now in the Indian summer of late September 1779 a pattern of happiness returned to her family. They arose at dawn to walk to the top of Penn's Hill and watch the glories of the sunrise. At breakfast the six Adamses and Billy's daughter sat digging their elbows into each other's sides while they made John and John Quincy give them descriptions of the palaces and cathedrals of France. By seven the Adams school was seated about the clients' table, from which all the merchandise had been removed, with John as headmaster. By eight-thirty school had recessed. Abigail watched her husband gather about him those state constitutions which had already been written, dissect them and bring forth for Massachusetts all that was wise and workable, tapping the resources of his own mind to make Massachusetts one of the most progressive commonwealths the world had known.

He followed the example of the Virginia Bill of Rights by first declaring that all men were born free and independent and had "certain natural, essential and unalienable rights, among which may be reckoned the right of enjoying and defending their lives and liberties; that of acquiring, possessing and protecting their property. . . ." It should be the duty of men in society publicly to worship the Supreme Being; to preserve good morals; "the people of this commonwealth have the sole and exclusive right of governing themselves as a free, sovereign and independent state." He wrote the statutes for free elections, for the equal right of all male inhabitants "having sufficient qualifications . . . to elect officers, and to be elected, for public employments," guaranteed every citizen of Massachusetts his "right to be fully heard in his defense"; underscored the right of trial by jury and the rights "to the freedom of speaking, writing and publishing their sentiments"; laid out the mechanisms for the setting aside of public funds for the education of the young as well as the encouragement of literature and the sciences.

The committee of thirty made some minor changes in John's constitution; the convention made a few as well. At the same time the delegates of eleven states at the Continental Congress in Philadelphia elected John Adams commissioner to negotiate treaties of peace and trade with Great Britain through England's ambassador to France. He was to return to Paris, instanter!

Once again they summoned their assets. The Congress had not yet approved John's vouchers for the first trip. Though Benjamin Franklin was ordered to pay John his expenses out of the French loan in Paris, there was no mention of how the salary of eleven thousand two hundred and fifty dollars a year would be paid. Aside from the four hundred dollars John received for his attendance at the Massachusetts convention meetings, they were as innocent of hard cash as they had been during their courtship, when John Adams had worried himself into dyspepsia over marrying without an adequate practice. He watched Abigail sell part of her dairy herd and poultry to meet the new Massachusetts tax. There was an even more crucial question, and Abigail knew she was going to have to be the one to ask it.

"John, how much longer is this war going on? We've been fighting for four and a half years now."

The Reverend Mr. Smith had just left, after once again bidding John good-by. They were lying in bed with the house quiet about them. John rose, donned his robe. Search as he might, he could think of no victory of the American arms that could suggest a quick peace. Since midsummer of 1779 each side had won small but indecisive victories; the British under Major General Sir Henry Clinton had captured New Haven, Fairfield and Norwalk, pillaging and burning those towns. The Patriots had defeated Clinton's men two weeks later by storming Stony Point under cover of night, shooting through the British abatis and killing, wounding or capturing the British force of over five hundred. In August, Major Henry Lee, Jr., had attacked the British at Paulus Hook near New York, capturing the British encampment; at the same time a Massachusetts expedition to Penobscot under Brigadier General Solomon Lovell and nineteen ships under Commodore Dudley Saltonstall was mauled so badly and so many of the ships were destroyed that the surviving Americans had to make their way back to Massachusetts on foot.

Unless other European countries besides France and Spain entered the contest against England the war could go on for years. There was no reason John could think of why the British should accept a peace commissioner, or the independence of the United States. That could not happen until after they had been soundly defeated, or until the English people would no longer support the war. The Americans had no choice.

In the end she had to let him go. It was more difficult now, for she knew how meaningless much of the separation could be, how fraught with controversy was his garbled commission. John Quincy had not been eager to leave with his father, yet she saw the progress he had made in his studies. She also garnered the courage to insist that Charley too be given the opportunity to travel and to absorb the foreign cultures. This was the only gift left in her poverty-stricken hands to give to her sons.

They sailed on *La Sensible* on November 13, 1779. She stood with Tommy in the little store, twisting a bolt of newly arrived French gauze in her hands. She had sent Nab into Boston for the winter season with Isaac and Elizabeth Smith. Even her mild-mannered young cousin John Thaxter had departed from the household, for the Congress had allowed John a secretary this time, and Thaxter had gone to do the work.

In the middle of January 1780 she summoned the will to write to John Quincy. Sitting at her desk, she poured out her heart to her oldest son:

"These are times in which a genius would wish to live. It is not in the still calm of life, or the repose of a pacific station, that great characters are formed. Would Cicero have shone so distinguished an orator if he had not been roused, kindled and inflamed by the tyranny of Catiline, Verres and Mark Antony? The habits of a vigorous mind are formed in contending with difficulties. All history will convince you of this, and that wisdom and penetration are the fruit of experience, not the lessons of retirement and leisure. Great necessities call out great virtues. When a mind is raised and animated by scenes that engage the heart, then those qualities which would otherwise lie dormant wake into life and form the character of the hero and the statesman. . . . It is your lot, my son, to be an eyewitness of these calamities in your own native land and, at the same time, to owe your existence among a people who have made a glorious defense of their invaded liberties and who, aided by a generous and powerful ally, with the blessing of Heaven, will transmit this inheritance to ages yet unborn."

4

During the first years of the conflict Abigail had asked herself, "When can we finish this war?" Now in moments of fatigue an unseen hand rubbed out the first word of the question, leaving behind:

"Can we finish this war?"

John Adams was asking a similar question in Paris. Member of a thorny breed, he did not like the subservient, near-toadying position into which the United States had fallen in relation to France, and set out singlehandedly to prove that, since France in beating down England was gaining as much as she was giving, the United States should not allow themselves to be treated as though they were a dependent colony of King Louis XVI. His personal antagonist was the Comte de Vergennes, French Foreign Minister. Vergennes did not like Commissioner Adams, finding him blunt, porcupinish, ungrateful and a busybody. He instructed John Adams not to inform the British of his treaty-making powers. For six months John obeyed, until he realized that he had allowed Vergennes to take over American foreign policy. He then demanded the right to negotiate with the British for a prospective peace. Vergennes refused, insisting that they submit their dispute to the Continental Congress. John was infuriated. It was impossible for him to concede that the affairs of the United States could be run from Paris.

He began a series of detailed communications to Vergennes:

"I am determined to omit no opportunity of communicating my sentiments to Your Excellency, upon everything that appears to me of importance to the common cause. . . ." Whereupon he instructed the Minister of Foreign Affairs on how to use the ships of the French navy in America, how to fight the war in the West Indies. Vergennes protested to Franklin, declaring that "he would enter into no further discussions with Mr. Adams, nor answer any more of his letters." Franklin agreed with Vergennes, observing that since John Adams had nothing to do "he seems to have endeavored to supply what he may suppose my negotiations defective in."

With this, John Adams and Benjamin Franklin came to a parting of the ways. John told Franklin, "America has been too free in expressions of gratitude to France for . . . she is more obliged to us than we to her; and . . . we should show spirit in our applications. . . . A little apparent stoutness and greater air of independence and boldness in our demands will procure us more ample assistance. . . ." Franklin, knowing how much of money, guns, ships, soldiers and sailors the United States still needed from France, replied that King Louis XVI liked to think of himself as a generous protector of the United States and "I think it right to increase this pleasure by our thankful acknowledgments, and that such an expression of gratitude is not only our duty but our interest."

John lost to Vergennes and Franklin.

He left for Holland in the hopes of securing a loan from the Dutch in order to lessen the United States' dependence on France. Vergennes retaliated by requesting that Franklin forward the entire correspondence between himself and Commissioner Adams to the Congress. Franklin wrote John to ask if he wanted to add anything by way of explanation. John declined; he had already sent copies of the communications to the Congress. When Vergennes's letters reached the Congress, John's exclusive commission to deal with the British for peace was revoked by the adding of four new members: Benjamin Franklin, John Jay, Henry Laurens and Thomas Jefferson. His power to negotiate a commercial treaty with Great Britain was revoked entirely. The Congress instructed the commissioners to "make the most candid and confidential communications upon all subjects to the ministers of our generous ally, the King of France; to undertake nothing in the negotiations for peace or truce without their knowledge and concurrence . . . and ultimately to govern yourselves by their advice and opinion."

It was not a situation under which John Adams could or would work. Congress knew it, Franklin knew it, Vergennes knew it. At home, Abigail reasoned that he might resign and return.

She should have known better. Her husband was not the resigning kind. He convinced a majority of the Congress that loans could be secured from Holland, millions of guilders; or at least that he should be allowed to try. John Adams was named minister plenipotentiary to the Netherlands and set up housekeeping in Amsterdam.

The dividing line between the past and the present became blurred for her because of the formlessness of the future. A full nine months went by without the receipt of a single line from her husband or either of her sons. During this time what had started as an American revolution against England had exploded into a world-wide war. French and Spanish fleets fought the British in the English Channel, the West Indies, Gibraltar. The Spanish defeated the British in Pensacola and captured West Florida. The French were contesting for the control of India. Russia, which had been assumed to be friendly to Britain, turned on her with a Declaration of Armed Neutrality, and was joined by Denmark, Sweden and Prussia, all of them determined to break England's blockade on France and Spain by sending in ships and goods. Holland ran naval stores to France, using its island of St. Eustatius in the West Indies to supply America so abundantly that England declared war on Holland. Their two navies fought to a standstill off the Dogger Bank in the North Sea. England's line of ships and men was now stretched thin to circle the globe; fleets that were intended to provision British troops in America or blockade major American ports were engaged with the enemy in other seas.

Now in the fall of 1781 news reached her which shocked her into a present from which she could never again recede. Fourteen-year-old John Quincy was on his way to St. Petersburg to serve as secretary to their friend Francis Dana, American minister to Russia. Charley was on his way home to Massachusetts.

The weeks and months were filled with the minutiae of struggle. Her shop was empty of merchandise. A shipment from John of Dutch china was sitting in Philadelphia, but she had no way of getting it to Boston. She had to pay sixty hard dollars as her state and county tax, and at the moment did not have it. Four months after eleven-year-old Charles was supposed to have started for America she learned that the boy was stranded with other Americans in Bilbao, Spain, unable to secure passage. There was not a syllable from or about John Quincy on his long and arduous journey to St. Petersburg; or any letter from her husband for months on end. She could learn nothing beyond the fact that the wet Netherlands climate was not agreeing with him.

She saw to her farm, took walks to the top of Penn's Hill, visited with her father and Cotton Tufts, kept her emotions keyed low. She pulled her hair back severely from her brow and behind her ears, tying it in place with any scrap of ribbon on hand to keep it out of the way. Though she was approaching thirty-seven an unintentional glimpse of herself in the mirror revealed her face to be outside the realm of time, indeterminable, as happens to people in hiatus. Her skin had been roughened by the weather, since she paid it little attention during the long season's work in the dairy and driving the cows. It was her eyes that seemed most strange to her: masked, uncommitted, the brightness and sensitivity muted, almost expressionless, a reflection of her banked fires and determination to react as little as possible in a world that had momentarily passed beyond her control.

She had no personal life but served as a stopgap, shoring up any breach in the little world around her. When Peter Adams's wife Mary died a few days after childbirth, Abigail took their eleven-year-old daughter into her home. She nursed John's mother when Mr. Hall died, and then her own father, who lived alone now in the Weymouth parsonage. When the *Essex*, carrying a dozen Braintree men, was captured by the British their families came to her to plead that she write to her husband to secure their release from prison. She did so. When Catharine Louisa was threatened with physical violence by a brute to whom Billy owed money, Abigail turned over the four hundred dollars she had received from Massachusetts for John's twenty-five days' attendance at their Constitutional Convention, money she had kept hidden in the attic Specie Bank against an emergency.

It was good to be needed, to be useful. Who knew better than she that loneliness was the most rackingly painful illness to which the body or mind could be subjected, a giant hand reaching out to strangle her as she went about her chores. She would move from room to room gasping for air, massaging the knifelike pain in her heart with downward sweeps of her tightly crooked arm. Demons flailed about her head with barbed wings that perforated her eyes, sending her up the pie-shaped stairs to fling herself face down on the bed, clutching a pillow over her head until the roaring receded from her ears, the needles eased themselves out of her breast, the air came back into her lungs. Then she would rise, wash her face in cool water, comb her hair back tidily and descend once again to her work, the attack over.

John was suffering from giant strangulations of his own. His efforts to be recognized in Holland as the minister plenipotentiary from the United States failed, along with his plan to borrow money for his government. He wrote to the Congress:

"My prospects both for the public and for myself are so dull, and the life I am likely to lead in Europe so gloomy and melancholy and of so little use to the public, that I cannot but wish it may suit with the views of Congress to recall me."

British General Cornwallis, in the winter of 1781, intervened to release the United States, John and Abigail Adams from their misery, to start the fledgling country on the long, sometimes tortuous road to strength, and Abigail and John to reunion.

5

The winter of 1780–1781 was the worst the American army had endured. General Washington's forces in camp in the Hudson Highlands around West Point were not as badly off as his Valley Forge troops two years earlier: they had more food and protection against the freezing winter. But morale was the lowest since the fighting on Lexington Green six years before: the men had enjoyed few victories, suffered a series of disasters and defeats. Their pay had been rendered near worthless by the inflation. Many who had enlisted for "three years or during the war," having served three years, felt they were being held unjustly.

Two mutinies erupted. Six Pennsylvania regiments at Morristown moved in strict military order toward Philadelphia, met with a congressional committee at Princeton and returned to camp peaceably when promised an investigation of their grievances and a discharge for the men who had served their full three years. Three New Jersey regiments which revolted near Pompton were forcibly crushed by General Washington, who used New England troops to take the mutineers into custody.

Benedict Arnold, victor of the battle of Lake Champlain, who had deserted the American forces and joined the British, invaded Virginia and captured Richmond. British Major General Phillips wiped out an American fleet on the James River. English Lieutenant Colonel Tarleton's legion captured Charlottesville, where the Virginia legislature was in session, took seven legislators prisoner, with Governor Thomas Jefferson barely escaping.

Washington sent the Marquis de Lafayette, twenty-three years old and already a major general, with twelve hundred New England troops to Virginia to destroy Benedict Arnold's forces. The two armies never met. French Admiral Destouches, who commanded the French fleet at Newport, sailed for Virginia to lift the siege. He was blocked by British Admiral Arbuthnot. A major battle was in the making but it would take months of troop movements. Cornwallis began concentrating his men around Yorktown, expecting to be reinforced by the British naval squadrons now reaching New York. In the late summer of 1781 Washington moved swiftly southward, being reinforced by French troops under Rochambeau.

The Patriot investment of Yorktown was a joint American and French venture, with General Washington as commander-in-chief and Major General Benjamin Lincoln, a Hingham friend of the Adamses, in command of the American forces. Under him were Lafayette and Von Steuben as division commanders. Rochambeau's French army, including General Marquis de St. Simon's forces, totaled nearly eight thousand trained troops. French Admiral de Grasse made available a detachment of battle-hardened French marines; he was also keeping his formidable French fleet of twenty-eight ships of the line anchored at the mouth of the Chesapeake Bay to block the expected British naval squadrons. General Cornwallis fortified the new British base at Yorktown with eight thousand soldiers and a thousand fighting sailors.

The campaign opened on September 28, when the allied forces marched together from Williamsburg to landlock the British inside their redoubts, their backs to the York River. Knox's artillery and heavy French siege guns were hauled forward to form batteries seven hundred yards from the British defenses. The fortifications took a week, after which the American-French army began to dig their first attack-parallel. On October ninth the French siege guns opened fire, followed immediately by the American batteries.

Cornwallis and the British were caught by surprise. Under the heavy volume of accurate artillery fire their guns were blown apart; those that remained intact stopped firing for lack of ammunition. Casualties were inordinately high.

On the night of October eleventh the Patriots built a second parallel, three hundred yards from the trenches east of Yorktown. Three days later American and French officers contended for the right to lead their troops into the British forts, where the fighting was heroic on both sides; officers and men fell mortally wounded from hand-to-hand combat. By ten o'clock that night the first forts had been captured. On the sixteenth, allied artillery flattened the remnants of the British defenses and Yorktown itself.

At nine-thirty the next morning, the anniversary of Burgoyne's surrender at Saratoga four years before, a British drummer appeared on the parapet, drumming a signal for a conference. A British officer waving a white handkerchief was blindfolded and led to Washington's headquarters with a note from Cornwallis asking for a "cessation of hostilities for twenty-four hours." Washington granted the British two hours and rejected their demand that all troops be allowed to return to Britain and Germany.

Four peace commissioners treated. On the morning of October nineteenth the papers were signed. At two o'clock, with the French and American troops lining the road to Yorktown, flags flying, the British and Hessian troops came out with their colors cased, their bands and drum corps playing muted marches. The officers laid down their arms in a field surrounded by French hussars. Over eight thousand enemy soldiers and sailors surrendered. In this decisive battle for the North American continent the Americans had lost some fifty men, with another sixty-five wounded; the French had lost sixty men and less than two hundred were wounded. The British killed, wounded and missing numbered close to five hundred.

It was a victory of staggering proportions. Braintree and Boston were intensely proud because their Massachusetts regiments had figured importantly in the storming of the British redoubts. This was General Washington's greatest victory, and that of the generals under him. A new wave of patriotic zeal swept the nation. The Tories were crushed.

The results in England were no less galvanic. Lord North, who had prosecuted the war for the King, was bitterly opposed in Parliament by the men who had been waiting for just such a serious setback. When he heard the news of Cornwallis's surrender, Lord North took long, agitated strides up and down his apartment, cried:

"Oh God. Oh God. It is all over. It is all over."

So it seemed to most of the world, though it would take months to move the last of the British troops and ships out of New York. In the Netherlands the Dutch, who had been resisting John Adams's blandishments to recognize the United States and provide them with a sizable loan, moved to an acknowledgment of American independence. He signed agreements with private banking firms which gave the new country five million guilders at five per cent interest, repayment not to begin for a full ten years. At last his work in Holland had been justified. He now hoped to begin the service for which he had been sent to Europe: to negotiate a treaty of peace with Great Britain.

Good news behaves like clover: it all comes up at once. At the end of January 1782, after having been away for two years and on the missing list for many months, Charles at last arrived on the ship *Cicero*. He was a full head taller than when he had left. He had suffered from homesickness and colds in the chest, but the experience abroad had turned him from a frolicsome boy to a poised youth. Though he carried no letters from his father, he had vivid tales to tell. Through Charley Abigail could see and feel the texture of John's days. Charley loved being the center of attention, grasping how important he was to the family as a link to its missing members. He moved back into the second bedroom with Tommy, assuming a lordly position as the older brother.

In the same blossoming, romance entered the Adams household, bringing lightness and humor and endless complications.

His name was Royall Tyler. He came from one of the best Massachusetts families. He was twenty-four years old, had earned degrees from Harvard and Yale, then studied law under Francis Dana. The boy's father had died when he was only thirteen, leaving young Tyler a handsome estate of £7000. There were rumors that he had been wild as a youth, dissipating his patrimony. But that seemed to be all over now; he had settled down as a boarder with the Richard Cranches, was studying intently and beginning to find a few clients.

Tyler had been living with the Cranches only a few weeks when Abigail's sister Mary came by, her cheeks flushed. The Cranches had been doing better since Richard had been elected as Braintree's representative to the General Court. When John was home he had secured an appointment for Richard as a local judge. Now that the fighting had stopped Cranch was importing watches and other fine merchandise from Holland, with John vouching for his credit.

"Sister, can you keep a secret?" asked Mary.

"I can try."

"You remember our new boarder, Mr. Royall Tyler? He and my Elizabeth have taken to walking out. He reads to her of evenings, poetry and plays. Don't you think that's a good sign? Elizabeth talks of nothing else. Sister, can I bring him to tea on Sunday? I want you to approve."

The Cranches brought Royall Tyler at four o'clock, Sunday teatime in Braintree. When Mary walked in with Richard and her son Billy at one side, the new young man between Elizabeth and young Lucy on the other, Abigail's mind flashed back to the days when Richard was courting and Mary the girl in love. How quickly the cycles spun themselves out! Marriage had brought Mary none of the external success she had promised herself: a mansion as big as Colonel Quincy's, frequent trips to England to visit Richard's family, a fine collection of silver. Their life together had been that of the itinerant watch seller and repairer, with successive shops in Salem, Boston and now Braintree. Yet no one could have known from Mary's attitude that she had not fulfilled the ambitions of her youth. Tall, stately, with a good deal of her mother's regal posture, Mary moved through the animadversions of fate as though she had decreed them.

Abigail glanced at her rather plain niece, then turned her attention to Royall Tyler. He was elegantly garbed in a scarlet broadcloth coat, white vest, ruffled shirt. He was, she decided, a handsome man, with black arching eyebrows, a short nose and trim mouth which he used facilely for the making of witticisms. He wore his thick dark hair as full as a wig, combed over the top half of his ear and curling down his neck. There was a touch of shadow beneath his eyes, which were as swift in transition as were his ideas. He had a cheerful musical voice.

Royall Tyler gave the impression of a man who could never find the time to utter half of the penetrating comments that came to his mind. He quoted from the latest volumes of plays he had been reading, declaimed whole verses of poetry. He kept the room filled with the stimulation of his overflowing mind. Abigail enjoyed his warmth and sparkling intellectualism. Everyone seemed to.

Everyone except Nab. She sat in a corner by the bowfat, hands crossed sedately in her lap, eyes down, exchanging no word with him.

"Didn't you like Elizabeth's young man?" Abigail asked when the company had left.

"Yes, I did."

"Then why were you so uncommunicative?"

"Did you find me so? I was merely listening."

The next day Abigail was writing letters at her desk when she heard the pounding of the front door clapper. Mrs. Newcomb mounted the stairs to announce Mr. Tyler. He was alone. In his hand he carried a book. His face lit up in a heart-warming smile when he saw her.

"Forgive me for intruding, Mrs. Adams. You expressed interest in a new play I mentioned yesterday. I took the liberty of bringing you a copy."

"That was kind. Won't you come in? I suspect it's teatime."

"I was devious about that, Mrs. Adams. I came at what I hoped would be the right moment. Tea and conversation make the workday bearable."

Nab came in.

"Oh, Mr. Tyler. Where is Cousin Elizabeth?"

"Safely at home, I would assume. Your mother was kind enough to invite me to tea."

"All neighbors are welcome to drink tea."

His ebullience was crushed. But not for long. Over the tea table he declared that he had come to ask for the loan of one of John Adams's lawbooks.

"Not meaning to flatter, Mrs. Adams, but I should like to become the kind of student of the law that Mr. Adams is. I've read his *Thoughts on Government.*"

"Truly?"

The impressionable entertainer vanished. In his place came a serious young man. He gave Abigail a résumé of his recent reading: Coke, Blackstone and Acherley through Selden, Hawkins and Hale. Abigail perceived that he had an absorbing and analytical mind and that, like the young John Adams, he had broadened his base by a careful study of the classical authors: Livy, Horace, Marcus Aurelius. She liked him and found him interesting. When she asked how he enjoyed living in Braintree, he replied:

"Exceeding well. Though I confess I had considerable opposition from my mother when I made the choice. She wanted me to open an office in Boston. I said that if Braintree was good enough for John Adams to make his start in, it was good enough for me. No intent to compare myself, ma'am, but every ambitious young man must have an idol, and John Adams is mine."

Abigail was flattered.

Nab gave Royall Tyler not one word of agreement, or a single appraising glance.

By the end of the week, when Tyler had presented himself at the door each day for tea bearing a beaming smile and a small gift, sweets or a slender volume of poetry, presenting them almost as his ticket of admission, his glance and conversation directed more and more to the reluctant and aloof Nab, Abigail decided that she had better get a few matters straightened out. Nab left the room on signal, after pouring a second cup. Abigail turned a serious face to her caller.

"Mr. Tyler, we enjoy your company . . ."

"Your daughter too? I'm afraid not."

". . . My sister, Mrs. Cranch, tells me that you are interested in Elizabeth."

"Only as a friend, Mrs. Adams."

"Nothing more?"

"Nothing more."

"Then why does Elizabeth think so, as well?"

"Perhaps I've been indiscreet. Since I live in their home, I've tried to become a brother to the two girls."

"Nothing more?"

"Upon my honor."

"May I ask you, in all confidence, why you have honored us with your presence for seven days running?"

"This is the most stimulating house in New England."

"For what, pray tell?"

"For delightful, infectious conversation."

"Nothing more?"

Royall Tyler flushed.

"Yes, something more. I am fascinated by your daughter. I have made no effort to conceal it."

"Then you are going to have to do so."

The young man blinked his eyes, asked formally:

"Am I permitted to know why?"

"Because you have been walking out with Elizabeth. Her mother believes the two of you are in love."

Royall Tyler jumped up from his chair, moved agitatedly about the sitting parlor.

"I've given no one reason to believe that! Not Elizabeth, not Mrs. Cranch, not Mr. Cranch."

"That is the impression they have received."

"Then I shall correct it. Mrs. Adams, may I then have your permission to become interested in Miss Nab?"

Abigail replied without inflection:

"Miss Nab makes her own decisions."

The next morning, early, brought Mary Cranch. Abigail had rarely seen her sister so angry.

"That young man, Royall Tyler: do you know what he had the effrontery to tell me? That his feelings for Elizabeth are only those of a brother!"

She sat down abruptly.

"But it's the best thing that could have happened. We've been hearing dreadful stories about his youth. He drank, gambled, associated with unsavory characters."

"I'm sorry to hear that, Sister."

"A man's character doesn't change. If he's wild and irresponsible in his youth he'll be wild and irresponsible all his life."

When Tyler showed up that afternoon and Abigail repeated the charges, he answered quietly:

"Much of it is true. I was unhappy after my mother remarried. We were a wild set, we did drink and gamble. In fact I lost half my inheritance before I awoke to what I was doing. But that ended five years ago. Since that time I have disciplined myself, worked hard . . ."

When the Cranches and Adamses came out of preaching the following Sunday, Mary Cranch was furious again. Richard Cranch had decreed with judicial calm that the young man had been within his rights; that he was to remain in their home.

Royall Tyler became a friend of the Adams family. No one could have said he was courting Nab; his enthusiasm for the Adams family embraced them all. He took the two boys hunting, using John's old fowling pieces, or fishing off Rainsford and Hangman's islands. He engaged Abigail in discussions of the place of law in past civilizations until, closing her eyes, she thought she was listening to the young John Adams. He delighted her with his poetic verse. Young Louisa Catherine could hardly tear herself from his presence, he was so unfailingly kind to her. With Nab he was reserved. Yet the day-by-day impact of his presence was having its effect on her. Tyler was hard to resist as he projected his human warmth and hearty laughter, his sonorous voice filling the little cottage for hours after he had reluctantly left.

One night in the bedroom she shared with her mother, a low dividing partition giving them privacy, Nab asked from her bed:

"Mother, have you written to Father about Mr. Tyler?"

"No. There didn't seem to be anything to write."

"Because I'm not encouraging him? Should I?"

"Only you can answer that question."

"How old were you when you met Father?"

"Your age."

"Did you encourage him?"

Abigail smiled in the darkness.

"He needed none. We became friends."

"You said that Father was your first spark."

"So he was."

"Is Royall Tyler my first spark?"

"He would like to be."

"He has never embarrassed me with his intentions."

"Have you any idea of how fortified you remain behind your uncommitted eyes?"

"I already love two men."

Abigail listened for clues to her daughter's uncharacteristic outbreak.

"My father and my brother." There was a silence. "I have felt . . . abandoned. Does my father love me? He's been gone so many years now. Johnny and I were dear friends. I haven't heard one word from him. I know why Mr. Tyler's here: he's waiting for the day when he can court me openly. Frankly, I like him. He's talented and diverse." Nab paused in the darkness, then asked, "But how can a girl begin to think of love if she does not know she's loved at home?"

Abigail wanted to go into Nab's narrow section of the room, take the girl in her arms and comfort her. She replied matter-of-factly:

"Why should you doubt their love? I don't doubt their love for me."

"That's different. You're a wife and mother. I'm only a daughter and sister."

The word "only" broke down Abigail's reserve.

"Nab, listen to me closely: your father and brother love you dearly. It is an accident of fate that keeps them away from us, the call of duty. Love is a weak thing if it cannot stand a physical separation."

"Mother, I have known your sacrifices and the unhappiness you have suffered."

Abigail had never felt closer to her daughter.

"Unhappiness, yes. Loneliness, more painful in all the points of the heart than neuralgia. But loss of faith in my love for my husband and our family, or our family for me, never! Nor must you doubt. I would stake my life on it that your father loves you with all the tenderness he has within him."

"I accept that. But I must see it, feel it."

"In the meanwhile, what about friendship?" asked Abigail. "That is what I sought, long before love. It is the only reliable road to love. I learned the lines from Dr. Young:

> "A *friend is worth all hazards we can run.*
> *Poor is the friendless master of a world;*
> A *world in purchase for a friend is gain.*"

She could envision Nab knitting her handsome brows, the eyes pools of puzzled reflection, even as John's were when confronted with an emotional problem.

"My dear child, friendship is not born whole and accomplished. It starts from a fragmentary base and takes months and years to reach full flower, longer perhaps than the love that follows."

"Then I can become friends with Mr. Tyler and let it grow by littles?"

"You are several years from love, I would venture."

Nab now welcomed Royall Tyler as heartily as the rest of the family, complimented him when he read well from Sheridan or Congreve and, in the full warmth of summer, went horseback riding with him each afternoon. Together she and Abigail sewed a new habit of nankeen faced with blue satin, her little blue hat topped with a cocky feather. She looked adorable. There was a warm, subtle coloring to her skin, much as Abigail's complexion had been.

Abigail grew fond of Tyler. It certainly made life less lonely.

6

During the months of 1782 Benjamin Franklin began exploratory talks towards a peace treaty with Britain's negotiator. John Jay arrived in France to participate, and behind him came John Adams from Holland. Henry Laurens, who had been captured by the British and imprisoned in the Tower of London, followed John Adams but Thomas Jefferson, fifth of the commissioners, could not leave the United States at the time. The ambition of the commissioners was to secure the best possible treaty whilst re-establishing friendship between the two countries. Widespread trade between Britain and the United States was imperative for American prosperity and progress. John recorded in his diary how well the four commissioners worked together to achieve the imperative demands of the Continental Congress: the independency of the United States to be recognized; all British troops to be removed from American territory; the British to leave without "carrying away any Negroes or other property of the American inhabitants." John secured New England's fishing rights to the waters off the Grand Bank and all other banks and coast of Newfoundland as well as the right to cure its fish on the shores of Newfoundland.

As word of the seven months' arbitration found its way across the Atlantic to Philadelphia and Boston, it was realized that the American commissioners had had to make certain important concessions: English creditors would be able to recover "the full value in sterling money of all bona fide debts heretofore contracted. . . . Congress shall earnestly recommend it to the legislatures of the respective states to provide for the restitution of all estates, rights and properties which have been confiscated" from the Tories. John approved these measures as legal and just.

So, finally, on January 14, 1784, peace was declared. The thirteen states set about establishing their state constitutions, the last of the soldiers returned home, the farms and businesses settled down to produce and prosper.

Anticipating the recognition of the United States by Holland, John Adams bought the first permanent American Embassy in Europe for fifteen thousand guilders, a splendid town house owned by the Comtesse de Quadt Wykeradt, located on "a fine situation and . . . a noble spot of ground." He had no authorization from the Congress to buy but the price was reasonable, and the United States was going to have to have a permanent minister at The Hague. For the purchase he paid down ten thousand guilders, most of it a loan from a Dutch banker and long-time friend to America, Jan de Neufville; when extra money was needed for the transfer fees, he paid the money out of his own pocket. If Congress failed to approve the purchase he would sell the house when he left Holland. Everyone agreed he had bought extremely well and so he had no fear. He furnished the house out of salary he had received.

Abigail now wrote to John offering to pack and come to Europe. Nab pleaded with her father to let her come to The Hague and keep house for him. John replied to his wife and daughter that he should be coming home soon. To Nab he wrote:

"I have received your charming letter, which you forgot to date, by Mrs. Rogers. Your proposal of coming to Europe to keep your papa's house and take care of his health is in a high strain of filial duty and affection, and the idea pleases me much in speculation, but not at all in practice. I have too much tenderness for you, my dear child, to permit you to cross the Atlantic. You know not what it is. If God shall spare me and your brother to return home, which I hope will be next spring, I never desire to know of any of my family crossing the seas again."

Young and pretty Mrs. Francis Dana, whose husband was American minister to Russia, and for whom Johnny was private secretary, came to dinner in Braintree and made no secret of her severe displeasure at being separated from her husband. Unlike Abigail, she saw no reason to keep her personal feelings to herself. There were times when Abigail agreed but she would have scissored her tongue off rather than say so in public. Asked by a Braintree selectman:

"If you had known that Mr. Adams would have remained so long abroad, would you have consented that he should have gone?" Abigail recollected for a moment, then spoke the dictates of her heart, accompanied by the jingling of washtubs and bird cages tied to the rafters of the general store:

"If I had known, sir, that Mr. Adams could have effected what he has done, I would not only have submitted to the absence I have endured, painful as it has been, but I would not have opposed it even though three years more should be added to the number, which Heaven avert! I feel a pleasure in being able to sacrifice my selfish passions to the general good, and in imitating the example which has taught me to consider myself and family but as the small dust of the balance when compared with the great community."

Yet for some of her friends the Revolution and victorious war had already turned to ashes. The Warrens had bought the former home of Governor Thomas Hutchinson in Milton—Governors Bernard and Hutchinson had both died in England—only a few miles from Braintree, a mansion surrounded by rolling greenswards and rich farmlands. When they came to Abigail for dinner it turned into a gloomy occasion. Mercy declared hotly that the passions of the Revolution had caused her brother, James Otis, to become irrational. James Warren was so embittered by the war years, during which he had risen to the rank of general, that, though he had twice been asked to represent Massachusetts in the Continental Congress, he had refused. He was now being asked a third time; there was a murmur against him in Suffolk County for his lack of interest in his country.

"It's quits now, for me," he declared as he spat a dry walnut into the palm of his huge hand. "I've had enough of this new democratical class that has come into power, men who formerly might have brushed my shoes."

Abigail could not help wondering what it was that had so soured this good man; yet she was meeting more and more such men in Boston as well as Braintree. Sometimes they were disgruntled office seekers, sometimes men who had lost their farms or trades or shops during the war; but by no means always. There were those who had gained rather than lost but were disillusioned with what they called their misguided idealism. These were the thorny ones for Abigail, for they gave the impression that they had lost faith in the Federation, ridiculing the idea that this group of independent states, already feuding over borders, specie, trade, debts, focalizing of power, could ever become a unified people or nation.

The saddest case of all was Samuel Adams. His had been the single most important voice in the Revolution but now that the United States had achieved its independence there seemed to be less and less need for Cousin Sam'l's particular gifts. He had continued to be elected to the Continental Congress and shared in the debates but when John Hancock resigned the presidency of the Congress and returned to Massachusetts to become its first governor, Samuel Adams's troubles began. John Hancock had been a close friend and working associate of Samuel Adams for many years; now they were mortal enemies, with each spending a major portion of his energies trying to destroy the other's political influence. Governor Hancock's political machine achieved total power in Boston, and Hancock turned on Samuel, accusing him of having opposed long-time enlistments in the United States Army, of having attempted to undermine George Washington's power over the army, of having upset the Congress by creating the Silas Deane–Arthur Lee controversy in France. Samuel had had to rush back to Boston from Philadelphia to defend himself in order that his political career might not be ended forever.

Abigail had seen little of Cousin Samuel and Betsy. Samuel had remained in the Congress for several years but he had returned to Boston to live the year before and was elected to the Massachusetts Senate. She decided the time had come to remedy the situation and sent a note to Betsy insisting that she bring Samuel out for a Saturday and Sunday so that they could talk. She would put the boys in the attic for the weekend.

Samuel's hair was white and disheveled, the tremor marked. His eyes were brooding, his face lined in deep grooves of disapproval. Saturday evening, as she sat with Betsy and Samuel before the fire in the sitting parlor where the four Adamses had enjoyed so many hours during the years of struggle and crisis, she decided to ask the question plainly:

"Cousin Samuel, what has gone so terribly wrong now that the war is over? We have the independence that you spent your life to achieve. Why are you not profoundly gratified?"

Samuel looked up at her with a flash of fire in his eyes.

"Come into Boston with me and you'll see nothing but new faces. Who is controlling our state now, and our nation? Patriots who led us to independence and fought the war? Assuredly not! It's the profiteers, the speculators. Our old merchants have been driven out of business. The mushroom gentry have taken over the Tories' mansions and seized their places in society. Stand on a Boston street corner and watch the scum go riding by in the most expensive coaches. Who are they? James Warren will tell you: 'fellows who would have cleaned my shoes five years ago.' And what are they doing? Pretending they are British in every idle amusement and expensive foppery. That's all we import today, British frippery and foppery. I loathe and detest the old Tories. I shall fight to the end against restoring them their properties but, in all honesty, what is there to choose between them and the new Patriots? Patriots indeed! Witness how John Hancock celebrated his inauguration as governor. With parties and dinners, balls and orgies the like of which Boston has not seen since the days of Bernard and Hutchinson. Boston once stood foremost in the cause of religion and liberty. John Hancock is in process of destroying our people's love of liberty with luxury and temptations for soft living. I tell you, dear Cousin, this is not what the Revolution was fought for. Don't you know that as Puritans we have lost this war?"

He sat on the edge of his chair, gripping its arms to stop the tremor in his hands.

"Surely, Sam'l, this is but a temporary phase? We have found the right leaders before, we will find them again."

"No, Cousin. When we lose our Puritanism we lose our virtue. Men have sacrificed and suffered and died; your husband has lived away from you and his children for years but the rewards have gone to the greedy and the corrupt. Greatness is dead in our land."

He excused himself and stumbled wearily up the stairs to the bedroom above. At length Abigail said:

"Cousin Betsy, your burdens are heavy. I have not known."

Betsy looked up at her, her face pale but her eyes clear.

"I mind it only when Samuel makes himself ill. Otherwise, has he not been a robustious fighter all his life? He is not without influence in Boston though he claims he is. He is president of the Senate now and he can still carry on his fight. I'm sad only when Samuel tells me that he has passed the peak of his life, that the people and the country no longer have need for his services."

"We would not be a free nation today without the mind and strategy of Samuel Adams," Abigail declared vehemently.

Betsy smiled wistfully, murmured:

"There are good moments. But he wants to play a determining part in this new country he has created." She rose. "If you'll forgive me, I had best go up to him."

Abigail remained owl-eyed, roaming the downstairs rooms of her house in the dark, desolate. Was it for this that she had given up her husband and her love for all these years? To have it end in ignominious squabbling and defeat?

7

She combined with the Cranches to hire young Mr. Thomas to tutor her two boys and Billy Cranch. He stayed for the equivalent of a school term, then left to go into business. Abigail found another teacher, son of a Plymouth clergyman, who used their infrequently stocked store as his classroom. After a few months young Robbins had the opportunity to be taken into a family that was opening an American business house in Bordeaux. She then began writing to private schools; her boys must be set in a permanent course of education. Andover replied that it was full. So did the others. Abigail despaired; unless she could get them disciplined training they would never be accepted at Harvard. The time was growing short. In this problem more than any that had arisen she missed her husband's qualified hand. But surely John must know that the future of his two youngest sons was being endangered?

Well, she would enable them to become landowning farmers at the very least. She bought five lots in Vermont, of three hundred and thirty acres each, but the fifty dollars a lot was more than she could accumulate and she had to give a note for the fifth parcel.

The twelve men off the *Essex* for whom she had asked John to intercede when they were taken prisoner by the British were returned safely to Braintree. They came with their families to the Adams home to pay court. Each brought the sum of money with which John Adams had provided them. Abigail accepted their gratitude in John's name but felt she could not take the money.

"Begging your pardon, ma'am," said Job Field, spokesman for the group, "why not?"

"I have no instructions from my husband. That may have been the Congress' money he gave you."

"That was no Congress money, Mrs. Adams."

"Please keep it, gentlemen," she insisted, "until Mr. Adams returns."

After the fall rains began Royall Tyler changed his schedule, rising at five to pore over his lawbooks so that he might have his evenings free to sit with the Adams family before a roaring fire. Abigail liked the young man more all the time. He was building a modest practice; when he had a particularly involved case he would borrow John's writ book. In return for their hospitality he asked permission to collect some of John's legal fees still owed by Tories or evasive merchants. He did in fact collect one or two sums.

It was not until the onset of winter that Abigail realized that she had been seriously remiss. Royall Tyler had been coming to the house for almost nine months now, but she had never written John one word about the young man. At first it was because Nab had been so reserved that Abigail had not thought anything would come of his visits; no need to alarm John unnecessarily. There were moments when she had thought she saw signs of Nab's thawing, but just as quickly the girl would flee inside herself and remain withdrawn. Now it was clear that Tyler had serious intentions of courting Nab and that Nab might be accepting the first approach of love. John would be right to be furious with her. Yet as long as there was the possibility that John would be returning soon from Europe, she put off writing, preferring to save the news for a personal relating.

But suppose Nab was really in love? Abigail would be in trouble with her husband, having to present him with a *fait accompli* a full year after the man had appeared on the scene and, by indirection at least, announced that he wished to marry Miss Adams.

She had procrastinated far too long; best to write the whole story to John immediately. Under the date of December 23, 1782, she gave him a full portrait of Mr. Tyler, telling how he had studied law with Mr. Dana, opened an office in Braintree nine months before and boarded with the Cranches.

"He has popular talents, and his behavior has been unexceptionable since his residence in town, in consequence of which his business daily increases. He cannot fail making a distinguished figure in his profession if he steadily pursues it. I am not acquainted with any young gentleman whose attainments in literature are equal to his, who judges with greater accuracy or discovers a more delicate and refined taste. I have frequently looked upon him with the idea that you would have taken much pleasure in such a pupil."

Then, because she was resolved that her husband know the complete truth about the young man, she related the story of his wild youth and wasted patrimony. She also rose to his defense:

"Even in his most dissipated state he always applied his mornings to study, by which means he has stored his mind with a fund of useful knowledge."

At this point she realized the enormity of her sin of omission. She swept into Nab's room, said abruptly:

"Child, I think you ought to spend the rest of the winter with Uncle Isaac and Aunt Elizabeth."

Nab declined to be upset by her mother's tone.

"I should like that."

"I shall tell Mr. Tyler myself."

"Very well, Mother."

She did so that very evening, painfully aware of her culpability.

"Mr. Tyler, I think my husband will return in the spring. I don't think it proper for my daughter to have her mind attached . . ."

"If she is attached she has given me no sign."

"As of today your law practice is not sufficiently large to think of a permanent . . . Be that as it may, I have but one voice, and that is Mr. Adams's. Until I hear from him about all of this, I am sending Nab into Boston for her winter visit."

"And I shall remain here, working. I shall do everything in the proper manner, so that you and Mr. Adams will approve. I know that I have a questionable youth to live down and for that reason I shall work twice as hard and live twice as austerely as any young man in New England."

John's answer was the outraged cry of the father who suddenly learns that he is about to lose his little girl. He had no idea that in the years of his absence his daughter had grown into a long-legged, deep-breasted woman. Because it brought severe reproof for Abigail, this exchange of letters was the swiftest she had ever known. John had written in such hot temper that Abigail's eyes managed to pick out, the first time over, only a line here and there:

". . . yours of the 23d was brought in. The contents have awakened all my sensibility and show in a stronger light than ever the necessity of my coming home. I confess I don't like the subject at all. My child is too young for such thoughts, and I don't like your word 'dissipation' at all. . . . A lawyer would be my choice, but it must be a lawyer who spends his midnight as well as evenings at his age over his books, not at any lady's fireside. . . ."

"O Heaven!" she thought. "Has John forgotten those wonderful long nights in my father's sitting parlor?"

"A youth who has been giddy enough to spend his fortune, or half his fortune, in gaieties is not the youth for me. . . . I am not looking out for a poet nor a professor of *belles-lettres*. . . . I positively forbid any connection between my daughter and any youth upon earth who does not totally eradicate every taste for gaiety and expense."

He added that he did not like this method of courting mothers!

She was stunned by the violence of his letter. Yet upon a second reading she had to acknowledge that from John's isolated point of view he was justified in his outbreak.

Three weeks later he wrote:

"The peace which sets the rest of the world at ease increases, I think, my perplexities and anxiety. I have written to Congress a resignation, but I foresee there will not be a speedy decision upon it, and I shall be left in a state of suspense that will be intolerable. . . . I shall certainly return home in the spring . . . so you have nothing to do but wait to receive your old friend."

By the time this letter reached Abigail the buds were out on her apple trees, the fields trilling sea-green lines above the furrows, and Nab was back in Braintree. What all of Royall Tyler's affection had been unable to bring out in Nab the separation had accomplished in full measure. What her father had called Nab's greatest glory, her reserve, had vanished.

"Mother, now that Father knows about Mr. Tyler there's no reason why he can't call, is there?"

Abigail hesitated. She had not told Nab of her father's vehement reply.

"You haven't heard anything derogatory about Mr. Tyler in the past month?" asked Nab.

"On the contrary, he has merely been a mole."

Royall Tyler's visits were limited to two a week, an hour's walk with Nab in the afternoon, a single cup of tea before returning to his studies. He was earning a few more of the simpler writs but acknowledged himself to be at least two years away from being self-supporting.

Abigail turned her attention once again to the dire plight of her two sons' education. They were now ten and twelve. There were still no private schools with available places. She had only one recourse, her brother-in-law, the Reverend Mr. Shaw, Elizabeth's husband.

Haverhill was an eight-hour ride by stage from Boston and expensive, the company charging eight shillings for Abigail and six each for the boys. The town had been settled by English Puritans of whom it was said "the Lord winnowed a whole nation for the planting of New England." The second wave of immigration was a fighting breed of Scots-Irish, whom the selectmen of Boston sent up to the northwesternmost farm in Massachusetts, a salient sticking straight into Indian country.

Haverhill was a compact, close-knit village of about two thousand. Having subdued the Indians, they continued to fight among themselves. The people were prosperous, the principal street running along the Merrimack River, which took its produce of salt beef and pork, barrel staves and hoops, cheeses and butter, pot and pearl ashes down to Newburyport on the Atlantic. Main Street ran up the hill with the Common on the left, dominated by the white church with the parade and drilling grounds around it. Cater-cornered was the parsonage on Pleasant Street, a white house with large windows, set back from the street. In the past few years the church had been one of the busier parts of the drilling field, for religious dissension had rocked the community. Five preachers in a row had failed to tranquilize the pulpit. The Reverend Mr. Shaw was not a forceful man but, being amiable and charitable, he had managed to inter the religious differences in the burying ground. Probably the most peaceable home in the town was the parsonage, with its four tall columns making it look more like a Virginia planter's mansion than the home of a clergyman living on £100 a year.

The Smith girls had been fortunate, Mary, Abigail and Elizabeth, for each had married the man of her choice. Abigail was still conscience-stricken for having opposed John Shaw. "Why did I really?" she asked herself as she embraced the Shaws' two young children. "Because I did not recognize the mature man in the young student?"

She apologized silently to Elizabeth, whose happiness precluded any such need, and thanked her slim, fast-thinking sister that John Shaw had never known of her opposition. She needed all of her brother-in-law's kindness and loyalty.

She pleaded her case plainly: there was no one else who could tutor Charles and Tommy, give them the necessary college preparation.

"Sister and Brother Shaw, will you take them to live with you for the next year or two?"

Elizabeth went about the room lighting the candles in her wall brackets.

"My husband must make the decision."

The Reverend Mr. Shaw was already a stooping figure at thirty-five. "You are not abandoned, Sister. I will teach them all I know."

Tears smarted behind Abigail's eyes. She curtsied genteelly.

"The Adams family will be in your debt forever."

"If families counted up their debts, usurers would coin fortunes," Shaw answered. "I will leave you sisters alone now to arrange the practicalities. I have my Sunday sermon to finish. I struggle like a fowl caught in a storm, pulling each sentence out of my mind the way a duck pulls his legs out of the mud."

8

John had been gone for three and a half years. She had been alone for so long that a numbness settled over her. She huddled inside her skull as sailors do inside their oilskins during a storm at sea. The summer heat served as a soporific. She did a lot of visiting: the Warrens, Mrs. Francis Dana in Boston, the Shaws in Haverhill, her failing father in Weymouth, Cotton Tufts, now a state senator, the Cranches for tea or supper since her own house seemed oppressive. How wonderful to escape longings and loneliness in idle, unguided chatter; miraculous how these sessions of pure tongue-clacking filled the void and put grease under the hours.

The fall changed her rhythm abruptly. By the beginning of September it was clear that the seventy-five-year-old Reverend William Smith was dying of uremia. Abigail summoned the family. Her father whispered, between his bouts of distress from the strangury:

"There is only one reason I wish God could spare my life a little longer: I should like to see the return of your dearest friend."

He died two days later, surrounded by his daughters and fourteen grandchildren. Only Billy was missing; not all the frantic efforts of the three sisters could locate the errant son. The Reverend Mr. Smith never mentioned Billy, but each time someone entered his room his eyes lighted up expectantly. The loss of Billy was the one failure and disappointment of his long and fruitful life. His good-bys to his family partook of the nature of a farewell sermon:

"I have endeavored to do all the good I could with the talents committed to me; and to honor God with my substance."

They wound up Burying Hill, six deacons of his church carrying the plain plank coffin. All of Weymouth and the surrounding countryside was there: several hundreds whom the minister had in his forty-nine years of the pastorate baptized, tutored, married and in turn baptized the children of. It was not a mournful hour, not even for Abigail; it seemed to be an occasion to rejoice that so good and fastidious a man could have lived and served so long.

The strongest impression was made on Nab. Now past eighteen, she decided that the time had come to take a stand with Royall Tyler. She told her mother nothing, but Tyler became ebullient, overflowing with high spirits and ambition. He succeeded so well in collecting John's old legal debts that Abigail found momentary relief in her finances.

One Sunday Nab and Tyler returned from an after-dinner walk in the cool November air, a sense of entrancement enveloping them both.

"Mrs. Adams, would you take a walk with us?" Tyler asked eagerly. "There's something we must show you."

Abigail put on her warm cloak and walked with the young couple up the Boston Road past the eleven-mile stone, the Liberty Tree, the schoolhouse, the Meeting House and burying ground. About a quarter of a mile past the ten-mile stone they turned west on another road and came to what was known as the Vassall-Borland house.

"Is this what we've come to see?"

"Yes. The Borlands were Tories whose house and farm were sequestered by the court. With the signing of the peace treaty, Mrs. Borland has been allowed to return. She has put the house and one hundred acres up for sale, as well as fifty acres of woodland. The price is high, £1000, but it's the finest property around."

They entered a white picket fence, walked up a path between overgrown bushes to the front stoop. Tyler had the key. He held the door open. Abigail stepped into an entry hall. To her right was the dining room, to her left the drawing room, paneled in San Domingo mahogany. Upstairs there were two bedrooms, and above them two small rooms with dormer windows. The house was connected by a short breezeway with the kitchen and servant quarters behind. It had been built in 1731 by Major Vassall, a wealthy West Indies sugar planter, and a good deal of money had been spent to keep out the heat and cold.

Although it was a rather narrow structure, only an entryway and perhaps two and a half rooms wide, it was tall and stately and gave the impression of being in the tradition of the Quincy home in Mount Wollaston. There were good fireplaces and mantels, a wide staircase, superbly carved banisters. Down the east side there was a stone wall with an opening large enough for carriages to enter and be driven into the carriage house at the rear. There were maples and elms at the back of the house, gravel walks and trimmed shrubs in front.

"I could live here myself," exclaimed Abigail. "It has a feeling of permanence and dignity. All I would need to add would be a library."

Tyler and Nab exchanged a smile.

"This farm can afford a good living to a family," Tyler rushed on, enthusiastically. "My knowledge of agriculture is unfortunately scant, but I intend to make myself good in husbandry." He studied Abigail's face as they climbed a slight rise to the road. "Do you think Mr. Adams might approve?"

Abigail was not going to be caught in that trap.

"Your decision must be your own, since it's your money and your future. But Mr. Adams knows the farm; it is good land."

"Thank you. I shall buy the place as soon as I can convert some of my Boston investments."

When they had returned home and were alone, Abigail decided to face Nab down.

"You like the Vassall-Borland house quite well?"

"Should I not?"

"Did you encourage Mr. Tyler to buy it?"

"Not exactly."

"Did he ask if you would like to live in the house?"

"Yes."

"Forgive me for sounding like your father on cross-examination but it seems to be the only way I can dredge any information out of you. Did Mr. Tyler propose marriage?"

"Yes."

"What did you answer?"

"That he be patient until I could see my father and be certain that he approved."

A culminating series of letters came from John. In the first he wrote that, with Charley and Tommy at Haverhill, "yourself and Mistress Nabby and Mr. John with me, I could bear to live in Europe another year or two. But I cannot live much longer without my wife and daughter, and I will not." After Congress restored his commission to negotiate a commercial treaty with Great Britain, he wrote: "This resolution of Congress deserves my gratitude. It is highly honorable to me and restores me my feelings which a former proceeding had taken away. I am now perfectly content to be recalled whenever they think fit, or to stay in Europe until this business is finished, provided you will come and live with me."

Three days later he added, "The negotiation of a treaty of commerce with Great Britain will detain me in Europe at least until next spring, perhaps longer. . . . I will hasten to receive you as soon as I hear of your arrival." On November eighth he wrote, "Come to Europe with Nabby as soon as possible and satisfy your curiosity, improve your taste by viewing these magnificent scenes. Go to the play. See the paintings and buildings. Visit the manufacturers for a few months. And then, if Congress pleases, return with me to reflect upon them." He also instructed her to bring two servants to run their house.

Time was no longer tenuous; it was in short supply. First, she made a wedding for Phoebe, who had been granted freedom in the Reverend Mr. Smith's will, and an annual allowance; Phoebe and her new husband would occupy the cottage as long as the Adamses were away. Next she came to satisfactory terms with her tenant to farm their land on "halves" for the duration of her absence. She turned over all of her account books, assets, forthcoming obligations and taxes to Cotton Tufts, who had in the last year become a shrewd investor in state notes, which he was buying for seven shillings on the pound. Cotton agreed to sell the produce of their farm, collect the rent on the Boston house and pay their bills.

As he had promised, her father had willed the Lincoln farm to Catharine Louisa. Abigail returned her young daughter, amidst a great shedding of tears. Then she went to Haverhill to arrange with the Shaws, with whom the Adamses had been left half shares in Mr. Smith's Medford farm, to manage the property as they saw fit and to use the Adams half of the receipts toward the expenses of her two sons. The Cranches had inherited the Weymouth Mansion and farm.

Royall Tyler had bought the Vassall-Borland property. He urged Abigail to look for outstanding furniture, rugs, art objects for the house while in Europe. Abigail closed down her store. Tyler turned it back into a law office, which he would use as his own, brought John's books down from the attic and replaced them on the shelves. For the house abroad, Abigail engaged John Briesler, about thirty, recommended by Richard Cranch's family as steady and virtuous. She also hired young Esther Field, a neighbor's daughter who had been helping her.

The news of their departure saturated the countryside. There began the parade of friends sending respects and duty to John; the women from her quilting days, the families of the men John had worked with as selectman, the Reverend Mr. Wibird, his frame twisted at oblique angles, saying prayers for their safety, her fellow church members and deacons, the members of her family from Mount Wollaston, Norton Quincy and Colonel Josiah Quincy's widow, Catharine Louisa and her children from Lincoln, the Cranches.

She was to proceed to London. John would direct her from there. Uncle Isaac urged her not to take a ship in which she would have to furnish her own food, tableware and cook. He would find one for her in which she would need to supply only her bedding. Friends and relatives who had been to Europe cautioned against taking trunks full of clothes which style and custom would not permit her to wear abroad.

Finally she closed her bedroom door behind her for the last time and circled lightly down the steps. Unbelievably, after four and a half years of separation, she would be reunited with her husband and oldest son, now returned to his father in The Hague. She was still half a year short of forty, and at this happy moment it was difficult for her to believe that she had been married almost twenty years and had four children. Would John notice the toll the last years had taken? Then she laughed, the two notes low and musical in her throat. But of course, John had aged the exact same number of years!

Nab was already waiting in the carriage. As she glanced at her beautiful daughter in her traveling cloak, and patted her own hair into place under her new velvet hat, she chose to ignore completely her dread of the ocean and John's comment:

"A lady cannot help being an odious creature at sea."

9

The *Active* was seaworthy, with a copper bottom and a knowledgeable captain. The Foster brothers who owned her, although charging a high price, a hundred and ten dollars a passenger, provided the "found" so that she would not have to assemble the quantities of foodstuffs she had had to prepare for John and the boys on their crossing.

They waited at her uncle Isaac's until the loading of oil and potash was completed, the tide and winds right for departure. Isaac's younger son, William, was in London. He would be awaiting their arrival. Joseph Foster, the younger of the owners, assured her she would have a stateroom to herself, and every accommodation and attention she could wish for. Captain Nathaniel Lyde, a roughhewn man, rolling in his walk as though on the bridge, also sought to reassure her, saying:

"The sea is never dull, ma'am. Always something interesting going on. With your permission, I'll teach you to take a trick at the wheel."

She met most of the other passengers: Mrs. Lovey Adams, the only Adams Abigail had ever met who was not kin to John, a pretty woman of about thirty-five whose husband, a doctor, had been settled and practicing in England since the beginning of the war; and with her a young brother named Lawrence, going to England for travel and further education. Colonel Beriah Norton, a grave man of fifty, was a member of the Massachusetts Senate. With him was a Mr. Spear, making jokes to amuse them. Dr. John Clark, a gentle person and world traveler, assured Abigail and Nab that he would take care of them on the voyage. A haughty Scotsman by the name of Green promptly informed Abigail on the social position and comparative wealth of each of her fellow passengers.

Early one morning when she was seated in her aunt Elizabeth's alcove Thomas Jefferson was announced. She descended to find him in her uncle's library, taking books down from the shelves and scanning sections of them. She studied him from the doorway while he stood with a book in each hand, the image on the screen of her mind flashing back twenty-three years to the picture of John Adams in her father's study, sniffing alternately at the two open books held in his eager, affectionate hands.

Jefferson was tall, slender, graceful, a "straight-up" man as his friends described him, about forty, with sandy hair, freckles on his high cheekbones, but not on the hollowed cheeks themselves, a high bony-ridged nose, a full-lipped compassionate mouth and a brow as noble as that sculptured on the marble bust of a Roman emperor. His dark eyes were melancholy, still reflecting the death of his beloved wife only twenty months before, following childbirth, and of two of his daughters and a son prior to his wife's passing. He was dressed in a plain black coat and ruffled white shirt; it was evident that he paid little attention to prevailing fashion. He did pay fascinated attention to almost everything else: to painting, architecture, music, literature on the one hand, all the diverse aspects of natural philosophy, science, geometry, astronomy on the other, and, at the center of his being, statesmanship, already proved by his brilliant writings for Virginia and the United States.

Beside Jefferson, gazing into a picture book, was his eleven-year-old daughter Martha, called Patsy, with her father's big eyes, high cheekbones, warm mouth and smooth round chin. Her dark hair was parted in the center, with short curls over her forehead.

Jefferson turned his head. The eyes lighted with pleasure. He bowed formally.

"Mrs. Adams! How good to see you."

"The pleasure is mine, Mr. Jefferson. Elbridge Gerry wrote me from the Congress that you were coming to Boston."

"I hastened myself on my journey in hopes of having the pleasure of attending you to Paris and lessening some of the difficulties to which you may be exposed."

"Would that it could be so, Mr. Jefferson. The *Active* sails for London in about two days. Would it be possible for you to accompany us?"

"Alas, that is too soon for me. I have arranged to spend a week in Portsmouth, then return to New York and take passage directly to France on a French packet. I have insured you your choice of accommodations should you care to join us, and the owners have promised that the departure of the vessel would be made agreeable to our movements."

Abigail did not relish the long trip into New York; better to use the time moving eastward across the Atlantic toward John.

"It was good of you to plan ahead for me. And I should like to have Patsy with me, the crossing could be more agreeable for her with two women as companions. But I have already paid four fares and I think the owners would not be able to find replacements for us at so late a date."

"I understand."

Abigail turned to Patsy, who seemed well poised for her years. They agreed that they would see each other in Paris and exchange stories of their adventures with the French.

On the morning of June twentieth Mr. Foster sent a carriage for them. Uncle Isaac, Aunt Elizabeth and Royall Tyler, who had come to Boston for the occasion, accompanied them.

The trip down Court Street into the State House Square was like a voyage through time, even as the *Active* would take them on a journey through space. Here John and Cousin Sam'l had been given the tumultuous farewell on their departure for the first Congress ten years before.

The *Active* was tied up at the wharf of their family friend John Rowe, four wharves east of Griffin's Wharf where she and Betsy had watched Samuel Adams's long-promised Tea Party. The *Active* was riding easy on her ropes, compact, more sturdy than graceful in line. She was a three-decker and three-master, painted over all a pitch black except for the deck, which the crew had holystoned to its natural light wood color. To Abigail, who had been looking at the ships tied up to the Boston wharves all her life, the *Active* seemed frighteningly small and frail to brave so vast an ocean.

Her farewells had already been spent. Royall Tyler, though he had gone along with Nab's reasoning, was now utterly crushed. He appeared half his size, shoulders hunched, eyes red. Uncle Isaac led him off the dock. Abigail and Nab were helped up the swaying gangplank, with its narrow bight of water below, by several strong hands which she recognized as belonging to Captain Lyde and the red-faced Scotsman, Mr. Green. They were escorted by a young lad across the narrow deck and down a flight of unguarded stairs, as narrow and steep as her own at home. On the deck below and forward was the galley, and on the opposite side a room with twelve bunks ranged about the walls in layers of three for the male passengers, with a square table in the center.

They were directed across this room to a door leading to their stateroom. Abigail stood at the threshold, eyes wide: the room was eight feet square, with two bunks on either side, each three feet wide, leaving a space between of two feet in which to move about. There was a small grated window, but it opened onto a companionway of the ship. The odor coming through was redolent of grease. There was no air, except that coming through the door to the men's sleeping quarters.

"It is also the dining room for passengers," the boy proffered.

Abigail, Nab and Esther, the young Braintree girl who was coming along to serve them, were to use three bunks. A few of their personal possessions could be laid out on the fourth. The trunks would have to remain outside, in the general quarters.

"With every accommodation you could wish for," mimicked Nab.

Esther had turned a yellow-green.

"Don't you feel us rolling?"

She sank onto a lower bunk and began to groan piteously.

"O Heaven!" exclaimed Abigail. "Esther is seasick and we're still in Brattle Square! Nab, let us go on deck and watch the sailing."

A warm fresh breeze was blowing. Abigail enjoyed the hurly-burly of the shouted orders, the sailors casting off ropes, the raising of the sails, the slow movement out into the bay, and then northward, with the buildings of Boston growing faint on the horizon, the thin border of land vanishing into air, and all about them the ocean, a clear noon-blue, immense, infinitely mysterious, unknown. Whatever sadness Nab had felt at leaving Royall Tyler behind was thrown off as she enjoyed the excitement of further sails being let out, amidst a jungle of ropes, to catch the strengthening wind.

That was the last enjoyment they were to know for many a day. Two hours out, when they had passed the light, Captain Lyde came to them and said:

"Ladies, please to put on your sea clothes and prepare for sickness."

Esther had already made a mess of their room. Stepping gingerly, they put on special oilcloth wrap-arounds, took off their shoes . . . and were instantly sick. They lay hunched in their bunks, the door to the general room closed behind them. The ship rolled from side to side unceasingly. Through the small window the smell of potash combined with that of the oil as the cargoes began to shift in their hold.

Night fell. The thought of food was repulsive. The air in the tiny room was stifling. Nab said:

"I saw a curtain on the other side of the door. It'll let in a little air."

Abigail stared at her daughter, muttered, "What would I have thought on shore to have laid myself down to sleep in common with half a dozen gentlemen?"

"Pay it no mind, Mother, they're as seasick as you are. Except Dr. Clark. I see him moving about trying to help the others. Shall I call him in?"

"Thank you no, child."

It was the most ghastly night of her life. They had only partly undressed, about as much as the Yankee bundlers. The curtains rolled with the ship. Truly a lady was an odious creature at sea; she could only be thankful that John was not there to see the spectacle.

Morning brought a little relief. Young Lawrence, who was sharing an equivalent stateroom with his sister, offered to sleep in the common room and give up his bunk to Nab. Abigail accepted gratefully; with only two of them in her stateroom there was a little more comfort, though the air was now compounded with the rancid smells of frying food from the galley.

Esther hung for hours with her head over the side of the bunk, retching.

"Mrs. Adams, please, ma'am, ask them to throw me overboard. Once more . . . I'll turn inside out. I'd rather be dead."

Dr. Clark knocked on the outside panel of the doorframe, took one look and went for Briesler. Briesler was wretchedly uncomfortable, but still able to walk. He helped Abigail put on her shoes, assisted her into her heavy camblet cloak and, with the help of Lawrence and Foster, carried her up the clifflike steps into the cold, salty air of the sea. She gasped with relief. Foster was conscience-stricken over Abigail's troubles. He could not steady the ship, but he did find a separate bunk for Esther, into which the steward and two boys carried her bodily like a bog-soaked log. As his last contribution before going under, Briesler scrubbed Abigail's stateroom. She did not see him again for five days; or Esther for a week.

Captain Lyde released a man to her in place of Briesler. Job Field brought her a little custard or a bit of fresh milk from the ship's cow, and for two nights slept outside her door on top of her trunks so that he could hear her if she called out. Abigail held to the sides of the bunk until her hands and wrists ached in order to keep from falling to the floor. Even so, she rejoiced at the strong winds which the captain assured her were driving them at good speed to England, and after a while found herself falling asleep in spite of the lashing of the waves and the tumbling of the vessel. When she was able she crawled on deck, but it was so cold and damp, even in her coat which was lined with heavy baize, that she could not remain long. Never more than once in twenty-four hours was she able to get across the general cabin unassisted. The other Mrs. Adams had similar trouble crossing from the opposite room.

Everyone was helpful. The gentlemen went on deck for an hour each day to allow the ladies to perform their ablutions. Dr. Clark gave her a quieting powder and told diverting stories of his travels in the Orient. He was attentive to Nab, as were Lawrence and Spear, the droll bachelor. All of the men behaved with scrupulous sensitivity, which saved embarrassment. Though she was eating no solid food, Abigail went occasionally into the big room for company. The square table was roped into place, the passengers frequently remaining in their chairs only by holding each other arm in arm, with their feet braced against the table so as not to go sliding off, one after the other, to crash their chairs into the bunks on the side.

On the eighth day she awakened to a calm sea. Esther was standing in the doorway looking wan but with an eager smile on her face.

"Good morning, Mrs. Adams. I thought I was going to die of the disease, but now I got it conquered. Can I bring you some breakfast?"

"Well, Esther, I never thought I'd see you standing on your ownsome legs again. No food, but you can open the trunks and get me clean undergarments. Not to mention a pail of warm water and my packet of soap."

She achieved the miracle of getting up on deck unassisted. It was a brilliantly clear day, the ship making less than its usual seven or eight knots because of the slack in wind. Captain Lyde reported that they were a good eight hundred miles out from Boston, more than a quarter of the journey. Nab joined them. Abigail took a long look at her daughter, with the color in her cheeks and her eyes clear, head held high.

At noon they went down for the main meal. It was the first time Abigail had attempted to eat at the square table. To her astonishment she saw that there were not enough knives or forks to go around, nor half enough cups. She was even more surprised when she was served the food. First the steward brought in from the galley a leg of pork all bristly; a quarter of an hour later there came a cake; a half an hour later the man triumphantly served a pair of roasted fowl, and twenty minutes later he produced a piece of beef. When everybody had finished eating there emerged a bowl of boiled potatoes.

For the most part Abigail sat with her teeth locked. When the steward brought in a pail of fresh milk, Mr. Foster pursed his lips disapprovingly, turned to Abigail and said:

"Mrs. Adams, could you tell us how rightly to get this milk pail clean? I don't think it's been scrubbed since we left Rowe's Wharf. It's my guess the cook just milks into it, each day onto the other."

"I'm surprised that you haven't all been poisoned by now. Let me have the pail. I shall scrub it myself."

She did, with a clean cloth and some powder from her own belongings. When she brought it back through the general room, Dr. Clark led the applause.

A few days later a delegation was sent to her by Captain Lyde to report that the cow had been disabled in the last storm. Colonel Norton of the Massachusetts Senate announced:

"It's up to you, Mrs. Adams. Shall we let the cow die a lingering death or put her out of her misery?" Everyone was watching.

"If you're all agreed that the poor thing must die . . . ?"

By herculean efforts they got the great bulk lifted out onto the deck. Captain Lyde read a funeral service. The cow was dropped overboard.

A storm came up, with thunder, lightning and rain. They retreated to a cabin where Mr. Foster and Colonel Norton played backgammon, Abigail read William Buchan's *Domestic Medicine*, or chatted with Nab and Mrs. Adams. The rest played whist. The ship began to pitch, which Abigail found more disagreeable than the rolling. Mr. Green rushed into the cabin with great news: the mate had reported that they were sixteen hundred miles on their way to England. Abigail kept repeating the good news all night as she held rigidly to the sides of her bunk.

The crossing took a precise month. They knew they were approaching the south of England when they saw twenty different sails. The skipper of a small boat bent on a smuggling expedition assured them they were close. The captain sounded and found bottom at fifty-five fathoms. A day or two of good wind would give them land. But the beauty of the windless day resulted in the *Active* becoming becalmed.

"Patience, patience, patience," recited Abigail, "is the first, second and third virtue of the seaman, as necessary to him as to the statesman."

The next morning they saw the cliffs of Dover, Dover Castle and the town. It was raining hard, but it was with joy that Abigail felt drenched at the thought that she was not only to be reunited with her husband but was at long last to see her Motherland. While the pilot boat came alongside, and the captain anchored his ship in the downs, with the little village of Deal before them, her mind went back to the days when they had loved England, the font of all that was good and permanent in their lives. She remembered how she had memorized parts of King George III's first speech to Parliament. She remembered during her first walk through the streets of Boston with John how he had commented that Boston must be a good deal like London. She recalled the travel books she had borrowed from her uncle Isaac's library, in which she had read descriptions of the gentle English countryside.

An emotional nostalgia swept over her; she had never been out of Massachusetts and now she quivered with excitement at the prospect of seeing the great world: first London, and then Paris. It was a moment of such intense realization of old dreams that she had to lean against the ship's wet railing to steady herself.

Captain Lyde came to advise them to put whatever they needed into small trunks. The *Active* would be a week in the Channel before she would be able to get up the river. He would land them at Deal and they could make the seventy-mile trip in post chaises to London.

They were wrapped in oilskins and lowered from the ship into a boat about as large as a Charlestown ferry. They would have to be run up on shore by the waves. The surf was six feet high. When they set off from their vessel they mounted on top of a wave as high as a steeple, then sank so low that she could not see the *Active* at all. Mr. Foster, just ahead of her, braced himself against the side of the boat, held her as she stood resolute, her face turned to the shore.

10

They slept restlessly in a small inn in Deal and were up at five to be handed into a series of post chaises and carried eighteen miles along smoothly cobbled roads to Canterbury. She was impressed by the vast fields of wheat, oats, beans, hops, everything cultivated like a garden right down to the road. Unlike New England, there were no fences.

At the Canterbury Inn new stages were ordered. While they were being prepared, the ship's passengers were served an opulent breakfast. Abigail was surprised to find Canterbury a larger town than Boston, with Gothic churches built of stone blocks. She noted their windows were covered with iron bars, as though they were prisons. Their stage was ready to carry them to Rochester, where they changed again for Chatham. As they drove into the yard of an elegant inn they were surrounded by footmen. The well-dressed hostess stepped forward. Abigail was given a bill of fare to mark. After a half hour of making their toilette the passengers sat down to dinner, the host serving the first course as a courtesy. There followed seven courses of fish, fowl, meat and vegetables.

The next drivers were urged to get them past Blackheath before dark, but even so a post chaise was held up. Two miles up the road they came upon the robber, who had been captured. He was a youth of about twenty, miserably clothed and abject in terror.

"The assize sits next month," cried his captor, "and then, my lad, you swing!"

At eight o'clock that night the last chaise set them down in front of Low's Hotel in Covent Garden. There was no John Adams to receive them, or even a note from her menfolk. She asked Mr. Spear, one of the passengers, to find her cousin William Smith. In less than half an hour William and Charles Storer, Elizabeth Smith's nephew, were waiting in her parlor. They had run the full mile from the Custom House to the hotel.

"We rejoice to see you," they cried.

They informed her that John Quincy had been in London a whole month awaiting their arrival but had returned to The Hague, discouraged. William had heard from his father of Abigail's impending arrival by a ship that had come in three days earlier. He had immediately reserved a pleasant suite of rooms for them at Osborne's New Family Hotel, and written to John Adams that Abigail and Nab were expected hourly. They were sure John would cross the Channel from The Hague on the first packet. The two young men moved Abigail and Nab to Osborne's the next morning. This was where John had stayed during an earlier visit to London. A dozen members of the American colony called to invite them to dinner, to tea, to go riding in the country.

The first to arrive were the Benjamin Hallowells; he was John's cousin, former comptroller of the customs for the Crown, whose home had been wrecked by the Boston mob. The Hallowells insisted that Abigail and Nab come to dinner, bringing William Smith and Charles Storer. Here she met still another of John's cousins, Thomas Boylston. They were served a typical New England dinner: salt fish, fried lamb, boiled tongue and fowl, pea soup, pudding. The Hallowells were living comfortably but in nowhere near the opulence of their Boston days before they had had to flee.

Abigail liked London. It was a much larger city than she had imagined, more beautiful, with its numerous open squares, and more sophisticated. She was impressed by the wide, regular streets with ladies walking very fast in the sunshine; the uniformity of the stone and brick houses in Grosvenor Square and along Hyde Park. In the shops she found the British manufactures superior to anything being produced in America. She walked for hours, the small flat stones of the sidewalk comfortable underfoot, to visit Copley, the American artist who had painted John's portrait, to Westminster and St. Paul's; along the Thames River where she watched the ships dock from all over the world, even the *Active*, which arrived five days later with her trunks and Briesler. She and Nab went by carriage to Kew and Windsor Castle. She realized now that she and John had been naïve to imagine that Boston was London "in little." London was a world metropolis, the public buildings were imposing, the great number of coaches the most luxurious she had seen.

Although the treaty of peace between England and the United States had been proclaimed some six months before, it had not made the English any more friendly to Americans. It was not so much hostility she perceived from their attitude, as indifference: a desire to ignore the late unpleasantness and anyone who had been involved in it.

She had been in London for eight days but there was no sign of John. Had he and Johnny already left for Paris before William Smith's note could reach them? In the meanwhile she kept hearing about old friends and relatives: Isaac Smith, Jr., had left for America shortly before, after nine years of a quiet life as a country schoolteacher and preacher in Devonshire. Samuel Quincy was in the West Indies as comptroller at Antigua. Jonathan and Esther Sewall were living in Bristol because it was cheaper there. Jonathan had been unable to acquire a law practice in England and the family had had to live sparsely on the income of £600 a year which had been granted to Jonathan by the Crown during his days of prominence in Boston, as judge commissary of the Vice Admiralty Court in Nova Scotia.

She was writing a letter to her sister Mary when Briesler came running in, puffing and red in the face.

"Madam, young Mr. Adams is come!"

"Johnny! Where is he?"

"In the next house, ma'am, he stopped to get his hair done."

"His hair done . . . !"

"Now, Mother, he wants to look his best," exclaimed Nab.

A few moments later a young man entered: tall, handsome, fastidiously groomed, the hair well powdered, with aristocratic features: high, exquisitely rounded brow, expressive eyes, a long Roman nose, full, sensual mouth. He reminded Abigail of someone she had met, but only the eyes were really familiar. She was unable to believe that this could be seventeen-year-old Johnny, when he cried:

"Oh my mama!"

This man was her son! Abigail went close to him. She wanted to hug him to her bosom, kiss him a dozen times. She did lean up and peck her oldest son on the cheek. He not only looked different, he smelled and felt different: the white powder on his hair, the cologne the barber had used on his face after the shave, even the manly texture of the well-cut coat and white cravat. Johnny was as much surprised by this kiss of reunion as his mother had been. His arms lifted as though they were about to return her embrace; his face was brimming with joy.

"Oh, Johnny, I've been remembering you all this time as the boy who sailed on the *Sensible*, while you've been working at growing up."

"It was just natural, Ma; it didn't take much work."

Nab had held back, shy. Abigail felt Johnny's and Nab's eyes searching each other out. She murmured:

"Look how Nab has changed."

Johnny took a step toward Nab, said quietly:

"I should have recognized my sister anywhere in the world."

They stood in the center of the room, big-eyed, lips quivering. Johnny bowed stiffly from the waist, asked how her crossing was. Nab curtsied slightly, allowed that it was supportable.

It was a tribute to Johnny's acumen that his father had commissioned him to buy the sturdiest English carriage he could find in London—they were expensive, the best ones costing as much as £150—in which to bring his mother and sister to The Hague, putting it on board ship at Harwich for Hellevoetsluis, a twenty-six-hour crossing if the weather was fair. Abigail wanted to leave for The Hague instantly. Johnny took over as the man of the family.

"Mother, one simply doesn't buy a carriage in an hour, the way one does a hat. European roads are notoriously bad, pocked with holes and half-buried stones."

A day later he had found a strongly built carriage that had been driven by an English gentleman for a short while. Because it was slightly used he was able to obtain it for a low price. Nevertheless he insisted upon waiting another day to bring in a veteran coachmaker to test its qualities, and on his assurance paid over the money.

Abigail had been hard put to contain her impatience. Only three days from John and still so far away! Yet she knew that Johnny's cautious method was the right one; in any event she would not have injured the young man by supplanting his authority.

She was packing her trunk in her hotel parlor when she heard quick, nervous, yet ponderous footsteps in the hallway. She barely had time to straighten up when the door was thrown open. Seeing her, John Adams's countenance became radiant. In the brief second before he strode into the room to clasp her in his arms, she was able to judge that he was leaner than she had ever seen him, and that there was a deep network of wrinkles radiating from the corner of his eyes. Then the years dissolved, time fled like a whipped cur, its tail between its legs. It was as though they had never been separated.

John held her face a few inches from his, so that he could study her. His eyes were alight with love.

"At last, my dear, we are together again. You haven't changed a particle. Just the sight of you makes me feel twenty years younger."

She could not bespeak her heart. It was too full. Instead she murmured, her lips close to his:

"What are you doing in London? We were leaving in the morning to join you in The Hague."

"I could not let you make the crossing without me. We are going directly to Paris." He placed his lips on hers, kissed her repeatedly, brushed her hair back fondly from her ears.

"Abigail, life is beginning all over for me now that we are together."

"Oh, John, I feel such a recruit of spirits. I am a young girl again, eager to begin my life and love."

BOOK SEVEN

ENEMY COUNTRY

1

THEY engaged a suite of three bedrooms and sitting parlor at the Hotel d'York on the Left Bank overlooking the narrow but trim Rue Jacob. The bedrooms faced the garden and ancient church of St. Germain des Prés.

Their travels in the new coach from London to Dover had been delightful. The English had provided excellent horses, handsomely harnessed, with postilion riders to set the pace. At the inns they had fared well, with neat apartments, genteel serving and good food, and they had been carefree as children in their joy at being together. From the moment they crossed from Dover to Calais a depressing ambience had forced itself upon them. They were given cart horses to pull their coach, tied with frayed ropes such as were used in America on plows. The postilions were ragged. They were obliged to change horses and gear every six miles. The inns were so odor-laden that Abigail and Nab ate their meals in the coach. There had been scenes of natural beauty, but the villages looked poor and mean, the narrow streets dirty. The low heavy farmhouses made of clay with thatched roofs were without glass in the windows. Whole families, including the children, were working in the fields; unlike the English farmers, the French seemed brutalized, stooped with hard labor, the expressions on their faces glum. The whole feeling had been one of poorness: the fields, the crops, the houses, the animals, the humans. The Channel was so narrow; yet to Abigail the two countries seemed separated by centuries.

The dirt and noxious odors of Paris assailed her nostrils. She was accustomed to the black soot of Boston chimneys settling on the snow of the sidewalks, but here the dirt seemed to be ingrained in the terribly old buildings. Debris lay about in the streets: night soil, refuse of the kitchens, a dead dog lying in the gutter with its four legs stretched out stiffly. Other odors seemed to emanate from the houses themselves, making the hot stagnant air so unbreathable that when she rode out in their coach she held a handkerchief to her nose to screen Paris through a scented cologne. She felt badly about reacting so provincially to one of the world's great centers of culture but if she expected John to admonish her she was mistaken. He asked:

"You don't feel you want to settle in the heart of Paris?"

"Not if there is a choice."

"A happy one. I have never enjoyed these putrid streets either. That's why I asked Thomas Barclay, our consul general, to negotiate for us to lease the house of the Comte de Rouault in Auteuil. It adjoins the Bois de Boulogne, overlooking the river Seine, and is surrounded by beautiful gardens. Yet it is inexpensive."

"It sounds lovely. But isn't it inconvenient?"

"Not excessively. Only four miles on the outskirts. Our carriage will bring us in to the theatre and opera or for dinner with friends in half an hour. We'll drive out tomorrow and see if you approve. Barclay himself had rented it for quite a time; in fact, he took me there when I was ill last year and nursed me back to health."

The château was known in the neighborhood as the Comte de Rouault's folly since its construction had come close to bankrupting the nobleman. It was built of white stone, three stories high, with decorative sculptures above the central windows and doorway. The semicircular wings projected toward a formal garden with crisp-cut hedges, elevated urns, graveled walks leading through green lawn, a variety of blooming flowers beyond a columned fence, and at the bottom of the garden several rows of arched trees taller than the house and so trimmed as to have their leaves almost touch, giving areas of deep cool shade.

"Why, it's formidable!" Abigail exclaimed. "We have no palaces like this in New England."

The downstairs was designed spaciously: the salon where they would receive was elegantly mirrored, a third larger than the great hall of the new Warren home in Milton, big enough to contain their entire salt-box house in Braintree. Two sets of glass doors admitted to the garden and to an enclosed court. On the other side of the foyer was the dining room, also completely mirrored. The kitchen beyond seemed too small to feed as many as the dining room would hold, but not so the long wing of servants' quarters with ten separate bedrooms.

The family apartments were upstairs. Here Abigail got a blow, for the stairs were so dirty that she had to hold up her skirts while ascending.

"As though I were passing through a cowyard," she said under her breath.

They came out into a long gallery with six windows facing on a quiet tree-lined street of Auteuil. Opposite each window was a separate apartment with a bed and sitting room. All four members of the family could have private quarters, with two guest apartments for friends. Abigail figured that with the side wings at least forty beds could be made at one time.

That evening John signed the lease. The next morning she and Nab drove out to engage the servants. John Briesler would be their *valet de chambre,* Esther their *femme de chambre;* but in quick succession Abigail had to hire first a *maître d'hôtel,* who would act as overseer and do the shopping for the family; a *femme de cuisine* to do the cooking, a serving girl, a gardener, a groom and finally a *frotteur*. She could not understand what a *frotteur* was supposed to do. The applicant showed her. There were no carpets in the house, the floors of the salon and the dining room being laid with red tiles. The man put some wax on the salon floor, then donned a pair of foot brushes and went dancing through the room like a Merry Andrew in a series of steps similar to ice skating, covering every inch of the floor and leaving it shining clean.

The *maître d'hôtel,* who spoke English, said, "Madame must have *le frotteur*. No one else can clean these floors."

"But eight servants!" Abigail gasped. "At home they will think I have become wanton."

The *maître d'hôtel* did not understand. He added, "It is the barest minimum allowed by good taste, madame. In truth, this house demands ten. I will serve Madame as footman providing you will give me a gentleman's suit of clothes. And Madame must have a *coiffeuse* to do the family's hair. I recommend Pauline here, she is young and sews well."

Abigail returned to Paris in a state of shock. John demonstrated that even with ten servants they could live in Auteuil more inexpensively than in Paris, and have the beautiful château and park for themselves. Since the house would be used for official entertaining it had to have a certain grandeur.

"*Mon Dieu,* if you will excuse my American accent," Abigail mourned; "it will take me all day just to keep track of them."

John Quincy came forward to add his reassurance. He had a quiet manner that was a balm to Abigail. Since his return from St. Petersburg he had been serving as volunteer secretary to John, writing much of his mail and making copies of necessary documents.

"It won't be difficult, Mother. I'll set up the account books and pay the bills for you. You'll have no trouble overseeing the servants because you will rarely lay eyes on them."

They moved in the following day. John and Abigail took the two master apartments with a connecting door, which the comte had built for himself, though John pointed out:

"You won't need your private bedroom. I've lain alone too many years."

Johnny and Nab took adjoining apartments at one end of the gallery which shared a common sitting parlor.

Only now did Abigail learn that this was one of the most famous villages in the valley of the Seine; here some of the greatest poets, philosophers and statesmen of France had lived or visited. Most enchanting of all were the views from the house and garden up the Seine, with Paris glowing in the distance, the peaks of Montmartre or Montparnasse visible in the clear summer air.

The château had come only partly furnished, for a little under a thousand dollars a year rent. John had a fully furnished house in The Hague, yet none of these valuables could they bring to Paris: the shipping costs would be exorbitant, French tariffs inordinately high; the Congress might prefer to repay John and keep the embassy intact. Abigail bought bed and table linen, three dozen sets of silver forks and spoons, tea furniture, china for the table, wineglasses, decanters.

She also learned why the stairs had been dirty in an otherwise clean house: they fell into no one's province. Each servant had a rigidly ceremonial set of duties. Though it appeared to Abigail that they were idle three quarters of the time, if she asked the young *coiffeuse* to dust her bedroom Pauline replied:

"It is not my business."

Another time she asked the groom to carry in some firewood. The man shook his head and said:

"It is not the fashion."

Esther and Briesler secured hot water from the cook and scrubbed down the stairs; they took care of all the upstairs rooms and were superb in the frequent crises of adjustment when one of the servants or another would cry:

"*Mais no! Ça ce n'est pas mon province!*"

The others made so much fun of Esther because of her straight unpowdered hair that she several times came to Abigail in tears. Finally Abigail said:

"I think we had best give in. The hair is the most important part of French life and fashion. The young man who comes to do Mr. Adams's and Mr. John's hair stops at the village shop every morning to have his own dressed. Pauline, who does my hair and Miss Nab's, pays a *friseur* to have her own done. I will speak to her about doing yours."

Esther was delighted with herself with her hair powdered brilliantly white and arranged high on a comb. Briesler was particularly enchanted. The staff embraced her. Then it was Briesler's turn to have Johnny's hairdresser attend him each day. No one laughed at the American help any more.

For her first dinner party Abigail invited Benjamin Franklin, who came from his villa at Passy only a mile away; and Tom Jefferson with his daughter Patsy. It was a fond reunion, for the three men had worked together in the Continental Congress and were responsible among them for much of the thinking and writing of the Articles of Confederation. These three were now the sole ministers of the United States in Europe to draw treaties as well as settle with the Barbary pirates who were seizing American shipping in the Mediterranean. John had the deepest admiration for Jefferson. Although he and Franklin had quarreled over methods of handling the French government, they had by now worked together through so many galling defeats that they were beginning to recognize each other's talents and forgive the idiosyncrasies.

After dinner the men remained at the table to smoke. Abigail and Nab went into the salon with Patsy, looking more than ever like her father, with freckles on her high cheekbones and a tinge of melancholy in the expressive eyes. To their astonishment, Patsy confided that they had made their crossing in nineteen days of sunlit, smooth seas.

Patsy was about to be placed in the ancient Abbaye de Panthemont, in the Rue de Grenelle. She was being admitted under the patronage of the Comtesse de Brion through the kind intervention of a friend of Jefferson's. It was one of the best convent schools in France. Patsy looked uncertain.

"Patsy dear, why are you unhappy?" asked Abigail. "Is it because it is Catholic and they must impart a good deal of religion along with other subjects?"

Patsy blurted:

"I do not speak a word of French."

Abigail put an arm about the child's shoulders.

"Would you like to come and live with us? Johnny could tutor you."

Patsy was her father's child. She held her head high on the slender swanlike neck.

"Thank you, Mrs. Adams, but I must go to a regular school. If there's no English to speak, I'll learn French the quicker. But I would like to come sometimes for holidays or Sundays. Father says I need not worry about the religion, the abbess in charge has had many Protestant girls. She understands that we are not to talk religion; and that I am to come out as good a Protestant as I go in."

The men came into the salon, oddly assorted in their external appearances: Jefferson tall, lean, sandy, the youngest at forty-one; Franklin much bothered by the stone, barrel-chested, growing close to seventy-nine; and John Adams approaching fifty.

They gathered in a small circle on gilded, red velvet chairs. It was a tight group huddled close together on foreign soil, with a good deal to say to each other of an urgent and troubled nature. Since Jefferson had served in the Congress for the six months previous, he reported on that harried and fast-disintegrating body. In his soft but articulate voice he told them of his drafting of thirty-one separate state papers, of which his "Notes on the Establishment of a Money Unit" was responsible for creating the dollar with its divisions into tenths and hundredths, which would soon supersede the existing American money. What he considered his most important recommendation was still unpassed: the abolition of slavery in all Western territory after 1800; and the illegality of secession on the part of any Western area. As Abigail listened to him read from his notes and efforts in the Congress, her mind went back to the State House Square on July 18, 1776, when she and her four children had heard Jefferson's Declaration of Independence read from the State House balcony. Then they had been at the beginning of their struggle; now independence had been won but the road ahead was rock-strewn, the hopeful title of the United States of America succumbing to the Separate States of America.

Now that England was no longer the enemy, the Continental Congress had become America's adversary, as had the concept of a strong central government which could control the freedom of action of the separate states. The central government, which all three of these men had served with the highest talents of their heads and hearts, was a shattered, quarreling, debt-ridden group of principalities which not only feared but frequently despised one another. The states no longer sent their best men to the Congress; often the best men refused to go. Certain groups wanted the Congress to wither away so that the few powers the states had given up would revert to them. The Articles of Confederation, drawn over eighteen months of patient exploration and debate, had held the new nation together loosely during the years of the war; but now they were ignored, abused, reviled. The concept of the affiliation of equal and sovereign states to create a strong nation appeared to be vanishing.

Independence was one thing, unity was another. Could a whole way of life, throwing off mankind's centuries-old shackles, a concept in which government was derived from the consent of the governed and from *no other source,* really obtain? Could a republic survive in a world of monarchy and autocracy where the vast majority of people eked out the barest existence as slaves of their hereditary betters? Hope had been kindled that something magnificent was being born in the New World: a world of vast lands and resources, where no man could become any other man's better except through his natural talents forged to his abilities to work and create. What had happened in so short a time, only eight years, since Abigail had stood in the square in Boston and the assembled thousands had wept and cheered for this glorious birth of freedom?

She had lived through the printing of unsecured money which had wiped out savings, through the profiteering, the exhaustions of the war and running down of idealism, the personal feuds, disappointments, jealousies among the founders; the loss of thousands of Tory families, not only the damage they had inflicted on the Patriot cause during the years of conflict but the deprivation of their accumulated talents, intellects, professional and technical skills; the sheer waste of war: young men killed, natural resources consumed: homes, shops, crops, materials destroyed.

All of these cruel losses the new United States could withstand, slowly healing its wounds, recouping its energies, building its goods and wealth. Americans were a young, vital, prodigiously active people. The cross on which they were crucifying themselves as a nation was internal jealousy and the fear, much of it ingrained, of giving up the individual freedoms of the states to a strong central government with powers to legislate over those states, possibly to control their actions and their properties. Now that hatred of a common enemy was no longer a congealing force, that hatred, seemingly omnipresent in the nature of man, had been pitted against each other: region against region, state against state, disputing over boundaries, indebtedness, how much freedom each would give up for how much security. None, apparently; at least not without an enemy at their door.

John and Benjamin Franklin took up the burden of exposition: they knew more about Europe than any other Americans alive. As seen from Russia on the east to Spain on the south, all Europe was against the United States remaining a strong, centrally governed nation. "Is that not equally the fault of England?" John demanded heatedly. Great Britain had signed a peace treaty with the United States but had refused to live up to its obligations, keeping troops in the Northern posts around Detroit and Buffalo after agreeing to remove them; keeping the Negroes taken at the close of hostilities, though signing to return them; refusing to negotiate a commercial treaty, tenaciously as John Adams had been battering at their diplomatic doors.

Nations which had been friendly during the war itself, not only allies such as France, Spain and Holland, were growing increasingly contemptuous of the fledgling nation which could neither resolve its inner problems nor pay its honorable debts. None of the nations wanted to lend more money to the disintegrating union of states and, aside from the treaties of amity and commerce which John had negotiated between Sweden, the Netherlands and the United States, not a single one would agree to a commercial treaty.

This attitude of contempt had in turn embittered the Continental Congress and the American people, many of whom resented sending representatives to Europe at all. Let them stay home! And let the foreign countries call back their ambassadors, who frequently interfered with the work of the Congress and set a bad example for simple democratic America with their wealth and ostentation, their jewelry and balls. There was a growing feeling in America, as Abigail could attest from New England, that the United States wished to live isolated from Europe.

To earn respect for their country, to negotiate most-favored-nation treaties with some twenty European and Mediterranean countries, to win such demonstrable advantages for the United States that the country would shake off its lethargy and enter into vigorous, profitable trade, this was the task these three diplomats faced. It was admittedly something of a vicious circle: Europe would not sign treaties with the United States until that country was strong enough to fulfill its agreements;

the United States could not resolve its inner struggles until it became an international power.

What to do? Franklin was old and ill, had several times requested the Congress to let him retire. Jefferson was new on the scene. And John Adams? Abigail surveyed her husband. He was showing the signs of incessant battle: from the very beginning of their marriage he had poured out his strength, giving unceasingly, sometimes almost wantonly, of his time and courage. Had he spilled his seed on the ground? After these years of struggle, of war, of defeat and victory, had they indeed exhausted themselves?

When their guests had gone, the Adamses walked in the warm summer garden, the scents of full-blooming flowers heavy in the night, following the mile or so of pebbled paths, bright in the moonlight. Abigail gazed inwardly with an equally fierce light from this new perspective three thousand miles distant from New England.

Her life was a trichotomy, to use one of John's favorite words out of Euclid's mathematics, divided into three equal and inseparable parts: her own day-by-day struggles, often alone, to resolve her personal problems for the past ten years; John's day-by-day contests in the Congress and Europe; and their nation's day-by-day battles to remain united and unconquered. For her own survival she had had to blend these elements skillfully, no one facet of her equilateral triangle becoming more important to her than the other, though at times she had lost sight of this as she plummeted to her private purgatory. Everything that had happened to John in Europe, everything the Congress did or failed to do in its internecine feuds directly affected the well-being of the Adams family. At the bottom of the trough Abigail had needed John's gift of looking into the future to see the whole of a development rather than the consequence of a single happening. John had had a vision, he had had it at the time of Concord and Lexington: that one day the United States of America would be a strong, independent, resourceful, flourishing nation, able to take its place as an equal at the international board. It was this vision which had sustained him through his years of discouragement and loneliness, a position which the Congregationalists described as a position of faith.

There was no question in her mind but that John's attitude and her own had a religious base. What they were trying to make of America was "a city that is set on a hill," even as the first settlers had tried to create of the Massachusetts Bay Colony a City on a Hill. Americans were to be Saints in the same way the members of the Congregation were known as Saints. If, to become a Congregationalist Saint, one had to achieve grace through moral and spiritual purity, just so America had to come into a state of grace through being a free society of free men: free to think, feel, speak, act, own, regulate for the good of all, a society in which every man would have a chance to grow, and those whose chances were lesser would be protected rather than exploited by representatives of the people who had been freely elected to serve their nation and the least of its citizens.

This was as vast a dream as the one which had driven the first Puritans and Pilgrims across an unknown ocean to an even more unknown wilderness; and perhaps more difficult to achieve. Men had struggled for religious liberty before and achieved it, at least in small groups; their English ancestors who had fled to Holland for religious freedom were proof of that. But to overthrow all the powers that had ruled since the Roman emperors: kings, princes, potentates, popes and bishops, lords of the domain, chieftains, warrior conquerors, to set tyranny aside forever, to force no man to obey a law not devised and approved by his fellows; to give him equal opportunity in the market places, the countinghouses, the legislatures and courts and town meetings . . . ! If successful, this would be the most significant movement and revolution in the history of mankind. It must be done; it would. The costs were high, but the results magnificently Messianic.

Matthew had said it in 5:14, "A city that is set on a hill cannot be hid."

2

Abigail rose early, with the sun streaming into her windows, though not quite as early as when she had had to feed the turkeys and geese and let the cows out of the barn. First she roused Nab, then knocked on Johnny's door. He greeted her with an open book in hand. They assembled at the breakfast table, made plans. Unless John had to go to Passy or Paris for a conference with Franklin or Jefferson he went into his study to work on his papers. Johnny translated Horace and Tacitus, Nab studied French grammar. Abigail returned to her bedroom to set forth the day's chores for the servants and write her letters home.

At noon John would emerge from his room to take Nab for a horseback ride on the French cavalry track in the Bois, a magnificent stretch, completely shaded, with sharp curves and turns for practice maneuvers.

Other days the four of them went walking in the Bois, picking wild flowers, staying out in the cool verdant forest until two when they returned for dinner. Frequently Nab and Johnny went into Paris to see an attraction. When they returned from a five o'clock performance at the Comédie du Bois de Boulogne, Abigail saw with a flush of pride what attractive young people they were.

"Did you enjoy the comedy?"

"The music was good, the actors and actresses only tolerable," Nab replied earnestly. "I am not fond of comedy, in general; I had rather be improved than amused."

"Spoken like a true New Englander," murmured John. "How did you react, Johnny?"

"I have lived in Europe long enough to learn that some of society's most mordant portraits are cast in comic rather than tragic form, all the way from Aristophanes to Molière. Comedy has been used to tear down civilizations as well as to summon up giggles."

After tea the table was covered with Johnny's mathematical instruments and books from which John was tutoring his son. The two women, trying to read, heard nothing but theorem, bisecting and dissecting until nine or ten o'clock, after which the table was cleared a second time and the men demanded a few hands of whist. They were wonderfully happy with each other. When Abigail went into Nab's bedroom to find her daughter brushing her waist-long brown hair, her eyes intensely alive, she said:

"Miss Adorable, you were never more radiant."

Nab whirled about on the fragile dressing bench.

"I've never felt more agitation of spirits in my life. My thoughts go back to Mr. Tyler more and more . . . affectionately."

"Has your father told you of the letter he wrote just before we sailed, and that we never received? He left it up to my judgment to give you a wedding in Braintree, if I thought you wanted it."

"I have not yet discussed Mr. Tyler with Father."

If Abigail's domestic life was tranquil, her exposure to French life was filled with tremors. The first came when the Adamses were invited to Saturday dinner by Benjamin Franklin in his home in Passy. Franklin had long enjoyed the reputation of being a romantic figure among the French women. At seventy-eight, Abigail reasoned, Franklin would be past all that; but she was quickly disabused. While waiting in the sitting parlor of the modest, much-used villa for Franklin to descend, a Madame Helvétius entered the room. She was a widow who had erected a monument to her husband and was now in process of erecting one to Benjamin Franklin.

Madame Helvétius, although sixty years old, flounced into the room with what Abigail thought a careless air, her chemise of tiffany looking as decayed as her own beauty. Over frizzled hair she wore a small straw hat with a dirty gauze half-handkerchief around it. Carrying her little lap dog in one arm and a black gauze scarf in the other, she ran to Franklin, caught him by the hand, then kissed him robustly on each cheek and on the forehead for good measure.

Abigail simply could not get over Madame Helvétius's conduct. In public no less! At table Madame Helvétius, seated between Franklin and John, carried on a gay conversation with both of them at the same time, half the time holding Franklin's hand, spreading her arms along the backs of both men's chairs or holding one arm affectionately about Franklin's neck. Back in the sitting parlor she threw herself down on the settee where she showed more than her feet. She kept kissing her lap dog, and when he wet the floor Madame Helvétius wiped up the puddle with her chemise.

Abigail's distaste must have shown; for when they were leaving Franklin said with a quiet smile:

"Madame Helvétius is a genuine Frenchwoman, wholly free from affectation or stiffness of behavior."

Abigail glanced at her husband and son; they had dined frequently with Madame Helvétius and were accustomed to her ways. Apparently they even liked her!

She suffered a second upset a few days later when the family went to the ballet. The beauty of the performers in their thinnest of silk and gauze dresses over short petticoats she found enchanting, but no sooner had the dance commenced than her delicacy was so wounded that she knew she should be ashamed to be seen looking at them. The dancers sprang two feet from the stage, poising themselves in the air, as perfectly showing their garters and drawers as though no petticoat had been worn. Abigail, who had seen no theatre except the illegal and unstaged singing of opera in Boston, could not put down her sense of outrage; at the same time she was admiring the exquisite art of the performance and astonishing light-as-air movements of the dancers who had been trained at the royal academy. When she remembered the stories she had read of these girls who took the highest bidders as lovers and protectors, she could not get over her abhorrence. She mentioned this to John in the carriage during the ride home.

"There is no relation between the delight of the ballet and the private lives of the girls," he said gently. "When the ballet becomes ragged you should be outraged, as all good Parisians are. The girls' private lives bear no relevancy to art."

"Word of honor," Abigail thought, "my family has become *sophisticated!*"

Her third upset was more profound, of a religious rather than a moral nature. Thomas Jefferson had invited her and Nab to come early of a morning to visit with Patsy at the convent, there to witness the ceremony of two nuns who were taking their vows. They rose at seven, dressed in the new florence and satin gowns which had been made for them by a dressmaker recommended by Mrs. Thomas Barclay, wife of the American consul general in France. After breakfast they went to the church. Patsy greeted them in the vestibule. She looked lovely in her uniform of crimson made like a frock laced behind, the tail hooked on like a *robe de cour,* with muslin cuffs and tuckers. She seemed well cared for. When Abigail asked if she was enjoying the convent Patsy said quietly:

"Very much. My French is really getting better by the day."

They went into the nave of the church and were admitted to seats facing the altar where the priests performed. Sunlight streamed through the stained-glass windows, the priests wore richly colorful robes; all about them were statues of the Madonna and Child, the Pietà, paintings of the Ascension. There was a large compartment behind a railing for the nuns and students of the convent. The floor in front of the altar was covered with an elegant carpet on which nuns were gathered together, praying.

A curtain was drawn, and the abbess, nuns and pensionnaires entered. Each nun held a lighted candle in her hand. The two novices who were to take the veil came forward attired in fine white woolen robes, loose and flowing, and white veils. Their hair had been shaved off. They knelt before the altar; there was a great deal of singing and chanting of prayers, alternate kneeling and rising, with the priest coming forward from the chancel to make many signs which Abigail did not understand. One of the priests delivered a sermon in French which the Adamses did understand fairly well, for he was expatiating on the goodness of the King and the excellence of every class of people from the throne to the footstool.

The two novices then lay down upon their faces on the carpet. Eight pensionnaires brought in a pall of black appliquéd with a white cross, which was held over the novices while a priest read another part of the ceremony and the nuns chanted prayers.

It was a moving sight. The two girls lay on their faces for half an hour. When they rose, to symbolize the resurrection, the abbess put upon them the nun's habit. A priest dusted their veils with holy water and perfumed them with frankincense. The two new nuns then kneeled before the abbess, who pinned upon each of their heads a wreath of flowers; a candle was put into their hands and a mass was said. The ceremony was over . . . except that the priest invited all the girls present to follow the example of these two nuns.

Mother and daughter rode home in stunned silence. They could not make out this religion which was the official religion of France. Neither could they understand why the two young girls, one of them French, the other Irish, had volunteered to pass the rest of their lives within the walls of the convent. Patsy had told them that the nuns took pleasure in contributing to the happiness of the students, that they were always cheerful and agreeable. Abigail wondered how this could be. She wondered about the whole ceremony, for it was the first time she had ever been inside a Catholic church. John had attended one in Philadelphia while at the Congress and had written her about the beautiful music and art works. Her mind crossed the Atlantic Ocean to the hanging pulpit of the Congregational Meeting House in Weymouth; she saw her father standing there in the icy cold delivering his brief sharp sermon from Luke or Matthew. God's Barn where the elders would allow not even the most modest organ or piano or the stalls to be painted. How different a world was this; how difficult to grasp.

Sunday, which in New England was devoted to holy walking and preaching, generally two sermons a day, with only tea drinking and decorous conversation, was in France devoted to the abandonments of joy. Early in the morning a procession of coaches and carts rumbled down the street in front of their château headed for the Bois. Abigail sat at a window watching the wagons go by, the horses frequently led rather than driven, their benches filled with well-dressed Parisians and countless children escaping the fetid city for the cool fresh air of the woods.

By midmorning the four Adamses were dressed and had joined the throngs. There was music and dancing, large families picnicking on the grass, booths where cake, fruit and wine were sold; children running and romping, shouting their games in high glee. The women were gaily dressed, wearing hoods or silk veils to protect their elaborate coiffures. The men carried their hats under their arms so as not to rumple heads as white as snowbanks. The paths were as thronged as the Boston Common on Commencement Day.

As they wound their way back through the crisscrossing paths toward Auteuil, Abigail observed:

"Pleasure is the business of life here."

"Puritans live to work," answered John, "the French work to live. Can we really say they're wrong? You saw on the journey from Calais how wretchedly the peasants exist: the thatched mud, windowless houses, earthen floors; plundered by their landlords, crushed by taxes a hundredfold more onerous than you paid in Braintree during the war. If they cannot pay, it's flogging or prison; generation after generation of serfs bound to the soil, illiterate and hopeless."

"Does this apply to the city laborers as well?"

"All the wealth is at the top, in the hands of, say, one or at the most two per cent of the French population. You saw Versailles, the estate of the Prince of Condé at Chantilly . . . The country landowners live as luxuriously as the nobility."

"Then for six days of the week," said Abigail, calculating, "America has a better civilization. Granted, our Sundays are harsh, with little lightheartedness for the people who toil all week. But those other six days they live and work much better as free men. The French must be a very patient people, or very resigned."

"They are also a very old people," said John. "The Ile de la Cité in the Seine was first settled before Christ. Americans have millions of acres of land, free for the taking by anyone with the energy to move west. The French people are trapped. They see no way to shake their crushing burdens from their shoulders. So they save their few coppers, have their hair frizzed and come to the Bois for their one free day. It may be all that makes life bearable for them."

Abigail glanced sidewise at her husband. How well he had matured during his six years in Europe; he had become a cosmopolite while she . . . for years confined at home as a housekeeper and dairywoman . . . She must not let John outgrow her; she too must leave the provinciality of New England behind.

She laughed to herself. That would be just about the most difficult task of her life. Given time, she might accomplish it; but oh! the trunkloads of prejudices she had brought over with her on the *Active!*

Her most profound shock came with her visit to Hôpital des Enfants Trouvés, an institution which housed six thousand of the illegitimate children born in Paris each year. There were nuns at the door night and day to receive the infants who were placed in boxes kept available in certain parts of Paris for the purpose, the mother never needing to be seen. Sisters of Charity took care of the babies. She was taken into a light and airy room with one hundred cribs affixed to the walls, two more rows down the center. Many of the children were asleep, a few were crying; but Abigail saw at once that they were fastidiously cared for. Every bed had white linen, each child looked well fed.

The Sister of Charity who was guiding her explained that they received twenty infants a day but lost about a third of them notwithstanding all their care, many of them so chilled with the cold and poorly clad that the Sisters could not get them warm again, even before the bright fires which were kept burning. Abigail Adams, her eyes wide, watched with awe as the Sisters in their floor-length robes and crisp all-covering hats dedicatedly went about their tasks.

"The first step in the education of a Puritan," she murmured to her husband and daughter when she had returned home. "I simply must applaud the charitable aspects of the work. The Sisters are wonderful. . . ."

"They are among the truly great souls of the earth," John agreed. "The nuns live a hard, relentless life: the unshapely robe is their only material possession. They sleep in tiny cells on hard narrow cots, eat the plainest of food, give unquestioned obedience. All they receive in return is the right to serve God. One must admire them."

"But, John, what debauchery necessitates this kind of charity! I've been told that half the babies born in Paris are illegitimate."

"We have our bundling," said Nab.

"But we oblige the parents to marry," said John. "That gives the child a name and a position in society. These thousands of 'found infants' are a natural result of the Frenchman's cavalier attitude toward marriage: every husband with his mistress, every wife with her lover."

Abigail blanched and glanced toward Nab.

"Travel is broadening," observed John sotto voce.

3

Abigail was having her tremors and quakes with the French morals and mores. John was having more serious problems with European diplomacy. The Spanish, who had been allies during the war, refused to discuss a trade agreement unless the United States returned a minister to Madrid. John Jay had spent two years there while Spain was at war with England, but the Spanish court had steadfastly refused to recognize the independence of the United States. England declined discussions of a commercial treaty until a minister plenipotentiary was stationed at the Court of St. James's. The Barbary pirates, operating out of Morocco, Algiers, Tunis and Tripoli, were still capturing American ships and enslaving American seamen. They wanted an annual cash bribe to let American ships do business in the Mediterranean. English shipping, released from its war function, had once again come to dominate the seas.

King Frederick of Prussia alone was willing to deal with the three commissioners. He wanted American cotton, tobacco, rice and grain and also saw a growing market in the United States for his Silesian linen. All the other hundreds of letters, proposals, analyses, documents, statements of the strength and manufacturies of America were seemingly wasted. The United States was suffering from the colonial system from which they had revolted: Spain and Portugal would not permit their colonies to trade with the new country; neither would Great Britain, including its lucrative West Indies. Thomas Jefferson, dining at Auteuil of a Saturday late in 1784, groused to his hosts:

"The European countries know little about us except as rebels who have succeeded in throwing off the yoke of the Mother Country. They are ignorant of our commerce and of the exchange of articles that could be profitable to both of us. They're all standing aloof."

John groaned sympathetically.

"We simply have to continue wooing them: Russia, Denmark, Saxony, Sicily. Once we can communicate our enthusiasm for the future of our country . . ."

Each Tuesday the three ministers had to attend the levee of King Louis XVI at Versailles. The families of the ministers were not invited, so Abigail saw the Dauphin only of a Sunday when his gardens were opened to the public. John disliked these Tuesday court assemblies. The King, whose custom it was to speak to each foreign minister, always asked the identical question:

"And have you come out from Paris today?"

John could not recall ever having been allowed to answer. He used his time to good advantage making friends with the other ministers, whom he invited for Saturday dinner. The Spanish ambassador came in a splendid carriage, accompanied by eight liveried servants. It was during these social dinners that John Adams, Jefferson and Franklin were able to preach the gospel of the nascent United States to friendly ears, to make some little progress in the reports the ambassadors were sending home to their monarchs and cabinets.

Many of these ambassadors were men of great wealth; even Franklin and Jefferson had considerable private income. Abigail soon learned how urgent this was. Upon the death of an eight-year-old prince whose father was in alliance with King Louis XVI, it was decreed that all who came to court wear mourning black. Jefferson hied himself to a tailor where for two hundred thirty-five dollars he had a fine outfit made, sable trimming being de rigueur. The Adamses could not afford a large outlay for an eleven-day mourning period; if someone else died a short while later the whole style would have changed and the recent clothes be equally worthless.

The court levee for that Tuesday was canceled. Jefferson, uninformed, arrived in a carriage with Colonel David Humphreys, the American secretary to the commissioners, to pick up John. Jefferson was exquisitely accoutered, his hair powdered and combed like a French dandy's. When he heard that he had gone to the trouble and expense for nothing, he cried:

"Hair! It is at the very center of French life. I am tempted to cut it all off. I do not expect to live above a dozen years and I shall lose one of them in hairdressing."

Abigail consoled him with tea. It turned out to be a festive day. Thomas Barclay came out with his wife, bringing as well wealthy financier William Bingham of Philadelphia and his exquisite twenty-year-old wife; William Short, a Virginian who was serving as secretary to Jefferson but living with a French family in the neighboring village of St. Germain in order to learn the language. Madame Helvétius arrived with Franklin. Abigail found her to be a delightful guest whose affection for her American friends was ample to light up the Comte de Rouault's château.

It was good for Abigail to have this tightly knit American circle, for she had almost no communication with the French. Aside from the fact that she could not carry on an intelligible conversation in French, the practice of card-leaving was a barrier as was the necessity for the visitor to make the first call. She finally summoned courage to make a planned journey, leaving cards at half a dozen homes. Within the next week or two the ladies returned the call, leaving their cards in the silver tray on the onyx table in the foyer. That was the end of the social intercourse.

Or so it would have been without the Marquise Adrienne de Lafayette. John had known the Marquis when he served as a general under Washington. Lafayette had on occasion brought letters to Abigail from John. The Adams women called to pay their compliments; their *maître d'hôtel*, riding with the groom, presented their cards. Their carriage was turning from the door when the servant came running out to inform them that the Marquise would be delighted to see them.

Indeed, the Marquise was at the front door. With the freedom of an old friend she caught Abigail by the hand and kissed her on each cheek.

"Mrs. Adams, I am most heartily rejoiced to see you. Won't you please come up to my bedroom where we are *en famille*."

In the spacious, sun-flooded room, with one end devoted to a chaise and comfortable chairs, the Marquise presented Abigail and Nab to her mother and sister, who were knitting. They were obviously not gowned for callers.

"But I could not let you leave. I have been waiting so long to meet you. I am strongly attached to all Americans; my husband so adores your country. He is there at this moment. Excuse me, I wish to bring in my two younger children to present them. They speak so fine an English; their father has insisted they study your language almost from the day they were born."

She returned with her daughter, seven, and her son, George Washington de Lafayette. They did indeed speak an almost unaccented English, and wanted to hear stories of their father's heroic battles in the United States. It was an informal family gathering such as might take place in Weymouth or Braintree.

It was also impossible for Abigail not to perceive that the Marquise adored her husband and had the profoundest love for her three children, whose education she directed herself, and for the sanctity of her home and marriage which had triumphed over long separations even as the Adamses' had. This youngish, middle-sized, sprightly, warmhearted, well-educated woman's character and reputation were beyond reproach. Her mother, the Duchesse d'Ayen, was a lady of honor to Queen Marie Antoinette. The Marquis came from the oldest and most revered French nobility with vast wealth, lands, jewelry. Yet they played no part in the amusements of the French court. The Marquise's family was her life.

"This is a new side of France for me," Abigail murmured as their carriage left the Lafayettes' town house. Had she been doing the French an injustice?

In a few days Adrienne de Lafayette returned their call. Nab and Johnny had gone into Paris to see the new sensation, *Figaro*, John had locked himself into his study where he was writing furiously in the margin of a book by a dissenting English minister, Dr. Richard Price, *Observations on the Importance of the American Revolution*. Dr. Price was an ardent supporter of the United States but he had unfortunately included in his pamphlet a letter written to him by Monsieur Turgot, former French Minister of Finance, in which Turgot attacked the American state constitutions as unworkable because of the balance of powers. This letter was circulating throughout Europe, thanks to Dr. Price, and would further undermine confidence in the Americans to govern themselves.

For their next dinner party, to which Abigail had invited several ambassadors and their wives as well as her official American family, she sent a card to the Marquise de Lafayette. The Marquise accepted by return messenger.

During the dinner the wife of an American whispered to Abigail:

"Oh dear! Is that the Marquise de Lafayette? How modestly she is dressed, and without jewelry. In the midst of all these glittering diamonds."

Abigail whispered in return, "The lady's rank sets her above such formalities."

As she sat at her table surrounded by the grandeur of the foreign uniforms and lavish gowns, Abigail thought:

"How far I have come in accepting the values of French society."

Her major problem here as at home was hard cash. She simply could not make ends meet. She elicited little sympathy; some of their neighbors in New England, learning that the Adamses were living in a château with eight servants, thought them to be emulating the princes of the realm. The Continental Congress, to indicate its displeasure at being obliged to keep ministers in Europe, had cut twenty-two hundred and fifty dollars off their salaries and allowances. The compensation of the commissioners now stood at nine thousand dollars a year. Economize as she would, entertaining only once a week, confining their visits to the opera and theatre to once a week, Johnny's totaling of her bills and outlays at the end of each month showed that they were spending more than John was receiving. Their income in America from their share of the crops of their home farm and the one they owned with the Shaws in Medford barely paid the taxes, upkeep and repair of the properties and the normal expenses of Charley and Tommy in Haverhill. She tried cutting down on food purchases and supplies for the house until she learned that the servants and neighbors were ridiculing her.

The commissioners could not get one dollar from the Congress. All expenses of the American officials in Paris, as well as the interest to be paid on the French debt, had to be secured by John from Holland under one of the loans he had negotiated. Franklin, who had attacked John Adams publicly when he went to Holland to see "whether something might not be done to render us less dependent on France," was now dependent on John Adams's credit in the Dutch banks for his upkeep in France. John enjoyed this innocent revenge: for the two men were working together in harmony again. John had not yet heard the line written by Franklin the year before to Robert Livingston, Secretary of Foreign Affairs, which would hurt him so severely in the future:

"He means well for his country, is always an honest man, often a wise one, but sometimes and in some things absolutely out of his senses."

Their economic life seemed to have become a succession of outstretched hands. In New England daily gratuities did not exist. Here they had to tip the servants at every house where they went for dinner or tea; the attendants at the shops and markets, theatre, opera, ballet, restaurants; the people who brought packages or performed services at the house. One was never able to leave the house without a purseful of coins to be distributed as though to omnipresent beggars. At holidays, and particularly at Christmas, every employed person whom the family had touched even remotely during their stay had to be given his annual due. This was a sum so hardened by custom that if a smaller sum were proffered, the correct amount was indignantly demanded. The lackeys at Versailles had stipulated sums that had to be paid to them at New Year's: the chefs, the coffee men, the porters, the liverymen, the *valets de chambre*. The hour-by-hour tipping added hundreds of unexpected dollars to their expenses.

It took a full month too to learn that she was being cheated at every turn by the tradesmen who provided goods and services. The methods of extracting more money than was warranted were so ingenious that Johnny could not uncover them, check the bills as he might. It was their French friends who rescued them, revealing the subtle centuries-old methods that tradespeople and servers had evolved to take advantage of their customers. Nor did the tradesmen seem to mind that their techniques had been exposed; it was a hoary tradition to cheat the rich, particularly if they were foreigners.

John shifted the entire burden of the family's finances to Abigail's shoulders. When he declined to examine the account books she was goaded to one of her rare complaints:

"Mr. Minister Plenipotentiary, you have been so long a statesman that I cannot get you to think enough about your domestic affairs."

"Why should I, dear soul, when you handle them so capably?"

"Then I am going to start being less capable. I have been adding and subtracting for ten solid years now."

"And always kept us solvent! If I had your talents the United States would already have most-favored-nation treaties with sixteen European countries."

She refused to be flattered.

"John, I am very willing to relieve you from every care in my power, yet I think all this has too much the appearance of wielding instead of sharing the scepter."

He was contrite. He left his desk in their sitting parlor, put his arm about her shoulders.

"It's true. I accept the criticism. Could I offer to treat with you on this subject?"

"No. You will treaty me out of my reasonable rights."

"Now, my dear, I have not been that successful as a negotiator. Suppose you run the château and keep our business straight with Cotton Tufts, Sister Elizabeth Shaw and the others. Within six months to a year we'll be back in Braintree. I promise to handle all our business forever after."

At times of crisis she practiced crisis measures, going against everything her father had taught her, and old New England traditions. She sold off some of her state notes and army certificates, even if she had to take a loss, then used her past savings to meet current expenses.

Though Abigail had written frequent letters home, they had received only an occasional note from her sisters. Then on the evening of January 4, 1785, while they were sitting before a cheerful fire, John reading his favorite author, Plato, and Abigail reading in French a play they had seen acted in Paris a few nights before, Molière's *Les Précieuses ridicules,* Briesler entered with two large packets. Abigail cried:

"From America! I know, from America!"

She seized her scissors and cut them open. A number of them were for Nab from Royall Tyler. She set these aside, then she and John took turns reading aloud. First Elizabeth's letter so that she could hear about their two sons. It was full of the homely details which she found a cordial to her soul. Charley had escaped his usual summer fever; both boys were doing well in dancing class; they were happy in the Shaw household.

Mary Cranch wrote the news of Braintree. Cotton Tufts, who was still serving in the Massachusettes Senate, had visited the Adams house and found that Phoebe and her husband were giving it good care, though the moths had got into some of Abigail's stored woolen clothing. He also reported that the large Alleyne home and farm were for sale. Might the Adamses be interested against the day when they would return?

At ten o'clock the young people came home. It was a dark stormy night, but there were lamps all the way out from Paris along the Seine. A dog barked, then the bell at the gate rang, indicating that the carriage had arrived. Nab came in first, hugging her deep-sea-green robe about her.

"Pray, what spectacle have you seen tonight?" asked John.

"A variety from the Palais Royal." Johnny then satirized some of Molière's titles. "We saw *The New Parvenu* and *The Intendant Comedian in Spite of Himself*."

"Nab, I have a New Year's present for you," exclaimed Abigail.

She dealt out Royall Tyler's letters, one by one. Nab retreated to a chair in the far corner of the room, engaged in chuckles, blushes, sighs. John had now accepted Tyler as Nab's suitor, and seemed satisfied with the reports on the young man.

John was very much interested in the Alleyne estate. He remembered it as a commodious house, fitted to his new stature. After living for seven or eight years in Dutch manor houses and French châteaux, he thought their cottage in Braintree might prove too small.

"Has the house shrunk, or have you expanded?" asked Abigail.

"That is the story of the minister to Queen Elizabeth whom she one day visited, observing that he had a very small and indifferent house. 'May it please Your Majesty,' said the minister, 'the house is big enough for the man, but you have made the man too big for the house.' "

"Very well, if the Continental Congress has made you too big for the cottage, how much money will be required to house you properly?"

"I should say the Alleyne estate would go for nine thousand dollars."

It took several days of perusing their assets, adjusting prices paid, improvements, increased growth values, but at last Johnny presented them with a bill of particulars:

Home and nine acres	$1,800
Peter's former home and thirty-five acres	2,000
Boston home	2,400
Furniture in The Hague	4,500
Abigail's half of the Medford farm	1,800
Assorted landholdings	1,350
Carriage and furnishings in Auteuil	1,200
	$15,050

Congress owed John money for back salary but it was impossible to get the members to commit themselves on the exact amount; for all practical purposes it had to be left out of the reckoning.

"By a series of sales," contributed Johnny, "you could put the nine thousand together."

"But if we sell all our furnishings here and in The Hague we will have nothing with which to furnish the Alleyne house," Abigail observed. "There will also be repairs and refurbishing and putting the farm into working order."

"You'd have to give up almost all your possessions," Johnny added, studying the sheets.

"Then how would we educate our three sons?" she asked hoarsely. "You all three must have college training, and that will cost us over a thousand dollars a year. You must also live through long apprenticeships. It simply makes no sense. We cannot gamble on our boys' future merely to live in a bigger house."

John nodded his head approvingly.

"I was right to insist you remain the Secretary of the Exchequer. From the present temper of the Congress we can expect to be left here only a short time. What am I to do for the rest of my life? Go back to the law? It's ten years since I have handled individual cases. Assuming that I have not lost my hard-won skills at drawing writs or pleading before juries, could I return now to the spite cases and other pettinesses that make up the bulk of a lawyer's practice? Yet if I sat in my office and said grandiloquently, 'I'll not take your case unless it is a serious and important cause,' I would not only offend New England but sit solitary for a very long time."

"Then it's back to our cottage?"

"Back to our cottage."

John sighed resignedly.

"Johnny, feed all those neat balance sheets of yours into the flames. Your mother has again kept the Adams family solvent."

4

Winter clamped down suddenly. The streets of Auteuil became a quagmire. No one could walk through them without boots or wooden shoes. The trees in the garden lost their leaves, the flowers had long since vanished, even their blooming shrubs were in hibernation, giving the garden an abandoned, desolate look. No member of the family ventured out there any more. The château would have been a monumental ice palace if not for the fact that every room had its own fire. The inclement weather kept their friends from driving out from Paris for impromptu visits.

To divert her, John insisted that they go into Paris several times a week. She had ceased to be shocked at the ballet girls' garters and drawers but particularly loved the French theatre where the tragedies were presented. Here she saw Racine's sacred drama, *Athalie,* and the plays of Corneille and Crébillon. Her French was now good enough to understand the unfolding beauty of the lines. Afterward they promenaded with the colorful crowds who seemed to enjoy walking the boulevards as much as they did the performances.

She found herself reconciled to the habits, customs and fashions of the French people, admitting that women's use of rouge made them more attractive. She was no longer embarrassed when ladies came into a salon, put their arms about their gentlemen friends and kissed them on both cheeks, nor was she any longer offended when gentlemen diners leaned over their partridge to smell it before tasting. However she never would get used to the men standing all close together before the fireplace, effectively cutting off the heat from the women seated at the other end of the room. She became reconciled to the incessant tipping when she learned that that was the only way the supplicants could support their families.

She had come to adore Madame Helvétius, learned that her prejudice against French men, whom she had imagined to be shallow and deceitful, was unwarranted. They proved to be warm, sincere, graced with an intelligence spiked with wit and urbanity. There were even times when, against all New England convention of general conversation at the dinner table, the conversations falling into tête-à-têtes of two by two, the voices subdued and glances lowered as though there were private conspiracies to transact, she found herself thinking heretically that the French men could be more interesting than the American.

Her greatest help in assimilating French life was Adrienne de Lafayette. They had become close friends. The Marquise understood how difficult it was to make the transition from one culture to another, in Abigail's case, of diametric opposites. She explained the French institution of marriage in which young boys and girls of ten to fourteen years were affianced by their parents without ever having met, seeing each other for the first time at the wedding, brought together in matrimony to preserve bloodlines and family fortunes. Yes, she too had been affianced in just such a fashion, but she had been fortunate enough to adore and be adored. Many of her friends were equally fortunate.

The end of January brought torrential rains. The daytime skies were charcoal. No one could venture more than a few feet from the fireplaces without freezing. The family read by candlelight or oil lamp, all desks and chairs cordoned up tight on the hearths.

The dead of winter also began a long series of illnesses, accidents, misfortunes and misunderstandings. Franklin was the first to be stricken, so tormented by his stone that he was confined to his house and bed. He feared he would not be able to survive long enough to die at home, in America.

Thomas Jefferson had rented what he called a "small hotel" in the Cul-de-sac Taitbout to give him privacy from the noise and clutter of Paris. He poured out almost five thousand dollars on the house, as well as money for lamps, china, silver, furniture. Since he was in the midst of Parisian society he had to employ several more servants than Abigail's eight.

Jefferson had made a manifest impression on the French owing to his gentle warmth, his intuitive wisdom and his training in all fields of man's endeavor. John Adams loved Thomas Jefferson as he had few men in his life. Never celebrated for his modesty, he was coming to the conclusion that Jefferson was perhaps the mightiest mind yet produced on the American continent, a considerable concession. This impression increased as Jefferson took over more and more of Franklin's work in the European negotiations.

Now the dark hand of death reached out to strike Thomas Jefferson still another blow. The Marquis de Lafayette, returning from America, brought him a letter from Virginia. Jefferson's two-year-old daughter Lucy, born a few months before her mother's death, had died at her maternal aunt's home from "the complicated evils of teething, worms and whooping cough." Jefferson had now lost three daughters, his only son and his beloved wife Martha. Though he still had robust Patsy and six-year-old Mary, called Polly, also living with her aunt in Virginia, the death of the child sent him to bed ill, disconsolate, unable to bring himself back to the working world.

The Adamses urged him to come to Auteuil to live with them. There was little else they could do for the stricken man. They sat by his bed holding his hand, wiping his fevered brow with a cool damp cloth. He gave up the Tuesday levees at Versailles, could not garner the moral strength to ride out to Auteuil for Sunday dinner, not even when Nab and Johnny rode in to the Abbaye de Panthemont to claim Patsy for the day. John was now the only American minister in Europe able to work.

Nab also was encountering difficulties. Her months in France had seemed to be the happiest of the girl's life. She and Johnny filled every moment with amusing games, were forever off to see the plays or the churches of Paris. It was Adrienne de Lafayette who noticed it first, asking Abigail in an aside, after dinner at the Lafayette town house on the Rue de Bourbon:

"What has happened to your beautiful daughter? She seems *triste*; no, not exactly sad, but *grave*."

It was true, Nab had lost some of her buoyancy. She had heard nothing from Royall Tyler except for the one packet of letters several weeks before. Although Richard Cranch reported Tyler to be slaving over his books, other family accounts suggested that he was melancholy and tormented, convinced that he would never see Nab again. Nab could not understand such faintheartedness.

"Can a man who truly loves be so apprehensive?" she asked her mother.

Abigail had a few questions of her own she would have liked to ask. Did Nab intend to return that spring or summer and marry Tyler? If so, she certainly had told no one. Would she like Tyler to come to Europe so that they could be married here? If so, Abigail had heard no such intimation. John would have accepted either of these alternatives. After all, Tyler had private means and would one day inherit his mother's considerable estate. He could support a wife and children. But Nab had seemed too happy in her new-found family life and the curiosities of France to think about it. Had Royall Tyler perhaps sensed this from her letters?

Next there came the matter of the balloon ascension. The Adams family, along with the scientifically interested Benjamin Franklin, had the previous September paid a crown each to be admitted to the garden of the Tuileries to see the event. The balloon was made of taffeta in the shape of an egg. Franklin explained how it contained the air, and that the platform below was for the balloonists and the ballast. At eleven o'clock the balloon was moved from its standing among the trees to an open situation, the ropes held by some of the most renowned men in the kingdom. The cords were cut, the balloon rose, remained in sight for considerable time as the balloonists experimented with the dropping of their ballast; and at six that evening came down at Bevre, fifty leagues from Paris.

The experiment was a *succès fou.* All of Paris applauded the courage and skill of the balloonists. Franklin entertained them by describing how they should all return home on balloons instead of ships, the winds carrying them from Paris to Boston in three days instead of thirty.

But it was a different story when Royall Tyler went up in a balloon in Boston. What had been a brave, venturesome experiment in science for the French balloonists became a foolhardy, irresponsible scrape for Tyler. New England disapproved, and so did John. When Abigail pointed out how he and Franklin had praised the French balloonists, he replied tartly:

"That is their profession. They built the balloon. They mean to demonstrate that people can travel considerable distances by air. Some of them will be killed trying to prove their scientific hypothesis. What has this to do with Royall Tyler, a lawyer preparing to be admitted to practice before the Superior Courts? For him it was a lark, something exciting and dangerous with which to beguile himself. I tell you, Abigail, I don't like it. It raises all my original doubts about the young man's seriousness."

Nab agreed with her mother but she suffered under her father's disapproval.

It was Abigail's turn to incur unhappiness, although the daughter of a Congregationalist clergyman could hardly admit that doing her bounden duty could make anyone unhappy. After several months of discussion she came to the conclusion that they must send near eighteen-year-old Johnny home that spring so that he could be admitted to

Harvard to complete his spotty academic education. Johnny would be missed. He was his father's secretary; he kept his mother's account books and participated in her heroic effort to support the château. He was Nab's closest friend and companion. Johnny held a special position in the household: all three adored him, trusted him, enjoyed him. Their lives would be bereft without him. Some tears were shed, separately and privately, but Abigail commented:

"America is the theatre for a young fellow who has any ambition to distinguish himself in knowledge and literature . . ."

"Or law!" John interrupted.

The miasma which had settled with the winter cold over the Americans seemed to hover over the French as well. The Adamses rode into Paris to watch Louis XVI and the entire court attend Notre Dame in order to give thanks for the birth of a prince, Louis Charles. The crowds of Parisians were grim-faced, sullen, seeming to resent every individual in the richly gowned parade of French nobility. There were more police forming a solid line on the Rue de Rivoli than the spectators whom they were guarding against. Assuredly these were not pleasure-loving people come to watch an entertaining spectacle. Abigail reflected that she had never seen such naked hatred on the faces in a crowd, certainly not on the English soldiers lining the Boston Common on the day they had watched their mortal enemies, John Adams, Samuel Adams, Thomas Cushing and Robert Treat Paine, depart for a Congress which might declare war on them. These people lining the streets of Paris were the King's countrymen but from their black looks it was apparent they thought of King Louis XVI, Queen Marie Antoinette and the royal court as enemies.

At last the clouds settled over John Adams. He had written a report to Livingston, Secretary of Foreign Affairs in the Continental Congress, in which he had strongly recommended that a minister plenipotentiary be appointed to Great Britain. He had then added his idea of the necessary qualifications for such an American minister to the Court of St. James's. It was a detailed and brilliant self-portrait which everybody instantly recognized as John Adams's recommendation of himself for the job. Everything he wrote was valid and true, but under the circumstances it would have fitted Benjamin Franklin's description of him as "sometimes and in some things absolutely out of his senses."

The debate in the Congress, which by the turn of 1785 had decided that John Adams was right in maintaining that no treaty could be negotiated with Britain without an American ambassador, had been protracted and acrimonious. Now the New York delegates rejected John Adams for the job on the grounds that he cared about nothing but New England fisheries; now the Southerners resisted on the grounds that since he was opposed to slavery he would not work to secure the return of the slaves carried away by the British; now the middle-state delegates demurred on the charge that, since he acknowledged the legality of American merchant debts to England which had been incurred before the outbreak of the war, he would not strive to have interest payments set aside. Many pointed to his letter as flagrant and outrageous vanity.

John Rutledge was proposed for the position, then Livingston was nominated. He had strong support. John Adams's New England friends worked hard and persuasively; even so the first ballot came out at five votes for John Adams, four for Livingston and two for Rutledge. For two days the debate continued. At last John's supporters, led by the able Elbridge Gerry, Francis Dana and Arthur Lee, were able to convince the Congress that he was the most experienced man in foreign affairs, indispensable to their cause. Nine states of the eleven represented voted for him, giving him a gratifying majority.

Thus success came to John Adams. He had been elected to the one and last office he desired. Yet it was a bittersweet victory. A long letter from Elbridge Gerry giving him a full account of what everybody had said for and against Minister Plenipotentiary John Adams of Massachusetts made noxious reading. It so galled him that he sat immobilized at his desk for several days writing a fiery and philosophic discourse on the nature of vanity, of which he claimed that he possessed the most creative kind: "proper love of self."

Abigail nodded in assent.

Their French adventure was over.

Benjamin Franklin was granted permission to return home. Thomas Jefferson was appointed minister plenipotentiary to France, which pleased him. He had become fond of the French, had begun to speak the language fluently and had been studying the history of French art. He was content to settle in Paris for a number of years, particularly if he could send for Polly to live with him and Patsy. No New Englander could feel the affinity for the French and their culture that Thomas Jefferson, the Virginian, enjoyed.

They gave splendid dinner parties, toasted each other in the best

French wines. The Adamses walked along the Seine amid the budding spring flowers, the trees coming to leaf, the sunshine sparkling on the streets and houses.

"How could I ever have thought Paris was dirty?" Abigail asked. "Or that it smelled? It is beautiful. Let's drive up to the top of Montmartre for one final view of the red tile rooftops that I can carry with me always."

"Nostalgia," murmured John; "the loveliest of all emotions."

It was time to depart.

Johnny went first, sailing on *Le Courier de l'Amérique* for New York, loaded with letters of introduction to his father's friends. Madame Helvétius came to embrace them and cover their cheeks with kisses. The Marquis and Marquise de Lafayette drove out on a brilliantly clear May day, bringing presents for all.

When they entered their carriage to start for Calais where they would take the boat across the Channel to Dover, the domestics gathered about them in tears. Abigail realized with a pang that she had grown fond of these assorted servants with whom she had lived peaceably for ten months. She said good-by to each warmly, conscious that she would never see them again, saddened by the thought that a colorful and stimulating part of her life had gone forever.

Now, at this parting moment, she grasped the genius of France: that it could take a granite-bound Massachusetts Puritan and in less than a year convert her into a tolerant, pleasure-loving citizen of the world.

5

London was crowded at the end of May, for Parliament was sitting, it was King George III's birthday, and there was a celebration of Handel's music at Westminster Abbey. There were no rooms to be had at the Adelphi Hotel, which they had requested. Fortunately Charles Storer had scoured the city and found them a suite of four rooms at the Bath Hotel in Piccadilly. It was in the court end of the city, not the most desirable because of the great concourse of carriages during the day and evening, which created a constant noise of carriage wheels over cobbles. A chambermaid, cook and waiter were included in the cost of a guinea a day, but they had to provide their own food. Each bedroom had its own drawing room, genteelly decorated in green bordered with gold, card tables, a dining table and wall mirrors.

"It's elegant," observed Abigail, "but a third more than the château at Auteuil cost. Can we afford it?"

"Not for long. We must find a proper house. Our home will be the first American Embassy in England. It must be distinguished, the kind of expensive, upper-class town house which so impresses the British."

"There's been no word yet from the Congress as to your increased salary as our first minister to England?"

"The Congress is not concerning itself with petty details."

"Then how will you know how much you can pay for the houses you will be inspecting?"

"I won't be. You will. I must begin work at once with the ministers and the court."

"It will be pleasant to be able to use my tongue handily with a language once again, instead of rolling it around in my mouth in those hopeless sounds I assumed to be French."

They were unpacking their trunks when there was a staccato knocking on the door. John opened it to admit a young man of about thirty, tall, slender, with a good figure and a naturally dark complexion burned a deeper shade by years of military service. He bowed formally, said in a deep voice:

"Ambassador Adams, permit me to present myself. I am Colonel William Smith, formerly aide-de-camp to your good friend General Washington; and now, by act of the Congress, secretary to the American legation in London. In short, your humble but I hope helpful assistant. I have with me your official commission from the Congress as minister plenipotentiary. May I present it to you, sir."

John welcomed the man, introduced him to Abigail and Nab. He was a romantic figure, easy-spoken, with a large-chested military bearing, apparently of a fond nature, carrying himself proud and erect.

Abigail ordered tea to be served in their parlor. The Colonel had a robustious appetite, dispatching a tray of bread and butter and cakes with his half a dozen cups of tea as he told them of conditions at home. He also remained long enough to reveal that he had come from a large and prosperous family of New York landowners, had joined the army and fought through the war as an aide to General Sullivan, and then to Washington, had participated in the successful evacuation of the troops from Brooklyn to Manhattan, leaving in the last boat with Washington; was wounded in the battle of Harlem Heights. He had been promoted to the lieutenant colonel for gallantry at the battle of Trenton, was made adjutant general under Lafayette, was on the committee that treated with the British on their withdrawal from the United States and as Washington's aide was the officer to whom New York City was surrendered.

When Colonel Smith finally rose and bowed his farewells, he left behind a bemused and stimulated Adams family. Nab asked:

"Father, what does the secretary of the legation do?"

John replied dryly, "There's an old saying that the secretary keeps the embassy and the ambassador keeps a mistress."

"My, haven't we become a worldly family!" exclaimed his wife.

The following day at one o'clock, accompanied by Colonel Smith, John presented a copy of his commission at the home of Britain's Foreign Secretary, Lord Carmarthen. He was politely received. His lordship informed John that on Wednesday next he would be presented to King George III in his closet, and there might deliver his letter of credence.

When the Adamses learned that evening that Jonathan and Esther Sewall had come up to London for a few days and were staying in a hostelry on the outskirts, John cried:

"We must call on them at once."

The Sewalls were astonished to find Minister Plenipotentiary Adams attending them. But were not nearly so taken aback as Abigail and John were when they saw Jonathan. The formerly handsome, flashing-eyed man who had created laughter in order to be refreshed was now an old and ugly man, his face bumpy with carbuncles, red ones adorning his nose. Abigail had heard the rumor that he had been drinking heavily for years. Esther was still pretty in the Quincy tradition but her face was a mask.

The two women embraced. John took Jonathan's hand in both of his.

"How do you do, my old friend. This is a happy moment."

Esther bustled about trying to arrange four chairs together in a bedchamber that had only one small window overlooking the stables and grooms' court.

"Forgive our modest surroundings," Jonathan said, "we are just up from Bristol for a day or two on business."

"How are you faring, Jonathan?" John asked.

Jonathan's creased eyelids fell most of the remaining distance over his mustard-yellow eyeballs. Bitterness spread over his mouth as palpably as breadcrumbs.

"Once the war was over, Lord North and his successors washed their hands of us Loyalists. They drove me to England and the devil has kept me here."

Abigail turned for a swift glance at Esther's face. Esther had not wanted to leave her family, friends, roots. Did this mean that Jonathan wanted to return to Massachusetts? Other Tories had been allowed to do so.

Jonathan caught the exchange.

"I have not changed my mind. You were wrong and I was right. The fortuitous outcome of the war does not change anything. John, you have a heart formed for friendship and are susceptible of its finest feelings, though perhaps rather implacable to those whom you think your enemies."

"I never thought you an enemy, Jonathan; only a valued friend who unfortunately passed out of my life."

Jonathan lowered his voice, expressing thoughts that had been rattling around in his skull for a decade.

"During the American contest an unbounded ambition and an enthusiastic zeal for the imagined or real glory of your country may have suspended the operation of your social and friendly principles; yet this visit proves they have not been eradicated. John, you have been gratified in the two darling wishes of your soul: the independence of America is acknowledged and you yourself have been placed on the very pinnacle of the temple of honor. Why, John Adams, the very devil himself would feel loving and good-natured after so complete a victory, much more a man in whose heart lay dormant every virtuous social and friendly principle."

John had the good grace to net the compliment and let the criticism escape. Esther wanted news of her family; John wanted some clue as to how he might help his oldest friend. Jonathan's tale was the typical one of the American Tory, enthusiastically received in England at first, then slowly abandoned as the war dragged on, as the pinch was felt at home, as more nations came in against England, as her ships went down, her troops were lost in a series of blunders and conflicting leaderships, her commerce was cut . . . until England came to hate the Tories as symbols of the futility and frustration of the wasted years. He had never been able to practice in England; his £600 annual grant as judge commissary of the Vice Admiralty Court of Nova Scotia had not been rescinded but he had had to pay over a quarter of the wage to his replacement since he had never served in Nova Scotia. They lived penuriously on a little over two thousand dollars a year, unable to afford London prices.

"Jonathan, our treaty of peace with England recommended payment for all properties seized in the United States."

"A recommendation! What does that mean? The Continental Congress cannot force Massachusetts . . ."

"No, but I firmly believe the state will pay for the condemned property. How much was yours worth, Jonathan?"

"My property losses amount to close to £6000."

"Well, you shan't get twenty-seven thousand dollars back but you'll get some of it, I promise."

"Esther, won't you and Jonathan come to us for dinner tomorrow?" Abigail urged. "You haven't seen Nab since she's grown up."

Jonathan responded for her. "Cousin Abigail, your invitation is so friendly that I am sorry I cannot comply but I resolved to make no visits nor accept any invitations in London . . . on the grounds that I have previously declined invitations to dine with Sir William Pepperell and other friends."

Tears sprang to Esther's eyes. "We're going back to Bristol, then you want to move to Nova Scotia. We may never see Cousin Abigail and Cousin John again."

"Oh, come, Jonathan," cried John, "we're not friends, we're family."

They did not arrive. In their place came the story of what Jonathan Sewall had said about John Adams, though he was only repeating what so many had said in London since word reached England that John Adams was to be the first American minister plenipotentiary. Now that Minister Adams had reached the summit of his ambition, he would find himself quite out of his element. He was not qualified by nature or education to shine in courts. His abilities were undoubtedly quite equal to the mechanical parts of his business as ambassador but that was not enough. He could not dance, drink, game, flatter, promise, dress, swear with the gentlemen, talk small talk and flirt with the ladies; in short, he had none of the essential arts or ornaments which constituted a courtier. There were thousands who, with a tenth part of his understanding and without a spark of his honesty, would distance him infinitely in any court in Europe.

Abigail smiled wearily at the two American friends who brought the report, feeling that the minister should be forewarned.

"John Adams is a Puritan Joan of Arc; he has been burned at the stake endless times. But like a true Phoenix he rises each dawn from his own ashes."

They had expected their residence in England to be painful. Jonathan Sewall had confirmed the depth of feeling against the first American ambassador. The most difficult of all moments arrived, on June first, when Minister Plenipotentiary John Adams had to be presented to King George III who, it was rumored, had long believed that the "brace of Adamses" had caused the American Revolution. It promised to be the most agonizing confrontation of John's life. His first inclination had been to deliver his credentials silently and retire, but Lord Carmarthen informed him that Minister Adams must make a speech to King George, one as complimentary as possible. John had written it painstakingly over the days, rehearsing it before Abigail. Now as he stood in their sitting parlor, his wig fastidiously powdered, dressed in the handsome coat the Duke of Dorset had advised him to have made in Paris for this great occasion, black silk breeches and silk stockings, silver buckles on his shoes, distractedly fiddling with sword and gloves, Abigail could hear his high, intense, emotion-packed voice reading the address on which so much of their residence here depended.

"Sir: The United States of America have appointed me their minister plenipotentiary to Your Majesty and have directed me to deliver to Your Majesty this letter which contains the evidence of it. It is in obedience to their express commands that I have the honor to assure Your Majesty of their unanimous disposition and desire to cultivate the most friendly and liberal intercourse between Your Majesty's subjects and their citizens, and of their best wishes for Your Majesty's health and happiness, and for that of your royal family. The appointment of a minister from the United States to Your Majesty's court will form an epoch in the history of England and of America. I think myself more fortunate than all my fellow citizens in having the distinguished honor to be the first to stand in Your Majesty's royal presence in a diplomatic character, and I shall esteem myself the happiest of men if I can be instrumental in recommending my country more and more to Your Majesty's royal benevolence, and of restoring an entire esteem, confidence and affection; or, in better words, the old good nature and the old good humor between people who, though separated by an ocean and under different governments, have the same language, a similar religion and kindred blood.

"I beg Your Majesty's permission to add that, although I have some time before been intrusted by my country, it was never in my whole life in a manner so agreeable to myself."

At one o'clock the Master of Ceremonies called for John at the Bath Hotel. Abigail assured John that he would be the most resplendent courtier at court. He was driven in the coach of Lord Carmarthen to St. James's. When they arrived in the antechamber the Minister of Foreign Affairs left to confer with the King. John stood on the spot where all ministers stand when they are first to be presented at court. As he looked about him he saw that the room was full of ministers of state, bishops, courtiers. He felt himself the focus of all eyes. He knew that a goodly portion of these people not only expected but actually wanted him to have a rough voyage to the King's closet. Lord Carmarthen returned, asked John to accompany him to His Majesty. John walked with his lordship through the length of the levee room and into the King's closet. The door was shut behind them.

Minister Plenipotentiary John Adams stood before His Majesty King George III in the almost bare hall. He had rehearsed the three reverences which he had to make, the first at the door, the second halfway across the room and the third before the presence of the King, a usage to which he had become accustomed in other courts of Europe. He could hear the strain and agitation in his own voice.

His speech finished, John looked directly at King George for the first time. He was a short, stockily built man, very much of the same figure as John Adams, dressed in elaborate blue satin with lace collar and cuffs. He had a red face, white eyebrows, thick lips and a plump underchin.

The King had listened to John's speech with an emotion apparently as great as John's own. When he answered, John found that there was even more tremor in the King's voice than there had been in his:

"Sir: The circumstances of this audience are so extraordinary, the language you have now held is so extremely proper, and the feelings you have discovered so justly adapted to the occasion that I must say that I not only receive with pleasure the assurance of the friendly dispositions of the United States but that I am very glad the choice has fallen upon you to be their minister. I wish you, sir, to believe that it may be understood in America that I have done nothing in the late contest but what I thought myself indispensably bound to do by the duty which I owed to my people. I will be very frank with you. I was the last to consent to the separation; but the separation having been made, and having become inevitable, I have always said, as I say now, that I would be the first to meet the friendship of the United States as an independent power. The moment I see such sentiments and language as yours prevail, and a disposition to give to this country the preference, that moment I shall say, let the circumstances of language, religion and blood have their natural and full effect."

There was a brief pause, a smile came to the King's lips. He asked informally:

"You last came from France, Mr. Adams?"

"I did, Your Majesty, just a few days since."

The King laughed gaily. "There is an opinion among some people that you are not the most attached of all your countrymen to the manners of France."

John was taken aback at the remark. His eyes sparkled, there was a half-smile on his lips as he responded firmly:

"That opinion, sir, is not mistaken. I must avow to Your Majesty I have no attachment but to my own country."

Quick as lightning King George replied:

"An honest man will never have any other."

The King turned to Lord Carmarthen, bowed his dismissal. John retreated, stepping backward as was the custom, made his last reverence at the door of the chamber. The Master of Ceremonies was waiting, escorted John through the levee and to the front door, where the lackeys called up the carriage. He drove back to the Bath Hotel.

Abigail, Nab and Colonel Smith, who were to be presented soon themselves, were waiting to hear every tiny detail of the ritual, but mostly to learn how John's speech had been received. After assuring them that he could not guarantee the King's precise words, he gave a very faithful reproduction of it. Abigail was elated. A cold reception would have been quickly translated through the Ministry and among the foreign ambassadors.

"I think we may now expect that our residence will be less painful than we anticipated," said John. "So marked an attention from the King will silence many grumblers. But we can infer nothing from all this concerning the success of my mission."

The results of the cordial interview were instantaneous. All through the afternoon and evening there were callers from the English Ministry, from members of Parliament, and a number of ambassadors, led by the sympathetic ones from Sweden and Holland.

Five days later a copy of the *Public Advertiser* was brought to their suite. They read:

"An Ambassador from America! Good heavens what a sound! The gazette surely never announced anything so extraordinary before, nor once on a day so little expected. This will be such a phenomenon in the *corps diplomatique* that 'tis hard to say which can excite indignation most, the insolence of those who appoint the character, or the meanness of those who receive it. Such a thing could never have happened in any former administration, not even that of Lord North."

They looked at each other in consternation. John's splendid reception had been little more than fanfare, the marching of the guard of honor around the Coliseum prior to the mortal struggle between the gladiators.

6

Abigail turned to her two most pressing problems. She redoubled her efforts to find a house and to resolve the difficulties of Nab's waning love affair. When Nab had received no letter from Tyler in half a year, Abigail pointed out to her daughter that she too had failed to receive letters from John for periods as long as half a year. Nab replied coolly:

"That was during the war. Ships' captains often destroyed the personal correspondence they were carrying when they thought they might be captured. No such condition prevails now. Mr. Tyler simply has not troubled to write to me."

"I asked Johnny to visit him immediately he reached Braintree. We should have his report in a few weeks."

Nab was clenching her fingers so tightly together that the knuckles were white, a gesture Abigail recognized as her own when perturbed.

"It is not only his failure to write: some people have difficulty putting their feelings on paper. But we have heard that Mr. Tyler is apparently behaving strangely, that he is moody and is not tending to his law business as he should. He knows that he has to set these things right before we can be married. I shall write to Mr. Tyler this very day and plainly tell him my mind."

"Have faith," said Abigail quietly. "Enjoy London."

Indeed Colonel William Smith was doing all in his power to make it more attractive. He was a sympathetic young man, well bred, his barely suppressed vitality filling the atmosphere around them. He served the Adamses with eagerness but was most attentive to Nab, letting his eyes rest upon her long and affectionately. Nab blushed a little at first, then said to Abigail, with the first smile her mother had seen for some time, "I must say that Colonel Smith is an extremely fine gentleman, and is capable of extending friendship."

The house hunting was more difficult, since the house would also serve as the American Embassy. She left the hotel early in the morning, pursued every lead but found nothing fit to inhabit under nine hundred dollars a year, plus the taxes, which amounted to another two hundred and seventy. Luck was finally with her. On June ninth she found a lovely house in the northeast angle of Grosvenor Square, a little out from the city. The rent was reasonable because it could be had for only the remainder of an existing lease, approximately twenty-one months, which John considered might very well fit the time of their residence in England. Since they were to be charged on the basis of seven hundred and twenty dollars a year, and the owners agreed to paint the two important downstairs rooms, John signed the lease at once.

Grosvenor Square was one of the finest squares in London, surrounded by sturdily built houses. In the middle of the square, enclosed with a grated fence and surrounded by sixty lamps which were lighted each night, and a hedge to give privacy, was a charmingly intimate park to which only the residents surrounding the square had a key. In the center of the green park was a statue of King George on horseback; around it were gravel walks with plots filled with clumps of low trees and thick shrubbery. Their opposite neighbor was Lord North, their near neighbor, Lord Carmarthen.

Their new home was constructed of long slabs of horizontal white stone on the first floor, and brick for the three floors above. There was a balcony over the first floor and banks of large windows. There was also a fifth dormer floor for the servants.

John sent to The Hague for his furniture. The Foreign Office arranged for the boxes and crates to be admitted through customs. Since he had informed her that he had no adequate tables coming, Abigail set about the task of having a set made which would dine sixteen to eighteen persons, all the dining room would hold. She would also have to replace her French kitchen utensils, which had been made for a hearth fire and could not be used on the English grates.

London's streets were full of people whose dress, gait and appearance indicated that their purpose in life was the pursuit of business, and this she recognized. The London ladies, wigless, in their muslin and lutestring dresses walked a great deal and she joined them on the flat stone sidewalks. Now it was John who complained of the city, its smoke and dampness, the smells emitting from the kitchens, cellars, stables onto the people using the narrow sidewalks. She felt that London gave an impression of greater wealth and grandeur than Paris; certainly the horses and carriages were superior. When they drove out into the country they found the fields richly cultivated, without the slavish peasantry that had disturbed them in France. It was a relief to be back in a country that had a Congregationalist church to attend, even though it was the "dissenting church," the clergy so restricted that they were not even allowed to perform marriages.

They learned that the pastor of the Hackney congregation, Dr. Richard Price, was John's old friend who had been identified since 1776 with the cause of American independence. Each Sunday morning they drove in their carriage the four miles to Hackney to hear familiar preaching which tasted good against the ear after their ten months in a Catholic country. Dr. Price's church was not as austere as God's Barn in Weymouth, but he preached from the closest thing to her father's hanging pulpit that Abigail had seen in a long time.

The day arrived when Abigail and Nab were to accompany John to court to be presented to the royal family. The gowns of the Englishwomen so presented were as elaborate as any of their French counterparts.

Abigail directed her mantuamaker to let her dress be elegant but plain as she could possibly appear. The gown was white lutestring full-trimmed with white crepe, festooned with lilac ribbon and mock point lace over a hoop of enormous extent. She was pleased with what she called her "rigging": ruffle cuffs, treble lace ruffles, a cap with long lace lappets and two white plumes, a blond lace handkerchief, two pearl pins in her hair and pearl earrings, all bought from London jewelers for the festive occasion. Nab's dress was also white, her train wholly of white crepe and trimmed with white ribbons.

They left the Bath Hotel shortly after one, Abigail and Nab in one carriage followed by John and Colonel Smith in another. At two o'clock they went to Queen Charlotte's circular drawing room, passing through several apartments lined with spectators. As they passed into the drawing room they were received by Lord Carmarthen and the Master of Ceremonies. Abigail did not recognize a single woman until the Countess of Effingham entered. There were three young ladies, the daughters of the Marquis of Lothian, who were to be presented, and two brides. All were placed in a circle around the drawing room, some two hundred people, the Adamses and Colonel Smith close to the door by which the King would enter. King George made the circle around to his right, the Queen and Princesses to their left. The King spoke briefly and pleasantly to John, then turned to Abigail. His voice was so low that it might have been considered a whisper. No one except the person standing next could hear what His Majesty had said.

Abigail drew off her right glove. George III saluted her left cheek.

"Mrs. Adams, have you taken a walk today?"

Abigail could have replied that she had spent all morning preparing to wait upon the royal family. Instead she answered:

"No, sire."

"Why? Don't you love walking?" the King asked.

"I am rather indolent in that respect, Your Majesty."

King George III bowed, was then introduced to Nab.

It was a full two hours later before Queen Charlotte, the Princess Royal and Princess Augusta, with their ladies-in-waiting behind them, made their way to the Adamses. The Queen's lady-in-waiting introduced Abigail to the Queen, who seemed to stiffen. Abigail felt that Charlotte was embarrassed; and she had to admit that she too had disagreeable feelings. Yet she had found the King quite personable. The Queen asked:

"Mrs. Adams, have you got into your house?"

"Not yet, Your Highness, but our furniture is expected daily from The Hague."

"Pray, how do you like the situation of it?"

"I find it most beautiful, Your Highness. Particularly the openness of Grosvenor Square and the lovely park."

The Queen bowed briefly and moved along. Abigail was then introduced to the Princess Royal, who said with a compassionate glance:

"Are you not much fatigued, Mrs. Adams?"

"A little. Thank you for your consideration, Princess."

"It is indeed a very full drawing room today."

It was another hour and a half before the reception was completed, the royal family had taken its leave and the Adams family could depart. Abigail was exhausted. Her feet hurt. John was delighted with her.

"His Majesty deigned to salute you, my dear Mrs. Adams. The entire drawing room was watching to see how he would receive you. It will be all over London by nightfall."

"I did not fare so well with the Queen."

"She spoke to you as cordially as to anyone else and that is the important thing. It may be fairly concluded from this afternoon's levee that it is the intention of the royal family and of the ministers to treat America like all other foreign powers. That is the one thing we most desire, and you have made your contribution to it."

Abigail sighed. "Oh dear, that means that I must attend twice a month during the summer and each week during the season?"

"Yes, it does. The greater part of a diplomat's life is spent observing protocol. Without it we will never achieve any kind of a treaty with the English."

"I am resigned. But did you know that neither Nab nor I is permitted to wear the same gown twice in one year? I won't tell you what these dresses cost."

"I am reconciled to the fact that we are going home bankrupt. But if I can go with a robust commercial treaty in my hand I shan't object."

The furniture arrived unscathed. Abigail installed it as rapidly as she could in order to get out of the expensive hotel. She was delighted with John's good taste. She liked particularly an apple-green bed, three chairs of green velvet, bureau with dressing glass above it and secretary which she placed in Nab's apartment. She added Bell's edition of the British poets and a leather-bound set of Shakespeare, a house-warming gift to Nab from her father. Abigail was shocked at the prodigality with which John had bought red velvet dining-room chairs, green sofas and deep lounge chairs for the drawing room.

Her house now livable, she went about engaging a staff. She found it incredible that she was required to have even more servants here in London than she had had in Auteuil; and at wages that were considerably higher. She found a butler whose task it was to take care of the wine, to market, to see to the table and sideboard and to polish the plate as well as oversee the other eight to ten servants. He was called Mister not only by the other servants but by the Adamses as well. Next in line came the lady's maid, who dressed their hair, took care of the linen and spent the remainder of her time at her needle; then the cook; then the housemaid. The butler suggested that she needed only three more in help, a housekeeper, a laundrymaid and a porter.

The Adamses also had to have a footman in livery, and then have livery made for Briesler, since they could not go out in their coach without the required two footmen in attendance. John managed to have their carriage put in first-class condition again but they had to pay over five hundred dollars a year for their horses and extra coachman. The coachman got drunk while John was drinking tea at a friend's house, fell down from his box, broke the two lights and split the forepart of the carriage. The footman who was to work with Briesler was a German who did not understand English. Since he was honest and quiet, Abigail decided to let him stay on. She missed Johnny. He could have taken much of this petty detail off her shoulders, as well as her account books. He had grown canny about tradespeople and she found that here in London, no less than in France, the butcher who provided her with meat sent over short weight. They kept hoping each day to receive word from Johnny that his ship had reached America and he was back in Braintree, but the weeks passed without any news of him.

The ambiguousness of their financial position was soon borne in upon her. The Congress failed to restore John to his original higher salary. To make available funds for her court gowns she tried cutting down on the cost of her food. Since she could not persuade the butler to buy more practically, she undertook the task herself, going out each morning as she had in Boston to shop for fresh fruits, vegetables and fish for the table. The bills came down sharply but the gossip went up at an even higher rate, and the newspapers began making remarks about Mrs. Adams's going to the market in her chaise. John suggested gently:

"I'm afraid, dear soul, this is a form of economy we cannot afford."

"I know," she replied mournfully; "the newspapers are also insinuating that the American minister has not yet given a diplomatic dinner for the other ministers."

"They are not attacking us personally, my dear, only as representatives of America. They receive fourteen to nineteen dollars for each half dozen lines to print the scurrilous stories, paid by interests in England who want to see America put down. We can understand now why King George seemed so foolish in his handling of the American colonies, forcing them to war and independence when all they wanted was to remain loyal and loving Englishmen. He must have been surrounded by a wall of obdurate flesh, his courtiers, ministers and advisers who never allowed the tiniest grain of truth about America to sift through their planned protection of him. However they are right about one thing, we must give a dinner for the ministers whatever the cost."

They made friends with a group of American painters, Benjamin West, John Singleton Copley and John Trumbull, who were having a great success in England and who loved to bring their wives to Grosvenor House after a day's work to sit *en famille* with the Adamses over a glass of wine and their pipes and talk about art. Mather Brown insisted that all three Adamses sit for their portraits. They went often to Shuter's Hill. Joshua Johnson, brother of the former governor of Maryland, had lived in England before the Revolution as a factor for an Annapolis firm, married an Englishwoman and produced a bevy of handsome daughters. Johnny had spent considerable time at Shuter's Hill that fruitless month during which he awaited the arrival of his mother and sister on the *Active*.

Abigail had known that the configurations of love move on their own peculiar time schedule, adhering to no protocol or logic, the boundaries of development and of regression obscured, hazy, determinable by neither mathematical instrument nor the law of Fenning's *Algebra*. Yet she was unable to give shape to the two swift moves that determined the rest of Nab's life. At the beginning of August it was fourteen months since she had parted with Royall Tyler and she had received only the one packet of four letters in France. Though John's appointment to England had been known in Massachusetts for many months, there was no word to her parents or herself of congratulation, or any suggestion looking toward a meeting.

Nab sought counsel of her parents. Since they were going to be in England for another two years, what sense was there in permitting the affair to drag on? It was bringing everyone discomfort. John was disturbed over Tyler's lack of emotional stability; apparently this was not a young man to whom one could entrust a daughter's life.

Nab wrote to Tyler:

Sir: Herewith you receive your letters and miniature with my desire that you would return mine to my uncle Cranch, and my hopes that you are well satisfied with the affair as is.

A. A.

No mention had been made in the dispatching of Royall Tyler of the omnipresence of Colonel William Smith, who had fallen in love with Nab at first enamored sight. To Abigail he appeared modest, worthy, suffering from occasional flashes of temper, but sensitive; from the beginning she had forseen that the family would have pleasure and comfort from their connection with him. He had his quarters a few squares away but ate his meals with the Adamses, frequently coming into their intimate breakfast chamber off the dining room to write memoranda and letters for John on a space cleared between the chocolate urn and trays of buns, butter and jam. He was not a profound man, nor did he read; in fact the English press had unfairly accused him of being illiterate. Yet he was energetic in making copies of John's letters and reports to the Congress for their official copybook. He was a man of independent spirit; he was splendidly virile, with a bony jutting nose and sensual mouth. He would not have been found reading poetry or reciting scenes from a play, yet he was captivatingly sentimental and impulsive with the ladies.

They had been in Grosvenor Square for only a week when Abigail and Nab were starting for a ride after dinner. Colonel Smith came up in his carriage with a General Stewart from America. Through the open window of their carriage, Abigail said:

"We had intended to ask you to accompany us, Colonel, but we knew that you had company."

Colonel Smith flashed his contagious grin, cried, "Coachman, open this door!"

Once inside their carriage, nestling his hard-muscled frame between them, he cried to his friend:

"General Stewart, you will find Ambassador Adams at home. Please to forgive me!"

As the weeks went by the three Adamses found that Colonel Smith's ideas fitted companionably with their own. He was domestically inclined, disliking the court receptions as thoroughly as they did. Despite his adoration for General Washington he had steadfastly refused to wear the insignia of the Order of the Cincinnati, which Washington and his officers had founded in America in 1783. John had considered the Order dangerous and undemocratic, since it carried the nucleus of a self-perpetuating military aristocracy—only children of the original founders could join—which John feared might one day take over the Congress and constitute itself the new American royalty.

Would Nab have terminated her engagement to Royall Tyler, Abigail wondered, if there had been no handsome, attentive young secretary of legation on hand night and day to let her know by every look and gesture that he adored her? Probably not. Or at least she would have waited, expressed a desire to return to Braintree herself, or asked permission to invite Tyler to England.

But Colonel William Smith was present; in fact, Abigail decided, too much in evidence: he rarely missed a meal in the embassy. It would not appear honorable for Nab to have thrown over the absent Royall Tyler for the ubiquitous William Smith. People in Massachusetts would resent it and talk. She decided she had better keep the young Colonel out of the house until Nab and Royall Tyler had definitely broken their engagement.

Fate was helpful. At the beginning of August, Colonel Smith spoke of the upcoming military maneuvers in Prussia. Would it not be a good idea to have a competent observer on hand to report back to the Congress? John agreed; he gave the Colonel permission to leave for the requisite month's journey.

The ebullient young man departed. Neither he nor Nab, as far as Abigail could perceive, was sad at the parting . . . from which Abigail inferred that they had reached an understanding. A few weeks later she received a letter from him from Berlin, urging her to plead his case with Mr. Adams. She did not show the note to Nab, but answered urging patience.

Abigail sent out cards of invitation to their first diplomatic dinner ten days in advance. Lord Carmarthen accepted at once, and was instantly followed by the full diplomatic corps, some fifteen foreign ministers. It was to be a three-course dinner, first the solid food, a second course of trifles and whipped syllabub, a third of fruits of the season and foreign sweetmeats. As luck would have it a friend, Captain Hay, returned from the West Indies several days before the dinner and presented the Adamses with a turtle weighing a hundred and fourteen pounds. Abigail had it prepared for the dinner.

Because it was not the custom for ladies to attend such an affair, Abigail begged dinner for herself and Nab from a friend, Mrs. Rogers. When she returned at nine o'clock she found that not all the gentlemen had yet left. They assured her the turtle had been a great success.

It was a matter of considerable pleasure for her to find that the English newspapers had a full account of the affair. They were most complimentary to Minister Plenipotentiary and Mrs. Adams for having given so bountiful a dinner; the table had been exquisitely set, the courses well served . . .

7

One section of the second floor of the house had been converted to offices, with John taking a large sunny corner room overlooking the park, and next to him a smaller room for his secretary, a job now filled on a volunteer basis by young Charles Storer. There was also a room for Abigail which had been fitted out with a desk, chair and scttee; here she kept her accounts and maintained her correspondence. Since there was no room in the house that was properly appointed for nighttime reading, she converted their bedroom into a gay sitting room with English chintz coverings on two comfortable chairs, and movable whale-oil lamps similar to the ones they had on their night tables in Braintree.

John worked doggedly at his two main tasks: to get England to observe the peace treaty and to negotiate for a most-favored-nation commercial treaty. He was received everywhere in official circles with courtesy, was invited to Windsor Castle for conversations with George III. The Prince of Wales came to the embassy for supper.

He accomplished precisely nothing.

England appeared to have as many legitimate protests to lodge against the conduct of the United States as John had against Great Britain. His discussions with Lord Carmarthen and his interview with Prime Minister William Pitt were of no avail. When he demanded that the British evacuate the Northwest forts as they had agreed to do, making it clear how disagreeable to Americans it was to have thousands of British troops still quartered in Detroit, Oswego and Buffalo, in all likelihood inciting the Indian raids, Lord Carmarthen replied that England would observe that part of the treaty when the various states rescinded their laws advising American merchants not to pay British merchants their millions of pounds of debts. That it was equally disagreeable for Britain to watch the state legislatures declaring that interest on such debts was illegal. When Minister Adams wrote a close-reasoned and legalistic request to the British government that they return the slaves taken from America, Lord Carmarthen took as much as three months to answer the letter, then stated that the slaves would be returned as soon as the United States allowed the Tories to return and be indemnified for their confiscated properties.

Their social position seesawed, depending on immediate happenings in the United States. If the British were pleased, Grosvenor Square was filled with cordial Englishmen; when the political weather turned foul they were left alone. Abigail slowly came to perceive that their major function in England was to serve as targets for the abuse which would have been heaped upon any first American minister plenipotentiary regardless of who he might have been. A majority of the English people, particularly those in high place, never would forgive Americans for winning their freedom. The American Tories, stranded and embittered in England, were happy to have someone on whom to take out their frustrations. The John Adamses were vulnerable with their Puritanism, their lack of ostentation. The press still took great joy in calling them "penny pinchers."

Yet John Adams enjoyed a unique position among the foreign diplomats at the Court of St. James's. He was the only one who had participated in the actual creation of government. The Articles of Confederation and his constitution for the state of Massachusetts were read and admired in certain English political circles. His books *Thoughts on Government* and *Dissertation on Canon and Feudal Law* were published in England and had been translated in a number of countries of Europe. If, as Jonathan Sewall had so rightly said, he could not dance, game, flatter, it was equally true that he was known and respected as a historian in the field of the political philosophy of government.

One of Abigail's more difficult tasks was keeping her temper with the English ladies whom she had to entertain while their husbands discussed business with Minister Adams. "Undoubtedly you prefer England to America? . . . Surely our culture is carried to a higher degree here than in America? . . . You must find a great difference between America and this country in general appearance, manners, customs, behavior. . . ."

On one such occasion Nab cried:

"If anything, I find a greater degree of politeness and civility in Americans than in the people of this country!"

When she apologized to her mother after the ladies had gone, thinking she might properly be reproved for her outburst, Abigail said musingly:

"I'm sore pressed to understand this need of the English to keep insisting on their superiority. When I was young I read that the English have suffered for centuries from a sense of their own inferiority. How can they be carrying around the two diseases at the same time?"

In their very stolidity as they absorbed the abuse of the newspapers and the gossip that went about the country, the Adamses served their country as well as any American family could have. They even managed to make a few staunch friends among the English, yet sometimes when they walked arm in arm in Hyde Park, talking out the events of the day, analyzing their minor successes and continuing failures, it seemed small compensation to have to admit that they were no closer to a commercial treaty than they had been on the day they landed and settled into the Bath Hotel half a year before.

"But why, John?" Abigail asked perplexedly. "We are no longer at war. Why can't we prosper together? We did so for a hundred years prior to the war."

"Their direct object is not so much the increase of their own wealth, ships or sailors," John explained, "as the diminution of ours. I believe they're motivated by a fear of our potential naval power and consider the United States as their most dangerous rival. That is why they have re-enacted their Navigation Acts of 1696. All of the goods that we produced and thrived on for so long, and shipped to the West Indies in our own bottoms: masts, bowsprits, staves, tar, pitch, turpentine, can now be transported to the British West Indies only in ships owned by His Majesty's subjects. Our cured meats, fish and dairy products are no longer allowed in. Oh, they'll let us ship some few products to Great Britain, but *upon the same terms as from a British colony*. They are less afraid of an augmentation of French ships and sailors than they are of American, foreseeing that, if the United States had the same markets for ready-built ships which they had ten years ago, we would be in so respectable a position that British seamen, manufacturers and merchants would hurry over to us. They do not want the United States to become a major world power."

She knitted her brows, asked, "Are the British trying to win the war they won't admit they've lost? How much good can it do them?"

"It has done them an enormous amount of good. New England shipbuilders are paralyzed. There is no call for their ships. We must find new markets for our products. We will, eventually. In the meanwhile the greater part of America's money is being spent for manufacturies and luxury goods, practically all of them made in England and sent to America in English bottoms. No other country can compete with them for taste or excellence of product. But unless we stop buying their goods while they don't buy ours, we are going to become a purely farming civilization again, more dependent upon them than we were as colonies!"

He was silent for a moment, his face grimly set.

"I tell you, Abigail, we will never have a treaty of commerce until England is made to feel the necessity of it."

She forced a little laugh.

"Then it looks as though we'll be in England for the rest of our lives."

By the beginning of December the Adams family was in a state of alarm about Colonel William Smith. They knew he had been in Berlin; it was also rumored that he had been denied permission by the King of Prussia to see the military maneuvers. All of this had been over three months before, and since that time he had neither written nor come back to his duties at the embassy. Minister Adams's permission to travel might have been stretched a little past a month but Colonel Smith was beginning his fifth month away, neglecting his tasks as secretary of legation and, since Charles Storer had returned to America, leaving John

Adams stranded with no one to carry on the considerable chores of the legation, to help with the mail and the reports. Smith was drawing full salary and there was no conceivable excuse for his behavior. John Adams was not visibly angry, though he was suffering from eyestrain doing all his writing himself and making his own copies. Nab missed the Colonel and was hurt that she had not heard from him during these months. She wondered whether she had somehow managed to find a blood brother to Royall Tyler. Abigail was the most upset. She had given her tacit approval to this match. Where were they all now?

On the evening of December fifth, returning from the theatre after seeing *The Confederacy,* they had settled in the small breakfast room for a hot drink when William Smith put his head into the room and exclaimed to John:

"I see you, sir! Here is Colonel Humphreys from Paris. I have brought your friend as a peace offering."

His exuberance kept them from asking any questions. Despite the unwarranted absence they were glad to see him. When he learned from Nab that she had terminated her relationship with Royall Tyler, he wrote Abigail a formal letter asking for Nab's hand in marriage, explaining that it was easier to communicate with her than with Minister Adams. He sent along a number of documents and letters which testified to his honorable service in the American army and to the excellence of his family. He admitted frankly:

"It is better to marry a gentleman always involved in business than one who has no profession at all," but asked indulgence on the ground that when he would have gone into a profession he had entered the army instead and served continuously for the length of the war.

Abigail was relieved to have the letter; for Royall Tyler had learned in Braintree of the presence of Smith and was inclined to blame his plight and Nab's renunciation of him on the young Colonel. She could not deny to herself that there was an element of truth in the charge; but she was also convinced that Tyler had been the author of his own misfortune. He had not behaved well in his long silence, had apparently lied about sending letters via The Hague which had been lost. The Cranches were disturbed; they had already suffered from Royall Tyler's vagaries, and now his conduct seemed irrational to them when he locked himself in his room for days at a time, and then came down to dinner with a batch of Nab's letters clutched in his hands, making a display of reading them with great emotion. Johnny's report from Boston was that, although he enjoyed Tyler and thought that he had a scholar's mind, he had been behaving erratically ever since Nab's departure and had lost a good many of his former friends. Abigail decided she would be glad when Nab and Colonel William Smith were married.

John approved the engagement. He liked Colonel William Smith. Nab had passed twenty, time to be married.

Special attention was paid to the Adamses on the Queen's birthday when they went to the reception in the afternoon and the ball in the evening. But John could get nowhere with the English Ministry. He did hold a series of successful conferences with the envoy from Portugal. He concluded the treaty with Prussia which was in process of being ratified by the Continental Congress and the King. He was also making progress on the Mediterranean piracy problem. The ambassador from Tripoli let it be known that his feelings were hurt because Minister Adams had not called on him. John went at once with the idea of leaving a card but was ushered into a room where there were two chairs before a fireplace. He was bade to sit down and for the sake of diplomacy smoke a pipe of which the stem was some two yards in length, the bowl resting on the carpet. He watched the Tripoline ambassador, took a whiff whenever His Eminence did, drank coffee to match, and in a *lingua franca* talked about a peace treaty.

A few days later the ambassador came to the American Embassy. Abigail caught a glimpse of him from an upstairs window. He had a long beard and in Turkish fashion was swathed in an orange-colored material tied loosely about the waist, sandals, and a turban on his head containing at least twenty yards of muslin. He was attended by two servants.

"He's not really talking about a treaty of peace," John confided when the ambassador had withdrawn. "He made it known to me that America can have friendly relations with all of the Barbary countries, who will stop seizing our ships and imprisoning our sailors, providing we agree to pay them something in the neighborhood of a million dollars a year."

"A million dollars a year! That is sheer blackmail."

"True. But on the profitable side, since we are losing many millions of dollars' worth of merchandise, bottoms and seamen. I am going to write to Mr. Jefferson and urge him to come to London for a visit. I think working together we can conclude the Portuguese treaty and also these negotiations with the Mediterranean pirates."

Thomas Jefferson came over from Paris. The Adamses were enchanted to see him again. Jefferson had come to love France, its literature, its politics and its learned philosophers and encyclopedists. He was also thoroughly exasperated with England. There were companionable lunches and suppers with the Adams family, Colonel Smith and Mr. Jefferson all nostalgically homesick, talking about New England, New York and Virginia. Jefferson disapproved of the proposed treaty with the Barbary States. He had worked up a mathematical formula proving that it would cost less to build and maintain a fleet which would protect American shipping in the Mediterranean than it would to pay the annual bribe. However he accepted the judgment of the Congress and he and John worked with the Tripoline ambassador to attempt to keep the charge as low as possible. It was humiliating work and went against the grain.

To recover, the two men set forth on a week's tour of England. Abigail remained at home, preparing Nab's trousseau and plotting to set aside a modest cash dowry, sewing additional collars and cuffs and shirts for her three sons in Massachusetts to relieve Elizabeth Shaw and Mary Cranch from the heavy duties of keeping the boys in clean and presentable linen.

There were several pieces of bad news from America: her aunt Lucy Tufts had been ill for a considerable time and finally passed away. Cotton was living alone in his house in Weymouth. Her brother Billy, who had several times been reported dead, was now in the most serious trouble of his life. He had been arrested for passing counterfeit notes and was being tried on criminal charges. Abigail gritted her teeth in despair at the disgrace to the family.

The trial was highly publicized. In the end Billy was acquitted by a jury on the grounds that he had not printed the notes himself. He was now a habitual alcoholic with no visible means of support. He no longer returned home for his annual visit. Neither did he see his sisters. Occasionally he wrote to neighbors asking about his children but never about his wife. After his acquittal he wrote to Catharine Louisa demanding to know if his children were supplied with the necessities of life, and what kind of education she was giving them. He assured her that as soon as he was able he was going to land a shipload of British goods, then he would be in a position to do something for his family.

Billy's ship never came in. The following year Mary Cranch had word from an acquaintance that Billy was dead of black jaundice. Abigail did not even know where he was buried. She wondered if perhaps Catharine Louisa had not been right in saying that it would have been better had Billy been killed leading the first charge across the Concord bridge.

Abigail was determined that no daughter of hers was going to be married by a Church of England clergyman in an Episcopal church. Neither would she stand through a ceremony performed by a clergyman who was hostile to America. Any marriage rites performed by the good Dr. Price would be illegal. In order to be married at home a special license had to be obtained from the Archbishop of Canterbury, one which was available only to members of Parliament and the nobility. Colonel William Smith was sent posthaste to the Archbishop, who was puzzled by the request, since Colonel Smith refrained from telling him that the Adamses were from the dissenting religion. He decided that since Mr. John Adams was a foreign minister he took rank with the bishops of the kingdom. His family therefore had a right to be granted the dispensation. Abigail then requested an appointment with the Bishop of St. Asaph, whom the Patriots had admired because in a speech written for Parliament in 1774 he had looked upon North America "as the only great nursery of freemen now left upon the face of the earth."

The bishop was kind enough to invite the Adamses to dinner, along with Dr. Price, happily agreeing to perform the marriage. Since he was about to leave for the country, the wedding was arranged to take place on June 12, 1786, a month short of Nab's twenty-first birthday.

The ceremony was held in the drawing room of the embassy, a small altar having been placed at the street end, before the windows. Abigail regretted that her three sons could not be present. She had invited the Copley family for tea, not telling them that they were to attend a wedding. As she stood listening to the service and looking at Nab standing beside William Smith, she was aware of a dual commentary running through her mind: the almost incredible belief that she could have a daughter old enough to be married, and a mild disparagement of the absurdities of the ritual. When Nab repeated after the bishop, "I, Abigail, take thee William," Abigail thought this rather more embarrassing than the curtsy of assent through which Congregationalist brides made their gesture of avowal. The genial and sympathetic bishop set her at ease by exclaiming:

"I have never married a couple with more pleasure, because I never saw a fairer prospect of happiness."

The young couple rented a small house in Wimpole Street, not far from Grosvenor Square. They took dinner at the embassy each day.

John wanted to speak to the Colonel immediately about a matter he considered urgent. Abigail suggested that it would be better if they were allowed a two-week honeymoon. On the third Sunday, after their family dinner, John pushed his chair back from the table, took a sip of claret from his glass and turned his full attention on his son-in-law.

"Colonel, Mrs. Adams and I have been thinking about your future. The dowry we were able to provide was perforce modest. I should like to add something to it of infinitely more value than the cash sum."

William Smith lifted his dark, handsome face to his father-in-law. "Yes, Mr. Ambassador?"

"I can add substantially to your free time by assuming some of your duties and thus afford you the magnificent opportunity of studying the law here, where our common law was born."

There was silence.

"You could enter yourself at the Temple and attend the courts at Westminster, a priceless experience. I would direct your studies. By the end of our stay you would be prepared to practice in New York or Boston."

The Colonel remained silent. Nab changed the subject. John sighed, defeated.

Abigail's thoughts turned to her absent sons. While the two younger ones had not written often, her sister Elizabeth and the Reverend Mr. Shaw had been faithful in reporting their well-being and progress. Apparently they were getting along splendidly. Johnny had been admitted to Harvard as a third-year student. Charley had entered as a freshman the previous autumn. Tommy was due to join his brothers at Cambridge within a few months.

Each winter John spoke of returning home in the spring; but he had been doing this far too long for her to take him seriously. Instead he took her for a month's vacation to Holland. He carried with him a copy of the treaty with Prussia, duly ratified by the Continental Congress, which he would exchange in The Hague for the Prussian copy, the King of Prussia having stipulated that the ceremony was to take place there.

John knew the country well, having lived in Holland for two years, and had many friends there. He moved them at a leisurely pace through Rotterdam, Delft, Haarlem, Leyden, which she particularly admired for its wide streets and neat brick houses, Amsterdam, Utrecht, the many other charming villages whose names she could not remember. They made excursions to Scheveningen from The Hague, sailed up to Saardam for the annual fair, to which the people wore their colorful holiday costumes, were struck by the silence and calm of traveling through Holland. Some of the roads having been made of sand, they could not even hear the wheels of their carriage. The people of the countryside appeared to be well fed, well clothed, contented. Many of the Dutch had been impressed by the revolutionary ideas of freedom which had been born in America.

Indeed the ablest men of Holland had been engaged for a considerable time in creating new constitutions for the seven separate states of the United Provinces, using the state constitutions of America as models. John and Abigail were at Utrecht on the day the new magistrates, who had been elected by the free suffrage of the people, took their oaths of office. The ceremony was conducted with striking dignity, in the presence of the whole city and many spectators from other cities as well. It was, as John commented to Abigail, a revolution conducted with decorum.

8

The letters and newspapers from home, accumulated during their month's absence, told the same disheartening story: in this year of 1786 the United States of America was on the verge of collapse.

They sat in the drawing room, the windows open to Grosvenor Square. The floor between them was as littered with sheets of letters as was the warm September air of the room with their half-finished sentences.

Massachusetts was the most severely affected. The state was bankrupt. There was no circulating medium with which to buy or sell. Apple orchards were left to rot. Wheat was allowed to wither in the fields. It was a waste of time and effort to harvest products for which there were no buyers. A little barter was carried on but the people seemed in a stupor. Since there was no cash to be had, creditors were foreclosing on the farms. In the hardest-hit sections of the state men had taken their fowling pieces off the wall, marched in military order on the towns, led by Revolutionary War officers, to prevent the courts from opening.

For John the uprisings had taken an even more serious note. When he finished the fourth letter from old political friends in Massachusetts, he rose and paced the long room, his hands behind his back gripping each other bruisingly. His voice was low and hoarse.

"Bad times come and go; we've all had our share. But the people who are hurt are blaming everything on the government. On the Massachusetts Constitution, to be more exact. They want to throw it out."

"Throw it out! What would hold them together?"

"They do not want to be held together. They want to outlaw the elected state Senate, cut the governor's office to a ceremonial role, leave total control in the hands of the House of Representatives. That would destroy all balance of power, without which a republican state cannot survive."

She felt sick at heart.

"No constitution can persevere if the many factions within a state are at war with each other," he continued. "Here, read these pages from James Warren, Tristram Dalton and Samuel Osgood."

He stooped down, angrily gathered together some scattered pages and thrust them at her. She read. The story of what was happening in Massachusetts was not pretty; it was also familiar to her. Samuel Adams had said it all. The remaining Tories were still being persecuted. In Boston the scarce hard money was being spent for what the rest of the state despised as "British gewgaws." Luxury was being paraded by newcomers who had played no part in the Revolution. The hatred of these parvenus was so strong in the countryside that a crisis was fast approaching which could end in bloodshed. The City on a Hill had degenerated into a usurious pleasure-mad metropolis. James Warren wrote that interest in self-government had vanished; few attended town meetings or bothered to vote.

She gazed at her husband, who had collapsed on a red velure chair, his head and hands trembling as she had remembered Cousin Samuel's in his darkest days.

"That Massachusetts Constitution is one of my offspring, as much as Nab or Johnny or Charley or Tommy. It must not be allowed to die or be destroyed. Abigail, could you brew me a dish of strong tea? I'm low in my mind."

"It will bring us both a recruit of spirits."

They sipped the inky-black hot beverage.

"Tea brings courage," said John. "That's what the British Empire is founded on. Had they kept their last tax against us on paint instead of tea we might still be an English colony. The Continental Congress is another of my children. It wants to disband."

He sorted out the letters, making marks in the margins.

"The Articles of Confederation are no longer working. The finances of the central government are a shambles. The Congress is growing more ineffectual every day. Only five states bother to send delegates, and Foreign Affairs Secretary John Jay cannot answer my questions because there is not a quorum to discuss his instruction. Each state insists on being a separate sovereignty. Their stubborn dignity will not allow them to tolerate a federal government strong enough to secure life, liberty and property. There's talk of men of property forming an army to take over the government . . ."

"O Heaven!"

"You may well appeal to Heaven. Yesterday I made the rounds of the ministers. They know of our condition from their Tory informants. As we grow weaker, they grow stronger. It has been made clear to me that I need no longer supplicate for a treaty. I will be allowed to accomplish nothing for the rest of my ministership."

"John, that's eighteen months! We can't just sit here for a year and a half."

"Exactly not!" He sprang out of his chair, stood hovering over her, his body quivering, his eyes as blue-black as coals. "I've had a year and a half to arrange a commercial treaty with the British which would have brought prosperity to the states, respect and power to our central government. I have failed. The fault is squarely mine. So everyone is saying in Massachusetts, and many in New York and Philadelphia. Very well, if I can't secure us the treaty that will save us, there is something I can do. . . ."

She gazed at him, her eyes asking, "What is that?"

"Write a book."

She shook her head as though she had not heard aright. Massachusetts was on the verge of civil war, with armed bands defying the militia; the Congress was in danger of being dissolved or taken over by the large property owners. Yet John Adams, three thousand miles away from home, was going to sit and write a book . . . !

He saw the incredulity in her eyes. He crouched before her, his elbows digging into her thighs while he held her face tightly between his tensed fingers.

"Yes, a book. A long one. In several volumes. It will take a year or more to write. You were never one to doubt the power of the printed word. It can flash through the air like a mighty scimitar, cutting through tissues of falsehood, evasion, ignorance."

"But, John, is there time?"

"This is the only way I can turn my failure into success. The Annapolis Convention which is meeting now to consider a uniform system between the states in their commercial regulations simply cannot stop with so simple an objective, not with the whole of America falling in on their heads. Some of our best men will be there, James Madison and

Edmund Randolph of Virginia, Alexander Hamilton of New York, brilliant men, and Patriots. They will see that they need to call a greater convention, to write a new, strong, workable federal constitution."

"You want to have your book ready in time for their consultations?"

"Precisely so. I will call it *A Defence of the Constitutions of Government of the United States of America.* It will be aimed as much at Massachusetts as the Continental Congress, or any other body meeting to write a federal constitution. I have to prove that only a balanced system of government, with a strong, independent executive, two separate legislative bodies and a judiciary, can keep a republic alive. I must demonstrate from the thousands of years of recorded history that, without a balance of the three powers, governments become tyrannies or oligarchies, with human freedoms destroyed."

Abigail felt a warm glow suffuse her. Now it was her turn to take his perspiring face in her hands and kiss him on each flaming red cheek.

"Forgive my incredulity. Every victory you have won has come through the word: spoken or printed. If it is possible for a book to conquer chaos . . ."

They made arrangements with Charles Dilly, bookseller and printer in London, from whom John had been buying books for some twenty years, to print the volumes. The Adamses guaranteed to buy sufficient copies to cover the larger part of Dilly's costs. Dilly would gamble on selling the balance of the stock in England.

"Is there any chance of Congress paying the costs?" asked Abigail hopefully, gazing at the lists written in John's nervous scrawl of fifty-odd books in German, Italian, Spanish, in addition to the English volumes which he would have to collect for his historical evidence.

"The work is not authorized. You will have to be the Chancellor of the Exchequer, as usual."

She sighed. "Ah well, as a descendant of shrewd Yankee traders it intrigues me that those members of Congress who least want your work will be paying you a salary while you write the book."

He asked Abigail to invite Dr. Richard Price for dinner, then barely let the old gentleman get started on his portion of rack of lamb before announcing, "Dr. Price, I have a favor to ask of you. Of a literary nature. I am going to write a book defending the American constitutional form of government. It is under attack at home and abroad."

"I have been reading of your political troubles."

"You will recall that in your book which you so kindly sent to me in France two years ago you published a letter of Monsieur Turgot to you. It was an attack on our government based on his readings in a French publication containing six American state constitutions. The introduction by Regnier said, 'These constitutions seem to me the finest monuments of human wisdom, representing the purest democracy that has ever existed.' However Monsieur Turgot attacked these constitutions because the three orders or powers of the government were to be kept in balance. Now the time has come to prove that such a constitution for the federal government of America is the only kind that can possibly work with a democratic people."

"A splendid project," Dr. Price replied. "But Monsieur Turgot is five years dead."

"What I wish to ask of you, my dear Dr. Price, is that you allow me to use your name on the title page. My defence will read: *Against the Attack of M. Turgot, in his Letter to Dr. Price.*"

Abigail converted his office into a working library, hiring a carpenter to build extra shelves for the books for which she and John, Nab and Colonel Smith scoured London and wrote to booksellers in Paris, Rome, Madrid. John already had a good many of his reference books: Montesquieu, Coxe's studies of the political conditions of Switzerland, Poland, Russia, Sweden, Denmark, Polybius, Mitford and Gillies on the history of Greece, Machiavelli. From each of these, and the new ones as they arrived, he compiled further bibliographies, aspiring to build around him all the available writings that spoke of the world's political failures and successes.

The family settled into a period of intense concentration. John was reading and annotating for close to twenty hours a day, begrudging even the few hours of sleep Abigail obliged him to take. Colonel Smith undertook the work of the embassy, receiving the Americans who had problems, taking them to the proper ministers, banks, merchants, visiting the other embassies when John Adams's presence was requested. Abigail undertook whatever entertaining was inescapable, carrying on without John, who no longer joined them even for meals. She also attended faithfully the levees at court, being particularly attentive to Queen Charlotte because Minister Adams was not paying his respects.

Nab was in circumstances. When she saw that her father's eyes were red from reading and his writing arm sore from the long hours of copying, she asked:

"Father, Johnny copied for you, why can't I?"

"Why not indeed? Here, I need these bracketed passages out of Algernon Sidney and King Stanislaus I. But you must not overtire yourself."

"I am not delicate. And think of how this will help your grandchild: he'll be born a political expert."

"We could use a few in America," he grumbled; "all we have now are experts in quarreling. Sit opposite me, here."

"Yes, Papa."

After a month of riotous reading in a dozen civilizations John began writing his Preface, which would stand as the justification and rationale of the thesis. Word reached London that the delegates to the Annapolis Convention had indeed issued a call for a larger convention to "devise such other provisions as shall appear to them necessary to render the constitution of the federal government adequate to the exigencies of the Union."

"You're a good prophet, Minister Adams," his wife told him.

"I'd have to be mighty stupid not to be. How long did it take those delegates in Annapolis to decide on the need? Precisely three days. Everybody knows we must have a new and stronger government."

"Does the Continental Congress?"

His pleasure was punctured. He sat down at his desk, pushed aside a mass of papers, rubbed his eyes with the back of his hand.

"No. They'll fight it. They'll say, 'Why can't we just repair the Articles we've got?' Even Tom Jefferson agrees that's all they need to do."

When Nab tired, Abigail took her place opposite John's extended desk, copying from the books that surrounded him. She enjoyed the work, felt transported to Braintree and Boston. She had always been at home in the world of ideas and found the stories of history more exciting and enthralling than those of literature.

Mostly John was quoting from historical sources under such chapter headings as "Democratic Republics" and "Aristocratic Republics." But he was organizing and analyzing the materials into the kind of book no one had ever attempted. She thought:

"If the primary purpose of a human being during his journey on earth is to grow, then John is entitled to be a Saint in the City on a Hill."

The other half of her task was not as pleasant. Money was pouring out at such a rate for the printer, for books and supplies, that she stopped all other expenditures. The cost of running the embassy in London had proved to be a quarter again as high as for the château at Auteuil, yet the Congress was paying him the nine thousand dollars he and Jefferson had been receiving as commissioners in France. However John was certain that the Congress, in all fairness, would restore him to the salary with which he had been sent abroad in 1779.

"I sincerely hope so," she replied, "because the accounts show that I'm spending closer to the eleven-thousand figure than the nine."

She took over the marketing, no longer caring that the newspapers might call her a penny pincher, and regulated the amount of food prepared in the kitchen. When two of the servants left she did not replace them. She stopped buying tickets for the theatre; John would not leave his desk in any event. Her only vacation from the rigorous routine was a short trip John insisted she and Nab take to Bath, where a Boylston cousin entertained them.

Abigail reproached herself when she returned in early January, for she found John gaunt, his eyes bleary, his face pale, his writing arm sore from the shoulder down. Yet he was happy with the progress he was making; the first volume had been completed in four months. He commented:

"Time must be spent prodigally. This is the one area in which a Puritan can be a wastrel: the dissipation of his strength and courage to achieve a desired end. Granted, I am as much a spendthrift of my time and vital forces as any profligate who squanders his patrimony on drink or cards. I love work with the same passion that an idler loves pleasure."

He dated his Preface on January 1, 1787. The key, she thought, was above the date:

"The institutions now made in America will not wholly wear out for thousands of years. It is of the last importance, then, that they should begin right."

She murmured, "Amen!" turned to page one and began to read aloud. John sat with a copy in his lap, making emendations as he heard the ring of his prose through the inflections of her voice. She was delighted with the colorful character of his presentation.

"'Without three orders and an effectual balance between them, in every American constitution, it must be destined to frequent unavoidable revolutions; though they are delayed a few years, they must come in time. The United States are large and populous nations in comparison with the Grecian commonwealths or even the Swiss cantons; and they are growing every day more disproportionate, and therefore less capable of being held together by simple governments. Countries that increase in population so rapidly as the States of America did, even during such an impoverishing and destructive war as the last was, are not to be long bound with silken threads; lions, young or old, will not be bound by cobwebs.' "

Only much later did she find an element which made her uneasy. It was John's plea for a single and continuing executive.

"John, they will think in America that you are setting up for a king."

His sober reply indicated that he had been concerned about this too.

"I am for delegating to the executive the same authority which the British King has under the British Constitution, balancing his powers by the other two branches. He must have the negative power over the legislature, otherwise he will be their servant. Why should not the people at large appoint him? Then he will truly be independent. He will confine his attention chiefly to the Assembly, and believe that if he can satisfy a majority of them, he has done his duty. *The executive power is in truth the government.*

"As for his tenure, if there are perpetual attacks in the press about the discharge of his functions, they will keep the nation anxious and irritated, with controversies which can never be decided nor ended. Therefore, to be above the clamor, the President should be selected for a long term and be allowed to succeed himself."

"Surely not to perpetuate himself?"

"My dear, we are employed in making establishments which will affect the happiness of a hundred millions of inhabitants in a period not very distant. We must have the ablest man in the land as our executive, and for considerable periods of time to assure us of equilibrium."

"But our people will fear that the executive, if he remains in power long, will become a monarch. It is open to such an interpretation."

"I must take the risk. We have been governed by a Congress, how badly you and I well know. Most of our people will want it to be our only central government. I must plump for the strongest possible executive in order to achieve a balance. If I am misunderstood, it will not be the first time a teacher has been stoned in the forum."

9

When Abigail heard that Royall Tyler's house, the old Vassall-Borland house, might be for sale, she saw before her eyes, as vividly as though she were standing in the road in Braintree, the tall and stately building which looked somewhat like the parson's Mansion in Weymouth where she had been raised. She remembered the wood paneling, the handsome fireplaces and broad staircase, the commodious carriage house at the rear and magnificent trees and flower garden, which looked a good deal like the English gardens. It was smaller than the Alleyne house which they had decided in France they could not afford, the farmlands were less extensive; yet it was a house and a farm which could be expanded as they had the need and the funds. It might also be an estate which they could afford to buy.

She chose a moment when they were walking home from a visit to Westminster Abbey to ask:

"John, you remember the Vassall-Borland house?"

"Yes, very well."

"I saw it with Nab and Royall Tyler before he purchased it." She flushed. "Tyler has given up his law practice and returned to his mother's house in Jamaica Plain. Do you think we might try to buy the place? I know by now that our cottage in Braintree is going to be too small for our possessions; not to mention our thoroughly corrupted addiction to luxury."

"Write to Cotton and ask him to investigate," John responded.

"Do you think I should mention it to Nab?"

"How could it conceivably matter to me?" demanded Nab, somewhat later. "That's all in the past."

Nab was getting along now, feeling a little heavy. She sat with a book on her lap, unopened, gazing into the future. It was, Abigail assured her daughter, a time to wait. Nab had moments of anxiety, when she asked her mother whether she would know how to take care of the baby when it became ill. What if it weren't born normal, if it had eleven fingers or toes? Abigail told her that she had asked the identical questions. For the last period of waiting wouldn't Nab like to move back into her old room in the embassy? It would save her the trip in the morning fog and then back at night in the rain and cold.

Mr. Dilly printed very fast. John would not take the time to correct the galley proofs. They were pleased with the binding. The *Defence* was a stout volume which could pass from hand to hand under intense discussion and not fall apart.

"I am sure that's equally true of its ideas," Abigail murmured after John had gone through his lover's ritual of fondling the book between his hands, turning the pages tenderly.

All four members of the family wrapped copies to be sent to Thomas Jefferson, Elbridge Gerry, Cotton Tufts, Samuel Adams, James Warren, Francis Dana, President Willard of Harvard, members of the Continental Congress and, proudly, to Johnny, Charley and Tommy. The remaining stock of thirty volumes, after he had sent review copies to the English journals, were shipped to Cotton Tufts, who was to turn them over to a Boston bookstore for sale.

The first English criticism was horrendous. John was accused of an "ostentatious display of learning," the book was described as "an embarrassed affection of elocution." The reviewer went on to write acidly, "Had the book been written by a youth with a view to obtain some academical prize, we should have said that it offered indications of an active mind that gave hope of future acquirements, but that the young man, too eager to discover the extent of his reading, had carelessly adopted some confused notions of government and hastily skimmed the surface of the subject without having taken time to investigate particulars and sift the matter to the bottom." Although the book might amuse the ignorant or mislead the unwary, it could "neither . . . inform nor entertain the philosopher or the man of letters."

Abigail spent twenty-four hours serving as a sympathetic ear for John's outpourings against waspish critics and news printers in general, whom she declared to be the fathers of all lies.

"I'm the first to agree that it was a hasty job," said John. "It had to be. A project of this kind is so ambitious that it would have taken the best scholar in the land seven years to complete it. Nevertheless my concepts are so valuable they deserve thoughtful consideration."

With that, and aided by the three rum punches Abigail had served him, he went to bed and slept the clock around.

She was always amazed at his recuperative powers. The next morning his face was clear. He had put the bad review behind him. He dawdled over an extra portion of biscuits and jam, went for a walk in the rain up to Hyde Park, took dry clothes from Abigail's hands and returned to his desk to start work on Volume Two.

Nab moved back into her room in the embassy in March. On the second of April she was delivered of a fine boy. Dr. Price came to the embassy to name him William after his father, and Steuben after the Prussian officer Colonel Smith admired. Abigail loved the little boy with a tenderness that she would not have thought possible. His presence lighted up the world for her with a soft, luminous glow. A nanny was brought in to care for Nab and the child, but Abigail cheated by bathing the infant in a little canvas tub of warm water, easing powder into his still red joints, slipping him into a long warm woolen shirt and holding him in her arms. Her love for the boy was unlike any emotion she had

had for her own children: there was less of concern in it, something strangely akin to exultation. John felt something of the same nature. Abigail suggested:

"Perhaps it's the sense of continuity? Now we know there will be another generation. The Smith-Adams blood will go on after we are gone."

It was a peculiar coincidence, Abigail learned later, that Royall Tyler too had had an offspring. In New York, shortly after Nab had had hers in London: the first comedy, called *The Contrast,* ever written and produced by Americans.

Nab had dismissed Royall Tyler from her mind completely. Not so her mother, for Abigail received mail from Massachusetts telling her that Tyler had never accepted Nab's dismissal, that in fact he kept protesting that he had never received her letter terminating their engagement and was convinced that he had been used badly by the Adams family. He was not loath to unburden himself to this effect to all New England.

The details of his accomplishment seeped in. After mooning about his mother's house, Tyler had gone to New York, fraternized with the American Company centering around the famous comedian Thomas Wignell. He had watched the production of Sheridan's *School for Scandal,* then locked himself in his boardinghouse room and written his play. Wignell and the other actors liked it so much that they mounted a handsome production at the John Street Theatre. According to one informant, *The Contrast* was brilliantly written and had been an instantaneous success, being repeated a number of times to enthusiastic audiences. The company was planning to play the piece in Philadelphia, Baltimore and even to invade sacrosanct Boston, where Theatricals were still illegal. Though the author's name was not on the playbill it was well known, and Royall Tyler was considered to have begun a new school of American writing. He was even now composing his second piece, a comic opera to be called *May-Day in Town, or New York in an Uproar*. Production was promised in the same John Street Theatre.

Abigail was not taken unaware by the report; she had always believed Tyler to be a gifted man. Many of the poems and scenes from possible plays which he had read aloud in the sitting parlor in Braintree had been of high if youthful quality. Now apparently he was settling down to a literary discipline.

Abigail was fond of William Smith, the more so because of this dear little boy studying his hands with intent wonder in his crib. There was only one niggling doubt in her mind, and this she took to her husband as she related to him the story of Tyler's astounding success.

"John, it's now six months since you wrote to Congress announcing your determination to return home. You've not changed your mind?"

"No. I'm resolute about it."

"Then Nab and Colonel Smith will be leaving with us?"

"Not necessarily. I'm writing the Congress not to appoint another minister in my place until England sends an ambassador to the Congress and agrees to a commercial treaty. I recommended that William remain as chargé d'affaires."

"But if he must return home, what does he work at? He loves the army best, but America has no army. Though the letters from his family in New York are cordial about receiving Nab and the baby, they evidently have no enterprise for the Colonel to enter, and not enough land to enable him to farm successfully."

"I tried to persuade him to study the law here in the English courts and he refused. However he is young, personable, has hundreds of friends throughout the states. Surely one of us will get him placed properly."

"I trust so."

"I'll write again to Secretary Jay. While you're worrying, what about giving some thought to your own poor husband, who is going to be jobless next spring?"

"I'm afraid I can't waste much worry on you, Mr. Minister. With Tom Jefferson remaining in Paris that will leave you the best political mind in all thirteen of the states."

John was happy writing his second volume about the Italian city-states and the analysis of what made a successful and stable, as against an unsuccessful and unstable, republic. The convention had begun its meeting in Philadelphia, ostensibly to repair the Articles of Confederation. However the meetings were secret and it was far too soon for any news to reach England. In the meanwhile American credit continued to founder, and so John went again to Holland, where he had a masterly touch with the Dutch bankers. He was able to borrow another million guilders at five per cent interest.

Abigail took the boy for walks in the Grosvenor Square park in his pram. In the fine weather she and Nab drove out into the country. The weeks passed. In Massachusetts the political climate grew increasingly stormy. The people were once again on the march, bringing to a head the problems that were besetting all the country's citizenry.

Beginning the previous fall, the harassed farmers of Massachusetts had asked the legislature for two measures: one authorizing paper money, the other putting a stop to the foreclosures on homes and farms. The legislature was dominated by lawyers and businessmen of a conservative persuasion; they adjourned without passing either measure, whereupon the populace rose in righteous indignation. There were inflamed town meetings, then a convention was called at Hatfield which declared the Massachusetts legislature motivated by selfishness, protested the inequitable taxes which fell heavily on the poorer classes, and demanded that the courts be closed until conditions improved and the farmers could pay their debts. The convention called by the farmers of Hampshire County had been seeking legal redresses to their grievances; but there were many who felt that only action could gain them relief. In towns like Worcester, Concord, Great Barrington and Northampton they prevented the courts from sitting, let prisoners out of jail, marched in numbers from three to fifteen hundred on the courthouses to make sure the judges and juries would not try cases. Governor James Bowdoin called out the Massachusetts militia, some sixteen hundred men. At this point the command of the protesters came under Captain Daniel Shays, who had fought well and honorably in the Revolution and who had lost his farm for back debts.

The militiamen were outnumbered. They did not attempt to fire on Shays's well-disciplined troops, who forcibly prevented the court from opening at Springfield. When Massachusetts declared Captain Shays and his followers outlaws, they set up a plan to seize guns from the United States arsenal at Springfield, move on to Boston and force the legislature to rescind the tax-debt laws at gun point. Once again Massachusetts raised an army of volunteers, the two forces met before the Springfield arsenal, the militia fired their cannon, several of Shays's men were hit and his force disbanded. Additional volunteer troops arrived under General Lincoln, also a Revolutionary War hero, strong enough to crush Shays's rebellion and arrest its ringleaders.

Samuel Adams wanted the leaders of the revolt executed. Though Abigail and John were distressed by the uprisings, fearing they might injure the federal government, they were hard pressed to understand the vindictiveness of Cousin Samuel's attitude. Slowly Abigail realized that Cousin Samuel would consider anyone who rose against his independent government an enemy. She was grateful that John had no such bloodthirsty instincts. He wrote strongly against the uprising, stating that it had to be put down with the firmest hand possible, but she had never heard him speak of harsh punishment for the leaders. John knew that to prevent further disturbances a return to economic prosperity was needed.

Two letters arrived from Cotton Tufts telling them that the Vassall-Borland house could be bought for twenty-seven hundred dollars. Royall Tyler had sold off some of the land for cash. The house had now reverted to the Borlands. Tufts was acidulous in his comments about Tyler's neglect of the property:

"The late occupant's time and attention is so fully taken up at New York in writing comedies for which he is become famous, that whether . . . we purchase the farm out of his hands cannot be an object of equal importance as that of acquiring the fame of a writer of comedies. . . ."

John told Abigail to have Cotton buy the house and lands. Cotton secured them at the price he had stipulated.

At the end of June a Captain Ramsay came to the embassy with little Polly Jefferson, younger sister to Patsy. Jefferson had written Abigail asking that she take the child in. Polly, just a month short of nine, her pretty face swimming in a sea of tears, was clinging to Captain Ramsay's hands as though she were about to be sold into slavery. The captain had to sneak out of the embassy by a rear door.

Abigail took Polly up to her bedroom and washed the girl's face, which strongly resembled both Patsy's and her father's, while telling her stories about Patsy in Paris.

"Now, Polly, I never saw your sister cry."

"She has her papa with her."

"I shall show you a picture of your papa. We had it painted when he was here by Mr. Brown, an American."

She brought out the portrait of Thomas Jefferson, a fine likeness with considerable vitality. Polly was unmoved.

"What's the matter, Polly?"

"I don't recognize him."

"Well, you're going to know him very soon now."

"Will you take me to him?"

Abigail hesitated, then replied:

"Yes, if there is no other way. But I will write to him immediately and ask him to come here to London, and then we'll all go on a trip through the country together. Wouldn't that be nice?"

"I don't know," replied Polly doggedly. "I've never been on a trip with one family, let alone two."

"Tomorrow or the next day I will take you to see the dancing dogs and high-wire walking at Sadler's Wells."

By the next morning Polly was all smiles. Abigail took the child to her mantuamaker to have an English dress and coat made. Polly enjoyed this. She asked Abigail if she might call her Mother.

Abigail began a hectic exchange of letters with Jefferson, assuring him that Polly could stay in the embassy as long as he wanted her to but that she felt very strongly he should come for the girl. She was determined that Polly must not travel from London to Paris in the hands of still another stranger. Jefferson had just returned to Paris from a tour of southern France and Italy.

A Frenchman by the name of Petit showed up at the house in Grosvenor Square. He was Jefferson's *maître d'hôtel,* a kind man and to be trusted. However he could not speak a single word of English. His instructions were to bring Polly back to Paris as quickly as possible. Abigail was aghast. She went to John's office, where he was completing work on his second volume.

"John, I simply cannot put Polly in the charge of a man who cannot exchange a single word with her, and let them take that week-long trip to Paris."

John gazed at her intently. "I agree, but what can we do? Would you want me to take her?"

"No, I think I should do it. I've already promised her that I would."

"It will mean a two-week trip for you. You'll have to come back alone."

Polly was bitterly unhappy. Abigail assured her that she would not let her go with Petit until she had heard from her father again. In the meanwhile she took the girl on daily excursions and to the bookstore, where she let her select another volume, for she was an avid reader.

By the end of a week Petit had worn out his patience. He did not like London, and he had been given a job to do. In a rush of French he showed Abigail that he had already bought two places on the stage for Dover. He cried quite volubly that the money could not be wasted, that it was not proper for Mrs. Adams to keep him from doing his duty.

"If Polly agrees to go, I will consent."

Polly was reconciled. "I know I have to go with Petit. I won't be able to help crying, so please don't ask me to."

"Think of this journey as just a bridge taking you from one part of your family to another," consoled Abigail.

Polly's face lighted in an intelligent smile. Her books were packed in one valise, her new clothes in another. She called to the Adams family from the carriage, "See, I'm not crying. Good-by, Friend Abigail."

In July, John sent the second volume of his *Defence* to the printer. He surprised Abigail by suggesting that they take a month's vacation to Devonshire, Southampton, Exeter, a sentimental pilgrimage to Weymouth to see what the original of Abigail's little town looked like. They would search out whatever Cranches, of whom there were many still living in England, they could find. It was to be a complete vacation and, as John explained it:

"Probably our last journey through England. Or anywhere else. Once we reach home we're going to stay there. Forever."

10

John's extreme haste and work under pressure proved to have been justified. Mail reaching them from the United States indicated that copies of the *Defence* had reached the members of the convention in good time. Editions were immediately printed in Boston, Philadelphia and New York. Although many disagreed with his approval of a limited monarchy and the need for a strong "*first magistrate, a head, a chief*" without which "the body politic cannot subsist, any more than the animal body, without a head," most of the delegates read the book carefully. It served as the starting point for probing discussions of the questions John had wanted raised. He had assured Abigail that his book would be the only comprehensive political survey available to the meeting, and so it appeared. While still three thousand miles away, immolated and isolated in a useless post, John Adams had been in Philadelphia behind the locked doors of the convention just as surely as though he had been a delegate from Massachusetts.

At the beginning of November they received from their faithful correspondent, Elbridge Gerry, a copy of the proposed new Constitution. A similar document was addressed to Thomas Jefferson. John Adams forwarded it to Paris at once.

As John took the papers out of their packet Abigail gingerly fingered the scant sheets between her thumb and right forefinger, murmuring:

"It can't be very long. Wouldn't they need more pages to make a full and complete Constitution?"

"Not necessarily. The shorter and clearer the better."

If her years in Braintree had been dominated by loneliness, their time in London had been characterized by frustration. Now as they sat together at John's desk, Briesler carrying fresh logs for the fire, John was pale and near to trembling, Abigail intent.

"Here, you read the opening," he said.

"Very well."

She read in a clear, firm voice. "'We the people of the United States, in order to form a more perfect union, establish justice, ensure domestic tranquillity, provide for the common defence, promote the general welfare, and secure the blessings of liberty to ourselves and our posterity, do ordain and establish this Constitution for the United States of America.'"

"Excellent!" John cried. "I couldn't have done better myself."

"'All legislative powers herein granted shall be vested in a Congress of the United States, which shall consist of a Senate and House of Representatives . . .'"

He seized the papers, hurriedly leafed through to Article Two, then read in his high pulsating voice:

"'The executive power shall be vested in a President of the United States of America. He shall hold his office during the term of four years, and, together with the Vice President, chosen for the same term, be elected as follows. . . .'"

He stopped reading aloud, swiftly swept through the balance of the article, his heavy head bobbing up and down in short jerky nods of approval. When he had completed the entire section once, he combined a reading with an analysis for Abigail: The President was to be commander-in-chief of the army, navy and the militia; he was to have power, "by and with the advice and consent of the Senate," to make treaties, provided two thirds of the senators present concurred; he was to have the power to nominate and appoint ambassadors, judges of the Supreme Court, and all other officers of the United States, again with the advice and consent of the Senate. He was to have the power to convene both Houses, to give Congress "information of the state of the Union, and recommend to their consideration, such measures as he shall judge necessary and expedient."

There was a moment of silence.

"The convention has written the articles as though you had been chairman of the committee," Abigail declared.

"Not quite," he said, though he was flushed with pleasure; "there's no mention here of the President's right to have executive councilors at the head of each department, whom he appoints and who serve him as assistants. Let's see what they've done about the legislature and judiciary."

The representatives, as well as direct taxes, would be apportioned among the several states according to their population. This House was to have the power to select its own Speaker and other officers, and have the sole power of impeachment. The Senate, on the other hand, was to be composed of two senators from each state, chosen by its local legislature.

"Here is an interesting development," said John. "Because the Senate is a new body it has to be given dignity and status. The elected Vice President is to sit as the president and chairman of the Senate, though he is to have no vote except in case of a tie."

"What are the Vice President's other duties?" she asked.

John swept through the document, then looked up.

"Nothing that I can find. But if he is well chosen he will make sure that the deliberations of the Senate are conducted on a high plain and that the proper legislation moves through that body with proper speed."

They interrupted their study for dinner, then continued, sometimes with sharp exclamations of pleasure, sometimes with considerable disappointment. For John the great lack of the document was a Declaration of Rights. There was no mention whatever of the freedom of the press, of speech, of assembly, of religious choice. When he voiced his regrets Abigail knitted her brows tightly.

"But isn't it a strange omission? You wrote a Declaration of Rights for the Massachusetts Constitution. George Mason wrote one for the Virginia Constitution."

"It is a grievous error, one that must be remedied immediately."

"Does that mean that you won't approve this Constitution?"

"Bless my soul, no! It's better that the states approve it now, and we make the addition of a Declaration of Rights later, than send it back into a convention again. The lack will certainly make its passage more difficult, but it is a sin of omission, not commission. So far I have not found anything in this Constitution that will not work for the best interests of a republic. Look, for example, how well they've done with Article Three. 'The judicial power of the United States shall be vested in one Supreme Court, and in such Inferior Courts as the Congress may, from time to time, ordain and establish.' "

He turned to the last page, glancing down at the list of signers. Many of the men he had worked with in the earlier Congresses. Even Benjamin Franklin had been there.

They could not sleep that night. John kept jumping up to light his reading lamp by the side of his bed and thumb through the document, looking for a specific item, checking the wording of a phrase or paragraph. Around two in the morning he began to worry about the powers of the Senate. Without looking to see if Abigail were asleep or awake, he declared:

"Abigail, giving the Senate the right to approve of the executive's appointments would make the President less independent, cut away from his power to act in his best judgment for the common interest of the country. I think that Senates and Assemblies should have nothing to do with executive power."

"But, John, isn't this just an architect's drawing?" she reassured him in sleepy tones. "As experience puts flesh and blood on the skeleton, these problems will work themselves out."

He was out of bed, pacing in his nightshirt, his hands locked behind his back.

"I only pray that the states will ratify it in quick order. It seems to be admirably calculated to preserve the Union, to increase affection and to bring us all into the same mode of thinking."

The following weeks were filled with excitements, all of them good. There seemed to be an updraft in their private affairs and in the affairs of their nation. It was heartily welcome.

Cotton Tufts wrote that they now were legal owners of the Borland house. The news brought a fresh sense of anticipation about returning home. Johnny became apprenticed to a lawyer in Newburyport. Impassioned letters went back and forth between the Adamses, Thomas Jefferson in Paris, their political friends in Boston and Philadelphia, everyone having his particular reservations about the Constitution, but all enthusiastic.

Thomas Jefferson, to John's surprise, was fearful that the two Houses of Congress would not be adequate to the management of either foreign or federal affairs. He was also concerned that the President seemed a bad edition of a Polish King. "He may be elected from four years to four years for life. Reason and experience prove to us that a chief magistrate, so continuable, is an office for life. . . . I wish that at the end of the four years they had made him forever ineligible a second time."

"Tom Jefferson is afraid of the one, I of the few," said John. "We agree perfectly that the many should have a full fair representation, but Jefferson is apprehensive of monarchy while I fear the aristocracy. I would have given more power to the President and less to the Senate. If we get our ablest man chosen to the presidency, I do not see why he could not continue through life. The people always have the right to defeat him, at four-year intervals, if he should turn bad."

Even the English, many of whom had been unrelenting opponents of American independence, were responding well. Abigail wrote to Cotton Tufts:

"The form of government by the late convention is esteemed here as a sublime work. They add that it is so good that they are persuaded that the Americans will not accept it. It may admit of some amendment, but it is certainly a great federal structure."

It had been a work well done.

December of 1787 brought them a sense of completion of their duty. John finished the third volume of *Defence* and sent it to the printer, anxious that, when the Declaration of Rights was called for and the constitutional government put into motion, this volume too would be available for discussion in the journals and amongst the legislators. At almost the identical moment he received word from Secretary of Foreign Affairs John Jay that the Congress had accepted his resignation as minister plenipotentiary upon the completion of his commission, which would be in February.

The time had come to prepare for their return to Braintree. Abigail drew rough sketches of the rooms of the Borland house as she remembered them, then walked about the embassy gazing at her assembled furnishings from Holland, France and England. For the sitting parlor, where she would put her red furniture, she thought a French gray paint would be best. If the mahogany paneling was not greatly abused, she would leave it in its native state, but she intended to cut two windows in the wall overlooking the garden. For the bedchamber over it, where she would install Nab's green furniture, she wanted a matching green wallpaper. She asked Cotton Tufts that iron backs be provided for the chimneys, brass locks for the doors, and all repairs made as quickly as possible so that they might move their furniture directly from Quincy Harbor into the house.

With the beginning of the new year, 1788, things grew more pleasant for them than they had been at any time during their residence. News came that Delaware, Pennsylvania and New Jersey had ratified the Constitution after only two months of discussion; Georgia, Connecticut and Massachusetts looked as though they might do so soon. New York had refused even to call a ratifying convention, but the best men were waging brilliant polemic battles for the ratification.

There was a speech in Parliament in favor of the United States by Lord Grenville. Lord Carmarthen summoned John to ask him whether, since he liked the Constitution and assumed it would be adopted, the time had not arrived when the two countries could begin serious discussions of the commercial treaty. When John reported this to Abigail she cried:

"A fine time to tell us, indeed. Just as we are about to leave."

"It was a bon voyage gesture."

In the embassy Abigail began the major task of packing. The furniture had to be crated so that the gold leaf and delicate fabrics would be amply protected against the long sea voyage; her collection of glassware adequately wrapped; John's books fitted by categories into numbered cases, with lists detailing their contents. Esther, who on and off had been in ill-health, insisted on doing her simple duties. When she fell ill again with a consistent nausea, Nab made an observation. Abigail asked:

"Esther, please forgive my intrusion but could it be possible that you are in circumstances?"

Esther was not offended. She replied, "No, madam. It's just some of the old sicknesses combining on me."

Abigail let it go but after another few weeks there was no longer any possibility of being mistaken.

"Esther, it's Briesler, isn't it?"

"Yes, ma'am, we've been in love. Ever since Auteuil."

"Then why didn't you marry?"

"Because by the time we wanted to be married we was here in England, and we didn't want to be married in the Episcopal Church."

"Perhaps I could have got special permission for you, as we did for Miss Nab."

Esther threw her a severe look.

"Begging your pardon, madam, the Bishop of St. Asaph would marry the daughter of the American minister. He would not come to the embassy to marry two servants."

Abigail flushed.

"We decided to wait until we got home to Braintree and be married there."

"Don't you think it's getting a little late for that?"

Esther shook her head sadly. "Then I guess we'll have to be married in their church. It won't be illegal in the United States, will it?"

"No, of course not. We'll have a little family party here at the house."

John left for a farewell ceremonial mission to Holland. He had not gone to secure another loan, but Jefferson had joined him there, urging him to try. He secured another million guilders for the United States.

She had made plans to have all of their possessions put aboard Captain Callahan's ship, the *Lucretia*, in February, but there were constant delays: the boxes and crates were not the right sizes, the packing materials failed to appear. By the eleventh of March she was still working desperately to get the last of her clothes, silver and dishware out of the Grosvenor Square house. Captain Callahan informed her that she had another week to complete the task.

She managed to accomplish it, though her activity was slowed when she learned that her uncle Isaac had died, having survived her aunt Elizabeth by only a year. He had been her stoutest friend. She grieved that she could not have said a last fond good-by to him.

John returned, the drays lined up in front of the house for several days to cart away his voluminous collections of art works, furnishings and the substantial library collected over a decade. With that they moved back into the Bath Hotel, from whence she had started her English sojourn.

There was one last disappointment. Despite John's many enthusiastic letters to the Congress they were not able to secure a post for Colonel William Smith. Neither as chargé d'affaires here in London, nor anywhere else. Colonel Smith had been sent to London to serve as secretary of legation to Minister John Adams, and he was being recalled as of the same moment. Colonel Smith decided that he had best not wait for the Adamses, or take ship to Boston. He wanted to get to New York as quickly as possible so that he could investigate his possibilities of appointments in the new government.

The Smiths were packed and ready to leave for Falmouth. It was a sad parting.

Their last audience with King George III was also a touching one. Abigail and John had often heard the short, plump, full-jowled sovereign described as a fool. His capacities were limited, he seemed to care more about husbandry than statecraft, but he had been consistently warm-hearted to Minister Adams and Mrs. Adams. He had gone to considerable pains to let them know that he admired them.

"Madam, I have always remembered your husband's first observation to me. When I suggested that perhaps he was not the most attached of his countrymen to France, Mr. Adams answered, 'I have no attachment but to my own country.'"

"And you, Your Majesty, answered, 'An honest man will never have any other.'"

King George saluted her cheek. They backed out of his presence.

Going down the steps of the palace to their carriage, Abigail felt an impulse to tears.

"Do you know how far back my mind goes? To the first Sunday supper you had in our house, when I quoted so admiringly from the King's first speech to Parliament. I thought him a Patriot King."

"In fact you admired him so much that I became jealous. I wrote to you, 'Although my allegiance has been hitherto inviolate, I shall endeavor all in my power to foment rebellion.'"

"So you did, John, so you did."

Four days later Abigail and John left for Portsmouth, hoping the winds would be favorable for an early departure. Everything was already on board; they had with them only a portmanteau of fresh linens and night clothes. Riding southward through the gently rolling country of Surrey, the spring crops just a line of brilliant green buttons studded through the buttonholes of raised ridges, Abigail said:

"I'm looking forward to making butter and cheese, and tending my garden."

He asked lightly, "Are you certain you can go back to the simple life?"

"Ah, I know of their fears in Braintree: that I shall come home with examples of luxury and extravagance. But I promise my dear countrywomen they shall have none from me. What about you, John?"

He turned from her, gazed out the window as the carriage which had carried them through France and England moved slowly over a rise into a woods beyond. When he turned back his face was serious but his eyes were as light green as the spring grasses of southern England.

"I mean to retire to Braintree as a private man. No one need fear that I will become a competitor with them for office."

"Surely you could have something?"

"I doubt me. I've always dealt too openly and candidly with my countrymen to be popular."

"New England knows your worth."

"Perhaps. But I've expended it in fourteen continuous years of service to our government. Besides, there are criticisms of my monarchial principles."

"They will dissipate."

"I can never conceal a sentiment of my heart from the people which I think it is in their interest or happiness to be acquainted with, even though I should forfeit by it the highest offices in the United States."

She studied his face intently.

"I believe you mean that, John."

"I do. I have been out of my own country for ten years now. I'll need time to settle in. I want to put our farm back in good working order, add a library to the Borland house when I've been paid what is due me in salary by the government. If we find ourselves in need of money to complete the boys' education, I shall find some special law work that I can handle. I have no further ambition, except to live out my life quietly with my family, as a farmer, and perhaps a writer of history."

She sat quietly, the wheels braking noisily beneath her while the carriage descended a hill. Then she murmured:

"We have had spirited years. Now we'll be together again in our own land. God has sent us a good deliverance."

BOOK EIGHT

WOMB OF MORNING

1

THE firing of cannon shattered their dream of peaceful retirement. Save for the birth of Esther's baby, the eight-week crossing had been uneventful. Now they were standing at the prow of the *Lucretia* with the Light just coming into view. After eight years John was nostalgic at the sight of his beloved Massachusetts; Abigail, after four, was barely able to suppress her emotion at the thought that she would see her sons again. The entire battery of artillery at the Castle was fired in their honor. As the ship approached her moorings the official barge left its dock carrying the Secretary of State and a welcoming committee sent by Governor John Hancock to congratulate the Adamses on their arrival and to invite them to stay at his home. There was to be a state dinner.

When they stepped onto the pier two thousand Bostonians cried their huzzas, thronging about Governor Hancock's carriage. The bells of Boston were ringing. The booming of the Castle cannon had summoned the rest of the city. They lined the streets, men, women and children waving handkerchiefs and hats as the triumphal carriage with its four matched bays rode slowly through the streets.

Abigail slipped her hand into John's. He gave a puzzled shake of his head.

"I never expected any part of it. Remembering my modest accomplishments and spectacular failures . . ."

"You looked better to the Massachusetts than you did to yourself."

The carriage drew up in front of the Hancock mansion on Beacon Street across from the Common. At the top of the stoop in front of the open door stood Governor Hancock in full regalia. His face was still handsome but his lean six-foot figure was bent from years of the gout.

His wife, Dorothy, had managed to remain the reigning beauty of Boston despite the fact that she had turned forty. Behind them in the noble hall that ran from the front door to the back of the house stood their old friend, now Lieutenant Governor, Benjamin Lincoln, who had been a general in the Revolution; Robert Treat Paine, now Attorney General of Massachusetts, with his warm welcoming smile; Samuel Adams, white-haired and dour, presently holding no official position but having managed to mend his fences with Governor Hancock. Surrounding them in a reception circle were the other heads of the Massachusetts government.

Henry Knox thrust his solid three-hundred-pound bulk forward, booming in an artillery voice:

"I have the best welcome of all, letters from your daughter in New York. They arrived safe after a good passage."

There were messages from Charley and Tommy as well. They would be in from Cambridge the following day.

Dorothy Quincy Hancock rescued her cousin from the political reception and took her up to the guest room over the great parlor. It was decorated in yellow damask, the mahogany four-poster, window curtains, upholstered chair and ten small chairs lining the wall, all of yellow damask. Mirrors reflected the light from the fireplace. Dorothy asked about her sister, Esther Sewall.

"Poor child," she murmured, "she never wanted to leave home."

Abigail had a luxurious soak in Dorothy's five-foot-long bathtub. The Hancock servants had taken John's ceremonial suit and Abigail's satin-striped *demi-saison* to be pressed.

There were fifty at dinner: the Governor's Council, the heads of the departments, Boston's leading selectmen, a variety of old friends including Francis Dana, now associate justice of the Massachusetts Supreme Court, Elbridge Gerry. Their ladies were gowned in silks and chambray gauzes. So many toasts were drunk to the returning Adamses that Abigail feared she might grow tipsy. She tried to catch John's eye as he talked excitedly to the men around him. Was this sumptuous banquet and resplendent official welcome a tribute for past services or an initiation dinner?

They had arrived home at a particularly auspicious moment. Before departing from London they had known of only three states which had ratified the Constitution: Delaware first, then Pennsylvania and New Jersey. News of the ratification by Georgia, Connecticut and Massachusetts had not reached them. Now they learned that Maryland had ratified in April and South Carolina in May. Only one more vote was needed for the federal government to come into being. The word in Boston was that their neighboring state, New Hampshire, was certain to sign in a matter of days, that Virginia too was poised to sign and that New York could come in within weeks. John Adams had reached home in June 1788, when the nation he had worked so long and heroically to create was about to be born.

"And that," Abigail decided in her mind, "is what I am celebrating at this reception."

The following day John was received in the Representatives' Hall of the State House by the General Court. Both Houses of the legislature assembled to pay him honor. A permanent chair had been assigned for his use "whenever he may please to attend the debates." The Acting Speaker of the House read a paper announcing that John Adams had been elected a representative to the Congress for a one-year term.

Back in the Hancock great parlor they found Charley and Tommy. Abigail was determined to gather both her little boys into her arms and cover them with kisses. But at the threshold she saw two young men garbed in spotless white shirts and gray smallclothes, their hair worn long and full over their heads. She stared, transfixed. Charley was now eighteen and a junior at Harvard College. His face, a replica of his sister Nab's, handsome and aristocratic, wore a warm and mischievous grin. Tommy, at fifteen and a half, was shorter, more compact; his face had the same plain open expression she remembered.

The moment for embraces passed. The boys approached their parents tentatively, bowed, shook hands, murmured their pleasure at seeing their mama and papa again. Johnny, they said, was well and would be in Boston as soon as he could find transportation from Newburyport, where he was apprenticed to Theophilus Parsons, a leading lawyer. They all seemed subdued here in the governor's house. Charley whispered:

"We can't wait till we all meet at home, Ma."

That evening when they had retired to their chamber and were resting on the handsome damask sofa, Abigail read from the report in the day's issue of the *Massachusetts Centinel:*

" 'Every countenance wore the expressions of joy—and everyone testified that approbation of the eminent services his Excellency has rendered his country, in a manner becoming freemen, federalists, and men alive to the sensations of gratitude.' "

"Most handsome," John murmured. His cheeks had been flushed since the first cannonading from the Castle. "I know that a man should not be rewarded for doing his plain duty, but I must say in all honesty that I enjoy it."

"Do I reship my furniture to New York?" she teased.

"Assuredly not."

"Might you find the Senate more tempting?"

"That has been proposed to me by friends. I think not. The Senate will be a smaller body but it is still part of the legislature. I have served my years in the legislature."

The following morning Francis Dana came to call. He had been ill and looked poorly.

"As an old friend, may I presume to make a suggestion?" he asked.

"Of course."

"Then I would urge you to repair to New York immediately. The Congress committee which will set up the apparatus of government will be appointed at the beginning of July. You must become a leader of those discussions. You have been out of the country for ten years now. Though we know you in New England, the rest of the country knows you less well. In this way you will become known to all and put yourself into position for the highest offices in the new government."

"You are not suggesting that I can be elected President?" John asked in mock seriousness.

"George Washington will be President. The people want it. They credit him with winning the war. As President of the convention his was the most ameliorating voice. Without him I doubt me we could have secured ratification. He is a genius in his ability to persuade people of divergent points of view to work together harmoniously. The idea of a federal union is acceptable to people who fear federation only because they know that General Washington will become our President."

A silence followed his outburst. Dana continued after a moment.

"But you see where this places you, John?"

That night as they lay in the four-poster in the spacious guest room, Abigail propped her head inquisitively on one elbow.

"When New Hampshire ratifies, how will our national elections commence?"

"We're not certain yet. For the House and Senate it's simple: each state legislature selects its two senators. The representatives will be elected by popular vote in each state: one representative for every thirty thousand of the population. That means over one million men may vote for their representatives in Congress. . . ."

"You never did accede to my request to remember the ladies," she murmured.

He blushed. "Even though women do not have the vote they will live in a republic where the laws of free men will protect them. . . ."

"Yes, John. . . . What about the President and Vice President?"

"The Constitution says each state shall appoint, in such manner as the legislature may direct, a number of electors equal to the whole number of senators and representatives to which the state may be entitled in the Congress. These electors will vote for the President and Vice President. The federal government can commence shortly after all the ballots are counted at the seat of the government."

"Which will be?"

"The Lord alone knows! From what I gather, sentiment is evenly divided between New York and Philadelphia. There will be anguished bloodletting before that issue is decided."

"Who nominates the candidates for the presidency and vice presidency? How much bloodletting will there be before that issue is decided?"

He jumped out of bed, began to pace the bedroom floor in his ankle-length linen nightgown, hands gripped tightly behind his back. She noticed how far his hairline had receded, how the oval bald spot gleamed in the lamplight.

"There are no nominating methods prescribed. Groups of men who want to advance a candidate will meet informally and chart procedures. So will the government leaders in each state. They will work to have those electors selected who will vote for their favorites. Individuals or groups will be free to advertise their choices in the newspapers. Sodalities will arise in each state to persuade their neighbors. I won't know until it's over and study the results as a historian just how the process will work. All I know at this point is that the Massachusetts General Court will choose two electors at large, then they will select eight more names from a list of twenty-four sent up from our eight congressional districts. These ten men, all of them outside of government, will meet in the Massachusetts Senate Chamber and by majority vote select men for the President and Vice President."

She did not consider it discreet to ask if he also knew who their final choices would be.

2

They were anxious to move into their new house. John preceded her to check its condition. Abigail was to use the day shopping and waiting for John Quincy.

"The governor has offered to escort us to Braintree," John announced, "attended by his light horse. Braintree had planned to form a reception at the Milton Bridge to greet us. But I have declined. I know my fellow townsmen too well. They can accept Boston honoring me; it's an honoring of themselves. But if they come to the Milton Bridge for a ceremonial and see us descend from Hancock's resplendent carriage they'll begin to think: 'Perhaps we've gone too far. Mr. Adams thinks well enough of himself already.' Your cousin William Smith has offered me the loan of a horse. I shall ride quietly into my birthplace like any other returning citizen."

He left shortly after dawn. By eight Abigail was out in one of the Hancock carriages to visit the shops. The June sun had clear warmth as she caught a view of the dozens of ships rolling gently at anchor in the bay. She breathed deeply, relishing the familiar scent of salt against her nostrils. Boston, in yet another of its fires, had the year before suffered its worst disaster since the Revolution. More than a hundred buildings on Beach Street leading toward the Neck had gone up in flames. So had the Hollis Street Meeting House. But Bostonians were indefatigable; by now the burned-over areas had been rebuilt, the Charles River Bridge had been completed; and the Hollis Street Meeting House had been redesigned by young Charles Bulfinch in an architectural style eschewing the old-fashioned God's Barn in favor of a blending of the classical traditions of England and New England, with a domed interior, twin cupolas and a Tuscan portico.

When she returned at half after ten she found Johnny waiting. This time, even after the separation of three years, he did not seem to her to have changed. His clothes were disheveled and his hair in disarray but he had been on the road for three hours. What Abigail had forgotten was what a tender soul he was.

"My dear mama. How good to see you. I feel as though I am being reunited with a near and dear friend after a long absence."

She held her son against her bosom, hid her head on his shoulder.

As a girl she had yearned for a friend, quoted to herself her favorite line, "A friend is worth all hazards we can run." She had found John Adams. They had been dearest friends all their married lives, running all manner of hazards. And now, a generation later, she had found another dear friend: her oldest son. She had run hazards for him too: let him cross the ocean during a dangerous war to be separated from her for five years while he traveled Europe all the way up to the Czar's Russia; then had sent him back to his necessary schooling for three more years of separation. But her son loved her deeply, as she did him.

Johnny was talking against her ear.

". . . absolutely no transportation. For two whole days, while I knew you were here . . . I kept crying the line from *Richard III*, 'A horse! a horse! my kingdom for a horse!' But, Mama, I have a whole month to spend with you and Papa. Mr. Parsons says I've made myself ill from working too hard."

The Borland house in Braintree, after their Auteuil palace and the town house in Grosvenor Square, was not the mansion she had remembered it. Its low ceilings made it seem more like a wren's cottage. Cotton Tufts had continued the building of a new kitchen ell attached to the house, the frame of which had been begun by Royall Tyler. An extra bedroom on the second floor and two on the third were being added. Cotton had pushed the work along, hoping to have the house renovated for their return, but Abigail arrived to find the place swarming with carpenters, masons and painters. Nothing was finished. She managed to clear one bedroom for herself and another for her three sons. The crates of furniture were carried up to the attic unopened.

She saw that the kitchen ell was not being built the way she wanted. Fortunately the carpenters were able to make the structural changes she desired. She also had them cut the large windows in the wall of the mahogany-paneled room, one on either side of the fireplace overlooking the sun-flooded west garden where she planted the rosebushes she had brought from England. The dark mahogany was then painted white. John built his own bookshelves in what had been the dining room, converting it to his library. The bedrooms were freshly wallpapered. When the crates in the attic were opened it was found that during the eight-week passage the gilt had chipped off the chairs and some of the coverings had become mildewed. Abigail cried:

"I wish I had left all the furniture behind."

In three weeks they made the house habitable, bringing over their marital bed and John's pigeonhole desk from his original office. Friday, July 11, 1788, was Johnny's twenty-first birthday. Their relatives would be coming to celebrate on Sunday.

Friday at sundown, John and the three boys bathed in the creek. Esther, whose baby was thriving, filled the ancestral oak tub in the kitchen for Abigail's bath. Then, dressed in their best clothes, they sat on the red damask chairs with Johnny on the red velvet sofa acknowledging their toasts with his raised glass of Madeira.

The Adamses glowed with pride over Johnny. He had been graduated high in his class and invited to give the Phi Beta Kappa address in Cambridge in September before the notables of New England. A sensitive person, he imitated his father in many of his tones and gestures.

"*Alors*, Johnny, how does it feel to be a man?" John asked.

Johnny answered wryly:

"It emancipates me from the yoke of parental authority which I have never felt, and places me on my own feet which have not strength enough to support me."

Charley and Tommy adored him but they could not have been more different in temperament if they had come from another set of parents. Charley was gay, full of a sunny humor. He was the handsomest of the three and knew it. He had been the favorite at the dancing classes at Haverhill while staying with the Shaws. There was a wisp of a rumor that he had been running with the crowd in Boston that liked gaming, drink and the ladies. Tommy was the most stolid of the boys and the plainest. Seeing what a success Charley had been as a prankster, he had deliberately set out to make himself amusing.

Briesler announced dinner. They went across the entrance hall to the dining room become library. The room was permeated by the smells of John's new bookshelves, his hundreds of books neatly arranged. The table Abigail had had made in London was set with the family's finest linen, silver and French glassware. The three sons stood in a semicircle behind their mother's chair while she sat down. Esther brought in a rare roast of beef from the kitchen.

As they sipped from a bottle of French wine, Johnny asked the key question:

"Father, have you decided what you will do?"

All eyes were on the master of the household.

"What is to become of me? At my age this ought not to be a question; but it is. I will tell you, my dear sons, that it appears to me your father does not stand very high in the esteem, admiration or respect of his country. I have got quite out of circulation."

"But, Papa," interrupted Tommy, "remember the cannon and church bells, Governor Hancock and the crowds cheering you when you came home."

John hesitated, decided to speak his heart to his young.

"Don't be fooled by my old friend Governor Hancock. He staged a theatrical show the better to conceal that he considers us in competition. Any office I may aspire to he has wanted longer and harder."

"Do you aspire, Father?" Charley asked.

Abigail listened to her husband conversing with himself. He had refused to accept the appointment to the Congress.

"Charley, the public judgment and the public voice seem to have decreed to others every public office that I could accept with honor. No alternative is left to me but private life at home, or to go again abroad."

"John, surely you wouldn't!" Abigail was amazed.

"No, I wouldn't accept another foreign post. But I will tell you one thing, my esteemed family, you will hear of me on a trading voyage to the East Indies or to Essequebo before you will hear of my descending as a public man beneath myself."

Sunday dawned clear and hot. The boys set up long planks on horses in the garden under the shade of the chestnut trees, two tables to seat thirty each. The first to arrive in midmorning was John's mother, seventy-nine now, her face an interlocking myriad of wrinkle patches. Her eyes danced mischievously as she exclaimed:

"Daughter Abigail, when you left I cried, 'Fatal day, I shall never see you again.' But I vowed, 'I won't die, not even once, until my children come home.'"

Peter Adams had brought his mother, along with his three daughters and one son. He had been a widower for eight years but had felt neither need nor inclination to remarry. His mother was managing his house and raising the young. Heavy-set and phlegmatic, he appeared content with life. He commented to Abigail:

"Remember when I got John elected selectman, I laid out my own program? I been climbing the ladder rung by rung: constable, Fisheries Committee, tithingman, selectman, moderator at town meeting. I practically run this town now."

Samuel Adams and Betsy arrived next, having left Boston early that morning. With them was Hannah, Samuel's daughter, who had married Betsy's younger brother. Samuel had obviously come early because he was spoiling for an argument. As a member of the Massachusetts Ratifying Convention he had voted for the Constitution but not without such severe reservations and attacks that he had alienated a large portion of the state. Samuel looked older than the passage of the years warranted. In the past years he had been defeated for the Senate and defeated in his bid for the post of lieutenant governor. Yet he always had some kind of job: justice of the peace or member of the governing Council. They gathered on the cool side of the carriage house.

"Sam'l, what disturbed you about the Constitution?" John asked immediately.

"As I enter the building I stumble at the threshold."

"But if you accept my thesis that the balance of powers assures freedom . . ."

"Not so fast, Cousin. I meet with a national government instead of a federal union of sovereign states. If the several states in the Union are to become one entire nation, under one legislature, the powers of which shall extend to every subject of legislation, and its laws be supreme and control the whole, the idea of sovereignty in these states must be lost. Can this national legislature be competent to make laws for the *free* internal government of one people . . . ?"

The discussion was interrupted by the arrival of Isaac Smith, Jr., and his brother William. William was a replica of his father, open-faced, blunt, shrewd, thoroughly trained by Abigail's uncle Isaac and expanding the family business by building two ships, one intended for the lucrative China trade. Isaac, Jr., was now approaching forty. Most of the mist of fine blond hair which used to fall like spray in front of his green eyes was gone, along with his finespun moral ideals which had caused him to send Lord Percy and his redcoats on the right road from Cambridge to Lexington. He had been eking out a living as a tutor in a boys' school.

"Next year he'll have his appointment as a librarian at Harvard," William confided. "It doesn't pay much but it's what he wants."

Abigail's eyes followed Isaac, Jr.

"Isaac is a casualty of the war," she murmured, "just as was my brother Billy and Mr. Adams's brother Elihu."

The Cranches arrived, tall broad-beamed Mary looking more than ever like her solid, imperious mother; Richard, after a series of long illnesses, appearing ten years older than his sixty-two. Their son Billy had been graduated from Harvard with Johnny and was apprenticed to a lawyer in Boston. Young Elizabeth was engaged to the Reverend Jacob Norton, who had taken the Reverend Mr. Smith's place in the Weymouth pulpit and had just purchased from his future mother-in-law the family home in which Mary, Abigail, Elizabeth and Billy had been born. Mary told Abigail that Richard, since his services as justice of the peace and state senator, was considered the patriarch of Braintree.

Elizabeth and the Reverend Mr. Shaw came out of the house. The boys welcomed them boisterously. Charley cried:

"After Uncle Shaw, Harvard was a Dame School."

Family arrived as fast as Abigail could receive them. Cotton Tufts astonished everyone by escorting Susanna Warner, twenty years younger than Cotton's fifty-six; a handsome, long-legged Gloucester woman, pink of cheek as she stole admiring glances at Cotton whenever he left her side. Cotton's hair was freshly cut, his spectacles concealed in their case. He was dressed in handsome new broadcloth and a fine ruffled shirt.

Hannah Storer arrived with Deacon Storer, whispering to Abigail that she was happier than she had ever been with the high-tempered Dr. Bela Lincoln. John Thaxter, who had sworn to his cousin Abigail that he would remain celibate, brought his young wife to meet the family.

Catharine Louisa arrived with her children. The oldest, Billy, was apprenticed to a storekeeper. Louisa, the next oldest, threw herself into Abigail's arms and wept for permission to return to the Adams house as a member of the family. Catharine Louisa did not expect she would marry again. Her sallow face was like bleached sailcloth stretched over bones.

"I am with God now, more now than ever. He talks to me night and day."

They sat down to dinner at midafternoon, the shade spreading a benevolent umbrella over the tables. The children were nineteen strong. The Reverend Mr. Wibird, old and tremulous now, said grace.

Richard Cranch pushed back his chair, rose and with raised glass exclaimed:

"To the first Vice President of the United States!"

Abigail glanced quickly over to John. His face was an expressionless mask.

3

She scoured the countryside for craftsmen who could regild her chairs and repair the damage to the fabrics. John threw himself into the restoration of the farm, working as many as ten men at a time to clear the fields of the stones thrown up by the frost, to build fences, plow the land, bring wagonloads of salt hay from the coast and compost wherever it could be bought. Late one afternoon he returned home with six Guernseys. He led them around to the kitchen door, called for Abigail and presented the herd to her.

"What in God's name are these?"

"Cows."

"Do tell! And what are we supposed to do with them?"

"Milk them."

"Has it occurred to you that we have no barn?"

"O Heaven, I forgot about the barn. We'll have to build one."

"By nightfall? Johnny and I are just adding up the cost of putting the house and farm into condition. We've spent five thousand dollars, close to the whole sum of back pay the government owes us."

John sank onto the kitchen stoop, his face covered with perspiration. "I'll lead them down to our old barn. Nabby, I was so starved to become a farmer again I just couldn't wait."

That night was the last before Johnny had to return to his law studies in Newburyport. The Adams family sat around the library-room table with their ledger, bills, receipts and official accountant. Johnny estimated that their physical properties, including houses, farms, furnishings and books, were now worth twenty thousand dollars. There was little income from any of the land; the Boston house brought a hundred and forty dollars a year in rent and was in need of repair. Abigail's half of the Medford farm covered Charley's and Tommy's costs at school. Their several thousand dollars invested in army and government notes would return no interest until and unless the new government assumed the payments.

"The one thing I do need," Abigail sighed, "is a dining room. John, if we built a dining room behind this library we could serve directly from the kitchen."

"It is a waiting time for us. Seven or eight months until the elections are settled."

"Couldn't you practice law, Papa?"

"No, Tommy. If I were elected to an office I'd have to desert my clients in the middle of their cases."

"Doesn't the same reasoning apply to the farm?" Abigail's voice had an insistent edge.

"I don't think so. The farm will bring us good crops. We can always hire hands, let it on halves."

Abigail thought of Pratt farming on halves at the old Adams houses; all he had managed to raise was a large brood of children.

She held her tongue. In the next few days John bought chickens, ducks, turkeys, geese. When practical Tommy asked if they did not have enough fowl, Abigail replied with a sigh:

"You know there is no saying nay."

It was a transition period for John. He read, filed his papers, unpacked the remaining crates of books until the fireplace wall was lined solidly with history, the east wall with law, adjusted himself to the thinking of his own country. When friends insisted that he become the presiding officer of the dying Congress he shook his head a vigorous no.

"If my future employment in public depends on the feather of being for a week or a day president of Congress, I will never have any other than private employments while I live. I am willing to serve the public on manly conditions but not on childish ones; on honorable principles, not mean ones."

Abigail went out to work around her rosebushes.

Nothing had happened to change John's sense of dedication, or her own; the United States was weaker today than it had been at any time since Bunker Hill. All who opposed the new federal Constitution—they were amazed at the number and virulence of the attacks by good people in every state in the Union—were afraid to let the new government come into being. They feared that, as Cousin Samuel had enunciated, state sovereignty would be annihilated; that under the "general welfare" clause those in office could create a tyranny.

Letters, journals, friends poured into the new house to argue this troublesome issue. John agreed that the federal powers had to be limited; he also believed that the projected Bill of Rights would protect all individuals. On these grounds he became a leader of the Federalist point of view, of those who approved federation and a strong central government. His years in Europe had taught him how urgent this need was. Those who opposed federation became known as Anti-Federalists. Though they were not organized, it appeared that there might be a full quota of them in the new Senate and House of Representatives.

Nab wrote from New York that everyone was speaking of John for Vice President or Chief Justice. Dr. Benjamin Rush wrote from Philadelphia that Pennsylvania would surely support him. General Henry Knox came as an emissary from Alexander Hamilton, powerful leader of the New York forces of the Federalists, to find out whether John Adams would accept anything less than the vice presidency. Knox reported he would not, and Hamilton then made it clear that he would support Adams for the post. More and more out-of-state journals spoke favorably of him. Since George Washington was from the South it was being strongly expressed that the Vice President had to be from the North. Since the beginning of the Revolution the North had meant New England. Yet John Jay and Governor George Clinton, both of New York, had to be taken into consideration.

Here in Massachusetts they knew that Governor John Hancock wanted the office. James Warren and Cousin Sam'l had been against adopting the Constitution, that let them out. Francis Dana, Henry Knox, Caleb Strong, Tristram Dalton, General Lincoln? Would any of these men impress the whole nation?

Nab's letters carried a different kind of news as well.

As a renowned Revolutionary War hero and friend of General Washington, as secretary of legation in London, Colonel William Smith had been an important and respected man. At home in Long Island he was a small boy, one of four sons and six daughters of an overbearing mother who both spoiled and dominated her children.

Nab liked William's brothers and sisters but was homesick for her parents, her brothers, for New England. She was in circumstances again; and this brought up an even more serious problem. Colonel William was neither working nor looking for a job. He was spending his days hunting for quail and partridge, jollying with his brothers. They had sufficient money to live on for a year, thanks to Nab's frugal managing of Colonel William's salary as secretary of legation. Apparently the Colonel was not going to concern himself about a job until the money was gone. In any event, Colonel Smith expected that as soon as his friend George Washington was elected to the presidency he would be named to a high post in government, preferably as minister to a European country.

Abigail comforted her daughter as best she could: Mrs. Smith, as the mother of the family, was entitled to Nab's respect; Nab must be patient and forbearing.

On the subject of Colonel William's future, John Adams was not so conciliatory. He wrote to Nab:

"My desire would be to hear of him at the Bar which, in my opinion, is the most independent place on earth. A seeker of public employments is, in my idea, one of the most unhappy of all men. . . . I had rather dig my subsistence out of the earth with my own hands than be dependent on any favor, public or private; and this has been the invariable maxim of my whole life."

John refused to campaign for the vice presidency, the position he now believed he should have. He made no speeches, attended no rallies or meetings, called no conclaves in his home. But his friends were working tirelessly for him. An intense crosshatch of letters passed from state to state. New England would be solidly in his electoral column, for John Hancock had made too many enemies. A letter from the president of Yale College told them that John had been awarded an honorary degree; it also stated that he should be elected to the second office. Dr. Rush was organizing Pennsylvania behind John Adams with the avowed hope that John would help bring the government back to Philadelphia. The great surprise was the solid support of the South. Arthur Lee, one of the strongest leaders of Virginia, wrote that his state found Mr. Adams eminently acceptable. Richard Henry Lee, another Virginia stalwart, considered that the vice presidency must go to John. David Ramsay of South Carolina wrote a friend that John Adams should have any office he desired, after General Washington as President. Alexander Hamilton of New York wrote James Madison of Virginia that John Adams must be chosen Vice President in order to keep the New Englanders content with the new federal government.

As far as Abigail could gather during the winter months before the electors were to meet, vote and send their results to the Congress, there remained no serious opposition to John Adams for Vice President. He was not likely to receive a unamimous vote as Washington would; there would be votes cast for Governor Clinton of New York, for John Jay, even for John Hancock. But all of them together could not add up to more than a dozen.

Not, that is, until something went subtly and mysteriously askew. Abigail heard the rumors of it from Boston friends: Alexander Hamilton was writing letters to a few of his confidential allies suggesting they "drop off," not vote for John Adams, so that he would not emerge with too outstanding a majority. If he did, John Adams would challenge Hamilton's behind-the-scenes control of the Federalists. Hamilton wanted Adams elected, but barely.

John moved calmly and resolutely during the weeks of trial. Dozens of his associates were in the house each day for dinner or tea and long political discussions of how the new government could be made to work. He never spoke of his desire for the vice presidency, or of his assets for the post, as he had to the Continental Congress when he yearned to become the first American ambassador to England. He was behaving with the dignity and detachment of a historian rather than a candidate in the heat of a campaign he could not wage. New England liked him in this refreshing and modest role. His wife was amused.

They drew off their cider, picked over the barrels of pears for repacking, slaughtered two cows and hung the beef in the cellar, purchased pork and made bacon. Some of Abigail's "out-of-door family" were plucked and stored in the coolest part of the cellar for winter eating.

By December the states were in the throes of electioneering for local offices as well as national. Samuel Adams ran for the federal House of Representatives from Suffolk County but Fisher Ames, an ardent Federalist, defeated him. Massachusetts chose its electors, who in turn would vote for the President and Vice President. After weeks of bitter wrangling in the Congress, New York was selected as the seat of government. John Adams and most Southerners had supported Philadelphia. However the Philadelphia enthusiasts could not assemble a majority and its supporters had to yield, as James Madison wrote to General Washington, for fear of "strangling the government in its birth."

On the first Wednesday in February 1789 the electors in eleven states met in their capitals to vote for the President and Vice President and then send their ballots by courier to the Congress in New York. George Washington received not one dissenting electoral vote from any state. By the harshest figuring of his political consultants, John Adams was certain to receive a majority of the sixty-nine votes cast.

He did not. When the first word reached them from Elbridge Gerry at the new Congress in New York, in a letter written March 4, 1789, they learned that John Adams had been elected only by virtue of receiving more votes than anyone else: thirty-four, less than half. Hamilton's strategy had worked exactly as he had planned it.

John felt angry and humiliated. Most of the pleasure went out of the election for him. It caused serious doubts in his mind whether or not he ought to accept the post.

"You can't refuse, John." Abigail's manner was firm. "You've been legally elected. The Constitution does not provide any other way for us to secure a Vice President."

"I know. But my tendons have been cut. I'll have little influence. Every day will bring up urgent matters for which we have no precedent. As a minority Vice President I cannot lead."

"You will lead from the basis of experience. No man has your years of training at the Congress, or abroad in foreign affairs."

He was consoled, but only a little. She had rarely seen him so crestfallen. The months of tranquillity fell away. His face was pale, there was a slight tremor apparent in his hand. She too had her worries: what to do with the house and farm and animals? They would need ready money with which to travel to New York and make a home there.

They were silent, anxious. The winter night was black about them. John went to the window overlooking Abigail's dormant rose garden. He spoke without turning:

"When the official notice comes of my election, I had best go down to New York alone. John Jay has offered me hospitality in his home. That way I'll be able to convene the Senate as soon as we have a quorum. When the Congress sets the President's salary and mine, I'll find a suitable house for us. . . ."

She felt her eyes fill with tears. No matter what happened it always came to this: she would be left behind, with crops to plant, labor to hire, debts to pay.

John crossed the room, crouched by her side.

"It won't be for long. Only a few months. Then we'll have a proper home in New York, with Nab and her two boys close by. My brother Peter has agreed to take care of the farm when you join me."

It was not until the twelfth of April that official word was brought to Braintree from the new Congress that John Adams was now Vice President of the United States. The following day he and Abigail rode into Boston, escorted by a troop of light horse. The moment they entered Boston through the Neck the church bells began to ring and the streets to fill with people. The Roxbury Light Horse had taken over from the Braintree guard of honor, formally escorting the Adams carriage to the Hancock mansion. John Hancock was a good loser; he had been fond of John since their school days in Braintree.

John bade farewell to Abigail on the porch of the Hancock house, their good-bys drowned in a salute of thirteen volleys of musket fire. As he left for the Connecticut Road the crowds cheered once again, all reminiscent to Abigail of the day John and Cousin Sam'l, Robert Treat Paine and Thomas Cushing had set out from the State House Square on August 10, 1774, for the first meeting of a Congress in Philadelphia.

She got into her carriage and started for home, alone.

4

The spring was backward and cold, the stock expensive to feed. She offered to sell some of the cows but there were no buyers. She planted twenty fruit trees which John sent her from New York, had the wall of the pasture poled because the sheep were getting out. When Briesler brought John's horse by boat from New York she tried to get its cost back, seventy dollars; no one would pay that much. It became her chore to go over to their old barn and lead the Guernseys to pasture. She did not mind the task because her butter and cheese were in demand. With this money she hired hands to plant but it would be five months till harvest time. Cotton Tufts bought three heifers and ten wethers to give her cash in hand.

A new tax bill was announced by the town selectmen. Peter came over that evening after supper, shuffled his feet under the kitchen table.

"Sister Abigail, I can't take over running this place."

"Peter, you promised."

"I will never get sufficient from it to pay the taxes."

"Then take part of the sheep."

"No, Sister, I'll help all I can, but I won't take responsibility. Brother John will think I should have done so much more than is possible, he will set me down for a fool or a knave."

She sighed.

"I am in the same position, Peter. We can only do things to the best of our judgment, then abide the consequences."

Peter left without answering. A heavy parish tax was assessed against them, one cow died, the others were late in calving, there were wages owed the hired hands, six months' salary due Briesler. Her sister Mary arrived in a melancholy mood. Richard Cranch's small farm could not afford them a living; Mary had already spent her equity in the Weymouth house. What to do?

Abigail went up to her bedroom and took from a drawer of her bureau a box of ten gold guineas.

"We will have John's salary coming in soon. You use these to help you out of trouble. Let's hear no more of it."

Although John had had a gratifying trip into New York, being met at the state line by the Westchester Light Horse, which provided an honor guard for him to King's Bridge at the north end of Manhattan, and then by an official reception committee of congressmen and private citizens in carriages and on horseback, he had never even been sworn into office. On April twenty-first he had gone to the recently redecorated Federal Hall and been escorted into the Senate Chamber by Senators Caleb Strong of Massachusetts and Ralph Izard of South Carolina. The Senate Chamber was architecturally fine, forty feet long by thirty feet wide, with a design of sun and stars on the ceiling. Each side wall had a beautiful fireplace of domestic marble; on the north wall were three tall windows draped in crimson damask. Under the middle window was the dais with the chair for the presiding officer set under a canopy of matching crimson. On the opposite wall were three doors, also draped in damask, leading to a portico on Wall Street. Here Senator John Langdon of New Hampshire said to John in front of the assembled senators:

"Sir: I have it in charge from the Senate to introduce you to the Chair of this House; and, also, to congratulate you on your appointment to the office of Vice President of the United States of America."

John gave his prepared speech to the Senate:

"It is with satisfaction that I congratulate the people of America on the formation of a national Constitution, and the fair prospect of a consistent administration of a government of laws. . . ."

His speech was applauded. The Senate thereupon adjourned for the day. John returned to John Jay's house to find a few old friends from Massachusetts assembled for a quiet celebration.

All this was in startling contrast to the reception and swearing in of President George Washington. The General had been received by a joint committee of Congress and given an artillery salute by the troops on the waterfront at Elizabeth Town Point in New Jersey where he boarded a brilliantly decorated barge. After the barge crossed Newark Bay and came opposite the end of Staten Island a whole flotilla of boats, flags flying, fell in behind in a great naval parade. New York City closed down for the day. Thousands of people jammed into the streets, a band played "God Save the King" and the American, Spanish and British ships lying in the bay fired a thirteen-gun salute. The tumultuous crowds were so great at Murray's Wharf at the bottom of Wall Street that the parade, after the General had been welcomed by Governor Clinton and hundreds of other dignitaries, took hours to start. All of the city's bells were ringing, there was a full-dress salute by the militia, and finally a banquet at Governor Clinton's home.

On April thirtieth, when Washington appeared before the two Houses assembled in the Senate Chamber, he traveled in a magnificent coach preceded by a massive parade of troops, congressmen, federal and New York officials. Vice President John Adams formally received him, then led him to the portico overlooking Wall and Broad streets. Before them was a sea of upturned faces. George Washington bowed. A tremendous cheer went up from the assembled citizenry. He moved forward to the iron railing. On either side of him stood Vice President Adams and Governor Clinton. Samuel Otis, secretary of the Senate, lifted the Bible and red cushion from the table. Chancellor Robert R. Livingston of New York administered the oath of office, then turned to the people in the street and cried, "Long live George Washington, President of the United States." The American flag was raised in the cupola of Federal Hall. There was sustained cheering, the ships in the harbor gave another thirteen-gun salute, the bells of the city rang. President Washington returned to the Senate Chamber to give his address and then the entire party walked through streets lined with militia to St. Paul's Chapel to hear divine service.

The presidency of the United States had been born.

It was a great and noble office, filled by a great and noble man. The vice presidency could no longer be regarded as the second most important office in the land, even by Abigail or John Adams. The Vice President was a stand-by, of importance only in the event of a dire tragedy.

John's problems were no more easily solved than Abigail's. Though the Jays were good hosts he felt he was imposing. The tremor of his right arm had increased, his eyes were troubling him. He had quarreled with the Senate, over which he was supposed to sit as an impartial parliamentarian who raised his voice only in the case of a tie vote, because he had attempted to lead it, to give advice to the senators on the innumerable elements of protocol.

He rented Mr. Montier's house on the North River a mile out of the city. The rent was reasonable because it was in the country. It had a good stable, coach house, garden and pasture for two cows, rooms for the family. Abigail must come at once and bring Esther and Briesler and her whole houseful of furniture. As soon as Charley had been graduated he must join them. To secure money she must sell off all the animals. If she could not sell them, she should give them away.

Abigail was furious. Why had he insisted on buying all those animals and farm tools, built fences and planted crops? Why had they not sat still, spent nothing until the final decisions were made? John assured her that they would live in New York for four years. He did not intend for them to keep running back and forth to Braintree, so even the improvements on the house could have waited.

There was one compensating factor: John had arranged for Nab, Colonel Smith and their two boys to move into the house with them. They were to bring their own furniture. That meant Abigail could leave several beds and a number of chairs and tables behind in case they ever wanted to come home to see how their new fruit trees were doing.

When she rode up the winding road of Richmond Hill, lined by forest trees, she drew in her breath at the sublime beauty of the view. The house had been built on the top of the hill; from the second-story terrace outside the sitting room she saw the majestic Hudson River glittering in the sun, sailing vessels plying up and down its silver waters. Beyond lay the country of the Jerseys covered with a lush green. To the north there were fertile plains where cattle grazed; to the south, through a clump of trees she could see the roofs of New York City.

John returned from the Senate. He exclaimed:

"From your expression I would say you like it."

"Oh, John, for natural beauty it vies with the most glorious panorama I've ever seen."

New York, like Boston, was inescapably a port town, the vista of each street ended with sailing masts swaying against the sky. Dutch was the second language, particularly in the shops and pulpits. The streets were cosmopolitan, filled with seamen, foreign merchants, large groups of French, Scotch, Irish, Jews, Poles, Portuguese, Negroes, all speaking in their native tongues. Yet in physical size the city was disappointingly small compared to Boston. Broadway, which began at the Battery, had well-built houses for only a mile before it trickled into open country. A half hour's walk in any direction exhausted the town's possibilities; a stroll along the East River brought them to a swamp, a walk from Wall Street quickly ended on somebody's farm. But the city had tremendous vitality. Dozens of new buildings were being hammered up, land was being made on the river by means of piles and dikes; new theatres, coffeehouses and shops were being opened. Most of the streets were unpaved. The two-foot-wide sidewalks of broken cobblestones were all but impassable, worse than Paris, cluttered with hitching posts, mud holes, garbage piles, rooting hogs, clusters of night soil thrown off front stoops.

By the time she completed her staff she found that her family consisted of eighteen members: they were three Adamses, with Charley, four Smiths, her niece Louisa, Briesler, who was major-domo (Esther had preferred to remain in Braintree with her child), another young girl, Polly Tailor from Braintree, the rest local servants. Food was high and not of a good quality. Abigail could not eat the butter. The white domestics she hired were constantly drunk, the Negroes worked well for a week or two, then vanished with their first pay. Briesler was the saving grace, riding into town several times a day to market. People in the city liked to take the lovely ride out to the Adamses' in the early morning for breakfast. New ones came for dinner, senators and representatives, some of John's long-time associates from the old Congress; and in the evening close family friends, sometimes of Colonel Smith, sometimes from New England.

She shuddered to think what the cost would be of feeding her retinue plus all the new government people and New York society who would be expected to be entertained by the Vice President of the United States. Better to stick her head in the hawthorn bush and not see; when Johnny came on vacation he would set up her books and tell her how much money she was spending.

As the frenzied activity continued, with servants coming and going as fast as the guests, she revolted. She and John were resting alone in the high-ceilinged, second-story sitting parlor surrounded by John's gilt chairs, once again chipped in travel.

"John, I feel as though I'm running a post road tavern."

"What can we do? It solidifies the position of the vice presidency to entertain people, gives a feeling of established authority which the office needs."

5

She chose one day in the week for her levee. Everyone was welcome. On the other six days they must go elsewhere. Mrs. Jay had Thursday, Mrs. Knox Wednesday and Lady Temple Tuesday.

She had called on Martha Custis Washington the very morning after her arrival at the Franklin house on Cherry Street, which had been official headquarters for the President of the Continental Congress. It was a good house, albeit small. During the war Mrs. Washington had sometimes visited the General's headquarters but she had remained so quietly in the background that no one knew anything about her.

Abigail took Nab with her. Martha Washington received them with ease and politeness. Abigail found her to be unassuming, with a becoming pleasantness on her countenance. Mrs. Washington led them to the drawing room, ordered morning coffee. She was plainly dressed, though Abigail noted that the materials were of the best. She was short of stature and somewhat inclined to plumpness. Her hair was white, her teeth beautifully regular. Her voice was warm.

"It is my great pleasure to have you in New York, Mrs. Adams. I have been awaiting your arrival. Mr. Washington has high regard for Mr. Adams and hopes they will achieve important ends for the new government by working together. In a modest fashion perhaps you and I can accomplish something as well."

"That is my dearest hope. As a beginning, might I ask if you have selected a day for your drawing room? I wish to put off my choice until I know your pleasure."

"I shall select Friday, I think."

"Then I shall take Monday."

"Agreed." She turned to Nab. "Mr. Washington is very fond of Colonel Smith. He feels that he should lend his considerable talents to the government."

Nab flushed with pleasure. She and Abigail excused themselves. The next afternoon Mrs. Washington arrived at the Richmond Hill house for tea, unannounced. Before she left she invited the Adamses to dinner.

"John, the more I see of Mrs. Washington, the more I esteem her. I am more deeply impressed than I ever was before Their Majesties of Great Britain."

"I feel the same way about the President. He received me with great cordiality, with affection and confidence. Everything has gone agreeably between us. We will need friendship to solve the myriad problems that the enemies of the government are hauling up before us like beached whales."

Abigail and Martha Washington saw each other nearly every day. They attended each other's receptions only fortnightly, for the crowds were large, but when they drank tea together privately they were able to set a course of action in many areas of activity that were new and strange to them. The Anti-Federalists were watching and commenting, hoping they would be arrogant, exclusive, seriously err. Neither lady gave them any consolation, though Mrs. Washington's dinners were elaborate, with powdered lackeys receiving the guests. At her drawing rooms Abigail had the seat of honor at Mrs. Washington's right. If the chair were inadvertently occupied, the President in his affable but dignified manner would have the person rise so that Abigail might take her acknowledged place.

The first time Abigail called at the presidential residence Washington had been down with a painful abscess. The second time he insisted that Mrs. Washington bring her into his chamber. He was lying upon a settee, obviously uncomfortable, but half raised himself to receive her. It was many years since she had first met him, at the Roxbury camp after he had taken command of the Revolutionary forces.

"Mrs. Adams, I beg you to forgive me for receiving you in this posture; but I did want to congratulate you on your arrival in New York."

"Thank you, Mr. President; but you need not have seen me while you are in distress."

Washington waved this aside. "Tell me, Mrs. Adams, how can you relish the simple manners of America after being accustomed to those of Europe?"

"Mr. President, where I find simple manners I esteem them."

When she wished him a speedy recovery so that he could go about again, Washington replied:

"Oh, I have a bed put in my carriage, and ride out."

"Splendid. The next time you are taking the air I hope you will make Richmond Hill your resting place."

The President arrived the very next afternoon. Though it was difficult for him to climb the flight of stairs, he insisted upon going up to the second-floor sitting parlor to drink tea and discuss problems of government with John.

The beginnings of the federal government had an impact on New York City. When the last congressmen arrived there would be twenty-two United States senators and fifty-nine representatives who could be seen moving through the streets for the ten o'clock convening in their separate chambers of Federal Hall, returning to their homes, taverns or boardinghouses for a four o'clock dinner.

For offices, President Washington used two downstairs rooms of the Franklin home, where he received his Department heads, envoys of foreign countries, visiting state officials trying to adjust the delicate balance between local and national authority. Here too he interviewed applicants for federal posts: tax collectors, port authorities, postmasters. Here his secretaries Lear, Colonel Humphreys and Major Jackson also lived and worked.

The Executive Departments were beginning to function. The choices had seemed almost inevitable: Thomas Jefferson as Secretary of State, Alexander Hamilton to head the Treasury, General Henry Knox in charge of War, and former Governor of Virginia and member of the Continental Congress Edmund Randolph, Attorney General. It would be his job to see that the Constitution was enforced. Hamilton had the largest department, with thirty-nine employees on his payroll. There were only five men in the Department of State but that was perhaps because Jefferson was still trying to get back from France. Knox needed only a couple of scriveners; the main part of his time was spent closeted with his commander-in-chief conferring on how they were to negotiate with the Indians, how they were to build a militia which was controlled by the individual states but owed its allegiance to a federal government.

Acting Secretary of State John Jay was constantly in attendance with dispatches from London, Madrid, Paris. President Washington read them all, then with Jay's help drafted answers, wrote communications to the heads of distant governments. The first news of the uprising in France was considered of so little interest that three weeks passed before anyone, aside from Thomas Jefferson in his confidential letters to John Jay, troubled to inform the United States about it. Even then, news that the Third Estate had proclaimed itself a National Assembly, taking its oath on the tennis court after being ejected from the palace at Versailles, and that the Bastille prison had been captured by a Parisian street mob was reported in a single paragraph on page two of the *New York Daily Advertiser*. John commented to Abigail on the item but neither of them had perceived a sign of revolution during their stay in France, and so they too dismissed the activities as a passing unrest.

When he felt sorely in need of counsel President Washington would pick up his hat and cloak, walk to the home of a Department head for discussion. On several occasions he arrived unannounced at the Adams house. Once he came seeking recommendations for the five Supreme Court justices and Chief Justice.

The presidency was an exhausting job. Almost every day a new bill was proposed by the Senate or the House which had to be studied and signed. The first signature was attached on June 1, 1789, to the initial bill passed by Congress prescribing how oaths of office were to be administered; after that even the neglected Vice President would be properly sworn into office. On July fourth the President approved the Import Bill which set tariffs on imported articles; on July twenty-seventh he signed the desperately needed and much-debated bill creating a Department of Foreign Affairs; on August seventh a bill creating a Department of War; on September second, after long study, the bill setting up a Department of the Treasury. He approved a House appropriation for twenty thousand dollars to treat with the Creek Indians. Toward the end of September he signed bills establishing federal courts. After consultation with the Vice President and Department heads he forwarded to the states the twelve resolutions of the Bill of Rights which guaranteed the freedom of religion, speech, press, assemblage, petition for redress of grievances; the right to keep and bear arms, be free from the quartering of troops; no unreasonable search or seizure; public trials; trial by jury. The Bill now went to the state legislatures for ratification.

Over that first summer Washington appointed qualified men from the different states as naval officers, surveyors, collectors of duties, then guided the appointments through the Senate. The country was prosperous, trade was booming, a thousand tasks were at hand: to appoint a new minister to France to replace Thomas Jefferson, a governor for the Western Territory, a comptroller for the government, a chargé d'affaires for Spain. There were treaties to be written. British troops still occupied American ports and gave Washington endless trouble. States were quarreling among themselves about boundaries, turning to the President for decisions; governors and judges of the outlying territories had to be approved or recalled. Hundreds of private citizens swarmed over his home demanding a resolution of their problems. Hundreds of others demanded to be entertained: at receptions, teas, levees, dinners. The machinery of government was being implemented. All executive officers were busily occupied.

All, that is, except Vice President John Adams. The Constitution had not given him anything to do but preside over the Senate. Each morning he left his home for the Senate Chamber, mounted the woolsack, but the Senate allowed him to do little but preserve order. Acting Secretary of State John Jay came to see him when he wanted to discuss a thorny problem about England or France. Friendly senators or representatives discussed pending bills. Nevertheless it was clear to everyone, most particularly to John and Abigail Adams, that Mr. Adams had been removed from the field of action.

The Congress, after considerable discussion, confirmed the salary of the President at twenty-five thousand dollars a year, including a suitable house in which to live. The Vice President was to receive five thousand dollars a year and no house or any other expenses, not even for a secretary. John was aghast at the news. Was it a slap at him personally? Or was it an expression of contempt for the office itself, though there was only the breath of one mortal between it and the presidency? These were rhetorical questions asked by a thoroughly angry man.

"I am certainly permitted to ask practical questions," John grumbled, pacing their bedroom overlooking the back garden; "how do we live in New York on that sum of money? Or meet the obligations thrust upon us by the office itself?"

Abigail put the best possible face on the matter.

"We can make it, John, entertaining at only one levee and one dinner a week, scrimping on our own diversions, no theatres or balls that require special gowns; few new books . . ."

He groaned. "This is the cycle of our lives."

She replied calmly. "With the President appointing Colonel William as marshal of the District of New York, Nab will be provided for. Peter can send us our meats, poultry, fruits and vegetables, butter and eggs, everything that is so expensive here. We'll survive."

"Barely!" he said, gritting his teeth.

"John, we're no worse off than we have been before. As you remarked some years ago, we milk our cows, not our government."

"But I am the cow getting milked!" Having made a joke, he felt better, some color came back into his puffy cheeks. "What can't be cured must be endured. My sympathies, dear Mrs. Adams, the burden of balancing our books will once again fall on you."

Their lot was made easier by the knowledge that their friend John Jay had accepted the post of Chief Justice at four thousand dollars a year. Alexander Hamilton, legal and financial wizard of the Federalists, as the first Secretary of the United States Treasury was to receive a salary of three thousand. Hamilton had just begun to earn large sums from his practice of the law. He was making a very considerable sacrifice.

John admired Alexander Hamilton. His magnificent papers, written alternately with Jefferson's young friend James Madison and John Jay, and published in *The Federalist*, had been the instrument of persuading recalcitrant New York to ratify the Constitution. He was supporting John loyally now, which made Abigail consider the rumor that it had been Hamilton who deliberately undermined John's vote as part of the wicked gossipmongering with which government circles were already infested.

To atone for her sin in believing evil she gave a dinner party for the Hamiltons to which she invited their intimate circle of Massachusetts friends, their two home senators, Caleb Strong and Tristram Dalton who had gone to Harvard College with John. Elizabeth Schuyler Hamilton was the daughter of one of the oldest, wealthiest and most influential families in New York. She was a thin-faced woman with a cleft chin and enormously expressive black eyes, modestly attractive but exquisitely gowned in the finest English fashions. She loved her husband almost fanatically, thinking him godlike.

It was soon made plain at the Adams dining table that this was an opinion Alexander Hamilton shared. He had been born with the brain of a genius and an insatiable appetite for intrigue. His broad, aristocratically handsome face, with majestic eyebrows over devouring eyes, a powerful Greek-god nose, strong albeit sensuous and indulgent mouth, was sparkling and attractive to men and women alike. A natural leader of men because of his combined magnetism and brilliance of mind, Hamilton had earned everything for himself on the journey up from his illegitimate birth in the West Indies (his mother was a respectable native French Huguenot, his father a Scot) and a penniless apprenticeship in a general store to becoming one of General George Washington's most trusted aides during the Revolutionary War. He was pyrotechnical and unstable, had resigned his commission during the war over an imagined slight by Washington, yet on sheer intellect worked his way back to become Washington's most trusted adviser. He was the behind-the-scenes organizer and manipulator of the Federalists.

He dominated the dinner at the Adamses' as a Hamlet dominated the stage during the acting of Shakespeare's play. The Massachusetts people were fascinated by him, also a little repelled. He was too gaudy of soul for these plain New Englanders. They felt uneasy about being charmed by him.

Abigail thought Mrs. Hamilton as genteel and educated a lady as she had ever met. But she was not deceived by her exterior fragility.

"She has a will of iron," she said to John when the company had left. And, once again considering the pre-election rumors, added, "I don't think the Hamiltons' plans include us. . . . Watch my word, we're not important enough to find a place in their circle. To Hamilton we're small-town yeomen fulfilling an insignificant post. He never means for us to go any further."

6

Life was simpler in New York than Abigail had found it in Boston. In spite of the city's reputation for wantonness, its society entertained less lavishly. At her own weekly dinners she entertained the President and Mrs. Washington and his heads of Departments; then in the following weeks those senators and representatives who had brought their wives to New York; subsequently those legislators, crowded into boardinghouses, who had been obliged to leave their families behind.

Many of the guests she now received she recognized from John's descriptions of them after his return from the Continental Congress in 1774. She could see and hear John filling their bedroom in Braintree with a whole assembly of legislators as she now welcomed them in New York.

"Richard Henry Lee of Virginia is tall and spare, a masterly man." He was now a senator. "Roger Sherman of Connecticut has a clear head and sound judgment, but when he moves a hand in anything like action, Hogarth's genius could not have invented a motion more opposite to grace." Sherman was now a leading voice in the House. "John Jay is a hard student and a good speaker." He was now Chief Justice.

Here too, eating and chatting comfortably at her table, were Senator John Langdon of New Hampshire, who had first told John, while he was trying a case in Portsmouth in late 1777, that the Congress was sending him to France. Here were such old associates of John's as Charles Carroll of Maryland, John Rutledge of South Carolina, George Clymer, the diffident, retiring merchant of Pennsylvania, many others with whom John had toiled to achieve this government. There was a strong bond between them, an unexpressed sentiment that this work of their heads, their hearts and their years must not vanish from the earth.

John's implacable sense of duty caused him never to miss one day of presiding over the prolonged and frequently acrimonious debates of the Senate. He had terminated his months of cockfights with the senators, learned to abstain from their discussions. Abigail knew the details of the contest well. Those who quarreled the loudest with John as he sat on his dais came to Richmond Hill for her annealing dinners and friendship. Their greatest complaint was:

"It is not his job to lead the Senate but to preside over it."

Nonetheless he became a pillar of strength, his short stocky jowled figure representing the Constitution and the government.

"In every congressional battle we've had so far," John confided to his family, "there are men who damn our government and say it will never last. I've heard it from New Englanders as well as Southerners. Yet every day that we continue to exist is another milestone on the road to permanence."

Charles, after graduation from Harvard, settled in New York and was working faithfully at his books in the John Laurance law office. Abigail learned that the stories she had heard about his errant behavior were true. He had been guilty of what Boston called "youthful follies"; his association with the roistering group, the very kind which had ruined Royall Tyler's reputation earlier, had caused considerable eyebrow lifting in New England.

Now he was making amends. He avoided worldly pleasures, walking his father in the morning to Federal Hall, continuing on to Laurance's, returning with his father at four for dinner. He spent the evenings in his room studying, went into company only with his father or Colonel Smith. Abigail wondered why Charles so frequently accompanied his sister to Long Island on Sundays to spend the day with the Colonel's family. And why Sally Smith was such a faithful visitor to Nab and the little boys at Richmond Hill. Sally was the fourth daughter of the Smiths, twenty years old, tall, with a fine figure and a pretty face, unaffected in her manners. It never occurred to Abigail that nineteen-year-old Charley, with three years of an apprenticeship to serve, and more years before he could earn an adequate living, would be so foolish as to get involved. But Charley was the most volatile of the Adams children, the least controlled by his rigid Puritan ancestry and precepts. He committed the indiscretion of falling in love.

Nab was happy to be living with her parents again. She managed the servants in capable fashion so that neither Abigail nor the guests knew of the recurrent difficulties. Colonel Smith, as marshal, was once again an important man, arresting those shipowners who tried to smuggle or defraud the federal government of its rightful duties. Nab was amused.

"I was raised on tales of how six generations of Quincys, Boylstons, Smiths and Adamses smuggled molasses past the British custom officers."

John had insisted that the senators create a high title for the presidency in order to impress European courts with the majesty of the office. The senators rebuffed him, saying that the Constitution declared the Chief Executive should be called the "President of the United States" and so they and the House ruled. John had wanted elaborate procedures for the President's visits to the Senate, based on the King of England's visits to Parliament, again to impress the world with the high solemnity of the occasion. The Senate agreed that the President could have a special chair, nothing more. John complained to Abigail, as they climbed down the steep path to the Hudson and he took her sailing in the warm September air:

"I have more power to control this boat than I do the direction of the Senate. The Vice President, I have learned, is the least important post in our new government. I have not the smallest degree of power to do any good either in the executive, legislative or judicial departments. I am a mere Doge of Venice, a mechanical tool to wind up a clock."

Abigail reclined in the stern, letting the sun beat on her face, staring at the Jersey shore.

"For a man who thinks so little of his office, you are faithful. You haven't missed one hour of the debates."

"Nor shall I. I know my duty. But the office is not adapted to my character. It is too inactive. Time and again I yearn to leave the woolsack, go down on the floor and throw some light on the subject. . . . But it cannot be done. Well, I wanted the office. . . ."

"I wouldn't say you were completely a non-participant. I have heard that some of those tie-breaking votes of yours caused quite a furor."

His eyes became as gray-green as the Hudson under the noon sun.

"Those are the days that bring me a recruit of spirits. Not to mention unabashed abuse."

The Senate was supposed to be federal in nature but in fact it was composed of men who were passionately determined to serve their local, regional interests. Everyone agreed that the central government needed money with which to operate; there was equal agreement that the other fellow should pay it. When John argued against the proposed tariff on molasses, Massachusetts' chief import, and it was subsequently lowered, he was hotly accused of being a Vice President for New England rather than the United States. It was not until he cast the deciding vote for a tariff on loaf sugar, which Pennsylvania produced, that the Pennsylvanians were satisfied with him; or until he killed a proposed tax on salt, which would have hurt the small farmer, that the frontier states accepted his judgment as honest and impartial. He was then plunged into a debate on the right of the President to remove his Department heads without the approval of the Senate. John had never heard such intemperate language, such shouting and ranting as was exhibited at what the Senate considered a further mulcting of their power over the Executive. By a series of private, eloquent and soundly based legal arguments, John broke down the opponents one by one until the vote was tied and he was able to cast the deciding ballot. The presidency was further strengthened.

The struggle brought strange repercussions. It was bruited about that John Adams was fighting for these added powers of the presidency because he expected to take over the office one day and wanted to build up its structure so that he would have established the legal power to control all phases of the American government. In short, become the Monarch of America!

Abigail was wide-eyed.

"John, is there any truth to this talk?"

"That I want to become a monarch?"

"That you may one day be President?"

"Hasn't the thought occurred to you?"

"Only in an idle moment, nibbling at the back of my mind without my willing it. It is a kind of trap, isn't it? Mrs. Washington told me yesterday that her comings and goings are so regulated that she feels like a state prisoner."

John leaned over the balustrade of the upstairs terrace scattering his words to the discreet wind.

"Is there a chance that I may become President? Who can tell? President Washington will be elected for as many terms as he wants. But will I be? And after four years of that Senate bear pit, will I be willing to sit over their discussions for another four years? That's a sentence I would not hand down to my worst enemy."

"No, only to yourself. If elected you will serve. There's no way to get off this road except at the end."

John sighed. He was laboring under intense emotion.

"Do I want to be President of the United States? Of course I do! A man would have to be a fool not to want the highest office his nation has to offer him."

He went back to his chair, balancing on its edge.

"Many of our relatives and oldest friends are bitter about me because I haven't been able to get them jobs in the government. They won't believe that President Washington appointed Colonel William as marshal because he was a trusted aide during the war; they accuse me of using my influence. . . ."

His voice trailed off. Abigail knew this was true. Mercy Warren was no longer communicating with her because of her anger over John's failure to secure for her husband James the high position to which Mercy felt his long service entitled him. Richard Cranch desperately needed a job. Dr. Cotton Tufts's brother, whom they had known very little, applied. So did their old friends Robert Treat Paine, who wanted a federal judgeship, James Lovell, who wanted to be collector of the port of Boston, Ebenezer Storer, General Lincoln, who had put down Shays's rebellion, Captain Lyde of the *Active*, who wanted to become a naval officer; dozens of entreating letters pouring in to John and even to her from men who had served long and well and needed the employment.

John had no jobs to give. The only one ostensibly at his command, secretary of the Senate, had been awarded to the man whom the Massachusetts senators knew John wanted: Samuel Otis, brother of James Otis and Mercy Warren. He was qualified, the Adamses hoped this appointment would mollify Mercy. It did not.

The Continental Congress had sat almost continuously but the new Senate and House were scheduled to adjourn at the end of September so that its members could go home to take care of their families, professions, businesses and farms. This termination point had two advantages for John Adams: some of the appointments and legislation which had been delayed by private and frequently senseless debate would now be acted upon. And it would make the Vice President his own man again.

7

Johnny came down for a month's vacation. He sat at his mother's French escritoire, which had made its pilgrimage from the Weymouth parsonage to the Adams cottage, the Borland house and now Richmond Hill, to post the family's accounts. He insisted that Charley join the bill-adding session so he could take over when Johnny returned to Newburyport.

"I don't love the practicalities," complained Charley; "I'll try. But don't bank on me to come out even."

Abigail was amused. "We have never come out even in your father's fifteen years of government service. Why should we start with you?"

Sometimes Johnny accompanied his father, going into the House to listen to the debates. The Senate was locked to all outsiders. He returned home at dusk with John and Charley, wide-eyed at the tumult, dissension, personal animosities and sectional feuds. At dinner he exclaimed:

"If one had to give an opinion at the end of a single day's session of the House, one would have to say that this government will never work; that after one more violent outburst by a member, the legislature will shatter into a thousand fragments."

"So the Senate seems too," replied John; "and don't for a moment imagine that there aren't people who want it to shatter."

"Then what holds the mechanism together?" Johnny queried.

"Many things: the reverence in which President Washington is held, the fact that able men are willing to serve, that both the Senate and the House have a few wise members who keep those less wise under control and oblige a compromise of differences; that eleven states have approved the Constitution and North Carolina is about to adopt."

"John, I've been thinking about this," said Abigail. "Isn't it also because *we have nowhere else to go?* If we allowed malcontents to break us up what could we become? A monarchy? An anarchy? A group of city-states, as in Italy? A Hanseatic League as with the German towns? We have to make this republic work because there is no other form of government we can live under."

"Hear! Hear!" It was Charley. John added:

"Mother is right: we have nowhere else to go. Every hour, every day we can keep this government together and working is that much more guarantee that we can survive. That's why President Washington is going to New England next month; they're grumbling in spite of all we've been able to do for their shipping and industries. The President wants to show himself there, renew old friendships, make new ones, assure New England that we are and must be a united nation. I know no one else who could accomplish that."

Abigail smiled.

"But the President has asked you to join him."

He would be gone only a few weeks. New York seemed quiet now with the government out of session. Abigail rode into town to bring the young Custis girl out for a visit: she was one of Martha Washington's grandchildren from a first marriage. That afternoon Mrs. Washington came to drink tea. A few days later she invited the Adams family for dinner and to hear the last concert of the season. Her regard for Abigail was not only a strong vote of confidence for the Adamses but a demonstration of intersectional confidence.

Letters arrived from John. President Washington had had a magnificent reception in Cambridge, where he had assumed command of the Continental Army in 1775. The New Englanders took to him again with enthusiasm. Was he not the man who had liberated Boston from the British? By his very presence he was able to dissolve antagonism, fears that the federal government was a potential enemy and despot.

Only Governor John Hancock's long retroussé nose was out of joint. Although he had invited the President to informal dinner at the governor's mansion, he failed to make the first ceremonial call on the President at his private inn on Court Street the afternoon of his arrival. Washington's modesty did not include an affront to the office of the presidency of the United States. He refused to go to Governor Hancock's dinner, turning instead to his old friends from the first Continental Congress, the "brace of Adamses." During the majestic parade into Boston, where State House Square was decorated with arches, he marched between John and Samuel Adams. On Sunday there again was the President seated between the two Adamses at King's Chapel.

John spent a few weeks with his mother and brother Peter, packing crates of books from their locked house to be shipped to New York. Abigail wrote a stream of instructions to John and to her sister Mary in the hopes of getting herself provisioned for the rest of the winter. She asked that a supply of firewood be cut off their land and shipped to New York because her purchases of oak and walnut had been so expensive.

"The porter which is in the cellar you will either have sent on or disposed of, as it will freeze. The red wine and any other you choose, you will direct Briesler to put on board . . . 200 weight of cheese and all the butter which can be procured. . . . The horse cart, horse sled and one saddle which the doctor has in his care, and the saw, should be put on board. We shall find them very useful. . . . Pray tell Briesler to bring me thirty or forty dozen of eggs. . . . Malt is another article that I should have been glad to have six bushels of. . . ." Briesler had returned to Braintree to be with his wife but had not been able to find employment paying as much as Abigail offered, two hundred dollars a year and keep, so was returning to New York with Esther and his children.

They could not have been more wrong about the French uprisings. As news trickled in from reliable observers it became clear that an overthrow of the existing regime had begun. By August of 1789 the Third Estate, composed of the middle class, merchants and artisans, had forced the nobles and clergy to relinquish their time-patined privileges. Louis XVI, though he had been permitted to remain King, had been forced to acknowledge that the French people, who had risen in every town and province to elect the Assembly, was the ruling power of the land. Serfdom was abolished, taxes were to be "paid by every individual in the kingdom in proportion to his income." There had been some violence, the burning of toll bridges, country houses; peasants had destroyed the seignorial deeds which had enslaved them, sometimes shooting recalcitrant landlords and cutting down their crops. Wandering bands of rioters clashed with the National Guards. But once a Declaration of Rights was passed which created a France in which all Frenchmen would be subject to the same laws, with all professions open to them, peace descended on the land. A new constitution was being written, accepted perforce by Louis XVI.

The Americans were jubilant. France was now their brother in freedom. Abigail had seen the brutalizing poverty of the peasants as she made the journey from the coast of Paris; she had felt the black wall of human hatred lining the streets as King Louis XVI moved with his entourage toward Notre Dame to return thanks for the birth of a prince. But the French had been an oppressed people for centuries, battened on by the nobility, the landowners, the Church, the King and his ruthless tax collectors. She had understood little French and had had limited contacts with the French people. Certainly her friendship with the Marquise de Lafayette could not have led her to believe that a revolt was imminent, or that Lafayette would become one of its leaders.

But John had spent almost a decade in France, he spoke and read the language fluently, he had had French friends among the nobility, clergy, army. He had discussed widely the works of the *philosophes*, the encyclopedists, Diderot, D'Alembert, Voltaire, Rousseau. Had he known there was a revolution in the making?

"In hindsight, yes. Then again, no. I knew that France was going deeper and deeper into debt, that she faced bankruptcy because she could find few buyers for her notes. I knew that the nobility despised the King and cuckolded him, politically as well as with his errant Queen. I knew that the extravagances of the court were crushing the people; that all pleas from the more humane priests and noblemen were being ignored. I knew there had been bread and salt uprisings in the provinces. Did I therefore know that the French would mount a revolution even as we did? I confess I did not. Nor can I remember Benjamin Franklin or Thomas Jefferson anticipating such an uprising. Perhaps one had to be French to feel in one's bones that revolt was brewing."

When the first reports of the new French Constitution reached New York, John Adams's enthusiasm was chilled. The French had not created a balanced government. The Assembly had debated and then rejected the idea of a second legislative house because it would not divide or share its power. No judicial system had been instituted to review the legality of the acts of the Assembly. The King as executive had been rendered powerless.

"This is the first dangerous flaw," he observed. "The Assembly has constituted itself the total government. Any deputy or group of deputies who can take control of this Assembly will rule France. That kind of rule means ruin."

As much as anyone in America, he wanted the French Revolution to be successful and for France to become a republic. Yet he felt that the road she was taking would lead only to bloodshed and destruction.

Congress reconvened on January 7, 1790. North Carolina had ratified the Constitution the previous November and been admitted to the Union. Neither John nor the Senate got into so many brawls as had characterized their first session. They had tested each other's mettle, established procedures of protocol, were abiding each other a bit better. Abigail settled into a harsh winter, feeding six fires to keep the house comfortable.

Instead of Johnny, she had Tommy at home for the holidays and the month of January, thin and pale from having overworked himself at his studies and from the recurrent bouts of rheumatism which he had inherited from his mother. He was the least bright of the three Adams boys but he had no intention of letting that minor handicap keep him from getting as good grades as his brothers. Abigail gave him a puke, after which he felt better; then she tried to fatten him up by making him eat alongside Charley, who had grown complacently plump. Charley remarked to Nab, his confidante in his love affair with Sally Smith:

"My two brothers make themselves ill by overwork. Thank heavens there's one male in this family who knows enough to enjoy life."

Abigail's family still consisted of eighteen. The materfamilias of so large a family is never without complications. Polly Tailor, the girl she had brought from Braintree, had a violent temper which she visited on the other help, causing Abigail to lose good servants. Her female cooks drank and when in their cups caused vulgar brawls. However there was

James, a bright-faced homeless fourteen-year-old Negro boy whom friends urged her to apprentice to the Adams family. He helped about the stables and gardens, in return for which he was to be given an education. James soon became the pet of the household. Each afternoon that she was free Abigail had him come to the sitting parlor for his lesson in reading and writing. He was eager, clever and learned fast. And there were Esther and Briesler, who occupied a little house on the hill below. Under their joint management the household ran reasonably smoothly.

She resumed her state dinners. One week she entertained the foreign diplomatic corps, the French chargé d'affaires, Louis Otto, the Spanish secretary of legation, José Ignacio de Viar, and the Netherlands minister resident, Pieter Johan van Berckel. The next week she gave a dinner for the five recently appointed Supreme Court justices, from Pennsylvania, South Carolina, Massachusetts, Virginia and Maryland; and as the guest of honor, their old friend Chief Justice John Jay. She entertained visiting governors and other high officials of the now twelve states.

On March 21, 1790, Thomas Jefferson finally arrived in New York to take over the post of Secretary of State. John Adams went round to the City Tavern where Jefferson was lodging, to bring him home for family dinner. It was a happy reunion after four years of separation. Jefferson quickly broke the news that Patsy was married. He appeared younger than he had in Paris or London. The hollows in his cheeks had deepened, the long, aristocratic nose was sharper, but his eyes seemed less sad, more compassionate now in their gentle, omnivorous gaze. He was pleased that John was Vice President, and told him so. John was pleased that Jefferson had at last joined the government in New York, which sorely needed his wisdom and talents; and told him so.

8

They went to church every Sunday morning the weather was affable. They were in as bad a way as when they had lived in France and England, for here in New York there was no Congregationalist Church. The Adams family were dissenters.

"I never would have thought it possible," Abigail sighed on their return home from the Presbyterian Church, "but every Sunday I regret the loss of Parson Wibird. I should really think it an entertainment to hear a discourse from him."

It had snowed the night before and they were in their sled, the one

John had brought home from storage in Cotton Tufts's barn. John spoke above the squeaking crunch of the runners.

"The only sermons I enjoyed were the three by the visiting New England clergymen. In a year or two we'll have enough New Englanders in New York to gather our own congregation. In the meanwhile better bad preaching than none at all."

Things were not going well for Nab and Colonel William. The job of marshal paid only a pittance. The Colonel was to receive a substantial portion of the fines assessed by the government against smugglers or shippers who falsified their cargo manifests. But few if any were misbehaving; the times were increasingly prosperous, there was a market for local produce as well the foreign imported goods, the shipowners and captains were scrupulously declaring their cargoes, the larger ships paying as much as thirty thousand dollars in duties. This was enormously helpful to the government but kept Colonel Smith from making a living.

"Why couldn't he have entered himself at the Temple in London?" John growled. "With an English law education he could have had a good practice in New York by now. Instead, what has he got?"

"A house in New York. He rented it yesterday. They move on May first, when all of New York moves."

John stared at her, incredulous.

"Did he tell you this?"

"No."

"Why is he moving?"

"Apparently living this far out of the city restricts his movements."

"To do what? Favor the punch bowl? If he is earning little to nothing, how is he going to support a household?"

"I don't know. His mother will help, I suppose."

"Nab won't like that."

"She's in circumstances again." When John went silent, she continued in a low voice, "I begged her not to have children so fast. This will be the third in four years."

President and Mrs. Washington were also moving. When the Macomb house on Broadway, formerly occupied by the French minister, became available, President Washington leased it and spent considerable money on refurbishing, adding lamps and green carpet, enlarging the stables to keep sixteen horses, making room for his fourteen white servants and seven slaves from Virginia. When he went abroad it was in a handsome carriage drawn by six matching cream-colored horses. No one accused him of monarchial tendencies; this charge was confined to the Vice President, who merely preached in the Senate what Washington was so brilliantly practicing, that this newest executive office on the world scene must be treated with respect and dignity.

Spring was harsh, cold and wet, with more snow than they had had through the whole winter. Abigail was confined to her bed with rheumatism and fever. An epidemic of influenza swept the city.

President Washington went down with a cold. A few days later it had developed into pneumonia. Reports were circulated that "the symptoms which attend the President's indisposition are not threatening"; at the same time an express was sent to Philadelphia to bring back a fourth doctor, a surgeon.

During the next three days the President sank rapidly. The calamitous news swept the city. All activity came to a standstill. Congressmen stood in the foyer of the Washington house, tears in their eyes. John and Abigail returned home on the afternoon of the fifth day, after a brief visit to the Washington house. One of the doctors had confided that the President's death was not improbable.

They went up to their bedroom. John closed the door as though to shut out the world. Perspiration streamed down his face. His speech was hurried, his thoughts disjointed as he poured out his feelings.

"It can't be. . . . We simply must not lose him . . . we have barely begun. . . . He makes the government work. . . . He will lay the foundation . . . we need him . . . for years. . . ."

He took a handkerchief from his waistcoat, wiped his dampened face. Abigail said slowly:

"I fear a thousand things which I pray I may never be called to experience."

Next morning she went to the Washington home to see if she could be of service. She was in the little sitting room when Mrs. Washington came out of the President's bedchamber.

"He is dying. I have just heard the rattle in his throat."

Tears sprang to Abigail's eyes. She put an arm about Martha Washington's shoulders. They stood for a moment so, then Mrs. Washington moved into the next room.

Abigail rode home. John was huddled in a big chair in the upstairs sitting room. One look at her and he buried his face in his hands. She sat opposite him, flooded with pity for the President, sorrow for his wife, with commiseration for the rest of the country, including themselves.

Millions of prayers commingled with the James's powders administered by the doctors. Late that afternoon the President broke out in a copious sweat. The crisis passed. The nation rejoiced.

Frustrated at being unable to speak in the Senate, John turned to the first sustained writing in the two years since he had finished *A Defence of the Constitutions of Government of the United States of America.* There were many things he had been thinking, annotations he had been making in the margins of his history books. Abigail was pleased to see him writing again, correlating the full powers of his knowledge and insight. She often thought him happier as a historian than as a politician.

The work was planned as a series for the *Gazette of the United States.* His major thesis was the imperfectibility of man: ambition, jealousy, envy, greed, vanity: mankind would never and could never rid itself of these attributes. The only way man could be forced to behave himself was by a government of laws which took into account these weaknesses and found a means to contain them. He did not believe that Utopia could be achieved on earth, neither did he believe that, as the Declaration of Independence stated, "All men are created equal." The most any government could do was give people the opportunity to be free and equal; in no society would all men be able to fulfill that opportunity equally. Abigail read in his vigorous scrawl:

"We are told that our friends, the National Assembly of France, have abolished all distinctions. But be not deceived, my dear countrymen. Impossibilities cannot be performed. Have they leveled all fortunes and equally divided all property? Have they made all men and women equally wise, elegant and beautiful? Have they annihilated the names of . . . Rochefoucauld and Noailles, Lafayette and Lamoignon, Necker and Mirabeau? Have they committed to the flames all the records, annals and histories of the nation? . . . Have they burned all their pictures and broken all their statues?"

She looked up from the sheets.

"John, is it wise to publish such sentiments in a democracy?"

"The historic truth must always be taken into account; how else can we build an enduring republic? Can every man in America serve as President, Chief Justice, Secretary of Finance and Foreign Affairs? Unthinkable! We have to find the men with the greatest training, talent. . . . They must find these men in France too, and distribute them through the Executive, the Assembly, the courts. The mob from the streets of Paris that captured the Bastille cannot rule the country. All men must be equal before the law but they cannot be equal in ability to run a complicated governmental structure."

"Granted. But it will renew the charges against you of believing in aristocracy."

"So I do: of the mind, the intellect, the spirit, the will."

What disturbed Abigail even more were John's speculative passages on the value of hereditary office. She had warned him in London, when she read the manuscript of the *Defence*, that his praise of good constitutional monarchs would bring charges of his being in favor of monarchy. She knew better than anyone else that this son of a yeoman and cobbler was merely making historical observations. This truth had not helped him when the book was published; the accusation of being a monarchist had been made by many then and had never quite died down. These new writings would reawaken those critics, expose him to the raking fire of his adversaries.

The outcry against the *Discourses*, when they were printed in Fenno's *Gazette of the United States*, was even more venomous than she had feared. Everyone now knew where John's sentiments lay. He was a monarchist! Had he not cast the tie-breaking vote in the Senate which gave the President the right to discharge heads of the Executive Departments? Had he not written letters to friends in various states urging the strengthening of the President's veto power? Had he not said again and again the President must be a protective screen against legislative excesses? His line about "a senator by hereditary descent" was coupled with a rancorous attack against what his critics claimed was his anti-French sentiment. He was against the French Revolution because it was a movement of the people, and John Adams was an aristocrat!

It was gratuitous ammunition. Angry and hurt, John returned to his desk to write protesting letters:

"I am a mortal and irreconcilable enemy to monarchy. . . . I am for having all three branches elected at stated periods."

If he cried out a warning did that make him an enemy of the French people, an advocate of their corrupt and impotent monarchy? On the contrary, he wanted France to achieve the same freedom and stability which the United States was slowly gaining. Let them take warning, then, and achieve a democratic balance of powers. All other roads led back through the ages to tyranny.

9

The public's general complaint was that Congress sat day after day and did nothing. This was an unfair charge, observed John; they held mountainous debates. It was simply that they accomplished almost nothing. There were two urgent measures that needed to be passed immediately: a funding bill in which the federal government would assume all state debts incurred in the war and in which there would be a unified plan for federal borrowing, to be followed by the payment of interest on all debts and their ultimate retirement. It was a bill prepared by Alexander Hamilton, who was giving inspired leadership to getting it approved. The second concerned the settling of the national government in a generally acceptable spot.

Abigail asked the question which all New York was pondering:

"Why not here? The people have already spent fifty thousand dollars to refurbish Federal Hall. Why do we all have to pack up and move again?"

John had always wanted to go back to Philadelphia, the scene of the birth of the government.

"The House has already voted for Philadelphia for the next ten years. Then we move to a permanent site on the Potomac River where a whole new federal city will be built. Jefferson and Madison are securing the Southern vote for our tax bill, most of which the South fears and hates, in return for having the capital located in the South. It appears a fair horse trade to me."

The summer turned hot. Nab suffered in her little boxlike house in the city. The Colonel was away most of the time; he was working on a scheme to make big money. Soon they would buy an estate on Long Island and live in luxury.

Elizabeth Shaw gave birth to a daughter. Elizabeth Cranch Norton had a son in the Weymouth parsonage. Nab gave birth to a third son. Tommy was graduated from Harvard. Abigail reflected ruefully that circumstances had kept her from the graduation of all three of her sons. Tommy started on a leisurely trip to New York and promptly got himself lost from his parents' view, his whereabouts unknown to them for weeks.

By the middle of August Johnny was settled in the front room of their home in Boston, ready to practice law in his father's old office. He boarded with a private family nearby. He wrote to his parents that he found the law profession crowded in Boston; he had no clients or prospects. When he finally did get a case, the older lawyer who was his opponent beat him badly. Johnny wanted to quit. He was also embarrassed to be taking money from his parents when he was already twenty-three years old.

At the end of August Abigail paid a last visit to the Washingtons in their house in New York. Mrs. Washington took her by the hand and said:

"God bless you, my dear madam. We will meet again at Philadelphia."

Abigail replied, "It is one of the occasions I shall look forward to, dear Mrs. Washington. In the meanwhile I trust you will find everything well at Mount Vernon and enjoy your hard-earned vacation."

Mrs. Washington smiled, wistfully.

"We must stop first at Philadelphia to find a proper house. I shall regret leaving New York. I have been as happy here as I could be at any place except Mount Vernon. If only the seat could have been on the Potomac now instead of ten years from now; how close we would have been to home. But the President is extremely happy with L'Enfant's first plans for the federal city. It is to be as beautiful as Versailles, as extensive as Paris, with broad tree-lined boulevards connecting the public buildings, all to be constructed of gleaming white stone; canals, fountains, parks. We have the opportunity to build the most beautiful city in the world."

John's apprehensions about the instability of the new French government appeared to be unwarranted. Their old friend the Marquis de Lafayette had initiated the demand for a second House in the Assembly. He helped draft France's Declaration of Rights based on the American Declaration, became mayor of the Tuileries and persuaded Louis XVI and Marie Antoinette to move into Paris where they would be under the control of the people. The King and Queen went before the Assembly to announce that they accepted the new constitutional government. The Church was reorganized, its extensive properties placed under the control of the State.

In September John returned from Philadelphia with the news that he had rented Bush Hill, an estate of three buildings strung out on a line at the crest of a hill overlooking the Schuylkill River, two and a half miles from the city. The main house was of brick, three stories high, with seven large windows lined up in orderly procession across the front, the formal entrance beneath the central window. Next came wooden stables and at the end of the regimental line a handsome carriage house with brick pillars. There was a grove of trees at the back, gravel walks and space for a garden.

Abigail listened, then exclaimed:

"I wish I knew a ladylike expletive with which to curse my bad judgment in sending for the rest of our furnishings when Nab moved out with hers. They have not been a month out of their crates and again they have to be boxed and shipped."

Though she sent the crates sufficiently in advance and John made provision to give the inside of the brick house a coat of paint, they arrived to find their dwelling as filled with painters and carpenters as it was empty of chairs or bedding. Since there were sixteen of them they could not afford to move into a tavern for more than the first night. The Bush Hill house had been unoccupied for four years and was cold and damp; the accumulated moisture in the bricks and plaster oozed through the fresh paint. Tommy, who had finally reached home, kept logs burning night and day in an effort to dry out the walls.

The furniture arrived, and with it dozens of well-wishers: friends of the family and the government to pay their respects. Philadelphia received the Adamses with its social arms wide open. John had made many friends there during his stays with the Continental Congress. There were invitations to tea and cards; to routs, to dinners, to dances. They went to one assembly with the Washingtons, the ministers of state and their wives, where Abigail found the dancing very good; and on their first trip to the theatre, as prettily decorated as any she had seen in France, the actors met them with the announcement that a box would always be available to the Vice President and his party. The play was *The School for Scandal*, wittily presented. Abigail's mind could not help but turn to Royall Tyler, who had based his play on the piece being acted before them. She heard his expressive voice reading scenes from the play to Nab and herself. Tyler was respected now at the Bar by clients and jurists alike; he was said to have as strong a grasp on the historical background of the law as any young man since John Adams. His plays continued to be produced successfully, and he was publishing poetry in the periodicals. In short, a fulfilled life, one which would grow in stature and accomplishment with the years. While Colonel William . . . Had she somehow failed her daughter?

The protective grove of trees at the front of the house had been cut down by British soldiers for firewood during their occupation of the city in 1777–1778, leaving the house naked against the world and the icy mid-November winds. Tommy was seized with such an acute rheumatism that he lost the use of his arms and legs for five weeks, having to be carried from his bed to a settee and fed like a child. Polly Tailor followed with a pleurisy fever which neither bleeding nor blistering could cure. Louisa went down next.

"What I need is a corps of nurses," mourned Abigail when Esther Briesler was bedded as well; "and all I get is invitations to formal balls in our honor. Look at me, John, I must have lost twenty pounds since I came to Philadelphia."

If she did not have any nurses she did have the services of the best, albeit most volatile doctor in town, Dr. Benjamin Rush. It was he who had first written to John about his becoming Vice President, in return for which John was to bring the government to Philadelphia. Now he made his rounds at the Adamses' Bush Hill hospital, elegant, sprightly, literate, effusive, intermingling prescriptions for his patients with bleedings, blisterings and purgings, and an analysis of why the second President of the United States would be none other than John Adams himself. Abigail exclaimed:

"O Heavens! I cannot project my thoughts years ahead when I hardly know how to get through the next hours."

Dr. Rush was a maverick who had established a new system of medicine, begun writing on medical and political matters and opened the country's first free clinic at the Pennsylvania Hospital. Abigail realized that he was fulfilling all the dreams on which Cotton Tufts had raised her.

Tommy recovered. John apprenticed him to a Philadelphia lawyer. Tommy's ambition was to practice with his father and two older brothers.

An express arrived from New York with a letter from Nab. Colonel William had just taken ship for England with no prior notice to his wife, or any explanation of why he was going except a vague reassurance that it was all part of his business plans. He would more than earn his costs by collecting some of his father's debts in England. As far as Abigail could learn he had left little or no resources for his wife and three children to live on. She was filled with concern for her daughter.

John was apoplectic. Abigail gathered from his sustained tirade that he had been coming to the painful conclusion that his daughter had married a fool, an incompetent and a wastrel. She let the outburst run its course, then said quietly:

"That marshal's job was a poor appointment. . . ."

"I didn't ask the President to give him that post," John protested. "It was the President's own idea. The Colonel was his aide and friend."

"Why did not the President offer him a more responsible job in the government?"

"You don't really want me to answer that question, do you?" His voice was heavy with bitterness.

"John, if we could get him an appointment that would satisfy his pride . . ."

"Nabby, I have steadfastly refused to be guilty of nepotism."

"I know, dear; I've read the disappointed letters from our friends. I'm only suggesting that you find the occasion to drop a subtle hint."

"That characterizes me perfectly: subtle John Adams, famous as such to friend and foe alike!"

The road from Bush Hill to Philadelphia was clay which turned into sticky mud in the winter months, sometimes up to the horses' knees. Yet she had to go into Philadelphia five days a week because John, who was immobilized on his dais at the Senate, found that as in Europe he could accomplish more over a dinner table or before a social fire in a friend's house than he could in the formality of his office.

"John, if we accept even half these invitations we shall spend a very dissipated winter."

"We must. That's how I make new friends and conciliate old opponents. It's good for the government, for the President and myself to meet frequently with congressmen, judges and diplomats; it gives everyone a sense of intimacy and participation."

"I insist upon keeping our Saturday nights and Sunday, then, for the family. Just close friends for tea."

"Very well. However you must give one dinner party a week, as you did in New York. And once a week the house must be open to strangers and friends alike. It is expected."

John took her on his favorite walks around Philadelphia, for he knew the city, largest in population in America with its forty-two thousand inhabitants. She found Philadelphia more like an English city than either Boston or New York despite the fact that on the streets she passed signs in German, and many Amish, Mennonites and Friends in their "broadbrims" and severe black dress. The city had been laid out by William Penn's engineer a century before. There was something comfortingly precise about the checkerboard streets which had been squared off between the Schuylkill and Delaware rivers, running for more than two miles along the shore back to the recently renamed Market Street where, on Wednesdays and Saturdays, Abigail bought delicious veal. The streets were well paved with pebbles, brick sidewalks were raised a foot high to protect the walkers. As the residents had proudly testified this past April at the funeral of their greatest son, Benjamin Franklin, Philadelphia was a city of firsts for America: the first magazine, the first daily newspaper, public hospital, library company, Philosophical Society. It was for this boldness of mind and imagination that John Adams had long admired it.

Philadelphia had rented for the Washingtons the best house in town, belonging to the financier Robert Morris, on Market Street. It was handsome, commodious and dignified, a proper residence for the Chief Executive of the United States, though Washington ordered at his own expense extensive changes, enlargements and decorations, even to the new curtains on the stairway. The public rooms reflected the good taste of their Virginia planter hosts. On Tuesdays from three to four the President had a levee to which came congressmen, Philadelphia's male society, visitors from other states and abroad. On Thursday nights the Washingtons gave a handsome dinner. On Friday evenings Martha Washington had a drawing room, entertaining with coffee, tea, cake, ice cream, lemonade. From seven to nine the well-bred ladies of Philadelphia came to swirl their exquisite gowns in the candlelight of the Presidential Mansion.

Chief Justice John Jay was the Adamses' house guest while the Supreme Court sat, and a delightful addition to their family circle. Samuel Otis, secretary of the Senate, kept Abigail informed about important people coming to the capital, particularly from New England, so that she was frequently able to have invitations to dinner or tea awaiting them on their arrival. Mrs. Bingham, their exquisite friend from Paris, and her equally lovely sisters were the arbiters of Philadelphia fashion; they decreed that Abigail's drawing room should become the center of a constellation of beauties dressed in the highest elegance.

She grew fond of Philadelphia. The city was accustomed to being the center of the national government. Its people did everything in their power to create a friendly milieu in which the components of the government could work harmoniously. As the snows vanished and the sun dried up the rains she came to enjoy Bush Hill as well. The rooms were spacious, there was a fine view of the city and the surrounding flatlands, with fields of wheat and grass stretching in front of the house. Her regret was being separated from Nab. She could not shake off a foreboding anxiety about her future.

Secretary of the Treasury Alexander Hamilton in December of 1790 and the winter of 1791 became the storm center of the country. The summer before he had driven through the legislature by force, cajolery and sheer weight of logic his funding bill consolidating all American debts, state and national, and allowing the government to borrow on a unified loan. Now he had taken what John described as the two next imperative steps: the establishment of a Bank of the United States with branches in the states, and the raising of federal funds through an excise tax on spirits. The bank was to be owned one fifth by the central government and the rest by private subscribers. Its function would be to serve as the fiscal agent for the United States at home and abroad, to control state bank issues by refusing to accept their paper as a medium of exchange unless it was backed by adequate specie.

The idea of an excise tax was lambasted by all local interests, but particularly the whisky distillers who would have to pay Hamilton's proposed tax. The government clearly needed the money and equally clearly the Constitution gave it the power to raise money through taxation. As a result the bill passed the House, apparently without serious dislocation. The bank bill was another matter. Jefferson considered it unconstitutional, since the Congress had not been given the power to create such national agencies. The basis of his judgment, with which Attorney General Randolph agreed and James Madison as well, was contained in the new Bill of Rights: "The powers not delegated to the United States by the Constitution, nor prohibited by it to the States, are reserved to the States respectively or to the people."

John Adams disagreed. He knew that American credit could be maintained only by a centrally controlled bank. He involved himself behind the scenes, making his experience and opinion available. The Senate gave the Bank of the United States a majority. The House also approved the measure. Jefferson recommended to President Washington that if the arguments in his mind were well balanced he should sign rather than veto the bill in respect for the wisdom of the legislature. Washington signed the bill. The United States now had a bank to care for its business. And Alexander Hamilton became firmly entrenched as the leader of the Federalists.

The offices of supervisor and inspector for the state of New York were now combined, and the post offered to Colonel William Smith. He had to be back by July first to be sworn in. Secretary of the Treasury Hamilton assured John he would write to Colonel Smith in London. John and Abigail could not forbear sending him urgent messages to return. The duties of the post would be arduous but the salary was a handsome one.

Congress recessed in May. The Adamses moved out of Bush Hill, sent a few pieces of furniture to Braintree and put the rest in storage. They would have six months on the farm.

Their fields were brilliantly green when they reached home. Peter had set out a vegetable garden beyond Abigail's rosebushes. The house was sorely underfurnished but they would make do.

Then unseasonal hot weather struck. The fields were robbed of their verdure; the vegetables drooped and died. Abigail went down with an attack of ague, the chills and fever so weakening her that she did not have the strength to walk about her bedroom. John was stricken with political ague. The attack came from an inconceivable source, his friend Thomas Jefferson, and would destroy not only their friendship but the national calm that had been growing during the years of patient plodding to achieve unity. Jefferson's attack would set up a strong contending party in the United States, absorb the Anti-Federalists, belabor John Adams as its natural antagonist, and attempt to remove him from the political scene.

10

A man in public life becomes inured to the carping of his critics; it is expected, he grasps the motives. The attack by Thomas Jefferson was the more painful because it was unexpected.

Thomas Paine, whose *Common Sense* had done so much to unify American sentiment during the Revolution, was writing a defense of the French Revolution. In the process he published in England a book called *Rights of Man*, a copy of which found its way to the House of Representatives in Philadelphia. The clerk loaned it to James Madison. After reading it, Madison sent it to Jefferson with a request that when Jefferson had finished reading it he send it to the printer in Philadelphia. In sending on the book, Thomas Jefferson added an accompanying note:

"I am extremely pleased to find it will be reprinted here, and that something is at length to be publicly said against the political heresies which have sprung up among us. I have no doubt our citizens will rally a second time round the standard of *Common Sense*."

The printer used these two sentences as the Introduction for his pamphlet. Copies were sent to the newspapers. Many of them seized on Jefferson's statement as an attack upon Vice President John Adams and the Federalists, reviving the cry of monarchist and the accusation that John Adams was against the French Revolution.

When John finished reading Jefferson's Introduction he handed it to Abigail across the fireplace of their wood-paneled sitting parlor.

"How can this be? We have never differed on political theory. There has always been confidence and trust between us. Why would Tom Jefferson set forth to accuse me of political heresy?"

"John, we must not convict Mr. Jefferson of a personal attack."

The Anti-Federalists now became known as the Republicans. Under this canopy they were able to bring together not only the former Anti-Federalists but all those who felt a discontent either with some specific measure of the Constitution or with the manner in which the burgeoning federal government was beginning to function. They bought or financed newspapers in most of the important cities, including one that was founded with Jefferson's help, Philip Freneau's *National Gazette*, which would represent the Republican point of view. These newspapers led an organized campaign to undercut the position of the Federalist Party, holding it to be an opponent of American democracy; and by the same token building themselves as the true representatives of the people. Since President George Washington was beyond personal criticism or abuse, except for an occasional sniping in the *New York Journal* or the *National Gazette*, a scapegoat was needed to set fire to the issue. Vice President John Adams seemed to have been born to the role. He had a talent for publishing material which left him a stout and open target.

The *Poughkeepsie Journal* claimed it was plain to see that John Adams was attached to "aristocratical and monarchical principles." The *New Haven Gazette* called Vice President Adams an enemy to freedom and to all republican institutions. The *Boston Independent Chronicle* suggested that he was an apostate from his original creed, that he would like to see a limited monarchy ruling the United States. He was satirized in the *Boston Centinel* as being stingy to his workmen, of complaining at the smallness of his salary. One Anti-Federalist paper caricatured him as the "Duke of Braintree."

As severe as was his shock at the attack by Jefferson, equally did he suffer when Cousin Samuel rose before both Houses of the Massachusetts legislature and delivered a sharp harangue against those who led the movement for hereditary powers in American government.

"Cousin Sam'l knows as well as Tom Jefferson that I am not in favor of hereditary powers!" John cried. "They know I am considering these elements from a historical point of view, and in light of what might be considered alternate possibilities if the Constitution fails."

They had recently been trying out possible names for their new home and farm. The one John liked best was Peacefield. No name could have been more malapropos, for their home became gloomy, torn by the accusations and the wounding quarrels which somehow had been conjured up. Abigail wondered why he had not been aware of the antagonism he had raised by the lines he had written in London praising the constitutional monarchy. She too felt that, with the Constitution so young and untried, it was not discreet to debate the possibility of its failure. The Constitution as it stood could be amended and was being amended; its basic structure had to be defended with the last drop of one's blood and the last iota of one's brainpower.

John Quincy was as outraged as his parents at the attack.

"Father, I know you have decided against taking up swords with Mr. Jefferson on this issue. You're right, it could only do harm for two high officers of the government to begin contesting each other in public. But what about me? I should like to defend the *Discourses*. I have a series of articles planned for the newspapers here. I would publish them under the name of 'Publicola.' Since no lawyer should defend himself in court, would you retain me as your counsel?"

John Quincy had not won many of his cases, but John's face lighted with the first smile Abigail had seen since the Paine pamphlet arrived.

In his defense of the *Discourses* in the *Boston Columbian Centinel* John Quincy necessarily linked the book with an attack on Tom Paine's pamphlet, based on the belief that France faced great upheaval and bloodshed if governed by a unicameral body. The American people recognized John Adams's stand. They concluded that John Adams had come out not only against the French Revolution but against Secretary of State Thomas Jefferson.

The summer was shattered.

Upset by the viciousness of the undertones which had been unleashed by his two sentences, Jefferson wrote to John explaining that in sending the pamphlet on to the printer, a stranger to him, he had added the lines about political heresies "to take off a little of the dryness of the note," and he had not meant to attack his old friend. "The friendship and confidence which has so long existed between us required this explanation from me, and I know you too well to fear any misconstruction of the motives of it. . . . Be so good as to present my respectful compliments to Mrs. Adams. . . ."

The depression which had settled into the household like a slate-gray fog lifted. The family read the letter over and over again. John sat down to draft a reply to his friend.

"I received your friendly letter of July seventeenth with great pleasure. I give full credit to your relation of the manner in which your note was written and prefixed to the Philadelphia edition of Mr. Paine's pamphlet on the *Rights of Man;* but the misconduct of the person who committed this breach of your confidence by making it public, whatever were his intentions, has sown the seeds of more evils than he can ever atone for."

Jefferson's answer was cold and formal. He insisted the whole unfortunate affair had been caused by the publication of the articles by "Publicola" and not by the two sentences which he had given for the Introduction. Abigail could not help exclaiming:

"What can Mr. Jefferson be thinking? Either his sense of time has vanished or he is being less than candid with us. His Introduction was published at least two months before Johnny's articles."

John rubbed his middle finger between his eyebrows until he had made the area a raw red. "Assuredly he would not mean to be false or dishonest. Mr. Jefferson is one of the fairest human beings I have ever known."

"Granted he *was* all of the things you say," exclaimed Johnny; "but what *is* he now?"

Abigail looked sharply at her son. "Why would you ask such a harsh question, Johnny?"

"Politics. Mr. Jefferson is an ambitious man. I know he talks about his desire to return to Monticello to be a farmer and scholar. Do not be deluded. He means to be the leader of this new Republican Party and to become its presidential candidate. Not this year, he too wants President Washington to be re-elected; but it is my opinion that he will cede second place to no one else in this country. I believe him when he says he did not intend those two sentences to be published; nevertheless they were in his mind, and I am sure he has spoken them and written them to his political friends. Nine out of ten of the attacks on the *Discourses* are launched by those who have not read it. What remains to be seen is precisely who is reading history accurately, Father, you or Mr. Jefferson."

Summer was over. Their plans for a relaxing vacation while putting the farm into good shape had gone askew. Richard Cranch had lain at death's door from a serious mortification of his leg. Knowing that her sister was again embarrassed for funds because of the long illness, Abigail asked Cotton Tufts to see that the Cranches were provided with firewood and all necessities over the winter without their being told from whom they came. Nab's third son, one-year-old Thomas, died suddenly in New York and caused a deep sadness in the house. Johnny had strained his eyes with so much reading that Abigail feared for his sight, prescribing an ounce of bark mixed with a portion of salt. John was so debilitated by the strife he could hardly make the trip south to Philadelphia. The one sustaining piece of news was that Colonel William Smith had returned to New York and taken up the post of supervisor of the state of New York.

The house they rented in the center of Philadelphia was expensive, almost a thousand dollars a year. The rooms were small and compact, but since no two of them opened into each other it made entertaining difficult. She needed only half the staff. Visitors called all day. She was fortunate in finding a Negro woman who was a fine cook, reliable and loyal to the family. The unruly Polly Tailor had been replaced by an amiable young Braintree girl called Ceilia. The Massachusetts state notes which she had bought cheaply at seven shillings sixpence on the pound, because interest rates were uncertain, were now paying their stipulated rate. This enabled her from time to time to use these sums for household purposes. It was obvious that the five thousand dollars a year salary would not cover the full session.

John went each day to the Senate Chamber. At home he assiduously followed the news from France. The French Assembly was torn by dissension. Feuds, conspiracies, betrayals splintered the single legislative body. The King and Queen fled the city, hoping to cause frightened royalty of other European countries to lead armies into France and put an end to the Revolution. They were captured and returned to Paris, where the crowds waved insults and guns at the royal pair. Blood lust was rising in France. However King Louis XVI signed the revised Constitution, an amnesty released all political prisoners and once again the middle class thought the Revolution peaceably concluded. John Adams still thought otherwise. Again he traced the course of the democratic party in France, saw the basis for a future civil war and said so. Again he was accused of wanting the Revolution to fail.

Abigail played her own role, stinting on nothing when it came to entertaining the hundreds of people who poured through her house. She had been a camp follower, moving to Richmond Hill outside New York, then Bush Hill outside of Philadelphia and now this house in the middle of the city.

She did not worry John or allow the fact that they were falling into debt to depress her. When they needed money to help Charley open his office in New York, provide for John Quincy, who was earning little, and Tommy, who was earning nothing, she would sell some tax certificates or the land left to her by her parents. Or she would write to Cotton Tufts to sell some of their livestock and stores of hay, grain, cider at any emergency price he could command. When she was really desperate she broke the last of the Puritan commandments, borrowing money from such old friends as General Lincoln in Massachusetts. At such times, when John realized how short she was of cash, he wrote strong letters to Secretary of the Treasury Hamilton demanding some of the money he had laid out of pocket in Europe; and once even went with his vouchers and notebooks to the Secretary's office to offer proof of how much in back expenses and salary the government owed. Occasionally his efforts resulted in a token repayment; even these Abigail was grateful to receive. Lack of money seemed to have become inextricably woven into the heavy rope which bound them to their calling: a self-evident evil to any sound New Englander but one they could not escape.

"Surely one term as Vice President is enough?" she thought. "Will we not have done our duty? I was once plump as a partridge, now I have no flesh left on my bones. Mr. Jefferson or Mr. Hamilton could serve equally well as Vice President. When the election comes at the end of the year, could not John simply retire? He has described the job as the meanest position ever invented by man. He is unhappy, misplaced, wasted. Why would he conceivably want another four years of such drudgery?"

She wrote to Cotton Tufts. Would he please repair the leak in the roof which her two carpenters had failed to find the summer before? Would he have them put new sashes in her bedroom window; find painters to give the exterior of the house a new coat? Would he try to buy beds at vendue; lay in hams, casks of tongues, barrels of cider in the cellar?

Nab came for a long visit with her oldest son William. One day Colonel William burst in upon his astonished wife. He was overflowing with confidence and excitement. Without an exchange of greetings he cried:

"Nab, we're going abroad. On the March packet out of New York."

"Might I ask what you've done with your position as supervisor for the state of New York?" his father-in-law demanded.

"I've resigned it," the Colonel answered airily.

"It was a good position. It paid well."

"A living. I want spectacular money. A fortune. I have it in the palm of my hand. Nab, we're going to be rich. I have our estate all marked out, hundreds of fertile acres."

Nab asked quietly, "Could we know what this plan is?"

It had something to do with the thousands of acres of land recently come onto the market in central New York through Governor Clinton's treaty with the Indians. The Colonel was planning to sell the land in England. He had wealthy American backers, options to sell whole townsites, had himself bought some of the best tracts . . .

Nab was convinced that at long last her husband had a magnificent opportunity. She was glad to be going abroad again. She would take letters of introduction from her father. . . .

Abigail and John were glum. Later that night he asked:

"Does he seem like a financier to you?"

"You were never of the opinion that it took genius to make money."

The great debate of the 1792 legislature was over reapportionment of representatives for the House. The country was growing, Vermont had been admitted as a state in 1791, Kentucky, part of Virginia's extensive western lands, was moving rapidly toward statehood. There were more states and more people, all of whom wanted to have a voice in government. Each state demanded more representatives in Congress, but not at the cost of giving other states a larger number. New England, the South, the East all wanted to enlarge their total geographic vote so that they could have sufficiently large blocks to put through their own bills while defeating legislation they considered to their disadvantage. The Constitution said that each state should have one representative for every thirty thousand; but what of those sizable fractions that were left over?

The Senate had the right to approve the House's decision. When a compromise bill was finally passed after several months of debate, its opponents decided that New England had gained the most votes.

President Washington negatived the bill on the advice of Jefferson, Madison and Randolph that it was unconstitutional. Since this was his first "negative" of a bill passed by Congress, he was embarrassed. How would Congress accept such a revocation of its will? Would there be outcries, wails of anguish, accusations of tyranny?

Washington's veto was accepted calmly. When the House failed to recruit the necessary two-thirds vote to override the negative, it passed a more satisfactory measure. The legislators were so pleased at their equable solution that, as John remarked jubilantly:

"They failed to notice that they have irrevocably set their approval on the executive power of veto. In the first three years not one piece of their legislation was rejected by the President. This was a time of test. Now we know it will work. If the Congress cannot override a presidential veto it must write a better bill, or at least reach a tenable compromise. For the purpose of a balanced government, this acceptance can be the most important decision we have made."

11

Spring came to Philadelphia in April. They grew homesick for their green fields and blue hills. She began packing her personal things for the trip north.

"John, how long do you think we'll be home this time?"

"Quite a spell. I don't want to be in Philadelphia during the voting; it would make it appear that I am seeking re-election to the vice presidency."

"The electors must all be named by December fourth?"

"Yes. I'll resume my seat on December third. The session should be brief. Both Houses want to conclude their debates before Installation Day, March fourth, and leave immediately after."

This last year had not been a good one for her. She had endured too much illness and turmoil. During the past months a feeling of debility had overtaken her, as though her body were waging inner conflicts over which her mind and will had scant control. It left her little reserve strength with which to fight off the epidemics that swept the city, the external sicknesses which one could talk about.

"Would you mind terribly if I took a sabbatic? I'd like to stay home for those three months. You'd be comfortable with the Samuel Otises. They've become like family."

"You have earned it. What would you suggest we do with this house and our furniture?"

"If you're not returning until December, the year's lease will already be up. I think we ought to put our furniture in storage, then turn the house back to the owner and see if he can rent it again, and return us the six months' rent."

John bobbed his head on his chest.

"There's a demand for houses," he said. "The owner is reasonable. Even if we only save enough to pay for the cartage and storage . . ."

They returned to their farm in time for John to take the burden of the fields off his brother Peter's still reluctant shoulders, leaving Tommy behind to continue his apprenticeship in Philadelphia. The town of Braintree had been divided in two and, at Richard Cranch's suggestion, their half had been named Quincy after Abigail's grandfather. Johnny came from Boston for a visit. Abigail worked lazily around her English rosebushes. The house was largely bare of furniture, with only the oilcloth on the floor of the sitting parlor which Mary Cranch had tacked down the spring before. Cousin Cotton had bought them some beds and bolsters; the cellar was well provisioned. She was pleased about this, for she had no stomach for the practicalities.

Their minds were preoccupied with the coming elections. Would John be re-elected? During the first election there had been essentially one party: the Federalists. The rest were skeptics, malcontents, states' rights battlers loosely roped together under a knot known as Anti-Federalism. There was now no new issue really. Yet this time there would be parties, and strife, the kind of altercation John feared as divisive to a country. Thomas Jefferson had made it clear that he would not contest the vice presidency with John. Alexander Hamilton did not aspire to the post. George Clinton was re-elected governor of New York and then decided that he would like to be the next Vice President. He proved to be a rallying point for those dissidents. A number of states had gathered around him.

In other years this would have disturbed John. Now he was determined to keep any controversy from invading their tranquillity. He refused to return to Philadelphia even when Alexander Hamilton wrote him a strong letter stating that his absence was hurting his chances, staying with his promise of early spring that he would assume his post only after all votes for the electors had been cast. On November second he cast his own ballot in the Braintree Meeting House. Abigail was not happy about the fact that she could not vote.

On November 19, 1792, they parted casually, as though John were going to Boston, agreeing to write each other a brimming letter of news each week. John would have Tommy in Philadelphia to keep him company and Briesler to serve him; for herself she had Louisa, now nineteen, who had become as a daughter to her. She had one hired hand, a reliable older man, not as strong as the farmwork sometimes required, and young James.

She settled into the quietness within herself, raising no issues, accepting no alarms. When the most severe snowstorm in years clamped down and she knew it would engulf John on the road, she did not worry about him but instead rescued the sheep on the hillsides and secured them in the converted carriage house. Time flowed easily about her. She remembered how she had felt, fourteen years before, with John three thousand miles away: time then had been a solid; each hour a skirmish inside the day's battle to fill the calendar.

All week she thought with pleasure of the grab bag of news she would send him, and lingered over the writing. The wood had been cut for the corncrib; it would be hauled in as soon as the snow permitted. The roads to the coast were a quagmire, but when they dried the wagons would bring salt hay for the fields. The pine trees they had found in their cedar swamp would be carried to the mill to be cut into boards.

John's letters brought her as much pleasure as writing her own. He had been well received when he resumed his chair in the Senate. He was comfortable at the Otis home, in a chamber with a southern exposure and a fire day and night. He obeyed Abigail's orders to lie warm, "for the damp and chill is very penetrating." But he could not get a complete night of sleep. He disliked lying alone.

The Federalists had been well organized and put on a spirited campaign backing John. Governor Clinton got the unanimous votes of the electors of New York, North Carolina, Virginia and Georgia. Jefferson won Kentucky, which had become a state in June of 1792. John ended with seventy-seven votes against Clinton's fifty, this time winning a clear majority.

Abigail held to the concept of lying fallow. Mary and Cousin Cotton came to drink tea. It was the only diversion she allowed herself except for Johnny's visits on Sundays to take his mother holy walking and to have midday dinner with her. He was not faring well. He had taken his father's advice and was participating in local politics, at this moment petitioning the Massachusetts legislature to rid itself of its obsolete anti-theatrical law. But he seemed lonely. He had ventured no romantic attachments since Abigail had discouraged an earlier one two years before. He did not always bother to take the best care of his clothes or hair.

She visited with him in Boston, listened to the successful lawyers in court. They did not seem to have the depth or insight Johnny had; yet they had clients and Johnny almost none. She wondered whether her son was perhaps overeducated for a tyro at the Bar, his learning and wide travel frightening off clients with minor problems to solve.

Since Boston was a hotbed of French sympathizers, Abigail was able to stay abreast of the news. There had been riots in Paris in front of food warehouses and grocery shops, at which times the merchants had been forced to lower their prices on rum, coffee and sugar. Pillaging in the provinces had become the order of the day. Mobs armed with pitchforks and muskets stopped grain boats, dividing the corn among themselves. In provincial cities the workmen marched under banners to force downward the prices of eggs, butter, cereals, wood and coal. When the merchants resisted, they were shot. In Paris the Tuileries was stormed, the Swiss Guard massacred; Lafayette, now out of favor as the Jacobin democrats rose in power, fled his country, only to be captured by the Austrians. Although new elections were called and a National Convention convened which established universal suffrage, this did not apply to the royal sympathizers, who were first jailed and then massacred without benefit of trial. As John had predicted, law and government had broken down in France. The Revolution still had a long and bloody road ahead.

Abigail said little, for most of her old friends rejoiced at the killing of the loyalists, believing that it led France closer to becoming a republic. But her heart was filled with sorrow for the French people she had come to know and love.

One of her reasons for remaining at home was to attempt to throw off the intermittent fever which had laid her low for three winters in succession. What helped to cure her was the unexpected return to New York in February of Nab and Colonel Smith. The Colonel had enjoyed a fantastic success in selling New York land and came home with a fortune in money. He bought Nab a carriage and four and, according to John's report, was bragging about his great wealth to everyone he met.

John wrote to ask if it might not be wise to take their furniture out of storage and send it home in time for his arrival the following month. Abigail had an idea. She wrote to Nab: if it made no difference to the Colonel in what city he carried on his business, why not Philadelphia? The Colonel was speaking of buying a large estate. If they would buy or rent in Philadelphia, Abigail and John could live with them for the few months that Congress sat, use their own furniture in their chambers and bear their share of the expenses. Did not Nab think it would be a fine thing for the family to be reunited for a portion of each year?

Nab certainly did. The Colonel thought otherwise. He wanted to live in New York, with the surrounding acreage of an estate. He was going to build a replica of Washington's Mount Vernon.

John was sworn in as Vice President on March 4, 1793. All attacks against him stopped. As leaders of the two parties, Thomas Jefferson and Alexander Hamilton became the antagonists, each partisan press berating its "enemy" in the shrillest of terms. The personal quarrels between Secretary of State Jefferson and Secretary of the Treasury Hamilton were based partly on personal animosity, partly on irreconcilable political differences. The raucous intensity of the row was so shattering that President Washington, for whose favor they were vying, declared that their quarrels were disrupting the federal government. He urged them to make "mutual yieldings," adding, "Mankind cannot think alike," and advised all officers of the Republic to compromise their differences to achieve a common goal.

The Adamses had a ringside seat at this cockfight. What they did not learn from the men themselves they read in the *Gazette of the United States,* the most widely read journal in America, which praised Hamilton while it damned Jefferson's every move. Through the voice of Freneau's *National Gazette,* which Jefferson and James Madison had created, Hamilton's reputation was in turn blackened as Jefferson was described as "that illustrious patriot, statesman and philosopher."

The government was now divided into two fanatical factions, each determined to destroy the other, apparently unconcerned if the Union fell in the process. The seeds of the uninterrupted quarreling were born with each morning's sun: should England be allowed to move its troops from the Northern United territories to fight the Spanish in the lower Mississippi? Should the Post Office be in Hamilton's jurisdiction or Jefferson's? Should the Mint be under the control of the Treasury Department, as Hamilton protested, or that of the Department of State? Who was to control the funding of the debt? Was the treasurer becoming a financial tyrant who had introduced poison into America with his Bank? Had Jefferson acquired the "French disease"?

Where before these quarrels had been conducted inside the government, known only to Washington, Adams and a portion of the Congress, now their mutual recriminations and hatreds were spread across the newspapers for all to read. Was Jefferson motivated by rancor and "lust for power"? Was the Republic in serious danger from each man, as the supporters of the other publicly charged?

The major effect of the internecine war was to diminish the stature of the two Secretaries as well as deepen the rift between the two parties. But something else was unmistakably clear: John Adams once again followed President Washington as the second man. The troubles into which his indiscretions had plunged him had been momentarily eradicated by the more serious indiscretions of his two most pressing rivals.

The session was over. John had lived economically in Philadelphia. When Abigail managed to get some cash from crops or rents she immediately bought more government certificates. Now that John was back home the farm would support them for the rest of the year providing he did not go in for any extensive improvements. He gave much of his time to Johnny, who needed his father's company and reassurance. Johnny was still obliged to accept money for his support. This killed his soul. He was an omnivorous reader, devouring Livy and Plato in the original, studying history as ardently as ever his father had. But there still appeared to be no place for a scholar at the Boston Bar.

The news from France continued to be heartbreaking. In January of 1793, a few months after the Convention had abolished its monarchy, King Louis XVI had been guillotined. The British dismissed the French ambassador. The French Assembly, announcing that its purpose was to annihilate kings and to free oppressed peoples everywhere, declared war on England and Holland on February 1, 1793. Among the French people there was exultation rather than fear at the prospect, for the French and British rarely missed an opportunity to declare war on each other. In the throes of its political and economic chaos France was not only on fire with the zeal of liberating Europe but was already waging a war with Austria.

The guillotine became the national symbol of France as Queen Marie Antoinette and her circle were all beheaded. Blood ran in the streets, oozed between the cobbles as the blade fell on thousands of Parisians and Frenchmen throughout the land, the example being set by the successive leaders of the Assembly who, in seizing power, unfailingly guillotined their predecessors. Everything John Adams had predicted had come true. The Assembly had destroyed itself, Robespierre's reign, known as the Terror, was in John's opinion the worst the civilized world had known. The French Revolution had still not evolved a government which could rule the country with peace and justice.

Boston's French sympathizers wore ornamental guillotines pinned onto their coats and dresses to indicate their pride in the French Republic. Their feelings rose higher against John Adams in direct ratio to the accuracy of his prediction.

Abigail settled into the cycles of the seasons. The weeks and months were blurred. Time was no longer a mountain but a river. She spent the winter before her fireplace, the spring in her flower garden. She was at that period in a woman's middle years when pains, fevers, mysterious malaises fogged her mind and spirit, made her content to remain inactive. On those days when she went down, Mary Cranch came to nurse her. When she was better she sat with Richard Cranch who, each year, was on the sere leaf-edge of death, or nursed John's mother, who grew so weak that it appeared nothing could bring her back. They survived, both of them.

"Nobody in New England dies easy," she commented to Mary. "We are all so cantankerous we refuse to answer the first half dozen blasts of Gabriel's horn."

Her problems on the farms were endemic. She felt as though she had been born with them and would die with them. It was an open winter with a pretty fall of snow but the oxen were unable to bring in loads of firewood or rails from the cedar swamps. They now owned three separated farms; the same hired hands could not tend all three nor could the tools: plow, spades, forks, shovels, axes, hoes, scythes had to be constantly borrowed back and forth, or duplicated. It was over thirty-two years since she had started walking out with John. They had been at the center of a tremendous amount of history, had in fact been responsible for a lot of it happening. Yet if they had played on history, history had also played on them.

She was forty-nine. She felt within herself tremendous reservoirs of energy. The Quincys and Smiths were long-lived. She walked up to the bedroom, her legs strong beneath her. In the mirror she saw her rich brown hair dusted with a becoming silver-gray, her eyes wide, strong, able to grasp the world about her, her face and figure lean now as when she had first walked the streets of Boston with John; her mouth warm, strong, her chin flashing the intelligence that Abigail Smith Adams would do her duty no matter where or how far it called her.

They would have problems with which to grapple, more history to spin. She would cope.

12

Wars, in Abigail's view, were rarely won; they were recessed. John Adams had maintained in Paris that France had joined the United States mainly to crush her ancient enemy. Now France was trying to pull the United States into her conflict against England. Citizen Genet, son of a family John had known in Paris, came to Philadelphia as the French ambassador and attempted to blackmail President Washington by appealing to the people over his head. Washington had him recalled. The Federalists, Washington, Adams, Hamilton, Jay, insisted upon remaining out of European wars. The Republicans, joined by citizens who still hated England because of the War for Independence, wanted the United States to repay its debt to France by siding with the French and fighting the British. The conflicts in Philadelphia became so destructive that Jefferson resigned and returned to rebuild his home in Monticello. Hamilton was planning to resign and resume his law practice. General Knox prepared to resign because administering a War Department was more difficult than moving pieces of artillery from Fort Ticonderoga to Boston in the middle of winter.

It was the job of which John Adams despaired, his vice presidency, which enabled him to cast a tie-breaking vote and defeat a harsh measure against Great Britain which might have made that war inevitable.

John and Abigail in their three years' residence in England had had contact with King George III, his Cabinet and members of Parliament. They had admired much about the British form of government. Now they were sought out for their knowledgeability. What made the English behave the way they did? Ten years after they had ratified the peace treaty they still had not evacuated their troops from the Northwest forts. A thousand redcoats were on American soil stirring up the Indians. They had adopted secret Orders in Council to seize all neutral ships and had captured two hundred and fifty American vessels, all of them condemned by Admiralty courts in the West Indies, their cargoes confiscated, the crews impressed into the British navy or imprisoned. Fever ran so high that Abigail read in a journal of the need for a Second War of Independence.

At a small dinner party given by Martha Washington for government officials the question was asked:

"Why would the British make this calamitous move when they know how hard we Federalists are working to keep us out of war on the side of France? Don't they know they're arming the Republicans who want to go to war against them?"

All eyes turned to John. He took time to organize the materials of his brief.

"The British are blockading France to starve it into defeat. It is logical for them to confiscate foodstuffs and materials of war from neutral vessels. We would do the same if pressed hard enough. The losses to our merchants are damaging, though not enough to go to war over. But when they start seizing our ships as well, impressing our sailors . . . *I just don't understand them.*"

Abigail was able to follow the maneuvers of the two American parties in the Boston papers which Johnny brought out twice a week, and in the journals sent to her by John from Philadelphia and New York. At the moment the Jefferson Republicans wanted to pass a bill prohibiting the importation of sizable amounts of British goods into the United States. Hamilton's forces were livid at the suggestion; the tariff paid on British goods was one of the largest sources of income to the Treasury, helping to support the United States Government and maintain its credit.

If John could not understand the British, Abigail was having equal difficulty following her fellow Americans. The attempt to keep out British goods caused such a split between the Northern and Southern states that John wrote, "Nearly one half the continent is in constant opposition to the other." Talk of separation could be heard at the levees and dinner tables of Philadelphia. Senator Rufus King of New York was reported to have told John Taylor of Virginia that since New England and the Southern states "never had and never would think alike, dissolution of the Union by mutual consent" was the only sensible solution to the differences of opinion.

The solution came out of the Senate. A group of Federalist senators asked President Washington to send a minister plenipotentiary to Great Britain to seek a comprehensive treaty which would put an end to British depredations on American shipping, secure a mutually beneficial trade pact and get the British soldiers off United States soil.

Washington chose Chief Justice John Jay, familiar with such negotiations in the past. The following week a Republican measure which provided for non-intercourse with Great Britain passed the House of Representatives and came to a tie vote in the Senate. John Adams cast his vote against the bill. Had it passed, Jay's peace mission to Great

Britain would have been destroyed, for the British Ministry would never have received him. As it was, Chief Justice Jay sailed in early May. A break with England was almost certainly averted.

The Republican papers again began to whip John through their journals as more British than American. French sympathizers who wanted America to war against England were hiding behind every tree on the Atlantic seaboard, tomahawks in hand, waiting for Jay's scalp if he brought back a treaty which bound the United States and England as allies. John Adams was still being proved right about the French government: Robespierre had had Danton guillotined, and now Barras had had Robespierre guillotined, while tens of thousands of French men and women continued to be slaughtered without recourse to legal procedure.

Abigail's own crises were minor. When there was sixteen dollars owed Savil for loads of firewood and she had not sixteen cents in cash, she put him off. When slugs crawled over the orchard she tarred the trees. When she needed clover seed she wrote to John to ship it from Philadelphia. She bought a cheese press; rubbed the throats of the sheep with goose oil when they got the mumps. When a tenant moved out of the old house of John's parents, leaving it as filthy as an Augean stable, she found a way to run a river through it. John showed his first agitation over the presidential election, still two years in the future, by developing an acute case of farm fever. Abigail was to establish a dairy at each of their three houses. She must buy as many yearlings and two-year-olds as she could find. Since she had no money, no barn, little help except the continuing stream of applicants for the older houses, she declined the invitation to add to her herd.

It was this spring and summer of 1794 that the Adams family had a stroke of good fortune, the sweetest to Abigail since Nab had achieved financial security. Johnny had at long last found clients and was earning a modest living. He enjoyed the proudest hour of his life when he came home to Quincy to say to his mother:

"I won't need this last of Father's drafts. I'm earning enough now to cover my keep. My affairs should go forward with good dispatch."

Without warning letters arrived for Abigail and Johnny announcing that President Washington, who had come to know Johnny in Philadelphia, had made inquiries about him, had apparently read some of his political writings in the journals, and now nominated John Quincy Adams to be the American resident minister to Holland, there to live and conduct his embassy in the very house which John Adams had bought as the first of the European embassies to be owned by the United States Government. The Senate gave its unanimous approval; the senators congratulated Vice President Adams and showed their happiness for him. There was no talk of nepotism. John Quincy had won the position on his considerable merit. Johnny would be filling his father's shoes.

"An end devoutly to be desired," he told his mother, pale with suppressed joy. "In all those years I watched Father and Francis Dana serve in France, Holland and Russia, I yearned to continue the work."

"Your father has always maintained that you have the best political education of any young man in America."

Johnny struggled against the emotion surging within him. He gave up the contest, put both arms about his mother and kissed her.

"Thanks to you for having been willing to let me sail for Europe during a war, face all kinds of terrifying dangers, leaving yourself without an older son who could have been of some help with Father away. Mother, where did you find the courage?"

She remained inside the sanctuary of her son's arms. It was a long time since Johnny had been able to put aside his heritage and show his love for her. She gazed up into his warm brown eyes.

"Courage, Johnny? I don't know. We just do blindly the thing we think is right. I wanted you to have the advantages of travel and knowledge of European cultures. What was it that moved me: love? duty? ambition? All three. Now I have my reward in full measure. Nothing that has happened in the years since your father was chosen Vice President has given me such a recruit of spirits."

"Mother, I never wanted to practice private law. I have always longed to serve our government. But I could not have accepted this appointment a year ago, before I was earning a living. For the rest of my life I would have said to myself, 'You took the post as minister to escape your failure at the Bar.' Now I know I can contend, so I go in pride."

Abigail crossed the room to the bowfat with its decanter of Madeira. She noticed a bemused expression in Johnny's eyes.

"Johnny, you're up to deviltry. What is it?"

A wholehearted grin enveloped his face.

"It's Tommy. I'd like to take him with me as my secretary. He's the only one of us who has not had the chance to see Europe. There's no salary allowance for a secretary to the embassy in Holland, but I'll pay his costs of travel out of my wage. If Father would continue the same allowance Tommy gets now I'm sure we'd make out."

Abigail gulped. Two of her four children would be away from her again. This too was a recurring pattern. Johnny was to receive four thousand five hundred dollars a year, almost as much as John Adams made as Vice President of the United States. John felt only pride; and that was what she felt now.

"Johnny, I'd know you for my son, no matter where we met."

The problem about which John Adams had worried, whether the federal government could stand up to a rebellion inside one of the states, now came into focus. Pennsylvania men walked the streets with placards reading "Liberty and no Excise. O, Whisky" and burned the home of the regional inspector of the excise taxes in a Whisky Rebellion against the federal taxation imposed by Secretary of the Treasury Hamilton.

President Washington sent in his army of militia and the threatened uprising was quickly extinguished. The strength of the Chief Executive, for which John Adams had labored so fruitfully, had preserved the dignity and power of the central government.

If John Jay returned with the kind of treaty John Adams had never been able to extract from the British, he would undoubtedly replace John Adams as second man of importance in the country. Instead Jay got a mauling.

President Washington received a copy of the treaty in March of 1795 and, being unhappy with its provisions, determined to keep it a secret until the Senate reconvened for a special ratifying session. The word "secrecy" had not been written into the Constitution and nobody in the government had to obey its stricture. A copy of the treaty was sneaked to Benjamin Bache of the *Aurora,* a Republican newspaper. Once again fat sputtered on the hearths of the fifteen states. President Washington exclaimed that the battle over the treaty was ". . . like that against a mad dog."

In April, John Jay returned home.

The ratifying session was called for June. Abigail traveled to New York with John en route to Philadelphia. It was a chance to visit with Nab and the children until the Senate either approved or rejected the Jay treaty. Nab had had a daughter, finally, after bearing three boys. She was in good health and spirits, the Colonel bursting with optimism and affluence. He insisted upon driving the Adamses to the Van Zandt farm to show them his superb acreage lying between the East River and the

Boston Post Road. It contained a variety of barns, ponds, outbuildings and had cost the Colonel "only £5000," a bargain. Since he had been elected to the presidency of the Society of the Cincinnati, replacing Baron Von Steuben, he needed a proper home in which to entertain. He showed Abigail the first portion of his transplanted Mount Vernon, a most distinguished carriage house. The mansion itself was going to be seventy-six feet long, with wide verandas, a promenade on the roof. Abigail asked tentatively:

"Colonel, have you an estimate of what this house will cost?"

"It doesn't matter," he replied. "Money is falling into my hands as though I were standing in an apple orchard in the overripe season. I buy big parcels of New York City and sell them for profit. I'm helping fit out two privateers for the Mediterranean trade; they return unbelievable sums. My future brother-in-law, Saint-Hilaire, and I are setting up an international business of staggering proportions. You know that I've been providing the French with supplies for several years?" He slipped an arm through Abigail's. "Did you ever suspect when you helped me win Nab's hand that you were bringing a veritable Croesus into the Adams family?"

John Jay had been dealt two foul blows which made his task a near hopeless one. First, Hamilton undermined his mission by confiding to the British ambassador that the United States would never join the French coalition in any case. Secondly, James Monroe, now American minister to France, was so passionately pro-French in his loyalties that he frightened the English. How could the United States remain neutral in any war in Europe if Minister Monroe was giving exhortatory speeches to the French National Assembly? Nevertheless John Adams considered that Chief Justice Jay had secured several important concessions: the British promised to get out of their Northwest forts by June of the following year; navigation of the Mississippi River to its mouth was granted to the United States; full and complete compensation was agreed upon for all American ships that had been seized and condemned. American ships were to be admitted to all British ports on a reciprocal tariff basis. In return America would not allow its ports to be used by Britain's enemies. The American government would repay the legitimate private debts of its merchants incurred before the War of Independence.

Jay had been unable to establish the freedom of the seas. American ships could still be stopped, searched and any portion of the cargo seized. Neither did the British agree to stop impressing American sailors; or to return the slaves who had been transported during the war, or their worth.

A large part of the citizenry became angry. The Republicans were outraged. The Southerners rejected the treaty in toto. Hamilton was stoned at a public meeting in New York when he tried to defend it. John Adams recognized that it was a step forward. At this moment Britain seized several American ships carrying food to France. President Washington determined not to sign the treaty. Then he learned that Secretary of State Randolph, who had strongly advised him not to sign, had been caught in secret negotiations with the French minister, Monsieur Fauchet, to upset relations between the United States and England.

On June 24, 1795, the Senate ratified the Jay treaty. President Washington affixed his signature on August eighteenth. There was no rejoicing. Abigail mused:

"John tried for years to secure just such a treaty and failed. Now because there has been a revolution in France and a war is being waged, John Jay is condemned and his career hurt for getting at least half of what we wanted. There can be no stranger world than politics."

The Reverend John Shaw died in Haverhill shortly after Johnny and Tommy sailed for England. Betsy grieved but within a matter of months married the Reverend Stephen Peabody, proving the New England adage that widowhood is like a pain in the elbow: sharp and short.

Abigail had thought during her visit to New York that Charley was behaving furtively. It was not until she and John had returned to Quincy after the Jay treaty session that they received word that Charley had married Sally Smith.

John went into squalls.

"He has just become a barrister. A premature marriage will hurt him. Why could he not wait until he was established and secure?"

Abigail was glad to see Charley in safe anchorage. She replied mildly:

"Were you totally established when you married me? I think not, if I can remember your terror-stricken weeks preceding the wedding. Can there not be some little element of adventure in marriage? Give Charley his chance, John. He's twenty-five, old enough to be a man."

John was mollified.

He returned to the latest reports that had come from Paris. The French were now coming around to John Adams's way of thinking. They created two elected legislative bodies, independent of each other. These two bodies had chosen a Directory of five members to serve as the nation's executive. It was a step forward, he agreed, but still a serious error.

"They will find their plural executive will be a fruitful source of division, faction and civil war."

The Directory would debate but it would not rule. Their failure to create a viable form of government for themselves would keep the French in constant trouble. It would also continue to serve as a source of harassment to the President of the United States.

13

It was President George Washington who opened the presidential election of 1796. He chose the beginning of the year to inform one of his secretaries, who confided it to John, that he was "solemnly determined to serve no longer than the end of his present period." At the same time Mrs. Washington took John aside at a dinner party and implied that there was nothing that could persuade either the President or herself to serve a third term. Washington did not wish to make this statement public or to have it generally known: he still had a full year in which to exercise executive power over recalcitrant groups.

Chief among them were the Republicans. They were determined to elect Thomas Jefferson as President to succeed Washington. Throwing a sop to John Adams, New England and the Federalists, they declared that they would be content to allow Mr. Adams to remain in his chair as Vice President. John wrote home to Abigail:

"You know the consequence of this to me and to yourself. Either we must enter upon ardors more trying than any ever yet experienced, or retire to Quincy, farmers for life. I am at least as determined not to serve under Jefferson as Washington is not to serve at all. I will not be frightened out of the public service, nor will I be disgraced in it."

Word of President Washington's intent spread through political circles. John found himself invited out each night to dine and to discuss the political prospect. As far as he could gather, the Federalists had no intention of overthrowing their line of succession. John Adams was still their Number Two man. If Washington retired, Adams would move up.

Abigail had to admit to herself that John's letters were a source of anxiety to her. Her ambition did not lead her to be the "first in Rome." Search her heart as she might, she could find neither a beam of light nor a shadow of comfort in the contemplation of being the President's wife. If her personal considerations were to be the only ones which counted she would ask John to retire. She wrote him in full candor:

"In a matter of such momentous concern, I dare not influence you. I must pray that you may have superior direction. As to holding the office of Vice President, there I will give you my opinion. Resign, retire. I would be second to no man but Washington."

It very soon became clear that the election would be bitterly contested. Thomas Jefferson's forces would make a strong bid. The treaty Thomas Pinckney had negotiated with the Spanish was so favorable to the United States in terms of the free navigation of the Mississippi River and the establishing of heretofore disputed boundaries that Pinckney too could become a formidable opponent. John still loved and admired Thomas Jefferson. He confided to Abigail that if Jefferson should be elected President and John Jay Vice President, or the other way around, he could retire to his farm in confidence, no longer needing to feel anxious for the fate of his country.

No successor could expect the support that President Washington had had. She knew of "the whips and scorpions, the thorns without roses," which constituted political life. She had to be honest with her husband and so she wrote him that the part he might have to play as President was not the only one that disturbed her:

"I am anxious for the proper discharge of that share which will devolve upon me. Whether I have patience, prudence, discretion sufficient to fill such a station so unexceptionably as the worthy lady who now holds it. I fear I have not. As second, I have had the happiness of steering clear of censure, as far as I know. . . . I should say that I have been so used to a freedom of sentiment that I know not how to place so many guards about me as will be indispensable. To look at every word before I utter it and to impose a silence upon myself when I long to talk. Here in this retired village I live beloved by my neighbors, and . . . I assume no state and practice no pageantry. Unenvied, I sit calm and easy, mixing very little with the world."

Her calm and ease referred only to the political aspect of her world, for the year 1796 opened disastrously for Colonel William Smith. The reversal was as sudden as an old barn roof caving in, and grew increasingly worse. Abigail received the dolorous news from her daughter in a series of tear-stained letters: the Colonel's two privateers had been seized and claimed as prizes; his investment was a total loss. His brother-in-law, Felix de Saint-Hilaire, with whom Colonel Smith had invested half his fortune, proved to be not merely a bad businessman but a swindler who absconded with the Colonel's money. Worse, he had held the Colonel's note for four thousand five hundred dollars, which he discounted before he fled. The bank called in the paper. Colonel Smith had no money. His creditors, from whom he had bought lavishly, descended upon him like the biblical swarms of locusts and ate up everything in sight: the still unfinished replica of Mount Vernon, the twenty-three acres of the Van Zandt farm, his holdings in Manhattan and Long Island.

Colonel Smith and his family were stripped bare, not only of money but of respect. The crushing blow for Nab was not the sudden impoverishment but the public proof that her husband had been a show-off, a wastrel and, in the end, a booby.

On June first, Tennessee was admitted to the Union, becoming the sixteenth state, adding the weight of its electors to the coming election. John's contribution to the campaign was confined to the building of a new barn, some fifty feet long, for which he had been hungering the past several years. In this way Abigail would be able to center her now separated herds of cows and carry on a profitable dairy business. It also accomplished the non-dairying purpose of proving to the world that John Adams did not need, did not even necessarily want, the presidency. By building the barn he made it apparent to all that he was preparing to retire to the life of a gentleman farmer in Quincy.

President Washington in mid-September published his farewell speech in the *American Daily Advertiser* to inform the nation that it must choose a new President. He then warned the people of their gravest danger:

"The unity of government which constitutes you one people is also now dear to you. It is justly so, for it is a main pillar in the edifice of your real independence, the support of your tranquillity at home, your peace abroad, of your safety, of your prosperity, of that very liberty which you so highly prize. . . ."

Thomas Jefferson and Aaron Burr of New York were running on the Republican ticket, Jefferson pursuing much the same tactics as John Adams: instead of erecting a barn he was trying to raise the walls of his remodeled home at Monticello.

Alexander Hamilton decided that he did not wish to run for the presidency. What he did most earnestly wish was to knock John Adams out of the running and elect a man whom he could control. A Federalist caucus during the summer of 1796 thought otherwise. It put up John Adams for President and Thomas Pinckney for Vice President. The voters would indicate their preference for two men, though not for the specific office. The men receiving the highest vote would become President and Vice President, even though they belonged to different parties. It became Hamilton's scheme to have Pinckney poll more votes than Adams, thus becoming President. This strategy could well bring about a majority for Jefferson, thus putting the Federalists out of power. Hamilton liked dangerous games.

The campaign was fought in the newspapers with no limit to the scurrility levied against the contenders. Jefferson was traduced for lacking firmness and moral courage, for twice having run out on important jobs, first as governor of Virginia when the British came in; and second as Secretary of State. He was accused of being an atheist, a man who had no religion or God, and hence was unequal to the trust of high office. The charges against John were that he wanted to install a monarchy in America, that he was an enemy of the French Revolution and hence of the freedom of all peoples; he was an aristocrat who did not believe in equality . . . his strong central government would deprive the states of the last of their sovereignty. . . .

Partisan pamphlets were printed and spread widely over the nation, attacking the aspirant on one page, praising his opponent on the other. To Abigail doing her daily chores in the new barn, it was a civil war of the press. No heads were broken, no guillotines were used to decapitate; the American prisons were not filled with one's political opponents. Nevertheless the air was filled with hatred of neighbor for neighbor. She decided there was no further purpose in reading these polemics. They were destructive by nature, containing little truth, either of praise or blame. It was like the yellow fever that had swept through Philadelphia in 1793, uncontrollable until the cold weather of November set in. Then the corpses would be buried, the pockmarked would be persuaded to go out into public, the wounds would be healed by the medicinal waters of time. That, at least, was her hope; if the wounds did not heal the Republic would founder, even as John Adams had early feared it might, on the virulence of popular elections. When she expressed this grave doubt to John, he replied in a heavy voice:

"You are the one who said we have no place else to go. If these two parties were sectional, all of the Federalists in the North and all of the Republicans in the South, then perhaps we could divide in half, become two nations. But every state, every county, every township has its Republicans and Federalists living next door to each other. Perhaps that's our greatest safety. All of us are going to have to live next door to our adversaries the day after election."

Samuel Adams, who had inherited the governorship of Massachusetts on John Hancock's death, and had since been elected on his own merits, not only came out against his cousin John but actually ran as a Republican elector, hoping to cast a ballot for Jefferson. Indeed, Boston and its *Chronicle* appeared to be the originating point of the worst calumnies against John. Abigail wrote to her two sons in Europe in an attempt to reassure them that "from the *Chronicle* you cannot expect truth. Falsehood and malevolence are its strongest features. It is the offspring of faction and nursed by sedition, the adopted bantling of party. It has been crying monarchy and aristocracy, and vociferating anathemas against the *Defence* as favoring monarchy, and making quotations of detached sentences. . . ."

The weeks and months dragged as slowly as oxen moving across a mud-bogged field. Abigail and John spoke little about the campaign, though they wrote letters to friends attempting to keep the record straight wherever an attack was particularly vitriolic. There was no way of knowing how the election would come out, thanks to the ingenuity and political intrigue of Alexander Hamilton. Had he supported John Adams there could never have been any doubt.

When French Ambassador Adet threatened war against the United States unless Thomas Jefferson were elected President, it appeared that many frightened Federalists might transfer their allegiance. The Adamses were reassured by a message from Samuel Otis, estimating that John might possibly squeak through with a three- or four-electoral-vote majority.

It was time for John to depart for Philadelphia so that he would be present when the Senate convened on the first Monday in December. They faced a dilemma. Should Abigail accompany him? The weather was freezing, the roads miserable. Where would they take up residence? If John were defeated he would remain only long enough to witness the swearing-in ceremonies of the new President and return home at once. Under these circumstances would it be worth while for her to make the long hard trip and spend three months in the wet and cold of Philadelphia?

And if John won?

"I *would* like to see the celebration if you win, my dear. The parades, the fireworks. I would like to give a reception and then a state dinner for President and Mrs. Washington. I would like to bring Nab and the children to Philadelphia for the occasion, Charley and his wife. . . . Is this vainglorious of me, wanting to be on hand if the hour should be ours?"

The last month of the campaign was harried and filled with tension. Abigail was shocked to learn that the Jeffersonian voters were openly wearing the French cockade. John was going to lose Pennsylvania to Jefferson because of "the audacious treaty we had the assurance to make with Great Britain." Apparently the election would be decided by whether the people favored France or England. The press was partisan and vituperative; few of the charges against the two leading candidates were new, but the constant repetition loaned them an air of credibility.

"Almost everyone's judgment," Abigail commented to her sister Mary, "is warped by faction."

John Adams remained an inactive spectator, living at the Francis Hotel in Philadelphia, and Thomas Jefferson stayed at his home in Virginia. By New Year's Eve, Abigail began to receive callers bringing congratulations on John's probable victory. The electors had met and cast their ballots. The newspapers reported that they would not be officially counted until the beginning of February, but that the vote would be so close that a single vote might decide whether Federalist John Adams or Republican Thomas Jefferson became President of the United States.

On February 8, 1797, Vice President John Adams rode to Independence Square, went up to the Senate Chamber on the second floor of Congress Hall, entered from the east room, made his way through the elegantly furnished chamber with its mahogany tables and elbow chairs, over the floor newly laid by the city of Philadelphia. He walked up to the podium, sat in the high-backed, upholstered chair, a caretaker regulating the venetian blinds behind him to admit the maximum of light. After a moment he let his gavel fall once, determinedly, on the small table before him. The combined Senate and House were called to order.

Absolute silence fell. Secretary of the Senate Samuel Otis approached the dais with a locked metal case. Inside were the heavily wax-sealed envelopes, one from each of the sixteen states of the Union, containing their notarized ballots. With a recording clerk on either side of him and the senators leaning forward tensely in their chairs, Vice President John

Adams broke each seal, took out the enclosed sheet of paper, read the recorded figures in a clear, firm voice. There were stirrings, muted groans, sibilances of pleasure as the vote tallies mounted.

John Adams showed no change of expression, no sign of emotion, as the vote turned for or against him. He moved slowly, read the figures deliberately, waited in complete quiescence while the clerks counted the final rows of figures. They checked each other, then turned to the Vice President and respectfully handed him the totals. The Vice President rose, holding the tally sheet before him; his hand trembled slightly now.

"The new President of the United States is John Adams, with seventy-one electoral votes. The new Vice President is Thomas Jefferson with sixty-eight."

There were seconds of silence, then the United States Congress rose and gave their presiding officer an ovation.

At that moment on February eighth, Abigail sat at John's desk in his office at Quincy with the unofficial votes from the state capitals before her. She came to the identical result her husband had just announced in Congress Hall. She picked up her pen, wrote:

"The sun is dressed in brightest beams,
To give thy honors to the day.

"You have this day to declare yourself head of a nation."

She slowly dropped her head onto her folded hands.

"And now, O Lord, my God, Thou hast made Thy servant ruler over the people. Give unto him an understanding heart that he may know how to go out and come in before this great people; that he may discern between good and bad. . . ."

She again took up her pen.

"My thoughts and my meditations are with you, though personally absent; and my petitions to Heaven are that 'the things which make for peace may not be hidden from your eyes.' My feelings are not those of pride or ostentation. They are solemnized by a sense of the obligations. . . . That you may be enabled to discharge them with honor to yourself, with justice and impartiality to your country, and with satisfaction to this great people, shall be the daily prayer of your

A.A."

BOOK NINE

THE KISS OF GOD

1

SHE awakened to an icy dawn. The sun rose but afforded no warmth. She was alone in the house except for Louisa in a near bedroom. As she snuggled deeper under the goose-feather comforter she remembered that this was a long-awaited day. In Philadelphia, John would be rising to prepare for the crucial transfer of power: inauguration, the papers had begun to call these ceremonies of March 4, 1797. John Adams had declined the six-horse carriage that had carried President Washington to his induction. He would arrive at the Hall of Congress in his own carriage, drawn by two horses and wearing a pearl-colored broadcloth suit he had had made for the occasion, a short sword and cockade. He would be sworn into office, deliver his acceptance speech and return to Francis's Inn. As far as she knew there was to be no celebration: no reception, no levee, no tea, no dinner, no parade, no fireworks. President Washington was being given a farewell dinner by the merchants of Philadelphia at Ricketts's Amphitheatre. John would possibly be invited to attend as a guest. But there would be no affair at which the second President of the United States would be the host, or be greeted as the new leader of the American people. There would be no cheering crowds, ringing of bells, the joyous festivities which had welcomed General Washington into New York eight years before as the first President.

He was going to be terribly alone. He would return to the inn, nurse his cold with the cough rhubarb and calomel she had recommended, light a fire in his bedroom, get into bed to read and write a letter, fall asleep as best he could. It was the New England way.

Should she have been in Philadelphia by her husband's side on this festive day? The President's house would not have been available to them, since the Washingtons still lived in it; but she could have gone to Francis's Inn, held a reception there, served rum punch and cake.

Looking back, she tried to sort out the many reasons why she was not in Philadelphia. First there was the closeness of the election. Unofficially, word had reached her in January that John Adams would be President. However if the state of Vermont's electoral votes were thrown out on a technicality, Jefferson could win the election by a single vote. In February the votes had been counted in the United States Senate but the intelligence had not reached her in Quincy until a week later.

Should she have left at once? She could have reached there by the end of the month. But she could not bring her mind to making the permanent move into Philadelphia yet. The weather was foul, the roads potholed from a severe winter. She had not made definite agreements with French and Burrell, who were working the other two farms on halves. Cotton Tufts was ailing; Peter reluctant. She had no one to install in Peacefield.

One of the more serious stumbling blocks was the President's house. The Morris mansion had deteriorated under its hard usage. The carpets were threadbare from the hundreds of guests who were entertained in the house each week. The coverings on the sofas were worn, sometimes cracked; the legs of the chairs had been kicked, the tables scarred, the wallpaper stained, the dishes and glassware chipped or broken. The Washingtons had had to replace these sets two to three times. President Washington would be returning to Mount Vernon, taking with him a few private possessions and auctioning off the rest. The necessary repairing, refurbishing and refurnishing would be the responsibility of his successor. In any event the President and Congress would be moving to Washington City late in 1800.

What would be asked of the incoming President? The Morris house would need many thousands of dollars before it could be put into proper condition. Would the Adamses be expected to spend this money out of their pockets, as President Washington frequently had? According to Abigail's estimate, it would take between ten and twenty thousand dollars to make the place beautiful again, furnished as the President's house properly should be. They would have to sell much of what they owned to raise this sum of money. Even if they had been willing to pour their savings into a building which would be left behind in three years, it would leave them little reserve with which to meet the high cost of being President: three thousand dollars a year for the rent of the house, the cost of the new carriage and horses required for state occasions, the salaries of servants, secretaries, running the Chief Executive's office, entertaining the nation. It would take considerable private means to carry on in the handsome tradition set by George and Martha Washington.

Though John Adams did not have to tell his wife that they simply could not afford to move into the President's house under these circumstances, he had made it abundantly clear in his letters that they had best be patient, wait for the Congress to act, endure the separation with fortitude. If Congress would not take care of the President's house, then the Adams family would not move in. Neither would they occupy a lesser house; that would be a blow to the office of the presidency. John would remain at the inn, Abigail at Peacefield, finding help when spring came round, tending her dairy and caring for their properties while John did his best to care for the nation. The old Congress would adjourn after inauguration, the new one did not convene until the next winter. John would come home in June, be reunited with his family, help with the harvest and run the office of the Chief Executive from his library.

It was the sensible way.

She rose, went into the adjoining room which she used for closeting her clothes, broke the thin sheet of ice on top of the water bowl, washed and brushed out her hair before a mirror. The face that she saw reflected was not the same one she had studied in the mirror over her chest of drawers in the Weymouth parsonage. At seventeen, there had been a symmetry of bone structure, her high and agreeably curved forehead balanced by prominent cheekbones, a slender but resolute oval of jawline and strongly molded chin. Now the face showed the thirty-five years that had passed over it since then, thinning the lips, putting hollows under the cheeks, accentuating the longish nose.

It was, she thought with a wry smile, the face of an "old fielder." That was what a Baltimore newspaper had just called John Adams. He had sent her the definition:

"An old fielder is a tough, hardy, laborious little horse that works very hard and lives upon very little. Very helpful to his master at small expense."

"It is a description that fits us both," she thought.

She combed a few curls onto her forehead, put on a warm dress, heavy boots, a wool scarf over her head, crunched through the snow to visit John's mother at Peter's house and to congratulate her.

Mrs. Hall was already dressed in her best dark blue gown with the lace collar and cuffs, and a white lace cap on her head. A week short of eighty-eight she was moving about spryly, her wrinkled face all smiles.

"Mother, do you know that you are only the second American woman to be the mother of a President?"

"That's the Boylston blood. Rises to the top every time! John always favored my side."

"Get some rest, you're coming this afternoon to drink tea with the ladies of the town."

At noon, when John was taking the oath of office in Philadelphia, she sat in his law library with her fingers intertwined in her lap. The dormant countryside was quiet about her. She was grateful for the resolution of the campaign, not merely because John had won, and it had been important to his *amour-propre* to do so, but because every step of the way had been distasteful. The charges on both sides had been scurrilous. In all fairness she had to admit Thomas Jefferson had suffered the most. The Republicans appeared to accept the verdict with good grace, and were helping to prepare for the orderly transfer of power.

Politics aside ("How can the wife of John Adams ever put politics aside?" she asked herself with a tiny smile), the three months of separation had passed quietly. She had lived suspended, without alarums or pressures; sleeping late in the morning, dawdling over tea with her sister Mary or neighbor friends. Louisa brought her a tray with a light supper, which she ate before the warm fire in the sitting parlor, then went early to bed with the "Virgin," a stone bottle filled with boiling water and wrapped in flannel which John had used for company while sleeping alone in Europe. She read for a while, and was soon asleep.

John Quincy, after nearly three years in The Hague, had been appointed by President Washington as minister plenipotentiary to Portugal at double the salary. He was now preparing to go to London to marry Louisa Johnson, daughter in the delightful family they had known during their London stay. He had courted Louisa during the fall of 1795 when he was sent to London to participate in the exchange of the Jay Treaty. From all accounts she would make him a fine wife. Tommy was studying French and enjoying his European experience as Johnny's secretary. Charley's practice was increasing in New York.

But today, at noon, she would become the wife of the President of her dearly beloved Union of American States. Soon she would be required to take Martha Washington's place, to become "first in Rome."

2

Philadelphia society, and the members of the government, insisted that President Adams move into the Morris mansion. When Washington moved out on March ninth, he had left behind a few scuffed pieces of furniture, enough for John to use as a "bachelors' hall," a couple of rooms which could serve as office and bedroom. In the interval between Washington's departure and John's moving in on March twenty-first, the house had been at the mercy of its caretakers. John wrote to her in anguish:

"Last night for the first time I slept in our new house. But what a scene! . . . There is not a chair fit to sit in. The beds and bedding are in a woeful pickle. This house has been a scene of the most scandalous drunkenness and disorder among the servants that ever I heard of."

She was in a kind of pickle herself. A tax collector had called at her house for the second time, trying to collect an assessment of two hundred and eleven dollars.

"I can't pay you," she told him, "but I will in the course of the month."

"If you can't pay, Mrs. President, who can?"

Abigail rose, went to John's desk. There lay a solitary dollar bill, all the cash she had on hand.

She borrowed four hundred dollars from their friend General Lincoln, signing a note. Mr. French, working the old Adams farm, insisted that Abigail buy him a mate for his ox. Burrell refused to plant their recently acquired Thayer farm unless she secured him a yoke of oxen and a cart. . . . She wondered if John were having as much trouble getting money to run his departments as she was hers. He wrote:

"My expenses are so enormous that my first quarter's salary will not discharge much more than half of them."

Their plans came into focus when President Adams proclaimed that the newly elected Congress must convene in May "in order to consult and determine on such measures as in their wisdom shall be deemed meet for the safety and welfare of the said United States." The cause for the emergency was the real and present danger of war with France, which had refused to accept Charles Cotesworth Pinckney as Washington's appointed American minister to France, insulting him in the process and threatening to arrest him. France also had been seizing American vessels in the West Indies. John felt the Congress should share the responsibility of handling the delicate, unpredictable problem. As a result there would be no possibility of his returning home that summer; in fact he might not get out of Philadelphia at all that year.

The retiring House, on the last day prior to inauguration, had appropriated fourteen thousand dollars for the repair and refurnishing of the President's house. With this money John was buying new furniture. Mrs. Otis, wife of their long-time secretary in the Senate, had selected the basic sets of dishware, glassware, table linens, kitchen equipment.

John wrote: "There are so many things to do in furnishing the house in which I want your advice and on so many other accounts it is improper we should live in a state of separation that I must entreat you to come on, in your coach with Louisa, Mrs. Briesler and her children. You must hire four horses in Boston and a coachman to bring you here upon as good terms as you can. . . . I am very unwell, a violent cold and cough fatigues me while I have everything else to harry me."

It never occurred to her to question his summons.

What to do with the multitudinous chores he had assigned to her, the houses and farms, the suit she should instigate against the Nightingale family who, without permission, had cut wood off four or five rods of their land? She was instructed to have her carriage freshly painted, to engage several reliable young girls in the neighborhood and bring them along, since the Philadelphia help practiced "brigandage." She had to resolve Esther Briesler's family problems so that she would come to Philadelphia with her children. She was to sell off as much of the livestock as possible for ready cash, leave responsible men on each of the farms, settle a reliable family in their home to care for it. She was to board Billings, their hired hand, with his brother Peter, leave his mother cared for . . .

There was no help for it, she would have to call on her uncle-cousin Cotton still once again. Tall, thin, white-thatched, bespectacled Cotton looked more than ever like a patriarchal schoolmaster. He was a few weeks short of sixty-five and suffering from his usual spring pain in the chest, but he had indomitable energy. He had married Susanna Warner seven years before, and for six years had been president of the Massachusetts Medical Society he had worked so long to establish. To everyone's surprise he had proved as skillful at investments as in bringing about the dissemination of medical knowledge.

"Cousin Cotton, I do not know of any person's property so unproductive as ours is. I do not believe that it yields us one per cent per annum. I have the vanity, however, to think that if Dr. Tufts and my ladyship had been left to the sole management of our affairs, they would have been upon a more profitable footing. In the first place I never desired so much land unless we could have lived upon it. The money paid for useless land I would have purchased public securities with, the interest of which, poorly as it is funded, would have been less troublesome to take charge of than land and much more productive. But in these ideas I have always been so unfortunate as to differ from my partner, who thinks he never saved anything but what he invested in land."

Cotton blinked his spectacles a hump lower down on his bony nose, said affectionately:

"This shall be a secret between us two: I hope that your husband is a better business President of the United States than he is a businessman on his farms."

"He will be a good President. Statecraft is his profession."

She laid out the complexity of her problems. How was she going to get them all solved and depart for Philadelphia at once?

"You're not. It will take a little while. But let's divide up the tasks. Our cousin William Smith is the best one to have your carriage painted in Boston, hire the horses and coachman. You cannot buy the Cranch farm now, even though it adjoins yours and Cranch wants desperately to sell. I know a couple, childless, by the name of Porter, who would take care of your home and garden as fastidiously as though you were here; I've only to help them rent their own little place first . . ."

They went down the list. There was little or no market for cattle. They would get the ox for the Thayer farm and finish the piece of wall to keep the stock in pasture; buy the yoke of oxen for French at the old Adams farm. Of her nineteen dairy cows she wanted to dispose of five. Unless the dairy products of the remaining fourteen were skillfully produced and marketed, they would end up with a feed bill of two hundred dollars and no profits to compensate.

"I'll have the meadows planted in hay," Cotton assured her. "If you need cash, you've only to tell me how much. Go down to Philadelphia and help the President manage our country."

John sent her six hundred dollars. She gave two hundred to her cousin William, who was in charge of the carriage; paid back wages to her hired hands, bought the necessary farm tools and seed, contracted for the wall. She searched for three or four energetic young girls to hire as domestics. Esther Briesler refused to budge unless her husband came to fetch her.

A sudden change in the weather and a snowstorm sent Mrs. Hall to bed.

"We'll have you up in no time, Mother," said Abigail, spending the night with her as a watcher.

Mrs. Hall lay motionless in the bed.

"Now that you're leaving me, child, I'm fixing to die."

She gave Abigail's hand a barely perceptible squeeze. Her head rolled to the wall. Four days later Dr. Phipps pronounced her dead. Abigail had her buried alongside John Adams, Sr., in the old burial ground. Since John had never become reconciled to her marriage to Mr. Hall, she was buried as Susanna Boylston Adams, everyone conveniently forgetting the second marriage.

Two days later Billy's second daughter, Mary, who had been living with the Cranches, died of consumption. Louisa had been her watcher for weeks. Abigail again arranged for funeral services and the burial.

John had sent Briesler posthaste to bring his family to Philadelphia. Her cousin William Smith offered to accompany the party to New York, which was en route to Philadelphia, as its good shepherd.

"I'm not really a lamb, William," said Abigail, thanking him. "I'm more like a kite with a long tail."

The tail was long indeed: thirteen people in all, William, Briesler and James riding horseback, Abigail in the carriage with Louisa, Esther, the three young girls from around Quincy alternating on the coachman's seat with the Briesler children.

The roads were intolerable, the rains having washed the stones bare. Yet the brilliant green fields of spring, the leafing forests of birch and maple as they traveled west across Massachusetts to Springfield, then south to Hartford and New Haven, were a joy to the eye. Cousin William engaged the rooms at the inn each night, ordered the meals, kept the bills in order. En route, Abigail would stop off briefly at Nab's farm in Eastchester, sending the rest of the party to Philadelphia, and then visit Charles in New York.

It was two years since she had seen her daughter and grandchildren. Out of his financial debacle of the year before, Colonel Smith had been able to save only this small farm and modest house twenty miles from New York and, according to Nab's description, completely isolated, the nearest neighbor several miles away. Abigail had plans. Although she could not ask John to give the Colonel an important job in the government, she was determined to take the entire family with her to Philadelphia and move them into the President's house, even as they had lived together on Richmond Hill seven years before. Colonel Smith would meet the world there and find an opportunity to utilize his talents.

Nab opened the door of the lonely farmhouse, puffy-eyed, heavy around the shoulders and hips. Running to the door to see who had come were William Steuben, aged ten, John Adams, eight and a half, Caroline, two. Abigail embraced the children, then walked into the barely furnished sitting parlor.

"Where is the Colonel?"

"Away."

"Away! Where?"

"Up to his lands. He left a fortnight ago."

"I didn't know he still had lands."

"He went with his brother Justus, who has tracts around the Chenango Valley. William is hoping to acquire options."

"I wanted so much to speak to him."

Nab threw her mother a stern glance. She was not to discuss the Colonel or criticize him even by implication.

Abigail spent two days in the forlorn house. There was a couple working the farm but to Abigail's trained eye they seemed incompetent. There was food to keep Nab and the children from hunger, firewood to keep them warm; nothing more. Nab's daughter was like dancing sunlight in the dark farmhouse; the two boys were completely without schooling.

Abigail's spirits were depressed. She had to rescue Nab. But she could not invite them to Philadelphia without the Colonel's consent.

"When Colonel William returns, will you all come for a visit to Philadelphia? I'll have the extra bedrooms furnished by then."

"I would like that, Mama."

Her next visit was to Charles, Sally and their baby daughter, whom they had named Susanna Boylston after John's mother. They were living at 91 Front Street, in a new house so near to the river that the rear windows framed a forest of masts. It was so much a part of the noise and clangor of navigation, Abigail felt the house might haul anchor at any moment and set sail. The rooms were commodious, Charles's book-lined office boasted clients all the day. To live up to his father's demands that he live frugally, Charley had sublet half the house. Sally was a good and prudent wife. Part of John Quincy's salary as minister was being paid over to Charles for investment.

"I hope you're being cautious with Johnny's money," Abigail said. "He'll need a competence when he returns to this country and has to set up in law again."

Charles averted his gaze. Abigail noted the beginnings of dark circles under his eyes.

"Charley, are you working too hard?"

"No, Ma, it's just that I'm not sleeping well."

They were alone in his office, the open window admitting the sounds of winches, moving cargoes, the operatic bustle of an active waterfront.

"What's worrying you, Charley?"

". . . nothing, Ma."

John had offered to send horses to meet her carriage at Paulus Hook, across the Hudson from New York City, but Briesler found a team for reasonable rent and since John had forwarded money to her at Charley's house, she decided to let the hired coachman drive the horses he was accustomed to. It proved a good decision: the heavy rains and six stages daily had so cut up the clay that she was knocked about in furrows a foot deep. Just after she had passed Trenton, about twenty-five miles out of Philadelphia, she saw John's carriage and horses blocking the road. President John Adams, with a broad, warm smile, was waiting to claim her.

It was one of their happiest reunions. After John had sent the coachman ahead they sat on the comfortable seat of John's carriage, exchanged hearty embraces and tender words to bridge their separation. At Bristol they enjoyed a leisurely meal at a front window of the inn overlooking the Delaware River. After dinner, with John puffing contentedly on his pipe, Abigail gave him the latest news about their farms, the sermon preached at his mother's funeral, the condition of Nab, alone in Eastchester.

In return, John confided his news. He had decided not to have John Quincy proceed to Portugal, but rather to become the minister to Prussia, with whom the United States, thanks to the original treaty John had drawn with King Frederick II, was building a lucrative trade. It would not be a promotion for Johnny, but he could do a more important job there. They were both happy about his impending marriage to Louisa Johnson. Joshua Johnson was now United States consul in London but was waiting only for his daughter's marriage to John Quincy to return home. It would be good for Johnny to have a wife when he settled in the remote city of Berlin where so few Americans ever ventured.

"What about the job of being President, John? How does it appear from the inside?"

The dining area of the inn was deserted now. John leaned across the table, spoke in the confiding voice he kept for her alone:

"Filled with problems. Thousands of letters from deserving people asking for jobs. The rejection of my inaugural speech, particularly the part in which I insisted we deal firmly with France, by the Republican press. Benjamin Bache praised the speech in the *Aurora*, but writes unbelievably virulent attacks on everything else I say and do."

Since Bache had accused President Washington of cankering the principles of republicanism, writing, "The man who is the source of all the misfortunes of our country . . . is no longer possessed of power to multiply evils upon the United States," the Adamses hardly expected him to do otherwise with them.

"But surely no one will listen to any word he writes," Abigail cried.

"No one but the Republicans," replied John with a wistful smile. "You know what a blow it was when France rejected our minister? I have wanted to send Vice President Jefferson or his friend, former Congressman James Madison, to France. Both have refused."

Thomas Jefferson was remaining aloof. He had taken exception to John's firm stand against the French in his inaugural speech, and apparently did not consider it politic to merge his party with the administration.

"Does that mean we cannot be friends with him?" She was distressed.

"Certainly he will be as welcome at the President's house as he was at Auteuil. But I think we shall consult very little together."

Abigail took the opportunity to bring up the question of the Secretaries John had inherited from the Washington regime: Secretary of State Pickering, Secretary of the Treasury Wolcott, Secretary of War McHenry. John had not asked for their resignations, nor had they offered them, though they were known to have been appointed through Hamilton's influence.

"Are they not still Hamilton's men?" she asked. "They are frequently in opposition to you. I doubt me they will speak their own minds."

"They could be disagreeing honestly. It does an executive little good to have men about him who only say, 'Yes.'"

Pickering was a harsh, humorless man who disliked the Adamses, even though he was a Massachusetts man. Wolcott rarely had a thought that did not originate in Hamilton's office in New York. McHenry was incompetent, he only got the job after four good men had said "No" to President Washington. Attorney General Charles Lee was a totally independent man.

"Would you not find it more productive if you had your own men as the heads of departments," she asked, "working together harmoniously? You would have fewer difficulties with Congress."

John bit the stem of his pipe.

"These men have the experience, they give the people a sense of continuity in their government. The best men no longer want to come to Philadelphia to suffer public attack and abuse. I can control the ones I have; they do me no harm."

John's greatest problem was his growing isolation from the world about him. He could not even tell where some of his fellow Federalists stood on important issues.

"There is no one to whom the President can give his confidences. Dear soul, can you know what it is like to be surrounded by a hundred people and not be able to reveal your inner thinking to any one of them? I have never needed you more than in this lonely office of the presidency."

3

When they arrived at the President's house the late afternoon sun shone through the new window curtains of the ground-floor rooms. John had covered the entrance hall and staircase with a Wilton carpet of an oriental design, its loops cut to furnish a soft pile underfoot. For the small dining room he had bought an oblong table and chairs of local make. The long table with the rounded edges and raised center "plateau," on which the Washingtons had displayed porcelain figurines, was in the state dining room.

Abigail did not go back through the steward's room or kitchen but ran excitedly upstairs. The state drawing room, a big room filled with mirrors, marble fireplace and a great chandelier, though not yet complete, was resplendent with a dozen crimson damask chairs and settees and damask draperies. In the smaller drawing room, which was at the front of the house overlooking Market Street, John had used the color scheme of her mother's sitting parlor in Weymouth. The windows were covered with soft yellow satin draperies, on the floor was a thick Brussels carpet, white ground with green leaves and lemon-yellow flowers. There was a yellow damask sofa in the corner beyond the fireplace, and chairs covered with green woven cloth. She stood motionless, suffused with thoughts of her parents. How proud they would have been of John's accomplishments and the honor their country had bestowed on him. She was touched by her husband's salute to her mother's memory.

John had taken the two rooms at the end of the long hall for his offices. There was a private entrance for visitors. The central bedroom was theirs, with a spacious canopied bed made in New England, and on either side of the room old Virginia chests for their personal clothing, night stands with lamps and books as there had been in her nuptial chamber in Braintree. He led her through a center door to her own quarters, which Mrs. Otis had furnished with an escritoire, bookcase, a comfortable chaise, dressing table and stately armoire large enough to hang her gowns. Upstairs, on the third floor, Louisa occupied a small room which General Washington had used for a private office; next door were the Brieslers, and beyond their suite, Samuel Malcom, John's secretary. The fourth floor was a beehive of small rooms for the girls she had brought down from Quincy, the cook and other personal servants. Abigail congratulated John on the beautiful furnishings.

"We knew what you liked, Mrs. Otis and I. We hoped you would be happy with us."

She rose at five each morning, donned a robe, went next door to John's presidential desk in a corner under three large windows to the south and a window to the east where the rising mid-May sun engulfed her with its light and warmth. She used the quiet time to plan her day, write letters to her family, make out invitation lists, suggest menus, read letters from political friends or memoranda handed to John by his Cabinet officers which he had set out for her to study.

Here too, in the quiet clarity of early morning, she read of the developments in France, apparently bent on conquering the world, England and the United States included. At seven John joined her, having already gone through his ablutions in the bathing room off the kitchen on the ground floor. With him arrived Briesler, coffee and a sheaf of papers.

Breakfast was at eight in the small dining room downstairs. Louisa was the only member of the family present. Young Samuel Malcom, who had been apprenticed to Charles in New York before serving John as a secretary, joined them to get approval of his appointments schedule for the day. Old friends dropped in for coffee. The breakfast period was largely committed to politics. Because of the charges of monarchist and aristocrat levied against him, John wanted to keep the President's house an example of complete democracy.

Complete democracy for Abigail was a complete day's schedule.

The hours until eleven she spent at her desk keeping her books and bills, settling problems among the servants. At eleven she dressed. From noon until two, and sometimes until four, she received. John had excused her until the fall, from the regular drawing room which Martha Washington had maintained, yet the day before there had been thirty-two ladies invited, and nearly as many gentlemen. Today the foreign ministers would call with their wives, as well as the Secretaries of State, Finance and War with their ladies. In the days ahead she would entertain at dinner the entire Senate and House. Hundreds of persons asked permission to call. All were assured a welcome. She would rise to greet each newcomer with a few words ("Have you come out from Paris today?" "Are you in your house in Grosvenor Square yet?"), make sure they met the President, were served lemonade and cake.

Each day after the reception or dinner she must ride out until seven, returning visits or leaving calling cards. This was expected if she was to keep the sophisticated society of Philadelphia happy.

She was rather more of a success as the President's hostess than she had anticipated; but the real surprise to her was John's affability. At General Washington's levees, the ones he had held for men only in the state dining room, all seats had been removed. The President had stood in front of the fireplace clad in black velvet, his hair in full dress, his coat framing a long sword with a finely wrought steel hilt. A secretary formally presented the caller to him. He received the visitor with a dignified bow, his hands so disposed as to indicate that the salutation was not to be accompanied by a shaking of hands.

John's levees were informal. He wore a plain gray or black suit, with a white ruffled shirt and collar, shook hands with each person as he arrived, spoke to him about home, family, local politics, the intricacies of national problems. Republican congressmen opposing him on the floor of the Senate or House were nettled by President Adams's performance. At the small informal drawing rooms Abigail made it a practice to give just an instant longer to the wives of the Republican members. John chuckled at this.

"Those Republican husbands are going to have a more difficult time damning me in front of the wives you have charmed."

President Adams was not having anything like a comparable success with the legislators when it came to backing his proposals with votes. He began working on his message to the special session soon after her arrival. It concerned itself with France's rejection of President Washington's chosen minister:

"It would have afforded me the highest satisfaction to have been able to congratulate you on a restoration of peace to the nations of Europe whose animosities have endangered our tranquillity. . . . While other states are desolated with foreign war or convulsed with intestine divisions, the United States present the pleasing prospect of a nation governed by mild and equal laws . . . flowing from the reason and resting on the only solid foundation—the affections of the people. . . .

"The right of embassy is well known and established by the law and usage of nations. The refusal on the part of France to receive our minister is, then, the denial of a right . . . the refusal to receive him until we have acceded to their demands without discussion . . . is to treat us neither as allies nor as friends, nor as a sovereign state."

He called for strong naval power; a revision of the laws for "organizing, arming and disciplining the militia"; and for public finances through direct taxation to protect the country's security.

"It must not be permitted to be doubted whether the people of the United States will support the government established by their voluntary consent and appointed by their free choice. . . ."

It appeared that the major task of John Adams's administration would be to keep the United States out of European quarrels, imbroglios and wars, to protect its ships on the high seas. Domestic matters pertaining to the states and their individual interests were drowned in the sea of acrimony between the Anglophiles and the Francophiles. The formal answers of the Senate and House to President Adams's message were cordial, but the two Houses spent the next weeks defeating most of his requests.

John Adams wanted a strong America. Vice President Thomas Jefferson, as leader of the opposition party, cried that such legislation as President Adams proposed would further infuriate France, bring on the war. The Congress was unwilling to approve the artillery company John had asked for, the cavalry, or a more rigidly organized militia. All he secured was the right to borrow up to eight hundred thousand dollars for defense purposes and to ask the governors of the several states to arm and keep at the ready eight thousand militia. He also managed to secure approval to send three commissioners to France to sue for a treaty.

The commissioners included Charles Cotesworth Pinckney, who was hovering in Holland after his shabby rejection by France; Francis Dana, who declined and was replaced by Elbridge Gerry; and John Marshall, a Virginia lawyer, fair and honorable, described as having one of the best-organized heads in the country.

"These three men are going to have to take the place of the army I was refused," John confided to Abigail.

A handsome portrait of John Quincy arrived as a gift from Mrs. Copley in England. Johnny had been painted with his hair worn long and loose over his ears and cut low on the neck; his brow was high and patrician, his eyes brilliantly animated; there was her father's long, aquiline, Roman senator nose; the strong mouth and chin. Abigail hung it in the small dining room.

"Johnny's true character shines out of that portrait," she murmured.

"It also shows that our son is an uncommonly handsome devil," replied John. "He looks very much as you did when I fell in love with you."

"Was I ever that beautiful?"

"Yes, dear friend, you were. And you are."

"Mr. President, that is the kindest proclamation you will issue today."

The height of her social season was the Fourth of July celebration of the Declaration of Independence. George Washington had established the custom of inviting the governor of Pennsylvania with his state officers, the City Council of Philadelphia, the heads of the business firms and social orders, the foreign legations, Secretaries and their wives.

"To which I will add the members of the Congress and their wives," Abigail commented to John. "That will be a hundred and fifty people more. We'll set out long tables in the garden as well as the house. Martha Washington used two hundredweight of cake, two quarter casks of wine, besides spirit. The day cost the Washingtons five hundred dollars; ours will run considerably higher."

John whistled tunelessly. "And last month the man who owns this house raised our rent to twice what the Washingtons paid."

"Since we are not permitted to pray to God for money, I shall confine my supplications to a plea for a cool Fourth," she replied with a chuckle.

The Comptroller of the Treasury sent a thousand dollars that was owed to John from the years of his vice presidency; and the Fourth dawned crisp, without a punishing glare. She was dressed at an early hour, in white lutestring with curls on her forehead, wearing the jewels she had bought for her first reception by Queen Charlotte in London, two pearl pins in her hair, a pearl necklace and earrings. John wore the suit in which he had been sworn into office.

The company first visited with the President in the state rooms below, partaking of cake, wine and punch with him. Then all who had brought their wives ascended the staircase to Abigail's smaller drawing room to present their compliments, after which the guests went out to the garden for conversation. The parade lasted from twelve until four o'clock. Briesler estimated that close to a thousand visitors had passed through the reception line. All were received graciously. It was, after all, the people's house. They had put the Adamses there.

4

They left Philadelphia for Quincy at the end of the special session.

The climate at Eastchester had deteriorated sharply since Abigail's earlier visit. The Colonel's fortnight trip had been extended to three months. It was now the end of July and his wife had not had a single word from him. Nab no longer pretended to know where he was or how long he would be away. Her two boys were running wild. She was too dispirited to tutor them effectively. The farmhouse had an abandoned air. Abigail murmured to John:

"Poor girl, she is one of the most alone creatures I know."

"Then let us take her and the three children home with us."

"Invite, yes. Take, no."

As they sat around the kitchen table at supper, the late July sun stabbing through the western window, Abigail asked:

"Nab, wouldn't you like to come with us for a few weeks, to be among old friends at Quincy?"

Nab lowered her head:

"Thank you, Mama, but I couldn't leave. The Colonel is expected home any day. I mustn't let him find an empty house."

"That's as you wish it, Nab." Abigail's voice became firm. "But you really must let me take the boys to your aunt Elizabeth and the Reverend Peabody. There's a good academy in Atkinson, where the reverend has his pulpit. Your aunt will take the boys into her home. The Reverend Peabody will oversee their education. We're bringing Aunt Elizabeth's son William to Peacefield to serve as your father's secretary."

Nab rose, went to the window to watch the sun sink beyond the tree-bordered field.

"Yes," she whispered, "the boys must be put in school. They've wasted two years of valuable time already. It will be hard for me to be left here with just Caroline, but I cannot sacrifice them further." She turned. "Thank you, Mama and Papa. I know the boys will be happy with Aunt Elizabeth and Uncle Peabody."

Later that night, sleepless, Abigail asked her husband:

"How can we save her?"

"By sheer nepotism. I'll find the wandering Colonel a job in Philadelphia, even if I have to invent it. . . . We will pay his salary out of our own pockets."

They left with the boys the following day.

The Porters had kept Peacefield meticulously, but mice had got into the locked storeroom, eaten part of the loaf sugar and nested in the rolled-up carpets. Mary Cranch had located the key, had the carpets scrubbed and aired, the loaf sugar scraped. The English rosebushes were blooming. Cotton Tufts had kept the hands at work; but there had been a hailstorm on July fourteenth which destroyed part of the vegetables, broke down the barley fields and tore part of the corn. They cut the barley for fodder and housed it.

Dispatch riders came up the road nearly every day from Philadelphia, bearing reports, letters, requests for policy. There were personal and official letters to be answered, salutes approving his conduct, diatribes condemning it, all of which John answered by his own hand, using each opportunity to persuade the people that they must remain "attached to the union of our American States, their constitutions of government and the federal administration . . . the happiest omen of the future peace, liberty, safety and prosperity of our country."

It was much too soon to know how the three commissioners to France would be received, or whether they could achieve a genuine treaty of friendship with the Directory. Seeing that there remained only day-by-day chores, and Louisa could receive the friends and delegations who arrived to pay their respects to the President, Abigail took her two grandsons and her sister Mary Cranch in the carriage to Atkinson. It would be the first time the three sisters had been together for several years.

The joyful reunion was tragically flawed. Charles Smith, Billy's youngest, working at Haverhill, near Atkinson, was in the last stages of the same consumption that had killed his sister. Catharine Louisa was there to watch but it was a hopeless cause. Abigail observed mournfully:

"Billy dead, one of his children dead and another dying."

"The ways of the Lord are inscrutable, Nabby," said Mary Cranch softly. "Why did my daughter Lucy marry John Greenleaf, a blind man? And why is she now about to be confined when I warned her that her children might be born blind? Why did my son Billy abandon the Bar, go into land speculation with the Greenleafs and end bankrupt? All the years wasted, his profession gone . . ."

"His profession isn't gone, Sister. John has loaned Billy two hundred dollars to buy a law library. He can be back at the Bar before long."

Elizabeth had married well, for the Reverend Mr. Peabody, first pastor of the gathering of the faithful in Atkinson, was a vigorous and intellectually alert man at fifty-seven. He enjoyed telling the story of how, upon being widowed, he went to Elizabeth Shaw to ask her recommendation for a new wife to "share his joys and his sorrows." Elizabeth recommended a lady in Newbury. While en route to Newbury to propose, the Reverend Mr. Peabody learned that the Reverend Mr. Shaw had died. He turned his horse around, got back to Haverhill in time for the funeral and, after a discreet wait—his detractors claimed he had proposed to Elizabeth at the funeral—married her.

Abigail and Mary went directly to the parsonage. It was a large two-storied, two-chimneyed house with enough spare bedrooms to house eight boarders from the nearby Academy. Peabody was a farmer as well as a clergyman, a tall, commanding figure with curly black hair who built his own stone walls and raised cattle, even as had the Reverend William Smith in Weymouth. He had had two children by his first marriage. Since only one of Elizabeth's children, Abigail Shaw, was still young enough at seven to require his supervision, he welcomed Nab's sons with considerable gusto.

He set off at once to register them at the Academy, leaving the sisters to draw chairs in the middle of the sitting parlor and talk with their heads close together of the fleeting years and the shifting fortunes of the younger generation. It was good to be once again in a tight circle of blood ties; Mary Cranch fifty-five, Abigail fifty-two and Elizabeth forty-seven, all that was left of the Reverend William Smith of Charlestown and Elizabeth Quincy of Mount Wollaston. They had remained close friends over the years, helping out in bad times, taking care of each other's young. They were held together, their voices low and confidential, by the knowledge that their parents would have been happy at this continuing bond. Abigail thought:

"It's strange how intensely we want to please our parents, even after they have been dead for years."

By the beginning of October they had to return to Philadelphia. Their home stay had been short, two months, but refreshing. The work around the farm, picking the fruit crop and starting a dry rock wall at the foot of Penn's Hill had renewed John's vitality. Companies of light horse at Hartford and New Haven met the presidential carriage a number of miles from the town to escort them to their lodgings and to afford an escort out of town the following morning. John accepted these gestures as an evidence of the loyalty to the continuing office of the Executive. He made this point plain to the gatherings in each city.

When they reached the inn closest to Eastchester they saw a uniformed horseman. He followed their carriage to Nab's house, delivered letters from New York City, and confirmed the reports that Philadelphia was stricken with an epidemic of yellow fever. Thousands were dead and dying, those who succumbed in the streets were left to lie, untended; fifty thousand inhabitants had fled to cooler, higher air, but the fever was raging in the crowded apartments of the recent Irish and Scotch immigrants.

"Well, Nab, we shall have to stay with you for several weeks, until the frost comes to Philadelphia and Congress will be willing to reconvene. Can you put up with us?"

"I not only can put up with you, I can put you up. And if you think that's not too good a pun, remember that I've hardly spoken to an adult since you left in July."

The Colonel had been gone for half a year now, without sending his wife one word of his whereabouts or one penny of his pocket. The humiliation and frustration had made Nab ill. Abigail gave her a vivid report on how enthusiastically her sons had been received by the Reverend Mr. Peabody. Suddenly Nab's façade of calm broke.

"Oh, Mama, maybe I should never have left you at all! I feel as though I have been abandoned."

Abigail took her daughter in her arms.

"Not by your family, you're not. If the Colonel is not back by the time we leave for Philadelphia, you and Caroline are coming with us."

"Yes, Mama. Oh, Papa, what have I done that's wrong?"

"Nothing, dear soul. Fate has been unkind to you."

Nab was not the only one of their children in trouble. John went into New York City twice a week for meetings and government business, staying with Charley. Abigail knew from his first visit that something was wrong. John was uncommunicative; she did not press him. Finally he reached the point where he could no longer contain himself.

"Abigail, would you accompany me into New York tomorrow? It's Charley. Something's wrong. He won't talk to me. Perhaps he will to you."

They arrived at Charles's house at midmorning, amidst the pleasant cacophony of ships being loaded. Sally said he was preparing a writ. Abigail knocked, asked if she could see him on a legal matter. Charley's eyes were red. He had developed a tic at the left side of his face. He was thin.

"Legal matter, Mother? Of course."

"It's not a matter for the courts, Charley. You see, I have a son. I love him very much. So does his father. He's in some kind of difficulty. We don't mean to pry, we only want to be helpful. We thought you might intercede for us, as counsel, and advise our son to open his heart to us."

Charles was too strained for subtlety.

"If you're talking about me, Mother, there is nothing to be concerned about: I have some thorny cases to handle. Nothing more."

That afternoon Abigail took Sally aside. She was an attractive girl, alert, with heavy-lidded eyes but warm, beautifully curved lips. She saw the logic of Abigail's approach.

"Yes. Charley sorely needs help. In his own conscience, at least. Though I don't know why; the fault was mine."

"Suppose you tell me the details."

"It had to do with the part of John Quincy's salary which was turned over to Charley for investment. For the first year, he had invested it in a mortgage. Apparently it was a poor one; he had to pay the interest out of his own pocket. But the following March my brother William fell into serious trouble, you remember."

"I remember Colonel William's troubles."

"What you did not know was that he was in danger of being confined in a debtors' prison. My brothers prevailed upon Charley to transfer the mortgage security for a note to save him. My brother Justus has the note but has been unable to pay any interest on it. That's what Charley couldn't tell you: he feels so humiliated at failing John Quincy. At the same time I think he felt obligated because of Nab and me. His mind is full of reproaches, even against Johnny for saddling him with the responsibility for the money in the first place."

"How much is involved?"

"About two thousand dollars, I would surmise."

That night they gathered in Nab's kitchen, mother, father and daughter enclosed intimately within the light of the whale-oil lamp. But Abigail could not get herself to reveal the troubles of one of her children to another; besides, the knowledge that her husband had got her brother into trouble would hurt Nab.

"John, could we sell one of the farms, or some certificates?" she asked when they lay side by side in the upstairs bedroom. "Give Charley back the two thousand dollars?"

"You know the answer to that."

"Yes, regrettably, I do. It would take the responsibility off the Colonel and Charley as well."

"If we bail Charley out now, we'll be bailing his boat all our lives. When I get the Colonel responsibly placed in Philadelphia, I shall personally oblige him to repay the debt."

"Poor Charley, he did in fact keep the Colonel out of debtors' prison. His repayment is to eat himself alive."

"Why is he so thin-skinned? We all make mistakes. We have to learn how to forgive ourselves so that we can move ahead with our work."

"Why is Charley thin-skinned and the Colonel thick-skinned? Isn't human nature the true riddle of the universe?"

It was November fifth. They would be leaving early the next morning for New York, and then go directly to Philadelphia where the Congress would reconvene by the middle of the month. Caroline was excited, dancing in and out of rooms. Not so her mother. Nab was dispirited; leaving her home was an admission of defeat.

Late in the afternoon a horseman came down the road, knocked loudly at the front door. He held a packet of letters.

"Mrs. Colonel William Smith at home?"

"Yes. Come in."

Nab came running to the front door.

"Letters from Mr. Justus Smith, ma'am. Bid me deliver them myself. I've just come down from the Chenango country."

"And my husband. Have you seen him?"

"Not lately, ma'am."

Nab went up to her bedroom, read the letters from her brother-in-law while her parents waited in apprehensive silence below. When she descended there was color in her cheeks.

"The Colonel's brother says that both he and the Colonel have written frequently by the post. They were astonished to learn I had not received any letters. They sent me some money by a private hand to New York. I'll ride in with you tomorrow and collect it."

Abigail and John stared at each other mutely.

"Oh, Father, these letters change everything. William's expected back at Chenango in a few days. After that he'll be coming home. I must be here to receive him."

It was a plea, almost a wail, asking that her parents buttress her belief that her husband was returning. Abigail sighed.

They rode into New York in the morning. While John visited with Charley and gathered his mail, Abigail took Nab in the carriage to the address of the man who had brought money for her from her husband. He had moved away. Nobody knew where to.

Nab was crushed. She had not seen a coin in months, yet the disappointment was a good deal more. If the man had not absconded with the money, it meant that the Colonel had not sent it.

"Won't you change your mind, dear? We can send someone to bring Caroline and the trunks . . ."

Nab interrupted. "No, Mother. I'll miss the money, but now I know my husband wrote, and is planning to return soon."

5

Briesler had fled with his wife and children to escape the plague but returned in time to get the President's house running smoothly. So many senators were still avoiding the city that no quorum could be counted. John used the days to write his First Annual Address. He needed the additional time, for upon his arrival in the city he had ridden in a military parade, yielded to persuasion to leave his carriage window down on the raw day, and caught cold. He was confined to the house, got good nursing from Abigail and the excellent staff of domestics Briesler had assembled; and rather enjoyed being pampered.

Abigail fluffed the pillows behind his back, then sat in a rocker by the side of his bed. As he read, his high, eager voice sounded exactly as it had on New Year's Day in 1762 when he had driven her from her grandfather Quincy's dinner to see his newly opened law office and had read to her from a plea in his commonplace book in which he was fighting for the right of apprentices to be taught to read, write and cipher. Now he was attempting to embolden the Congress to stand foursquare against all foreign encroachments. After informing the members that their three envoys had reached Paris, he said:

"Whatever may be the result of this mission, I trust that nothing will have been omitted on my part to conduct the negotiation to a successful conclusion, on such equitable terms as may be compatible with the safety, honor and interest of the United States. Nothing, in the meantime, will contribute so much to the peace and the attainment of justice as a manifestation of that energy and unanimity of . . . the people of the United States . . . and the exertion of those resources for national defense which a beneficent Providence has kindly placed within their power."

The major part of Congress, fretful and anxious over how their envoys would be received by the French Directory, favored President Adams's leading from a position of strength. The pro-French Republicans continued to call him a war-worshiper who was attempting to goad France into hostilities.

Abigail opened her now completed upstairs drawing room. She could tell how widely the reputation of the United States was spreading by the burgeoning costumes in the reception line. Added to English, French, Italian, Spanish were the colorful fashions of Greece, Turkey, Tripolitania, Russia, China, India. More and more the distant, exotic, largely unknown world was coming to the new nation to pay its respects, and to see how this ridiculous and impossible experiment in self-government worked.

It worked: fumblingly, stumblingly, with battles and brawls, but it worked. While John was writing and sending to the Senate a treaty with the Seneca nation of Indians and a message to the Congress asking for a change in the time for holding circuit court in Delaware, Abigail entertained thirty gentlemen for dinner, including Vice President Thomas Jefferson, who had arrived in Philadelphia the night before. When President Adams felt forced to fire such government officials as Tench Coxe for obstructing the course of the government, or John Lamb and William Jarvis for peculation, only to be accused of firing all Republicans indiscriminately in order to surround himself with sycophants, Abigail invited to their home the men who could document the cases against Coxe, Lamb or Jarvis. When Bache published scurrilous articles about the "Duke of Braintree" in the *Philadelphia Aurora,* Abigail pored over the Federalist press, perusing dozens of papers each week to find well-stated, refuting material which she clipped and sent to sympathetic papers to offset the attacks.

"It's like trying to drive a sleigh over a swamp," she confessed to John, who found her at her desk in her sitting parlor, fingers black from the newsprint. "The wider we spread the truth, the more frantic becomes Bache's distortions. Is there no way to stop him? Don't the laws protect the President of the United States against outright libel?"

"The *Aurora* affords us a new suit with each issue. My record will defend me better than lawsuits."

Abigail pushed aside that day's paper, smudging her cheek with the ink from her fingertips.

John was not the only target of the "miserable rag." The Federalists were being damned, and Alexander Hamilton in particular. Hamilton was still achieving a measure of control over the Chief Executive through Secretaries Pickering and McHenry. One of Hamilton's bitterest enemies, Beckley, a discharged clerk of the House of Representatives, revenged himself on Hamilton by inciting a book called *The History of the United States for the Year 1796*, the story of Hamilton's love affair with a Mrs. Reynolds and his plot with the lady's husband to mulct the Treasury by buying up veterans' notes cheaply, knowing they would be redeemed at par. Abigail and John had heard of the charges but refused to dignify them by reading the book. Now in the fall Hamilton published his defense: he was able to document his political integrity but admitted to his adulterous affair with Mrs. Reynolds. It was a blow to the Federalist Party.

The holidays were gruesome. Nab wrote from Eastchester that although the Colonel still had not arrived, she could not come to Philadelphia for Christmas. There were no letters from Johnny or Tommy. Abigail had written to John Quincy: "Without any disparagement to your brother, whom I doubt not will do the best he can with your property, I would advise you to employ our old tried and faithful friend Dr. Tufts." But it would be a considerable time before the letter reached him. Meanwhile his savings were still being paid over to his brother. They learned that Charley, in an effort to recoup Johnny's first loss, was taking greater gambles in high interest with unsecured notes. This was anathema to the Yankee tradition of doing business. But the Adamses would have to wait for Johnny himself to cut off the funds.

They heard too that Charley was mixing with a wild set in New York, drinking and carousing. Abigail asked herself, "Why?" Charley had had so many advantages; the handsomest of the three boys, he had made friends most easily, had not suffered the years of rebuff John Quincy had gone through in Boston before he could secure clients. He had married the woman of his choice, had a respected position at the New York Bar. He had maintained a disciplined life for years. Could one financial setback have destroyed that discipline?

A shard of reason flashed across her mind. Charley's nature could not withstand reverses. He was geared to success. Failure had never been part of his pattern. She was frightened for her son.

She went down with an attack of intermittent fever. Dr. Rush blistered and bled her.

"It's gout, you know," he proffered. "The same as the Roman emperors had."

"Dr. Rush, please! If Ben Bache hears you, he'll accuse us of acquiring monarchical diseases."

She had to be up for New Year's Day: hundreds of diplomats, government officials, congressmen, visitors would throng the house drinking punch, eating cake, wishing the President, Mrs. President and the nation a felicitous 1798.

The French armies under General Napoleon Bonaparte were everywhere victorious. Italy was conquered. Austria surrendered. Prussia, Spain, Holland and Tuscany were forced to make peace. France had also conquered and acquired Belgium. A French force had invaded neutral Switzerland and captured Basle. Only England was continuing its war. The latest rumor was that France was about to cross the Channel and invade England. The Republicans celebrated the possibility with wild acclaim. For the Federalists, and particularly for President Adams, it was a portent of tragedy.

As a result of their widespread victories, the French Directory had refused to receive John's three commissioners. John had relied heavily on these men to persuade the Directory that the United States and France had everything to gain as allies, everything to lose as combatants. Now the French increased their activities against American shipping, seizing vessels and cargoes, putting sailors ashore on the nearest beach without provisions or arms with which to defend themselves. The Republicans were livid with anger at President Adams.

They lived in the ambience of a brawling Congress. It started with the seemingly uncontroversial Foreign Intercourse Bill to establish a world-wide diplomatic and consular service. It was the House's right to debate the appropriation of the monies; in a stormy session Federalist Roger Griswold of Connecticut insulted Republican Matthew Lyon of Vermont, decrying his Revolutionary War record. Lyon spat in Griswold's face. Griswold attacked Lyon with a cane. Lyon picked up a pair of fire tongs. The two men rolled on the floor of the House chamber. John was aghast.

"This is the single worst thing that has yet happened to our federal government. We've had elected councils and legislatures since we founded our first colonies. We fought the British governors, not each other! When we formed this government we worried about the Chief Executive, never the legislature. The presidency is working. But if we have violence in the legislature, how can we persevere?"

"You feared that strong political parties would breed this kind of party strife. It's growing worse by the day."

Abigail felt as though she had been forced into the company of unsavory characters. In a moment of despair she wrote to Elizabeth Peabody:

"My dear sister, I am sick, sick, sick of public life, however enviable it may appear to others, and if the end of creation was not best answered by the most good we can do, I should wish to hide . . . in the shades of Peacefield, secured from the noise of the world, its power and ambition. Public service becomes wearisome to all men of talents and to men in years who are worn out by continual opposition and by constant exertions to support order, harmony and peace against ambition, disorder and anarchy. I hope we may be held together, but I know not how long, for oil and water are not more contrary in their natures than North and South."

One morning she opened the wax seal of a message to read that "The President, Lady and Family" were invited to an Assembly and Ball to celebrate General George Washington's birthday, February twenty-second, at Concert Hall. She waited until John rose from his desk, having annotated a long document from the Treasury, handed him the invitation.

"John, is it proper for the President and family to be invited as private citizens to public balls? Why didn't the committee come to you and ask you to be the official sponsor?"

He flicked his index finger against the invitation.

"It isn't deliberate, my dear. Most of these sponsors are Federalists."

He took up a pen, scrawled "Declined" across it.

The rejection was printed in the *Aurora* on the day of the ball. Though Vice President Jefferson also did not attend, the refusal caused a furor in the newspapers. John stood his ground.

She was confined to her room by Dr. Rush. He stayed for tea every afternoon, more ebullient than ever, for John had appointed him Treasurer of the United States Mint. In her enforced idleness she planned to move John's library out of her dining room in Quincy. She wrote to Cotton Tufts to remove the connecting wall between two small rooms and line them with bookshelves. Also to build an outside staircase so that couriers and visitors would not have to trek through the house. She kept it a secret from John.

He was thoroughly occupied. In between advising the House on the amount of losses recovered by United States citizens under the Jay Treaty, sending his Tunisian treaty to the Senate for confirmation, sending Congress a report from the committee directing the building of Washington City, he managed to find the money, over two thousand dollars, to buy the farm that Richard Cranch had been saving for him. When she learned that John had actually sent the cash through Cotton Tufts, she wrote to Mary:

"I want to say a word to you by way of advice. The farm which has been disposed of, I hope may prove a relief to Mr. Cranch as well as an advantage to him and that the income from the money if vested in public securities will yield you more real profit than the land. . . . My request is that the sum during Brother's life may not be broken in upon with an idea of assisting children. They are young and can better bear hardships and care, than those who are advanced in life."

At almost the same moment she learned that Colonel William was at home with Nab and had summoned his creditors to make a settlement of his debts. Soon after came letters from John Quincy to Secretary of State Pickering telling him that he and his wife were settled in Berlin and were no longer disappointed over losing the Lisbon post.

She called for warm water for a bath, dressed in an attractive wool dress and went down to dinner with John and their circle of intimates.

"Humans are resilient earth," she thought as she listened to the pleasant hum of conversation about the table.

On March fourth the Adamses celebrated the anniversary of John's becoming President. In the middle of dinner the first of several messages were brought to John from the Secretary of State. They had been received in code from the three commissioners in Paris. John grew grimmer and grimmer as the decoded reports arrived.

"Am I not to know their content?" she asked quietly.

"I dare not tell you. Only the three Secretaries and the Attorney General have seen them. It's my painful duty to ask these four gentlemen whether I ought to recommend to Congress an immediate declaration of war."

"War! John, have the French so far incited you that you can go against all your principles and declare for war?"

"You will scc. I dare not send these reports to the Congress or I will fear for the lives of our envoys. I know not if they have left Paris yet."

She had her mouth open to speak but shut it precipitately. She kept it shut during the ensuing days while John wrote a strong message for Congress from which his Secretaries demurred. He finally sent to the Congress Secretary of the Treasury Wolcott's version, with his own changes, asking for a defensive plan "for the protection of our seafaring and commercial citizens, for the defense of any exposed portions of our territory, for replenishing our arsenals, establishing foundries and military manufactures, and to provide such efficient revenue as will be necessary to defray extraordinary expenses and supply the deficiencies which may be occasioned by depredations on our commerce."

Congress, not provided with the coded messages, refused to act. The Republicans in the House demanded, and secured, a set of the messages.

By now it was early April. The secret had been the best preserved in the history of the young nation. The explosion was all the more violent when the country and Congress finally pored over the messages and learned that French Minister of Foreign Affairs Talleyrand had informed the American commissioners that "the Directory were greatly exasperated at some parts" of President Adams's speech to the special session of the Congress. That before the commissioners could have an audience certain parts of the speech would have to be modified; but more important, to assuage their hurt pride, Talleyrand would have to be paid privately a sum of two hundred and fifty thousand dollars in cash. The United States would also be obliged to afford France a loan of almost thirteen million dollars. These payments would make possible friendly negotiations between the disputing countries.

The demands for private bribes and public blood money were the worst insult one sovereign nation could inflict upon another. The Republicans were shocked into silence. They had thought to embarrass the President but now, with the predominantly Federalist Senate insisting upon publication of the papers, the entire nation suffered a convulsion of anti-French feeling, repudiated the Republican leaders and swung passionately behind their President. At long last John Adams had become President of all the people.

With little opposition from the immobilized Republicans, President Adams's bills were debated and passed by the Congress every few days: for building twelve armed vessels; additional regiments of artillerists and engineers; a Navy Department; erection of additional fortifications; an act to procure arms and ammunition; authorization to raise a Provisional Army of not more than ten thousand non-commissioned officers and rank; permission for the navy to seize French ships hovering off the United States coast or those that had seized United States ships.

The bribery scandal became known to the American public as the XYZ affair because John Adams, asked by the American commissioners in France not to divulge the names of Talleyrand's three unofficial envoys, had labeled them in his report X, Y and Z.

"XYZ," Abigail murmured, "a strange way to spell a three-lettered word called WAR."

"The French almost defeated me in the election of 1796," he rejoined. "And now they've made me a hero to my people. I've never really been a hero before."

"How does it feel?"

"It has a strange consistency: halfway between a banana and a rock."

6

A surge of patriotism swept the country such as it had not shown since the days of the Massachusetts war: Concord, Lexington, Breed's Hill. Abigail attended the theatre with the Samuel Otises where a crowded audience cheered the newly written words to the *President's March*. Over a thousand young men between the ages of eighteen and twenty-five paraded to the President's House, passing in procession through an assemblage of ten thousand which filled the streets as far as Abigail could see from her second-story window. The President received their committee in his levee room, dressed in his uniform as commander-in-chief, where he heard a rousing testament of their loyalty and devotion to the Union. Similar meetings took place in many of the cities, composed of the young men who would fight any war France might push them into. France had become the mightiest military power in Europe. The United States army and navy were bivouacked in congressional bills. How could a nation with only a fledgling military machine fight the conqueror of Austria, Italy, Belgium, Switzerland, and the genius of General Bonaparte? These young men singing the words of patriotic songs under their President's windows were the answer.

There were those who remained outside the embrace. When John called for a national fast on May ninth as "a day of solemn humiliation, fasting and prayer," anonymous letters reached the President that Philadelphia would be burned to the ground. Light horse patrolled the streets all night.

The *Boston Chronicle* charged father and son with having extorted eighty thousand dollars from the federal government in two years, accusing John of having nominated John Quincy to negotiate a new treaty with Sweden solely to provide John Quincy with the money for a new outfit and extra salary.

Nor was Ben Bache silenced. He called the President "blind, bald, crippled, toothless, querulous Adams."

John's hair was pure white at the sides now. He wore it full and long down his cheeks, making an interesting contrast to his strong eyebrows, still a slashing black above the big, tired, intensely aware eyes. There were few wrinkles in his face, his nose, mouth and chin remained firmly molded; but as he had slimmed with age the jowls at either side had broken into an extra looping layer of flesh. His figure had changed little: he was still stocky, sturdy, a small man of enormous inner power and physical force, the kind that seemingly never grows old.

When the Speaker of the House announced that the formidable, all-conquering French army which had been preparing to invade England was instead setting sail for America, the President's House became the nerve center of the country. The influx of government officials began by six in the morning and continued past midnight. Whoever might be working with John at breakfast, dinner or teatime was provided food and drink.

No matter what room Abigail went into she found a conference of tense men, huddled about one of the tables and poring over sheafs of papers. She came to understand how it happened that Martha Washington's furnishings had been worn out three times during her occupancy of the house. Though each department had its own offices scattered about the city, they were all now concentrated here. The leaders of the Senate and House arrived for consultations before their sessions opened at ten, and were back at four to report progress on the bills which John felt to be imperative; determining ways of getting their three envoys back from Paris; the appointment of commanders of the newly adopted army. General Washington was the first choice to command; there were arguments over who was to be second in command; Alexander Hamilton, Henry Knox, Charles Cotesworth Pinckney, one of the three commissioners in the XYZ Affair.

Abigail saw on one of John's scribbled lists the name of Colonel William Smith as adjutant general. It was late at night. John rubbed his bloodshot eyes. He had not been out of the house, even for a walk, for days. He commented doggedly:

"He's a good man for the job. General Washington respects him."

There was a sense in which these times were like those of the early Revolution when the Patriots were surrounded by Tories. Today the Tories were aliens, Frenchmen or French sympathizers who dedicated their considerable resources to tearing down the Adams administration, newspapers which became known as the "Gallic faction," led by Bache's *Aurora.* There was no crime of which they did not accuse President Adams: warmongering, criminal nepotism, looting of public funds, the building of an army with which to suppress the people and convert the United States to a monarchy with himself as King John I and his consort as Queen Abigail.

The Adamses were sensitive to the poisoned atmosphere of plot and intrigue, with its distribution of seditious literature, the secret meetings, the hiding, as former Massachusetts Senator Fisher Ames, described it, "like serpents in winter, the better to concoct their venom."

"I'm like Charley," John confessed, "thin-skinned."

If the aliens were the instruments through which a "flood of Jacobinic filth" was spewed over the country, there was little doubt in the President's House who were the instigators of what they were now convinced was a pernicious plot to destroy the union. It was the Republicans, led by Thomas Jefferson. They again opposed every measure designed for national security; bills for the army, the navy, for fortifications passed only by the Federalist majority. Without these measures, President Adams maintained, the United States would be defenseless against an invading French army. Stephen Higginson of Massachusetts, who was acting Secretary of the Navy, cried:

"There is yet a wicked and a vile spirit visible in Congress, which opposes everything energetic and dignified, but it must be subdued or expelled."

John's fear was that many Republicans who appeared to feel a greater allegiance to France than to America would join the invading French army, even as the Tories had fought with the British against the Patriots in the Revolutionary War.

It was an early June night, hot and airless. John and Abigail walked arm in arm in the back garden at two in the morning, whispering their confidences in the darkness.

"There's nothing we can do about the Republican congressmen," he said; "they're legally elected representatives of their people. We must outthink them and outvote them. But Massachusetts Representative Harrison Gray Otis and Robert Goodloe Harper of South Carolina are right; there is something we can do about the Frenchmen and other aliens who are working to subvert our government."

"Invite them to return home?"

"The bills now being discussed both inside and out of Congress are fourfold: first, to make it difficult, a longer residence in point of fact, before aliens can become American citizens. Second, to secure the right to hunt down, prosecute and expel such men who are actively engaging in sedition. Third, in time of war to give the President power to deport resident aliens of the enemy country. Fourth, to give the President the right to deport any alien he considers dangerous to the peace and safety of the country."

"Can we get these acts passed?"

"Yes. There is a French party in the United States and an English party; but as one French observer in Philadelphia has informed his government in Paris, there is also a third party 'composed of the most estimable men of the two other parties. This party, whose existence we have not even suspected, is the American party which loves its country above all and for whom preferences either for France or England are only accessory and passing affections.'"

"Glory be to God! If the French Directory really believes that, there will never be an attempt to invade us." She held herself against him, the night having stirred its first cool breeze. "John, will there be a war? Will our former allies try to accomplish what the British failed at?"

There was no want of crises; interlarded with the national dangers were their personal problems. At this moment a long-time friend in Boston, Dr. Thomas Welsh, went bankrupt. The Welsh family lost every penny of its possessions. Their doleful plight was outlined in Mary Cranch's letter. John Quincy, before he left the country, had given Dr. Welsh his savings to invest. Poor Johnny! He had lived economically, made sacrifices, saved religiously; now the fruits of his rigorous management were gone. Plus the present earnings which Charley had lost. . . .

Johnny had tried so hard to accumulate a fund against the day he would return home to begin anew his practice of the law.

She put two letters side by side on her desk. The first was from Tommy, pleading piteously that he wanted to come home. Could Abigail find a replacement for him in Berlin? The second letter told her that young Thomas, Dr. Welsh's son, just about to finish at Harvard, would have to find immediate employment. She wrote to her cousin William Smith in Boston asking his opinion of sending young Welsh to Berlin. Cousin William approved. John issued the proper orders: Thomas Welsh was to proceed to Berlin and Thomas Adams was to return to his parents' home in Philadelphia.

At least she would have one of her children home with her again.

It was late afternoon of June 19, 1798, that John Marshall, outstanding member of the three commissioners to France, arrived in Philadelphia. He was met at an outlying village by Pickering with a detachment of cavalry and given a parade through Philadelphia which was routed past the President's House. The American public had learned that Marshall was the true hero of the XYZ Affair in France. It was Marshall who, although he treated with Talleyrand's emissaries with frontier friendliness, had opposed them with such enormous resolution that the Directory began to suspect that the United States would be neither blackmailed nor bullied.

John Marshall was at the President's house for breakfast at eight the next morning. John and Abigail received him in the family dining room. Marshall was forty-two, a man with high color, sturdily built and in magnificent physical health. He had spent his early years in the open, which had given him the easy alert poise of the woodsman. His rich black hair was parted on the left side and worn very short. He had big dark eyes, wrinkles about the eyes, a cherry-red mouth filled with humor. John Marshall had grown up in Virginia. He was without formal education but had trained himself on Pope and Blackstone. Friend and opponent alike said that he had one of the most comprehensive legal minds in the country.

Abigail knew that the Virginia frontiersman favored a hearty breakfast. She ordered a thick ham steak for John Marshall, with half a dozen eggs, wheat and Indian bread and a big jar of honey. Marshall ate with enormous appetite, yet in his thinking he was a moderate man. Though he came down on his mother's side from the Jeffersons, Randolphs and

Lees, his father had been a poor man who had to make his own way. Along the route, the father had become a neighbor of George Washington, had worked for the General and come to know him. The moment news of Lexington and Concord reached them, both John and his father had taken their guns off the fireplace and joined the Virginia Army. Marshall had fought at Brandywine, Monmouth, and had spent the winter at Valley Forge with Washington. During these years he had considered "America as my country and Congress as my government."

For all of these reasons, and because they considered him incorruptible, the Adamses listened intently to John Marshall's report. To their surprise he did not feel that war was imminent. He said in his warm, attractive voice:

"Sir, in my opinion France is trying to frighten us. I tried to leave behind the impression that we don't scare all that easily. If you'll continue to remain strong and resolute, Mr. President, she will declare no war against us."

Marshall finished a plate of cucumbers, a last thick slice of wheat bread buttered with fresh butter. He wiped his mouth vigorously on his doily, sat up formally in his chair, said:

"Sir, I ask permission to say something in disagreement with your views."

The Adamses were surprised. John Marshall had been one of their most ardent supporters. They had been sorely disappointed when he turned down President Washington's offer to become Attorney General. President Adams replied, "Mr. Marshall, any view you express is respected in this house."

"Then, sir, it is my understanding that you are about to sign the Alien Bill."

"You do not approve?"

"Mr. President, it not only violates Amendment One of the Bill of Rights, which prohibits Congress from abridging the freedom of speech or of the press, but goes contrary to Amendment Five: 'No person shall be held to answer for a capital or otherwise infamous crime unless on a presentment or indictment of a grand jury . . . nor be deprived of life, liberty or property without due process.'"

"In time of war? When they are treasonable we must expel them. That is sheer self-defense."

"Is our country so weak that we cannot defend ourselves against a few aliens? When we deprive even the least of them of due process, we weaken the fiber of due process for our own citizens."

John stiffened.

"There is no parallel. The full rights of citizens are protected. Aliens are visitors, here on our sufferance. It is the government's task to send them back before they do us harm. The bill is enforceable for only two years. If there has been no war it will expire."

Marshall bowed his head to indicate that he yielded to his superior officer.

"Sir, might I ask indulgence on one more issue?"

"Certainly."

"Then, respectfully, I hear that you approve the Sedition Act that is being debated in the Congress. May I warn you against the terrible danger inherent in that Act? The Alien Bill is a bad precedent, it will injure the concept of our Republic abroad. It hurts our own citizens only inferentially. But a Sedition Act! Against our own citizens. There, sir, is the single most dangerous piece of legislation in the brief history of our nation. If the people who are against us are not allowed to speak or print their opinions, they will gag us just as brutally when they come into power. And it shall be we who are responsible because we afforded them the legal tools."

"Such an act could not be passed except in time of war."

"And who is to determine legally the border line between peace and war? With the unceasing wars and turmoils in Europe, this nation may spend much of its time in that shadowy sphere which is neither peace nor war, but only the threat of war. Even as now. Mr. President, the genius of America lies in its ability to let everyone worship his own God, speak his own mind, assemble with his own friends and print his own heresies. You spoke out strongly for a Declaration of Rights. I beseech you not to abandon its principles now. Any tyrant rising in the land can use such a Sedition Act to close every critical mouth. The worst fears of those who fought federation and the Constitution will have been realized."

Abigail had been sitting quietly; now she begged permission of the gentlemen to speak.

"Mr. Marshall, you have been out of the country for almost a year. You have not experienced the mounting venalities and grotesqueness of the enemy press . . ."

". . . opposition press, ma'am," Marshall interrupted.

"Very well. We are informed that their system is to calumniate the President, his family, his administration until they have obliged him to resign. Then they will reign triumphant. Thomas Jefferson will be the man of the people! We are come now to a crisis too important to be languid, too dangerous to slumber. . . . I can prove this to you in a matter of minutes."

She went into her own sitting room and assembled the articles which she had marked each day for Louisa to cut out for her: from the *Aurora*, the *Chronicle* of Boston, the *Argus*, *Albany Register*, *Richmond Examiner*.

"Mr. Marshall, please read these attacks. Do they come from honest men? Or are they written by evildoers and incendiaries?"

Marshall spread out her lexicon of abuse. His normally ruddy cheeks paled as he read the savage attacks. When he lifted his eyes they were filled with shame and apology.

"Now you will agree that we need this Sedition Act? It is plain to you?"

"Mrs. President, I am horrified! But what is plain is that we need more stringent libel laws. A Sedition Act will never go down with our people. Sir, you are a historian, and you should know: if you sign these repressive measures, history will treat you harshly. If you negative them, history will add this brave act to your luster."

"That may be, Mr. Marshall. I find myself in the unhappy position of a client who must reject the advice of his able and honest counsel. I haven't time to speculate about this possible judgment of history. I have two clear and urgent tasks: first, to try to prevent a war with France, second, to make sure we win it if France invades us. All else is commentary."

Marshall took the President's proffered hand.

"My services are yours for either eventuality, Mr. President."

John Adams signed two Alien Bills in June, and in July a stringent Sedition Act passed by both Houses of the Congress.

He believed that the courts would now have the proper tools with which to silence the traitors and traducers.

7

Oppressive heat struck the city. Abigail found the streets so "nauseous" that she sensed a return of the yellow fever. All around people were going down with complaints of the bowels and inflammatory sore throat. Congress wanted to adjourn and make its way home. So did the President, and what John Adams called his "Presidente." But despite John Marshall's optimism, every day brought new war measures that had to be passed by the Congress and signed by the President; and on June twenty-fifth the bill authorizing "the defense of the merchant vessels." Within a week John sent General Washington's name to the Senate as commander of the army. The government was to buy thirty thousand stands of arms which could be sold to the state militia at a price to be set by the President. The treaties between the United States and France were no longer to be binding. He signed bills creating a Marine Corps; informed the French consul that he was no longer recognized. A direct tax of two million dollars was laid on the states; the President was to be permitted to borrow five million dollars from the Bank of the United States. So high did the invasion fears continue to rise that Congress raised the number of authorized regiments from eight to twelve.

Abigail's secret about her preparations for John's library was exposed when Mr. Soper, a neighbor from Quincy, "spilled the beans." John seemed quite happy.

"I have needed more room desperately. It's a question I hardly dare ask anybody in the government: how do we pay the bills?"

"When we were in Auteuil I asked Cousin Cotton to buy me £100 of army certificates. It took thirteen years but the government finally redeemed them at par."

He took her in his arms, smoothed her graying hair back from her temples and kissed her gently.

"'Parson Smith's girls, are they frank or fond or even candid?' Remember my confessing my doubts to you that first day we went to Rainsford Island? That was thirty-six years ago! Do you know, dear friend, a man can be an idiot all the days of his youth but if he makes the one right decision he is instantly converted into a genius?"

The Senate confirmed General Washington as commander. President John Adams sent Secretary of War McHenry to Mount Vernon to ask him whom he would recommend for his General Staff. He also sent with McHenry a tentative list of officers for Washington's consideration: Lincoln, Morgan, Knox, Hamilton, Gates, Pinckney, Lee, Muhlenberg, Burr and William Smith. The House adjourned but the Senate remained to approve the list of officers whom Washington would propose. General Washington threw out the Republicans Muhlenberg and Burr, added a few names, to make a staff of ten top officers. John sent for Abigail, exclaimed excitedly:

"Look, General Washington has nominated Colonel Smith to be a brigadier general. It is the one move that can repatriate our son-in-law.

I shall suggest the Colonel be made adjutant general. I think he is perhaps more qualified in that department."

The next day John sent the list to the Senate for confirmation. Within a matter of hours a committee of three senators appeared at the President's house. They were embarrassed; but they wanted to save him from even greater embarrassment. Would not the President remove the name of Colonel William Smith from the recommended list? The Senate simply could not confirm him. Their reasons? He was a "speculator . . . a bankrupt, and an Anti-Federalist." The President would not. All the other names on the list were approved. Colonel William Smith was rejected. Abigail was crestfallen. Her husband was furious.

"How could it have happened?" she demanded.

"I warned our good Colonel against ostentation and preening during his short period of prosperity. During his financial difficulties he walked out on his obligations to his closest associates."

"But, John, he did have a meeting of his creditors last February. Didn't anything good come of that?"

"Nothing that I've heard of."

"Is there absolutely nothing we can do? How will we face the Colonel with the news?"

"Perhaps we won't have to. Frankly, I think he was home for a short time and has been gone ever since. We'll break the news to Nab as gently as possible when we pick her up and take her to Quincy with us."

The yellow fever was spreading hundreds of deaths every day throughout Philadelphia. The Senate recessed and hurriedly left the city. Abigail ordered the Brieslers to go into the country. When the Adamses finally left on July twenty-fifth, the heat and dust of the roads was so oppressive that Abigail had to have the carriage stopped twice within a few hours while she went into an inn to undress herself and lie down on a bed.

The trip home was ghastly. The air inside the carriage was suffocating. Despite the fact that she had Nab and Louisa to care for her, it was the worst journey of her life. When they reached Quincy she had to be half carried up the stairs to her bedroom.

Here she remained for eleven weeks. She suffered bouts of chills and fever. No one could tell precisely what was wrong. Dr. Cotton Tufts called on her every day. He brought with him Dr. Benjamin Waterhouse and Dr. John Warren from Boston, hoping they could diagnose the illness. At first it was thought to be the yellow fever, but the possibility of that passed. As the heat grew worse her strength ebbed. When several days elapsed of which she could remember only a few moments, she was convinced that her time had come. She made her peace with God, summoned her husband and her daughter to say her farewells. She was unhappy that she could not say good-by to John Quincy and Tommy and Charles, but they were far away. It was her sister Mary Cranch who brought her up sharply.

"Sister Abigail, I am surprised at you. You have said we Puritans die hard, that we refuse to hear Gabriel the first half a dozen times he blasts on his trumpet."

Abigail could see her sister's face only dimly. She said in a voice made hoarse by fever:

"You can see that I am dying."

"I can see that you think you are dying. That's a very different thing."

"I am reduced to skin and bone and I am growing weaker all the time."

"You were plump to start with. That gives you a lot of shrinking space. I don't doubt me you will get sicker and sicker until the cold weather comes. When that happens you will be out of bed."

Mary was right. Nab and Louisa took turns at nursing her. John was heartbroken at her illness and frightened at the possibility of her death. Working in his upstairs library, he received dispatches and correspondence from all over the country, as well as the delegations that came to see him. He tried to answer the more important mail but could accomplish little more. When his Secretaries urged him to return to Philadelphia, stressing the need for the Chief Executive to be on hand, he wrote to Secretary of War McHenry in Philadelphia:

"I cannot go to that city . . . very soon. Mrs. Adams's health is so low and her life so precarious that it will be impossible for me to force myself away from her till the last moment. The last has been the most gloomy summer of my life, and the prospect of the winter is more dismal still. . . ."

That day he found her feeling a little better. He divulged the contents of his letter to the Secretary of War. Abigail said sternly:

"You must return to Philadelphia, or Trenton, if the government is going to sit there until the yellow fever passes. They need you. I'll be all right here. I'll come just as soon as I can."

The last intramural clash before John left had to do with the chain of command under Washington. President Adams believed the confirmed officers should have the same order of status they had enjoyed at the close of the Revolutionary War. He wanted Knox's commission dated the first day, Pinckney's the second, Hamilton's the third, giving them that order of command. Alexander Hamilton demanded that he be first under Washington. Secretaries Pickering and McHenry worked indefatigably to get him this post, going to General Washington, who then insisted on Hamilton being named to the top post.

John heard of the machinations in Quincy. He was at last convinced that these men felt a stronger allegiance to Hamilton than to their President. Nevertheless he yielded.

Abigail had been bedridden all summer, and John too distraught to pay any attention to the farm, yet they had their best crop in years. Cousin William Smith came out from Boston with buyers and secured them an excellent cash deal.

On her first day out she worked in her rose garden. Thinking back over her illness, she realized that it had much in common with her collapse in Boston just before her marriage to John Adams, when her aunt Elizabeth had been so alarmed she had suggested that the wedding be postponed. The doctors had not known what was wrong with her then, any more than they had now. She suspected that the world and her troubles had been a little too much with her, at both times.

Four of their regular retainers had died of the yellow fever over the summer. Benjamin Bache had been arrested in June on charges of libeling the President but had been released on bail. He too had succumbed to the yellow fever. It took all of the Adamses' Christian charity to mourn him.

No two periods of being alone were identical. She had been broken to the routine as a bride, when John went out circuit riding. Then had followed the years of service in the Continental Congress, beginning with the merest three months' absence and extending to eleven months. These had been the veriest prologue to John's absences in Europe: the first trip of eighteen months, home for three, then away and separated for nearly five years. After that she was a seasoned campaigner who could come out alive at the far end of any Thirty Years' War.

By the end of two weeks of cold weather she had regained her humor and was so invigorated that she was able to think back to her role as hostess in the Presidential House. She wrote John:

"Tell me who and who inquires after me as if they cared for me. The New York paper and Porcupine have undertaken to regret my necessary absence from the seat of government. I suppose they think you will want somebody to keep you warm and knowing that you are not a David, commiserate your lonely situation. The paragraph from the New York paper is a very precious one to me. Remember me to all my female friends. I have the vanity to think that the federal Reps. and Senators will miss me this winter."

Philadelphia did indeed miss her. With Abigail gone from the President's House, John made no attempt to entertain the women of the city's high social strata, or even the wives of the congressmen or ambassadors. Young William Shaw, John's apprentice secretary, wrote to his aunt Abigail:

"Briesler says he has no encouragement now to make good dinners. . . . There are no ladies, and if everything is ever so good, gentlemen never give any credit."

At Quincy she entertained not at all. When one of her brother Billy's daughters, Betsy, was to be married, she had the dinner and celebration in her home. At Thanksgiving Richard Cranch and John's nephew Boylston Adams were both down with illness, so she had the Porters, and Phoebe, "the only surviving parent I have," join her at the kitchen table to share the "bounties of Providence."

By December she was going for walks over the snow-covered fields. Her strength rose as the temperature went down.

"Heat is your natural enemy," Cotton Tufts advised her; "from now on you must flee it as you would the devil tempting you to sin!"

"Now, Cousin Cotton, what sins are available to a woman of fifty-four?"

The farms lay fallow under the snow. She lay fallow under a comforter enjoying each afternoon when a few relatives or friends visited, the president of Harvard, the lieutenant governor of Massachusetts. There were letters from the Reverend Mr. Peabody to assure her that Nab's two sons were doing well in school. There was no news from Charley; she wanted to worry about him but her mind veered away. She did worry a little over Tommy, who was long overdue in the United States, and Johnny's wife, Louisa, in Berlin: the poor girl had already suffered two miscarriages. About Nab, John wrote:

"The lieutenant general and major generals have recommended Colonel Smith to the command of a regiment. This is a degradation of him to which I would not consent without his consent. I have written to him hoping that he would forbid the nomination. But his pride is humbled to that degree that he writes me he will accept. . . . His situation will be miserable under the command of his former equals and inferiors. . . .

Happy Washington! Happy to be childless! My children give me more pain than all my enemies."

Abigail sat gazing at the fateful sentence. If John had said, "My child gives me more pain," that could have applied to Colonel Smith alone. But he had used the plural. Since they were deeply gratified by John Quincy's brilliant performance abroad, and Tommy had acquitted himself well, the plural could only mean Charley.

"How foolish of me," she thought, "not to have realized that John knew Charley was drinking hard. After all my husband is the President of the United States. He has countless contacts. He has probably concealed more from me than I have from him. But it's out in the open now. We must do something about him. We must arrange for Charley and Sally to live with us in Philadelphia. John can make him his secretary, his legal adviser. No one could object, if Charley doesn't draw a public salary."

Whatever had happened to her laughter-loving boy? No one but Jonathan Sewall—may he rest in peace!—ever loved to make laughter more than Charley.

If the first to laugh were the first to cry; if the fun and festivity makers were the first to learn that life was a cruel joke of which they were the victims, could it be that they created laughter originally out of their fear and dread of the gloom that invaded their hearts and heads like vandals?

She brushed the thought aside. Time enough to cope with Charley when she had recovered her own land legs. As for Colonel William, now that the United States planned a permanent army there was no reason why he could not serve for the rest of his life with fidelity and distinction. He might not be good at much else, but everyone from Washington down agreed that he was a good man to have around in a fight. It would mean that he would live in army camps, be ordered to distant frontiers.

She determined to take Nab and Caroline with her to Philadelphia. John Quincy's family would also move in when they finally returned to America, at least until Johnny decided where his future lay. There would certainly be plenty of room in the President's Mansion in Washington City for all their children. She would have her entire family under one roof again. Not since November of 1779 when John had set sail the second time for Europe, taking Johnny and Charley with him, had this happened. Nineteen years during which the family had been spread thin over the world.

John wrote to her frequently, but she had other sources of news. One of the first acts Congress had passed was a law which said that once the House and Senate had approved a specific bill, and the President had signed it, it must immediately be made available to one newspaper in every state. This law was a help to her here in Quincy; the newspapers sent to her by John and Samuel Otis, or brought out from Boston by her friends and relatives, gave a running account of what the government was doing. There were a good many bread and butter acts, domestic and even local in nature: appointing commissioners to settle the accounts between the United States and the several states in relation to debts owed to the federal treasury; an application of the laws of the United States within the latest state to come into the Union, Tennessee; acts appropriating substantial sums to carry into effect the Indian treaties among the several tribes and nations; acts fixing the pay of practically everybody in the government, beginning with commanders of the United States ships of war; providing the compensations of marshals, attorneys, jurors and witnesses in the United States courts; regulating the collection of duties on imports and tonnage; regulating the distillers; the medical establishment; the grants of land appropriated for military services; providing for the security of bail; authorization for the sale of Western lands . . .

The Congress was working hard. In addition to the domestic measures a number of strong acts in the field of foreign relations were passed. One arose from the circumstance of Vice President Jefferson's having given a letter of introduction to George Logan to friends in France. Logan used the letter as a means of gaining admission to the French government, beginning private, unauthorized negotiations looking toward a possible peace. This enraged President Adams and the Congress, which promptly made it a crime for a private citizen of the United States to attempt to settle disputes or controversies with any foreign power.

Although the record was productive, Abigail knew from her private correspondence that there was considerable turmoil inside the Congress, with its members split sharply between the Federalists and the Republicans. The Republicans continued to defeat bills which had to do with the building up of the federal strength, a standing army or increased taxes, any of the acts by means of which the central government might weaken the powers of the states. They also wanted the Alien and Sedition Acts declared unconstitutional for fear they would be used to suppress the Republican newspapers and writers. Jefferson and his political lieutenant, James Madison, drew up what were called the Kentucky and Virginia Resolutions, claiming that the states had the right to judge the constitutionality of federal acts, and asking that other state legislatures join in condemning the Alien and Sedition Acts in order to get them off the statute books. No other legislature would agree.

Assessing the news in the quiet of Peacefield, Abigail surmised how much John was harassed and chevied. As always his troubles were augmented by his own Federalists. Having helped to build an American machine of war, Hamilton appeared eager to use it.

8

Tommy was delayed in returning home because his parents insisted he travel only on an armed United States vessel. It would have been too inconvenient to have a French cruiser capture the son of the President. He sailed into New York in January 1799, visited with his father in Philadelphia, then joined his mother in Quincy.

Tommy held a special place in his mother's affection. He was the baby of the lot, though at twenty-six he was considerable of a man: short of stature, but with a powerful physique. He was the steady one, without fluctuating moods. He had taken care of the barnyard fowl when the older children tired; had helped her fix up the store in John's law office and keep it in running order. If he did not have the intellectual gifts of Johnny or Charley, he had tenacity and a sense of family duty. He had stayed with John Quincy in Berlin for a year beyond his impatient desire to come home, simply because Johnny needed him and would have been lonely without him.

Tommy installed himself in his father's library. She was delighted to have him at home. She recalled William Shaw's description of the meeting of Tommy and his father in Philadelphia. John Adams had taken his youngest son in his arms, the tears running down his cheeks, and said, "I thank my God, my son, that you have returned again to your native country." Could his mother do less?

They had dinner on a small table before the sitting-parlor fireplace. Abigail wanted her packet of news from Berlin but first she wanted to know about Tommy's plans.

"Ma, I want to open a law office in Philadelphia. Oh, you won't see too much of me around the President's House. I wouldn't want anyone to give me a case because I'm the President's son."

"Have you kept up your studies in the law, Tommy?"

Tommy ate his beef stew methodically. He had never been one to claim much for himself, either aspirations or accomplishments.

"I'm not really good at abstract thought, Ma. What Johnny calls the universals of the law. I could never write a constitution the way Pa has, or the kind of analytical reports Johnny has been submitting to the Secretary of State. I have no gift for philosophy."

"That's because you have a practical mind. You were the one who got things done, while Johnny and Charley were philosophizing about the implications of a problem."

Tommy flushed with pleasure. The plodder had rarely received the credit.

"For a long time I thought I had best go into business. But all our family are lawyers . . ."

"A majority of law cases have to do with business. Why can't you be a businessman's lawyer? Our trade is expanding, our country growing more populous all the time. Let Father write his constitutions, Johnny his European reports. You write contracts."

Tommy's eyes lighted.

"You think there's a place for me? Not as the President's son, but as Thomas Boylston Adams, unknown." He rose, concealed his expression by poking at the logs in the fireplace. "Ma, you just put me in business."

"You saw Charley in New York?"

"Yes, Ma."

"Did you see any signs of reformation?"

Tommy clenched and unclenched his hands. He would not utter a syllable about his brother whom he had always idolized.

"When you return through New York, straighten out his business papers."

"I'll do what I can."

Tommy was not one to give false hopes. He did, however, confide that he wanted a wife.

"I know I'm several years away from being able to support one. And who she may be I haven't the slightest idea, not having met any of the eligibles as yet. But a man is not a man until he has a wife, that much I know. . . . In the meanwhile I can be your business manager. French has agreed to pay a hundred and seventy-five dollars to work his portion of the farm, and pay the taxes. Burrell has agreed to remain through the year. You're short of cash, there are wages to be paid. According to your books, Cousin Cotton borrowed from General Lincoln last year. Do you want me to borrow five hundred dollars this time? That will meet your obligations. Pa can pay the note when the Treasury sends him the next quarterly voucher."

She leaned back in her chair, smiling to herself, for she could hear Johnny's voice in Auteuil going over their accounts.

The end of February froze the rivers and bay, the snow falling with violence. Tommy returned from Boston chuckling. He had been told a good story.

President Adams, sensing that France was ready for a conciliatory gesture, had appointed an old associate, William Vans Murray, a Marylander, as minister plenipotentiary to France. Murray had served in the Congress for six years, then had been appointed by President Washington to succeed John Quincy as minister to The Hague, where he now resided. The French Directory had seemed to like him. John had not consulted his Cabinet about the appointment. He had a good reason: the war wing of the Federalists would be outraged at any conciliatory gesture toward France.

"Some of the Federalists did not like Pa taking them by surprise that way," Tommy related. "They said, 'We wish the old woman had been there. We don't believe the appointment would have taken place if she had been in Philadelphia!' "

"That was pretty saucy of them, Tommy, but the 'old woman' can tell them they are mistaken. I consider the measure a master stroke of policy. The one thing your father most ardently wants to accomplish during his administration is the avoidance of war with France."

Tommy's eyes were dancing.

"I'm glad the old woman approves."

"Now, Tommy, it's you who is saucy."

John's appraisal of the French situation proved sound. Talleyrand was no longer so eager to fight the whole world, particularly now that the United States and England were considering the signing of an agreement to send troops into the Floridas and Louisiana. British Admiral Nelson had already defeated a French fleet. Talleyrand made life easier for President Adams by making a public apology for the XYZ Affair. Surely this was an indication that Talleyrand and France wanted peace?

But President Adams had underestimated the power of Hamilton, who used his influence in the Senate to set up a peace commission of three men, hoping to control at least one of them. John accepted the Senate's compromise. Now his popularity soared even higher than after the XYZ scandal. When he had been hardest pressed by the war

Federalists, he used the magnificent lines from Washington's farewell address:

"Every part of our country . . . must derive from union an exemption from those broils and wars between themselves which so frequently afflict neighboring countries not tied together by the same governments. . . . In the execution of such a plan nothing is more essential than that permanent, inveterate antipathies against particular nations and passionate attachments for others should be excluded, and that in place of them just and amicable feelings toward all should be cultivated. The nation which indulges toward another an habitual hatred or an habitual fondness is in some degree a slave."

The Republicans became convinced that he meant to have no war with France, admitting that his strong military preparations had been in part the cause of France's suing for peace. Only one enemy remained: Alexander Hamilton.

With the cessation of foreign war fears, domestic rebellion reared its head once again. In Bethlehem, Pennyslvania, where there was resentment among the Pennyslvania Dutch over the paying of direct taxes, a United States marshal arrested two tax dodgers. An auctioneer named John Fries, aided by two henchmen and backed by a crowd of a hundred armed residents, forced the marshal to release the two prisoners. When President Adams heard of it he sent in cavalry and militia who captured Fries and his two co-conspirators. They were brought to Philadelphia to be tried before United States Supreme Court justices for treason. A hanging verdict would be asked.

"Shades of Shays's Rebellion back in '86," Abigail commented to Tommy, "and the Whisky Rebellion in '94. What do we do with people who take up arms to defeat the federal law?"

John returned to Quincy earlier than she had expected. She sometimes forgot how greatly he thrived on opposition. The truth about John Adams, she decided as she watched him go about the building of another barn and cider house at Peacefield, was that he was indestructible. That magnificent contingent of men with whom he had started a revolution, carrying it through to the creation of a wholly new and noble form of government, had been kissed by God. Otherwise, how could they have accomplished so much in the course of their own generation?

Her nephew William Shaw arrived with the President. The Adamses were training William as one of their sons, even as their aunt Elizabeth had raised Charley and Tommy at Haverhill, and was now keeping Nab's two sons. Abigail sent home with him the quarter's advance for the children's board, as well as new clothing. She had been supporting the boys for two years now, ever since their departure from Eastchester. Colonel Smith had not made the slightest attempt to contribute to their expenses. Nab was as parsimonious as any other New Englander, but the Puritan's first duty, after his worship of God, was to rear and educate his children. Nab had still another of her tendons cut.

John rejoiced to see Abigail so well after the winter of hibernation. She was even ready to entertain, something they had not done the previous summer.

"I've planned a dinner each week."

"That will be good," he exclaimed quickly. "We need all the support we can get right now, particularly from our own people. They are cranky with me because I believe that a Chief Executive must sometimes act on his own."

They finished the barn, which caused Peter Adams's son Boylston, the wit of Quincy, to exclaim, "It's high time the President's cattle were better lodged!" They gave the house a coat of paint but made no repairs because they were planning a new wing, which would give them a drawing room of some twenty by twenty-seven feet, and above it a magnificent study for John, with windows facing in three directions, and a beautiful fireplace. This was the first time Abigail would not have to scrounge for the money. She had accumulated considerable sums of stock certificates and had used the interest to buy still more; at long last they could consider themselves comfortable.

John went about a good deal, to the Harvard commencement, to political dinners, to the riotous Fourth of July celebration in Boston. She invited to Peacefield all their old friends. Most came, even Cousin Samuel and Betsy. Sam'l was retired now, old, ruminative and ill. He had opposed his cousin's election to the presidency, but once John was in office Samuel had girded the loins of his pride and written:

"I congratulate you as the first citizen of the United States—I may add of the world. I am, my dear sir, notwithstanding I have been otherwise represented in party papers, your old and unvaried friend."

Mercy Warren too had swallowed her pride and sent congratulations to the Adamses, but her husband James had refused to sign a Plymouth resolution thanking President Adams for his vigilance in the XYZ matter. He remained embittered because the Revolution had not rewarded him more suitably. In every letter Abigail wrote she invited Mercy and

James to stop off on the road from Plymouth to Boston. Mercy wrote letters, but never set foot in the Adams house. Later, in her *History of the Rise, Progress and Termination of the American Revolution*, their old friend revenged herself on the inequities of fate by publishing a scathing indictment of John Adams's career.

The country was awaiting Talleyrand's official summons to the three commissioners. Couriers came in from Philadelphia several times a week. How large a standing army should be ordered into existence, now that peace with France looked favorable? Who were the best men in the sixteen states to be appointed officers of the army? Could the ruler of Santo Domingo be recognized without alienating Holland, Spain and France? A letter was sent to the American minister to England, Rufus King, urging him to protest strongly the continued British impressment of American seamen, an issue Lawyer Adams thought he had disposed of in 1769 in the Panton case. What to do with the letters from friends in Philadelphia warning him that his Secretaries were taking too much power upon themselves and using it to implement Hamilton's policies?

He was certain of the loyalty of Benjamin Stoddert, Secretary of the Navy, who was his own appointee; he had faith in Attorney General Charles Lee and Secretary of the Treasury Oliver Wolcott. To Abigail he confided:

"I shall discharge Pickering and McHenry one day, and put in my own men. But I shall do it at the time I think proper."

The holocaust of the yellow fever had once again swept Philadelphia. The government moved to Trenton, New Jersey. From Trenton, in August, came a pouch from Secretary of State Pickering forwarding Talleyrand's letter to Minister Murray giving assurance that the Directory "will receive the envoys in the official character with which they are invested."

John's elation was short-lived. Reports reached him of an upheaval in the French government. Talleyrand and the Directory could well be on their way out! Then, dated September eleventh, came a report from Pickering affirming that Talleyrand was indeed out; the Directory had collapsed. Two days later Secretary of the Navy Stoddert wrote in considerable alarm, urging President Adams to return in all haste:

"I have been apprehensive that artful designing men might make such use of your absence from the seat of government, when things so important to restore peace with one country, and to preserve it with another, were transacting, as to make your next election less honorable than it would otherwise be."

Stoddert feared the Hamilton clique would prevent the commissioners from leaving for France. Most importantly, "It appears to me that the decision in question would be better supported throughout the country if it be taken when you are surrounded by the officers of government and the ministers, even if it should be against their unanimous advice."

John would have to leave for the capital in Trenton at once. Abigail would follow with Louisa, stopping off at Eastchester. The Colonel had gone at the head of his regiment to the main encampment in New Jersey. Abigail found Sally at Nab's with her two children, having fled the yellow fever of New York.

"How is Charley faring?" she asked.

"He said he has clients and causes he cannot abandon."

Nab gave her mother a letter from John dated from Trenton. When she read his lines, her heart sank. John, who loved his children as much as any man alive, had disowned his son!

"Sally opened her mind to me for the first time. I pitied her, I grieved, I mourned, but could do no more. A madman possessed of the devil . . . I renounce him. David's Absalom had some ambitions and some enterprise. Mine is a mere rake, buck, blood and beast."

Charley was drinking. When he drank, he gambled; when he gambled, he lost, signed notes. . . .

That had been her brother Billy's pattern. "Oh dear God, no," she cried; "don't let Charley destroy himself as Billy did!" When Johnny had written to his mother insisting that she try to get an accounting from Charley, since his letters from Germany remained unanswered, Abigail had replied:

"What shall I say that will not pain us both? . . . How sharper than a serpent's tooth it is to have a graceless child. . . ."

She went to her bedroom, sat blindly on the bed, breathing hard. There was pity, remorse, guilt in her for she knew not what. "A madman possessed of the devil," John had said. Surely there must be some way to exorcise the devil?

A few days later was her thirty-fifth wedding anniversary, October 25, 1799. Nab was happier than Abigail had seen her in years. She was to accompany her mother to Philadelphia, stopping off to see her husband at the winter camp in New Jersey. She made a fine plum pudding and invited Samuel and Mary Otis to the party. Abigail was toasted for many happy returns. Charley did not travel the twenty miles to participate in the celebration. John wrote a loving letter the day of the anniversary. She answered:

"I received last evening yours of the twenty-fifth with a heart filled with gratitude for the many blessings I have enjoyed through the thirty-five years of our union. I would not look upon a single shade in the picture. . . ."

Colonel William was in fine fettle. The Congress had appropriated money for new uniforms but they were not yet available. He made a valiant effort to stuff his forty-four-year-old figure into a uniform he had worn in his twenties, escorted the party along the road to Brunswick, New Jersey, where John met them.

The President had ordered the three commissioners to France in spite of the upheaval.

This would be the last season of presidential drawing rooms in Philadelphia. The original congressional Act passed nine years before decreed that the government had to move to Washington City by the first Monday in December 1800. Philadelphia made the most of it. The social tempo accelerated. Wives of government officials who had never visited Philadelphia wanted to experience its sophistication before the Congress and President moved away. At Abigail's first drawing room the ladies arrived in more brilliant gowns and jewelry than she had seen at the Court of St. James's. She revolted against the display of wealth, the gowns were much too tight, showed too much of the whole form. When she herself changed from muslin to the proper winter silk, there was an instant upsurge of business for the local mantuamakers.

One of the kingmakers of Philadelphia society was missing: Mrs. Robert Morris, former owner of this President's House. Robert Morris, his vast fortune having perished in land speculations and other hazardous investment, was in debtors' prison. Abigail remembered Maria Morris as a remarkably fine-looking woman, gay as a bird and faithful to Abigail in her loyalties. She called at Mrs. Morris's modest dwelling. Maria was pale, dispirited, but on seeing Abigail tried to smile away her melancholy.

"Mrs. Morris, you must come and take tea with me." She took Maria by the hand. "Adversity should not cost us our friends."

"Mrs. President, I do not visit, but I will not refuse myself the pleasure of coming someday."

Mrs. Morris turned away, unable to stop the flow of tears before the front door closed. Abigail continued down the street, trembling. She thought:

"This is what Charley saved Nab from: being the wife of a man locked in prison for years."

By November it was clear that electioneering for the 1800 contest had begun. Little else was spoken about: in Abigail's drawing rooms, in the Congress, in the newspapers. John addressed the new Congress on December third. There was virtual treason within his official family. Secretary of State Pickering, long an adversary, now took an implacable stand, dictating the policy of his department without consulting the President, and undermining the mission to France.

George Washington's death on December fourteenth, from a cold and severe ague he contracted while riding on his plantation during snow and hail, momentarily united the nation. The country went into mourning: bells were muffled and rung sadly for days, there were funeral processions with the citizens wearing crepe around their arms. Congress Hall was draped in black. There were perorations from the pulpits, eulogies in the papers, ceremonial services for this man who had served so well and so long. John Adams had succeeded him, but no one could ever replace him.

Abigail's drawing room of December 27, 1799, was the most crowded she had ever had, a hundred gentlemen, all in black. "The ladies' grief has not deprived them of ingenuity in ornamenting their white dresses," she commented to John. They wore epaulettes of black silk trimmed with fringe on each shoulder, crepe hats with black plumes or black flowers, black gloves and fans; or two yards of narrow black cloth crossing in the back in the form of a military sash and tied at one side.

Abigail gave a dinner for the congressmen from New Hampshire, Massachusetts and Connecticut and their wives. A few days later it was the Supreme Court justices and their wives, with all visiting judges. She did not deceive herself; this entertaining was important to the well-being of the Union. It was also important for the forthcoming election.

John was already deep in the campaign. Republican Congressman John Randolph, claiming that he had been insulted by two army officers, wrote the President a stiff note claiming that the army was attempting to intimidate the legislature. John declared the note pure partisan politics. When a seaman named Jonathan Robbins, alias Thomas Nash, was arrested in South Carolina on a charge of committing murder on a British warship, he claimed citizenship in Danbury, Connecticut, which Danbury denied. The judge in South Carolina refused to surrender Nash. The case was referred to President Adams. John ordered the man released to the British under the terms of the Jay Treaty. The Republicans screamed, "Surrender to the British!" John commented, "Purer politics. Everything I eat for breakfast from now on will become a political issue."

New York was preparing for its legislative elections. If the Federalists won they would name John Adams electors.

"And if the Republicans win?" queried Abigail. "The reports are that Aaron Burr is waging a brilliant campaign against Hamilton and the Federalists."

John's eyes clouded.

"Can we lose New York and still win? Yes. But it will be difficult."

9

Nab and her daughter Caroline were using Abigail's dressing room and office as their bedroom. On February 20, 1800, President Adams signed a congressional act to suspend further enlistments in the army. Abigail did not tell Nab that Congress was planning to disband the army in a month or two and that President Adams would sign the bill. The Colonel would be out of work.

She sat for a portrait by Gilbert Stuart. Catherine Johnson, mother of Johnny's wife, visited as a house guest. Tommy was living with his parents but scrupulously avoiding clients or causes which might originate from the fact that he was the President's son. One day he invited twenty-eight young unmarried ladies and gentlemen to dine. Just before Abigail rose from the table he came around to her and whispered:

"Have you any objection to my having a dance this evening?"

"None in the world, Tommy, providing it comes thus accidental."

The company went up to the drawing room for tea while the tables were removed downstairs and the lights lighted. At eight o'clock the dancing commenced. The young people danced until midnight. John came in for an hour; Abigail stayed on as chaperon. When she and Tommy had said good night to the last guest, Tommy took her by the arm and walked her upstairs.

"How nice that was of you, Mother." They had reached the top of the steps. "By the by, how did you like Miss M.?"

"Her manners are perfectly affable and agreeable. However I cannot but lament that the uncovered bosom should display what ought to have been veiled. I wish she had left more to the imagination and less to the eye."

"She is not yet seventeen, Mother, and it is the fashion in Philadelphia to show off one's charms."

Abigail glanced at her son. He had grown up.

Congress decreed that they would convene in Washington City on the third Monday of November 1800 for their next session. Designers, and then workmen, had been at the construction for close to a decade. John had not wanted the government to move to Washington City, in what had been named the District of Columbia; it was so plaguedly far from Quincy. But now he was looking forward to the change with enthusiasm.

"In a certain sense it will make us a full-fledged nation," he declared, "to have a permanent home and seat of government. It is being carved out of a wilderness. I am proud that I will be the first President to reign there. It will bring me a recruit of spirits to have the opportunity to leave my imprint on it."

Congress passed an act appropriating fifteen thousand dollars with which to furnish the President's House in Washington. John signed the bill with a flourish.

"We will need our New England shrewdness to make that sum do," Abigail commented. "They gave us fourteen thousand to refurbish this house. The President's Mansion must be at least four times as large."

"I'll measure it when I make my first trip there next month. I understand that only a few of the rooms are finished. It will be another year before the whole house is completed. Congress will be there to know what's needed."

"Will we be there to know what's needed?" she asked softly.

John quivered like a ship suddenly hit by a high wave.

"Problematical."

She returned to the practicalities.

"All of this furniture needs to be packed and sent to Washington City. I mean to get out of the way of that. Perhaps I can have your big study finished by the time you reach home. Cousin Cotton says there is a great deal of activity. I just shipped the marble for the fireplace."

Abigail gave her last Philadelphia drawing room, for two hundred people, friends and government associates.

A caucus of Federalist congressmen met in the Senate chambers and selected John Adams and Charles Cotesworth Pinckney to head their party in the presidential race. In New York, Hamilton, who had tried hard to hold the state for the Federalists, lost it to Burr. He now declared his support of Adams and Pinckney equally, vowed that the Federalist Party would wage its campaign as a unified force. The naming of Pinckney should bring in certain compensating Southern states, particularly his native South Carolina.

The election news was good: in May the Federalist consensus was that John would defeat Jefferson by seventy-two votes to sixty-six. In June the expectations ran even higher, for Adams was assured of seventy-nine votes to Jefferson's fifty-nine.

She almost got away on this bright note.

Secretary of War McHenry was the cause of the uproar. Her husband chose this moment to give in to his temper. He had confided to her that it would be the wiser part of politics not to oust McHenry or Pickering. When the election had been decided he would ask for their resignations. He had appeared to take the defeat of Hamilton and the Federalists in New York calmly. Actually he was in a boil. He summoned McHenry to his office, accused him of opposing and frustrating the administration, of endangering their chances of re-election, threatened that he would not be allowed to retain his office after the election; then launched into a diatribe against Alexander Hamilton, uttering all the reproaches he had repressed these many years over Hamilton's schemings, double-dealings and betrayals. He cried:

"He is an intriguant, the greatest intriguant in the world. A man devoid of every moral principle, a bastard and a foreigner."

McHenry resigned at once. A few days later John asked for Secretary Pickering's resignation. When Pickering refused, John dismissed him. Two days later in New York, Alexander Hamilton heard not only of the dismissals of these Secretaries whom he had been controlling, but also of the names he had been called.

It was clear that he would strike back.

On her way to New York Abigail stopped at the encampment at Scotch Plains. The Colonel was outraged at the disbanding of the army. Nab was indignant. Her husband's troops had been well trained. He had done a fine job. Now he had lost his profession. General Hamilton was also at the encampment. He and Abigail agreed to have breakfast together the next morning. She found him charming, affable, noncommittal.

She was taking Charley's oldest daughter, Susan, home to Quincy. She was also dropping Caroline at Colonel Smith's mother's. Seeing the stricken look on Nab's face now that her third child was being lodged elsewhere, herself without a home, Abigail said gently:

"Every soul knows its own bitterness."

John Adams's firing of his two Secretaries—though John Marshall had been confirmed as Secretary of State, and his presence would give John solid comfort—Nab's and the Colonel's abandonment without job or income; the tense situation in Charley's house, all made her trip home an anxious one. She could not help wonder what the future held for her children—and found herself for the moment including John Adams in that category.

She rejoiced to hear that John had pardoned John Fries and the two men of the Pennyslvania insurrection who had been condemned to hang with him. It was an act of clemency which would make up for some of the unease caused by the Sedition Act trials. In May and June of 1800 the Sedition Act had been put to the test. First, Thomas Cooper, editor of the *Northumberland Gazette,* was prosecuted for publishing material which charged that President John Adams was a power-mad despot, a destroyer of the rights of man and an increasingly dangerous enemy to the Republic. Shortly after, James Callender, a Scotsman expelled from Great Britain, wrote in a pamphlet called *The Prospect Before Us* that the Adams administration was "one continual tempest of malignant passions. . . . The grand object of his administration has been . . . to calumniate and destroy every man who differs from his opinions." Callender called the President "a repulsive pedant, a gross hypocrite, an unprincipled oppressor . . . one of the most egregious fools upon the continent." Both men were convicted by juries of criminal libel, fined and imprisoned.

The new library-study in Quincy was completed. She covered the floor with a figured carpet, put a high-backed upholstered armchair in the corner next to the fireplace, brought up his heavy, sliding-top desk with its pigeonholes, and as a special gift bought him a handsome new writing desk and comfortable leather chair for the center of the room. When John reached home at the beginning of July, bringing Nab and Caroline, he was enchanted.

"This is a proper study for a scholar!" he exclaimed. "I could spend the rest of my life here studying and writing books on history."

"Good. You may have to."

"I know that. But the canvass is coming along quite well; our chances are looking up."

The papers were carrying a strange story indeed: President Adams had dismissed Pickering and McHenry in a bargain with Thomas Jefferson. John Adams would be re-elected for the presidency in 1800; in 1804 he would withdraw in favor of Jefferson. It all sounded highly unlikely to Abigail; but was not politics the most unlikely of all man's sciences?

She was eager to hear about Washington City. He wondered how much it would be prudent to tell her, for he had found the mansion and the city in an incredible state of unreadiness. He looked at her out of the corner of his eye.

"The President's Mansion will be . . . habitable. The Senate and House will each have a chamber in which to meet. The department files and papers are arriving; they are setting up shop in separate buildings."

"You don't sound very enthusiastic."

"The challenge will be greater than I had anticipated," he said with a crooked smile. Then quickly he told her that he had appointed Colonel Smith supervisor and inspector of the Port of New York. Colonel William was already working at his job, though he would have to be confirmed by the Senate when it met that winter.

The country was becoming thoroughly caught up in the election. Massachusetts politicians were in constant attendance. Everywhere there was campaigning, stump speaking; pamphlets were printed and distributed, passionate newspaper diatribes against either Jefferson and Burr on the one side, or Adams and Pinckney on the other. It was not possible to avoid Alexander Hamilton. He wrote John for an explanation of his charge that Hamilton was a member of a "British faction in this country." John did not see fit to answer. Their friends and advisers now found the electors throughout the sixteen states so minutely balanced that John Adams would just squeak by.

Alexander Hamilton did not mean that to happen. With his associates he combed John Adams's career from the earliest days of the Revolution, then wrote a long, devastating letter aimed at securing a solid vote for Pinckney for President, and the dropping off of Adams. The letter, which he claimed was only for the eyes of the Federalists, soon found its way into the hands of Aaron Burr, who delightedly printed excerpts in the Republican newspapers:

"Not denying to Mr. Adams patriotism and integrity, and even talents of a certain kind, I should be deficient in candor were I to conceal the conviction that he does not possess the talents adapted to the *admin-*

istration of government, and that there are great and intrinsic defects in his character which unfit him for the office of chief magistrate."

Hamilton next published his letter in book form. It would be distributed at the end of October and the beginning of November, when the majority of electors were being chosen.

John began his preparations to return to Washington City. Abigail looked forward to moving there, though she had learned by littles during the summer that she would be faced by the hardships that went with a frontier post. John decided to go ahead by the fastest route, the kind of horseback journey through dramatically changing country that had been part of his life as a circuit-riding lawyer. She would follow by coach, stopping off in New York to see Charley and picking up Tommy in Philadelphia for the hazardous five-day trip to Washington.

She found Charley in a boardinghouse on the waterfront. Nab took her to the room. Sally was living at her mother's house. Charley had been in bed a week. His skin had a soiled jaundice color; beneath the surface were masses of tiny dilated blood vessels. He was feverish, perspiring profusely, coughing blood. When they tried to clean him up he lashed out at them in temper. The doctor arrived, a short-necked man with a small face set disproportionately in a big head. He seemed disinterested; he had apparently had enough of Charles Adams. When Abigail inquired what Charley's illness was, he replied with a shrug:

"A dropsy in his chest. An infection of the liver."

"Are you certain it is not tuberculosis? We have a history of that on the Quincy side of my family."

"That too, perhaps."

"What can we do? We don't just stand by and watch young men die."

"I do, Mrs. Adams. It is my grisly profession."

He tucked his small features into their big setting, muttering that he should have become a sea captain since ships never willfully destroyed themselves; that that privilege was reserved to man.

Charley began coughing, vomiting blood onto the floor. Nab put a soiled towel over the mess. Abigail took a handkerchief from her purse, dipped it into a bowl of water and cleaned Charley's wasted face. She cried in agony:

"Nab, there must be something we can do to save him."

"I thought so too, Mother. But it's a clash of wills. Charley wants to die."

"Here's money. Take the carriage. Buy bed linens, fresh nightshirts."

"I'll bring them from my house. It's only a few minutes from here."

Abigail pulled a chair to Charley's bedside.

"Son, listen to me. I'm going to stay here with you until you're well enough to travel. Then I'm going to take you and Sally to Washington City with me. You'll live with us until you're well."

Charley's eyelids fluttered open.

"What would you do with a drunken sot in the new President's Mansion?"

"You can help your father; he needs people in whom he has confidence."

"My father has disowned me."

"He didn't mean it. He loves you."

"I'm finished, a used-up man."

"It is a sin to take one's life, Charley. God appoints that hour. You are usurping His prerogative. Aren't you afraid of the punishment?"

"I've had my hell on earth. Anything after this will be peaceful limbo. I yearn for it."

"But why, Charley?"

"I sour the lives of the people I love best, you and Sally and Nab and Johnny."

"If you love us why would you hurt us so deeply? You made life gay for us."

He put out a hand, touching hers.

"You must move on to the new Washington City. You must open the President's House, help Father receive the foreign diplomats at formal dinners. You have a job in the world."

"And you, Charley? Have you no job? To support your children, give them a father? To save us all from this senseless tragedy?"

Charley closed his eyes wearily.

"There must be a purpose in it, somewhere."

Abigail thought of her second daughter, the little child who had lived so short a time; some part of her had withered as Susanna had; then there was the infant who had had no chance to experience life at all, and another area of her being had dried up. Now the part of her life that was Charles died within her.

Nab appeared in the doorway. Behind her were Abigail's coachman and a burly laborer from the docks.

"I'm taking Charley home with me, Mother. He'll not want for care. Gentlemen, be so kind as to pick my brother up and take him down to the carriage."

10

The party, including Louisa and Susan, Charley's daughter, stayed over a day in Philadelphia to rest the horses for the hundred-and-fifty-mile ride to Washington City. Tommy had a letter for her from John. He had arrived safely, moved into the President's House and was eagerly awaiting her arrival. He wrote to her from the great depths of his feeling:

"I pray heaven to bestow the best of blessings on this house and on all that shall hereafter inhabit it. May none but honest and wise men ever rule under this roof!"

They left Philadelphia early in the morning. With the onset of winter the roads were deplorable. They could not hope to make more than twenty-five to thirty miles a day. For four days they were jounced and jostled against the sides of the carriage. Tommy arranged for the rooms, the meals, stabling of the horses. When they reached Baltimore an old friend, Justice Chase, came to the inn with a letter of invitation from Major Thomas Snowden, who owned a comfortable plantation twenty-one miles from Washington.

"Thank you, Judge Chase, but tomorrow we will push through to Washington City," said Abigail.

"Please don't try, Mrs. Adams. It's a long journey of thirty-six miles to an inn, and the roughest part of the road. You won't make it before dark. Best to rest at Major Snowden's. Their hospitality is the pride of this new country."

From Baltimore the country through which they traveled was a wilderness, the roads badly marked. There was only an occasional mud-walled hut with a group of Negro children playing before it. The roads were little more than ruts through the dark forest. Not a soul or cart appeared on the route. Tommy walked in front of the carriage, bending and breaking branches of trees overhanging the path.

"Ma, I think we must be lost."

A Negro appeared with a horse and cart. He offered to guide them to the post road. They had wasted two hours. Soon they came to an inn where they paused for a hasty midday dinner. She had sent a courier ahead to ask John if he would please come out in his chariot with a change of horses to meet her. Now they saw a chariot coming down the road with three extra horses and riders. Abigail was disappointed to find that John was not with them. There was a note telling her that he was in Cabinet meetings, but awaiting her arrival with great anticipation. Their horses were changed, they went on at the best speed the roads allowed. However they were still thirty miles from their destination.

The early dark of a November afternoon was falling by the time they came to the entrance to the Snowden plantation. Tommy ordered the carriage stopped.

"Mother, I must insist we stop the night here. I don't want us riding these rut-rimmed tracks in the dark. The carriage could be overthrown."

"Tommy, I can't impose these numbers on Major Snowden. It isn't proper. We'll just have to continue."

Major Snowden had been waiting at the front of his house, had heard the cavalcade come down the road and raced out on his horse to meet them. When Abigail protested that she could not impose nine people on him, he replied heartily:

"We can take care of double that number, Mrs. Adams. This is a privilege you would not deny Mrs. Snowden and me."

They were received by Mrs. Snowden, their two lovely daughters and a son who had dined at the Adams home in Philadelphia. The Snowdens were English, living in a handsome house, possessing the ability to give kindness without ceremony. Abigail and Tommy ate with the family before a roaring fireplace, then slept better than they had since leaving Philadelphia. Early the following morning they took to the road again.

It was one o'clock when they arrived in Washington City at the President's Mansion, a large structure of white sandstone gleaming in the pale winter sun. It stood raw against the elements, without enclosing fence, lawn, garden or walk. She could see nothing but the shacks of the workers and the pits of the now abandoned brick kilns.

A courier had brought news of their approach. As the carriage drew up, Abigail saw John standing on the wooden steps in front of the house, with her nephews Billy Cranch and Billy Shaw behind him, all grinning broadly, and behind them Briesler, Betsy Howard and Becky, two girls she had sent ahead, Shipley and Richard, two men who had been signed up in Quincy.

The old law which said that by the first Monday in December 1800 the seat of the government of the United States should be transferred to a district on the Potomac apparently had not been taken seriously. Nevertheless it was a happy reunion. John took one of Abigail's arms, Tommy the other, and they escorted her in royal fashion through the front door, the President murmuring:

"Mrs. Abigail Smith Adams, I welcome you to the new President's Mansion."

She chuckled, two notes low in her throat. Then she took a quick look around her, barely suppressing a gasp of dismay. The foyer was bare studding, the principal stairs were not built and would not be that winter. Only four rooms had been finished and made comfortable, John's temporary office, and an adjoining office for William Shaw, his secretary; a common parlor and a levee room. The rest of the first floor had not yet been plastered.

John saw her expression, said quietly:

"I don't think we'll be using this floor very much, although the builders assure me it will be plastered and finished, everything except paint, within three months, weather permitting. But you will find things more cozy upstairs. The Oval Room is finished and ready for your entertaining. We have two bedrooms, a little one for Susan, where we've even managed to get a coat of paint on the walls."

John was right, the upstairs apartments were charming. The damask chairs and settees had arrived from Philadelphia and been placed about the Oval Room. There were no curtains on the windows since they were too tall to take the old ones from Philadelphia. Some of the oldest pieces left over from the Washington administration had been crated and shipped, though Abigail had not thought them worth the cost. Now she was glad to have the extra furniture. There was carpeting, also from the Philadelphia house, on the floors. From the windows Abigail had a splendid view of the Potomac River. She could see vessels passing and repassing on their way down to Alexandria. Mrs. Johnson, Johnny's mother-in-law, was announced. She lived nearby and had come to welcome Abigail to her new home.

They were having tea in the common parlor which Briesler had dried out by burning logs in it for several days, chatting animatedly about the problems of living in a half-finished palace, when Betsy Howard appeared at the door and asked if she could speak to Mrs. Adams privately. Abigail went into the unfinished foyer with her.

"Mrs. Adams, I got a problem. We had to wash, we ran out of towels and sheets and personal things too. The wrangle you ordered hasn't come, we washed in tubs in the kitchen and now it's laying in baskets sopping wet, and no place outside to hang it. Not a pole or a line set up yet."

Abigail walked to the entrance of the East Room, turned to Betsy with an amused smile and said:

"I'm sure it wasn't designed as such, and this is going to be one of the beautiful rooms of America when it is finished, but right now, Betsy, I think it's our drying room."

"Ma'am, you mean we're going to hang a clothesline in here?"

"We certainly are. Providing we can find rope."

She walked to the extreme corner of the room, searched and found a nail jutting out from one of the studs.

"Betsy, go get young Mr. Adams, Mr. Shaw and Mr. Cranch. We need their help."

Tommy and his two cousins found a workman's kit in the cellar, brought up a hammer, nails and a tall pole with which to prop the center of the line. Billy Cranch tied one end of the rope to the nail at the east end of the room and, while Tommy guided it on top of the prop, Billy Shaw hammered a nail into the west corner, pulling the rope taut. Becky and Betsy started taking clothes out of the rattan hampers, shaking them sharply to stretch them, putting them on the rope, the sheets, pillowcases and towels at either end and the underwear, shirts and socks toward the middle where the rope dipped on either side of the pole. The room was cold and damp until Briesler came in with Shipley and Richard, carrying logs. He piled shavings on the hearth. The fire caught quickly. Everyone exclaimed with pleasure when it began to draw. Logs were put on the fire and the family stood with their backs to the flames, triumphantly looking at what was probably the longest clothesline that had ever been strung in an American home. They heard a laugh. Abigail turned to see John and Mrs. Johnson standing in the entranceway. He was shaking his head in incredulity.

"The first in Rome hanging out the family wash on her first day in the President's Mansion, in the great East Room where foreign ambassadors are to be received."

Mrs. Johnson offered to come the next day and help them locate the best place for the clothesline out of doors.

They slept warm in their big bed from Philadelphia. It was exciting and gratifying to be in the new house. They talked about it for a considerable time. William Shaw had managed to rustle up a supply of logs from which John kept replenishing the fire. He told her:

"You must not think that any of the unfinished work here or any of the faults are those of the builders. The problem has been that Congress refused to appropriate the money to pay the bills. However they are supposed to meet tomorrow in regular session. They have seen the condition of their own half-finished Capitol. Those who have arrived have assured me that ample funds will be made available."

The next morning she was taken on a tour of the city. It had been built in the marshes contained in a crotch of the Potomac River, an attractive spot but ridden by ague and fever. The early plans of L'Enfant and the commissioners for the city had envisaged a broad tree-lined avenue connecting the President's House with the Capitol, where both Houses of Congress were to meet, something over a mile away. However Pennsylvania Avenue, as it was called on paper, was a deep morass covered with alder bushes. Roads radiating in every direction were muddy and unimproved. A sidewalk had been attempted by using the stone chips from the Capitol but in dry weather the sharp fragments cut people's shoes and in wet weather covered them with white mortar.

Abigail saw half a dozen houses, taverns and office structures. The Post Office building was a three-story house leased from Dr. John Crocker, on the northeast corner of Ninth and E streets. The largest building, John explained, was occupied by the Treasury Department, some sixty-nine persons working there amidst the furniture and records which had come up the Potomac River on sailing vessels from Philadelphia. The State Department was located in one of the six buildings on Pennsylvania Avenue. Opposite was a three-story house leased from Joseph Hodgson in which the War Department had established itself with eighteen employees. Only one road had been built, New Jersey Avenue, which had two houses on either side of it. There were but two comfortable homes within the city, one of which belonged to Daniel Carroll and the other to Notley Young.

Many businessmen had been attracted by land speculation. Tobias Lear, President Washington's private secretary, was a leading merchant, Robert Brent had opened a quarry at Acquia, Virginia, which furnished some of the stone for the Capitol. A newspaper had been established called the *National Intelligencer*, edited by Samuel Harrison Smith, who had settled in the city. There were three architects: Dr. William Thornton, who had designed the Capitol and the Octagon House at New York Avenue and Eighteenth Street, George Hatfield, and James Hoban, who had designed the Executive Mansion. There were also several lawyers, physicians and pastors, a small church which the Episcopalians had bought for a trifle because the small frame building at the bottom of Capitol Hill had formerly been a tobacco house.

The north wing was the only portion of the Capitol that had been constructed, though the foundations had been laid for the central dome section. The Capitol, Abigail now learned, had been planned to resemble a palace of the Italian Renaissance, and the President's Mansion had been largely copied from an Irish palace.

"Does anyone know why Italian and Irish?" she asked her menfolk.

"No. All our plans evaporated when L'Enfant quarreled with the government commissioners, and they all had themselves fired. What we have now is two stone buildings in a rude frontier town in the midst of a wilderness." He added wistfully, "Given another four years, I should like to make something of it. Not a Versailles or Paris, as we were promised, but perhaps the most beautiful city in all America."

"Given four years, I could turn the unfinished President's House into one of the finest mansions in the country. The Chief Executive, whoever he may be, deserves to have it. The country needs it. A national home to look up to with pride, to stand as a symbol of the country's greatness. And, John," she added quietly, "it seems only right and proper. We helped create a permanent nation. Why should we not have the opportunity to help create a permanent capital?"

She took the glove off her left hand, slipped the hand into his. He was cold; she warmed him.

11

She drove the mile into Georgetown. It was a good settlement, but the road was a pothole. There were vegetables to be had and some eggs and milk but no fruit of any kind closer than Baltimore or Norfolk. For everything beyond the bare necessities she had to wait until the arrival of the vessel which Cotton Tufts had loaded for her, their clothing, boxes of fruit, a modest supply of wines and cider, extra blankets. She found a man with a coal and feed store in Germantown, and tried to arrange for a permanent supply of wood. He offered her a limited amount at nine dollars a cord, which was catastrophic, considering the number of firerooms there were in the mansion. Even at that price he despaired of finding workmen to go into the forest to fell the trees.

When she arrived home Mrs. Johnson was waiting in the outer room of John's office.

"Mrs. Adams, I know the difficulties involved, but I must tell you that the ladies of this neighborhood have been waiting on tenterhooks for your arrival. They need a society desperately here. As you can see, there is nothing this side of Baltimore. I have been pressed into service to ask if you would commence a round of entertainments. I shall give a dinner and ball in your honor at our home, if you will permit me, and there are a half a dozen other ladies who wish to receive you and the President. However, I must tell you that they cannot do so, according to protocol, until you open this Mansion to them and receive them as guests."

Abigail was amused.

"Wherever shall I put them? After all, I cannot hang them on the line the way I did the wet wash in the East Room. But you are right. I shall send out cards."

Though the ladies from Georgetown called upon her, and she returned fifteen visits, sometimes leaving cards, the President's Mansion was so unfurnished and filled with workmen throughout the week that she could do little more than bring back a couple or two for Sunday dinner after preaching in the Representatives' chamber of the Capitol. She had received an invitation to visit Martha Washington at Mount Vernon. Mrs. Washington's granddaughter dropped in for tea, as did Mrs. Benjamin Stoddert, Mrs. Harrison Smith, Mrs. William Thornton. It was a time for waiting, a penultimate time.

Politics were a "turn penny." The presidential election could go either way. Everyone in the country was speculating widely. Alexander Hamilton had destroyed himself by his polemics, and very possibly had destroyed the Federalist Party in the process. Would John Adams be re-elected President, or would the "Antis," as Abigail still called them, elect Thomas Jefferson? John Adams had his solid New England, Jefferson his solid South, except for Pinckney's South Carolina. John had lost New York, but he had taken New Jersey and Delaware. From all accounts, Pennsylvania and Maryland would be evenly divided. If the eight South Carolina electoral votes went to Pinckney and Adams, John Adams would be President by an electoral vote or two.

At the beginning of December, after Federalist senators from Pennsylvania achieved a compromise which earned John Adams seven of the state's electoral votes, the editor of the *United States Gazette* wrote, "They have saved a falling world." Word reached them from Boston that the *Columbian Centinel* would report: "There cannot be a doubt" of the election of Adams and Pinckney.

"We will not talk of it yet," said John. "The votes will all be in soon. We cannot alter them or add to them. I have enough to do making certain the Departments have made a good transfer to Washington."

Abigail uttered a silent prayer.

"If we win we will have four more years to complete our work. I will furnish this house, plant rosebushes, put up a fence. If we lose, we shall participate in the orderly transfer of power and retire to Peacefield. God grant a good deliverance."

Tommy had gone back to Philadelphia to continue his practice. He returned unexpectedly, his eyes heavy-lidded from lack of sleep. They summoned John and the three Adamses sat alone behind the closed door of their bedroom.

"Mother, Father, it's Charley. I could not let you hear the news from anyone else. He's dead. I reached New York only in time to say good-by. He sent you his dying words."

". . . yes, son." It was John, visibly shaken.

"He begged forgiveness. Asked you to pray for his immortal soul. Said that he never meant to hurt you . . ."

Abigail was grief-stricken. John went to the window, gazed like a blind man at the bare grounds and river below. He spoke without turning.

"You gave him a proper funeral?"

"I came on at once. He will have been buried by now."

John said from the window, hoarsely:

"A son who was once the delight of my eyes and a darling of my heart, cut off in the flower of his days . . . by causes which have been the greatest grief of my heart and the deepest affliction of my life . . ."

He was able to express his grief in words. Not so Abigail. The death of her son left her mind a hollow echoing chamber. Later that night, when Tommy came to say good night, she asked:

"Will he have a good grave, Tommy?"

"Yes, Mother. I'll take you there when you're on your way home."

"Perhaps we could take Charley home too. He should not lie among strangers, in alien ground. He should be buried in Quincy, surrounded by his kin."

On December 12, 1800, the *National Intelligencer* announced that South Carolina had rejected its native son, Charles Cotesworth Pinckney, giving its eight electoral votes to Jefferson and Burr. They would make the difference. John Adams was running considerably ahead of his party, which had managed to elect only forty-one representatives against sixty-five for the Republicans; but their hour of defeat was at hand.

The people had rejected John Adams for a second term.

Within an hour of their reading of the political death knell, Governor Davie of North Carolina, one of the commissioners to France, arrived with a treaty of peace and friendship with France. It was too late.

They went into the Oval Room, where Abigail had introduced the first society of Washington City. Facing the southeast window were one of the red damask settees and two of the matching chairs from Philadelphia. From here they overlooked the Capitol and Tiber Creek which flowed into the Potomac. It was the most private place in the house. No one except Briesler, who had lighted a fire for them, entered without invitation. They sat close together on the red settee, crushed, but determined that once they had spoken their minds to each other the outside world would see nothing of their disappointment. Abigail turned full face to her husband, noting how pale he was, the fatigue in his eyes.

"How did this happen to us, John?"

John Adams made no attempt to conceal his bitter chagrin.

"How many components are there to our defeat? Probably hundreds. Hamilton is one key; he split our party. The country has become tired of the war talk, of the taxes, of the growing strength of the central government. I have been victimized by a foul campaign and irresponsible personal charges. The Republicans have built a brilliant political organization, the first this country has known. They tarred us as being the party of business, banking, wealth, whilst parading themselves as the party of the people. They convinced sectors of our voters that the Federalists distrust the people, that we think government should be carried on only by the wealthy and the wise."

He smiled wryly.

"Since the majority of the people in America are neither wealthy nor wise, they have moved over to the new camp. We could promise only a continuation of government as we have known it for twelve years. The Republicans have promised that the federal government would fade into the shadows."

He raised his left shoulder in a gesture of futility, rose and began to pace the floor.

"The country has been told that the Republican way is the way to the future, a second American Revolution to rid them of the Federalist counterrevolution; that the Federalists represent a dying past. The North has given way to New York and the South. Part of it has been our fault. I made no secret of the fact that I believed the High Federalists dangerous. Hamilton made no secret that 'Jefferson should be preferred to Adams.' John Marshall was right. The Alien and Sedition Acts, even though they have already expired, did not go down with the people."

He returned to the sofa.

"We have been part of an old movement and we are being retired to pasture. Even as it came to Cousin Sam'l. Our four years in the presidency have been rejected."

She had listened to him exorcise his almost unbearable hurt. But this last turn of the screw she would not permit him.

"Without your strength in the presidency, John, there might not have been an independent United States to turn over to Jefferson and the Republicans."

The empty room echoed her cry of protest. He flashed her a look of endearment, rose again and walked the length of the Oval Room, stopping at the fireplace, his hands locked behind his back. Now his face flamed with indignation.

"What folly! I am being condemned for being the most possible President, in favor of a man who has assured the people he will be the least possible President."

"Mr. Jefferson has always favored a weak Chief Executive. When you sent him his copy of the Constitution from London, he replied that he was frightened by the implied powers of the President."

"He will soon learn differently."

He buried his face in his hands.

"The ingratitude kills my soul. All I wanted was one more term. A peaceful four years to prove our country can expand, grow prosperous. To be part of this new capital city. Then I could have retired to Quincy in honor. I feel humiliated, dismissed."

"We have wanted to serve, John. And we have served. There is now a capital called Washington City, of a nation called the United States; it is a long way from the injustices of the Stamp Act. Your courage, your vision, your dedication have brought us far from the Massachusetts Bay Colony. With His help you have been part of building the freest civilization the world has ever known. It's all there for the world to read: the documents, the reports, the constitutions, the treaties, the laws. All that King George's 'brace of Adamses' fought for and won. You are a historian, John. You know history will say that."

"I will say that!" A sparkle came to his eyes, the corner of his lips twitched in a reluctant smile. "In that beautiful library you built for me. The Republicans are not the only ones who have ink. It will take several volumes . . ."

"Would you like me to leave a little early, to prepare the house and your study against your arrival? I could have the ink in the inkpot, pens and writing paper on your desk . . ."

"Thank you, Miss Abigail, for the wonderful gifts of life you have brought me over the years."

She replied softly, "Life is for those who love."

There was a knock on the door. William Shaw was summoning him. When John had closed the door behind him, she wept.

12

This new Washington City had been built in the South. The Age of New England was over, the control of the federal government by the South would begin.

The age of John and Abigail Adams was over. They knew it. It was thirty years since he had defended the soldiers in the Boston Massacre, twenty-six since he had departed for his first service in the Continental Congress, drafted his first constitutions. Now it was time to go home to write the story of all he had been and all he had done. Abigail did not imagine that they would be easy years. John Adams had his detractors and his foes. But they had lived most of their married lives under attack. They knew how to survive; it was a Puritan trait.

Meanwhile their jobs were by no means finished.

She visited Martha Washington in Mount Vernon, both women sensing that this would be the last time they would meet. On New Year's Day she gave a formal reception. Beautifully gowned women came from miles around, their escorts in newly cut black suits. She gave dinner parties for the ladies, for the Supreme Court judges and John's new heads of the Executive Departments. The family went to hear preaching on Sundays at the Capitol.

When Secretary Oliver Wolcott resigned, President Adams moved Samuel Dexter over from the War Department to the Treasury Department. He appointed their nephew William Cranch to be a commissioner of the city of Washington; signed a congressional bill for a better organization of the courts and sent numerous names to the Senate for confirmation. He persuaded John Marshall to become Chief Justice of the Supreme Court. He shepherded the Paris treaty through the Senate. And, finally, had Secretary of State Marshall prepare recall papers for John Quincy.

She decided to return to Quincy at the beginning of February, as soon as the roads were passable: to her dairy, her pear and apple orchards, her children and her innumerable grandchildren, to John's voluminous books and the eternal spring planting. John would remain until the morning of March fourth, when Jefferson assumed power.

"Not one hour longer than the Constitution calls for!" he exclaimed.

When word got out that she was about to depart, Thomas Jefferson came to call. She received him in the Oval Room. He was staying at Conrad and McMunn's, a boardinghouse frequented by congressmen. His hair was now a long, snowy white cap on the well-sculptured head, his lips closed a little tighter against the intransigencies of the world, his all-encompassing eyes still beautiful.

"Mrs. Adams, I came to take leave and wish you a good journey."

"It is more than I expected, Mr. Jefferson. May I explain some things about the running of this house?"

"I should be very happy to retain all the domestics you can recommend. Mrs. Adams, I beg to assure you that nothing can so much contribute to my happiness as to be able in any way to be of service to Mr. Adams, to you or to any member of your family."

"Thank you, Mr. Jefferson."

Jefferson leaned forward.

"I want to inquire particularly about Mr. John Quincy Adams. Does he like his residence in Berlin? Would he care to stay?"

"I expect that John Quincy will return to America."

"Then you must give him my warmest regards." He rose, held out his hand. "The Jefferson family will always think of you with affection."

When she reported the meeting to John, she added, "The King is dead, long live the King. Do you think the day will come when we can return his affection?"

"If he does not ruin the country during his administration," said John grimly. "Or, for that matter, if he becomes President."

Nobody had "dropped off" a vote for Aaron Burr; he and Jefferson were tied with the identical seventy-three electoral votes. The election was now up to the House, which would have to select one of the men as President. Though everyone knew that Burr had run for the vice presidency, he refused to withdraw his name. Many die-hard Federalists in the Congress were helping to create mischief by voting for Burr for President. John feared Burr as an opportunist, far more dangerous than Jefferson.

The day finally arrived for Abigail to leave, February 13, 1801. She rose at dawn, was dressed and ready at an early hour. She opened the front door of the house, walked down the steps, stood looking at the unfinished President's Mansion. She was reminded of a time when she and John were traveling in Maryland, and a venerable white-haired man had asked to be admitted to the President. He entered the room, bowed respectfully, said: "Sir, I came many miles on purpose. Be this your lady?" John replied: "Yes, this is Mrs. Adams." The man was triumphant. "I told my wife this morning that I would come and she said, 'Why ain't you afraid?' No," said I, "why do you think I should be afraid to go and see my father?"

The face of the father would change. The face of the ideal, never. They had contributed to that. It was a gratifying thought.

She and John said their quiet farewells in the privacy of the bedroom. He held her close, stroked her hair, kissed her on both cheeks.

"Good-by, dear soul. In a few weeks we shall be together, never again to be parted."

"That is an end devoutly to be wished."

Everyone had gathered on the front steps to see her off: her nephews, a number of her friends and servants. John handed her into the carriage. Susan and Louisa sat backwards. The coachman cracked his whip. The horses started with a lurch. There were cries of farewell. She leaned out the window to wave, saw John Adams standing there, waving to her, his eyes sad but his shoulders resolute.

As the carriage carried her down the road toward Baltimore, and John Adams's figure receded in the distance, grew dimmer and dimmer, another image of him arose, as vivid and lifelike as though she had seen it that very morning. She was sitting in the middle of her bed in the parsonage in Weymouth, writing a letter to her cousin Hannah Quincy telling her how difficult friends were to find, when her sister Mary had called from downstairs, "Nabby, Richard is here. Brought company. That lawyer from Braintree." She had gone dancing down the stairs, seen John Adams standing in her father's library holding two volumes spread wide, sniffing from one and then the other. Startled, John Adams had turned, the color mounting in his cheeks. He had held out both arms to her, an open book in each hand.

And her life had begun.

NOTE

This biographical novel of Abigail and John Adams took four and a half years of concentrated research and writing. The only time taken out was for a four-month trip through Europe, Yugoslavia, Poland and the U.S.S.R. for the United States State Department under the Cultural Exchange Program. The material is as historically accurate and solidly based on the documents of the period as my enthusiasm and training made possible.

It must be acknowledged at the outset that a book of this kind would be impossible to write were it not for the scholarly research and writing by the men and women who have so brilliantly illuminated the period: Perry Miller, Samuel Eliot Morison, Arthur M. Schlesinger, Samuel Flagg Bemis, John C. Miller, Carl Bridenbaugh, Clinton Rossiter, Adrienne Koch and many others. The biographers too have given us marvelous volumes: Douglas Southall Freeman, Dumas Malone, Irving Brant, Claude G. Bowers, Esther Forbes, Catherine Drinker Bowen, Page Smith, to name but a few.

Quotations from the Adams Papers are from the microfilm edition, by permission of the Massachusetts Historical Society. Grateful acknowledgment is made to the Belknap Press of Harvard University Press, for permission to quote from the first four volumes of *The Adams Papers, Diary and Autobiography of John Adams* (copyright 1961 by the Massachusetts Historical Society), and the first two volumes of *Adams Family Correspondence* (copyright 1963 by the Massachusetts Historical Society). Special attention is called to the indispensable work done by Lyman H. Butterfield, editor of the Adams Papers, and Wendell D. Garrett, assistant editor, for their detailed, lucid footnotes, which do so much to illuminate the people and events of the times.

Grateful acknowledgment is further made to the American Antiquarian Society for permission to quote from *New Letters of Abigail Adams, 1788–1801*, Stewart Mitchell, editor; to the Library of Congress and the Massachusetts Historical Society for the use of material from the Library of Congress Collection of Letters from Abigail Adams to Elizabeth Smith Shaw Peabody; to the Massachusetts Historical Society for use of material from *The Warren-Adams Letters*, Vol. I; and to the University of North Carolina Press for the use of material from *The Adams-Jefferson Letters,* Vol. I, Lester J. Cappon, editor.

I also wish to express gratitude to the editors who are publishing the collected papers of the great figures of the time: Julian P. Boyd of the Jefferson Papers, Harold C. Syrett of the Hamilton Papers, Leonard W. Labaree of the Franklin Papers, Lyman H. Butterfield of the Adams Papers.

Franklin, Hamilton, Jefferson and the other characters are portrayed as they were seen and felt by Abigail and John Adams. The Adamses' views do not always, or necessarily, represent the opinions of the author.

The language of the day was flowery. The letters are filled with capitals and sprinkled with an abundant pepper of punctuation. Dictionaries were rare in New England. None of the three private libraries in Abigail Smith Adams's family appeared to have one. Her spelling was experimental.

In the Foreword of *The American Puritans: Their Prose and Poetry,* edited by Perry Miller, Mr. Miller says:

"Following the lead of Samuel Eliot Morison in his edition of William Bradford, I assumed as regards [Roger] Williams the privileges of an editor and prepared a modern—*not* 'modernized'—text. Here I have again exercised that prerogative. I have regularized the spelling and capitalization, omitted italics, broken up long paragraphs, and endeavored to refashion the punctuation so as at once to remain faithful to the spirit of the text and yet to assist the modern reader."

I have followed Perry Miller's example. However, aside from punctuation, spelling and capitals, all quotations from published letters and from the Adams Papers microfilm are faithfully reproduced.

In Boston I am indebted to Zoltán Haraszti, Lyman H. Butterfield and Wendell Garrett of the Adams Trust, Thomas Boylston Adams, Walter Muir Whitehill, Dana Cotton, the Reverend Francis Sweeney, S.J., and the highly co-operative staff of the Massachusetts Historical Society.

In Weymouth I am indebted to the Reverend David Haskell Eaton, Mr. Carroll M. Bill and the members of the Abigail Adams Society: Mr. and Mrs. E. Biden Whitney, Homer A. Clouter, Mrs. Wade Shorter, Theron I. Cain, Mrs. Alice Wallace, Mrs. James E. Giles, Jr., Mrs. Leo McCarthy, Mrs. Charles Flynn, Mrs. Ruth Connors and Mrs. Bell. In Quincy I am indebted to William C. Edwards, the city historian, and Wilhelmina S. Harris, superintendent of the Adams National Historical

Site. In Hingham I am indebted to Mason A. Foley. In Lincoln I am indebted to Mrs. Margaret Flint and to Robert D. Ronsheim of the National Park Service; in Concord, to Mrs. Caleb Wheeler; in Haverhill to Mrs. Vera Lindsley; in Atkinson to Mrs. Beatrice Reynolds. In New York I am indebted to Agatha Walsh of the British Information Services. At home I am indebted to Dr. Emil Krahulik for advice on the practice of medicine in our early years, to Mrs. Virginia Drasnin for architectural studies of the period, to Mrs. Esther Euler of the U.C.L.A. Interlibrary Loan; and to Mrs. Jean Stone, who was the editor on the entire project.

IRVING STONE

June 6, 1965

BIBLIOGRAPHY

BOOKS CONTAINING LETTERS BY ABIGAIL ADAMS

Letters of Mrs. Adams, the Wife of John Adams, ed. Charles Francis Adams, 2 vols., 1841; *Familiar Letters of John Adams and His Wife Abigail Adams, During the Revolution,* ed. Charles Francis Adams, 1875; *Warren-Adams Letters,* 2 vols., 1917; "Abigail Adams, Commentator," ed. Allyn B. Forbes, *Proceedings* of the Massachusetts Historical Society, LXVI, 1942; *New Letters of Abigail Adams, 1788–1801,* ed. Stewart Mitchell, 1947; *The Adams Family in Auteuil, 1784–1785,* ed. Howard C. Rice, Jr., 1956; *The Adams-Jefferson Letters,* ed. Lester J. Cappon, 2 vols., 1959; *Adams Family Correspondence,* ed. L. H. Butterfield, 2 vols., 1963; *The Adams Manuscript Trust,* Microfilm; *Turner Collection* of Letters from Abigail Adams; *Library of Congress Collection* of Letters of Abigail Adams to Mrs. Elizabeth (Smith) [Shaw] Peabody.

BOOKS ABOUT ABIGAIL ADAMS

Lydia L. Gordon, *From Lady Washington to Mrs. Cleveland,* 1889; Laura Richards, *Abigail Adams and Her Times,* 1917; Gamaliel Bradford, *Portraits of American Women,* 1919; Meade Minnigerode, "Abigail Adams," *Some American Ladies: Seven Informal Biographies,* 1926; Dorothie Bobbé, *Abigail Adams: The Second First Lady,* 1929; Janet Whitney, *Abigail Adams,* 1947.

BOOKS BY JOHN ADAMS

Novanglus and Massachusettensis, 1819; *Wemms–The Trial of the British Soldiers,* 1824; *Letters of John Adams, Addressed to His Wife,* ed. Charles Francis Adams, 2 vols., 1841; *The Works of John Adams,* ed. and with A *Life of the Author* by Charles Francis Adams, 10 vols., 1850–1856; *Familiar Letters of John Adams and His Wife Abigail Adams, During the Revolution,* ed. Charles Francis Adams, 1875; "Correspondence Between John Adams and Mercy Warren," *Collections* of the Massachusetts Historical Society, IV, Series 5, pt. 3, 1878; A *Compilation of the Messages and Papers of the Presidents, 1789–1902,* I, ed. James D. Richardson, 1903; *Warren-Adams Letters,* 2 vols., 1917; *Statesman and Friend, Correspondence of John Adams with Benjamin Waterhouse, 1784–1822,* ed. Worthington Chauncey Ford, 1927; *The Adams-Jefferson Letters,* ed. Lester J. Cappon, 2 vols., 1959; *Diary and Autobiography of John Adams,* ed. L. H. Butterfield, 4 vols., 1961; *Adams Family Correspondence,* ed. L. H. Butterfield, 2 vols., 1963; *The Adams Manuscript Trust,* Microfilm.

BOOKS ABOUT JOHN ADAMS

John Wood, *The History of the Administration of John Adams,* 1802; John T. Morse, Jr., *John Adams,* 1886; Correa M. Walsh, *The Political Science of John Adams,* 1915; James Truslow Adams, *The Adams Family,* 1930; Gilbert Chinard, *Honest John Adams,* 1933; Catherine Drinker Bowen, *John Adams and the American Revolution,* 1950; Zoltán Haraszti, *John Adams and the Prophets of Progress,* 1952; Manning J. Dauer, *The Adams Federalists,* 1953; Stephen G. Kurtz, *The Presidency of John Adams: The Collapse of Federalism, 1795–1800,* 1957; Page Smith, *John Adams,* 2 vols., 1962.

DOCUMENTS AND GOVERNMENT PUBLICATIONS

The Diplomatic Correspondence of the American Revolution, ed. Jared Sparks, 12 vols., 1829; *The Diplomatic Correspondence of the United States . . . 1783–1789,* 3 vols., 1837; *Journals of the Continental Congress, 1774–1789,* ed. Gaillard Hunt, 34 vols., 1904–1936; *Annals of the Congress of the United States,* compiled by Joseph Gales, Sr., 1834–1851.

HISTORY: GENERAL: UNITED STATES

John Bach McMaster, *A History of the People of the United States,* 8 vols., 1883–1913; George Bancroft, *History of the United States of America,* 10 vols., 1834–1874; Woodrow Wilson, *A History of the American People,* 5 vols., 1901; Charles A. and Mary R. Beard, *The Rise of American Civilization,* 1927; J. H. Denison, *Emotional Currents in American History,* 1932; Dixon Wecter, *The Saga of American Society,* 1937; W. E. Woodward, *A New American History,* 1938; Homer Carey Hockett, *Political and Social Growth of the American People, 1492–1865,* 3rd ed., 1940; Homer Carey Hockett and Arthur Meier Schlesinger, *Land of the Free,* 1944; John H. Ferguson and Dean E. McHenry, *The American Federal Government,* 1947; Henry Steele Commager and Allan Nevins, ed., *The Heritage of America,* rev. ed., 1949.

HISTORY: GENERAL: ENGLAND

Henry Thomas Buckle, *History of Civilization in England,* 2 vols., 1863; Thomas Erskine May, *The Constitutional History of England . . . 1760–1860,* 2 vols., 1863; William Edward Hartpole Lecky, *A History of England in the Eighteenth Century,* 8 vols., 1878–1890.

HISTORY: 1761–1776

George Richards Minot, *Continuation of the History of the Province of Massachusetts Bay,* 2 vols., 1798, 1803; Alden Bradford, *History of Mas-*

sachusetts, 1822; Caleb H. Snow, *A History of Boston*, 1825; *A Short Narrative of the Horrid Massacre in Boston*, 1849; W. H. Carpenter, *The History of Massachusetts*, 1853; Frederic Kidder, *History of the Boston Massacre, March 5, 1770*, 1870; Richard Frothingham, *The Rise of the Republic of the United States*, 1873; William Edward Hartpole Lecky, *A History of England in the Eighteenth Century*, 8 vols., 1878–1890; Justin Winsor, ed., *The Memorial History of Boston*, III, 1882; George Bancroft, *History of the United States of America*, II–IV, 1890; James Truslow Adams, *Revolutionary New England*, 1927; Albert Bushnell Hart, ed., *Commonwealth History of Massachusetts*, II, III, 1928, 1929; S. E. Morison, ed., *Sources and Documents Illustrating the American Revolution*, 1929; Thomas Hutchinson, *The History of the Colony and Province of Massachusetts Bay*, III, ed. Lawrence Shaw Mayo, 1936; Edmund Cody Burnett, *The Continental Congress*, 1941; John C. Miller, *Origins of the American Revolution*, 1943; John C. Wahlke, ed., *The Causes of the American Revolution*, 1950; Edmund S. and Helen M. Morgan, *The Stamp Act Crisis*, 1953; Lawrence Henry Gipson, *The Coming of the Revolution, 1763–1775*, 1954; Merrill Jensen, ed., *American Colonial Documents to 1776 (English Historical Documents*, IX), 1955; Edmund S. Morgan, *The Birth of the Republic*, 1956; Randolph G. Adams, *Political Ideas of the American Revolution*, 3rd ed., 1958; Oscar Theodore Barck, Jr., and Hugh Talmage Lefler, *Colonial America*, 1958; Henry Steele Commager, ed., *Documents of American History*, 1958; Benjamin Woods Labaree, *The Boston Tea Party*, 1964.

HISTORY: 1776–1789

George Richards Minot, *The History of the Insurrections, In Massachusetts, In the Year 1786*, 1788; Alden Bradford, *History of Massachusetts*, 1825; Alexander Hamilton, James Madison and John Jay, *The Federalist*; George Bancroft, *History of the United States of America*, V, VI, 1890; John H. Hazelton, *The Declaration of Independence*, 1906; *National Documents*, 1908; Edward Elliot, *Biographical Story of the Constitution*, 1910; Carl Becker, *The Declaration of Independence*, 1922; Albert Bushnell Hart, ed., *Commonwealth History of Massachusetts*, III, 1929; Samuel Flagg Bemis, *The Diplomacy of the American Revolution*, 1935; Burton J. Hendrick, *Bulwark of the Republic: A Biography of the Constitution*, 1937; Edmund Cody Burnett, *The Continental Congress*, 1941; John H. Latané and David W. Wainhouse, *A History of American Foreign Policy, 1776–1940*, 1941; Carl Van Doren, *The Great Rehearsal*, 1948; Merrill Jensen, *The New Nation . . . 1781–1789*, 1950; William Evan Davies, *Patriotism on Parade . . . 1783–1900*, 1955; Elisha P. Douglas, *Rebels and Democrats*, 1955; Edmund S. Morgan, *The Birth of the Republic*, 1956; Oscar Theodore Barck, Jr., and Hugh Talmage Lefler, *Colonial America*, 1958; Henry Steele Commager, ed., *Documents of American History*, 1958; Forrest McDonald, *We the People*, 1958; Jackson Turner Main, *The Antifederalists . . . 1781–1788*, 1961.

HISTORY: 1789–1801

George Gibbs, *Memoirs of the Administrations of Washington and John Adams, Edited from the Papers of Oliver Wolcott*, 2 vols., 1846; Samuel Flagg Bemis, *Jay's Treaty*, 1923; Samuel Flagg Bemis, *Pinckney's Treaty*, 1926; Edward Stanwood, *A History of the Presidency*, 1926; John H. Latané and David W. Wainhouse, *A History of American Foreign Policy, 1776–1940*, 1941; John C. Miller, *Crisis in Freedom: The Alien and Sedition Acts*, 1951; Robert Allen Rutland, *The Birth of the Bill of Rights, 1776–1791*, 1955; Joseph Charles, *The Origins of the American Party System*, 1956; James Morton Smith, *Freedom's Fetters: The Alien and Sedition Laws*, 1956; Noble E. Cunningham, Jr., *The Jeffersonian Republicans . . . 1789–1801*, 1957; Henry Steele Commager, ed., *Documents of American History*, 1958; Alexander DeConde, *Entangling Alliance*, 1958; Ray Allen Billington, *Westward Expansion*, 1960; John C. Miller, *The Federalist Era, 1789–1801*, 1960.

TORIES

George Atkinson Ward, *Journal and Letters of the Late Samuel Curwen . . .* , 1842; Lorenzo Sabine, *The American Loyalists*, 1847; James H. Stark, *Loyalists of Massachusetts*, 1910; Lawrence Shaw Mayo, "The Massachusetts Loyalists," *Commonwealth History of Massachusetts*, III, ed. Albert Bushnell Hart, 1929; North Callahan, *Royal Raiders*, 1963.

REVOLUTIONARY WAR, GENERAL

Henry Cabot Lodge, *The Story of the Revolution*, 2 vols., 1898; George Otto Trevelyan, *The American Revolution*, 3 vols., 1898; James Truslow Adams, ed., *Atlas of American History*, 1943; John C. Miller, *Triumph of Freedom, 1775–1783*, 1948; Lynn Montross, *Rag, Tag and Bobtail*, 1952; Christopher Ward, *The War of the Revolution*, ed. John Richard Alden, 2 vols., 1952; John Richard Alden, *The American Revolution, 1775–1783*, 1954; Bruce Lancaster, *From Lexington to Liberty*, 1955; Richard M. Ketchum, ed., *The American Heritage Book of the Revolution*, 1958; R. Ernest and Trevor N. Dupuy, *The Compact History of the Revolutionary War*, 1963; Piers Mackesy, *The War for America, 1775–1783*, 1964; Hugh F. Rankin, *The American Revolution*, 1964.

REVOLUTIONARY WAR, SPECIALIZED STUDIES

Mrs. Ellet, *Domestic History of the American Revolution*, 1850; Elizabeth F. Ellet, *The Eminent and Heroic Women of America*, 1873; Richard Frothingham, *History of the Siege of Boston*, 1873; Allen French, *The Day of Concord and Lexington*, 1925; Frank Wilson Hersey, *Heroes of the Battle Road*, 1930; Allen French, *The First Year of the American Revolution*, 1934; Carl Van Doren, *Secret History of the American Revolution*, 1941;

Carl Van Doren, *Mutiny in January*, 1943; Fred J. Cook, *What Manner of Men*, 1959; *Interim Report of the Boston National Historic Sites Commission Pertaining to the Lexington–Concord Battle Road*, 86th Congress, 1st Session, House Document No. 57, 1959; Arthur Bernon Tourtellot, *William Diamond's Drum*, 1959; Richard M. Ketchum, *The Battle for Bunker Hill*, 1962; Thomas J. Fleming, *Beat the Last Drum*, 1963; George Athan Billias, ed., *George Washington's Generals*, 1964; Harold A. Larrabee, *Decision at the Chesapeake*, 1964.

THE FRENCH REVOLUTION

Thomas Carlyle, "The French Revolution," 3 vols., *Thomas Carlyle's Collected Works*; Albert Mathiez, *The French Revolution*, trans. Catherine Alison Phillips, 1928; Georges Lefebvre, *The French Revolution, From Its Origins to 1793*, trans. Elizabeth Moss Evanson, 1962; Georges Lefebvre, *The French Revolution, From 1793 to 1799*, trans. John Hall Stewart and James Friguglietti, 1965.

CITIES

Massachusetts:

BOSTON: Caleb H. Snow, *A History of Boston*, 1825; Josiah Quincy, *A Municipal History of the Town and City of Boston*, 1852; Justin Winsor, ed., *The Memorial History of Boston . . . 1630–1880*, 4 vols., 1882; *King's Hand Book of Boston*, 1889; James H. Stark, *Antique Views of Ye Towne of Boston*, 1907; M. A. DeWolfe Howe, *Boston: The Place and the People*, 1912; Carl Bridenbaugh, *Cities in the Wilderness*, 1938; Carl Bridenbaugh, *Cities in Revolt*, 1955; Walter Muir Whitehill, *Boston: A Topographical History*; Harold and James Kirker, *Bulfinch's Boston*, 1964.

BRAINTREE: Samuel A. Bates, ed., *Records of the Town of Braintree, 1640–1793*, 1886; Charles Francis Adams, *Three Episodes of Massachusetts History*, 2 vols., 1892; Daniel Munro Wilson, *Three Hundred Years of Quincy, 1625–1925*, 1926; Henry Adams 2d, *The Adams Mansion: The Home of John Adams and John Quincy Adams*, 1929; Henry Adams, *The Birthplaces of Presidents John and John Quincy Adams in Quincy, Massachusetts*, 1936; William Churchill Edwards, *Historic Quincy, Massachusetts*, 1957; Waldo Chamberlain Sprague, *The President John Adams and President John Quincy Adams Birthplaces, Quincy, Massachusetts*, 1959.

HAVERHILL: George Wingate Chase, *The History of Haverhill, Massachusetts*, 1861; Albert LeRoy Bartlett, *Some Memories of Old Haverhill*, 1915; James Duncan Phillips, "Folks in Haverhill in 1783," *Haverhill Sunday Record*, September 1, 1946.

HINGHAM: Mason A. Foley, *Hingham: Old and New*, 1935.

LINCOLN: *Old Time New England: Bulletin of The Society for the Preservation of New England Antiquities*, XXIX, No. 3, January 1939; *Bicentennial Celebration of the Town of Lincoln, Massachusetts, 1754–1954.*

WEYMOUTH: Charles Francis Adams, *Proceedings on the Two Hundred and Fiftieth Anniversary of the Permanent Settlement of Weymouth*, 1874; Gilbert Nash, *Historical Sketch of the Town of Weymouth, Massachusetts, from 1622 to 1884*, 1885; *History of Weymouth*, 4 vols., 1923; *The First Church in Weymouth.*

New Hampshire:

ATKINSON: *An Address . . . by Hon. William Cogswell*, 1887; Harriet Webster Marr, *Atkinson Academy: The Early Years*, 1940.

New York:

NEW YORK CITY: Frank Monaghan and Marvin Lowenthal, *This Was New York: The Nation's Capital in 1789*, 1943.

Pennsylvania:

PHILADELPHIA: Elizabeth Drinker, *Extracts from the Journal of Elizabeth Drinker, from 1759 to 1807. A.D.*, ed. Henry D. Biddle, 1889; *Moreau de St. Méry's American Journey, 1793–1798*, trans. and ed. Kenneth Roberts and Anna M. Roberts, 1947; Luther P. Eisenhart, ed., *Historic Philadelphia* (*Transactions* of the American Philosophical Society, Vol. 43, Part 1), 1953.

District of Columbia:

WASHINGTON: Laura C. Holloway, *The Ladies of the White House*, 1881; William V. Cox, *Celebration of the One Hundredth Anniversary of the Establishment of the Seat of Government in the District of Columbia*, 1901; Anne Hollingsworth Wharton, *Social Life in the Early Republic*, 1902; *Restoration of the White House*, 1903; Mrs. Samuel Harrison Smith, *The First Forty Years of Washington Society*, ed. Gaillard Hunt, 1906; Wilhelmus Bogart Bryan, *A History of the National Capital*, I, 1914; Edna M. Colman, *Seventy-five Years of White House Gossip*, 1925; H. P. Caemmerer, *Washington: The National Capital*, 1932; Chalmers M. Roberts, *Washington, Past and Present*, 1949–1950; Constance McLaughlin Green, *Washington: Village and Capital, 1800–1878*, 1962.

RELIGION

GENERAL: Brooks Adams, *The Emancipation of Massachusetts*, 1887; Evarts B. Greene, *Religion and the State*, 1941; Leonard J. Trinterud, *The Forming of an American Tradition*, 1949; Edmund W. Sinnott, *Meetinghouse and Church in Early New England*, 1963.

CONGREGATIONALISM: *The Holy Bible . . . King James Version*, 1611; Douglas Campbell, *The Puritan in Holland, England and America*, 2 vols., 1892; Rev. Albert E. Dunning, *Congregationalists in America*, 1894; John Cuckson, *A Brief History of the First Church in Plymouth, from 1606 to 1901*, 1902; *The First Church in Weymouth*; William Haller, *The Rise of Puritanism*, 1938; Gaius Glenn Atkins and Frederick L. Fagley, *History of American Congregationalism*, 1942; Ola Elizabeth Winslow, *Meetinghouse*

Hill: 1630–1783, 1952; Perry Miller, *The New England Mind: From Colony to Province*, 1953; Edmund S. Morgan, *The Puritan Family*, 1956; Emil Oberholzer, Jr., *Delinquent Saints*, 1956; Edwin Scott Gaustad, *The Great Awakening in New England*, 1957; Emil Oberholzer, Jr., "The Church in New England Society," *Seventeenth-Century America*, ed. James Morton Smith, 1959.

Leaders:

ANNE HUTCHINSON: Winnifred King Rugg, *Unafraid: A Life of Anne Hutchinson*, 1930; Emery Battis, *Saints and Sectaries*, 1962.

COTTON MATHER: *Diary of Cotton Mather*, 2 vols.; Ralph and Louis Boas, *Cotton Mather*, 1928.

ROGER WILLIAMS: Emily Easton, *Roger Williams*, 1930; Ola Elizabeth Winslow, *Master Roger Williams*, 1957.

JOHN WINTHROP: Edmund S. Morgan, *The Puritan Dilemma*, 1958.

AMERICAN THOUGHT

Samuel Eliot Morison, *The Intellectual Life of Colonial New England*, 1936; Herbert W. Schneider, *A History of American Philosophy*, 1946; Harvey Wish, *Society and Thought in Early America*, 1950; Merle Curti, *The Growth of American Thought*, 2nd ed., 1951; Clinton Rossiter, *Seedtime of the Republic*, 1953; Saul K. Padover, ed., *The World of the Founding Fathers*, 1960; Adrienne Koch, *Power, Morals and the Founding Fathers*, 1961.

ARCHITECTURE

Hugh Morrison, *Early American Architecture*, 1952.

CLOTHING

Elisabeth McClellan, *Historic Dress in America: 1607–1800*, 1904; Alice Morse Earle, *Two Centuries of Costumes in America*, 2 vols., 1910; Alice Morse Earle, *Costume of Colonial Times*, 1917; Mary Evans, *Costume Throughout the Ages*, 1930.

COMMERCE AND INDUSTRY

Arthur Meier Schlesinger, *The Colonial Merchants and the American Revolution, 1763–1776*, 1918; James Truslow Adams, *Provincial Society, 1690–1763*, 1927; Charles M. Andrews, *The Colonial Period of American History*, IV, 1938; Bernard Bailyn, *The New England Merchants in the Seventeenth Century*, 1955; Edmund Fuller, *Tinkers and Genius*, 1955; Constance McL. Green, *Eli Whitney and the Birth of American Technology*, 1956; Richard Pares, *Yankees and Creoles*, 1956.

EDUCATION

Paul Leicester Ford, ed., *The New England Primer*, 1897; Alice Morse Earle, *Child Life in Colonial Days*, 1899.

LAW

Hastings Lyon and Herman Block, *Edward Coke: Oracle of the Law*, 1929; James Willard Hurst, *The Growth of American Law*, 1950.

LIFE IN NEW ENGLAND

Joseph B. Felt, *The Customs of New England*, 1853; Elias Nason, *Sir Charles Henry Frankland, Baronet*, 1865; Josiah Quincy, *Figures of the Past*, 1883; Charles Francis Adams, *Three Episodes of Massachusetts History*, 2 vols., 1892; Alice Morse Earle, ed., *Diary of Anna Green Winslow*, 1894; Alice Morse Earle, *Colonial Dames and Good Wives*, 1895; Rev. N. H. Chamberlain, *Samuel Sewall and the World He Lived In*, 1897; Alice Morse Earle, *Home Life in Colonial Days*, 1898; Rufus Rockwell Wilson, *Rambles in Colonial Byways*, II, 1901; Anne Rowe Cunningham, ed., *Letters and Diary of John Rowe, Boston Merchant, 1759–1762, 1764–1779*, 1903; Sidney Geo. Fisher, *Men, Women and Manners in Colonial Times*, 1908; Mary Caroline Crawford, *Social Life in Old New England*, 1914; Charles M. Andrews, *Colonial Folkways: A Chronicle of American Life in the Reign of the Georges*, 1919; Albert Bushnell Hart, ed., *Commonwealth History of Massachusetts*, I–III, 1927–1928; James Truslow Adams, ed., *Album of American History: Colonial Period*, 1944; Clifton Johnson, collector, *What They Say in New England and Other American Folklore*, 1963; Elizabeth George Speare, *Life in Colonial America*, 1963.

LITERATURE AND CULTURAL LIFE

Moses Coit Tyler, *A History of American Literature, 1607–1765*, 1878; Edmund Clarence Stedman and Ellen Mackay Hutchinson, *A Library of American Literature from the Earliest Settlement to the Present Time*, 11 vols., 1890; Vernon Louis Parrington, *Main Currents in American Thought*, 1927; Allan Nevins, ed., *American Press Opinion: Washington to Coolidge*, 1928; Frank Luther Mott, *A History of American Magazines, 1741–1850*, 1930; Evarts Boutell Greene, *The Revolutionary Generation, 1763–1790*, 1943; John Allen Krout and Dixon Ryan Fox, *The Completion of Independence, 1790–1830*, 1944; Kenneth B. Murdock, *Literature and Theology in Colonial New England*, 1949; Robert E. Spiller, Willard Thorp, Thomas H. Johnson and Henry Canby, eds., *Literary History of the United States*, rev. ed., 1953; Perry Miller, ed., *The American Puritans: Their Prose and Poetry*, 1956; Arthur M. Schlesinger, *Prelude to Independence: The Newspaper War on Britain, 1764–1776*, 1958; Russel Blaine Nye, *The Cultural Life of the New Nation, 1776–1830*, 1960; Leonard W. Levy, *Legacy of Suppression*, 1960; Frank Luther Mott, *American Journalism: A History: 1690–1960*, 3rd ed., 1962.

MUSIC

Gilbert Chase, *America's Music*, 1955; W. Thomas Marrocco and Harold Gleason, eds., *Music in America*, 1964.

NEW ENGLAND HOUSES

Anne Hollingsworth Wharton, *Through Colonial Doorways*, 1893; Mary C. Crawford, *The Romance of Old New England Rooftrees*, 1903; *Old Time New England, Bulletin* of the Society for the Preservation of New England Antiquities.

SCIENCE AND MEDICINE

Henry R. Viets, A *Brief History of Medicine in Massachusetts*, 1930; Otho T. Beall, Jr., and Richard H. Shryock, *Cotton Mather*, 1954; Whitfield J. Bell, Jr., *Early American Science*, 1955; Brooke Hindle, *The Pursuit of Science in Revolutionary America*, 1956.

SLAVERY AND SERVITUDE

John Hope Franklin, *From Slavery to Freedom*, 1947; Abbot Emerson Smith, *Colonists in Bondage . . . 1607–1776*, 1947.

TRAVEL

Seymour Dunbar, A *History of Travel in America*, 4 vols., 1915; E. Keble Chatterton, *Ships and Ways of Other Days*, 1924; Elise Lathrop, *Early American Inns and Taverns*, 1935; Val Hart, *The Story of American Roads*, 1950; Christopher Lloyd and J. Douglas-Henry, *Ships and Seamen*, 1961.

BIOGRAPHIES, AUTOBIOGRAPHIES AND WRITINGS

Charles Adams: *The Adams Manuscript Trust*, Microfilm.

John Quincy Adams: *Life in a New England Town, 1787, 1788: Diary of John Quincy Adams . . .*, 1903; Worthington Chauncey Ford, ed., *Writings of John Quincy Adams*, 7 vols., 1913; Allan Nevins, ed., *The Diary of John Quincy Adams, 1794–1845*, 1928; *The Adams Manuscript Trust*, Microfilm; William H. Seward, *Life and Public Services of John Quincy Adams*, 1849; Josiah Quincy, *Memoir of the Life of John Quincy Adams*, 1860; James Truslow Adams, *The Adams Family*, 1930; Dorothie Bobbé, *Mr. and Mrs. John Quincy Adams*, 1930; Samuel Flagg Bemis, *John Quincy Adams and the Foundations of American Foreign Policy*, 1949; Samuel Flagg Bemis, *John Quincy Adams and the Union*, 1956; Robert A. East, *John Quincy Adams: The Critical Years, 1785–1794*, 1962.

Samuel Adams: Harry Alonzo Cushing, ed., *The Writings of Samuel Adams*, 4 vols., 1904; William Vincent Wells, *The Life and Public Services of Samuel Adams*, 3 vols., 1865; James K. Hosmer, *Samuel Adams*, 1896; John C. Miller, *Sam Adams: Pioneer in Propaganda*, 1936; Clifford K. Shipton, "Samuel Adams," *Sibley's Harvard Graduates*, X, 1958.

THOMAS BOYLSTON ADAMS: *The Adams Manuscript Trust*, Microfilm.

ETHAN ALLEN: John Pell, *Ethan Allen*, 1929.

BENJAMIN BACHE: Bernard Fäy, *The Two Franklins: Fathers of American Democracy*, 1933.

SIR FRANCIS BERNARD: George Richards Minot, *Continuation of the History of the Province of Massachusetts Bay, from the Year 1748*, II, 1803; Alden Bradford, *History of Massachusetts, from 1764, to July, 1775*, 1822; Thomas Hutchinson, *The History of the Colony and Province of Massachusetts-Bay*, III, ed. Lawrence Shaw Mayo, 1936; "Sir Francis Bernard," *Dictionary of American Biography*, II, ed. Allen Johnson, 1943.

RICHARD CRANCH: Clifford K. Shipton, "Richard Cranch," *Sibley's Harvard Graduates*, XI, 1960.

FRANCIS DANA: W. P. Cresson, *Francis Dana: A Puritan Diplomat at the Court of Catherine the Great*, 1930.

BENJAMIN FRANKLIN: Carl Van Doren, ed., *Benjamin Franklin's Autobiographical Writings*, 1945; *Benjamin Franklin's Letters to the Press, 1758–1775*, 1950; Leonard W. Labaree, ed., *Papers*, 7 vols., 1959– ; Carl Van Doren, *Benjamin Franklin*, 1938.

ELBRIDGE GERRY: Jas. T. Austin, *The Life of Elbridge Gerry*, 2 vols., 1828–1829; Samuel Eliot Morison, "Elbridge Gerry, Gentleman Diplomat," *New England Quarterly*, Vol. 2, 1929.

ALEXANDER HAMILTON: Henry Cabot Lodge, ed., *The Works of Alexander Hamilton*, 12 vols.; Richard B. Morris, ed., *Alexander Hamilton and the Founding of the Nation*, 1957; Harold C. Syrett, ed., *The Papers of Alexander Hamilton*, 7 vols., 1961–1963; Arthur Hendrick Vandenberg, *The Greatest American: Alexander Hamilton*, 1921; Nathan Schachner, *Alexander Hamilton*, 1946; John C. Miller, *Alexander Hamilton: Portrait in Paradox*, 1959; Clinton Rossiter, *Alexander Hamilton and the Constitution*, 1964; Samuel J. Konefsky, *John Marshall and Alexander Hamilton: Architects of the American Constitution*, 1964.

JOHN HANCOCK: John R. Musick, *John Hancock: A Character Sketch*, 1898; Lorenzo Sears, *John Hancock, the Picturesque Patriot*, 1912; Mabel M. Carleton, *John Hancock: Great American Patriot*, 1922; W. T. Baxter, *The House of Hancock*, 1945; Herbert Allan, *John Hancock: Portrait in Purple*, 1953.

THOMAS HUTCHINSON: Thomas Hutchinson, *The History of the Colony and Province of Massachusetts-Bay*, III, ed. Lawrence Shaw Mayo, 1936; Alden Bradford, *History of Massachusetts from 1764, to July, 1775*, 1822; Clifford K. Shipton, "Thomas Hutchinson," *Sibley's Harvard Graduates*, VIII, 1951.

JOHN JAY: Henry P. Johnston, *Correspondence and Public Papers of John Jay*, 4 vols., 1890–1893; William Jay, *The Life of John Jay*, 2 vols., 1833; George Pellew, *John Jay*, 1890; Frank Monaghan, *John Jay, Defender of Liberty*, 1935.

THOMAS JEFFERSON: Paul Leicester Ford, ed., *The Writings of Thomas Jefferson*, 10 vols., 1894; Saul K. Padover, ed., *The Complete Jefferson*, 1943; Adrienne Koch and William Peden, eds., *The Life and Selected Writings of Thomas Jefferson*, 1944; Julian P. Boyd, ed., *Papers*, 17 vols., 1950– ; Lester J. Cappon, ed., *The Adams-Jefferson Letters*, 2 vols., 1959; Claude G. Bowers, *Jefferson and Hamilton: The Struggle for Democracy in America*, 1925; Gilbert Chinard, *Thomas Jefferson: The Apostle of Americanism*, 1929; Claude G. Bowers, *Jefferson in Power: The Death Struggle of the Federalists*, 1936; Adrienne Koch, *The Philosophy of Thomas Jefferson*, 1943; Claude G. Bowers, *The Young Jefferson: 1743–1789*, 1945; Dumas Malone, *Jefferson the Virginian*, 1948; Marie Kimball, *Jefferson: The Scene of Europe, 1784 to 1789*, 1950; Adrienne Koch, *Jefferson and Madison: The Great Collaboration*, 1950; Dumas Malone, *Jefferson and the Rights of Man*, 1951; Nathan Schachner, *Thomas Jefferson: A Biography*, 2 vols., 1951; Dumas Malone, *Jefferson and the Ordeal of Liberty*, 1962; Leonard W. Levy, *Jefferson and Civil Liberties: The Darker Side*, 1963.

HENRY KNOX: Francis S. Drake, *Life of Henry Knox*, 1873; Noah Brooks, *Henry Knox, A Soldier of the Revolution*, 1900; North Callahan, *Henry Knox: General Washington's General*, 1958.

MARQUISE DE LAFAYETTE: André Maurois, *Adrienne: The Life of the Marquise de La Fayette*, trans. Gerard Hopkins, 1961.

JAMES MADISON: Irving Brant, *James Madison: The Nationalist, 1780–1787*, 1948; Irving Brant, *James Madison: Father of the Constitution, 1787–1800*, 1950.

JOHN MARSHALL: Albert J. Beveridge, *The Life of John Marshall*, 4 vols., 1916; Samuel J. Konefsky, *John Marshall and Alexander Hamilton: Architects of the American Constitution*, 1964.

JAMES OTIS: William Tudor, *The Life of James Otis of Massachusetts*, 1823; Clifford K. Shipton, "James Otis," *Sibley's Harvard Graduates*, XI, 1960.

THOMAS PAINE: Philip S. Foner, ed., *The Complete Writings of Thomas Paine*, 2 vols., 1945; W. E. Woodward, *Tom Paine: America's Godfather, 1737–1809*, 1945.

JOSIAH QUINCY, JR.: Josiah Quincy, *Memoir of the Life of Josiah Quincy, Jr. of Massachusetts*, 1874.

PAUL REVERE: Elbridge Henry Goss, *The Life of Colonel Paul Revere*, 2 vols., 1899; Esther Forbes, *Paul Revere and the World He Lived In*, 1942.

BENJAMIN RUSH: George W. Corner, ed., *The Autobiography of Benjamin Rush: His* "Travels Through Life" *Together with His* COMMONPLACE BOOK, *for 1789–1813*, 1948.

JONATHAN SEWALL: John Adams, "Introduction," *Novanglus and Massachusettensis*, 1819; George Atkinson Ward, *Journal and Letters of the Late Samuel Curwen . . .*, 1842; James H. Stark, *Loyalists of Massachusetts*, 1910; Clifford K. Shipton, "Jonathan Sewall," *Sibley's Harvard Graduates*, XII, 1962.

ABIGAIL (ADAMS) SMITH AND COLONEL WILLIAM STEPHENS SMITH: Caroline (Smith) DeWindt, ed., *Journal and Correspondence of Miss Adams, Daughter of John Adams*, 2 vols., 1841–1842; Katharine M. Roof, *Colonel William Smith and Lady*, 1929.

REVEREND WILLIAM SMITH: "Diaries of Rev. William Smith and Dr. Cotton Tufts, 1738–1784," *Proceedings* of the Massachusetts Historical Society, Third Series, Vol. II, 1909; Clifford K. Shipton, "William Smith," *Sibley's Harvard Graduates*, VII, 1945.

COTTON TUFTS: "Diaries of Rev. William Smith and Dr. Cotton Tufts, 1738–1784," *Proceedings* of the Massachusetts Historical Society, Third Series, Vol. II, 1909; Gilbert Nash, *Historical Sketch of the Town of Weymouth, Massachusetts*, 1885; *History of Weymouth, Massachusetts*, II, 1923; Henry R. Viets, A *Brief History of Medicine in Massachusetts*, 1930; "Cotton Tufts," *Dictionary of American Biography*, XIX, ed. Dumas Malone, 1943; Clifford K. Shipton, "Cotton Tufts," *Sibley's Harvard Graduates*, XII, 1962.

ROYALL TYLER: "The Contrast," *American Plays . . .*, by Allan Gates Halline, 1935; Arthur Hobson Quinn, *A History of the American Drama from the Beginning to the Civil War*, 1923; Mary Palmer Tyler, *Grandmother Tyler's Book . . . 1775–1866*, ed. Frederick Tupper and Helen Tyler Brown, 1925; Frederick Tupper, "Royall Tyler: Man of Law and Man of Letters," *Proceedings* of the Vermont Historical Society for the Years 1926–1927–1928, 1928; "Royall Tyler," *Dictionary of American Biography*, XIX, ed. Dumas Malone, 1943.

JOSEPH WARREN: John Cary, *Joseph Warren: Physician, Politician, Patriot*, 1961.

MERCY OTIS WARREN AND JAMES WARREN: *Warren-Adams Letters*, 2 vols., 1917; Katharine Anthony, *First Lady of the Revolution: The Life of Mercy Otis Warren*, 1958; Clifford K. Shipton, "James Warren," *Sibley's Harvard Graduates*, XI, 1960.

GEORGE WASHINGTON: Jos. A. Hoskins, Compiler, *President Washington's Diaries, 1791 to 1799*, 1921; Jared Sparks, *The Life of George Washington*, 1842; Charles Moore, *The Family Life of George Washington*, 1922; Eugene E. Prussing, *George Washington in Love and Otherwise*, 1925; Stephen Decatur, Jr., *Private Affairs of George Washington . . .*, 1933; Shelby Little, *George Washington*, 1943; Douglas Southall Freeman (Vols. 1–6) and John Alexander Carroll and Mary Wells Ashworth (Vol. 7), *George Washington: A Biography*, 7 vols., 1948–1957; John Tebbel, *George Washington's America*, 1954; Marcus Cunliffe, *George Washington: Man and Monument*, 1958.